"YOU WILL ASSIST US?" THE MAN ASKED, HIS VOICE DEEP AND CONFIDENT.

Himmler sighed. "You leave me no choice. If I refuse to assist you, there are others you will turn to."

"It will be sanctuary for you as well. You understand that?"

"Yes."

In silence they climbed the castle's steps. At the top the SS Reichsführer turned and looked at the other man. "Is it true that all this is finished?" he asked, indicating the gray walls, the emblems, the flags, the castle itself . . . and, beyond it, perhaps something more.

The man nodded. "Yes," he said. "It is finished. Believe me."

Himmler looked at him and shivered.

"But not forever," said the man. "Not forever."

THE FINEST IN FICTION
FROM ZEBRA BOOKS!

DANIEL EASTERMAN
THE SEVENTH SANCTUARY

ZEBRA BOOKS
KENSINGTON PUBLISHING CORP.

ZEBRA BOOKS

are published by

Kensington Publishing Corp.
475 Park Avenue South
New York, NY 10016

First Zebra Books printing: September, 1988

Printed in the United States of America

This is for Beth, Nancy, and Sammy;
the first because I love her,
the second because we both love her,
and the third because he bites me.

PROLOGUE

27 April 1944

In a long, stone-walled corridor in Wewelsburg Castle, Westphalia, Heinrich Himmler was pacing nervously. In the shadows around him he could see yet more shadows. Dawn was still a long time away. Outside the castle, night birds howled but the sky was silent. Clouds covered a sickly moon. Guards stood on the turrets and at the gates, thin men in black, shivering in the night air.

Himmler wore a brocade dressing gown and heavy slippers lined with fur. It was cold, but he could not sleep. He walked down the corridor and out of his private apartments in the southern wing. A guard saw him, recognized him, and drew himself rigidly to attention. He did not notice the man or acknowledge his presence. He walked to the ornate dining room, then down a flight of stairs leading to the stone crypt underneath. It felt like an icebox. Or a tomb. He shivered. Down here, tonight, he did not feel like lord of this castle or Reichsführer SS.

Footsteps sounded on the stone stairs behind him. He turned. A tall man stood there, quietly watching him. Himmler said nothing. He recognized the man, guessed why he had come.

"It is late, Heinrich," the man said. "Can't you sleep?"

Himmler shook his head, but the gesture was lost in the shadows.

"Have you decided yet?" the man asked. The voice was deep and confident.

"What else can I do?" said Himmler. "You leave me no choice. If I refuse to assist you, there are others you will turn to."

7

"But you will assist us?"

"Of course."

"It will be sanctuary for you as well. You understand that?"

"Yes. And the Führer too."

The man seemed to shake his head.

"No," he said, "not the Führer. That is what you must tell him, of course. But he must have no sanctuary. We will not allow it. It has already been decided. Don't worry, I shall take care of it. He may leave Germany, but he must not live."

"May I ask why not?" whispered Himmler. His heart was constricted with fear and the creeping cold. Shadows seemed to gather in it.

"He has failed us," the man replied. "Is that not enough?"

What answer could there be?

"Come to bed, Heinrich," the man went on. "You must be cold. It's like a morgue down here. There will be enough of such places when the time comes."

Himmler sighed. He wanted to stay in the cold and dark, here in his own castle, his own stronghold. But the man beckoned and he followed. Together they climbed the steps. At the top he turned and looked at the other man.

"Is it true that all this is finished?" he asked, indicating the gray walls, the emblems, the flags, the castle itself . . . and, beyond it, perhaps something more.

The man nodded.

"Yes," he said. "It is finished. Believe me."

Himmler looked at him and shivered.

"But not forever," said the man. "Not forever."

ONE

Have you not seen how your Lord dealt with Ad, at Iram of the Pillars, the like of which had not been created in any land?

Qur'an 87:7

Then ye shall appoint you cities to be cities of refuge for you; that the slayer may flee thither. . . .

Numbers 35:11

ONE

Cambridge, 198-

A low gray mist lingered on the fringes of the river and hovered about the balustrade of the humped and pillared bridge. It clung to him with an air of faint menace as he approached the tall iron gates that lead to Butt Close and the eastern court of Clare College, where it huddles discreetly between Trinity Hall and King's. His feet crunched the cold gray stones of the gravel path beneath him, and he shivered again as the cold November air wrapped him in its damp embrace. To his right, beyond the river and above the mist, the great west window of King's Chapel hung in its frame of ancient stone, catching and transmuting in its colored panes the light of the sinking sun. Seen from the other side, the window would be a blaze of blue and gold light, the rays of the sun bent and torn and shaken like pools of translucent ink across the pale limestone slabs that stretch to the foot of the heavy west door.

He walked on and the walls of Clare blocked out the view, reduced his horizon to the confines of the tiny court. Lights had already flickered on in silent rooms all around him. As evening closed and the shadows darkened, the stillness, the confident intimacy of college life, asserted itself as it had always done against the coming of the night. It was a moment few visitors ever saw, the quiet assumption of its unquestioned privileges that academic Cambridge reserved for itself through the frozen nights of its long winter when the wind came off the fens and the river turned to ice.

John Gates felt cold and stupid and alone in that comfortable world of twinkling lights and softly shifting fires. He had arrived in Cambridge four years earlier when he was twenty-one, the print still damp on his first-class degree in archaeology from Manchester, acutely conscious of his provincialism and his lack of academic experience, unloved, unresolved, uncertain of the future. Within his first term at King's he had found love, and it had, in a measure, reconciled him to whatever it was had first dismayed him with life. Louise had stayed, had endured him longer than anyone had ever done, had lived through his brooding uncertainties, brought out warmth from his sterile and bookish interior, and in the end departed as her own doubts, fomented by him, had grown. That had been almost a year ago. Since then he had traveled furiously and written the last chapter of his doctoral dissertation in a haze of regret, filled with a brooding sense of pointlessness. His parents could not help, he had no close friends, his world was empty except for his books and his research.

He looked back and shivered. Behind him, shadows clung to the walls, empty and fading with the light. Ghosts? Christmas past and Christmas present and Christmas yet to come. It would be Christmas soon and white snow would fall and cover the lawns and courts and pathways. All the ghosts of Cambridge would assemble in the streets to gaze at the lighted windows and listen to carols sung by candlelight. Generation upon generation of ghosts, a succession of men and women who had taken their day in the groves of academe and gone, the taste of cream teas still lingering on their tongues, the frost of a May Ball morning still rimed upon their long-dead hair. This year he would join them, a disembodied presence drifting silently past the festivities of the living.

His thoughts over two thousand miles away among the ruins of a vanished empire, he walked on past Clare porter's lodge and out beneath the low archway of the main gate down to Trinity Lane, where it runs behind the Old Schools. There he turned sharply right to pass a moment later through the little gate that gives onto the west end of King's Chapel. Behind him, a don on an ancient bicycle rolled merrily out of Senate House Passage as he had done every evening for the past fifty years. Shifting his small pile of books and files from his left hand to his right, John skirted the back of the chapel and turned into the opening between it and the gray flank of the Gibbs Building. As he came level with the south door, the

12

silence faltered and gave way before the muffled sussuration of the choir within, their voices held tightly by the bindings of the heavy stone. He looked at his watch. It was almost four o'clock—choir practice had started about ten minutes ago. They would be rehearsing for the Advent carol service on Sunday, only a few days away now.

The small iron gate to the chapel porch was locked against visitors until five-fifteen, when it would be opened for choral evensong. Suddenly, without knowing why, he vaulted it and pushed open the lower part of the door that led into the chapel proper. The vast and hollow nave into which he stepped was in darkness, the wide fan vaulting above his head almost indiscernible in the dimness. But to his right candles flickered in the choir, their flames and shadows bobbing gently as if in time to the music. For a moment there was silence in which echoes hovered, then the voices rose into the stillness, carrying another tune. He recognized it at once: Ravenscroft's setting of the sixteenth-century carol, "Remember, O thou man." He stood and looked at the decorated pillars rising to the dim ceiling and thought of Christmas.

> Remember, O thou man,
> O thou man, O thou man,
> Remember, O thou man,
> Thy time is spent.

This evening his oral examination would take place. His fate would be decided. Until today he had been confident, but now, this evening, here in the melancholy darkness of the old chapel, he was no longer certain of his own merit or the value of the work he had done during the past four years. It seemed to him as he stood there, the music drifting to him across the vaulted space of the nave, that when Sunday came he might not be among those at the carol service, that his life in Cambridge might have come to an abrupt end. And if that happened, what else was there?

He went back out into the night, vaulted the little gate once more, and set off toward his supervisor's room in Bodley's Building down near the river. Dr. Greatbatch had told him to call about four to have sherry with him and the two examiners before settling down to the more arduous task of grilling him on his thesis. Here in

Cambridge, torture was civilized. The lamps had gone on round the front court, and already townspeople were beginning to pass through the gate on King's Parade to cut through the college on their way home. Footsteps rang out on the icy pathways. The door of the Wilkins Building opened and closed as students rushed in and out of the common room. He felt like a ghost walking past, unnoticed, indistinct, his thin frame little more than a shadow, hugging his thesis to his chest like an amulet, as if to ward off some impending evil.

At Bodley's, he hurried up the stairs of Y staircase to Greatbatch's rooms on the third floor. Greatbatch was an odd character: a college fellow for some twenty years, he had been married briefly—so it was rumored—and then suffered some curious tragedy, following which he had moved into these rooms, where he had lived ever since. Morose at times, frequently introspective and touchy, Gates had found in him a much-needed friend and mentor. He had interfered little in Gates's work, but his long conversations, rambling on as often as not until midnight or beyond, had subtly guided him and tuned him to the nuances of his field. Greatbatch's Arabic was extraordinary for a man who had never once set foot in the East, his knowledge of South Arabian archaeological sites astonishing for one who had never been on a dig or wielded a trowel. Greatbatch lived in and through other men's explorations, other men's books. But from them he extracted things that those with the direct experience had failed to observe, made correlations they were incapable of making. Without them, Gates felt, he would have remained little more than a competent but plodding scholar, but from him he had imbibed enthusiasm and imagination so that even dry texts had charmed him and the dust of a routine dig acquired a patina of life.

He opened the outer door, then the baize partition, and knocked briefly on the inner door. It was opened immediately by Greatbatch, tall, lunatic, disheveled, every inch the donnish figure of ripe eccentricity that jaded schoolmasters and aspiring under-graduate girls dream of in the long summer months before term begins. The gaunt man looked at Gates quizzically, almost adoringly, then raised an eyebrow and drew him in.

"John," he whispered, as if they indulged a secret together, "hurry on in. It must be freezing out there. I've had to turn my fire

14

up once already, it's going to get stuffy."

Gates slipped inside and shut the door carefully behind him. The sudden warmth of the room gathered about him in a moment of flushed self-consciousness as he caught sight of two men by the far windows turning to glance at him. Before he had a chance to recover, Greatbatch had him by the arm and was steering him at breakneck speed in the direction of the two strangers, one a dark-haired man of about thirty-five, the other aged and white-haired and, Gates thought, oddly familiar.

"John, let me introduce you to your examiners," Greatbatch said. With his right hand, he gestured toward the old man. "You will, of course, know by reputation Professor Paul Haushofer. He arrived from Heidelberg this afternoon, and I've persuaded him to stay at least until the carols on Sunday."

The old man looked ill, his face pale and strained and his frame sagging within clothes that seemed several sizes too large for him. As he reached a hand in his direction, John had difficulty connecting the face, with its huge, staring eyes, to the photographs he had seen. Haushofer must have aged rapidly, John thought, to have changed so much. The thought went through his mind that the old man was dying. Yet the hand that took his was firm, and the eyes that met and probed his were clear and filled with energy.

"Well," said the old man, his voice weak but distinct. "I am privileged to meet you at last, Mr. Gates. The illustrious Dr. Greatbatch here has told me much about you. And how I have read your thesis. Such an impressive piece of work. I have told several colleagues about it. You make me jealous."

Gates's head spun. He had not expected this. Of all the men to choose to examine his thesis, Greatbatch had gone to Haushofer! Was Greatbatch mad after all? John smiled and frowned simultaneously and clutched the old man's hand. What a fool he felt, to come here among these people, with his pretensions and his raw ambitions. He felt Greatbatch's hand on his arm again and turned to greet the younger man.

"John," Greatbatch said, "you know Peter Micklejohn, but I don't think you've actually seen a lot of each other, have you?"

John shook his head.

"No," he said, "Dr. Micklejohn was on sabbatical the year I arrived, then I was away on field trips, and we never met except at occasional sherry parties."

Micklejohn chuckled. He was a short, thick man with an enormous beard like a small shrub. His friends called him "The Gnome," his detractors "The Cro-Magnon."

"Well," he said, "maybe there'll be a chance to rectify that after all this nonsense is over. I'm going out to Buraimi this vacation, and I'd like your opinion on something before I leave. There's plenty of time. We'll fix up something later this evening."

Detecting a pause, Greatbatch swooped.

"You'll have a sherry, John, won't you? Course you will. Before we get down to the serious business." He said it with a smile, but it did little to cheer John up. Get him drunk first, that was the idea.

Without waiting for John's reply, the don swept off to the side table where he kept his Persian decanter with the portrait of Nasir al-Din Shah and half a dozen antique sherry glasses. Gates smiled nervously and sighed inwardly. In the four years he had been here, he had never plucked up the courage to tell anyone, least of all the insistent Greatbatch, that he really hated sherry, or at least the uncompromisingly dry variety served up in so many college combination rooms.

Glasses in hand, the four men seated themselves around Greatbatch's dining table. The highly polished wood caught and held fast the soft glow of the yellow wall lights; the reflection seemed to lie deep beneath the surface of the wood, in another world, contiguous to yet curiously remote from the world in which they sat, four modern European men whose lives and thoughts were hostage to another age and another part of the globe. On the table in front of them they arranged four copies of Gates's thesis, together with the notes and papers they required for the evening's work. Greatbatch muttered a few words by way of introduction to the business at hand, then turned the meeting over to Haushofer. The old man gazed at the table, then lifted his eyes and looked at John.

"Mr. Gates," he began, "I told you when we were introduced that I had found your thesis impressive. That was not mere flattery. I have neither the need nor the wish to flatter. What I said was true, I was impressed." He paused for a moment, breathing deeply. "I'm an old man," he went on, "and quite recently I've become very ill. You see how I am becoming wasted. I shall be dead soon, perhaps even before Christmas."

The room hushed around him. He continued.

"But I'm not worried about that. It has to happen, doesn't it? Still, I'm glad I've read your thesis. You have promise, Mr. Gates, you'll go far. It is good to think I shall be leaving scholarship in hands such as yours. It makes it easier.

"Now, there really are some very remarkable things in this piece of work. You have made some interesting discoveries and put forward some extremely provocative theories. I don't agree with all of them, of course, but I find them well argued. And there is one discovery that is truly exciting, if it leads to what you hope—I'm sure you know what I'm referring to. Well, before we discuss that, I think we should look at more routine matters. Let me see. Yes, on page fifteen you mention the problem of late Kassite ware in the Umm al-Nar tombs at Abu Dhabi. . . ."

So it began.

In the warm room, lulled by soft voices and shadows that dipped and swayed around him, John Gates saw his future being born, his life shaped and patterned for him in the space of an evening. He knew now that he would be given his doctorate, encouraged perhaps to apply for a fellowship, helped to find funding, enabled to make the discovery that he was certain lay in wait for him, if only he could take men and equipment and dig for it. If digging were even necessary. And he knew his name would become synonymous with that discovery, like Schliemann and Troy, Woolley and Ur. He would be more than a mere weaver of theories about the past, more than a plunderer in dark ruins: he would bring part of the past to life again.

A clock ticked tidily on the wall by the fireplace. The gas hissed as the fire glowed cheerily into the old, comfortable room. It only wanted to snow outside, white flakes to fall across the river and lie on the lawns, for all to be perfect. The questions and the long, detailed explanations that followed hardly mattered. What mattered was the stillness, the sense of belonging, the simple security. John wished the evening would never end, that darkness could lie endlessly over Cambridge and the world so that he might sit like this, watching the lights shine on surfaces of polished wood about the room forever.

No one noticed the door as it opened slightly inward. It is a

17

college custom to leave rooms unlocked when the occupant is at home. People often call. There was a soft sound as the door swung back again. A man stood there, indistinct in the gloom, his face masked by a long shadow that ran across the doorway. Greatbatch lifted his head, squinting in the direction of the door.

"Yes," he called, "who is it? Is it Jonathan? Look, I'm afraid I can't see you at the moment, Jonathan; we're in the middle of a viva, and I don't expect we'll finish for an hour or two. We might be in time for hall, so perhaps I'll see you there."

The man by the door said nothing. Then he stepped out of the shadows. It was not Jonathan. It was not anyone from Y staircase. He was a young man, but old in the way he stood, in his facial expression. It was a serious face, remote, more a shield than a border with the world. The skin was pale, almost like alabaster. He reminded Greatbatch of a South Arabian statuette, a pale alabaster god. He was above average height and slender, but well built, not thin or weak. His eyes observed everything, revealed nothing. He was dressed in pale colors, as if to match his skin. It made the resemblance to a doll all the more complete. A light-colored trenchcoat hung unbuttoned to reveal the pale suit and shirt underneath. He was not dressed well for winter; but in spite of his pale skin he showed no signs of cold. He carried a large briefcase in his left hand.

Greatbatch rose, his hand on the back of the chair, an odd sensation taking hold of him. It felt like fear, but he knew no reason for such an emotion.

"Look here," he said, "you really can't just come into someone's room like this. Perhaps it's someone else you want to see. As you can tell, we're very busy right now. You'd be better off at the porter's lodge." But, of course, the man would not want to walk all the way back to the front of college.

By now everyone had turned to stare at the intruder. He could see their round, surprised faces bent toward him, their eyes curious, impatient at interruption. He put his briefcase on the floor. It was black and seemed heavy, as if it contained documents of great importance.

Greatbatch was on his feet now, approaching the man, the beginnings of anger taking him.

"I'm sorry, you'll have to leave," he said. Perhaps the man was a foreigner, an out-of-season tourist without English, sheltering from unaccustomed frost. "If you need directions," he said deliberately, "the porter will be pleased to help you." He did not like the look of the man. There was something about the eyes, a sneering sort of look, almost icy, like a cat that has taken a dislike to you. And the way he just stared, standing there saying nothing. It was unsettling.

The man slowly peeled off the tight leather glove from his right hand and slipped the hand inside his jacket. When he drew it out again, he held a pistol, a long black affair tipped with a matt black silencer. Greatbatch stared in disbelief as the gunman raised his heavy, ridiculous weapon in two hands and leveled it at his head. It seemed like a stunt, but it was a long way from rag day. Behind him, Greatbatch's three colleagues started in amazement. Micklejohn stood, pushing back his chair in a decisive manner. "An armed robbery," thought Greatbatch, unable to believe the enormity of what was happening. The police would have to be informed, college security tightened at once.

The man's finger moved gently on the trigger of the gun, easing it back effortlessly in a practiced motion. There was a low noise and blood rushed out of the back of Greatbatch's head. The gun recoiled slightly as the killer lifted it up and away from his target. The hole in Greatbatch's forehead reddened. His eyes stared in a last seizure of horror and disbelief. He made no sound as his legs buckled and he fell lifeless to the carpeted floor, staining it.

In John Gates's head, irrelevant, insistent, the words of the carol began to echo:

Remember, O thou man.

It was a nightmare. A wordless killer, Greatbatch shot in his sanctuary, death in the room. Micklejohn made toward the man, uncertain how to proceed, nervous of the gun, but frightened and angry.

"What the hell's going on?" he shouted. It sounded weak and silly, the sort of thing people say in amateur dramatics. But what do you say to a man who has just shot your friend in cold blood? Who still holds a gun in a hand that is not even shaking?

There was no time to think. The man raised his gun a second time and aimed at Micklejohn. The bearded man shouted out,

19

something incoherent, something final. There was no time for words. The gun popped obscenely and the bullet took him fully between the eyes, just where his nose had joined his forehead. It passed directly through his brain and sped out again, diminished by the impact with bone. Micklejohn fell like a tree.

O thou man, O thou man.

Still unsmiling, showing no emotions of either joy or sadness, the man went about his task. He pointed the gun at Haushofer. A wisp of blue smoke escaped from the end of the silencer. The old man sat very still, knowing he was about to die, not understanding why. He had understood the cancer, even accepted it, but not this. The pale finger caressed the trigger once again and a bullet smashed through the German's skull. Blood washing his white hair crimson, he slumped forward across the table.

Remember, O thou man.

John Gates struggled to put his thoughts in order, to think of a means of escape. This could not be happening, there was no reason, no logic, no motive. A moment ago he had seen his future stretch before him, a long vista of research and discovery. And now madness threatened to take that away with the casual movement of a gunman's finger. The blood rushed through his head. He felt sick and he wanted to cry. He tried to speak.

"I . . ." he said, but he could not say more. The words stuck in his throat. Was not that simple declaration of personal existence enough? What more could anyone say in the face of death?

The man faced him and smiled. It was a strange smile, cold yet somehow understanding. Surely it indicated hope. Why did the man not speak? It occurred to John that perhaps he was dumb, chosen for that reason to be another man's secret killer. He wondered if all killers were dumb, if perpetual silence was a qualification for murder. It seemed important suddenly to know about such things, but now that he stood face to face with his own killer, there was no time any longer to ask the questions that rose in his mind.

He noticed that the man had a long, pale scar down his left cheek.

20

It seemed somehow trite that a killer should boast a scar on his face. Shouldn't his killer have been less stereotyped? The smile caused the scar to wrinkle. The eyes narrowed as the gun was leveled at his face and steadied. John watched the hands, fascinated. They were rock-steady, there was not a trace of nervousness. The man had done all this before, would do it again. John watched the trigger finger. His mind raced, out of control, singing.

Thy time is spent.

The bullet tore a pathway through Gates's singing head, tearing the carols and cribs and reindeers and all the sights and sounds of Christmases past and present and yet to come into a tangled mass of dying tissue. His body fell against the table and drops of blood fell like berries of holly on the white open pages of his thesis.

TWO

Ebla/Tell Mardikh, Syria

The clay tablet collapsed and fragmented in his hand. One moment it was there, a piece of history, four and a half thousand years old, the next it was mere clay again, wet shards that crumbled into even smaller pieces as they fell, dust that joined the ocher deposit at his feet. David Rosen sighed, dropped his trowel, and eased himself painfully into a standing position. A light rain still fell. He was cold, cold to the bone. He had been working at that tablet for almost an hour, scraping, brushing, gently working it out from the earth in which it had been lodged with hundreds of others for over four millennia. The rain had started again last night, heavy, pitiless rain, and sometime during the downpour the tarpaulin over the archive pit had collapsed, exposing a section of the unexcavated tablets to the storm. By morning, whole chunks of history had been melted down into a featureless mass of dull-colored mud. And the rain still fell.

Through the gray drizzle the low ruins of Ebla lay all about him, dark, wet, and sepulchral. He had only ever seen them in the summer before, when the heat of August shimmered across the baked stones and sand out of the desert blew into the cracks and crevices of the newly excavated courts and walls and gates of the ancient city. Now, as he dug there in the deepening November gloom, he tried to visualize the site as he had seen it in the sun, with the warm light flowing like liquid over the stones and filling them with life after their long sleep underground. Walls and doors and

22

stairways had acquired shape and identity once more, the light and shadows limning them against the blue sky. But since the rain began in October, the ruins had lost their contours, returning to their primal condition of rock and sand and mud. The rain and cold had been unaccustomed this year, relentless and depressing. Digging out of season, alone but for the Arab, had filled him with a quiet despair. He thought he would go mad if the rain went on much longer. It was insidious, numbing, like the cold that ate into his bones as he worked hunched over the tablets, like the bleak landscape that held nothing but drab men and even drabber women, sorry, bedraggled sheep, and even sorrier, more bedraggled children. And yet Ebla and its broken stones had somehow seeped inside him during the last month more deeply than they had penetrated him in any of his previous digs. The original inhabitants, after all, had known winter as well as summer, rain as well as sun. Here, without the others, he could feel the old ghosts around him.

The Arab was still digging to his left, the bent figure crouched wearily on the earth. He resented Rosen. And, David thought, suspected him. He had certainly been sent from Aleppo less to help with the excavation of the tablets than to watch over Rosen and report his movements back to Syrian security. They shared a tiny hut in Tell Mardikh village, whitewashed and shaped like a giant beehive. It was windowless and gloomy, illumined only by an oil lamp, and it felt like prison in the long winter nights. They talked little. Rosen sat through the hours of darkness, reconstructing, collating, transcribing, sometimes translating the tablets dug up in the course of the day. The Arab helped, but he was surly and taciturn, and David spoke little with him. He wanted to finish the work by Christmas, return to Cambridge, and get back to his book on Eblaite chancery records of the Mardikh IIB1 period. But before he could do that he had unfinished business here in Syria, at a military installation five miles west of Sefire. He would have to lose the Arab for a while, but that was easier thought than done: the man was a human leech, soft, pliable, and clinging.

At thirty-four, David Rosen was already acknowledged as the rising star of Eblaite research. An archaeology graduate from Columbia, his imagination had been irrevocably captured by Paolo Matthiae's discovery in the mid-seventies of the lost city and empire of Ebla, hidden from the eyes of men for countless centuries

23

beneath the Syrian hill known as Tell Mardikh. Tells are man-made hills formed from the rise and fall of towns built, one on top of the other, on the same site, the debris of generations growing until the ground is abandoned by nature or covered by the latest series of buildings. Ebla had first been built around the time of the foundations of the First Dynasty of Egypt, toward the end of the fourth millennium B.C. It had risen to greatness in the middle of the next millennium, only to be destroyed by Naram-Sin of Akkad about 2300. Twice again it had risen and been destroyed even before the days of Abraham, to lie almost unoccupied as the years and the weeds and the sands of the desert grew thick upon its stones and ashes.

David had set eyes on the site for the first time in 1977, shortly after beginning his graduate studies at Chicago. It had no soaring columns like Palmyra to the southeast, no treasure trove like Tutankhamen's tomb, no monumental carvings like Persepolis. But he had not gone there in search of such things. Between 1974 and David's arrival in 1977, Matthiae and his team had uncovered major caches of clay tablets in the second-period palace. Giovanni Pettinato had deciphered the Eblaite language, and a new world had begun to reveal itself. For David Rosen, it had been the right world, and he had thrown himself into the study of Eblaite with all the passion of a long-thwarted lover. It was as if he had lost something precious and had to scrabble recklessly for it in the dust, lest it vanish forever.

To look at, David Rosen possessed none of the trademarks of the conventional scholar. No glasses, no stoop, no pallor. When he was not in the library or back home in his study, he would be out jogging or weight-training in the Nautilus gym near the campus. Thick, curly black hair framed a face Burne-Jones would have enjoyed painting had it not been for the perpetually defiant expression in the eyes and the line of the chin, pushed forward as if to meet trouble halfway. His father and grandfather had worn black and ruined their eyes poring over Talmudic texts in half-lighted *yeshivas*. In David, all that had been altered. In him, the passivity, the brooding acceptance of suffering and death, had given way to confidence in life and resilience.

The Arab coughed. He had been coughing a lot recently. David hoped he would fall ill and be forced to leave. He knew they would

24

send another one to take his place, but what he had to do up there at Sefire would not take long, not long at all. Perhaps there would be just enough time between watchdogs for him to go there and make it back safely. If he was not caught and shot at Sefire itself, of course.

Israeli intelligence had got wind of something puzzling there. It was a military base remote from any town, inaccessible, except for permanent personnel, to anyone below the rank of brigadier, and leave permits from it were never granted. No conscripts served there, and tours of duty lasted two years with occasional R and R breaks at a high-security beach complex near Latakia. So far half a dozen MOSSAD agents had been captured trying to penetrate the base, and each time security had been tightened. They did not want Rosen to try to get inside—that would have been suicide—but they did want photographs, good, high-resolution shots of the latest security measures. Frankly, he thought that would be suicidal as well.

The Arab coughed again. It sounded dry, centered somewhere deep in the chest cavity. "Perhaps it's something fatal," David thought. He hoped it was. He had spent over a month in constant closeness to the man and he did not think he could last out the year. The Arab was about thirty, anemic, given to sulks, and obsessively hygienic. He washed and shaved every morning in cold water, dressed meticulously underneath the long robe he wore for outdoor work, and prayed with infuriating regularity after lengthy ablutions. He was small, thickset, with shifty eyes and a furtive manner. He was the sort who masturbated without enjoying it. David guessed that he fantasized about two-hundred-pound women with massive breasts and pouting lips called Fatima. His left foot had been twisted slightly inward and he walked a little like Ratso in *Midnight Cowboy*. On the second day, even before the rest of the team left, he had taken Rosen aside.

"Excuse me, Professor," he had said in a petulant voice, "but I understand that Rosen is a Jewish name. Is this correct?"

David had looked him straight in the eye for about ten seconds, then turned around and walked away slowly. The subject had never come up again, but David knew it had not been forgotten, that the question hovered, unspoken, at every meeting between them. And he knew it had not been idle curiosity that impelled the Arab to ask.

The man was looking for a Jew, a spy, a saboteur, a target for some gnawing hatred he carried inside him like a woman with a deformed child she will give birth to one day. He would be dangerous.

Bending, David tapped him on the shoulder.

"Time to go. The light will be gone soon."

The Arab began to stand, then coughed loudly, bending double, his chest wracked with the spasms, his eyes watering. David watched him until the coughs subsided. The Arab had refused to see a doctor.

"Why don't you see a doctor?" David asked for the hundredth time. "I think you should. I think it's getting worse. It won't go away on its own."

The Arab shook his head. He wiped his eyes with the back of one hand and straightened his back.

"No," he said, "it will go. I have had a cough before."

"You could die," said David, almost wishing it on him. "I'd be no use to you. I wouldn't be able to help you."

"I don't need help. It will go with time. It's God's will. It will be gone tomorrow, *insha'allah.*"

David headed for the jeep, carrying with him the box containing the tablets he had extricated during the day's digging. He had refastened the tarpaulin, securing it against even the heaviest fall of rain the night might bring. He could not face another day like that again. The Arab followed him with another box. Rosen almost hoped he would cough and drop it; it might give him a good excuse to get rid of him.

Somewhere in the fields beyond the tell, a bustard called, its cry forlorn as the landscape in which it sought some ragged shelter. They drove back to the village in silence. Above them, the light began to drain out of the sky, as if squeezed out of the clouds with the rain. David thought of the sunsets he had seen here in the summer and wished again that he were in Cambridge. The weather would be almost as lousy there by now as it was here, and he had heard that the low mists that rose from the Cam could be poison to the chest, but there were compensations. And London was only half an hour away by train. Here, even if he could go somewhere, there was nowhere to go. The way he felt, even Alaska and a fish-canning factory would be preferable to Syria and its puritan bleakness. At least there he could go to the john without worrying

26

whether somebody took a morbid interest in his lack of a foreskin. He glanced at the Arab. The man had declined. It was small comfort. On the right, they passed the site base camp, closed down until the next short season. There had been no point in keeping it open just for David and his assistant.

David had been hauled out of the seclusion of a sabbatical in Cambridge toward the end of the season. Alessandro Bertalloni had been sinking a sondage, a long trench, to the north of the public court of the royal palace, looking for traces of sacred buildings dating from the earliest period. At the level of the IIB1 period he had encountered the remains of a building that seemed to correspond to the temple of the later IIIA-B era. And he had immediately uncovered a layer of densely packed tablets. Widening the trench, he had discovered row after row of them, an archive at least as big as the main hoard found in 1975. There was enough work there to take them through to the next season, but all the chief excavators had unbreakable commitments throughout the coming academic year. But to leave the archive unexcavated was to run far too many risks of theft or senseless destruction, so a rapid search had been made for someone to act as caretaker excavator until the summer. David had been the obvious choice and had agreed to come after very little persuasion. A sabbatical was a sabbatical, but a discovery like this happened once in a lifetime. Enough digging had been done by October to allow him to concentrate on the task of indexing and transcribing the tablets that had been brought to light. If it had not been for the Arab, he would have been quite happy.

As they drove up to the village, the wheels of the jeep spun a little in the thin mud that covered the so-called road. They could hear the sounds of early evening grow about them. From the balcony of Hajj Sulayman's house a transistor reverberated with the voice of Umm Kulthum. The song, recorded twenty years earlier in Cairo, was loud and undulating and oozed with a desperate sort of sexuality that raised goose pimples all across David's back: Umm Kulthum had weighed in at about two hundred and eighty pounds, and he could never hear her ubiquitous squawkings without feeling queasy.

To their left, a small circle of young women draped in long Arab dresses and swathed in headscarves chattered loudly as they waited

in the thin rain outside Ahmad al-Khartumi's bakehouse for their
evening bread. In the center of the village a crowd of muddy dogs
and small boys barked and screamed at one another and ran like
lunatics after a long-deceased football. Here and there groups of
men stood or sat outside their houses, smoking, talking, and
laughing at old, well-polished jokes. They scarcely turned their
heads as the familiar jeep drew up outside the hut now occupied by
the two archaeologists.

David and the Arab carried the two boxes of tablets, along with
cameras, tripods, and measuring equipment, into the hut. It was
warm inside, the hut kept at a more or less constant temperature by
a small kerosene heater in order to prevent the tablets stored there
from cracking with the cold. The Arab lit the portable gas lamp on
the table and threw himself into the only half-comfortable chair. He
began to cough again. David set down the last box and reached for
the bottle of arrack he kept on a dusty shelf beside the primitive
stove. The bottle was low—he would have to get some more soon.
This one had lasted only two weeks: the weather could turn anyone
into an alcoholic. He poured himself a small glass, then offered the
bottle to the Arab. He knew what the response would be. It was the
same every night, a ritual they went through, pointless though it
was.

The Arab shook his head irritably.

"It'll help your cough," David said.

The Arab ignored him. David downed his glass and poured
another, adding water this time to turn the spirit milky white. It was
a personal superstition that the arrack would render the water safe
to drink. So far it had worked. If the water had made him ill, he had
not noticed.

After the usual meal of stale pita bread and *ful,* they settled down
to the evening's work. Two hurricane lamps hissed bravely against
the darkness. Outside, the rain grew again to a downpour. The
village was silent, its inhabitants confined to their homes, wrapped
up against the chill night air. From time to time the Arab coughed
as he measured and recorded the day's finds. At intervals his eyes
flashed in the light of the lamp as he glanced up at David where he
worked at the other table.

David paid no attention. His eyes were fixed on the tablet that lay
on the table before him, its clear and precise cuneiform dappled

with shadows by the hissing lamp. He had found it two days earlier under a heap of smaller, broken tablets. It was unusually large, 37 by 35 centimeters, with thirty-two columns of finely inscribed writing—a style of tablet normally reserved for texts dealing with commercial affairs. A cursory examination the previous evening had, however, quickly revealed that it dealt with quite other matters. The few lines he had deciphered had made him eager to continue with the task of translating it. A stack of dictionaries and glossaries perched precariously at the back of the rickety table, ready for him to consult, he began to read.

It told the story of Ishme-Adad, a *du-zu-zu* or scribe who had fallen in love with Immeriyya, a thirteen-year-old princess of the royal blood. She had returned his attentions and he had visited her for three nights in her room in the palace, but on the fourth night the lovers had been discovered and seized by the palace guards. Immeriyya had been walled up alive and Ishme-Adad taken to the temple of Damu, the god of healing and magic. There he was tortured to the point of death and then revived by the healing arts of the priests time after time. It had taken him a year to die.

The tale had a profound effect on David. The tablet had been written by Ishme-Adad himself, shortly before his death; there was a brief codicil in the hand of one of the priests of Damu, setting out the circumstances of Ishme-Adad's punishment and his eventual release from it. Holding the clay tablet in his hand, David felt a sense of disquiet run through all his limbs. For four millennia, Ishme-Adad and Immeriyya and their tragedy had slept beneath the dust of Ebla undisturbed. Now, with his trowel and his pen, David had awakened them again.

He sat back. The Arab had fallen asleep at his work. His low snoring mingled with the hissing of the lamps. Outside, the rain droned on against the roof, its dull beat unvarying and hypnotic. To David's right, the old kerosene stove released wave upon wave of muggy, stultifying heat. The hut smelled of damp and kerosene. He felt depressed. Partly it was the story he had just translated. Partly it was the hut and the rain outside. And partly it was himself, the sense of futility and meaninglessness that had been growing in him for over a year now. He sat and looked at the tablet and drank more of the arrack.

29

THREE

Dawn was pale and watery. The rain had stopped during the night, but the air still held moisture like a cold sponge. There was frost on the soil, a soft white caul that crackled beneath the feet of fellaheen going out to the thin, barren fields. Their breath hung above their heads in frozen droplets as they panted through the low mist, and the cold air stabbed their lungs as they drew it in in harsh, jagged mouthfuls. Somewhere a sheep bell rang tinnily as a shepherd brought his flock out to the field to graze on what little they could find.

David Rosen was already up. He liked to rise early, partly for the pleasure it gave him to wake the Arab. Breakfast consisted of thin coffee, fresh bread collected from al-Khartumi's shop, and a watery damson jam that seemed to be all that was ever on sale in Aleppo. At least the bread was warm. Over breakfast they discussed the work remaining at the tell. David wanted to complete the outside work as quickly as possible. Damp and cold were damaging the tablets and he wanted to get them indoors in the next few days. It would mean a trip to Aleppo to buy an arc light, but with that they could dig after dark, leaving the work of indexing and collating until all the tablets were safely in the hut.

"Listen," David said. "I can go up to Aleppo for the lamp. I'll leave you here to do some indexing, then we can get back to digging tomorrow."

There might just be time to get near Sefire before he returned. He had his photographic equipment ready in a waterproof bag clamped underneath the jeep. Israeli intelligence had given him a trick camera. The main reel contained 35mm film exposed at the Tell Mardikh site—if opened and developed it would reveal nothing to incriminate him. The working reel carried several feet of miniature film in a hidden compartment at the top of the camera. If that was found, he could be shot on the spot.

The Arab coughed into his hand and shook his head.

"Impossible. We have to finish the section from yesterday. The wet tablets may have frozen. Perhaps we shall go together tomorrow."

David shrugged. The Arab was right as far as the tablets were concerned. But he knew that that had not been his motive in seeking to prevent David from leaving alone. A professional agent would have found a way round the problem, removed the Arab without arousing his suspicions or alerting his superiors. But David was not a professional. Despite the intensive training he had received at the Bet Eshel camp in the Negev, despite his annual winter vacations there, despite his frequent perusal of MOSSAD and Shin Beth manuals, he still felt acutely conscious of his amateur status. It irked him because it contrasted so sharply with his mastery in the archaeological field. And he felt profound unease about the use of his archaeological work as a cover for his occasional intelligence activities. Perhaps his conscience was too tender. The two trades had much in common: in a way, the archaeologist was a detective, an intelligence agent, digging through layers of information, separating bricks from rubble, ashes from ordure, reconstructing scattered shards into pots, decoding buried messages, and as often as not remaking the past to fit the data at his disposal. The bones and bodies of the dead were to them both little more than grist to an ever circling mill. Other men's dreams and tragedies passed through their hands like used and crumpled bills. They lied and stole, they betrayed one another and sold themselves for the sake of some superior truth, some higher loyalty that made it all right in the end, made smooth the rough edges and rounded the jagged corners of hate and greed and envy. It was the betrayal that stuck in his throat, like a chicken bone that had become lodged there years before and refused to be coughed out. To dig in places such as Syria, archaeologists depended on the trust and confidence of the authorities, a trust that was hard to win and easy to forfeit. The Baathist regime in Damascus was inordinately suspicious of foreigners, wary of the tricks of the imperial powers, and quick to act against anything or anyone it saw as a threat to its continued existence. Rosen knew that, if he were exposed, the entire expedition would be expelled from Syria, if not for good at least for a decade or more.

And for what? For a few miserable photographs, a sketch of a desert track, a Xerox of documents stolen from the home of a low-grade civil servant and replaced the next day. No one had ever told him what use, if any, had been made of the intelligence transmitted by him to Jerusalem. Had any lives been saved, injustices righted, terrorists brought to book? He doubted it. At the back of his mind lay the image of a small black file marked "Rosen." It sat at the back of a filing cabinet in a side office at MOSSAD headquarters, and every now and then it was brought out, his latest documents tossed in, and the drawer closed on it again.

The Arab stood up and led the way out to the jeep. David followed, pausing only to lock the door. The villagers were basically honest people, but the tablets could be a temptation. There had been some illegal digging before the Italians arrived in 1964, and there was still a ready market for artifacts in Damascus. The lock could be broken, of course, but David knew that no one would actually attempt to do so; its mere presence was enough to tell people the hut was out of bounds.

David got into the driver's seat without a word. He twisted the ignition key, but the engine only coughed and died. "First the Arab, now the goddamn jeep," thought David. It took ten attempts before the engine admitted defeat and reluctantly burst into life. David pushed in the gas pedal and the jeep skidded off, narrowly missing one of the numerous potholes with which the village street was riddled. Already the cold had begun to seep back into their flesh. On both sides of the road stunted bushes of genista and tamarisk sparkled with rime frost. But beneath the thin layer of ice the road was still wet with dark, silted mud. Overhead the sky held a threat of further rain. The cold air smelled dank and rotten. As they drove, the Arab cast furtive glances at David. He had found the waterproof bag with the camera and film fastened under the jeep two days earlier, but he wanted to catch Rosen using them; his people needed to know what the Zionists were after.

The tarpaulin had held through the night, but the ground around it was soaked, and the frost had frozen the tablets beneath it, together with the earth in which they lay. They would have to be thawed gently to prevent further cracking. David brought a small dry-air heater from the jeep, connected it to their portable generator, and set it to blow evenly across the surface of the tablets. He turned to the Arab.

"Keep an eye on this, will you? I want to look at something down in the palace. Call me when they've dried out—but don't for God's sake let them get brittle."

He knew he should watch the tablets himself; he did not trust the Arab to do the job properly. But he had no heart for it today. Last night's depression had not yet lifted. Ishme-Adad was still at the center of his thoughts.

It was a short walk to the main palace complex, a little higher up on the western flank of the Acropolis area. All around him, basalt, limestone, and baked mud brick formed bewildering outlines of long-collapsed buildings. Once he slipped on a damp basalt slab, falling awkwardly on his side. The ground was uneven, treacherous. He came into the audience court of the palace by way of the narrow ceremonial stairway in the north facade. All was quiet. The sky lowered and seemed to meet the gray stones.

This must be the court to which Ishme-Adad referred at the beginning of his testimony. Here he had been judged and condemned by the king of Ebla, Ibbi-Sipish. The dais on which the king's throne had sat was still there, fronted by empty holes that had once held the bases of tall columns. They had found eyes of carved limestone scattered across the pavement of the court, great eyes that had once hung, heavy and baleful, from a wooden frieze running along the upper half of the surrounding walls. They had been the eyes of the god Dagon. They had haunted Ishme-Adad as a child and again as a man, after the judgment at the foot of Ibbi-Sipish's throne.

David stood in the middle of the court, trying to picture the scene, bringing to life in his mind's eye the pillars flanked by guards, the king beneath his canopy of linen, gold, and cedarwood, the court officials rank upon rank before him, bowing on the polished flagstones. But all he could see was Ishme-Adad beaten and bleeding, as they carried him to his long punishment in the temple of Damu. They had brought the girl to him on the first evening, lovely as ever, her small breasts painted with henna and perfume in her hair, and in his presence they had stood her in an alcove and proceeded to brick her into it. Brick by brick he had watched until she vanished forever from his sight. Drugged on the seeds of poppies, she had remained silent as the world was taken from her. But he had entered the darkness with her and passed into insanity.

David stood in the courtyard lost in thought. The tablet had made horribly clear something he had known from the first day he had worked on a dig, though he had never before formulated it to himself. All archaeology was built on strata of war, violent death, and endless misery. The layers bent and cracked, but the cement that held them together was made of blood and ashes. Cities rose and died by fire and sword, children were born and were fortunate to live out their allotted span. He felt he stood on the edge of an abyss. Death and plunder lay beneath his feet, a deposit of centuries. And the last deposit was here and now, its dust accumulating day after day. Jewish blood and Arab blood—what did it matter? In a thousand years, two thousand, who would know or care? When the blood had dried and the bones crumbled and the ashes turned to black clay, who would remember the Six Day War or the Yom Kippur War or any other war still to come?

The only meaning lay in the lives and deaths of individuals. Ishme-Adad's tablet and its contents had reminded him of that. And they had filled him with a sense of dread and foreboding he could not explain to himself. It was irrational, but since the night before he had not been able to shake it off.

He sighed and turned back to the stairway out of the courtyard. Forebodings or not, he had to get to Sefire soon, even at the risk of drawing attention to himself. From here he could see far across the countryside, right to the dim horizon. A few birds flew languidly beneath the cold white sky. He shivered and walked on. As he drew within sight of the archive pit, he noticed that the tarpaulin had collapsed again. The Arab was nowhere in sight. Why hadn't the idiot come to find him or even tried to reerect the canvas on his own?

David jumped down into the pit. His feet squelched unpleasantly in the clinging mud of the cleared area. He reached out for the edge of the tarpaulin and as he did so noticed that the mud around it had been stained crimson. And then he noticed that the stain was spreading and darkening. Uneasy, he lifted the tarpaulin by its edge, pulling it away to his left. The Arab lay underneath, his body awkward, fixed in the mud and broken tablets. His throat had been cut from ear to ear, deeply; the head was all but severed from the torso. The eyes stared fixedly, dilated with horror. David's pulse raced and his head spun. He had been gone no more than a quarter of an hour.

There was a faint sound behind him. David spun and looked up. On the lip of the pit, silhouetted against the sky, a man stood. He wore a long black anorak with the hood pulled over his head against the cold. His hands hung by his side and he was smiling. In his right hand he held a knife. The metal seemed dull and somehow soft in the faded light. David did not think he was Syrian. His eyes were blue and his fair skin soft, almost like a woman's. David noticed that the man's teeth were perfect. His tongue went around his own teeth and he observed detachedly that his mouth was dry. The man beckoned to him to climb out of the pit.

As if snatched suddenly out of a dream, David pivoted on his heel, straddled the Arab's body, and hauled himself out of the far side of the pit. His adversary had been waiting for such a move and was there behind him as he emerged on his knees. David turned his head to see the knife descending, a blur shot with silver. His whole body twisted, pain searing into his ribs as he threw himself away from the blade. It caught him awkwardly on the shoulder, cutting away cloth and flesh, slipping off him as he rolled away from it. An effort took him to his feet, still crouched, one hand on the ground pushing. The man in the anorak recovered balance, swung toward him, lunged with the knife again, but David kicked out under the blade and connected with the stranger's kneecap. The man winced, and the knife was again deflected as David stood and dashed back toward the other side of the pit. He had to make it to the jeep. Or else find something with which to defend himself. The killer slewed around in the mud, his knife raised again, like a talisman. The smile had left his face. David ran, but it felt as if he was running on ice. His feet slithered on the mud, finding little purchase. His breath rasped in the sharp air, his chest heaved.

An arm grabbed him by the throat from behind, pulled him off

35

balance, and dragged him back. He lost his footing, and as he fell jabbed back and sideways with his right elbow. He fell, pulling his assailant on top of him, kicking and struggling as the man tried to gain leverage and pin him to the ground. Both men were gasping for breath now, winded by the struggle and the cold. David jabbed upward with his knee, striking the man full in the groin. There was a loud grunt and the pressure slackened. The knife dropped to the ground. David freed an arm and pushed hard to the side of the other man's head. The killer rocked, then caught his balance and thudded a fist repeatedly into David's chest. David screamed in pain. He couldn't breathe. The man's face was right up against his, the breath stale and heavy in his nostrils, his eyes hard and staring. David could sense him fumbling for the knife, then it was in his hand. The blade came up to his side and the man shifted to find the proper angle for the kill. David leaned up into the pain, his chest in torment, twisting his head to the side so that his mouth found his opponent's nose and fastened round it. He bit down hard and felt flesh and cartilage give as his teeth sank in deeply. The man screamed and dropped the knife again. David pulled and felt part of the man's nose come away in his teeth. He felt sick. Turning, he spat out whatever was in his mouth, then pushed the man off and rolled aside.

Both men lay in the mud, David gasping to draw a proper lungful of air, the other howling, hands clasped to his face. They were covered in stinking mud from head to foot. There was no time to think, no time for questions. Now it was a matter of survival, nothing else. His shoulder burning and his chest aching, David dragged himself to his feet and staggered off toward the jeep. Each step brought renewed agony and every breath made fresh tears come to his eyes. Behind him, he could hear the man still yelling in pain. At last he made it to the vehicle. The heater was still running, attached to the generator in the back of the jeep. David yanked out the connecting lead and threw it aside. His only thought was of escape. His head felt as if it was splitting, and his vision was blurred. He felt his way around to the driver's door and pulled at the handle. The door opened toward him and he climbed in. The key was still in the ignition. Slumped against the wheel, he turned the key. Nothing happened. He tried again. Nothing. The engine felt dead. Desperate, he turned and turned the key, twisting it hopelessly. Not even a flicker.

Without warning, the door of the jeep was yanked open and a powerful hand grabbed David's upper arm. The man stood there, his face a bloody mess where the nose had been torn away. Blood still poured copiously from the open wound. David pulled back, struggling, but the man reached in and caught hold of his left leg, pulling him off balance. David snatched despairingly for the wheel, but it slid from his hand as the man hauled him from the cab. His head crashed against the doorframe, then he crashed to the ground, the breath slamming out of his lungs again. Within seconds the stranger had thrown himself on him, hands fumbling for his throat, strong fingers pressing into his windpipe. David was sick and breathless and dizzy, the world was spinning around him, he could feel his hold on consciousness slipping away. In a last desperate effort he grabbed for his opponent's hood, yanking it off his head and pulling it backward with all the force he could muster. The cord in front was knotted and jammed up hard against the thin neck. The head tilted backward and the man rose slightly, away from the pressure. It was David's last chance. He rammed his knee hard into the man's testicles and, as his grip loosened, pulled back as hard as possible on the hood with one hand while bringing the other around to push the head back. His fingers found the wound where the tip of the nose had been. The man screamed again and David struggled free.

Now the killer was between him and the jeep. The man looked up at David, savage anger, blind fury filling his eyes. But something else too—cunning, a cold intelligence struggling for mastery over the pain and the anger. Suddenly he stood, glancing about him, his quick eyes darting everywhere. Just to his right he caught sight of the pile of digging tools David and the Arab had been using in the pit. He moved quickly, snatching up a heavy-handed trenching spade, hefting it between his hands like an ax. With careful, deliberate motions he swung it through the air, getting the balance right, making it sing. He advanced toward David, the spade hissing as it swung, heavy and deadly.

David staggered, moving to the man's left, his eyes fixed on the spade. The man rushed suddenly, the spade raised above his shoulder. David sidestepped, moving in toward the weapon, but it caught him a glancing blow on the hip as it sliced down. He felt his flesh tear. Quickly, he ran past the man to the pile of tools. Without thinking, desperate, he grabbed a short-handled pick and lifted it. The man had turned and was running toward him. David swung the pick and threw it hard, taking the man with bone-cracking force across the shins. He staggered and swayed. David ran in, grabbed for the spade, and caught hold of it. They struggled and fell again, the spade between them. David let go, fumbled, and found the pick.

The long-handled spade was awkward to use for close-in fighting. As the man tried to swing it down on his head, David brought the pick down. The point entered his stomach, sinking in deeply. There was a cry of anguish and the man dropped the spade. Screaming, he grabbed the pick. For what seemed an age, they struggled for possession of it . . . and for life itself. Suddenly David's assailant weakened and the pick swung down and backward. There was a crunching sound and the man went limp. David looked up and saw that the pick had struck him full in the face, penetrating the skull just between the eyes. He was dead. David relaxed his grip and slumped forward across the body.

38

FOUR

He had no idea how long he lay there, in a semistupor. When he came to at last, cold and aching, it seemed like late morning. He glanced at his wristwatch, but it had been smashed in the struggle. Beneath him the man's body lay stiffening rapidly in the cold and damp. The pick was still lodged in his skull. The face was a mass of jellied blood. Painfully, smarting from his cuts and aching from his bruises, David clambered to his feet and looked about him. The site was still deserted; no one else had come.

Who had the man been? Where had he come from? David bent down and took the pick from the skull, turning his eyes away as he did so. He then began to search the man's pockets. There was nothing in the anorak, nothing in the trousers. He unzipped the anorak. Underneath, the man wore a heavy jumper, and beneath that a shirt. There were no more pockets. The killer had carried nothing to identify him or who had sent him. His hair was dark beneath the hood, but the face could tell him nothing now.

It was just his luck, David thought, that he was left with two bodies to hide right in the middle of the tell. An archaeological dig was probably the worst place in the world in which to dispose of a corpse. By next summer there would be scores of people all over the site, digging with spades and picks and trowels, as eager for old bones as a pack of terriers. He would be gone by then, of course, but if he was to have any life at all after this he would prefer it if the bodies stayed put for a while longer. He thought hurriedly, then remembered the wells. There were two deep wells in the palace courtyard. They had already been excavated, and nobody was likely to want to go back down them now. David thought they would do.

It was difficult dragging the bodies to the courtyard. He could not use the jeep; there were too many trenches in the way. One at a time, he hauled the corpses across the wet ground. It was heavy work, and his body protested agonizingly at being abused in such a way after so much punishment. But at last he had them both in the courtyard.

Headfirst, he dropped the Arab down the well beside the north facade. The stranger went neatly into the second well, on the east side of the court. David went back to the current dig and collected as much rubble as he could carry in the tarpaulin, pulling it behind him like a sack. He made two trips, dumping stones and earth into the wells to cover the bodies. It was far from perfect, but the shafts were deep and dark enough to make it unlikely that anyone would notice what had been done. He went back to the pit, carrying the tarpaulin. The archive was a mess—tablets smashed and flattened, blood congealing over everything. Using a trowel, he did what he could to clear away all traces of the blood. There was nothing he could do about the tablets, apart from reerecting the tarpaulin and hoping it would at least keep off the rain until someone could come to take care of the site.

As he drove back to the village, it was already early afternoon. It would be dark in a few hours. His wounds were painful but, as far as he could tell, they were superficial. His clothes were beyond salvage—he would have to change them back at the hut. He still had not formulated any plan, but he knew he had to get out of Tell Mardikh. He could hazard no guesses as to the stranger's identity or motives, and that worried him. There might be rivalries within the Syrian intelligence establishment that could lie behind today's events. God knew there were plenty of tensions in the country, not least between the Alawi elite and the Sunni majority. David did not want to wait around to find out. And there were other questions that clamored for an answer. Why had the man used a knife and not a gun? His clothes had not been cheap, he was obviously not a peasant. Had it been his intention to kill David and the Arab with a knife in order to make their deaths look like the work of local bandits? But even the bandits used guns sometimes.

He could wait until dark before going to the village but there was

40

probably no advantage in doing so. He would have to explain to someone that the Arab had left, gone to Aleppo or Damascus, and would not be returning. And he had to leave Tell Mardikh that night. There might be others looking for him. They might even be in the village already, waiting. Perhaps someone else had taken David's assailant out to the tell before doubling back to the village. It did not matter who they were if they carried knives or guns. David drove back down the rutted road, his stomach tight with nervous apprehension.

The village was quiet. Everyone was resting indoors after lunch, even the children were quiet for once. A dog barked and ran after the jeep for a bit, then grew tired of the chase and slunk back to its corner beside a ruined hut. Somewhere a cock crowed, confused by the dim winter light. A chicken scratched petulantly in the dust, looking for food. David stopped at the hut and killed the engine. There was no one about. He got out quickly, rushed to the door, and went inside. It was dark in the hut, as in all the huts of the village, as though light were something too precious for common use. David found the hurricane lamp and lit it. As he adjusted the flame, the lamp hissed at him like a snake, its voice sibilant and monotonous, filling the small, hateful room.

As if entering the hut had helped him make up his mind, David knew what he had to do. If the man on the tell had been a government agent, they would soon be looking for him at the airports and the Mediterranean harbors. The loss of an agent would trigger alarms between here and every border post in the country. He would be easily identified in a country that had precious few foreign residents and next to no tourists. He had no ready means of disguising himself or obtaining false papers, no knowledge of where Israeli agents were located or how to make contact with them. He was trapped.

Unless, that was, he could succeed in crossing the border quickly in the jeep or on foot. And there was no question which border it would have to be: the frontier with the territories still controlled by the Israeli military, west of Quneitra. David had only the haziest idea of what the border region was like, but one thing he knew for certain: nothing living passed that frontier in either direction, not even a lizard. It was death to attempt it. It was death not to. He might be nothing more than a part-time spy—but nobody keeps toy

41

bullets for the amateurs.

Quickly, he changed into fresh clothes. There was no time to waste, and he had no adhesive tape for his wounds. It took him less than a minute to pack everything he might need for the journey. The papers and tablets were important, but there was no time for them now.

The street was still deserted. There was something about the quiet that David did not like: it was too complete, too protracted. Nothing disturbed it now, not even a dog barking. Had someone warned people to stay indoors, aware that there was trouble in the offing? He tossed his bag into the back of the jeep and jumped behind the wheel. With luck, there would be enough gasolene in the cans at the back to take him to the end of his journey. What happened after that mattered very little, if at all. He switched on the engine, startling the sleepy village into life, then drove out fast into the growing gloom of late afternoon. As he reached the outskirts of the village the first drops of a gray and miserable rain began to fall against his windshield.

FIVE

The wipers fought desperately to keep the windshield clear of rain and mud. David had to screw up his eyes to see through the brown film on the glass, driving by feel as much as by sight. The road was a notion, an idea in the mud, something no mapmaker would engrave on his plates. The reality was mud and rock—mud under the wheels when the jeep was on the right path, rocks when it veered too far. The jeep bucked and rolled mercilessly, the four-wheel drive just holding it to the ground as he steered blindly through the driving rain, heading in the direction of the main Damascus highway.

In this weather it would be futile to attempt driving across open country. He would be lost within the first few miles, or bogged down. But there was only one proper road: through Damascus, on to Quneitra, and a few hundred yards farther to the border. It was about a hundred and sixty miles to Damascus, another fifty to Quneitra—a good two hundred in all. The road to Damascus would be crawling with troops as usual. There would be roadblocks. And there would be two major towns and several villages before he even got as far as Damascus.

He turned onto the main road just before Ma'arret al-Nu'man and headed south. A group of heavy trucks swirled past in the direction of Aleppo. A single car, a battered gray Volvo, passed him heading for Hama, its horn blaring briefly as it rushed by and was swallowed up in the rain ahead. A motorcyclist roared by, his single headlight stabbing through the gloom, raucous and cyclopean, on his way from nowhere to nowhere. David gave the jeep its head, pressing on the gas, his lights turned on like bright charms against

43

the storm. It was a dangerous road. In the rain, cars aquaplaned, crashing into one another without control or mercy. The torrential water washed the mud from the windshield, but visibility was little improved. He passed through Ma'arret al-Nu'man almost without seeing it. The streets were deserted. In a teahouse, jaundiced electric lights showed old men drinking coffee and playing backgammon. Then the road again, a colorless ribbon that stretched into the deepening gloom.

He bypassed Hama. David knew there had been a heavy troop presence in and around the city ever since the autumn, following the coup led by Mas'ud al-Hashimi. A few years earlier, Hama had been a center for the Ikhwan al-Muslimun, the fundamentalist Muslim Brothers. Armed by Arafat's PLO, they had risen in rebellion against the Baathist regime of Hafiz Asad. Asad had sent his brother Rif'at into the city with Alawi-controlled forces. Some reports said that as many as twenty-five thousand people had died in the massacre that followed. Part of the city had been razed to the ground. Shortly after his arrival in Syria that year, David had heard the widespread rumor that the troops had pumped cyanide gas into buildings through rubber hoses. And that had been the second massacre in Hama inside a year.

Now, the city was still a potential trouble spot. There had been great jubilation when al-Hashimi and his National People's Party overthrew the Baathists, but as yet nobody knew quite what to make of the new leader. He was said to be popular, and so far his policies had been liberal. There had even been talk of a settlement of some kind with Israel, although no one seemed willing to confirm or deny the notion. But whatever the long term held for al-Hashimi and his new government, things were still tense. It was safest to take no risks.

He rejoined the highway ten miles past Hama. Shortly afterward he passed a military convoy going toward the city: tanks, half-trucks, trucks, all grinding through the rain like a grim funeral procession headed for the cemetery. Behind them, a line of cars hung back, afraid to risk dashing past in this weather. A tank commander peered out from his turret at the dismal landscape, then dropped down again, like a snail retreating into its shell.

He passed through Homs without stopping. The street lights had come on. It was growing dark, but the rain showed no signs of abating. The road improved a little, but the traffic grew heavier here, on the long stretch to Damascus. The jeep climbed into the foothills of Anti-Lebanon, continuing on the high, wind-lashed passage through to al-Nebk, before the final descent that led past Qutayba to the capital. David swung right at al-Salihiyya to avoid Damascus proper, heading toward Lebanon for several miles before turning back past Qatana onto the Quneitra road.

He came into Quneitra in the early evening. Nothing moved. The town had been systematically bulldozed and shelled by the Israelis in 1974, before they handed it back to the Syrians as part of the cease-fire agreement of the previous year. It was a ghost town now, a monument to human insanity. It had taken a week to destroy. The population had been evacuated, then the demolition squads had moved in. Now it was nothing but a wasteland, dotted with the shells of ruined buildings: a church, a mosque, an abandoned cemetery. To David, it seemed more ancient than any site he had ever dug on. He had heard people speak of it often, his Israeli friends referring to it in low voices, embarrassed.

David found a house with part of its roof still intact, on the outskirts of the town. The UN peace-keeping force had quarters farther in, but he wanted to keep out of their way. He brought food and blankets from the jeep and cleared a space for himself in a corner of the empty room. Rain dripped through holes in the roof. On a glassless window a tattered piece of canvas flapped back and forward as the wind gusted past. Briefly David shone his flashlight on the walls. Moldy wallpaper with what looked like a pattern of roses still hung there. A cracked photograph still dangled from its rusty nail; it was a portrait, but the face was indecipherable. David switched off the light.

He lay there until well after midnight, resting, waiting for perfect darkness. The rain slackened to a weak drizzle. David rose reluctantly and went out into the darkness. He made his way stumbling through piles of debris to the southern edge of town. There was no point in going along the road. There were three posts, each two hundred yards from the next: Syrian, UN, and Israeli. He would never get through that way.

A thick coil of rusting barbed wire loomed up out of the darkness, snaking away on either side of him for an unknown distance. Not far from it, David found a large sheet of corrugated iron. He placed it across the wire like a bridge, flattening it to crawl across. To his right, he could see the lights in the Syrian border post. There was a gun emplacement, sandbagged and lonely-looking, with a single sentry shivering in the cold.

He began to crawl over the wet, muddy ground. There was a dank smell of decay everywhere. He felt as if he were swimming in a sea of mud. Suddenly a searchlight flared into life on top of the Syrian emplacement. It swung around in his direction, sweeping back and forward like a scythe, a cone of pure white light. David threw himself flat, praying it would pass over him. The light swung close, then away, then back again, catching him, coming to a standstill. A voice grated into the darkness, magnified and distorted by a loudhailer. The words were Arabic, incomprehensible to David in their amplified deformity.

The loudhailer barked again, louder this time. A light shone out from the UN post up ahead. There was the sound of a jeep traveling toward him behind the barbed wire.

"Algham," the voice said, but David did not understand. The word meant nothing to him. He shouted out in English, to no one in particular:

"I don't understand! Do you hear me? I don't understand!"

None of it made sense. Yesterday he had been deep in the past, today, tonight, he was here in the very worst of presents, dying in a muddy field on the Syrian border. He wondered why they did not fire.

A second loudhailer crackled, this time from the UN position. The words were English, the accent Irish.

"Stay where you are. You're in a minefield. Don't move. They'll take you out. If you're armed, throw away your weapons."

The jeep had stopped at the wire. Behind him, an Arab voice shouted instructions.

Suddenly a second searchlight blazed out, from the Israeli side. It mated briefly with the Syrian light, then began to traverse a straight line back to the Israeli side of the border. Simultaneously, a machine gun opened up, tearing into the mud along the line traced by the light. A mine exploded, then a second and a third.

Voices shouted behind David. There was a rifle shot, then a burst of automatic fire. He began to crawl toward the spot where the first mine had gone up. It was only a few yards away. Now he began to pull himself forward, keeping his eyes on the Israeli searchlight that held steady on the other side. He kept a straight line toward it, praying the mines had been evenly and widely spaced. Behind him, the machine gun fired burst after burst into the darkness. The Syrian searchlight had lost him. It danced about, trying to pin him down. Suddenly it had him. There was a voice from the UN post, a little behind him now.

"Run, man, run for God's sake!"

He picked himself up and ran. The machine gun chattered behind him. From the gun emplacement a second opened up. He twisted as much as he dared, keeping to the path cleared by the Israelis. Suddenly he tripped and fell into a mass of wire. It tore at his face and arms, cutting him in a dozen places. He heard voices. He looked up. An Israeli soldier was standing over him, a rifle in his hand. He was pointing the rifle at David and he wasn't smiling.

SIX

Jerusalem was Jerusalem: a city perched on the edge of a sort of madness, the capital of a country not quite real, as much in the mind as on the map. David was taken there in a van without windows and put in a small gray room with bars on the windows and a heavy lock on the door. The skullcaps and Hebrew were reassuring, but the manner of his escort was not. They left him alone for hours. Sometimes footsteps sounded in a corridor outside, but they never stopped at his door. At times David's flesh crawled, wondering what code or statute he had infringed that even his own people shut him up like this. He had explained all he could to the Israeli commander at Quneitra, a man of about forty with traces of pomade in thinning hair. Part of him had expected the man to pat him on the back—was he not, in a sense, a soldier escaped from enemy lines, a hero almost? But the Israeli had only stared at him with eyes that scarcely blinked and asked questions down through the small hours of the morning until the sun rose and tiredness fell on them both.

It took a day in Jerusalem to satisfy whoever checked such things that David was indeed who he said he was. No one whom he knew came to visit him—he had been recruited in America and trained in the Negev: in Jerusalem he was a name and a photograph in a file. They fed him and watched him and let him sleep long into the second day.

He was wakened from the presence of dreams by the sound of a door opening. David sensed that the man was there before he actually saw him. The empty room seemed to have taken into itself a fullness. The man was dressed in civilian clothes, but he held himself with the bearing of a professional soldier. He looked about fifty, but where most soldiers of his age show traces in the face or body of the ambushes, skirmishes, and battles they have passed through, this man seemed scarred by something other than bullets or shrapnel. David had seen that look before in the eyes of men who had trained him in the air of espionage. All of them had fought at some time with guns, but their real battles had been quieter affairs, infinitely more destructive of the man himself, of that core that physical combat usually leaves untouched.

"Good morning, Professor Rosen," the man said. His voice, like his hair, was thin and gray. "My name is Colonel Scholem; I'm in charge of our counterintelligence division dealing with Syria. My main work is antiterrorism, but I was asked to look into your case. I went over the details of your report earlier this morning, but there are still things we need to talk about. May I sit down?"

There was a flimsy chair by the side of the bed. David nodded and Scholem sat in it, turning it slightly to face him.

"I'm sorry you've been left in this room for so long," Scholem went on. "Suspicion breeds . . . a certain kind of thoughtlessness. You were guilty until found innocent, I'm afraid. Now tell me what happened. Don't worry, I'm not trying to catch you out with inconsistencies—this isn't a police investigation."

David told him, leaving nothing out. Scholem sat immobile, listening. He was a man of middle height with sad brown eyes and tight, sun-tanned skin. Thin fingers played unconsciously with the crease of his right trouser leg, but the rest of him remained quite still through David's monologue. He asked no questions, made no gestures. And yet behind the eyes David could see that a quick intelligence weighed the information it received. When David finished, Scholem smiled, a quick, perfunctory smile like that of a doctor who sympathizes with your sickness but treats you as just another case all the same. And then the questioning began.

It was not a murder investigation as such, but Scholem probed for details in a way no policeman would have done. He wasn't looking for a killer. He had two of them: a dead one and a live one. And if a crime had been committed it had taken place in Syria, a country with which Israel had nothing even resembling an extradition agreement. Scholem was interested in what, if any-

49

thing, the incident meant to Israeli intelligence; but the deeper he probed the less sense it seemed to make.

"Could he have been working for an art smuggling ring?" Scholem asked. He meant the man David had killed on the tell. In the end, it seemed the most likely solution.

David shrugged.

"Yes," he said, "it's possible." Word had probably got out that there had been a major find at Ebla. Art dealers wouldn't be interested in clay tablets. But if they thought there were uncatalogued artifacts of a more sellable variety, then it would make sense to send someone to snoop about.

Scholem stood at last. Beneath the raked skin and the tired eyes, David could sense a quiet, tightly wound energy. It was not the energy of a nervous, busy man, who squanders as much as he uses, but that of someone who knows exactly how much he has to spend and conserves it until he is ready to act. David guessed that it would take a great deal to rouse Scholem but that, when he did act, he would be decisive and purposeful.

"I think you can go home now, Professor. There's no point in our keeping you here indefinitely. It would serve no purpose. If we need you, we can get in touch with you. Where do you plan to go from here? Back to Cambridge?"

David nodded.

"First I'll go to Haifa for a few days. To visit my parents. They've been living there for five years now. I haven't seen them in a while. I ought to visit them, spend some time with them while I'm here. They're getting on. We don't see much of each other now."

Scholem looked across the small room at David. He seemed tired, not from lack of sleep or overexertion, but from something deeper, something from within. When he spoke again, his voice was different, less brusque, less formal.

"Are you a practicing Jew, Professor?"

The question surprised David. Scholem wasn't even wearing a *yarmulkah*. He did not even seem the type to care. A refugee from the Holocaust, David thought. His Hebrew was perfect. They must have brought him straight out from Europe as a child. His parents, all his relatives, were probably dead. He was a Zionist, but not a Jew, not in the religious sense. Why should David's practice concern him?

David shook his head.

"No. Not since university. Before that, yes. My father's an Orthodox rabbi. I was brought up religiously. Why do you ask?"

Scholem shrugged.

"No particular reason. Sometimes it helps. When you kill a man, when you come close to death yourself. For some people it's a means of coming to grips with things. Coming to terms." He stopped and there was silence for a while. Then he looked at David again.

"So why do you do it?"

"Do it?" David creased his forehead, puzzled.

"Spy for us. It isn't your job. You're an archaeologist, you have other priorities. We don't like people like you in this work. You suffer from bad consciences. You come to despise us." He paused and looked down. "You come to despise yourselves." He looked up. "You haven't answered my question."

David did not know how to answer. He had asked himself the same question when approached by MOSSAD during his first trip to Israel ten years earlier. And he had gone on asking it time after time since then. It was always unresolved, always nagging, like an irritation that refuses to leave the flesh.

"What can I tell you?" he asked. "How can I explain it to you when I don't really understand it myself?"

No, perhaps that was untrue. He did understand it in a part of himself, but it was a private place that even he knew better than to probe or question most of the time. He looked at Scholem again.

"I was brought up in an Orthodox family," he said. "We were post-Holocaust Orthodox, lost, confused, scared. Mostly just scared. Scared the things that were here today wouldn't be here tomorrow. They'd seen it, of course. My parents were in their mid-twenties when they were taken to Belsen. I don't know what happened to them there, they would never talk about it. Of course, I know generally what took place in the camps, I can guess. I grew up familiar with the numbers tattooed on their arms. I was ten when they told me what they were. I'd always thought they were a regular Jewish custom, like phylacteries or ringlocks. So many of the older people I knew had the numbers. And I grew up with my mother's screams. She would scream sometimes in the middle of the night, so loud it woke everyone. It used to frighten me."

He stopped.

"What am I telling you this for? You know it. It's part of all of us."

Scholem nodded.

"Yes, I know it," he said in a quiet voice. "Go on."

David continued.

"We were observant Jews. We kept *shabbat* to the letter. My father would take me to *shul* on Friday evening. When we came home my mother would have the table ready, the wine and the *challah* loaves. She would light the candles. It was her favorite moment of the week. 'Light in darkness,' she would say. It made her happy; that was the happiest I ever saw her, on *shabbat*. We observed *kashrut* and kept the festivals. My father and my brothers and I wore our hair in *pe'ot*. They still do."

David's hand brushed absently against his temple. He paused, thoughtful. Did Scholem understand what he was saying, what he was trying to say?

"I cut my ringlocks during my first year at Columbia. I fought to go there, really fought. And my father struggled to keep me out. I thought at the time he just didn't understand, but I know now that he did, a lot better than I. Perhaps if I'd done law, medicine, a science subject, it wouldn't have been so bad. I might still have cut my *pe'ot*, shaved my beard, changed my dress a bit just to mix more easily with non-Jews."

David paused again.

"I used to call them *goyim,*" he said. "How one changes. I can't do that now. Anyway, if I'd studied something like that, I might still have remained religious. Not so Orthodox, but privately pious, a little observant. I might have married, had a family, brought them up in the faith.

"But I wanted to be an archaeologist. And not just any sort, I wanted to do biblical archaeology. It was a teacher at school. He was Orthodox, of course, it was that sort of school, but he was clever and aware of things outside the *yeshiva*. And he didn't see archaeology as a threat, the way my father did. He thought it could strengthen faith, confirm the truth of the Torah, bring us closer to our Jewish past. He'd even been on digs a few times with Yigael Yadin and written one or two articles on the subject for the Jewish press. But he was an amateur, he'd never faced the sort of problems the academic has to confront, never looked at the real issues head on. When I started at Columbia, I didn't guess just how serious some of those issues really were.

"By the time I took my first degree, more than my *pe'ot* had gone. I'd lost my faith. There in university I learned a new way of thinking, and the more I used it the more I came to rely on it, the less I could use the old ways. And I couldn't get the two methods to agree. Some people can do it. But I'm not one of them. So what was I? I was still a Jew, I couldn't undo that, it was birth, family, those numbers on my mother's forearm. I could do all the things Jews do, but I couldn't believe in them, couldn't make the old connections. I used to go to *shul* with my father during vacations, and I thought how beautiful it was, but I couldn't really feel it any longer. It was part of me, but I couldn't experience the emotions, not the way I used to, the way I did when I was a child. At Simchath Torah I'd watch the other men singing and dancing, and some of them would have tears in their eyes, but I couldn't feel anything. Not a goddam thing. I didn't believe in God anymore, you see, and without that there's no heart in any of it."

He paused again briefly. Scholem was still listening.

"Things got bad between my father and myself," he continued. "They're still bad, but at least we speak to one another now. There was a time, from around my third year at Columbia till after I took my Ph.D., when he wouldn't talk to me, wouldn't even have me in the house. He said my studies were something from the *Sitra Achra*, the other side, satanic devices for the destruction of faith. My faith, he meant. That's passed, but he still won't talk about such things. And where does that leave me? I'm not a believing Jew; I can't be a family Jew; but I can't not be a Jew.

"So I went for everybody's solution: Israel. If being a Jew wasn't a matter of faith or family, maybe it could be something simpler than that. I couldn't believe in the religion, but I could believe in the people, in the blood. Does that explain it? Does that excuse it?"

Scholem sat in silence for a while, looking at David, yet not really looking at him. His thoughts elsewhere, yet his eyes held David's firmly, the sadness still uppermost in them, as if there was nothing else.

"You're not unusual," he said at last in a low voice tinged with tiredness. "How do you think Zionism got started? There are thousands like you. Especially here, especially in *Eretz Israel*. This place is their God, their religion."

He motioned to the ground, an unwashed concrete floor. This too was the Land; below it lay Jerusalem.

"Let me tell you something," Scholem continued, a low anger in his voice that David could not understand. "It's the nonreligious Jews who got us where we are. When being a Jew was a matter of religion, a man could escape, he could become a Christian or a Muslim or an atheist, he could leave it all behind him. But once it became a matter of blood, something in the genes, there was no way out. The Nazis didn't apply a religious test before they sent people to the camps, they asked, 'Who were your parents, who were your grandparents?' Atheists went into the camps with Hassidim, died cheek to cheek with them. Every time a bomb explodes here in Jerusalem or in Tel Aviv, the chances are an atheist planted it and that at least one atheist will be killed by it. Does it solve anything, this blood of yours?"

David sat in silence. There was nothing to say. He had heard all this before, and he understood it and agreed with it. This was why he had chosen not to live in Israel, not because he did not love the country, but because he feared that he would cease to believe in it too if he became part of it. It made sense to him only at second remove, within the mirror of the Diaspora.

Scholem stood up. He reached out his hand and grasped David's, tightly, as if he would have embraced him but could not.

"I'm sorry I spoke angrily," he said. "You have a right. And in spite of what I said, we need you, we rely on your help." He paused.

"You say you'll visit your parents in Haifa. We'll contact you there if we discover anything or if we need you again. Let me know when you plan to leave for Cambridge."

David nodded and stood up as well. He watched Scholem go to the door in silence. The colonel seemed like a man who has been beaten all his life, but who refuses to admit it, who struggles on as if life means something after all. At the door, he turned.

"My father was a rabbi too. A Hassid, a brilliant man. He considers me dead. In his heart, he buried me twenty years ago. I haven't seen him since then."

That was all he said. He opened the door as if it was heavy, like lead. Why had Rosen come? he wondered. He felt uneasy, as if he had a premonition of evil yet to come, of danger for himself. It felt close, unavoidable. He shivered and looked at David, standing facing him in the gray room. Softly he closed the door and left David alone in the silence.

54

SEVEN

He arrived in Haifa that night by *sherut*. He shared the big communal taxi—a black 1975 Mercedes—with five other passengers, four men and a woman, who smoked and argued with each other in voluble Hebrew throughout the two hours of the journey. Seated by a window in the back seat, David watched the darkness roll by, mile after inky mile of it, endless darkness. Cars passed them headed for Jerusalem, and twice a military convoy rumbled by, gray and featureless as the landscape through which they drove. They passed through Ramallah, Nablus, and Jenin, a few minutes each of lights and noise and crowds, then back out into the darkness again.

They reached Haifa about eight o'clock. From the Aviv *sherut* office on Nordau, David took a cab to his parents' home in Central Carmel. Haifa had grown over the years from a small fishing village at the foot of Mount Carmel to a vast port and industrial center that spread up and around the mountain on all sides. To get to Central Carmel, they had to climb the mountain, the cab negotiating at high speed the bends in the road as it twisted and turned toward the long, flat summit. When they reached the top, David asked the driver to stop. The view from where they sat was breathtaking, a sea of white, yellow, red, and green lights all down the face of the mountain and round the crescent of the bay. To David's left, halfway down the slope, the sacred buildings of the Baha'i world center stood bathed in light, the golden dome of their shrine dominating the city. Across the bay, he could make out the dimmer lights of Acre, the white-walled city of the Crusaders. Between the two towns lay the sea, purple and silent; over its surface a ship moved, outlined by lights that seemed to shimmer like St. Elmo's fire.

There had been light on the water three years earlier, when David was last there: a summer night bathed in starlight, as if earth and sky were rivals, the full moon rising behind the hill, pouring its light on the Italian marble of the shrines below. Was Rachel still in Haifa? he wondered. Did she ever come up here to stand and look out over the bay? His heart heavy, he turned and got back into the cab.

His parents were waiting for him, and in the first hour or so after his arrival it almost seemed as if time had stood still. Except that his father and mother had aged perceptibly since his last visit, it was as if he had never been away. This wasn't their old New York apartment, but it had been made as like it as possible. He recognized the books that lined the walls, the rows of Talmud, Midrash, Mishnah, and Haggadah, the commentaries by Rashi and Maimonides, the old seventeenth-century copy of the *Shulchan Arukh* that was his father's most prized possession. There were no paintings, in observance of the rules of the *Halakah* prohibiting images, but his father had made one concession to the world in the form of a photograph of his famous teacher, Moses Epstein, himself a pupil of Hirsch. A patch on one wall had been left unplastered, in token of mourning for the destruction of the Jerusalem Temple almost two thousand years earlier: it seemed identical to the patch in the wall of their New York apartment. And in the moment David saw it he understood his parents as he had never understood them before: their need for security, their craving for stability and a sense of order in a world that had gone awry all those years ago.

His mother had cooked a lavish meal in honor of his arrival: *knaydl* soup with matzo dumplings, *knishes* filled with potatoes, onions, and liver, *blintzes* with black cherry jam. After so long on beans and bread, it seemed rich and dangerous to David, a fullness repugnant to him in spite of its temptations. His mother presided at the table like a priestess in a temple, serving, replenishing, pressing food on him and his father, a formal, serious thing, like a religious ceremony. Her tongue was endlessly occupied; it ran free of her, words and sentences flowing in an agile stream out into the warm room as if to save it from some nameless catastrophe of silence. Her talk was mostly of family and friends, of brothers, sisters, aunts, uncles, and cousins, the old and new generations that made sense of time and place for her.

David listened to her talk and felt both pity and love for her. She had covered her wounds and her vulnerability with a mask of motherhood, her love devouring in its intensity, demanding a love and devotion in return that he was incapable of giving. Like the food she served, her love was too rich for him. He looked at her, at her thin, kind face, her gray hair tied back in a bun, her long, flowered, slightly faded dress, her nervous, mobile hands that reached and reached and never found what they sought. She was growing old, he thought, as if he had never noticed it till then, although she had been growing older all his life; he realized that he did not know her. She was a stranger to him, an old woman serving *latkes,* a mother without children. He ate and smiled and replied to her questions, but his thoughts were elsewhere. He thought of Ishme-Adad and Immeriyya and the Arab and the man he had killed with the pick: none of them thoughts he could share with his mother.

His father did not say much, and David sensed that time had done little to heal the breach between them. There were no questions about his work, no interest was shown in that part of his life he considered most his own. The old man sat in the chair like a stringless puppet, his limbs moving as if in a dream. His face was wrinkled and ashen, the eyes sunken into their sockets as if he was retreating from the world. Somewhere in there was the father David remembered from his childhood, like the rings of a sapling at the heart of an ancient oak; but David could not relate the two, could not make the old man his father or see the young man at the table beside him. The old rabbi talked of his new life in Eretz Israel, of visits to the Wailing Wall, of his classes in the *Pirke Aboth* at the principal *yeshiva* in Haifa. He still studied the Babylonian Talmud for two hours every day, engaged in *pilpul* or theological debate with his pupils and fellow teachers, and was busy writing a commentary on Maimonides' *Yad Ha-Chazakah.* In his concern with his own intellectual development, David had forgotten that his father was, in his own right, a brilliant man. His books had been published by leading Jewish presses, he had lectured widely, his opinions were sought by rabbinic authorities at the highest level.

When his mother went into the kitchen after dinner, David tried to steer the conversation into the old channels, though he knew it was perhaps foolish to do so.

"Did you read the book I sent you last year?" he asked, referring to Thompson's *Historicity of the Patriarchal Narratives.*

His father nodded.

"A few chapters," he said. "But you must have known I could not read such a book. This business of sources, this inbuilt skepticism, these childish games they play with the book of God . . ."

"But they are scholars, Father, serious men. They aren't writing for amusement. They have reasons for the things they say, just as you have reasons. *Pilpul* is like a game sometimes, but the arguments serve a purpose."

"*Pilpul* is argumentation between pious men. Your books are not written by rabbis, they form no part of the traditions of the faith; they are the works of *goyim.*"

"There are pious *goyim,* Father. And there are scholars among them. I don't want you to agree with what they write, I just want you to see that they reach their conclusions through scholarship, not through impiety or evil designs. They love truth just as you do, just as I do."

His father's face seemed sad, sad and worn by something more than the years. He was a small man, bent now, with a balding head on which wisps of thin gray hair struggled to survive. He wore heavy glasses, almost as much to shield his eyes from the world as to allow him to see it better. He shook his head gently.

"You do not love the truth, David. You love yourself, you love freedom, you love the world. Being a Jew is not about any of those things. I tried to teach you that and I failed, may the Lord of the Universe forgive me. You can't find your own truth by destroying other people's truths; you can find it only through humility, through obedience to the law and the traditions that have been passed down. Do you think you know more than all the scholars of the past? More than Maimonides? More than Rashi?"

It was the old argument and it would end in the old way. Between them there was only this distance, this vast, brooding silence that words could never fill. They talked and their voices grew loud and their arguments went in circles, round and round, never meeting, never touching. David could see only stubbornness and conservatism in his father's position, his father could see only willfulness and anarchy in his.

They were at their most heated when David's mother came into the room, an old apron still tied about her waist, her voice pleading.

"Stop it, please stop it. Aaron, you promised you would leave such matters, talk only of other things. And, David, you are our guest here, this is not your home any longer—it is your father's and mine. If you want arguments, this is not the place. This is not a seminar room, it is a Jewish home. If you want to stay, don't mention these things again."

David looked up and saw the tears in her eyes, real tears born of deep unhappiness and pain that he, in all the safety and innocence of his secluded world, could never understand. He stood up and crossed the room to her. Beside him, she seemed small, a little old woman who had been his mother so many years ago. He embraced her and held her tightly to him, and as he did so realized it was the first time he had held her since he was a child. Suddenly he felt tired, tired and dull and wasted, and he remembered the moment, it seemed like months ago now, when he had turned and seen the pickax protrude from the skull of the man who had tried to kill him on Tell Mardikh, on the muddy border between past and present.

He had wanted to sleep late, but his mother woke him with a light knock. She came into his room looking faintly worried; in her hand she held a telegram.

"This just arrived, David. I thought it might be important, so I woke you. Perhaps you would rather go back to sleep."

"No, Mother, that's all right. I'm awake now. I have things to do, I prefer to get up early."

She said nothing and started to go to the door. Halfway there, she turned and came back to sit at the foot of his bed.

"David," she started, her voice uncertain. "What happened last night . . . I'm sorry if I spoke harshly to you. I'm sorry if I seemed to be scolding you. You aren't a child any longer; sometimes I forget."

"It was nothing, Mother, nothing. You were right to correct me. This is your house, not a place for foolish arguments."

She shook her head sadly, as if it pained her to do so.

"No, David, not foolish. Very serious arguments about very

serious matters. A foolish argument can't be helped, it's nothing, a thing best forgotten. But these arguments with your father . . . They hurt me because I love you and I love him. I can't take sides, I can only stand and watch you shout at each other, watch you hurt one another. I feel helpless. It shouldn't be like this, David, in a family; so much hurting, such a distance between people. I don't know who is right or wrong in these things, but when I hear you arguing together I think you are both wrong."

"Mother, I . . ."

"No, David, listen to me. I have to say things, things that have not been said before. Your father loves you. Did you know that? He is proud of you—oh yes, very proud. And you hurt him, you give him pain. Not just these great things you argue about, but so many small things: you enter the house without touching the *mezuzah;* indoors, outdoors, you wear no hat, not even a *yarmulkah;* you don't pray, you keep *shabbat* only when you have to, you probably don't observe *kashrut* when you eat. David, you live like a *goy,* and your father believes that one day he will have to answer to the Master of the Universe for all this."

"But he isn't responsible for me. I'm an adult, I have to find my own way. The *Halakah*'s a path, not a prison."

She looked at him, holding his eyes with hers.

"His love makes him responsible," she said. "And mine makes me responsible. For both of you. David, I want you to find some way to make things up with your father, to come to an understanding, before it's too late. He's an old man now, David. A sick old man. Try to understand him."

Alarm gripped him. Was his father ill? No one had mentioned anything. How long had he been sick?

His mother nodded, her face suddenly worn and gray again, as it had been the night before.

"He's dying, David. There's no reason you shouldn't know, but please keep it to yourself. No one else in the family has been told. He has cancer of the liver. The doctors at Blumental give him a year, maybe less. He knows and he accepts it. In the camp, a year was like a lifetime. But some things still worry him. You worry him, you more than anything."

She stood up.

"Don't leave it too long, David. He wants some time with you."

There was nothing more to say. *Aroysgeverfoneh verter.* Wasted words. So many wasted words. She felt empty again, empty of words, of hopes, of dreams. Only this remained, the life of a stranger in Eretz Israel. The door opened and closed and she was gone, but the weight of her emotions lay heavily upon the room.

David breathed in deeply, struggling to accept what he had just heard, to understand that his father was dying, would soon be dead. His own death mocked him at times from a distance, but in the past few days it had come close enough to touch and smell, and somehow that made the possibility of his father's death more real, more imminent. Almost absent-mindedly, he opened the envelope and drew out the telegram.

Before leaving Jerusalem, he had arranged for a telex to be sent to the Department of Archaeology in Cambridge, explaining that he had been forced to leave the dig in Syria and that he planned to return to England within the week. This was the reply. And the second blow of that morning.

NEWS OF DEPARTURE RECEIVED. WILL NOTIFY ROME CHANGE IN PLANS. EARLY ARRIVAL ANTICIPATED. DEEPLY REGRET TO INFORM YOU TRAGIC INCIDENT CAMBRIDGE. MICHAEL GREATBATCH, PETER MICKLEJOHN, PAUL HAUSHOFER, JOHN GATES ALL KILLED BY GUNMAN EARLY LAST WEEK. MOTIVE STILL UNKNOWN. MURDERER STILL UNAPPREHENDED. FUNERALS FOLLOW POST-MORTEM NEXT MONTH. EARNESTLY REQUEST YOU TO COME.

The telegram was signed by Richard Halstead, head of the department.

David held his breath tightly until it pained his chest and made the blood pound in his temples. He had known Michael Greatbatch for about ten years, Micklejohn and Gates since the beginning of the summer. Haushofer he had known and respected by reputation. All dead? How was it possible? He thought of Cambridge, its weathered walls and deep-set gateways like ageless guarantees of security to those behind them. Who could have breached those walls to gun down innocent men?

And at once he thought of Tell Mardikh, its walls broken, its gates rubble, and the man standing near him with a knife. Was it

61

coincidence or fate that had brought him and those four others face to face with violent death in the space of a few days? He would have to contact Jerusalem at once. If there was a link between the incidents, it would have to be identified and investigated immediately.

Even as he thought about Jerusalem he remembered something. It had been eight or nine years ago, he wasn't sure. A professor at the Hebrew University, Yigael Bar-Adon, had been gunned down in his office late one evening by an unknown assassin. Some papers had been taken, all of them connected with the professor's research, but no one was sure what they had contained, and no motive could be construed from the fact of their disappearance. Bar-Adon had been a man of about fifty, married, with three children. And he had been an archaeologist. It had been conjectured at the time that the professor had been secretly involved in intelligence work: his digs often took him into the Negev and Sinai, and he had made visits to Jordan. David for one had no *a priori* grounds for doubting such a conjecture. But he had no reason either to believe that Greatbatch or any of the others killed in Cambridge had had similar involvements. On the face of it, it seemed highly unlikely. He would have to go to Jerusalem to find out.

His father had gone to the local synagogue for morning prayers. He was one of those who formed a regular *minyan,* a quorum of ten men essential for worship. He would go directly to the *yeshiva* where he taught after that, and would not return until early evening. Curiously, David felt a little hurt that he had not asked him to accompany him to the *shul.* Perhaps he would suggest it himself when he came back from Jerusalem: it would be a beginning.

After breakfast he explained to his mother that he planned to return to Jerusalem for a few days but that he would try to be back in time for *shabbat* on Friday evening. He packed a small bag, then waited until after eleven o'clock. In Cambridge it was now after nine, and with luck he would be able to contact Halstead in his office. A direct line took him through to the university switchboard, from which he was transferred to the departmental secretary. A few moments later Halstead's voice came on the line, a slightly lazy, low-pitched English voice that concealed enormous reserves of energy.

"Hello, Halstead here. Who's speaking?"

"Professor Halstead? This is David Rosen. I'm ringing from Haifa. I've just received your telegram."

"Ah, yes, David. How are you? You got my telegram, did you? That's not bad, I sent it yesterday. I hope it was clear."

"Yes," David replied, "very clear." He hesitated. "I don't quite know what to say. About the killings, I mean."

There was a pause on the other end. Then Halstead spoke again, his voice changed. It was duller and flatter.

"The killings. Yes. A very bad business. Very bad."

"I'd like to know the details, if that's possible."

"Yes, certainly. There's not much to tell, really. We don't know very much."

Without wasting words, Halstead filled David in on what had happened: the discovery of the bodies by Greatbatch's bedder, the police investigation that had so far met only a blank wall, the lack of clues or possible motives. No one had seen any suspicious stranger enter or leave Bodley's Building. At the time of day the shootings were thought to have taken place, local people pass through the college in large numbers, taking a short cut home from work. Every member of the department had been questioned, but so far there had been no leads or, if there were, the police weren't saying.

"Was anything taken?" David asked. "Papers, files, anything like that?"

Halstead paused again. David could picture him: tall, lean, with bushy eyebrows and a mop of tangled gray hair he cut once a year and combed twice a week.

"How did you guess?" Halstead asked. "Yes, we think some papers must have been taken. As I said, it was Gates's viva, so there must have been plenty of notes on the table, as well as copies of his thesis. When the bedder found the bodies, the table was clean as a whistle, so she says. No dissertation, no folders, no notes, nothing. Except some blood. It ruined a very good table, French Directoire, very elegant. You may have seen it."

There was a moment's silence, then the voice again, altered once more.

"I'm sorry, that was in bad taste. Please forgive me. This whole business has been the most terrible strain. I knew old Greatbatch

63

very well; he was a close friend, an old friend, an old friend. It's been very upsetting."

"I understand. You don't need to apologize. What about Gates's apartment? Was it broken into? Was anything stolen?"

"No, I don't think so. The police examined it, of course, but they haven't mentioned that anything was taken. Why do you ask?"

"Well, if we assume that taking the notes and dissertations was the motive for the killings, then we have to conclude that whoever was responsible was after something in Gates's work. In that case, he might have taken stuff from his apartment as well. Unless, of course, he already had what he was looking for."

Halstead made a humming noise.

"Yes," he said, "I see what you mean. We already thought the stolen papers might be a clue, but the police in their widsom have dismissed it all as a blind. Academics may get hot under the collar about their work or other people's, but they don't kill one another over it. And nobody else is likely to have found much to interest them in a dissertation like that. If Gates had been a nuclear physicist or doing research into new energy sources or something like that, something with an economic or military application, it might have made some sense. The police think it was a lunatic, someone who wants publicity for his crime. They've kept reports out of the press in the hope the killer will be forced to show his hand, write to the television, the papers, that sort of thing."

"Or kill someone else?"

Halstead breathed heavily.

"Yes, there is that risk. But, in any case, I don't think there can be any motive. A rational one, I mean. Unless . . ."

There was another pause. The line crackled twice and was silent. Halstead spoke again.

"David, you know Israel and you know the region Gates was researching. Is there anything down there he might have stumbled on by accident, anything . . . well, sensitive? Something the intelligence people might have got edgy about?"

It was plausible. David knew that Gates's work had taken him to Sinai and along the edge of the Straits of Tiran and the Gulf of Aqaba. It was a sensitive region and Gates had been something of an innocent.

"Yes," he said. "It's possible. But I think it's unlikely. I can make inquiries if you like. I'm going to Jerusalem today. I have contacts there who may be able to help. Unofficially, of course."

"I understand."

The line crackled again, and Halstead's voice became faint. His next words were barely audible.

"Are you able to come to the funerals?"

"Yes, I hope so."

"Good, I'll let you know the date when it's fixed. Look, we'd better hang up, this line's impossible now. Thanks for ringing."

"Thank you, Professor. I'll be in touch."

Halstead hung up. The line clicked again and was silent. David replaced the receiver and went to pick up his bag. He could be in Jerusalem in under two hours if he hurried.

EIGHT

He rented a car and drove out along the northeastern flank of the long Carmel range. As he left Haifa behind, the heavy white smoke rising from the cement works at Nesher blotted the city from sight. The smoke filled his rear-view mirror like a frozen cloud.

He arrived in Jerusalem just before two o'clock. It was years since he had seen the city properly by daylight, but he felt the old thrill of mingled excitement and loathing as he walked through the streets of the Old City. He did not want to go directly to Scholem's office. There was more to Jerusalem than the bare concrete floor in that little gray-painted room.

Jerusalem was like any holy city he had ever visited or read of: piety rubbing shoulders with blatant commercialism, worship doing business with trade. Holy Land soil and Holy Land water were on sale everywhere, earth and water for seeds and thirsts of an unearthly substance. Beads and crucifixes hung in cluttered ecumenicity with *tallits, tefillin,* and pictures of the Aqsa Mosque. Bibles and Qur'ans, breviaries and Haggadahs ranged themselves in old shopwindows all along the Via Dolorosa and beyond. Pieces of the true cross, nails from the hands and feet of the dead god, hairs from the tail of Buraq, the beast on which the Prophet rode from Mecca to Jerusalem, stones from the Temple of Herod—the body of the city had been sold over and over as if it were a whore, and still they came for relics.

David felt it press in on him, a presence, a discord in time, centuries of faith and rank hypocrisy crowding in from all sides. He walked surrounded by people. Old men, their faces semaphores of

66

memory, sat in even older doorways, recalling the days when the Turks had ruled here. Regret? Insouciance? It had all changed, it would change again. The winding streets and twisting bric-a-brac bazaars were never empty of moving feet. David was pushed along, like flotsam being pushed by the sea.

Suddenly he felt a wave of loneliness come over him, cold, bitter, and panicking, a vertigo of the spirit. He had lived for so many weeks all but alone at Tell Mardikh, occupied with his own thoughts, his own moods, his own presence, with only the Arab to talk to, and that but little. The Arab had died and left him alone on the hill with the man he had killed.

Now, abruptly, he had been set down in the middle of a vast, crowded, and noisy city, surrounded by tired and angry faces, by bodies running and turning and standing still. And among them, his heart told him, one face, one pair of hands that sought him among the crowd. He staggered and fell against a wall as a wave of sickness passed through him suddenly and was gone. No one stopped, no one even paused to stare. He was invisible almost, or tiny, a fragment among so many fragments. His mouth tasted sour and his throat ached suddenly.

He stood there for long moments, each distinct, detachable from the moment before and the moment after, then minutes passed and he was still alone in the crowded street. At last, by stages, the dizziness lifted and his head cleared, though his throat still ached and his limbs felt curiously weak. Tension and excitement had caught up with him. He breathed deeply, looked about him, and moved off again; he needed sleep and at least a day's rest. He was to have neither.

Scholem saw him straight away. He looked tireder and grayer than the day before, and his small office was cold. Beside the *Magen David* on the wall, David noticed a photograph of an old man in Hasid dress. Glass on the photograph caught the afternoon sun and blurred the sitter's wrinkled features.

"*Shalom,* Professor Rosen. So soon? I understood you had gone to Haifa. Perhaps Jerusalem still has some attractions. But please, sit down."

David sat without replying. The chair was hard; cold metal conveyed its touch to his flesh through the cloth of his trousers. In a quiet voice he began to explain what had brought him back to

Jerusalem. Even as he spoke, it sounded implausible to him. Granted, it was almost unknown for academics to be assassinated without some obvious political or religious motive, but it was not unprecedented. There were cases on record of failed students taking out their feelings of resentment with a gun. Granted, too, that it was stretching coincidence to the limit for two such incidents to have involved Middle East archaeologists, nevertheless the region was an unstable one with more than its fair share of terrorists and other fanatics: it could well bear the weight of more than one such coincidence. Yet Scholem said nothing, neither to prompt nor to interrupt, until David had finished his narrative. Perhaps nothing surprised or captivated him after so many years in such a trade. The cross and the nails and the crown of thorns would be to him nothing but wood and metal and dried vegetation. At last David finished. He waited for Scholem to respond.

A minute passed in silence. Scholem's face showed neither impatience nor amusement. It remained deadpan. He had long ago acquired the skill of giving nothing away.

"Is that all?"

David nodded. Had it been so unsubstantial, so inconsequential after all?

"It's interesting," Scholem said. "But what made you come to me with it? It's a matter for the British police, isn't it?"

"I thought you might know about Bar-Adon. He wasn't killed for academic jealousy. Or academic espionage. I'll stake my life on it. We kill our rivals with words, Colonel Scholem. Only your people do it for real. That had to be the reason for Bar-Adon's death. And perhaps the reason for John Gates's too. The answer isn't over there in Cambridge or down in Sinai or wherever else Gates went last summer. It's here, here in Jerusalem, perhaps right in this office."

"No, Professor, I don't think so. Not in this office, certainly. I have no knowledge of Gates. I have only a hazy memory of Bar-Adon's death. Let me assure you that neither had anything to do with our activities here."

"How can you be sure of that? Perhaps another department, another control . . ."

Scholem paused, propping his chin in his hands, his fingers brushing the bristle on his cheeks.

"Yes," he said, "that's possible. But within these walls things get talked about, rumors fly. I have heard no rumors. Never once have I heard the name of Bar-Adon mentioned. There was no investigation by us."

"But there may be files. Can't you at least check?"

Sunlight fumbled through the grimy window behind Scholem, attenuated, like the light of a flashlight whose battery is about to give out. David could see a patch of sky through the window. It was pale purple, pearllike and translucent, like the inside of a lichee shell. Scholem pondered, a finger tapping absent-mindedly on the cluttered desk in front of him. With a sigh he put his hands together and began to pick his nails, carefully, one at a time.

"Why do you want to know? Why is it so important to you?"

David stared at him, at the careful fingers, at the papers on the desk.

"I don't know," he said. "I'm uneasy, I need some answers. There must be some."

Scholem sighed again.

"All right," he said at last. "There may be something. I'll find out what I can. It may take awhile. Can you wait?"

David nodded.

"Very well. Wait here. I'll ask someone to bring you coffee, something to eat. I'll do what I can."

David wanted to ask if there was somewhere else to wait, but it seemed importunate so he said nothing. Scholem was gone a long time, and the room grew colder as evening fell outside. A girl brought coffee and *felafels* in *pita* bread. She was young and pretty, and her smile was warm, but she did not respond to his attempt to engage her in conversation. He had no status here, he realized; he was merely a passerby, an informant, perhaps even a suspect, nothing more. An hour passed and Scholem did not return. The chair was uncomfortable, his limbs cold, but he sat waiting, as if frozen in place, all activity suspended in the other's absence. Another half hour passed.

The door opened and Scholem entered alone. In his right hand he carried several thin buff folders, in his left a key. He smiled at David and walked across to his desk.

"It's cold in here," he said. "You should have put on the heater." He reached toward a switch on the wall behind him and flicked it up. A low hum began to vibrate through the room. But David could feel no heat, he heard only the steady drumming of the machinery.

"It's as I thought," Scholem began. "We have a record of Mr. Gates having been in Sinai, but as far as the files in question are concerned, everything was straightforward. To the best of our knowledge he never put a foot wrong, not with us, not with the Egyptians. We can fish for information from Cairo, of course. I'll let you know if we get anything—but, to be frank, I don't think we will.

"Bar-Adon was not like you, Professor. We approached him, of course, several times. He refused to cooperate. I have some letters in this folder, in which he makes his position very clear. I won't show them to you, they might upset you. There was an investigation of his death by Shin Beth, but they turned up nothing—absolutely nothing. I can assure you that the inquiries were thorough, both Shin Beth's and those of the police. There were no clues, no serious suspects, no motives that made any sense. The police file on his death is still open, but they don't expect to close it. You're wasting your time, Professor."

David shifted in his chair. His left leg had gone numb. His throat was dry.

"May I see the folders?"

Scholem's head moved twice from side to side.

"No, I'm sorry. You'd need to be cleared for that. If you think it's really necessary, if you insist, yes, I think clearance could be arranged. But I assure you, you'd be wasting your time. There's nothing. If there had been something, anything, however trivial, I would have told you. You don't matter to me, not personally. You're a drop in my ocean, Professor. But connections like these matter, incidents like these matter. I do my job. I look for the links, I join the disparate pieces until they cohere and become a whole. Your pieces are merely pieces, parts belonging to different jigsaws: there is no picture, no pattern, simply fortuitous resemblances. Go home, Professor, go back to your libraries and your books."

David looked at him, an unaccustomed anger welling up.

"And if they come for me again? If I step outside your doors downstairs into the hands of a gunman or another man with a knife? Do I just start all over again—kill him, leave him for your cleaners to dispose of?"

He stood up. Blood began to rush back into his leg, bringing pins and needles and a sensation of burning cold.

Scholem looked at him sadly, like a father disappointed in his son. David remembered that his father would be home by now. He should have been there in Haifa to greet him.

He shook hands briskly with Scholem and went to the door. A guard was waiting to take him to the exit. The corridor was cold. Outside, an icy wind blew across the street. He stepped out into the darkness.

Five minutes later he telephoned Abraham Steinhardt, a professor at the Hebrew University whom David had met several times at conferences. Steinhardt had been a colleague of Bar-Adon. David was surprised when he said he remembered him and relieved when he told him he could see him that evening.

"Listen," Steinhardt mumbled down the receiver as if trying to chew it. "Don't come here. It's one big mess. I never see anyone here, not even my children. I have to eat, you have to eat. We'll meet in Fink's, eat something, drink a little, talk. I assume that's what you want to do: talk. Fink's, eight o'clock."

David arrived at the little restaurant in King George Road just before eight, but Steinhardt was already waiting for him. He recognized the old man at once: silver hair down to his shoulders, an unruly beard still streaked with black hairs that he clipped once a year on Yom Kippur, a jacket and trousers several sizes too big for him. Even in a restaurant that had its fair share of eccentrics, he stood out. To David's surprise, Steinhardt proved that he remembered him by waving, shouting loudly, and beckoning him to his table. Before he could even sit, Steinhardt began talking in his accurate but heavily accented English.

"I've ordered, so we don't have to waste time with the menu. At my age, time is precious. You came out of the blue, David Rosen. A phone call, 'Shalom, ma shlom-kha, this is Rosen, I'm in Jerusalem.' I thought you were in Tell Mardikh."

"He might be old," David thought, "but his wits are all about him."

"How do you know that?" he asked.

"Pah! Of course I know. We all heard about the archive find, then we heard they'd tracked you down in London or somewhere and dragged you out there. You need a doctor for your brain.

71

Winter in that place! When you could be in a warm library somewhere reading lovely old texts and writing articles nobody will ever read. What are you, Rosen, a masochist?"

"It was Cambridge. I was in Cambridge on sabbatical."

Steinhardt grimaced.

"All the worse," he burst out. "Cambridge is a pretty place. Civilized. I spent a sabbatical there once, seven years ago. I went punting and fell in the river, what do they call it? The Cam. I had cream tea at Granchester every Sunday afternoon during the summer. And I fell in love with a beautiful little librarian in the manuscripts room at the library. You know the place, you go up in a lift. Imagine, at my age to do such a thing. She was married, of course; they always are."

"What, librarians?" David asked, wondering where the conversation would turn next.

"No, of course not, most of them are spinsters. And no wonder. I meant pretty young women. There are always husbands in the background. Or boyfriends nowadays."

Abruptly, he changed the subject.

"What will you have to drink? Adon Atik? Okay, it's coming."

He turned to a passing waiter. *"Meltzar, ha-yayin, b'vakasha."* Then, before the waiter had a chance to reply, back to David.

"Revolting language," he said. "Only the Sabras speak it properly, us older folk just make laughingstocks of ourselves."

This sounded strange, coming from one of the foremost authorities on ancient Hebrew texts. Steinhardt put up a hand as if to ward off David's question.

"No," he said, "you don't have to say it, it's been said often enough before. Why does Abraham Steinhardt dislike Hebrew so much? Pah! Of course I dislike it. I was brought up to read it, not order wine in it."

As he spoke, the waiter approached stealthily with the wine bottle, opened it, and left it on the table. Steinhardt had long ago told him to dispense with the formality of pouring a little into his glass.

"I have no palate," he said, "this is Israeli wine, and life is short. *L'hayim.*"

Behind the bar, someone turned up the radio. The music program had been interrupted by a special announcement. The diners fell silent without anyone needing to hush them. In Israel, listening to news broadcasts and radio bulletins is no casual matter: everyone listens. Half the men in the restaurant were, in one capacity or another, soldiers, either regulars or reservists, and in an emergency the radio would give first warning of a call-up. The announcer cleared his throat, then started the bulletin:

"We have interrupted the concert from Mann Auditorium to bring you a special bulletin. The Foreign Minister, Yitzhak Avi-Zohar, has just issued an official communiqué. Mr. Mas'ud al-Hashimi, the new President of Syria, who took office on September 14 following the deposition of Hafiz Asad, has just concluded talks with representatives of the Israeli government. These talks have followed secret negotiations by the United States Embassy in Damascus and the personal intervention of the American President. Mr. al-Hashimi has expressed his willingness and that of his government to hold full-scale talks with the Israeli Prime Minister and members of the Cabinet. As of 9 P.M. this evening, Syria formally recognizes the existence of the state of Israel. The two countries are no longer in a state of undeclared war, and immediate steps are to be taken to pave the way for the signing of a peace settlement sometime in the spring.

"No details are as yet available about the precise terms of the proposed agreement, but it is understood that the Syrians have made no demands likely to jeopardize the security of Israel or its borders. It is understood that the provisional terms of the agreement are entirely reasonable ones that are likely to prove acceptable to this country.

"We will be coming back to you with further information as it is made available. We hope to be able to interview government officials and political commentators in the studio this evening. The Prime Minister will be appearing on Israel Television at nine-thirty, when he will be talking with Absalom Agam about the proposed agreement. In the meantime, we are returning you to the Israel Philharmonic at the Mann Auditorium in Tel Aviv. . . ."

In the restaurant, no one spoke. The music returned, then was dimmed as the headwaiter turned the radio down again. As if at a signal, excited chatter broke out at every table. No one could quite believe it. Of all countries, Syria. David looked at Abraham Steinhardt. He raised his glass for the second time.

"I think your toast is more appropriate than ever, Abraham," he said. *"L'hayim."*

No sooner had they taken the first sips from their glasses than the soup arrived. More chicken soup with dumplings: David took a deep breath and silently asked his stomach to forgive him.

They talked through the meal, a long, comfortable affair punctuated by glasses of the dry red wine. The conversation was of digs, of the recent finds at Tell Mardikh, of mutual friends and rivals. Steinhardt for his part did not allude again to the mystery of David's sudden appearance in Jerusalem; as far as David could tell, he had completely forgotten about it. At last, brandy was brought, small glasses of calvados: they kept a bottle in the kitchen for Steinhardt's personal use. It was time to ask about Bar-Adon. David cleared his throat.

"When I was in Cambridge," he began, "I came across some books by Yigael Bar-Adon. His thing on the Moabites and the articles on the Amorites that they collected and published after his death. I thought it was very good work, but a bit incomplete. It's a tragedy he was killed before he could write more."

Steinhardt, a little maudlin with so much wine inside him and the neat brandy coming down on top of it, nodded in agreement.

"A good man, Bar-Adon. I liked him. Not a fool—I can't stand fools. A sound man, wrote well. Even in Hebrew. But then his people came to Israel in the second *aliyah*. That's a long way back."

"Did you know what he was researching before he was killed?" David pursued. "What the papers were that were stolen?"

Steinhardt looked astutely into David's eyes. The brandy had made him maudlin, but it had not dulled his mind in the least.

"It now becomes clear why David Rosen appears in Jerusalem out of season and contacts his old friend. You want information." He sighed. "I've heard about Greatbatch and the others, David. Most things pass down the grapevine. I made the connection you've made, but it hasn't helped. I still can't see a motive."

"I think it was the papers," David exclaimed.

Steinhardt nodded sagely.

"Yes, of course, that's obvious. The police are fools. I've been

74

told they think the papers are irrelevant. This wasn't the work of a lunatic: it was clean, efficient. Just like Yigael's death."

"What do you mean?"

"You don't know? No, perhaps you had no opportunity. They were all shot with a small-caliber bullet in the head. A single shot. With a silencer."

It made the link become more plausible, more certain. David became impatient. He had to know about the papers. What did Steinhardt know?

"Bar-Adon's papers. Do you know what was in them?"

The old man frowned, detecting the edge of impatience in the other's voice.

"Please," he said. "Sit still, relax. You've been under some sort of strain, I can tell. Why do you want to know about Yigael's papers so much? Why not tell the police, ask them to investigate?"

"I can't explain. I'm sorry. I'd like to, but it's not possible. It's better for you not to know."

Steinhardt frowned again. The young delighted in secrets, life was still a mystery to them. He grew irritated. There were too many secrets here in Israel. Whisper, whisper, whisper—everyone crouched down to your ear when they spoke to you. It was a national vice. "Have you heard what's really going on in Lebanon?" "Do you know the truth about the West Bank settlements?" What was Rosen's secret? Why was he so afraid?

There was a long silence. David realized he had pressed too quickly, lost his chance perhaps for good. Perhaps he should tell Steinhardt the truth after all. At last the old man spoke.

"The answer is, I don't know. Nobody knows what was in those papers. Yigael was a good man, as I said, but he kept things to himself, just like you. All I know is that they were documents connected with his most recent work. That much you seemed to guess or know. So now you want to ask again, what sort of research was that? Well, that much I can tell you. He was trying to identify the sites of a number of places referred to in ancient texts but never actually located. Mostly, he was concerned with unidentified biblical sites, like Masrekah, Enan, and Gittaim. It's better in my opinion to choose a tell, dig it, and see if you find something that helps identify the site. But he was on to something, I think. Just before he was killed, he told me he'd made an important discovery relating to the site of a place called Iram. It's not biblical. I think it's mentioned in the Qur'an: *Iram dhat al-'imad,* Iram of the lofty pillars. He didn't tell me what he'd found—as I say, he was secretive. But I could see that he was bursting to tell me. I think he had found a real lead, but what it was I can't tell you because I don't know. And if it had anything to do with his death, I'd be very surprised indeed."

"I've heard of Iram," David said. "The name, or something very like it, occurs in an Ebla text along with some others from the Qur'an: Shamutu and Ad, I think. Was there anything else he was working on? Had he visited anywhere . . . let's say sensitive? Border areas?"

"Of course, he was often in those places. He'd been in the Negev and Sinai a few months earlier, and I think he made a short trip along the Jordanian border. Nothing unusual in that."

"No, there isn't." But it was still the most likely explanation.

Steinhardt asked for more calvados, and the mood relaxed. They chatted about other matters, about books and music and life in the Goldener Medineh of America, a country Steinhardt loved, he said, for one thing only—its *bagels* and *lox.* By comparison, he said, the Israeli variety were *khaloshes,* rubbish food fit only for Sabras. He had been in America once, and nothing could persuade him to risk it again. It had been too much for his blood pressure. But the *bagels!*

They left the restaurant at midnight. David pretended he had reserved a room at the King David Hotel. Steinhardt snorted, "Rich Americans!" and shook hands. He would walk home, he said. He hated motorcars, had ever since one ran over his pet rabbit when he was a little boy. David tried to imagine Abraham Steinhardt with a pet rabbit and failed. He said good-bye, then found a cab. Giving way to exhaustion, he told the driver to head for the King David.

NINE

David woke late the next morning. His bed was comfortable, his room was warm, his head still ached from the effects of the wine and brandy of the previous evening, and the management had been considerate. His sleep had helped. The nausea of the day before had not returned, and he felt more himself again, more in control of things. He showered quickly, dressed, and ordered breakfast in his room. While he ate, he asked the hotel switchboard to connect him with Cambridge. It would add a small fortune to his bill, but it would save a lot of time.

It took a little longer to raise Halstead this time, and when he finally did come on the line he sounded tired.

"Halstead speaking."

"Hello, Professor, this is David Rosen again. I'm in Jerusalem. I traveled here yesterday to make those inquiries I mentioned."

The line crackled and Halstead's voice dipped and soared as it came to David across the miles.

"That was quick of you. And did you find anything? Or is this just a social chat at peak time?"

"It's not a social chat, sir, but I'm afraid I can't report much either. I don't think Israeli intelligence had anything to do with it. Maybe your people can do some poking about in Egypt. I did find out that before he was killed Yigael Bar-Adon had visited some of those same border areas Gates had been in. They may have stumbled across the same thing, though I can't guess what it might have been. Can't have been a military installation—they're much too well guarded, nobody gets near them."

77

"What's your next step, then? Sounds to me as if you're up against a wall. Leave it to the police, shall we?"

"No, I think I may be able to turn something up. Listen, can you discover exactly where Gates went on his last field trip? Would that be on record anywhere?"

There was a long pause, punctuated only by faint hissing sounds. Then Halstead came on again.

"No, I'm afraid not. There might have been something in poor old Michael's supervision file on Gates, but that was one of the things taken, you know. There's just a chance the postgraduate grants committee might have a note: they provided some funding toward the trip and probably asked for a report."

"Fine, let me know if they come up with anything. Or perhaps some of Gates's friends will have a rough idea of the places he went. The only other thing that might help would be details of Gates's research. I don't mean his overall topic, but have you any idea what he was working on during that last trip?"

Halstead paused again, then spoke.

"Not precisely, no. I only spoke to him once or twice last term. He was extremely busy when he got back from his trip at the end of May. He finished the thesis sooner than we expected, you know. I remember Michael saying something about his working like a slave to put in his new material and get the bound copies off to the Board of Graduate Studies. But I don't recall anyone saying what the new stuff was."

There was yet another pause, then the languid voice came back on the line again.

"Wait a minute, though. I am a bit of a fool. I've just remembered, there was a start-of-term party for the new undergrads, and Michael was there. I remember now he said Gates's thesis had gone off to the examiners and that he was extremely confident the young man would have his doctorate. Something about a chapter on an Arab city, I can't quite get the name, but he said it would set people by the ears. Hot stuff, he said. Make the boy's career. Can't think why I didn't remember before this. Just a tick, I think I've got it. Irash . . . the place was called Irash. No, it wasn't, I'm thinking of that other place, what's it called now, Jerash. Ah, it's come back to me now. Iram. Iram of the Pillars, Michael called it. Ever heard of it?"

David was conscious of his heart beating loudly as he answered in a calm voice, "Yes, Professor, I've heard of it."

"Think it'll be of any help?"

"I don't suppose so. It doesn't make much sense."

"What, Iram? No, made no sense to me either. Never heard of it myself, not till Michael told me. I'll try to remember that conversation, see if I can recall anything else. Don't think we talked about Gates for very long, though. Probably not."

David sighed inaudibly. It didn't much matter, he thought. Whatever it was, Iram was the link. His problem now was to find the connection to himself. Was it that obscure reference to the place in the Eblaite text he had seen once? It had been a name, just a name, among other long-forgotten names. No one even knew where Iram was. It was nothing to kill for.

"Thanks, Professor Halstead," David said. "You've been a tremendous help. I'll see if I can dig up something more here in Jerusalem."

"Not literally, I hope. Too many of us archaeologists there as it is. Place is falling down. Look after yourself and let me know when to expect you. We can have dinner some evening in my college. There are some interesting old birds at high table and we can have a long chat afterward. Away from the wife. Best thing. She was awfully upset by everything, still is. Anyway, mustn't keep you talking. Just a second, though. Did you get the package I sent?"

"Package?" David responded, puzzled. "No, I haven't gotten any package."

"Oh dear. It should have reached you by now. I sent it special delivery on Monday. Well, of course, you've been in Jerusalem, haven't you? I posted it to your Haifa address. It's probably waiting there for you now."

"What is it?" David asked.

"Ah, nothing to get excited about. It's a bit of a puzzle, really. Gates sent it to you originally not long after you left for Syria. It had his name on it and the postmark. Anyway, looks as if the post office people in Damascus can't read or something, because it came back a while ago marked 'address unknown.' Well, that was nonsense. Probably too much trouble to have it carted out to you out of season. It was a bit battered when it got back, so the secretary repacked it ready to send back again, but I told her we'd best hang on to it till you got back. Then I got your telegram with your Haifa address. I thought you'd better see it while you're out there in case you need to take a look at anything, so I sent it Monday morning as I said. It went express. With any luck, it'll be waiting for you when you get back."

"What was in it, do you know?"

"Not sure. The girl said it held about one hundred typed pages. At a guess, it was a couple of chapters from his thesis."

David was silent.

"Yes," he said at last, "it may have been. Before I left, he said he'd send some of it on to me. He wanted my opinion on some things relating to Eblaite texts. Probably gave up when I didn't reply. I'd forgotten about it."

"Funny he didn't mention the Iram business to you."

"Yes, I suppose so." He paused. "No, on second thoughts, not really. I think Greatbatch was being a trifle indiscreet when he told you about it. Gates was tight-lipped. I remember now—he swore me to secrecy when I agreed to look at the chapters he planned to send. But he wouldn't tell me a word about what I'd find in them."

And then it hit him, like a solid blow in the pit of his stomach, so hard that he stood stunned, speechless, hearing not a word of Halstead's response. It wasn't possible . . . but if it was, there was a terrible danger. He had to leave, he had to get to Haifa immediately. There wasn't a moment to spare.

"Professor," he said, hoping his voice sounded calm, though he knew it couldn't possibly be so, "something has just come up here. I'm afraid I'll have to hang up now, but I'll be in touch again as soon as I have more to report. I'll be back in Haifa if you want to contact me."

"Oh! Very good. I'll hear from you then. Thanks for ringing."

The connection was broken, and again David heard a sound like branches rubbing against telephone wires. Except that international lines go under-, not over-ground. He replaced the receiver, lifted it again at once, and asked for Reception.

"Reception. Can I help you?"

"This is Professor Rosen, Room 529. I have to leave immediately. Have my bill ready in five minutes. And I want to hire a car, a fast car. It's extremely urgent; I want it waiting for me once I've paid my bill. I'll sign the forms when I come down."

He packed his small case, retrieved his key from the bedside table, and ran out into the corridor, crashing into the laden arms of a passing chambermaid. Sheets and towels swooped in a white torrent to the floor. He muttered apologies, turned, and headed at full speed for the lift.

If he was right—and he prayed he was not—the man at Tell Mardikh had been after Gates's parcel. Gates may have left a note somewhere indicating that he had sent some parts of his thesis to David in Syria. It was not impossible that Halstead's phone had been tapped. And if that was the case, there might, just might, be someone already on his way to Haifa to retrieve the parcel from his parents' apartment.

Reception was quick. It was more than five minutes but less than ten. He signed for the car, paid by American Express, and rushed out of the hotel, key in hand. The car, a 1986 Volvo, was waiting for him outside. BAT, the car-hire firm, was less than a minute's drive away, in Shelomzion Ha-Malka. He accelerated out of the forecourt, turned sharp right, then right again. Within minutes he was speeding north on the Derekh Shekhem highway. He could have gone west to Petah Tikva and joined the motorway, but this was the road he knew best and he decided to stick to it.

He took risks all the way. Israeli highways are dangerous, but David took none of the precautions he would normally have taken. Sometimes the road seemed to slip away from his wheels as it took him up to Ramallah. To his left, the country fell away toward the sea, to his right, buff hills marched down toward the rugged expanse of the Jordan Valley. His greatest fear as he passed through the small Arab settlements of the West Bank was that he might hit a child. Almost any other kind of accident would mean trouble, but to hurt or kill a child could prove fatal for the driver of the car involved. There would be angry crowds who might beat him to death. Whenever he saw anything like human habitation ahead, he pumped the horn and kept a foot hovering near the brake. His tires threw up small stones in a constant patter as the road hurled itself down and past him. Three times he had to stop for military checks, but none kept him for more than a few minutes. Nablus was packed, the faces of the people hostile as he drove through. Shops were already closing for Thursday evening, the beginning of the Muslim Sabbath. Snatches of oriental music came to him and faded as quickly away, donkeys laden with heavy panniers strayed across his path, Israeli soldiers, their eyes tense and watchful, patrolled the streets uneasily.

The last stretch, from Jenin down to Haifa along the edge of the Plain of Yisreel, was the fastest and easiest part of the journey. He passed Megiddo: it filled him with a sense of foreboding. Mount Carmel appeared on his left, its long slopes blocking him from the sea a few miles away.

At its northern end, Carmel issues in a blunt promontory jutting into the Mediterranean like an elbow. Entering Haifa from the southeast, David climbed rapidly onto the wooded slopes of the mountain. Around him, the emptiness of Carmel's outer flanks gave way to the ever growing suburbs of the city—apartment blocks, shops, and schools set among rock and tenacious mountain trees. He raced through Kiryat Hatechnion, the sprawling modern campus of the Technological Institute, down Hankin into Moria Boulevard and Central Carmel. Vradim Street, where his parents lived, was only minutes away now.

As he came into Lotus Street from Tzafririm, his vision was blocked for a moment and he almost missed the dark blue Mercedes traveling at speed straight toward him. It seemed to take minutes, but it was actually seconds: the squeal of brakes as both drivers slammed their feet to the floor and turned their wheels frantically, the smoke rising from overheated tires, the rush of adrenaline crashing into his body, the sheer unbelief on the other driver's face and on that of his passenger, an Oriental-looking man, then the thudding halt as the car stopped halfway up the pavement. It had been a matter of millimeters. His heart pounding, he sat hunched over the wheel, pumping air into his lungs slowly in an attempt to calm himself. He should get out, he thought, and check on the other driver. Then he heard the sound of an engine being started. It was the Mercedes turning back into the road and driving off. He slumped at the wheel again—Israeli drivers might have the cool to handle such a situation every day, but he would need a nerve transplant first.

The explosion came less than half a minute later. It was earsplitting, a dull thudding sound that seemed to rock the car. Passersby, about to check that David was unhurt, turned in their tracks and looked about, frightened. A terrorist attack? Or the beginnings of another Arab onslaught? David glanced up. In front of him and slightly to his left, a plume of smoke had started to rise over the low rooftops. His heart tripped and his hand reached automatically for the ignition key. With a roar that tore at the car's insides, he gunned the Volvo out into the road again and kept his foot down the rest of the way to Vradim.

The road was littered with debris. People stood shouting and screaming, some in pain, some in panic. Smoke and flames belched in an ugly stream from the remains of his parents' apartment house. The third floor had been blown out by the bomb, the fourth and fifth floors collapsing on top of it, the two lower floors sagging beneath their combined weight. Girders stuck into the air at crazy angles, thin metal reinforcing rods poked out of slabs of split concrete. His parents' apartment had taken up the front portion of the third story. In the garden, a tree had caught fire and was burning convulsively, like a torch.

He slammed to a halt and threw open the car door, half jumping, half falling into the road. Not even aware that he was shouting their names, he ran toward the building in search of his mother and father. All around him, others were doing the same, desperately trying to locate and rescue the survivors, if there were any. Flames kept them back, angry red flames that leaped out of fissures and broken windows, struggling to be free. Had his parents been indoors when the bomb exploded? He turned to an old woman beside him. She wore a dressing gown and her thin gray hair streamed out around her face in coils, like the Medusa. Her eyes were wild with fear and loathing, her mouth toothless and sunken. Cold, bloodless lips moved like those of someone at prayer, mouthing over and over some private litany of desolation. David grasped her by the shoulder, speaking loudly in her ear over the din of the fire and the onlookers.

"The Rosens from the third floor! Have you seen them? Hannah and Aaron Rosen. They lived upstairs."

She looked at him blankly, struggling for words, tears streaming uninterruptedly down her cheeks, like rain on a windowpane. Her face was lined and creased with sorrows of a dark past, but the anguish of the present wove her wrinkles freshly into a network of pain. When she spoke, it was in a mixture of Hebrew, Yiddish, and German, the words mumbled, inarticulate. He could understand only a little.

"Mitzi," she cried, "have you seen Mitzi anywhere? She was with me when . . . It's started again . . . the bombs . . . all that darkness. There's no time, no time. . . . What are you waiting for? Leave. Leave while it's safe. . . . We should have gone fifty years ago. . . . Can you see Mitzi? She must be here. They wouldn't hurt Mitzi. . . . Are they still here? Have they gone? Did they take Mitzi?"

David held her firmly by her arms, thin, weightless arms, like sticks, so fragile he felt he could break them without even trying. He tried to stop the ceaseless shifting of her eyes, to hold her gaze long enough to make her understand.

"The Rosens," he repeated. "They lived on the third floor. He's a rabbi. Elderly people. Did you know them?"

The panic still had hold of her, panic and memories. The dark days in Germany had become entangled in her mind with today's bombing, like an old wound reopened by a fresh blow of the knife. For the second time in her life she had lost everything: her home, her possessions, her dog. The rest had gone long ago—husband, children, friends. There had been nothing else. And now there was nothing at all. She looked at David with crazed eyes, as if seeing him for the first time.

"The Rosens are dead," she intoned in a flat voice. "Everybody's dead. They never forget. They're here, even in Eretz Israel. . . . There's nowhere to go, nowhere to run. . . . I heard them, I know."

"What did you hear?" David asked, pressing her, urging sanity on her. "Who are you talking about?"

Her eyes grew calmer for a moment. She put a bony hand on his, pulling him to her, her face close to his, her breath stale in his nostrils.

"There were two men," she whispered. "One was yellow, like a Chinaman. The other was from the old country. They came in a blue car. The yellow one went into the building carrying a box, a case of some kind. Then he came running out again and they drove off. I knew when I heard them. I knew there was danger. . . ."

"What did you hear?" David insisted. He wanted to shake her, as if he could make sanity tumble out of her like salt from a box.

She looked at him again, but he had lost her; her eyes had grown wild again. Her grip tightened.

84

"Have you seen Mitzi?" she asked, like a little girl who has lost her favorite doll and cannot believe it was crushed by a truck. Suddenly her grip loosened and she turned away from him to stagger off among the crowd. Her voice came to him out of the uproar, like a voice from hell.

"Mitzi! I'm here, Mitzi, don't be frightened."

David was frightened. Could she have had a reason for saying his parents were dead? All around him there was madness. Men and women shouted and screamed in a chaos of fear and bewilderment. From somewhere inside the building he could hear a woman's voice crying desperately for help. He ran forward, trying to enter the house. If there were still stairs, perhaps he could make it to the third floor, perhaps he could find his parents if they were still there. They might have survived, it might be his mother's voice he could hear imploring assistance. Faintly, behind him, he could hear the sound of sirens drawing near, like fresh demons rushing to the inferno.

He dashed through the bent and broken doorway that led into the building's central passageway. Someone shouted behind him, but he could not make out the words. As if deaf, he pushed on. Through a cloud of smoke he could make out the stairs, choked with rubble and twisted. Gasping for breath, he ran to them and started to climb, covering his mouth with part of his shirt. A wave of intense heat hit him from somewhere. Above him, red and yellow flames danced obscenely in darkness. There was a roaring sound mixed with the crash of falling stones and timber. The acrid smoke grew heavier and denser as he climbed higher, forcing him to his knees, filling his throat and lungs with foul, unbreathable gases. A spasm of coughing wracked his chest. His eyes blurred and his head swam. He was like a man in deep water, drowning. He sank into the fumes, the air crushed from his body by the weight of them. A voice called in the distance, light-years away, remote and abstract. He was carried away on the tide of smoke, submersed in the thick, swirling whirlpool, taken down without sight or touch or hearing into its black, inescapable depths.

TEN

It was Friday afternoon, about two hours before sunset. David Rosen was being questioned by the inspector in charge of the bomb investigations at the Central Carmel Police Station on Elchanan Street. He had been there since late morning, explaining how he had come to be in Haifa, why he had come back from Jerusalem when he did. His story was that he had come from Syria via Cyprus (as his MOSSAD-doctored passport now showed) on hearing of his father's illness (which the hospital would confirm). He had gone to Jerusalem at short notice to see Professor Steinhardt on an urgent matter relating to his work and had hurried back to Haifa on hearing from him about the tragedy in Cambridge. It was obvious to him that a little diligent checking would disconfirm much of his account, but he hoped to be out of Haifa and possibly out of Israel by then.

He had spent the previous night at the home of friends of his parents, people called Kolek. He had not slept. The smoke had not had time to damage him before he was pulled out, but he still had a throbbing headache and his chest felt tight and painful. The doctor had recommended that he spend at least one day in bed, but that had been out of the question.

The early morning had been harrowing. During the night, after the fire had been extinguished, the rescue services had retrieved several bodies from the rubble, including two from what remained of his parents' apartment. The remains had been too badly charred for any hope of direct identification, and he was not asked to view them. There had, however, been some items found with the bodies that he was asked to examine: a gold wedding ring and a silver *Magen David* on a short chain. He recognized the ring, damaged though it was, as his mother's because of the thin wavy line chased along its upper edge. It had been made in Jerusalem from the gold of rings found in the camp she and his father had been held in. It had been a symbol: of rebirth, of hope, of trust. Now it lay blackened and twisted in a small tin tray, as if it had returned to its original state.

The Star of David caused him to turn away in acute pain. In all the days and nights that were to follow, it was the image of that small, partly melted pendant that was to return again and again to his mind's eye. He had given it to his father as a birthday present when he was about fourteen: he had saved for about two months to gather together enough money. That was the first time his father had really hurt him, refusing to wear the pendant.

"A Jew does not wear *kemi'ot,*" his father had said, treating the Star as a talisman. "They are relics of paganism. My son should know better."

David had carried the pain of that rebuff with him for years afterward. And all the time he had assumed that his father had thrown the amulet away. Now he understood something that had always eluded him before: that his father, in his reverence for the law and the joy he had in it, had crushed and denatured his own deepest loves and yearnings.

David had identified the ring and the star and signed to take them away.

"Professor Rosen," the inspector said, his voice bringing David out of the reverie into which he had fallen.

"I'm sorry," David said. "I was thinking."

"That's all right. I understand." The inspector's name was Ilan Gaon. He was about thirty, bearded, and intelligent. He had been sympathetic and kind, though David did not think he believed very much of his story.

"I just wanted to ask if you were planning to stay in Haifa," he said.

David shook his head.

"For the funeral, yes, of course. But after that . . . I have some other funerals to attend, in England."

"Ah." There was a pause. Gaon clasped and then unclasped his long, delicate fingers. A musician's fingers, David thought.

"I would prefer it," he went on, stressing the verb, "if you could find a way to stay here a little longer, Professor. At least during the course of the investigation, if that's possible."

"But why? I can't help you any further. You know I would if I were able, but I've told you everything I know."

Gaon shook his head.

"No, Professor, I don't think you have. I don't know why, but I mean to find out. Oh, I think much of what you tell me is the truth. But I don't think it's the whole truth. You know more than you're saying."

"I assure you . . ."

"No, let's not waste time like this. You met Professor Steinhardt the night before last, after a phone call made in Jerusalem. You arrived at the King David Hotel late that night without a reservation. You left yesterday morning with five minutes' notice, hired a car, and drove to Haifa at what I can only imagine was a speed well in excess of the 90-kph limit. The receptionist we spoke to says you were in a distracted state and described your need for a car as 'urgent.' You arrived here mere minutes before the bomb exploded. We're reasonably certain the bomb was actually planted in or near your parents' apartment. And you expect me to believe you know nothing about what happened? If anyone knows, Professor, you do."

David felt torn. He wanted his parents' killers found and arrested and, if possible, through them the killers of Greatbatch and the others. But he had to act alone. Since Tell Mardikh, it had become his personal struggle, as personal as that in which he had engaged in the frozen mud of the dig. Now, by killing his father and mother, they had struck a blow at him more direct even than that. He would let the police carry out their investigations, but he had his own methods and would use them on his own. He would find Iram, or whatever it was about Iram that John Gates had discovered, and he would let it lead him to the killers. That was as far as his thoughts went. He would decide where to go from there once he had found them. It was like writing an article or a monograph: you took care of the research and the basic structure and the conclusion usually took care of themselves.

Gaon continued in a low but implacable voice. The sympathy

was still there, and the kindness, but David could detect a hardness that it would not be easy to defy.

"I don't want to keep you any longer, Professor. You've been through quite a lot, and I think you should have some time to yourself to chew things over. I advise you to think very, very carefully. Stay in Haifa. If I have any reason to think you won't obey that advice, I'll have to issue an official order. Please don't make that necessary. I'll see you out."

Gaon rose, pushing his heavy chair back with a rough scraping sound. It grated in David's ears, like fingernails traversing a blackboard. He shivered and stood as well. The inspector took him through the station to the entrance hall, shook hands with a solemnity David had not observed before in a Sabra, and turned on his heel.

David still had the car, but he preferred to walk. If he drove, where would he go? What would he do? He needed time to be alone and think, as Gaon had said. He had to organize his still jumbled thoughts and plan his next course of action. The sky was clear, and there was still an hour or two of daylight: he would walk and let the streets determine which way he went.

In the event, it was not quite that simple. Haifa is not a city designed for thoughtful strolls: its streets wind and twist about, clinging to the sometimes precipitous slopes of the mountain, negotiating the sheer drops and sudden inclines that give the town its drama and its character, and that cause its inhabitants enough headaches to make the marvelous views less than exciting for them. There are almost as many stairways as there are streets, short cuts like those in Montmartre, that descend hundreds of feet in a single flight. The agony of Haifa is that the same steps that take you down so quickly also serve to bring you up again . . . slowly.

From Yafe Nof, David made his way gradually down the hill. About midway, he came to the ornamented gate that leads to the Persian gardens set about the holy buildings belonging to the Baha'i sect. The gardens are open to the public, and David had been in them many times.

A path of dusty red gravel took him down through palms and dark cypresses into the heart of the gardens. Between low hedges of thyme, flower-filled Chinese vases stood on tall pedestals of stone; peacocks and eagles of iron gazed with unseeing eyes into the green shadows. He passed through a low gate and walked down another pathway shaded by tall trees until he reached the marble shrine that lay at the center of the miniature paradise. The shrine itself, burial place of the martyr-prophet of the religion, was a strange building. At its heart stood a square stone construction of nine rooms. Above this, like an iced wedding cake, rose a later marble superstructure, gilded and balustraded and topped by an elegant dome of gold-plated tiles. In the sharp afternoon sun the dome seemed to vibrate, jeweled and incandescent. But the marble was icy cold to his touch.

Today the door of the shrine was locked, but he passed around to the north side where the building faced out over the mountain, looking across the bay to Acre. At his feet a steep flight of steps flanked by tall cypresses led down to Carmel Boulevard and the sea. Here, high above the city, all was silence, a green and fragile peace filled with light and deep, crisscrossing shadows. Far below, the sea shook in a million broken pieces, forming, reforming, remote and beckoning. Behind, to his left, the sun began its descent toward the Mediterranean. The golden dome seemed to catch fire. In the port, lights began to flicker, and across the bay the rays of the sinking sun fell on the walls of the white buildings, painting them red. Tell Mardikh, its dark stones, its ruined gateways, and its deep sunken wells, seemed an age and a world away. The explosion and the screams were taken from him and swallowed up by the long, vast silence. He closed his eyes and breathed in the dizzying scent of the gardens. When he opened them again, tears like undissipated memories blurred his vision. They were the first he had shed since his parents' deaths.

When his eyes cleared, he looked out across the bay at the white walls of Acre. In the sunshine the little city was beautiful. It looked so white and perfect and mysterious, a tiny world hidden beyond the short stretch of blue water. He remembered how it often looked at sunset: as if it was full of fire. A city on fire, like a bush, burning yet unconsumed. But inside it was a maze with gray walls and filthy little streets filled with an ancient stench.

The sun was a dull winter red now, turning the world to copper as it flowed across the western flanks of Carmel and began to redden the sea. David stood lost in thought beneath the arcade of the shrine until the pearl-shaped yellow hanging lamps came on and the lights in the gardens flickered into life, casting strange shadows among the trees and bushes. The gardens were beautiful, but there was something about them that he disliked. They were too formal, too well cared for, too oriental. It was as if anything wild had to be cut out. Order became everything. Keeping things tidy grew to be an end in itself. Was that what someone had been trying to do in Cambridge and Haifa? To keep something tidy?

The sky was growing purple. Stars had appeared, so slowly, so uncertainly at first that their coming had gone unnoticed until now they seemed to stream across the heavens. He walked down the first flight of steps, then vaulted the little gate to the main descent all the way through the terraces to Carmel Boulevard. He moved slowly, his feet heavy on the stone, a step at a time. Behind him, the mausoleum sprang into life, illuminated by spotlights like a tall white ghost, its dome invisible from where he stood. Beneath him, the green and white lights of Haifa sparkled like jewels. The long straight bay stretched like a necklace all the way to Acre at the other side.

He stood halfway down the steps, feeling tiny and alone again, uncertain what to do or where to go when he reached the bottom. As if alerted by a sixth sense, he turned round and looked up the steps in the direction of the shrine. Someone stood silhouetted against the white backdrop of the edifice, a shadow watching him. David felt fear rise within him like the taste of sour vomit. The watcher did not move: he simply stood there gazing down at David, his face invisible in the darkness. It was then that David decided what he would do. He turned his back on the man above and started down the steps again, slowly, ever so slowly. If the stranger knew what he was doing, he would shoot him now: David wasn't going to give him another chance.

ELEVEN

They brought the coffins down early the next morning, all the way from the synagogue to the cemetery, lower down the mountain. The coffins were long and rectangular, draped in the Israeli flag, gaudy almost, blue and white, the *Magen David* on top. David watched them come down through the wrought-iron gates, through the trees, the long procession, men in dark suits and *tallits,* the coffins on their shoulders. His brothers Benjamin and Samuel were among them, his young brothers whom he had helped to raise, whom he scarcely knew now, strangers with the weight of his father's coffin on their shoulders. His sister Sara was beside him, big-eyed, awkward, her dress still torn in mourning. He wanted to put his arm around her, hold her, give support, but his body felt rigid, he could only stand and watch as the men made their way toward the open grave.

When the coffins had been lowered into the grave, the *hazzan* began to chant in Hebrew, the *Tziduk ha-Din,* plaintive, the words rising and falling like swallows in flight, lifting and dropping again. Men and women, strangers to David, stood all about him, their faces impassive or stained with grief. The grave was deep and ugly, like a wound in the earth, an emptiness no amount of rock or soil could ever fill.

He wondered why he felt nothing, no grief, no pain, not even guilt. The absence of guilt surprised and dismayed him most of all. He had expected to feel it, like something eating him from within, yet there was nothing there. Unwittingly, but just as surely as if he had known, he had brought about his parents' deaths. A little thought, a little foresight on his part, and they would still be alive. His father had had a right to one last year, time in which to make his peace. Perhaps even with David. Why, then, could he feel nothing?

Sara, beside him, was distraught; she might never recover from her grief. Benjamin had broken down the night before. Samuel had spent several hours since his arrival praying. He, David, seemed to be alone in his numbness.

It was time to recite the *Kaddish*. The eldest son, he stepped forward to the graveside and began to read the prayer out loud in Aramaic, his voice scarcely rising above a whisper.

"Magnified and sanctified be the Name of God . . ."

He seemed to follow the words down into the grave, a great, unending depth, descending and descending forever. The Kaddish was for him, for the death inside him, for the funeral that was taking place this very moment in his heart. And he went on down, deeper and deeper into the grave.

"Magnified"

It was as if all that had been most alive in him was being buried here. His mouth spoke the words of the prayer, and the other mourners recited it with him, praising their God, but he seemed to be elsewhere, disembodied, remote. The prayer shawl hung like a massive weight on his head. His hands held the prayer book as if it was a stone. The words of the prayer seemed to go round and round, never changing.

"Sanctified"

Somehow the short prayer ended, somehow he bent and found earth and cast it into the grave. As he straightened up, David's eye caught sight of something moving just beyond the graves, in the trees that bordered the cemetery. It was a man, watching from a distance, his face hidden in the shadows. Even as David looked, the man slipped away into the trees and was gone. He looked down again into the grave, at the coffins disappearing beneath the earth, then abruptly turned and walked away. His brothers and sister watched him uncomprehendingly as he strode off down the path, taking the *tallit* from his head and shoulders, alone.

*　　　*　　　*

Several days after the funeral a letter arrived from Halstead. Accompanying it was a postcard found a few days earlier among Michael Greatbatch's papers. Posted the previous spring from Jerusalem and signed "John," he consisted of a brief itinerary of several places in Sinai he had received official permission to visit:

Dear Mike:

You'll be pleased to hear your letters did the trick. They've given me a general permit and fixed up special visits to Pelusium, Ostracine, Rhinocolorum, Raphia, El-Kuntilla, Ein Kadeirat, Serabit al-Khadim, and Dahab. I'm particularly excited about seeing the Proto-Sinaitic inscriptions at Serabit, not to mention the Temple of Hathor. I've also got your letters of introduction to St. Catherine's and St. Nilus' in Wadi al-Ruhban. I don't know how long the monks will let me stay in either place, but I hope to get time to look over one or two manuscripts—they may have what I'm looking for. See you in a couple of months. Visit Waffles for me; give Patrick my regards.

Yours,
John

Waffles was a well-known Cambridge cafe run by a Canadian couple. David remembered its spiced apple waffles, its crème chantilly, and its eccentric white-haired owner Patrick. That was another world now. Reality was here and at some place called Iram.

He telegraphed Halstead immediately, asking him to obtain official clearance with his contacts in Cairo for David to visit Sinai. The Israeli withdrawal from the peninsula had gone ahead almost without a hitch, and cross-border traffic was not particularly problematic; but David knew the Middle East and wanted leverage in case someone in Cairo had reason to object to his proposed journey.

He also asked Halstead to send him photographs of Gates and a general description to supplement his own memory of the man. There was no question of his using the telephone now: he was convinced that Halstead's line was tapped and had already written to tell him so.

Nor did he imagine he was free from surveillance himself. From time to time since the day in the Persian gardens he had caught glimpses of a man—or possibly different men—tailing him. There had been the mysterious figure at the funeral. David knew they were waiting for his next move, to see if he would reveal whether he knew anything, to observe where he went and whom he met. He could not head for Sinai directly, not without leaving his tracks wide open and leading them straight to whatever it was Gates had found there. It would be better if they thought he knew nothing and had gone back to his studies, chastened and frightened but no wiser. They would be mistaken if they thought that, and he would be a step ahead of them for once.

His parents' deaths had changed him, turned him finally into the killer he had become momentarily on Tell Mardikh. All the softness had been burned out of him, all the weakness and the fine gestures of cloistered academia. As he watched his mother and father being buried, he had gone down into the grave with them. He had realized that he was alone against something remorseless and uncaring. If he was to survive, he had to enter the horror within himself and master it. With the help of a friend at the Haifa Technion, he had obtained a gun, a black Sauer automatic that he carried with him everywhere, loaded at all times.

He planned his departure from Haifa carefully and well in advance. On the morning of December 12 he drove to the local office of El Al airlines on Derekh Ha'atzma'ut, where he collected a one-way ticket from Tel Aviv to Rome. He drove straight back to the Kolek apartment and disappeared inside. Fifteen minutes later he reappeared, carrying two suitcases, got into the car, and drove off. Except that it wasn't David who came out but Danny Bernstein, the friend who had found him the gun. Bernstein was approximately David's height, build, and color, and in David's clothes could pass for him at a distance. The ticket to Rome carried Bernstein's name and was now in his pocket: he would take a short break there, speak with David's colleagues at the university, and return to Haifa at the end of the week. He knew nothing of what was going on, except that someone had killed David's parents and that David planned to do something about it. That was enough. About thirty seconds after Danny moved off a second car slipped softly away from the curb and headed after him.

David paused only long enough to say good-bye to the Koleks

before leaving by the fire escape at the back of the building. Outside, a Jeep was waiting, already packed with equipment Danny had purchased for David's trip into Sinai. In just over an hour he was entering the Egyptian Embassy in the Hilton Hotel in Tel Aviv. Halstead must have had high-powered contacts in Cairo: it took less than two hours to arrange the visas and permits he would need for his journey. Ordinarily it could have taken days.

By midafternoon he was in Jerusalem, knocking at the gate of the Greek Orthodox Patriarchate on the Via Dolorosa in the western quarter of the Old City. Halstead's mysterious powers extended even past those austere walls. David was ushered in to smiling faces and small glasses of fine brandy. Men in black robes and tall circular hats hovered about him and spoke in earnest tones of the pleasures of scholarship. Greek letters of introduction to Father Nikandros, Archimandrite of St. Catherine's, and Father Andreas of St. Nilus' were ready for him. The Patriarch at Jerusalem had no direct authority over St. Catherine's or its dependency, but his letters would serve to have David admitted to both houses, something as difficult in the days of mass tourism as it had been in the times of unrestricted banditry.

He slept that night in the Panorama Hotel on the Hill of Gethsemane, just outside the eastern walls. Before retiring, he stood on his balcony and looked out over the Old City at his feet. It was quiet now, bracing its ancient stones for the shuffling crowds of pilgrims who would arrive, en route for Bethlehem, in a couple of weeks. Lights shimmered in the silence. He could see the Golden Gate and the Dome of the Rock rising behind it. The spires and domes of churches and the slender minarets of mosques were just visible in the labile darkness. He breathed the cold air into his lungs, smelling the city, filling himself with it. He gripped the balustrade tightly, shivering momentarily in the cold. Below him lay the Wailing Wall, the western wall of Herod's Temple, the magnet that had drawn his father to this place. He would pray there soon, when he had completed the task he had set himself. Whatever lay ahead of him in Sinai or elsewhere, he felt free tonight and secure from prying eyes.

He had not seen the second man watching him leave from the rear of the Kolek apartment or the car that had slipped into the traffic behind him as he headed into the coast road toward Tel Aviv.

TWO

The same day came they into the wilderness of Sinai.

Exodus 19:1

TWELVE

The journey from Jerusalem began badly. Several days before leaving Haifa, David had asked Abraham Steinhardt to find him an Arabic-speaking guide at the Hebrew University, someone who knew Sinai and its people well. Once in Jerusalem, he had contacted the old scholar by telephone. After mutters and mumbles and much deliberate vagueness, Steinhardt had told him his guide would be waiting for him in the hotel foyer at eight o'clock the following morning

"How will I know him?" David had asked.

"You wont need to. I've supplied a full description of you; you'll be recognized. Be in the lobby at eight, these guides don't wait about."

So David went down as instructed in the morning, just before eight o'clock. The lobby was almost deserted and he could see no guide anywhere. Shrugging, he turned to the desk to ask for a newspaper. There was a movement behind him, then a voice spoke his name. It was a woman's voice, speaking softly in English.

He turned to find himself face to face with a small, dark-haired girl of about twenty-five. She was slender, elflike, and unbelievably pretty. His heart did a flip, lay down, and gasped for breath. He knew Steinhardt well enough to recognize that something was up. It was horribly likely that this was his guide. He asked and she said she was.

"My name's Leyla Rashid," she said. "Professor Steinhardt said you needed an Arab guide to Sinai. He didn't say what for." She looked him up and down, then smiled. The way she smiled, it was hard to believe he had woken up that morning at all. "Not for tourism, I think," she said in the same seductively soft tones.

He scrutinized her in return. It would have been hard not to. He couldn't believe what the old fox Steinhardt had done; he had asked for an experienced Arabic-speaking guide to take him through some of the most difficult and dangerous terrain in the entire region, and the man had sent him a slip of a girl dressed in clothes that had been designed to be worn in the Faubourg St. Honoré—and probably had been bought there.

"I'm sorry," he began, "there must be some mistake. I plan to go into some very tough country. I won't be staying at hotels. It may be dangerous, there may even be some trouble. I need someone who knows the peninsula inside and out, not—if you'll forgive me—one of Steinhardt's coeds taking a vacation break. Besides, I plan to go places a woman wouldn't be welcome, where she might even be in danger. I'm sorry, Miss . . . Rashid, but my trip is very important and I don't have much time. If it was a dinner date, believe me, I'd take you anywhere. Perhaps when I get back . . ."

She gave him what could only be described as a withering glance.

"Don't patronize me, Professor Rosen," she said. Her voice was no longer soft or seductive. "I'm not a coed and I'm not an amateur. I do this for a living. For the record, I'm twenty-six years old, I'm an anthropologist with the Hebrew University, and I supplement my paltry income there by taking people like you for trips into Sinai. I'm Palestinian: my parents owned land near Haifa. They left by sea in 1948, when the Haganah's Carmeli Brigade moved in. They landed at Port Said and were moved within the week to al-Arish in the north of Sinai. They've been there ever since, doing business with the Sherafa merchants there, trading with the Bedouin as far as the south. Since I was a child I've traveled with my father evrywhere in Sinai, even into al-Tih by camel. I know the tribes like family—Tarabin, Muzeina, Tuwara, Aleigat, Tiyaha—I have friends among them all. I would be in much less danger there than you, Professor. I can assure you of that. You wouldn't have to look out for me. I'd be looking after you."

He felt his color rise.

"I'm sorry, Miss Rashid. I . . . I didn't understand. You . . . you don't look like a Palestinian."

He knew he had said the wrong thing as soon as the words left his lips. Somehow, he was glad they weren't on the top floor of the hotel: it was a long way down from there. The glint in her eyes became a glare. Her voice was even harder when she spoke again.

"Just what do you think a Palestinian woman should look like, Mr. American Professor? Yassir Arafat in drag? Or a refugee, like the ones you've seen in the camps, poor but proud? I'm sorry to disappoint your preconceptions. We wash our faces, we put on makeup, we go to hairdressers, we like pretty clothes. Would you prefer me to put on army fatigues? Or a veil? If you don't want me as your guide, that's okay with me. I'm not offering my services as a favor, you aren't under any obligation. This is business, Professor Rosen: take it or leave it."

He wondered if she was this touchy with everyone or whether he had been unusually maladroit. What could he do? He had to leave that day and he had to have a guide. Perhaps he could leave her with her parents in al-Arish and find someone else there.

"All right," he said. "I apologize. You'll do. I have bags to collect upstairs. You'll find my jeep in the parking lot out front. Here's the key."

She took it in silence, turned without another word, and went out.

They drove south out of Jerusalem, taking the road through Bethlehem and Hebron. The West Bank was tense. There had been riots in Hebron a few days earlier, two Arab students had been killed by Israeli soldiers, the mood of the people was ugly. They drove in silence, David at the wheel, the girl beside him, impassive, her eyes fixed on the road ahead. The squat gray houses of Hebron passed, crowded and forlorn. Outside the town they drove past rows of tumbling shanties, a refugee camp built under the old Jordanian administration. The sight of the sprawling slum did nothing to ease the tension between David and the girl. He put his foot down hard and drove on. Somewhere behind them a child shouted, a thin, anxious cry that shank rapidly and was swallowed up in the roar of the jeep's engine.

The road continued south, out of the West Bank and on toward Beersheba and the Negev. Cultivated fields gave way to scruffy sand and shrub as the desert took control. Every now and then they passed a family of Bedouin huddled beneath a thin tent away from the wind, their camels and scrawny black goats watched by a child not far off. Farther south they came to Nizana, the former frontier post between Palestine and Sinai. Barbed wire lay in rusty coils along the old border. The customs depot and the police station stood empty, slowly crumbling back into the desert sand; geckos and small green lizards scuttled in and out of the vacant doorways, pausing only briefly to watch the jeep rush past them and away.

The Egyptian border post lay a few miles beyond Nizana. Even carrying the right papers, David felt uneasy about the crossing. He wondered if the Syrians would have passed a description of him to the Egyptians. It was unlikely, given the present climate between the two countries, but one never knew. The customs officials at the post were surly and uncooperative. They seemed bored and listless, with unshaven chins and unpressed uniforms, men for whom life had given up what little it had to offer by the time they reached the age of fifteen. The man in charge, a middle-aged official with thin, almost bloodless lips and red, staring eyes, seemed the sort to make trouble if only to prove he was indeed in charge. He sat behind a heavy wooden desk beneath a slow-turning fan that did little more than move the hot air in sluggish circles.

Leyla dealt with the papers, speaking quietly in Arabic with the man while two of his assistants searched the luggage. At the nearby guard post soldiers lounged about, eyeing her like farmers at a cattle auction, rifles slung over their shoulders, tense with repressed libido and the uneventfulness of duty in this no man's land.

David heard raised voices suddenly and realized that Leyla was arguing with the man behind the desk. He could see his papers spread out on the desk top. They appeared to be the topic of conversation, but he was unable to follow the rapid Arabic. At the very least, he feared, there would be a question of money passing hands.

Almost as quickly as it had begun, the argument died down. The soldiers seemed to look away. David watched as the man gathered up the scattered papers and handed them back to Leyla without a word. She took them and walked back to the jeep.

"What was that about?" he asked.

She shrugged.

"A little contretemps," she murmured. "He tried to tell me your papers weren't in order. He's new here, fresh from Tanta. I put him right; he won't try it with me again." She got into the jeep and closed the door. David started the engine.

"And who is Leyla Rashid that he's willing to listen to you?" he asked.

She looked at him as if wondering whether to answer or not.

"No one," she said as they moved off. "A Palestinian. A woman. Twenty-six years old. Single. Around here, that equals 'nobody.'"

"So why does a creep of a customs officer take advice from a nobody?"

She shrugged again. The gesture caught his eye and he looked at her briefly. Short hair, a long neck, features so fine they might have been carved. She held her distance by means of that special reserve emancipated Muslim women learn to adopt if they want to stay emancipated. Men make assumptions about such women. Even going into a cafe alone is seen as provocative: to sip a cup of coffee in the shade is a man's prerogative and a whore's trademark. David looked away again.

"I'm no one," she repeated. "But my father is someone. The man knew. He understood."

"Understood what?" David spun the wheel to avoid a clump of genista that had grown across the road.

"That my father has influence in this area. That it was easier for him not to make trouble."

"Just who is your father?" David asked.

She brushed a spray of sand from her sleeve.

"A nobody who became a somebody," she said. "His name is Ahmad Rashid. He's a poet. Surely you've heard of him."

David shook his head.

"No," he said. "I'm the Jew from New York, remember? We don't read too much Arabic poetry there."

"Don't be clever," she retorted. "My father's a well-known poet. He writes about Palestine—about the land, the people, their sufferings. They call him *Sawt Filastin,* 'the Voice of Palestine.' His poems have been published widely in the Arab press—in *Al-Ahram* here in Egypt, in the Lebanese papers before the civil war, in Kuwait, in Iraq. Everywhere but Palestine."

He spun the wheel again, as much to avoid the last remark as the mound of loose sand that had been blown across the highway.

"Don't tell me that creature back there is a lover of poetry," he said.

She smiled for the first time, then remembered the need for reserve and returned to her serious expression. For a second David caught a glimpse of someone else underneath the cool exterior.

"No, but he'd heard of my father," she replied. "Poets mean something to Arabs. My father was mayor of al-Arish for a time. He has influence, he knows everyone who matters in Sinai. He's still a poor man, but he has respect. Believe me, that's important here. If word got out that a border official had tried to make trouble for Ahmad Rashid's daughter, he'd soon find himself thinking about Sinai the way people in Sinai think about the fleshpots of Cairo."

David looked round at the harsh landscape that was rapidly swallowing them up.

"Where could they send him that could be worse than this?" he asked.

She answered without looking at him.

"There are worse places than this," she said. "Much worse. He knows that. Be glad that you don't."

David said nothing. He headed southwest, down toward al-Kuseima and their first stop. Ahead of them, on a broad horizon, tall mountains grew toward the sky. They were toffee-colored, rich and golden in the thick afternoon sun. At Umm Katef the road became a dirt track, rough and potholed. To their left, a great swath of black flintstone covered the sand, creating the mirage of a dark and waveless lake. Sunlight fell on it flatly and was swallowed up. The desert echoed all around them, vast and weird and empty.

They turned a bend in the track. Ahead, David could make out the stunted palms and acacias of an oasis. They had reached al-Kuseima. They were in Sinai.

THIRTEEN

By night the desert is brutal. In summer the nights are cold, in winter they freeze so fiercely they can kill. Icy and dark and infinitely vast, the desert rings like a tense, highly tempered bell, vibrating deep inside with its own hard music. Frost glistens over the waves of sand like diamonds crushed and scattered by a giant hand. Above, the moon is vast and silent, hanging low enough to stroke with half-lifted fingers. The stars gleam like pieces of broken ice, remote, inaccessible, frozen forever in their places. Like a furnace all summer long, the mountains of southern Sinai are crisp and hard and bitterly cold during the long winter nights. Nothing in them is able to retain heat. The cold is everything.

It was their fifteenth night in the peninsula. They lay side by side in sleeping bags, huddled like tiny animals against the cold. David shifted uneasily, sleepless again, his left hip aching where it pressed against the stony ground. Beside him, she murmured in her sleep. He smiled, then winced again as he rolled over and discovered yet another hidden rock.

Leyla had not ceased to puzzle and amaze him ever since the day he met her. She traveled through the desert dressed in bright, fashionable clothes and seemed to possess the power of repelling dirt and dust. Every night she would remove her makeup, wash and tone her face, and every morning she would wash her hair and then sit applying cosmetics as if she were in her bedroom at home.

"There's enough water," she would say when he protested, and she was always right.

She knew the desert as he knew broken pots and clay tablets, intimately, as a child knows its mother. When he got lost she would point a well-manicured finger and in minutes they would be on the track again. She knew the Bedouin as friends, and they seemed to accept her, a woman in a man's world, roaming unveiled through their desert. Her toughness surprised him. She never seemed to tire or wilt, she could sleep like a log on the stoniest ground, she could walk in bare feet over rough pebbles that he stumbled on in his boots. And yet at the end of every day, when he felt exhausted, unshaven and red-eyed, she would be as fresh and pretty as she had been that morning when setting out. The fragility of her body appealed to him more and more, but he kept his distance. He still scarcely knew her, she talked so seldom, asked so few questions, invited none. She knew what David had come to Sinai for, but she refused to draw him out and he preferred to keep things to himself as much as possible. They grew to like one another's company, but neither sought nor encouraged any deeper friendship or any sharing of confidences that might have led to one.

In fourteen days Sinai had changed him. There had been time to reflect in the open spaces and empty wastes through which they had been driving. Sinai is a no man's land, an arid testing ground for men and beasts alike, and the home of an angry god. David took it seriously, every inch of it, every scarred hillside and eroded gully. It was his wilderness in a way that it could never be Leyla's, however intimate she was with its flesh and bones. His people had been punished there for forty years by the angry god, brooding on his mountaintop amidst smoke and thunder, and the fit of wandering had been on them ever since. It was not a place in which to go in search of anything but pain and guilt. It looked as if the old mountain god had built it expressly for that purpose.

The first Christian monks had discovered that long ago. The lure of the simple desert had drawn them in flocks out of the cities of Egypt and Syria to isolated cells and remote monasteries or tall pillars of stone where they would sit in the fierce sun among the nomads, listening to the voice of God. Thin-robed ascetics, wild-eyed hermits, clutches of anchorites, stylites, cenobites, and Apotactites, they had come in search of some sort of tranquillity and brought with them instead self-inflicted torments that allowed neither body nor soul to rest. They had blinded their eyes in the sun by too much dull staring, they had lacerated their skin and torn their flesh on the thorns of tall acacia trees. Their bones had returned to the desert or lay moldering in the silent ossuaries of St. Catherine's and St. Nilus', and now only a handful of their descendants hung on in Sinai and elsewhere, devout old men with ragged beards, fearful novices with the taste of the world still fresh on their lips and tongues, cut off from the outside by more than walls or hills or sand.

David and Leyla had spent two days in St. Catherine's monastery at the foot of Jabal Musa, long believed by monks and pilgrims to be Mount Sinai itself. Father Nikandros had welcomed them in person, an affable old man whose kindly manner to guests concealed a disciplinarian who ruled his monastery with a rod of iron. He had known Gates and spoken with him several times during the young scholar's visit the previous spring. He was shocked and troubled to learn of his death but knew of nothing that might shed light on it. David was introduced to Father Spiros, the librarian, who remembered Gates well and, what was more remarkable, remembered clearly which manuscripts he had consulted.

They had spent hours together closeted in the ancient library, David and the old librarian with his grizzled beard and thick, dusty spectacles. All around them in the main gallery where they sat, the walls were covered with gilded icons, triptychs, and richly colored panels. Everywhere the face of Christ, stern and bearded, stared out at them from the shadows, the gospels in his left hand, his right extended upward to bless or damn, it was not clear which. The Virgin and her child, martyrs, saints, and angels stood rank on rank along the shelves, the gold of their robes and halos catching the light of the flickering lamp by which the scholars read.

Behind a tall wire fence thousands of manuscripts were stacked, centuries of learning and pious copying locked away from the eyes of all but a few. No wonder someone would come to this place in the hope of finding an undiscovered text. For hours on end David had sat with Father Spiros, leafing through manuscripts in Greek, Latin, Syriac, and Hebrew. There were few clues, few references to places Gates might have gone. Buried in the little-used library, the task had seemed futile to David after all, the problems insurmountable. Why had he come on such a wild goose chase? What had made him think he could find anything here but dust and vellum?

But late on the second day, when they had come to the end of the last codex and David was being shown some of the library's treasures by Father Spiros, the monk had mentioned to him that Gates had been particularly eager to get to St. Nilus'. Spiros had told him of the existence there of a unique manuscript, an early Arabic travel narrative called *Al-tariq al-mubin min al-Sham ila'l-balad al-amin. (The Clear Path from Damascus to Mecca),* written in the eighth century by a certain Abu 'Abd Allah Muhammad ibn Sirin al-Halabi. Gates had been excited beyond measure to learn of the existence of this manuscript: he had come across references to it in several places, but there was no record of an extant copy anywhere. Brockelmann, the standard authority, did not even mention it.

Now David and Leyla were on the last stage of their journey. They had visited all the sites mentioned by Gates in his postcard, they had talked with people who had met and spoken with him, they had traced his movements through the peninsula to this spot. On the morning of the third day at St. Catherine's they had set out on horseback toward St. Nilus', more than a day's journey to the north, in the Shi'b al-Ruhban, a long and tortuous offshoot of the longer Wade Beirak. Hidden deep in the mountains, the monastery was inaccessible except on foot or by horse or camel. The passage itself was narrow, with high, sheer walls of granite and a treacherous floor of boulders, rubble, and loose sand. The going was difficult.

David had never ridden before and found the journey tiring and painful. The saddle rubbed his thighs and his back ached intolerably. They had to stop several times to allow him to dismount and rest. Leyla was unsure of the way, and their pace became increasingly slow. Soon they had begun to lose time, and by late afternoon it had become apparent that they would be unable to reach the monastery before dark. As darkness fell, they decided to stop where they were and camp for the night. Exhausted and still fully dressed, they had rolled up in their sleeping bags and huddled themselves against the deadly, penetrating cold. Beside them the horses, wrapped in heavy blankets, had stood shivering.

It was dark in the gorge. The tall cliffs on either side blotted out most of the sky. Only a few stars, ethereally bright in the clear desert air, flickered remotely above them. David tossed and turned, his thoughts anxious and filled with nighttime fears. One thought above all worried him: if it rained, they were as good as dead, trapped here in the center of the gully. Leyla had told him that in winter a sudden downpour can generate a flash flood in a matter of hours. They might not even know it had rained some distance away: the only warning would be the sound of roaring water swelling into the narrow channel and bearing down on them with the speed and the bulk of an express train. The Bedouin stayed out of the wadis and the gullies in winter. Leyla was nervous, though she had said very little to David on the subject. His thoughts still troubled, he fell at last into an uneasy and dream-filled sleep.

They woke before sunrise. The air was cold and they knew that, even when the sun did eventually climb above the walls of the passage, very little heat would come this far down. Shivering, blowing into their hands for warmth, they set about preparing breakfast. The previous evening, Leyla had lit a fire of acacia wood. A few embers still glowed, and she was soon able to make it blaze again. In Bedouin fashion, she made some yeastless dough, flattened it into a rough circular sheet, and laid it over the fire. Within minutes they had hot bread. With sweet black tea it made an acceptable if somewhat ascetic meal. David began to revive, though his body still protested at the treatment of the day before.

As they finished breakfast, thin gray light began to ooze into the *shi'b*, touching the rocks with dull, undefined shadows and bringing the bleak canyon into view once more. It was poor light, flat and wan. The sky out of which it came had turned gray and ponderous, like a slate ceiling above their heads. It seemed to press down on them, reaching as far as the canyon walls, boxing them in. Nothing stirred. A heavy, enervating silence hung over everything. Nothing lived there but snakes, lizards, and scorpions. Leyla had warned David about the snakes before turning in the night before. The thought of vipers had not helped his sleep. Leyla looked up at the grim walls of the *shi'b* and shivered. It was too quiet, like a valley of the dead.

"I don't like it here," she said. "This gorge has a bad name. People stay out of it when they can. It's like a prison, those walls. They give me the creeps. Your monks must be funny people to live here

109

voluntarily. The Tuwara keep well clear."

She had a polite disdain for the monks. At St. Catherine's she had spent her time in conversation with the numerous Jabali Bedouin who lived there, serving the monastery as laborers and craftsmen. With the monks she had spoken only briefly. For all the antiquity of their confraternity, she regarded them as interlopers in her desert. They for their part were uneasy to have a woman in their midst. St. Catherine's was not on Athos, and a woman could enter the monastery precincts, but the monks did not like it all the same.

They fed the horses, packed their equipment, and loaded the huge saddlebags again. It was time to be on their way. Though she did not show it, David sensed that Leyla was worried about the weather. The sky was not clearing, and rain might already be falling on the mountains. The sooner they were up in the monastery the better. The horses would not move at first. They were sullen and unresponsive. They had eaten saltwort in the night and were thirsty, but the water in the rock pools of the ravine was hard and brackish, and they turned up their noses at it. Leyla spoke to them in a quiet voice, coaxing them, stroking their necks, feeding them oats from a bag the monks had given them, but they moved only slowly, recalcitrant as ever.

For more than a mile they picked their way through the boulders and scattered rubble of the canyon. David ached throughout his body and his thighs felt raw and tender: he refused to ride again and walked instead, holding his horse's bridle in one hand. The narrow gorge twisted like a corkscrew, the enclosed, sightless bends increasing the sense of imprisonment and claustrophobia. Even the air felt stale and used, as if trapped here for centuries. They were too cold to speak. David was irritable and flared up easily. His head ached, and a small vein in his left temple pounded. Leyla felt useless, lost, her skills of the northern and central deserts redundant here amidst ancient, brutal rock.

Then they turned a last bend and it was there in front of them, at the end of the gorge, high up on the wall of a second, smaller passage that ran at right angles across the Shi'b al-Ruhban. The cliff face was stepped and broken here and had been cut back to allow the small monastery to be built. Constructed from stone taken from the cliff itself, it blended into the background, gray and forbidding in the murky light. Built in the eighth century by a group of monks from St. Catherine's who had sought greater seclusion in

110

their life of prayer and penance, it had stood untouched by time, wars, or invasions, a testimony to faith and endurance. The main building seemed to hang from the cliff like an aerie, precarious yet solidly buttressed. Above and to the side of it, subsidiary structures had been built on large outcrops, connected with the main building and with each other by narrow paths and stairs. Safely raised more than one hundred feet above the floor of the ravine, the monastery was immune to floods, bandit raids, and the intrusions of casual travelers alike. It was a sanctuary, a dark, almost windowless retreat that wound its way deep into solid rock and turned its back on the world outside.

Access to the monastery was by means of a primitive wooden elevator, like that at St. Catherine's, on which it was modeled. It was operated by a hand winch above. When David and Leyla arrived at the junction of the two canyons they saw that the elevator—little more than a stout wooden box—was perched high above on a rickety-looking platform. There was no sign of life anywhere: no face at any of the tiny windows that looked into the Shi'b al-Ruhban, no movement on the stairs or walkways, no sound of bells or voices. David had been told that seven monks lived here now, contemplatives given to a life of silent retreat. They would not be pleased to be disturbed, and they might well refuse Leyla admission. Hesitantly, he called out in a loud voice. Half a minute passed and there was no reply. He called again, louder, sending sharp little echoes round in circles through the enclosed space of the canyon. The echoes faded and the silence returned.

Then Leyla caught sight of a thin cord that hung from the winch platform down almost to ground level. She stepped up to it and pulled once, hard. Far above their heads an agitated jangling answered her tug and died away as quickly as it had come. She waited, then pulled again, harder this time, twice, three times. Above them the mass of the monastery lowered, mocking the tinkling of the tiny bells. It seemed to lean over them, its dark bulk massive and threatening at this distance. David called again, startling the horses, who had grown nervous in the narrow confines of the valley. He turned to Leyla and shrugged, but his voice expressed more honestly his uneasiness.

"They don't seem very keen on visitors. What do you think?"

She looked up at the platform far above, then back at David. "I don't like it," she said. "Something's wrong. It's too quiet."

"You don't suppose this is some sort of holy day?" he suggested. Leyla shook her head.

"They would have warned us at St. Catherine's. No, I think something's wrong. Sickness perhaps. Even a small thing like food poisoning could have serious effects in a place like this."

She pulled on the rope again, ringing the bell fiercely. One of the horses shifted and whinnied gently. High above, a raven winged its way across the canyon, a black shape against the gray sky. No one answered the summons. The monastery remained silent.

"What do we do now?" Leyla asked. She was worried. The thought of the journey back to St. Catherine's along the *shi'b* with rain threatening was disturbing in the extreme.

David did not want to turn back. Something told him the end of his journey lay here in St. Nilus', and he would not leave without finding what he had come for. He looked up at the monastery, then at the sheer walls of the cliff on either side. There was no obvious path from ground level to any part of the structure above them. The granite was rough and offered projections on which one might find handholds, but such an ascent was clearly a task for an experienced and well-equipped climber. There was a rope and a grappling hook in one of the saddlebags, for use in emergencies, but from where they stood the building was well out of reach.

"We need to get into the monastery," David said. "We've got to find a way of getting above it and then come down by rope. The passage has to end somewhere, and there's got to be a way up to the cliff top. I suggest we start right now."

Leyla nodded in agreement. She was eager to get out of the canyon. The sight of the monastery and the forbidding silence with which it had greeted them had done nothing to increase her enthusiasm for the place.

"Can you ride yet?" she asked.

David grimaced, then nodded. His body still ached, but he desperately wanted to hurry now. He went up to his horse and hauled himself up into the saddle with difficulty. As he shuffled onto the beast's back, ungainly and uncomfortable, Leyla laughed. The laugh bounced off the walls of the canyon, a weird, distorted echo, and was swallowed up into the rocks. Leyla shivered and mounted her horse, frightened by the echo as much as she had been by the silence that preceded it.

FOURTEEN

The narrow pass came abruptly to an end, opening out onto a broad river valley that ran for miles between tall rugged hills of red granite. The small gully had been cut, as it were, like a trench between two of these hills. All David and Leyla had to do was climb the hill on the monastery side of the canyon, then make their way across the rough, mesalike terrain skirting the top of the cliff. They found a spot where a shallow gully led gently into the slope of the hill before starting to climb more steeply. It seemed easy at first, but as they went higher the going became progressively rougher.

The horses could go no farther than the point where the gully gave way to the hill proper. Accustomed as they were to the rugged terrain of southern Sinai, they knew when they were beaten. Weighed down by the heavy saddlebags and edgy after their journey through the dark valley, they would go no higher. Leyla sat down on a rock beside them and sighed.

"They won't go any farther, David. And I think it would be risky to make them try. If one of them breaks a leg, we'll be in trouble. One of us will have to stay here to keep an eye on them while the other checks the monastery. I'm willing to go on if you want to rest for a bit."

David shook his head.

"No, there might be a problem with your being a woman. If they're ill, the sight of a strange young lady shinning down a rope into their sanctuary might give them all relapses. And if they're not ill they might throw you off the cliff before you get a chance to explain. I'll go on alone. I'll try to make it back today if I can, but

113

don't worry if I don't turn up. If something's wrong, I may have to sort things out there before I can get back to you."

He packed some equipment into a rucksack—rope, hammer, grappling hook, his revolver, and a little food. Inwardly, he was anxious. The silent monastery had filled him with misgivings. Something unusual had happened, he was sure of it.

"Take care, David," Leyla said as he set off. It was the first time in their brief acquaintance that she had addressed him with anything appproaching affection in her voice. He looked back at her, observing how she sat with the horses, small and feminine, incongruous among the sharp rocks. Her face was drawn and tense, and he could sense the nervousness in her eyes. He smiled, a forced, tired smile, then turned and began to climb.

It took him just over fifteen minutes to reach the top. From where he stood he could see for miles in every direction. It was the most breathtaking landscape he had ever seen: like a giant's battlefield, it rose and fell in jagged hills and flat, waterless valleys, gray and red and dun. It all seemed primitive, coarse, unfinished, as if God had not had time to complete his work here, so near his home. From tiny rocks to tremendous hills, every inch was overlaid with the same patina of vast and wrinkled age. Aeons of sun and rain had eroded the mountain and torn deep fissures in the solid rock, as if a canker had eaten it all away, ruining flesh and exposing dark, ancient bones. David felt dwarfed and insignificant, the only living thing in an immensity of lifeless stone, a vast, inhuman graveyard in which nothing could live for long.

It took him over an hour to reach the spot where the cliff overhung the monastery. From above, it was difficult to make out easily the configuration of the jumbled buildings below. Seen from the gorge, the basic organization of the monastery had been reasonably clear. It was built on three levels, each corresponding to a broad ledge in the cliff, cut back and given vertical clearance in order to accommodate the tall, flat-fronted buildings. On the bottom level stood the main structure of the complex, a featureless building some twenty feet high and thirty long. This, David had guessed, must be the principal residential section, the earliest part of the monastery, built in the eighth century and extending deep inside the cliff face. Beside it was another long low building, probably the refectory. Above these was a single building with a flat roof and small pointed windows: the library. On the third level stood two more buildings: the church, a small replica of the sixth-century basilica at St. Catherine's, and a low domed structure, whitewashed and windowless. The ossuary.

From where David stood now, he saw that he could make his descent onto a small paved area that lay between the ossuary and the church. Once there, he could use the stairs and walkways that connected one part of the monastery with another. Behind and to the left of him was a small olive grove like several other plantations he had seen in the vicinity of St. Catherine's. It was obviously cultivated by the monks, but how they reached it he had no idea. Making his way to the trees, he fastened one end of the rope about the gnarled but sturdy trunk of the nearest. He then walked back to the cliff, hammered a long metal pin into the ground about two feet from the edge at a spot overlooking the little square below, and turned the rope about it. Rock climbing was not one of the skills he had acquired in life and, glancing down into the gully far beneath him, he wryly thought that it was probably not the most sensible of skills to teach oneself. Eyes closed and hands clenched tightly round the rope, he lowered himself over the edge.

The slight overhang of the cliff meant that he swung out over the void. One slip and he would plummet onto the rocks of the canyon below. Hands and feet clinging to the snaking, twisting rope, he inched his way painfully down. Opening his eyes, he found that he was spinning, gently but dangerously, and hanging about five feet out from and seven feet above the area on which he wanted to drop. It was too late to go back and lengthen the rope: he feared his courage might fail him if he had to launch himself into space a second time. By dint of moving his legs slowly, then the rest of his body, he began to swing himself in the right direction. But as his swings gained momentum, so too did the circular movements of the rope. Watching for the paved square to come into view, preparing to throw himself onto it, he began to grow dizzy as the ground, the buildings, and the ledge spun underneath him, in and out of his range of vision. It was now or never: if he did not jump, he would lose his balance and fall. He jumped and landed awkwardly on the worn flags in front of the church.

His left ankle hurt and his right elbow was badly grazed. Bruised and winded, he lay for a time where he had fallen, recovering his breath and tentatively trying out the different parts of his body.

Satisfied that all was in reasonable working order, though aching more than ever, he rolled onto his hands and knees and pushed himself to his feet. As he straightened, he caught sight of the rope, swinging teasingly above his head, several feet beyond his reach. There would be no returning that way, he thought. Gingerly, he stepped to the edge of the paved area and looked down. The canyon floor looked far away and curiously compelling. It seemed to call him, urging him to lose his footing and tumble to it. This was no place for anyone with a fear of heights, he thought. It was not a comfortable thought, for he was nervous anywhere above the third story himself. But he had no choice in the matter.

His voice still a little shaky after the fall, he called out.

"Is anyone here? Can anyone hear me?"

The words dropped like lead into the valley and were lost. No one answered. A light wind gusted up the *shi'b* and was gone. He called again, this time in Arabic, and another breeze came and carried his words away with it. Cold. He watched the sky and felt the rain in the air and called out for a third time into the silence. Nothing but echoes, flat and lifeless. He approached the door of the church.

The plain wooden portal opened to his touch and led directly into the narthex, a broad vestibule that acted as an intermediary stage between the world outside and the church proper within. Intricately carved and inlaid doors faced him. Above them, a small oil lamp flickered, its burnished copper twisting and containing the soft yellow light of its flame, limning the doors with shadows and dark, shifting lines. Palm trees and lions, sycamores and small, delicate angels were carved in the smooth rectangular panels of the doors. Age and the pious rubbing of endless hands had worn them down and mellowed them, but in the light of the single lamp they seemed untouched, pristine. David stood facing the doors for a long time, silent and uncertain. Were the monks inside in silent prayer? Would his uninvited presence disturb and offend them? He hesitated a moment longer, then grasped the round metal handle of the door on the right and turned it. The door fell open and he stepped into the nave of the church.

Riches upon riches. Christ on the walls, Christ on the pillars, Christ above the altar crucified, Christ on the ceiling, Pantocrater. Lights suspended everywhere, their flames enrapturing and gilding all they touched. Gold in excess, silver in abundance, a surfeit of light. Incense like veils, swirling, drifting, hanging suspended in pools of red and yellow light. Before the iconostasis burning candles in tall candlesticks of polished brass. Hanging at the ends of long exquisite chains, ostrich eggs chased and ornamented in copper and silver filigree. The floor paved and carpeted, marble and rich rugs, mosaics of oriental geometry, flecked and grained. Across the nave, gilded and festooned with color, the tall iconostasis, painted and robed in red and black and gold, covered in icons, holy and set apart, shielding the altar from the profane eyes of the world. Paradise brought down, Byzantium in the desert, dark shadows and pale flickering lamps, Earth made Heaven.

The smell of incense, musky and dense, filled David's nostrils as he stood and stared. For long minutes he was dazzled by the splendor of what he saw, so unexpected here in this dark valley. His presence seemed an intrusion, an unwanted sacrilege. His skin crawled with the holiness of the place, he felt embarrassed, Jewish, alien. He dared not call out to announce his presence, kept even his breathing low and gentle lest it draw attention to him. His heart beat loudly in his chest and his temples pounded.

Slowly his eyes grew accustomed to the strange, shadow-filled light. He could see the body of the church clearly now and realized it was empty. Hushed and still, it was like a great ship that had been abandoned on the high seas, its incense burning, its lamps and candles lit, its icons in their places. All that was missing was the sound of voices chanting the Trisagion. Was a service about to begin? David felt uneasy. Something was wrong. He looked again at the iconostasis, the great gilded screen separating the lower nave from the sanctuary. The central door was partly open, and at its foot, on the threshold, lay a robed figure prostrate in prayer.

Hesitantly, David walked down the nave, his footsteps light but audible enough to warn the monk of his approach. The figure did not move, so David went closer, uncertain what to do. He was about twenty paces away when he saw something that was wholly out of place. A dark red stream ran down from the threshold of the iconostasis and across the marble floor, staining its whiteness and disrupting the symmetry of its pattern. Less hesitant now of sacrilege, more apprehensive of mundane terror, David approached the prone figure guardedly. The legs were askew, the arms twisted, the head and shoulders wedged in the open doorway. The crimson stream ran from a great wound on the side of the head, clotted and dried now. David stepped up to the body and rolled it over onto its back. Part of the face fell away where the wound had sliced open the skull; he turned away quickly, sickened. Violence was stalking him again and he felt lost and frightened.

His eye fell on an embroidered cloth that lay across a table to his left. He picked it up and placed it over the upper half of the dead man, covering the bloody, severed face. Sidestepping the remains, he pushed open the small iconostasis door and entered the sanctuary. Ahead of him, the altar, inlaid and ornate in front of a bright mosaic-covered apse. In front of the altar lay a second monk, his blood smeared on the altar cloth and jellied on the steps. David approached and caught sight of a great wound that had cleft the neck between ear and shoulder.

He bent and touched the body, that of an old man, white-bearded and gentle in expression, a saint rendered obscene by his open, ghostly wound. The eyes stared at him, dull, startled at the intrusion of death here in what must have seemed to the old man an inviolable place, a center of ultimate sanctuary. It was difficult to judge, but David thought he had been dead for several hours: the flesh was cold, but complete rigor had not yet set in. But, he dimly recalled, was it not possible for rigor to be delayed even for days in cold weather? And did it not wear off after twenty-four hours? It was not the sort of problem that usually preoccupied archaeologists. He looked at the blood again. It seemed fresh. Reluctantly, he traced it with a finger: it was still quite moist in places.

On the altar a small candle sputtered briefly and went out. David looked around and noticed that several others had already done the same and that yet more had burned low and would soon be extinguished. In their rich filigree cages, the oil lamps still gave forth a warm, uninterrupted light. From a panel above the altar the face of Christ gazed down at him. Grim and ascetic, it bore that look of pain, that lined and tortured expression that is found only in the Eastern tradition. David could not bear to look at it and turned away. He caught sight of another icon hanging on a pillar near the altar. It was strange and desolate, and under the circumstances profoundly unsettling. In the middle of the painting was a white, domed building filled with bones and dead men in shrouds, the ossuary: out of its door, the dead were being plucked by angels. Some were being carried up to heaven, becoming transformed as they ascended into figures of light. Others were cast down into a pit below, tended by foul-looking demons and filled with flames. Those who had already fallen into the pit were being consumed by fire, like living torches. David stood for a while gazing at the grim painting, then turned his back on it and made toward the iconostasis.

As he left the sanctuary, he became aware of a low drumming sound. It seemed at first to come from far away, then it suddenly swelled in volume and he recognized it. The rain had come. It was falling in torrents on the lead roof of the church, shattering the silence, like millions of tiny stones hurled down from heaven in outrage at the sacrilege.

There were no side chapels, no sacristy, no secret places where a murderer might hide. David could not stay in the church, waiting for someone to find him. He walked back through the nave and into the narthex, his back crawling with every step he took away from the horrors he had found. Opening the door, he stepped out into a roaring, blinding world of ice-cold water. The rain tore down at an angle, lashing the walls of the church and streaming across the ground, cascading everywhere as if rushing to do in a matter of hours the work of years. In seconds he was soaked to the skin and chilled to the bone. He could see only inches in front of his face; like a dense liquid veil, the water covered him on every side. Bit by bit, he moved toward the stairs that led down to the next level. The monastery had become a death trap in more ways than one. A single false step in the rain would send him plummeting over the edge and down into the gorge below. It might be safer to stay in the church, but if there was a maniac loose in the monastery there would be little to gain by remaining in one place. He could not escape back up the cliff face. There was only one way out, and that was down.

He found the steps more by accident than design. All down the front of the ledge, rain cascaded like a waterfall, pouring over the worn steps in a constant stream. The stone beneath his feet felt smooth and treacherous, moving almost, as if trying to escape from him. He began his descent, taking each step in turn, moving sideways, hands on the stair above. The valley was filled with a loud roaring. The sky was blotted out and a strange, crepuscular darkness lay on everything. Suddenly he slipped and fell on his knees on the edge of a step. For more than a minute he lay there, inches from sliding out into the gloom. The rain lashed him, froze his weakly clinging fingers, stung his face. His ears were filled with the loud plashing and gurgling of the water as it rushed past him, as if trying desperately to dislodge him. At last his feet made contact with the steps again, and he resumed his descent. The forty steps seemed like four hundred. He could not tell how long he was on the stairs: fifteen or twenty minutes perhaps, but it felt like hours.

Once on the ledge, he moved in toward the cliff, and made for the low wooden door of the library. It opened inward into darkness. There were no windows, no lamps or candles burning, the light that came through the door was weak and ineffectual. A musty, bookish smell. Silence. Nothing moved or shone or breathed. David held his breath and stepped inside. Was the killer here, hiding among old books and gilded icons in the brooding dark? Holding the door open for what little illumination trickled in, he looked about him for a light. On a small wooden stand to his left stood an oil lamp and beside it a box of matches. Leaving the door, he lit the lamp and held it aloft. As the door closed emphatically behind him, the lamp flared up, then settled down to shed a buttery yellow light into the darkness. Holding it high, David strained to make out his surroundings.

A high beamed ceiling was dimly visible overhead. Above the beams lurked ancient, vaguely shifting shadows, like small indecent nightmares waiting to drop on his shoulders and embrace him. He shuddered and walked forward, the lamp held stiffly out in front of him. On either side of him he could make out the dim shapes of bookcases. Bringing the light closer to the shelves on his right, he saw that there were six of them, low, heavy cases of old wood, covered in thick white dust. The monks here were not scholars, and the books were seldom read. He walked on down the central passage of the room, awakening shadows on all sides. The silence seemed to grip him like a hand. He felt hollow, as if not there within himself. Blood rushed through his head, but the sound seemed to come from far away. His clothes clung to him, wet and cold, and he shivered.

On the floor at the back of the library, in front of the heavy reading table, lay the body of a third monk. His head had been crushed by a massive leather-bound volume that lay, smeared with white hairs and blood, on the floor beside him. As David passed the lamp over the corpse, examining the man and his surroundings, he seemed to move, but it was only a trick of the light: he had been dead for hours like the others. Some dark evil was loose in the monastery, and David now knew what he could expect to find elsewhere.

Near the body, the contents of one of the bookcases had been spilled on the floor. Bound volumes and loose manuscript leaves lay scattered everywhere. For a moment David was reminded of the archive pit at Ebla and the body of the Arab, bleeding into the mud. He bent down and picked up one of the volumes. It was in Arabic, a commentary on the Qur'an by al-Tabari. Replacing it on the nearest shelf, he picked up another. A Christian text this time, an infancy gospel, it was also in Arabic. Putting it on the same shelf, David noticed a small sign at the top of the case. It was in Greek and said simply ARABIC TEXTS. The next case contained Coptic manuscripts, the one after it works in Syriac. The empty case was the only one to contain Arabic manuscripts.

It took David almost an hour to reach the conclusion that the manuscript he had come in search of, al-Halabi's *Al-Tariq al-mubin,* was not there. Had it ever been there at all? He found a large volume bound in calf that contained a catalogue of the books in the library. All the Arabic titles were together, and he found al-Halabi's book among them. There could be little doubt. It was too much of a coincidence. Whoever had killed John Gates and taken his thesis, whoever had killed David's parents and destroyed the papers in their apartment, had come here, killed again, and taken with him the last piece of evidence. Whether one man was involved or a dozen mattered very little to David.

By the time he left the library the rain had already slackened considerably and was now a weak gray drizzle that seemed to seep down rather than pour into the gully. A pale exhausted light accompanied it. David looked at his watch: it was after two o'clock. Sunset was not very far away. He made his way carefully down the steps to the lowest level.

The small kitchen and refectory were empty. From three windows near the roof, patches of light fell over the low wooden tables: seven places were set at one table, apparently for the noon meal, but none of them had been touched. The same brooding silence lay over the refectory as over the rest of the monastery: the stones of the Shi'b al-Ruhban had returned to their slumber after centuries of human disturbance. David had heard such a silence only once before. He had been present when a great rock tomb was uncovered in northern Syria. The sound of picks, one by one, had died away and the door of the tomb had been opened to reveal a bent human skeleton surrounded by the pitiful remains of earthly existence: gold and faience jewelry, pots of kohl and antimony, a polished bronze mirror, and tiny turquoise beads. Still fastened about the dead woman's skull had been a chaplet of finely worked gold leaves, still bright and gay-looking, though the flesh beneath had long since rotted away. Everyone had stood silent in the presence of that small unendurable death.

David closed the door of the refectory and crossed to the main building. The door was half open and a pool of water lay behind it, where the rain had been driven in by gusts of wind. David still held the oil lamp he had found in the library. He relit it and stepped across the water. Holding the lamp up, he found himself in a square reception room with rough bare walls along which ran a plain wooden bench. The room was empty. At the back a doorway led into a long dark corridor that plunged into living rock after only a few yards. On either side of the corridor were storerooms containing food and other supplies. There was no one in any of them.

The corridor led David down into the heart of the building, branching off several times into the darkness. It was cold and oppressive, with low stone ceilings, like a mine. Somewhere water dripped, where rain had somehow found a way down through deep fissures in the rock into the man-made caves. David's light flickered and burned low in the heavy atmosphere, casting his shadow on the floor and walls behind him. He entered a branch corridor containing the cells in which the monks slept, most of them long deserted. As he walked along he grew more and more uneasy. He threw open the doors of the cells as he passed them, fearful of what he was sure he would find, nervous of what might be following him. Old, worm-eaten pallet beds, rush mats covered in mold, cobwebs, abandoned icons gathering dust, candlesticks rusting, a breviary bent with damp, a knotted prayer string on a low table, held in place by long white threads, a mournful, deserted smell.

The fourth monk was in a cell at the end of the corridor. His hands were bound and he had been hanged by the neck from a hook set in the ceiling of the tiny room. When David touched the body to take it down a bell rang, jarring and remote in the stillness. The man had been strung up with the main bell rope, and the bell still hung on it, out of sight behind the body.

The remaining three monks were together in a small gray chamber beyond the cells, at the foot of a tall, thin crucifix that dominated the far wall. David saw them standing there, facing him, their eyes wide open, staring at him as he approached them. He opened his mouth to speak and then he saw what had been done to them. With a cry of horror and revulsion, he dropped the lamp and staggered back, gagging. The lamp burst into flames, illuminating with sharp brilliance the foul scene that had already been etched forever on David's memory. Clutching a wall for support, he threw up twice, bright beads of sweat breaking out on his forehead. Behind him, the flames of the lamp flared uselessly against solid rock and began to die. Straightening, frightened beyond endurance by this last insanity, he staggered out of the room into the darkness beyond, his feet ringing on the worn flags, his breath harsh and panting as he groped his way down the corridor past the empty cells. Behind him, the flames gave a last flicker and died. All around him was pitching darkness, total and impenetrable. No light came from anywhere. He pressed on, confused and uncertain. Several times he crashed into a wall and was forced to turn back. He was not sure how long he spent blindly groping in the dark, but at last he stopped and stood still. A cold hand seemed to clutch at his heart as he realized he was lost. Without a light, he could wander for days in here, making false turns at every move losing himself more and more deeply in the catacombs beneath the cliff. He had no idea how far they extended. He dreaded more than anything coming back in the dark to the room in which the three monks stood. All around him was darkness. The crowding, implacable silence pressed in on him more heavily than ever here. He felt more claustrophobically alone than he had ever felt in his life, like someone buried alive. He wanted to shout, to scream, to send echoes flying down the long, dark corridors, to give way to the madness that was nibbling at his nerves. But he could only stand as if frozen to the spot, listening.

It was then that he came closest to insanity. As if in a nightmare, he heard behind him the soft unmistakable sound of low, rhythmical breathing.

FIFTEEN

David opened his eyes into darkness once more. His head ached intolerably, and strange little lights bobbed and danced behind his eyeballs. He was lying on his back on a rough stone floor. Something heavy and awkward lay across his legs, and there was a peculiar, musty smell in his nostrils. Had he slipped in the corridor, concussed himself against the floor? Then he remembered the breathing. Someone must have come up behind him and struck him, though he could not remember either a struggle or a blow. He wondered how long he had lain there. His clothes still felt damp against his skin, but when he brushed his hand over the cloth it felt considerably drier than it had previously. His throat was sore and his nose felt blocked: it would go badly with him if his chill developed into something more serious.

Raising himself to a sitting position, he winced with pain as the blood rushed back out of his brain. Gingerly, he put a hand to the back of his head and felt carefully for a lump. His fingers came away sticky: the blow had opened a small wound behind his left ear. The wound and the area round it throbbed painfully. His whole body seemed to ache, some parts more than others, but all in some degree. He was dizzy and disoriented. But he remembered the darkness and his sense of hopelessness at being lost without a light in the mazelike chambers of the monastery.

Then, as he shifted, he felt something in the back pocket of his trousers, and a dim memory drifted back to him. He reached a hand into the pocket and drew out a rather battered box of matches. Now he remembered that he had absentmindedly pocketed the box he had discovered in the library. There were still several matches inside it. With their help, he might be able to find his way out of the maze. Shifting his legs, he pushed the weight that lay across them: something unpleasntly limp and heavy rolled to the floor. He stood slowly, his bones protesting, his legs shaky and uncertain. With a sharp scraping sound that seemed gratuitously loud in the silence, he struck a match.

It took several bewildered seconds before the full horror of what he saw penetrated David's mind. The shadows shifted and bent and took on shapes before his eyes. The shapes gathered themselves and coalesced into solid fragments of nightmare. He had, he was in no doubt of it, gone insane after all. He was in a charnel house, a low chamber filled from floor almost to ceiling with the contents of a large and ancient graveyard. At his feet lay the body of one of the monks he had found in the church. Just beyond him lay arranged the corpses of the other six victims. And on every side decayed and ruined corpses sat or lay in all the postures of death.

The match sputtered against his fingers and went out. Darkness rushed back, mercifully blotting out the scene that had hung before his eyes a moment before. David stood there stunned, unable to move or breathe or think. His mind quite simply refused to function. His consciousness had received so many shocks that it could register no more, least of all this final madness. Minutes dragged past, and with every minute the horror grew within him until it became uncontainable. The darkness was worse than anything the light could show him. His flesh crept as he saw in his mind's eye each individual corpse stir into life and crawl toward him. He could almost hear the rustling and cracking of old bones.

He struck a second match. Nothing had changed. They were all in their places staring at him. The little flame bobbed up and down, casting more shadows than light, gleaming on the polished bones all around giving a queer sort of puppet life to the dim figures. He glanced round, fearful of what might be behind him. He could just make out a short flight of stone steps leading up to a door before the match burned down to his fingers and extinguished itself. Fear gripped him and panic began to grow inside like a fever. His breath came in jerks, shallow and spasmodic, speeding up the rate of his heartbeats alarmingly. It could not be real. He was dreaming or insane, or perhaps he was lying somewhere in a fever brought on by the soaking he had suffered in the rain. With difficulty, he controlled himself forcing his lungs to take in deep, slow breaths, expelling them gradually, slowing his heartbeat, calming himself. And as he grew calmer the truth dawned on him. It was not a dream or a delirium-produced nightmare. He was really there, in the monastery's ossuary, surrounded by the bones of thirteen centuries. Someone must have carried him there, together with the bodies of the seven monks.

And as the reality of his situation came home to him, the physical sensation of his surrounding grew in him: the chill, the stale, unbreathed atmosphere, the clinging dark. But the horror was not lessened. It had a new dimension now. His nightmare of the present had been dissipated only to be replaced by all the nightmares of his past. Childhood fears of death and graveyards, ghouls and rotting flesh flooded back into his mind as if they had never been away. The darkness became the darkness of his childhood bedroom at home, peopled with old, musty fears. His reason told him he was in no danger, but his imagination threatened him with all the fears he had ever known.

Slowly he turned until he was facing in the direction of the steps. He struck another match. It flared up briefly, giving him enough light to make out the door at the top. In the darkness again, he climbed the steps carefully and put his hand against the door. It would not budge. Groping with both hands, he found a round metal handle like a ring and turned. It moved, but the door would give way to neither pushing nor pulling. Desperate, he crashed his shoulder against it time after time. The ancient timbers shook but held fast. He was firmly incarcerated.

He stood for what seemed an age by the door, his mind numb, his body cold and exhausted. He had to find a way out before he collapsed from cold and hunger. Leyla might come in a day or two, though for all he knew she had already been and gone. He had no idea how long he had been lying in the ossuary.

A stray thought nudged him and vanished. He struggled to recapture it, but it had gone. Disconsolate, he sat down in front of the door and buried his face in his hands. He had only one match left in the box—scarcely enough with which to conduct a search of the ossuary for another way out. And then the stray thought returned and remained. On a low stone pillar at the foot of the stairs he had seen the stumps of a number of wax candles. If he could find and light them, he would be able to carry out a proper search of his prison.

He went back down the steps into the body of the ossuary. In the darkness it would be easy to misjudge directions and distances. He could miss the pillar, find himself lost among decaying flesh and bones—and he could not waste his one remaining match to find his way back again. Slowly, delicately, his hand groping nervously in the dark in front of him, fearful of what he might touch, he inched his way forward in what he hoped was the direction of the pillar. There was nothing but empty air. Back and forth he swept his hand through the blackness ahead of him, a tiny pinprick of panic swelling inside him. If he had missed it he was finished. He shuffled his feet another inch forward and cracked his shins against something. Reaching down, he touched the pillar, lower than he had remembered it. He fumbled for a moment, found a candle, and set it straight on the uneven surface of the pillar. Holding his breath, he took the match out of the box. It felt small and fragile in his fingers, a thing easily dropped or snapped in two. He struck it against the box, turned its head down, and let it catch fire properly. Then, with a shaking hand, he stretched it toward the candle.

It would not light. The wick had been bent back into the wax below and would not catch. The match was already half consumed and beginning to die. Hurriedly he scrabbled for a second candle, picked it up in his left hand at an angle, and held the dying flame to it. The match flickered and went out, leaving a tiny, vulnerable touch of flame on the wick. David dared not move his hand or breathe. The slightest motion, the merest current of air, would extinguish it. Feebly the flame trembled, sank, flickered again, and began at last to grow, widening and lengthening as it moved down the wick. Turning his face away, David let out a long, shuddering breath and sucked in air again, dizzy with tension. Still shaking, he lit a second candle on the pillar as a safety measure in case the first should be accidentally extinguished.

In the light of the twin candles he could at last begin to make out more clearly the configuration of the building in which he was trapped. The basic shape was circular, topped by a low, shadow-filled dome. A narrow central aisle ran from the steps toward the wall at the far end, reaching its limit at the opening to a sort of cage filled from bottom to top with a jumbled heap of honey-colored skulls, some intact, some lacking a lower jaw. On either side of the aisle the floor had been cut down into a deep pit—just how deep David could not tell. These two pits were filled with a tangle of human bones. David could make out shin and chest bones, vertebrae, mandibles, ribs, whole hands and feet, the bones still joined grotequely by ribbons of dried flesh and muscle. The flesh, where it still adhered to the bones, had become hard and brittle like parchment. Dust lay thick and heavy over everything, and all through the bones ran matted strands of ancient cobwebs.

Lying or sitting on top of the bone pits were several badly decomposed but otherwise intact bodies. David remembered now what he had been told at St. Catherine's about the disposal of the dead. When monks or pilgrims died, they were buried initially in the small monastic graveyard. After a number of years, however, their remains would be exhumed, for soil is scarce in Sinai and pious people in several countries longed to be buried there. The bodies were taken from the graveyard to the ossuary, where they would continue to decay until their bones collapsed into the heap along with those of every previous generation. The skulls would be removed and stored separately.

Much the same must happen here, David thought, although, from the state of some of the remains he suspected that many were placed directly in the ossuary. Out of more than a dozen corpses, at least three seemed to have been there little more than a year. Their heads had fallen back and their mouths were wide open, as if they were screaming in the silence. Hair still clung to their heads and matted beards to their chins.

In front of the cage of skulls sat several figures dressed in the robes of monks. David went closer and saw that they were mummified remains, saints perhaps, set up to watch over the other dead. One of them held a staff, another a book, and between the wizened fingers of a third hung a Greek rosary of black knotted wool. This last corpse peered out at David from beneath an ancient cowl, the eye sockets hidden in deep shadow, terrible and menacing. Above the breast was written in Greek the word "Nilus." So this, David thought, was the saint after whom the monastery was named. After sixteen hundred years his bones were still the object of pious devotion.

David looked systematically for some sign of an alternative way out, but there was none. The floor was solid rock, the walls windowless and doorless. He sat down, putting the candle on the ground beside him. He felt hopelessness rush over him, wave after dull wave of it, sapping him, draining him of all energy. A deep lethargy mounted in him, destroying his will to think or act. He wanted to blow out the candle and lie there in the dark until he joined the dead. In some ways he already felt he belonged to them. What was the point of attempting what he knew to be impossible? He was already as good as dead, the latest victim in a grim tragedy whose meaning he still could not even guess at. Why had the killer chosen this death for him, the slowest of deaths, under the gaze of those already dead? He looked round at the contorted bodies, worm-eaten, brittle. They were like a welcoming party, assembled for his benefit. He bent down to blow out the candle.

Something moved. Out of the corner of his eye he had caught a glimpse of brief movement. There was a rustling sound, faint and all but inaudible even in that stillness. He sat without moving, listening. A dry rattling came from his left. Slowly he turned his head. At first he saw nothing, then he caught sight of another movement. Out of a black gap between a jawbone and a sternum a large spider scuttled into view. Along with God knew how many others, it had its nest down among the crumbling bones. The light had drawn it to the surface. It was as big as a large tarantula, but pale and with a bulbous, speckled anterior section. Its long jointed legs arced above its body, moving as if hinged across the uneven surface of the bones.

David froze. He had a horror of spiders—it was a phobia he had known since childhood, something years of archaeological work had never cured. It was the one fear that haunted his worst nightmares, something he dreaded more than physical danger or pain. Even as he watched it crawl in the direction of the candle, he heard another rattling sound and saw a second monster come into sight behind the first, its pale legs clicking against one another. In his mind's eye, David could see the place come alive with spiders, and he felt blind terror grip him, worse than any he had known up to that point. He had to get out. Nothing could make him sit there in the dark now. There had to be a way.

As if terror had spawned it, the solution came to him. It would be desperate and it probably would not work, but it was all the chance he had. In his fear he had somehow remembered the icon he had seen near the altar in the church: the bodies of the dead being consumed in the flames of hell, like brands burning in the hands of the demons who wielded them. He looked at the cadavers in front of the cage of skulls. As he had thought, several of them showed signs of having been mummified. That was, in itself, unusual. David knew that the early Christian Fathers, including St. Anthony, the founder of monasticism, had strongly disapproved of the artificial preservation of the dead. But he also knew that the Coptic Christians of Egypt had continued to embalm their dead in the ancient fashion. Mummies of the late Roman period were poor enough specimens, exercises in bandaging more than anything. But the embalming process still involved the use of a number of substances that rendered the body inflammable. Dehydrated in natron, mummies might be partly filled with resin or bitumen and impregnated with rich oils. They burned like torches, and even in recent times Arabs had used them to keep themselves warm in winter.

It was distasteful, but David had no choice. Hoping nothing would crawl out from underneath the robes, and praying the limbs would remain intact, he picked up the body of Nilus. It was surprisingly light. One hand supporting the thighs, the other beneath the thin neck, David carried the saint to the steps. As he started to climb them, the cowl fell back, exposing a bald pate with a few wisps of dried hair. Without the hood, Nilus seemed less menacing, just a pathetic, shrunken old man in David's arms. He carried him to the top and laid him down by the door. The little, shriveled saint seemed to look up at him with his sightless sockets, mortally offended by the sacrilege of such treatment. David patted the leathery bald head.

"I'm sorry, Nilus, my friend," he said, "but I have no choice. It's either you or me."

He pulled the cowl back over the withered head and went back down the stairs.

One by one, he brought the other mummies, seven in all, and stacked them on top of Nilus. Everywhere, the bones were coming alive as spiders crawled out into the unaccustomed light. He needed more tinder. The bodies on the bone pits were not mummified, but they had dried out thoroughly in their hot sand graves and would burn well, once alight. David reached out for one and drew it toward him. The arm came away in his hand and the body collapsed in a heap of withered limbs. Shutting his mind to the horror of what he was doing, David gathered up what he could like firewood in his arms and tossed it on the heap by the door.

He returned to the pit and took hold of the legs of a second corpse. The whole body shifted and came toward him. He stretched forward to pick it up and even as he did so felt something soft and hairy climb onto his left hand. It was a large black tarantula, and David knew its bite could kill. His legs felt like water, every nerve in his body shuddered, and his skin crawled. His instinct was to fling it off, but he knew that an unwary movement could provoke it to bite. Horror-struck, he watched it creep slowly onto his wrist and then along his forearm. Reaching down with his right hand, he fumbled among the bones, taking hold of a long, thin one. The spider was at his elbow now and still climbing. Lifting the bone, he put it to his left shoulder, then swept abruptly down along the arm, sending the spider flying into the air.

Shuddering, he reached again for the corpse and pulled it toward him, keeping a careful watch for any movement. When he had added the body to the pile, he returned for a few final items—several more arms and legs, bits of dried cloth from shrouds and winding sheets, and the wooden chair on which the remains of Nilus had been seated.

Taking a long shinbone out of one of the heaps, David wrapped pieces of cloth around it to make a torch. He held a candle flame to it and watched it flare up instantly. Quickly, he ran the brand along the bottom of the pile of corpses. They took fire straight away, long flames rolling along the twisted limbs. Empty eye sockets stared out at him, gaping mouths grinned and snarled, hands seemed to claw and grasp the smoke. The pile shifted, as if the bodies were trying to escape from the flames. David stepped back, revolted. He thought of his parents in the death camp, the corpses piled up ready for the crematoria, the flames in the ovens red and greedy.

Thick, acrid smoke billowed out from the heap of corpses, swirling into the small chamber. Choking, his eyes watering, David stepped back to the cage of skulls. He had to choose his moment well. If he rushed too soon, the door might not have caught fire

131

sufficiently to be broken. But if he left it too long he would be overpowered by the smoke as it filled the ossuary with black, poisonous fumes. The flames crackled and sang, feeding on dried flesh and the spices of ancient embalmers. Limbs burst and bent and twisted, then crumpled into ashes. Smoke poured out in a thickening cloud through which David could scarcely see. His eyes stung fiercely, his chest burned and heaved with wracking coughs. His head began to spin, filled with the sound of crackling, the roar of the flames magnified. Every nerve, every fiber of his body screamed at him to run, to break out, now while he could still breathe.

But a corner of his mind resisted. He had to hold on. The smoke was everywhere now, like a thick, deadly blanket. Every tearing breath was a torment. He couldn't last much longer. His chest was in agony, his throat was filled with a searing, cutting pain. Get out! Now!

He resisted, fighting himself, holding out against the overwhelming urge to run. Bending low, he tried to suck what little oxygen was left at ground level, but only smoke entered his lungs. It was now or not at all.

Staggering, his knees buckling as he pushed himself forward, he made his way down the aisle in the direction of the flames, dim behind the pall of smoke. His right foot slipped, crashing down among bones into the pit. He fell, rolled to the left, and picked himself up. He could feel himself giving way. Up the steps, one after the other, dragging his feet like lead weights. There were the flames, a great wall of fire now. The door was alight and burning fiercely.

He stumbled into the pile of charred corpses, throwing himself against the door. It groaned but would not give. Stepping back, he flung himself at it again. He heard it cracking but it held firm. His head spun. There was no more air. With a last despairing effort, he fell backward against the wood. There was a splintering sound and he felt himself crash through the burning timbers, out onto the ground beneath. Cold air like ice rushed into his lungs. He rolled away from the flames, sucking in air, and came to a standstill. Black, spinning oblivion rushed up and carried him away. But just before he lost consciousness he was sure he saw someone standing beside him, watching him.

132

SIXTEEN

When David woke, the purple sky of dawn was turning blue. He rolled over, coughed, and felt a searing pain in his chest that doubled him up in agony. The pain subsided and he opened his eyes again. The light still stung, but not as fiercely as it had when he first opened his eyes. His head throbbed, and his chest ached, as if a steel band had been fastened round it and was being further tightened. Slowly, he sat up.

He had been lying several yards away from the door of the ossuary. The wood had burned right through now, and there were no flames at the entrance, although a few wisps of smoke still floated out of the opening. He realized that what he had thought was the figure of a man standing over him as he fell unconscious was a lifesize icon painted on one side of the door, a saint keeping watch over the dead within, as if they had been the Seven Sleepers of Ephesus. He felt sick and tired. He had no idea how long he had lain there. His memory of the time he had spent in the charnel house was like the memory of a dream.

For a long while he lay there, enjoying the light, breathing the clear air deep into his lungs. He was weaker than ever, desperately hungry, and extremely thirsty. If he did not find food soon he would no longer have enough strength to move. Standing, he staggered to the steps. The descent looked more precipitous than ever, but at least the steps were dry. If he went down backward, he should be able to make it.

Even with frequent rests, it took all his energy to get down. He looked up once, saw the cliff soar above him into the sky, and felt a wave of vertigo run through him. He reached the bottom at last and made his way into the refectory. Nothing could take him back into the dark maze of the main building. He assumed that the killer had by now vacated the monastery, though he could not be sure; but somehow it did not matter. Even if the killer was there inside the refectory, he had to go in to look for food.

In the small kitchen there were ample provisions. The food was plain—bread, dried fruit, and grains—but it looked delicious to David. He drank deeply from a flagon of water, then stuffed raisins into his mouth while he set about lighting the primitive stove. He was soon able to make himself porridge, to which he added brimming handfuls of raisins.

When he had eaten and drunk his fill, he sat back, tired but not sleepy. The food and drink had revived him and cleared his mind. He had to leave. There was nothing more he could do here, nothing anyone could do. He had run out of options, out of strength, out of the will to carry on. He would leave the monastery, find Leyla, make the journey back to St. Catherine's, and from there travel to Israel to recuperate.

Since there was a chance that Leyla had already tried to find him and failed, he could not depend on discovering her and the saddlebags. He filled a sack with food and water, then tied the top with cord. He still felt tired and wanted to stay where he was for the rest of the day to recover as much strength as possible before beginning his journey; but he had no desire to spend the night in the monastery, even in the open. He knew he could not return to the end of the ravine by the way he had come, but perhaps he could climb down the rope that held the old lift. The platform was a few yards away on his right. From where he stood, he could see that the lift was no longer where it had been when he and Leyla had arrived at the monastery. But when he clambered up onto the platform and looked down through the central aperture, he saw that the rope had been cut and the wooden box of the lift could be seen nowhere.

Could he perhaps stack some of the furniture from the church underneath the rope he had left hanging at the top of the cliff? He climbed the stairs again to the highest level. In an instant all his reveries were shattered. The rope was gone. The killer must have climbed out that way and taken the rope with him. David looked at the cliff face above him. It was cut back a little, with a slight overhang, and almost perfectly smooth: no one could climb it without equipment. He would have to try to find a rope in order to get down into the ravine. Despondently, he descended the stairs again to the bottom level.

It took all his courage to reenter the main building. He knew there would be no danger, that the killer had gone, that he was unlikely to find any more bodies. But to go back into the dark, with just a lamp from the refectory, demanded every ounce of spiritual strength he still possessed. With each step, terrible memories flooded back. Every echo caused his pulse to race, every unexpected shadow startled him. He found a long coil of rope in the third storeroom, shoved down between old black metal boxes. The room was small and musty, and from the look of it had not been entered for a very long time. Heavy dust and cobwebs covered everything in a thick pall. He shuddered, thinking of the spiders he had disturbed in the ossuary. But he had to have the rope. In a single, determined motion, he pulled it. As he did so, one of the boxes, beneath which the rope had caught, shifted about a foot. The rope came away in a cloud of dust. David prepared to leave, then caught sight of something.

Underneath the box that had moved was another, identical in size and color. But, unlike the top box, the lid of this one was clear of dust. David could make out some marks and lettering, somehow uneasily familiar yet unclear. Putting down the rope, he took hold of handles on the upper box and hefted it gently. It was not too heavy, and he lifted it clear, placing it on the ground behind him.

A large spider scuttled away into the darkness as its web was torn. David shuddered and stepped back, but he did not leave the room. The lid of the bottom box held all his attention. A gold, stylized eagle stretched its wings across it. The eagle faced out over its left shoulder, presenting to David a single round eye. Sharp, articulated claws gripped a circular wreath. And in the center of the wreath was drawn a silver swastika, scraped and tarnished, but unmistakable. Beneath the eagle, in heavy Gothic letters, were the words *Expedition Ulrich von Meiers: Papiere, Bücher, und Filme* (The Ulrich von Meier Expedition: Papers, Books, and Films).

Bewildered and disturbed, as if he had found a freak among nature, David pushed the lid. It was not locked, but it moved grudgingly, rusted hinges grating as if angry to be roused from a long sleep. Bringing the lamp closer, he looked inside. Whatever it had once contained, the box now held little else but mold. The books and papers had long rotted. Here and there, odd sheets had survived in part, but the mass of the box's contents had decayed into an unreadable mass. Nevertheless, David could not resist the challenge of retrieving something from the mess, just as he had taken tablets from the mud at Tell Mardikh. Carefully, he sifted through the pile of rotting paper: books and papers crumbled between his fingers. Near the bottom, however, he touched something hard and cold. Gently, he grasped it and drew it out: it was a flat metal box, sealed all along its lid with heavy tape and wax.

It took him several minutes to break the seal, which had remained firm and unbroken. He lifted the lid to reveal a small book about six by four inches, bound in red leather, together with a canister of 35mm film. On the cover of the book was stamped the word *"Tagebuch* [Journal]." He lifted the cover and looked at the first page: the paper was yellow and somewhat brittle, and the ink had faded, but the writing was still clear. The script was Arabic, a legible *ruq'a* hand, but David could make no sense of it. He leafed through the stiff yellow pages. There were about fifty in all, covered in the same careful hand. He closed the book gently, replaced it, together with the film, in the small box, closed the lid, and put it down on the floor.

He brushed the coating of dust from the box that had originally sat on top. Another eagle appeared, grimy and badly worn. The wording underneath was too badly effaced to read. The lid would not budge at first, sticking as if it had been welded to the box. Suddenly, it yielded and flew up. David looked down in astonishment at what lay on top. Moth-eaten, but still neatly folded, an SS officer's dress tunic, finely stitched and braided, rested beneath a black cap with a silver death's-head badge. David put the cap to one side and lifted out the tunic. The shoulder tab was embroidered with three plaited silver threads—the owner had been an officer of middle rank. Beneath it lay the rest of the uniform: black trousers, jackboots, a brown shirt with black leather buttons, a black tie, and a black Sam Browne belt. Farther down David found more clothes, civilian clothes that might have been worn by an explorer around the 1930s. The labels indicated that they had all been tailored by Richard Schultz of the Kurfürstendamm in Berlin. Beneath the clothes lay a framed photograph of a young woman, an automatic pistol, a box of bullets, and a music box. David picked up the little box. It was shaped like a small Bavarian house, with a long sloping roof out of which a small handle protruded. He turned the handle and at once the little room was filled with the eerie strains of a song from the past, the old Nazi anthem, the *"Horst Wessel Lied."* The tune ground out into silence, shaking echoes from the cold stone walls. David shivered and stopped cranking the handle. Silence fell abruptly.

He closed the lid of the box and sat down on it. It was as if time and space had warped all around him. Here in the darkness of a monastery in the heart of nowhere, among stones that had not changed in ten centuries, remote, forgotten, ageless, lay relics of a modern cult of death and hatred. It made no sense, not the swastikas, not the Arabic writing in the journal, not the photograph of the primly smiling woman, not the song chiming from the little house-shaped box. The cobwebs and the blind, gradual dust had hidden a darker mystery than David had ever guessed at. Had this been what young John Gates had discovered? Had he learned something he was not supposed to learn, threatened to reveal it in his research? David looked round at the bent and crippled shadows hemming him in. What else lay undiscovered here, in this room, in the other rooms? He picked up the lamp wearily and began to search.

Two hours later he concluded that there was nothing else, unless it was hidden in some other, less accessible part of the monastery. Only a proper search would be able to determine that. He had gone through the main storerooms one by one and found them empty or stocked with sacks of food, vestments, icons, and the small, indispensable sundries of monastic life: candles and oil, scissors, jars of fish glue to stiffen the tall black hats, brooms, brushes, wine for the festivals, a roll of coarse black cloth, crosses of wood and gold and silver, tightly knotted rosaries. In the end he had returned to the room in which he had found the boxes. Perhaps he would be able to return. For the moment he would take with him the only thing that offered any hope of information: the box containing the diary and the roll of film. He put the small box in his sack, picked up the coil of rope, and went out.

The rope was very long and reasonably supple, though its fibers were impregnated with decades of dust; David was uncertain that it would hold his weight. He had no option, however. There had been no other rope, there was no other way out unless he could sprout wings. The winch for the elevator was extremely simple—a thick, six-foot-high, vertical column from which four long branches radiated at right angles, by means of which two or more men could turn it and lift or lower the wooden box. Since his rope was more than twice the length needed to reach the bottom, David simply looped it round the column and tied one end firmly to his waist. By paying the rope out slowly through his hands, he would be able to rappel down the cliff face. He fastened the sack to his belt, gripped the rope tightly, and swung out into the void.

It was an easy decent, but nightmarish, for at every moment he sensed the strain on the old rope. If even a small fraction of it had rotted, it would snap without warning and he would be unable to do anything to save himself. Freud would have been proud of him, he thought: he had replaced his irrational fear of heights by an entirely rational terror of falling.

At the bottom, relieved but shaky, he stood for a while debating with himself whether or not to retrieve the rope and take it with him, in case it proved useful. In the end, he decided against it: it would have been too heavy and cumbersome to carry any real distance, would probably not be needed in the end, and would make reentry to the monastery a lot easier if for any reason he found he did have to come back. He wondered where the wooden elevator had gone, then looked about at the still glistening rocks and the tiny pools of water that sparkled in every hollow and crevice and realized that there must have been a flash flood. A feeling of unease tugged at the back of his mind. He hoped Leyla was still safe. She knew how to take care of herself, but he still felt anxious for her. He smiled and thought of Freud again: the anxiety he felt probably took care of a hell of a lot of displaced libido. Leyla was very pretty and very untouchable.

He set off down the passage in the direction he and Leyla had taken . . . how many days ago? Assuming he had not been unconscious long inside the ossuary or after escaping from it, perhaps two days, but he could not be sure. His biggest worry was that Leyla might have gone. She could not be expected to stay at the

138

end of the canyon indefinitely.

He almost passed it without noticing. At first it seemed like just another boulder, rather oddly shaped. Then he saw that it was one of the saddlebags they had brought from St. Catherine's. It was lying pressed up against a boulder, waterlogged and heavy. David's heart beat quickly in fierce little blows. The flash flood must have carried it here, but surely not from the other end of the pass.

The horse was lying just round the next bend, its body stranded behind an outcrop of the cliff. Its lips were drawn back from yellow teeth in a macabre grimace, and its legs stuck out inelegantly, stiff and awkward. Insects and small animals were already picking at its flesh, although they had made few inroads as yet. David now felt genuinely frightened. Leyla must have entered the defile with the horses and been caught by the flood. Frantically, he looked about, running up and down the small stretch of canyon. She was nowhere to be seen.

He continued on down the *shi'b,* scouring the ground for a sign of her presence, hoping she had been able to find a high rock or ledge on which to shelter, but there was nothing. He came out at last onto the broad wadi and made for the slope on which he had left her. He found the remains of a fire, various cooking utensils, and her sleeping bag still unrolled, but she was not in sight. Then he caught sight of a white handkerchief on which words had been scrawled in charcoal. The message was brief: "Horses stolen; investigating; wait for me here." But when had she written this? It was clear from the state of the fire that she had not been here for some time.

He called her name loudly, time after time, but it only echoed faintly among the hills and was swallowed up again. Despairing, he sat down. Suddenly, without knowing why, he began to weep. He was not shedding tears for Leyla particularly or for himself or for anyone else. There had been too many deaths for that. He was weeping out of simple despair, out of a sense of waste that filled him with its emptiness. He wanted to vomit, to get rid of the sour taste in his stomach, but nothing would come. He picked up the sack of food, rolled Leyla's sleeping bag, slung it on his back, and started back down the narrow gorge.

SEVENTEEN

He noticed the elevator box just as he was turning from the pass
into the Shi'b al-Ruhban proper. It was a crude wooden box, about
four feet deep and five square. It had obviously been lifted by the
flood and carried some two hundred yards past the monastery,
where it now lay on its side, partly concealed by several large
branches that had been trapped against it. Something lay on top of
the structure, something sickeningly familiar. David ran down to it,
his heart in his mouth.

Leyla's body lay awkwardly across the planking, one arm
dangling limply down the side of the elevator. David jumped and
pulled himself up beside her. Her clothes were damp and torn, and
her skin was badly bruised and lacerated in several places. He felt
anguish and rage take hold of him. He wanted to swear at God, tear
Him down from wherever He sat watching all this. A murdering
God, smug in His omnipotence.

He bent down and touched Leyla's cheek. It was cold, like stone.
He could not tell how long she had lain there, how long she had
been dead. What could he do with her? There was nowhere to bury
her, here among acres of solid rock, and he could not carry her back
to St. Catherine's or up to St. Nilus'. He was not Moses, to strike
the rock with his staff and cause it to open. He touched her cheek
again, brushing back a strand of hair that had fallen across it. She
moaned.

At first he could not be certain, it was such a faint, almost
inaudible sound. Then it came again, louder this time. He grabbed
her wrist and felt frantically for a pulse. There was nothing at first,

140

then he found it, weak and irregular.

He realized at once what must have happened. If she had been with the horse in the gorge, she would have been swept along by the flood to this point. Just before reaching the spot where the elevator lay, the flood would have lost much of its force, a large portion of it being deflected out into the main Shi'b al-Ruhban channel. Leyla must have caught hold of the wooden structure as she was being dragged past and been able to keep her grip as the floodwaters subsided.

Rummaging in his sack, he brought out the brandy flask, unscrewed it and held it to Leyla's lips, letting a thin trickle of the pale liquid run through them into her mouth. She coughed and spluttered, and her eyelids quivered briefly. He cradled her head in his left hand. She seemed small and fragile and very near death. He had to make a decision, and quickly. There were three courses of action he could take: he could try somehow to get Leyla into St. Nilus', make her as comfortable as possible, and go for help; he could stay with her in the monastery, nursing her until she was strong enough to make the journey to St. Catherine's with him; or he could risk taking her with him as soon as she recovered consciousness, perhaps the next morning. There were objections to each of these options. If he abandoned Leyla in her present condition, it was highly likely she would die before he could bring help. But if he stayed and became ill himself—as was not impossible—they would both be trapped up there and he could do nothing except watch her die before dying himself. If he took her with him, she would slow him down, and the journey, relatively short though it was, might kill her.

She moaned again, more plainly this time. He poured a little more brandy into her mouth. Her lips moved and she coughed again, her head jerking forward as she did so. Her eyelids flickered, opened for a fraction of a second, then closed again. She was coming round. He opened a flask of water and splashed some gently on her face. She did not seem to respond at first, but gradually a barely perceptible trace of color crept into her face. Her eyes opened, unfocused and blurred. He stroked her forehead and whispered her name.

"Leyla, can you hear me?" he asked.

She coughed and her eyes filled with pain. That was good, David thought. Pain was consciousness, pain was awareness; only the unconscious and the dead were free of it.

"Here," he said, "try to drink some more of this." He raised the brandy to her lips once more and tilted a little into her mouth. This time she sipped and it did not choke her. She smiled. It wasn't much as smiles go, more of a grimace, but it was a step in the right direction. She shifted a little and the smile vanished: a cry of pain shuddered out of her throat and her eyes came wide open. It took more than a minute for the agony to subside. When at last she seemed calm again, he poured more brandy between her lips.

"Where does it hurt?" he asked.

Half a minute passed, then the answer came in jagged, pain-wracked bursts.

"My . . . side. . . . It feels . . . as if . . . something's . . . broken."

Carefully, he unbuttoned her heavy outer jacket and peeled it back. He touched her left side, but she did not respond, then her right side. She winced in pain. Gently, afraid of hurting her, knowing he did so, he rolled up her sweater and shirt. The skin beneath was a mass of bruises, and in places it had been torn severely. As lightly as possible, he touched the area around her ribs. She was raw and bruised, but he could see no sign of a broken bone.

"I don't think you've broken anything," he told her, "but you're badly bruised and you may have cracked a rib or two." He buttoned her up again, raised her head once more, and gave her a little brandy. In a voice that was little more than a weak whisper, she spoke again.

"Is . . . that . . . you . . . Professor Rosen?"

"Who the hell did you think it would be? A St. Bernard? And for God's sake call me David. Even my friends call me that."

She smiled.

"I wish . . ." she began.

He put a finger against her mouth.

"Don't wish. You aren't well enough to wish. Just lie here until we can move you."

"We . . . ?"

He sighed.

"No, just me. I'll explain later. Rest for the moment."

She closed her eyes and lay back on the planks. He did not like the look of her. Her skin was an unhealthy color, gray with patches

142

of dull red put there by the brandy. Moving her any distance was out of the question. So was leaving her. She lapsed into unconsciousness again. David held her hand for a while, so she would know she was not alone.

She woke about an hour after sunset, cold and shivering. In spite of the pain, David helped her climb down from the top of the box onto the ground. The large crate would serve as a rough shelter. He put Leyla in the sleeping bag and placed her partly inside and partly outside the elevator cage. He had gathered pieces of driftwood left by the flood and built a large fire in front of the box. It burned brightly, as much a talisman against the darkness he had come to hate so vehemently as a source of heat and light. Nevertheless, even fire itself now held for David grim associations he could not easily shake off.

Leyla ate a little—some bread and figs—and threw it up again two minutes later. She could not even keep down water. Her temperature was higher, but she still shivered frequently and fiercely. Without a sleeping bag, David was bitterly cold, even with the fire. He huddled close to it, afraid his supply of wood would be exhausted before the night was through. He slept briefly, around midnight, but was awakened by Leyla coughing, a hard, dry cough that remained unaffected by sips of water. She lapsed into sleep or unconsciousness—he could not tell which—several times during the long night. From time to time she cried out in pain and once in terror, waking in a cold sweat. He did what he could to comfort her, but he had nothing with which to treat her wounds or her other symptoms. His only hope lay in finding some medical supplies in the monastery the next day.

Dawn brought no relief to Leyla. In the brightening sunlight, David could see that her color had risen in the night. Her face and neck were red, with a bluish tinge, and her temperature was extremely high. As the morning wore on, her breathing became more and more shallow, broken by bouts of dry coughing. She began to cough up sputum, a light pink in color, with occasional specks of blood. She slept intermittently, but when she was awake she complained of pain, especially in her chest, which had not been bruised. David talked to her, trying to distract her, but her attention could not be held. He did not tell her about what had happened in the monastery. She seemed to have forgotten the

143

place, to be centered in her pain, in the present moment. From time to time she held him tightly to her, as if afraid. She cried often, sometimes from the pain, sometimes out of fear. She knew she was dying.

David felt more helpless than he had ever felt in his life. Help was perhaps a day's journey away, but it might as well have been a month. He could not leave her. She was terrified of being left alone. He slipped away when she was asleep, but twice he returned to find her in a state of panic, crying and breathing fast. It took him several trips up and down the two canyons to find enough wood for that evening's fire. With enormous difficulty he succeeded in climbing back into the monastery, tying one end of the rope around his waist and rappeling in reverse, using the other half. It took him some time to find the monastery's meager medical supply, consisting of bandages, what looked like antiseptic, creams, numerous jars of herbs, and vials of tiny white tablets whose labels made no sense to him. He took the bandages and the creams and used them to ease Leyla's cuts and bruises. But he could find nothing to give her for her chest and lungs. He knew she had pneumonia and that there was nothing he could do. He put a dressing on her wounds and it seemed like mockery.

In the afternoon her sputum became more profuse and dark rust in color. The area round her mouth was white, and she was hot to touch all over. Once she woke from a troubled sleep to find him beside her. She burst into tears and clutched him fiercely.

"I can't stand this," she said. "I've . . . wet myself . . . and I need . . . the toilet . . . and I don't . . . want you . . . to see me . . . like this. . . . Help me. . . . Please, help me."

He wanted to help her change, to nurse her, but she would not let him. She made him take her behind the shelter. With rocks, he made a rough toilet she could use. A jar of water served in place of paper. He left her, frightened of her weakness, embarrassed by her craving for dignity. Minutes passed, then he heard a cry. Finished, she had fallen trying to get up; she lay on the ground, breathless and in pain. He picked her up and carried her back to the front of their narrow, broken hut.

Her fever continued to rise. He sat with her through the night, watching until she slept, keeping her cool in sleep. About two hours before dawn he fell asleep himself, a deep, remote sleep in

144

which all was blotted out. He dreamed, but he could not remember what he had dreamed when he woke again.

The next day was worse. He wondered if she would die that day. She was hot, as if a fire raged inside her. He dared not leave her for a moment. There was no wood left for the fire, none within gathering distance: the coming night would be long and cold. Leyla tossed and turned all day, knowing little rest, coughing angry gobbets of bloody sputum and lying back exhausted. Once she became lucid and asked him what day it was, how long she had been like this.

"I don't know," he said.

"You . . . must know," she protested. "How . . . long were you . . . in the monastery? Why don't . . . the monks . . . come? Why . . . don't they . . . help . . . us?"

What could he say? Would a lie make any sense? Would the truth harm her now?

"They're dead," he told her. "I found them dead. Someone killed them. He tried to kill me. I was unconscious for a while. I don't know what day it is."

She was silent for a long time after that. Then, just as he thought she had gone to sleep, he heard her say in a weak voice:

"I wish . . . I wish I . . . knew . . . what day . . . it was."

She became silent after that, but increasingly agitated, as if the need to know the date was paramount in her. She seemed tortured, troubled by something more than the pain. Her pulse was rapid and her color bad. David did not know whether she would last the night.

About midnight the fever began. Wracked with the pain of drawing breath, she was drenched in heavy, sour-smelling sweat. Her mind was gone, filled with delirium. She shook and trembled, raving in Arabic, a man's name shouted again and again: "Muhsin, Muhsin, *la tatrukni, la tatrukni* [Don't leave me, don't leave me]." Beside her, David shivered with cold. Her raving allowed him no sleep. He wondered how she held out so long. Her tiny frame seemed almost torn apart by the fever and the constant convulsions. It was wasting her by the minute. And still she clung on.

By morning she was still burning with fever but she was so weak now that she scarcely moved, and he knew she would not last the day. He ate a little and slept just after dawn. When he woke he

145

thought she was dead, she had become so still and quiet. But she still breathed, barely. He wished she would die now. He could not bear to watch her suffer much longer. But he felt a terrible guilt for her death. He had brought her here on a quest that had no meaning for her. He carried no responsibility for the other deaths, except perhaps those of his parents, but hers would always be on his conscience.

Just after noon a horse whinnied somewhere up the valley. David looked up. It seemed to come from near St. Nilus'. He strained his eyes but could see nothing. The sound came again, a little clearer this time. David stood up and began to walk toward it. Leyla had told him about the stolen horse. Had the killer returned for some reason? David was sure it was he who had taken the horses. As he drew near the entrance to the Shi'b al-Ruhban, he heard the sound of slowly moving hooves and the voices of two men. He flattened himself against the wall and waited.

Two horses appeared, ridden by two men dressed in black, monks. David rushed forward, calling. He recognized one of them, Father Gregorios from St. Catherine's, a kindly old monk famous for his sermons and his jam making. The other was a small man of about fifty with a broad black beard and a weathered face out of which two shrewd eyes watched him approach. It was as if all the tension and exhaustion of the past days had been wound up in him in a tight little ball. As he came near the monks, the ball seemed to burst and expand through his veins and arteries. He reached Father Gregorios' horse and clasped the rein, looking up into the old man's face. Tears started in his eyes and suddenly he burst out weeping, overwhelmed by a sense of anguish he had held back until now. The old man dismounted and held him in his arms until the sobbing subsided and he was able to speak.

It did not take him long to explain what had happened. The monks exchanged looks of astonishment and unbelief, but neither appeared frightened by what David told them. They had come to St. Nilus', they said, to celebrate Christmas with their fellow monks. It was an annual visit whose origins dated back to the tenth century. David felt confused at first: surely he and Leyla had arrived here on December 28. Then he remembered that, among the churches of the Eastern rite, the Russians, Serbians, some of those on Mount Athos, and those of Jerusalem and Sinai still kept to the old Julian calendar. Christmas Day was on the seventh of January. Today, they told him, was the second.

The younger monk had already dismounted. He reached up to his saddlebag and lifted down a small leather case.

"Quickly," he said. "Where is the girl?"

David led him down the small pass to where she lay. Without a word, the man bent down and began to examine her. From his manner, it was obvious that he was a trained doctor. This, David thought, must be Father Symeon, the physician monk at St. Catherine's, whom he had heard of but not met. He watched as the man carried out routine checks, then answered a range of detailed questions about the course of Leyla's illness. Satisfied, the doctor turned to his case and took out a small glass vial of tiny pills. David noticed that the case was full of similar vials, perhaps a hundred or more of them. Father Symeon carefully tipped out two pills, resealed the vial, and placed them in Leyla's mouth.

"What are you giving her?" David asked. "An antibiotic?"

The monk shook his head.

"No," he said, "that is not my way. I treat homeopathically. This is a potentization of phosphorus. I'll repeat the dose every hour at first, then perhaps every two hours. It will bring her fever down, slow her pulse, allow her to sleep. I shall want her moved as soon as possible, perhaps tonight, perhaps in the morning. But first I think you will need some treatment yourself."

David was also given two tiny sugar pills, impregnated with something Father Symeon called aconite. In less than an hour he felt much better and was able to sleep. When he woke it was dark. A fire had been lit: Father Gregorios had traveled far in search of wood. There was a smell of food cooking, hot and aromatic. David realized suddenly that he was extremely hungry. He sat up, rubbing sleep from his eyes. The two monks were seated by the fire. Father Gregorios was cooking, while Father Symeon knelt beside Leyla in prayer. He had administered the sacrament of *euchelaion*, anointing her with oil: it was not a last rite for the dying but an essential element in prayer for the recovery of the sick. When David asked later, Symeon told him it did not matter that Leyla was a Muslim: there was a mosque in the courtyard of St. Catherine's; the Dome of the Rock and the Aqsa Mosque both stood on the site of the Temple of Jerusalem; he himself had seen miracles performed at the tomb of Nabi Salih near the Watiya Pass. What did a man's religion matter? It was life that was sacred.

David spoke quietly to Gregorios. The old man smiled at him. It seemed like a dream, the old monk by the fire, meat roasting, a warm silence.

"This is part of our Christmas lunch," Gregorios said in a low voice. "We bring meat each year for our brethren in St. Nilus'. I hope you like lamb." He turned the meat on its makeshift spit and sat for a while gazing into the flames. Then he looked up at David. He was no longer smiling.

"They are all dead, you say?"

David nodded.

"Murdered, you say?"

David nodded again.

"Where are they now? Can we go to them?"

David explained about the ossuary. He hesitated when he came to explain how he had escaped. Now that the whole thing seemed more like a nightmare than reality, he felt awkward about his treatment of the corpses. Reluctantly, he told Gregorios how he had burned down the door.

"And what about St. Nilus?" asked the old man. "Did you burn him as well?"

Shamefacedly, David nodded.

To his surprise, Gregorios smiled. David thought he could detect amusement in the gentle, lined eyes.

"Don't worry about it," the old monk said. "We have too many saints as it is. All those old ossuaries full of bones and dried flesh. No need for them. It would be the best thing if we burned the lot of them."

The smile faded.

"No," he went on, "you did the right thing. What is a saint's body worth compared to a life?"

He looked at Leyla, in the shadows.

"Two lives. She would not be alive if you had not escaped. And"—again he smiled, a mischievous twinkle in his eye—"if you and she were to marry and have children, how many more would that be? And grandchildren. Old Nilus would be pleased. He had a son himself."

David looked at Gregorios, puzzled.

148

"A son?" he exclaimed. "But I thought he was a hermit, that he was celibate."

Gregorios nodded and smiled.

"He was, but not to begin with. As a young man, he was married to a lady of noble blood in Constantinople. They had two children, a boy and a girl. Later they came to live in the monasteries of Egypt, his wife with the girl, Nilus with his son, Theodulos. After that the father and son came to live with the monks in Sinai. But Theodulos was taken captive by the pagan Arabs and prepared for sacrifice to their goddess, Venus. He prayed and God saved him, so he was sold as a slave in the market of Suka. At last he was returned to his father and came to live in his colony here in Sinai. Even saints have children, David. Didn't your own holy men have sons and daughters, didn't they love their families? So what is an old corpse? If we find the ashes, we can still enshrine them as a relic. The charred bones of a saint may prove just as powerful as his skin."

Symeon ended his prayer and joined them. He said that Leyla was making good progress and that they might be able to move her into the monastery in the morning, if they could repair the elevator. He examined David again, gave him more pills, and told him he could eat once they had entered his system, in about fifteen minutes.

After the meal they talked. Nothing was said about the killings or David's experiences in the monastery. For his part, he kept quiet about the boxes he had found and the tin with the diary and film, which he kept in his sack.

In the next few days David learned much by watching Father Symeon treat Leyla. She was already much recovered by the afternoon of the second day. With the help of the horses, they were able to rehang the elevator and haul Leyla up to the monastery, where she was made comfortable in the reception room of the main building. Symeon watched her every symptom, spoke with her gently once she was able to answer his questions, took note of her mood and her state of mind, and consulted a thick volume entitled *Materia Medica* kept in the monastery library. He seemed in tune with her, employing empathy rather than detachment, sifting and pondering even the smallest and strangest indications. He turned to

David at one point, just as he had selected a fresh remedy.

"You see," he said, "I am still learning. But she will be well. Her basic constitution is extremely robust. Her vital force is strong. My remedies will not suppress her symptoms, merely allow her body to recover balance. That is what illness is, the organism's efforts to throw off dangerous influences. Sometimes it doesn't know how to regain equilibrium: the remedies help."

By the third day Leyla was fit enough to talk. David came to know her well during the hours and days they spent together in the monastery. He did most of the talking—trivia, details about himself that came closer and closer to his closely guarded center. He told her about his parents, about his father and the amulet, about his Bar Mitzvah and his studies and his loss of faith. She told him about the home that had never been home, her father's love and his fits of rage, her simultaneous and irreconcilable hungers for the desert and the city. Neither spoke of what had happened, but each knew they had shared an intimacy closer than if they had slept together.

"We need have no secrets from one another now," he said, but he kept silent about the hardest things, and she followed his example.

The two monks spent their time restoring the ossuary, library, and church. On Christmas Eve they brought the bodies of the seven murdered monks into the church to perform the burial service. Both David and Leyla attended, standing at the back, unbelievers watching from behind the tall iconostasis through the central "royal" door, listening to the psalms and canticles rising toward the gilded and shadowy roof.

"I weep and mourn when I look upon death, and when I see our beauty, created according to the image of God, laid in the grave, formless, shapeless and without glory. What is this mystery which is our lot? Why are we given to corruption and yoked together with death?"

The voices of the monks rose and fell in the fecund semidarkness, filling the church with a strange, rich music. Candles flickered, lighting the icons, bringing the faces of saints and angels into sharp relief.

"I lie voiceless and deprived of breath. Beholding me, bewail

150

me, for yesterday I spake with you and suddenly on me came the dread hour of death."

David heard behind their voices the voice of the *hazzan* at his parents' funeral, chanting from the Book of Job:

"Man dies, and lies low; man perishes, and where is he? As the waters fall from the sea, and the river is drained dry, so man, when he falls asleep, shall not rise again. Until the heavens are no more he shall not awake, nor rise up out of his sleep."

Above them, the wounded figure of Christ hung limp from his cross. David looked at the bodies laid before the altar. They seemed calm and peaceful now, their arms folded, their eyes closed at last, all obscenity gone. Clouds of incense hung around them, wreathing the golden altar in a sweet-smelling veil. Father Gregorios and Father Symeon, in their ceremonial vestments, seemed to David like strangers, alien beings performing the rites of an alien creed. They sang in Greek, dark music, tragic, the voices of men in the face of unnecessary death.

> "*Kyrie eleison.*
> *Lord have mercy.*
> *Christe eleison.*
> *Christ have mercy.*
> *Kyrie eleison.*
> *Lord have mercy.*"

The bodies were so still, death had never seemed so complete before. Leyla stood like a statue, unmoving, silent, her thoughts far away. David put his arm around her shoulders, but she remained unaware of him. Beyond the iconostasis the voices wove the litany. Leyla broke away abruptly, turned, and headed for the door. David followed her into the narthex, into the darkness. She turned to him, emotions struggling in her face and eyes.

"I'm sorry," she said at last. "When I was ill, I kept thinking about today, thinking it was already today, that I would die."

"Why today?" he asked.

She looked at him, though he was only a shadow in the darkness.

"It was a year ago today that Muhsin died."

"Muhsin." It was the name she had murmured in her fever.

There was a period of silence before she spoke.

"My husband."

At last David began to understand, to see beneath the veils she had wrapped about herself.

"How did he die?" he asked.

She hesitated, then told him in a low voice.

"He became involved in politics at Bir Zeit University. There was a demonstration last year when Israeli troops came in to close down the campus again. Some people threw petrol bombs at an armored car, the troops fired back. Muhsin was in the crowd, trying to control them. A stray bullet hit him. In the back." She paused. "First they take away my home, then my husband. They've left me nothing."

Inside, the chanting ended. David held her, but she was not with him, not in the church.

The next day was Christmas. The monks lit lamps and candles in the church and celebrated the birth of Christ with songs and incense. David and Leyla stayed in the reception room and talked of the past. Christ came into the world once more, God become flesh, the Word descended incarnate. The monks sang and gave praise, saved from the darkness, redeemed to a world of light. But for David and Leyla there had been no birth, no incarnation, no angelic host, only the drab continuation of the unchanging darkness. For Jew and Muslim there could be no redemption in the body and blood of the dying God.

152

EIGHTEEN

They left the following day. In just under a week, Leyla had recovered almost completely. Even her wounds and bruises had healed with remarkable speed and no longer troubled her. She was able to ride, but David preferred to walk alongside her rather than go on horseback again. Father Gregorios rode ahead, engrossed in thoughts of his own. David had seen the old man become serious in the past few days, his normally outgoing qualities replaced by those of brooding and introspection. David thought he knew more than he admitted, that the deaths meant something to him. Once he had seen him come out of the storeroom in which the boxes were kept, his face troubled and drawn.

Father Symeon, on the other hand, though distressed and puzzled by the deaths, showed no signs of knowing any more about them than either David or Leyla. David had a good idea why that should be the case. Symeon was a relative newcomer here, whereas Gregorios had been in this region since his youth, a great many years ago. If David's guess was right, what had just happened here had its roots in events stretching back forty or fifty years.

Sometimes Leyla would ride ahead with Gregorios, engaging him in conversation, lightening his mood with her presence. She had developed a strong affection for the old man, and he for his part returned it, more in the fashion of one who had seen the world than a monk long out of it. During those times David would talk earnestly with Father Symeon, unburdening himself with growing candor. He told Symeon at last of what had brought him to Sinai and St. Nilus', and for the first time he talked about the man he

153

killed at Tell Mardikh. The monk listened in silence, nodding from time to time. He gave no advice, offered no rebuke, passed no judgment. What was there to condemn? he asked. David was not responsible for any of the deaths, he should not blame himself. But equally he had a duty not to give up. If he could find the killers by any means at his disposal, he should do so.

"Weakness is strength," Symeon said. "That is something those who are hungry for power never understand. A gun doesn't make a man strong, it weakens him because he comes to rely on it. Nuclear weapons don't make countries powerful, they sap them financially and morally. Look at my remedies. They are extremely strong. You have seen how effective they are. But they are prepared by diluting the orignial substance, sometimes thousands of times. Yet the more they are diluted the stronger they become as long as they are shaken at each step. Each time they are shaken the energy in them is increased.

"That is where your own strength lies. They think you have no power, so they will take no precautions against you. They think you are dead, so they will not be looking for you. They think you know nothing, but already you have identified the missing manuscript and . . ." He paused. "You have whatever it is you keep so well hidden in your sack."

David started, but the monk ignored him and went on.

"Don't worry. I don't know what you found, and I have no desire to know. You have been summoned to this task; I have no part in it."

He stopped and looked directly at David. His dark eyes were troubled and his lips drawn tight.

"This is something evil, David. What took place in St. Nilus' was the darkest blasphemy. A very great evil has been unloosed. I can sense it, I can feel it in my heart. Gregorios feels it too. He knows something, but he will not talk to me about it. He is frightened, deeply frightened. But it centers in you, David. It has found you and attempted to destroy you. It has taken the lives of people you loved. It is still there, waiting to take other lives, I am sure of it. Now it is your turn to find it and do all in your power to destroy it."

They reached St. Catherine's late on the second day, having traveled slowly with frequent rests. Leyla wanted to travel straight on to al-Arish, but Father Symeon made her stay a full week until she was well enough for the longer journey. She and David explored the monastery together or sat and talked while the monks went about their work around them.

On the morning of their last day she insisted on going with David to climb Jabal Musa, the mountain that towered over the monastery. For centuries, pilgrims had gone there, in the belief that it was Mount Sinai, the mountain on which Moses had received the tablets of the law from God. They started in the early hours of the morning, well before dawn, in order to see the sun rise from the mountain peak. The climb was rough and steep, winding up the side of the mountain along a narrow path. By the time they reached the top, tired and footsore, their enthusiasm had evaporated and they wanted to do nothing but lie down and rest.

And then the sun rose. Out of the east, the light came bouncing across endless miles of sand and stone, climbing and dancing into the sky. Before their eyes, darkness gave way to living sunlight and the world was reborn. The barren landscape that had seemed to them dull and monochrome came alive with vivid, singing colors: purples and reds and blues and greens and yellows, a whole rainbow stretched across the world. Leyla held David's hand and gazed in wonder as Sinai unrolled itself beneath her feet. Below them, mountains and hills and valleys stretched for miles to the horizon. To the north, the great wilderness of the Tih plateau lay like a golden, sun-washed sea, its desolation redeemed by light. Here and there great swaths of black flintstones covered the sand, transforming it into dark, waveless lakes. Sunlight fell on them and was swallowed up.

He heard Leyla whisper beside him, soft phrases of Arabic, incomprehensible.

"Salabu minni 'l-bayta wa babahu
salabu minni 'l-haqla wa 'ushbahu."

The words went on, sweet-sounding, sad and delicate, line after line, a gentle rhyme tying them together like a fine thread joining pearls. When she fell silent at last, he turned and looked at her. Tears were streaming down her face.

"Your father's?" he asked.

She nodded.

"It sounded beautiful," he said. "But I didn't understand a word of it."

She was silent, wiping away her tears.

"You wouldn't understand it," she said at last, "not even if you spoke perfect Arabic."

"Why not?"

She hesitated.

"Because you're a Jew," she said. "Because you're an American."

"I can't help that," he said. "I was born a Jew. Don't blame me for that."

"I'm not blaming you," she said.

"Then let me try to understand."

There was a longer silence, then she began again hesitantly, in English.

> "They have taken my house, and its door;
> they have taken my field, and its grass;
> they have taken my land, and its people.
> The stream I bathed in
> and the tree I sheltered beneath,
> the hill I grazed goats on
> and the flowers at its foot,
> the shrine of Abu Ahmad
> and my mother's grave—
> they have taken them all
> in the name of a strange God.
> Here, amidst sand and rocks,
> blinded by summer sun
> and cold with winter rains,
> I wander like the lost tribes
> in search of their angry God
> and the promise of another land."

She stopped, but her voice seemed to echo in his ears, the words tumbling like stones among the hills and valleys below.

"It was one of his first poems," she said. "He wrote it soon after he arrived in Sinai. He's still searching for your Jewish God. There's so much he wants to know, so many questions he wants answers to. If you ever meet your God, tell him my father's still waiting. It'll

156

soon be forty years. Even the Children of Israel got their Promised Land after that long."

David held her hand more tightly, but he said nothing. What was there to say after all? If they were ever to meet the God responsible for all this, it would be here, on this mountain. But wherever David looked, he saw only empty sand and stone.

They reached al-Arish toward noon, traveling by the western coast road as far as Wadi Sudr, then branching northeast through Bir Tamada and Bir Hasana. During the journey David had begun to hope that Leyla might agree to travel on to Jerusalem with him. He had no reason to expect it, there was nothing between them more than friendship, but he hoped it nevertheless. They came at last to the turnoff, where the road joined the coastal highway that led through the Gaza Strip to Eretz Israel. David stopped the jeep and turned off the engine.

"This is where we part company," he said.

She stared ahead through the windshield. The streets were familiar, the buildings numbered and tallied deep in her unconscious: acres of mud brick dotted with palm trees, above them the minaret of the principal mosque. She could smell the sea air. Gulls flew in from the Mediterranean.

"I have to go on today," he said. "I don't think there's time to waste any longer. I must go to Jerusalem. There are those things I said I had to do there."

"I know," she said. There was a pause. Children shouted in the street, an old man on a donkey passed them, incurious. "Don't ask me to come with you. Later, perhaps, but not now. I can't think of Jerusalem at the moment."

"Don't you have things to do there too?" he asked, pushing too much. He knew he should switch on the engine and leave. There was a cool breeze from the sea. He could taste the salt on his tongue.

She went on looking out the windshield, measuring, surveying.

"It seems far away," she said. "I can't explain it. I'm living two lives, two identities: Leyla Rashid the academic, Leyla Rashid the guide. I have to decide. All that seems unreal from here. This is my world, David; it's where I was brought up, where I belong. My father always wanted me to go back, back to Palestine. After the

157

Israelis occupied Sinai, I could go there, study, live like one of them . . . marry." There was a long pause. The wind tossed her hair like waves caressing seaweed among the rocks.

"But it wasn't Palestine," she said. "It wasn't home."

He looked at her. In profile her face was distant, two-dimensional.

"Palestine is just make believe, David," she went on. "It's what keeps us going, like a promise of candy to a spoiled child. I've never been there, I never will be. It doesn't exist any longer, the Palestine they remember, the Palestine they all talk about, my father and his friends. All those poems about Palestine, all those speeches, all that blood. For what? For a never-never land, a land of Oz. I'm tired of it, David. In the canyon, when I thought I was dying, I was able to see things a lot more clearly. I need time to think now. It's too soon for Jerusalem. Maybe never; I don't know."

A loudspeaker on the minaret crackled awkwardly into life. The words of the call to prayer cranked out: flat, distorted, mingling bleakly with the cries of the gulls.

"Allahu akbar, allahu akbar."

"David." Leyla turned in her seat.

"Allahu akbar, allahu akbar."

"I can't come with you. Please understand."

"Ashhadu an la ilaha illa 'llah."

He said nothing.

"It wouldn't work, David," She stared out the window. "Nothing works."

"Ashhadu an la ilaha illa 'llah."

David stretched out his hand to touch her, but she drew away.

"Ashhadu anna Muhammadan rasul Allah."

"I have to go, David." She pulled her bag from the back of the Jeep and opened the door.

"Ashhadu anna Muhammadan rasul Allah."

The tape was old and worn, the words unclear. David switched on the ignition; the engine roared into life, drowning out the call to prayer.

"Good-bye, David," she said. "Take care."

He smiled and let in the clutch. The Jeep moved forward slowly, then picked up speed as he turned onto the Via Maris.

He drove on, past palms and eucalyptus trees, skirting the sea, until al-Arish had vanished beneath the horizon. Several miles before Sadot, the road came down close to the ocean. David stopped the Jeep and switched off the engine. There was very little traffic. A great silence seemed to hang over everything, broken only by the sound of waves crashing on the beach below. He opened the door of the Jeep and stepped out into the stiffening breeze. Behind him, almond trees bordered the road. He crossed the bank and walked down a gentle slope onto the beach. White sand stretched away on either side. He went down to the water's edge, looking out across the sea, watching the waves sweep down to the beach in an endless cycle.

He stepped from the shore into the sea. It seemed so unclear to him, to pass without obvious transition from the one to the other, from element to element, as it were. They seemed to merge, one eating into the other, the constant coming and going of the tides. And yet the words were so distinct, like hard crystal, "sea" and "shore," "water" and "land." There could be no middle ground.

He walked out into the waves, letting them rise up to his loins, then to his waist, and finally to his chest. His feet felt insecure on the shifting surface of pebbles underneath, as if an undertow would come and uproot him at any moment. He would sink and drift, like so much flotsam tossed on the waves. He would be cast up finally on the beach, a piece of driftwood among bones and shells and all the weed-encrusted refuse of the sea.

He stood like that for a long time, letting the waves baptize him with their salt and foam, gazing out to the distance, as if waiting for something or someone to appear from beyond the long horizon. But there was only the sea and the wind. He turned at last and made his way back to the beach.

THREE

Thy holy cities are a wilderness,
Zion is a wilderness,
Jerusalem a desolation.

Isaiah 64:10

Jerusalem was desolate, stranded between festivals. The lights of Chanukah had been extinguished. Christmas had gone, both Western and Eastern. Purim, with its joy and drunkenness, was still some two months away, Easter and Pesach further still. The streets were filled with ordinary people. The only processions were for weddings and funerals, and sometimes they would cross one another's paths. At the Wailing Wall bearded men swayed back and forth in prayer, day after day, week after week, the great stones dwarfing them, all proportion gone. Above them, the Muslim faithful worshiped and discoursed in the Dome of the Rock and the Aqsa Mosque, the abomination of desolation, the feet of Gentiles walking upon the stones of the fallen Temple, treading underfoot the Holy of Holies.

Leaving the Temple Mount behind him, David Rosen crossed the Via Dolorosa and plunged into the Muslim Quarter of the Old City. He left the tourist shops behind and skirted the *suq*, heading away from the crowds into quiet, narrow streets and dingy alleyways. Several times he lost his way, but each time he succeeded in retracing his steps and locating the right turning. He passed old men at a coffee shop, smoking *nargilas* and playing backgammon, moving the black and red counters around the boards with astonishing speed. They gazed at him, their faces incurious, their thoughts far away.

This was a dangerous part of the city. Seedy hotels and cheap shops lined the streets. Men lounged about, sizing up the passersby. The children did not play but stood in small groups, serious, intent on mastering the menaces of the street. David felt conspicuous and vulnerable. He should not have come alone. A cassette recorder blared somewhere, loud Arab music, an *oud* in the background, small drums beaten rapidly; it was a love song, *"Ahdayt li warda,"* the shrill voice of a young girl oozing with saccharine passion. An army jeep turned into the street and drove past slowly. David could feel tension rise as it passed, could sense the resentment. Two young soldiers stood in the back, guns at an angle, ready for trouble, their faces tense. One of them called to him in Hebrew, "Are you lost?" but David ignored him and walked on. The jeep drove away and disappeared into the crowds.

The house dated from the late Ottoman period. The white granite facade was grimy and in need of repair. Someone had urinated against the wall. Old PLO slogans could still be made out, partly scrubbed away, beneath torn posters advertising concerts of Arab music. A thin dog ambled past, sniffed the wall attentively for a moment, and was gone. David hesitated. People were staring in his direction, their eyes hostile. He took hold of the heavy brass knocker and banged it twice against the door. The thick wood absorbed the sound. He knocked again. A voice came, a single woman's voice, in guttural Arabic. The door opened, a crack only, to reveal part of an old woman's face, wizened and suspicious.

"Shu fi? What's up?" she asked, as if no one would call at the door unless something were wrong. Without waiting for an answer, she went on, "There's no one here. You're wasting your time. Go away."

She began to close the door, but David had his hand against it, holding it open.

"I want to see Hasan," he said.

"No one here called Hasan. Go away." She pushed the door with surprising strength. David put one hand against it and held it open. He glanced at the number on the wall above the door, a white Arabic numeral enameled on blue. He looked back at the crone. Tiny, red-rimmed eyes glared at him.

"This is number 10 Shari' al-Najjarin?" he asked, although he could see for himself it was.

She nodded, frowning. Even she could not deny it.

"I was told I would find Hasan al-Yunani here. I have business with him. Tell him my name is David Rosen, Professor Rosen, and

164

that I want to speak with him. There's money in it."

The old woman sniffed but stood her ground.

"Money?" she exclaimed with a squeak. "I don't see any money. Go away." It was her favorite phrase and she planned to get it in as often as she could before circumstances forced her to give in. She pushed even harder against the door. It nearly closed.

From his pocket, David drew out five hundred-shekel notes and held them at the crack, in front of the woman's face. A withered hand snaked out and the notes were gone. The oldest conjuring trick in the world, in one of the oldest currencies. The door opened and David stepped through.

He was in a low, dark vestibule at the end of which stood another heavy, studded door. The old woman closed the street door and they were in virtual darkness, save for some thin rays of light that managed to creep down through cracks in the ancient wooden ceiling overhead. He smelled her beside him, old and fetid. The left-hand wall was cut back at hip level, providing a stone bench on which visitors had waited in the old days. It was cluttered now with rags and broken pots and old rusted cans of kerosene. In a dirty cobweb near the door a fat old spider sat waiting for flies to satisfy his never ending hunger.

The woman hobbled to the inner door. Lifting a rusty latch, she opened it and walked ahead of David into a square courtyard. David followed, closing the door behind him. The courtyard was empty. The old woman had vanished. David glanced around him. In the center of the courtyard sat an old tiled fountain, railed in wrought iron. The fountain was dry, bone-dry. From the look of it, it had not flowed with water in years, perhaps decades. The colored tiles around its base and central column were cracked and broken; some had fallen off completely. They were little Turkish tiles, whose lustrous glaze of turquoise and cinnamon and saffron had grown dull and mottled. The railing was bent and rusted. Weeds crawled over everything, weak, dust-covered weeds and starved, jaundice-yellow grasses. All around the courtyard, cracked and pitted flagstones and faded tiles were giving way to the choking weeds. The walls of the house itself were gray and spotted with lichen; plaster peeled away in spots, leaving sickly spaces of old, crumbling brick. The windows were shuttered and dead. Nothing moved.

David could not understand it. The man he had come to visit was one of the wealthiest men in Jerusalem. Hasan al-Yunani was a Greek Cypriot by birth: his real name was Stavros Kyriakides. He had arrived in Jerusalem illegally in 1946, at the age of twenty-three: some said he had been forced to leave Famagusta because of a family feud in which he had been responsible for the death of a relative.

Following the establishment of the state of Israel, he had left his small apartment on David Street on the edge of the Christian Quarter and moved to a small house on the Muslim side of the Damascus Gate, not far from the Mawlawiyya Mosque. During the next few years he had left behind his previous identity and taken a new one.

In 1951 he had converted to Islam and changed his name to Hasan, although he was still known in the quarter as "al-Yunani [the Greek]." Over the years that followed, Hasan al-Yunani became untouchable. He knew everyone and he knew everyone's weakness. It was said there were no secrets in Jerusalem to which he was not privy. He had ears and eyes everywhere, listening, watching, taking note. As time went on, no one was safe from him, not even the city's most powerful men. He had more enemies than friends, yet he was the safest man in Israel for the simple reason that he was the most dangerous. And if he was dangerous, he was also useful. He traded information. He had no scruples, no loyalties. For the right price or a suitable favor, he would tell a man whatever he needed to know or supply him with anything he wanted: power, money, a woman, a man, a life . . . a book.

There was a harsh whisper. David spun around. The old woman had returned. She stood staring at him beside an open door.

"He will see you now," she said. "Come." Her voice was no warmer than it had been, her expression no sweeter.

David stepped carefully across the worn tiles of the courtyard. The woman stood aside and let him pass through the open doorway. He stepped into a short, dark corridor lit by a single candle. She closed the door, then hobbled past him along the narrow corridor to another door on the left.

"He will come soon," she said. "Wait here." Bending, she opened the door to let him into the room. He went inside and the door was closed behind him.

Gray light filtered through grime-coated windows, diffuse and colorless. Everything in the room seemed washed out, faded. Dust was everywhere, on the ancient, high-backed chairs and carved oriental tables, on the thick Persian rugs that carpeted the floor, on the heavy velvet curtains that hung, rotten with age, on the walls by the windows. The corners of the room were lost in shadow. High up, David could see cobwebs weighed down with dust. There was a strong smell of mildew, an unpleasant odor that caught in David's throat. The walls were covered from top to bottom with old framed photographs, portraits of men and women and children, a gallery of faces, blank, formal expressions, sad eyes. It was like a butterfly collection, human faces pinned to al-Yunani's wall forever. In one of the chairs a large porcelain doll sat, dust-covered and ragged, its once golden hair tangled and barbed with spiders' webs. The sightless eyes gazed at David, following him everywhere as he paced the room, examining the photographs. There was a scraping at the door, then a fumbling sound. David turned.

The man who entered contradicted all David's earlier expectations. He had imagined al-Yunani as a small fat man with brilliantined hair brushed flat, and soft, fleshy hands encrusted with jade and crystal rings, wearing a silk tie and patent shoes: a Levantine godfather of the old school. The real al-Yunani was another thing entirely. He was a tall, thin, wasted man whose white hair fell, greasy and unkempt, across sunken shoulders. He wore a threadbare morning robe with wide, stained lapels and a faded silk cord. But David noticed none of this at first. All his attention was drawn to the man's face, to his eyes. The Greek was blind. His left eye was permanently closed, covered with a thick layer of scar tissue. The right eye was missing, its socket wadded with a ball of cotton wool.

Al-Yunani stretched out his hand. David stepped forward to take it, looking down, away from the unseeing eyes. He started and stepped back. The floor was alive, crawling with fur. Al-Yunani was surrounded by a sea of cats, cats of all colors and sizes. Like a priest, the Greek came forward, followed by his feline congregation. David watched them and wondered why it was that they were so silent, so utterly soundless. It was unnatural and somehow deeply disquieting.

"Good morning, Professor," the blind man said in heavily

accented English. *"Ahlan wa sahlan. Marhaba.* Please, do not mind my cats. They will not trouble you. Sit down, make yourself comfortable if you can."

David found a chair, removed some unsavory-looking rags from it, and sat down with distaste on the outer edge of the dusty seat. Al-Yunani followed suit, settling into a dirty-looking armchair as if guided there by radar. The cats came after him, some favored ones leaping onto his thin lap, others springing up onto the arms and back of the chair, yet others curling up on the floor at his feet. Still they were silent, as if dumb.

Al-Yunani spoke again. His voice was thin and grainy, gray but sharp, like a rusty blade that can still draw blood.

"What does David Rosen want with me?" he asked.

"You speak as if you know me," David said.

The Greek nodded.

"Yes, I know of you. You came to my attention recently. There was some trouble with MOSSAD, a border crossing, a fatality. You have been in Sinai since then. Was the desert good to you?"

David began to speak, but the blind man interrupted him.

"I do not mean the deaths. The deaths at St. Nilus' benefitted no one. But did you find whatever it was you went into Sinai to find? Did the mountains show favor?"

"How do you know so much? How do you know about St. Nilus'?"

"You do not ask me questions, Professor. That is my province. Did the desert show its goodness?"

David shook his head. He thought he understood.

"No," he said. "I failed to find what I was looking for if that's what you mean. That is why I have come to you."

Al-Yunani nodded. He had heard the sentence so many times before: "That is why I have come to you." The doctor to whom patients turn when all other treatments have failed, the surgeon, the phlebotomist. He leaned forward a little.

"Why did you go into the desert? The desert does not invite. Men do not go there for pleasure. You had reasons."

"That is my business."

"You are bandying words with me. I cannot work like this. Good day."

He made as if to stand up. The cats on his lap stirred. David stretched a hand out toward him, but it fell short, and he let it drop down again by his side.

"I don't mean to seem secretive, Mr. Kyriakides. I have reasons for my silence."

Al-Yunani's face changed.

"My name is Hasan," he said. "You will remember that." He paused briefly. "Why did you go into the desert?"

David sighed.

"To find the answer to a riddle."

"And did you find your answer?"

"No."

"What did you find?"

"More questions."

"And that is why you have come to me."

David paused, then nodded.

"Yes, that is why I have come to you."

The blind man smiled and leaned back in his chair. His thin left hand stoked one of the cats on his lap, a large white beast with green eyes and thick fur. With his right hand he played absent-mindedly with the cotton wool in his eye socket, tugging it compulsively, teasing the fibers into little stranded tufts. David felt sick, afraid the cotton wool would work itself loose, exposing the empty socket. He wondered what had happened to the man. Al-Yunani spoke again, his voice harder than before.

"Very well. Let us dispense with your reasons for the moment. We shall return to them if it seems necessary. How can I answer the questions you found in the desert?"

"By finding something for me," David said. "A book. The answer to my riddle may lie in a book. That was why I went to St. Nilus', but the copy that had been there is now missing. When I returned to St. Catherine's, I spoke with Father Spiros, the librarian, and he told me that many years ago a copy of the book in question had been made by a young monk and taken to Jerusalem. That copy was left for several years in the Greek Patriarchate here, but along with several others it vanished around 1930. Spiros had heard rumors that it had found its way into a private library here in Jerusalem. I do not know where this library is or who owns it. Spiros could only tell me that it was situated somewhere in the Muslim Quarter and that it was rumored that many valuable books and manuscripts had vanished into it in the years before the Second World War. According to Spiros, no one has ever been able to enter this library or consult the books in it. But he did know one thing about it. During the war years the contents of the library were kept in a cellar beneath the Dome of the Rock."

The Greek raised his head, as if looking up at David. An old habit, useless now. He brought his hands together beneath his chin.

"I know the library. Go on."

"That's all there is," said David. "Spiros knew nothing more. I told all this to the guide who took me to Sinai, Leyla Rashid. She said that you might be able to obtain the book for me. The original or a copy, it doesn't matter."

"What is so precious about this book that you are willing to risk your reputation stealing it? I say 'stealing' because that's the only way you'll get hold of a copy."

David shook his head. The cats watched him. Their black pupils were vast in the dim light.

"I won't risk my reputation. That's why I've come to you. I was told that you can guarantee discretion."

"Discretion will cost you more."

"I'm willing to pay." He paused. "For you and whomever you employ."

Al-Yunani said nothing at first. With his hand he stroked the cat again.

"Do you know why my cats are silent?" he asked.

David looked at them. They filled the room, silent shapes, gray and black and dappled, their eyes luminous in the semidarkness. Did al-Yunani keep them because they could see in the dark? David shook his head, as if the Greek could see him.

"I have had them doctored," the blind man said, answering his own question. "A small operation on their vocal cords. Less painful than neutering. Their bodies give me comfort. They are soft and warm, and they ask for nothing but comfort in return. But their cries used to distract me, so I silenced them. Silence is easy to arrange. Do you understand?"

"Yes," David said. "I understand."

He looked up at the photographs on the wall. So many unknown faces, all in al-Yunani's grasp, like the fetishes of sympathetic magic: hair and nails and wax dolls. The cats and the photographs, all silent, all in one man's power.

"What is the book called?" al-Yunani asked.

"It's an Arabic book. *Al-Tariq al-mubin min al-Sham ila 'l-balad al-amin*. The author was Abu 'Abd Allah Muhammad ibn Sirin al-Halabi."

Al-Yunani nodded.

"I will remember it. Blindness makes the memory sharp."

There was a pause. The blind man stood up.

"Did you see the bones?" he asked.

David looked at him. His face was turned away.

"Yes," he answered in a quiet voice. "I saw the bones."

Al-Yunani nodded absently, as if he had not heard.

"The bones are everything," he said. "They call the monks 'The Living Dead.' That is why they keep the bones so near at hand: to remind them of their mortality. I would have been a monk, once, when I was a young man. I had a vocation. There is not much difference between holiness and . . . what I do. One is a betrayal of the flesh, the other of the spirit."

He walked to the door. David got up and followed him, like an acolyte. They stood side by side in the doorway. David shrank from the Greek's eyeless face. Al-Yunani pointed to the spots where his eyes had once been.

"Do you pity me because I cannot see?" he asked.

"Yes," said David. "Of course."

"Then you are wrong. That is no reason to pity a man. Sight is not everything. There are worse things than blindness." He fell silent for a moment.

"The worst thing," he said in a quiet voice tinged with bitterness, "is not to be able to shed tears."

Turning, he went ahead of David to the door.

"Come back in two days' time," he said. "I'll have the book for you then. Bring five thousand dollars with you."

TWENTY

David closed the little notebook in despair and switched off his desk lamp. Since returning to Jerusalem several days earlier, he had been struggling to make sense of the Arabic diary he had found in St. Nilus'. He was living incognito in a small room he had rented in Me'a She'arim, near the Mandelbaum Gate. Here, in the heart of Jewish Orthodoxy, surrounded by synagogues and *yeshivot*, by bleary-eyed Talmudists and grizzled rabbis, cut off from the outside world by a wall of silent witness to the past, he felt reassuringly safe. He had told none of his acquaintances he was in the city: there was to be no repetition of the events in Haifa. He lived alone, bought kosher food in a little shop on the corner of his street, and ate it by himself in his room. Observing *kashrut* made him feel in harmony with his surroundings. He was growing a beard, and he had had his hair trimmed, leaving it uncut in *pe'ot* in front of his ears. He wore a *yarmulkah* when he went out. Sometimes he forgot and wore it indoors as well.

Time after time he had gone back to the first line of the diary, and still it made no sense, apart from the date at the top, which he could decipher: 30 August 1935. The word "August" was written as in English, *Agust,* instead of the more normal form *Aghustus.* But that was as far as David could get. No matter where he looked in the diary, it made no sense. His Arabic was poor, but with the help of a dictionary he should have been able to make some headway by now. He had taken a course in written Arabic for two years at Chicago and could read a clear text slowly. He looked at the first line again. As far as he could tell, it read like nonsense:

Hāwat zand wayr in bi-lastīn anjukumanna.

That was, of course, his own attempt to insert the correct vowels, which Arabic lacks. It could equally have read:

Hāwit zind wīr an bi-lastīn injakmin.

And there were several other possibilities. But they all had one thing in common: they made absolutely no sense.

His desk was covered in dictionaries and textbooks: Wehr, al-Fara'id, Wright, a complete set of Lane he had picked up cheaply in a small bookshop in the *suq*. He had bought some Persian and Ottoman dictionaries as well, but for every word that made sense on its own, a dozen others lapsed into gobbledegook.

He put down the Wehr and picked up the small, rather battered copy of Brünnow and Fischer's *Arabische Chrestomathie* that he had picked up for a few shekels in the same shop where he had found the Lane. He had read through parts of the texts as reading practice and used the glossary at the back as a supplement to his large dictionaries. The book fell open at the front, at the Arabic title page of the 1966 edition. *Tashī al-taḥsīl,* he read, "The Facilitation of Education," a play on words dreamed up for the Arabic title. Then his eye fell a few lines lower. He stopped and read it again, then the line at the very bottom. He sat quite still, staring at the page. The cover rose up and fell shut of its own accord. Why hadn't he thought of it right away? he wondered. Was it because it was so obvious?

The title page had been in Arabic, except for five words: *al-Libsīghiyya* (belonging to Leipzig); *ūghūst* (August); *fīshir* (Fischer); *insīklūbīdī* (Enzyklopädie); and the somewhat inconsistent *Libzīgh* for Leipzig. It was, in fact, the inconsistency between the Arabic transliteration for "belonging to Leipzig" and that for "Leipaig," the *s* in the one and the *z* in the other, that gave him the clue. He wasn't reading a code, he was reading a foreign language in Arabic script, with all the inconsistencies that would involve. And he was one hundred per cent certain the language was German. Feverishly, he opened the diary again. His hand shook slightly as he took up his pen and began to transliterate the letters before him:

Heute sind wir in Palästina angekommen.

"Today we arrived in Palestine."

He stood up, barely able to contain himself. Several times he paced around the room. Crossing to the little stove that sat in one corner, he put his coffee pot on the burner and heated it. He poured a large mug, added sugar, and went back to his desk. Writing out the text in German as he did so, he began to read the diary.

[Editor's note: The following extracts have been prepared from the manuscript text of the German diary, the original of which is currently in the keeping of the Institut für Orientforschung of the Akademie der Wissenschaften in Wiesbaden, who kindly supplied me with a microfilm copy. Lacunae are represented by dots in the present text. Editorial comments have been added in square brackets. D.E.]

30 August 1935

Today we arrived in Palestine. Our steamer, the *Heraklion*, sailed from the Piraeus at four o'clock two days ago, and we reached Haifa early this morning. The crossing was smooth, as it usually is at this time of year, but what we would have given for a breeze! Hartmann kept saying we should have waited in Greece until the weather grew cooler, but the great man said no, it was impossible to wait any longer. He's impatient to get to his destination and won't let anything stand in our way. Haifa is a small town at the foot of Mount Carmel, where Elijah once defeated the priests of Baal. It's quite picturesque, but full of Jews. The town is well laid out: straight streets and a sense of order—quite unlike anything I've seen in the East before. German influence, of course. The Templar colony here has done a great deal to raise standards and set an example, though there are few signs that the Jews and Arabs want to follow suit, as is only to be expected. The *Tempel Gesellschaft [the Society of Templars: a Christian organization founded by Christoph Hoffmann in the 1850s. Their principal aim was to establish colonies in Palestine in order to prepare the Holy Land for Christ's second coming]* dates back to the last century, of course, and is very well established here.

We are staying tonight at one of the Templar houses. It is owned by one of their leaders, Otto Schellenberg. He was brought to Haifa as a child in the early days and knew Christoph Hoffmann, who founded the colonies here and in

174

Jaffa. Schellenberg is a member of the Party, as are most of the Templars here: we shall be meeting them all tonight. This afternoon we were shown around the port and the town by Schellenberg's son, Rudi, who manages a large export/import firm. He told us of his troubles with the Haavara, a Jewish organization that holds a near monopoly on the import of German goods into Palestine. The settlers here would like something done about it back home. I have made a note of the matter.

Things were quiet in the town. It's Friday today, and the Muslims had all shut up shop. The Jews go off later for their Sabbath. I wish Anna were here—she would enjoy it all so much. I must write to her—I said I would do so every day. I have decided to keep this diary in code, using Arabic script so only I among the party will be able to read it. It may come in useful when compiling my reports, and it exercises my mind to write it like this.

31 August 1935

Herr von Meier was on form last night. The Party members came to Schellenberg's house as arranged. There were dozens of them in all, mostly younger men. The Templars are among the Reich's greatest assets in the Middle East. If war ever comes, as some of us think it will, they will be of immense service. The *Auslandsorganization [the Nazi organization responsible for the establishment of National Socialist Party branches outside Germany]* is very active here. Schellenberg talked to us for a while about the Templars and how they came to be in Palestine. He's an impressive old man, very lively for his years—he's over seventy—and extremely well read. His parents came from Ludwigsberg, where Hoffmann taught at the salon. They came out here in 1868 and stayed on with a man called Hardegg when Hoffmann went to fund the colony in Jaffa. Schellenberg says the Tempel Gesellschaft was founded to make Palestine ready for the return of Christ. Apart from the colonies, some of them wanted to restore the Temple in Jerusalem. Von Meier seemed to be extremely interested in that idea. There are almost two thousand Templars now. They keep in touch with the Fatherland, and

175

several have paid visits there since 1933. . . .

A telegram from Anna's mother today. Anna is very ill. The doctor thinks she may lose the child. I asked von Meier if I could return. He said it was out of the question, that I am essential to the mission. I know he is right, but my heart wishes to be with Anna. I pray she will recover. . . .

The next entry was dated 3 September 1935:

We've been having trouble with permits. The British authorities here say we have to go to Jerusalem for extra papers. We explained that this is just an archaeological expedition, but they pretended not to understand. Von Meier has gone off with Schellenberg—they expect to be away a couple of days. We've telegraphed the *Auswärtiges Amt [the German Foreign Office, whose political Bureau VII dealt with Palestinian affairs at this period]*, of course, and with luck they should be able to put some pressure on the High Commissioner. The Führer will be furious if there is a delay, but he can't be seen to be involved.

I've been brushing up my Arabic with the local cadi. He's a friend of A.H. They went to school together. He'd heard the Führer's favorable comments about Islam, that it was more compatible with the German military spirit than Christianity and so on. Of course, I didn't tell him what the Führer also said, that, if the Germans had been converted to Mahommedanism, they would have subjugated the Arabs, who are racially inferior to us. That's the sort of information it's best to keep to oneself. Not even A.H. knows about it. . . .

No news about Anna yet. I'm extremely worried.

5 September 1935; Jerusalem

We've all had to go to Jerusalem to get our papers sorted out. We spent the day at the British Secretariat in the King David Hotel. Döhle, our consul general, paid a personal visit, but it still took us hours to get through all the red tape. I feel exhausted, but von Meier wants us to start tomorrow. . . .

Telegraphed Berlin this evening.

10 September 1935

My first chance to write in days. We left Jerusalem on the 6th and traveled to Sinai by motorcar. The cars had to be left at Eilat, where we obtained camels for the rest of the journey. I've always hated camels: they smell, they're vicious, they're stubborn, and riding on them crushes your balls to powder. But I wouldn't want to travel in the desert without one all the same. We went down the coast as far as Ain al-Furtaga, stayed there for a night, then went up into mountain country through Wadi Ghazala. The Arab guides said they knew the way, but we got lost and it was rough going at times. The others were worse off than I was, of course. Most of them had never been on a camel before.

I suppose I'd better jot down some notes about the rest of the expedition. Our leader is Professor Ulrich von Meier of the Archaeology Department at Munich University. The expedition was his idea, and he had overall authority although, strictly speaking, he's only in charge of the archaeological side of things. He's a tall man with broad shoulders and he looks very strong. He has a distinguished face with sad, heavy eyes, a little bit like a spaniel. He reminds me of Otto Gebühr in his role of Frederick the Great. He must be in his early forties. Hartmann tells me von Meier belongs to an old family from Hanover. He's a regular aristocrat. Apparently he's not a Party member, although he's said to be a very close friend of the Führer. A bit of an odd fish, though. Keeps himself to himself a lot, although he seems quite thick with Keitel and Lorenz.

Walther Keitel is an epigraphist from Saarbrüchen, a wizened little man of about forty who's a health-food freak. He carries little packets of *Heil Erd* and *Heil Tee [*"Whole Earth" and "Whole Tea": two popular German health products of the 1930s]* and makes a fuss about the water. He's done all his work until now in a little room in Leipzig University, and this is his first expedition. He specializes in Hebrew inscriptions, which I found suspicious at first, but it seems he's a Protestant who studied theology at Tübingen for a while, hence his interest in biblical languages. His job is

177

to look out for signs of Proto-Sinaitic inscriptions, like the ones found at Serabit al-Khadim in 1904. He's already been working for years on the Serabit al-Khadim inscriptions and is writing a refutation of Grimme's *Althebraïsche Inschriften vom Sinai*. Basically, he disagrees with the view that the language of the inscriptions is Hebrew *[Modern scholarship tends to confirm Keitel's theory, although his work on the subject does not seem to have been completed. See J. Friedrich,* Entzifferung verschollner Schriften und Sprachen, *2nd ed.(Berlin, 1966), pp. 140ff.]*—which is, of course, one of the basic theories behind this expedition. Keitel has been a friend of von Meier's since his days at Tübingen. They spend a lot of time talking in private. I came into von Meier's tent a couple of days ago and found they engrossed in an old document of some kind. They seemed very put out, and Keitel tried to cover up the paper. Von Meier was furious at first, but he controlled himself quickly and avoided a scene. I shall have to keep an eye on them. The incident will go into my report, of course.

Our anthropologist is Dr. Felix Hartmann, from Breslau. I get on well with him. He's a tall man, well over two meters, full of energy and intellectual brilliance. Not that he makes a thing about his intellect. He's not one of those puffed-up academics, "Graeculi" as Walter Frank calls them *[Walter Frank was a leading Nazi historian, head of the Institute for Research on the Jewish Question at Litzmannstadt; "Graeculi" (little Greeks) was a term of scorn he reserved for professional academics],* who think you have to have half a dozen degrees before you can express an opinion on how to boil an egg. Hartmann gave a speech during the book-burning ceremony at Breslau back in '33: I was there myself, and it was afterward that I made a point of getting to know him. He has collaborated closely with Professor Hirt of the Strasburg Anatomical Institute, whose work on the skull measurements of Jews and other *untermenschen* has been so informative. He recently set up a Breslau branch of Herr Himmler's *Ahnenerbe [the Ahnenerbe Forschungs- und Lehrgemeinschaft, the Society for Research into and Teaching of Ancestral Heritage, was an organization founded by Heinrich Himmler].* I expect he'll make some fascinating discoveries here.

The rest of the part consists of Hans Fläschner from Berlin, the expedition photographer; Hans Neumann, whose job is to keep the records; and Heinrich Lorenz, who doesn't seem to perform any function except moan. Lorenz is a banker, a member of the Vorstand of the Deutsche Bank, and a partner in the private bank of Delbruch, Schickler. My uncle Hjalmar has told me about him. He says Lorenz is a clever man who has made a lot of money through the rearmament program, but he thinks he has low cunning rather than real intelligence, and I'm inclined to agree. He claims to be a member of Kranefuss' "Friends of the Reichsführer-SS," *[a club formed by wealthy industrialists and financiers who wished to show their loyalty to Himmler and the SS. Fritz Kranefuss was its secretary],* and I suppose he must be—but it seems a disgrace to me all the same. He has put up most of the money for the expedition, so von Meier has allowed him to come along. I find him a rather stupid man, a typical bourgeois, fat, ill-mannered, and bumptious. He's rich, of course, but I don't think that's any reason for him to be given a place on a scientific expedition. The odd thing is, he's very close to von Meier and Keitel, with whom he really has nothing in common. I've asked headquarters for information on him, but I don't expect it will ever reach me here. I'm anxious about being cut off so thoroughly, especially after the worrying news about Anna. Perhaps one of the guides can be persuaded to act as courier for me. . . .

The landscapes here are stunning. I wish Anna could see them. The mountains are cracked and broken and very old-looking. In the heat you would think the whole place is about to overheat, to split apart. Ain al-Furtaga, where we stayed two nights ago, was beautiful. It's a huge oasis right in the middle of a vast plain—palm trees, water, a regular paradise! The Bedouin have small gardens there, which they water by bringing channels in from a small stream. There was a spot of tension between them and our guides—something about a feud over water rights—but von Meier sorted it out, with me as interpreter. The man has an uncanny effect on people, almost hypnotic—the Bedouin wanted him to stay on afterward. They seem to think he's some sort of prophet.

With luck we'll reach St. Catherine's tomorrow. I'm looking forward to it. I feel very cut off here, very lonely.

11 September 1935

Arrived at St. Catherine's just before noon. The monks were a bit unfriendly at first and didn't want to let any of us in. But von Meier showed them the letters of introduction, including the one from the Patriarch of Constantinople. They've allowed us to stay three nights—the statutory period for guests—but von Meier hopes an agreement can be reached for a more permanent stay—otherwise we'll have to camp in the hills, and none of us much fancies that. Lorenz wanted to offer the monks money, but von Meier vetoed his suggestion. Quite rightly too, in my opinion. All the same, he was allowed in with von Meier to see the Archimandrite, which is more than the rest of us were, including myself. Just what is Lorenz's position on this expedition?

David closed the diary and leaned back in his chair, rubbing his eyes. He felt dizzy, perplexed. He had never heard of a German archaeological expedition to southern Sinai in the thirties. What had they gone to find? And who was this Professor Ulrich von Meier? David had never heard of him. Who was the writer of the diary? An Arabist clearly, but evidently more than that, and a convinced Nazi to boot. David didn't like the sound of it.

He stood and paced the room. It was late and he knew he should go to bed, but he also knew that, if he did, sleep would not come. There were too many questions to which he wanted answers. He poured himself another mug of coffee and sat down once more at his desk.

TWENTY-ONE

On the afternoon of the following day David picked up the book from al-Yunani. The Greek seemed brittle and anxious. He sat in the dark, cat-filled room playing nervously with a small string of worry beads.

"I had trouble getting this for you," he said, holding the book out to David. "I can't let you keep it. Please make a copy and return it to me as soon as possible. Tomorrow if you can."

David took it from him and examined it. It was a leather-bound volume of about two hundred finely written pages in the *naskhi* style and without much vocalization. The paper and ink were modern. On the flyleaf was the seal of the Greek Patriarchate and beneath that a smaller Arabic seal. As far as David could make out, the name in the second seal was Amin Al-Husayni. Was that the name of the owner of the library? The name seemed familiar, as if he had heard it somewhere before, but he could not place it.

He gave al-Yunani his money and thanked him.

"I'll have a copy made today," he said. "Don't worry, I'll take care of it. It'll be with you again tomorrow."

The blind man accompanied him to the street door. As he turned to go, al-Yunani took his shoulder tightly in his hand.

"Be very careful," he said in a tense voice. "Don't get mixed up in this. Satisfy your curiosity. Find an answer to your riddle. But leave it there. You don't understand the danger you're in. You don't know what's involved. Stay clear if you want to remain alive."

"What do you know?" David asked him.

Al-Yunani turned his blind eyes away from him.

181

"I can't tell you," he said. "I've taken enough of a risk getting this book for you. You'll have to leave now. Take care. Watch your back."

That was all. He closed the door and bolted it from inside. David heard his footsteps recede across the weed-choked courtyard.

He took the book to a photocopying service in Kiryat Shmuel, near Jabotinsky Avenue. The machine he was shown was an old, rather slow model, and it took him all afternoon to copy the complete text. It was six in the evening before he got back to his room.

He put the book and the copy, tucked into a large manila envelope, in the drawer of his desk. He would return the book to al-Yunani the next day and then begin the immense task of scanning the copy for the information he sought. By now he thought he knew what that information referred to, but finding it would still take time. And something made him think that time might be something in short supply.

All that morning he had been transcribing the diary and translating it into English. If even half of what he had read in it was true, something very disturbing indeed had taken place in Sinai during the last months of 1935. He took his translation down from the small blue shelf over the desk. It was not yet complete, but he wanted to read over what he had done so far before going further.

14 September 1935

At St. Catherine's four days now. The Archimandrite has agreed to let us stay on condition that we interfere as little as possible in the daily life of the monastery. We have agreed in return to do some restoration work in the library. Fläschner says he will make a photographic record of the more important icons.

A planning meeting this morning. Von Meier set out the two principal objectives of the expedition once more and assigned us individual tasks. This will be as good a place as any to make a note of the objectives as they now stand.

First: discover evidence in support of Professor von Meier's theory that the so-called "Children of Israel" who entered Sinai under the leadership of Moses were, in fact, a band of runaway Egyptian slaves and that the Jews of the present day are the descendants of those slaves. If this is true, von Meier argues, the authentic representatives of the line of Abraham are the Arab peoples, descended from his eldest son Ishmael. Keitel's theories concerning the non-Hebrew character of the Sinai inscriptions will be a starting point for this investigation, which is centered initially around Jabal Musa.

Second: carry out anthropological research into the racial characteristics of the Jabaliyya Arabs of St. Catherine's and the surrounding region. These Arabs—of whom we have now seen numerous examples—are taller than the other Bedouin of the region, and many have brown hair and blue eyes. It is said that they are the descendants of one hundred Wallachian slaves sent to Sinai by the Emperor Justinian to serve the monks of St. Catherine's—a function they still perform—but Hartmann is of the opinion that they are, in fact, of Germanic origin.

I am almost certain that von Meier has additional objectives and that only he and Keitel—and possibly Lorenz—know what these are. When our work routine was arranged today, von Meier told us that he and Keitel would be working together on Jabal Musa. I have been assigned to work with Hartmann in obtaining the cooperation of the Jabalis in our survey. Fläschner has already started work photographing the library, and Neumann will be busy in a day or two writing up our various reports. The fat man Lorenz spends his time doing what he wants, which generally means talking with the monks. It appears he speaks Greek fluently. Far from reassuring me about the man, that fact somehow makes me all the more uneasy.

20 September 1935

An argument with von Meier this afternoon. Over Lorenz, what else? I asked von Meier outright what Lorenz's position on the expedition is: I said I had a right to know since I have to report back to the *Auslandsnachrichtendienst [the intelligence service covering foreign countries, Bureau VI of the Central Security Department of the Reich (RSHA), run by the SS Security Service (SD)]* and the *Reichsführung* SS

[Supreme Command of the SS]. He was positively rude. He said I might be an SS Sturmbannführer back home, but out here I'm employed as an Arabic interpreter. I told him my authority extended outside the Reich and that I was responsible for ensuring the expedition and its members conformed to Party standards in all matters. He just laughed at me. He actually laughed at me and told me to get out. Later in the day I saw him with Keitel and Lorenz, the three of them together in one of the guest rooms, talking earnestly. I will send a full report tomorrow with one of the Jabalis, a young lad called Ahmad who seems to be trustworthy. There will have to be an investigation. And a reckoning.

27 September 1935

I haven't written anything for several days. On the 21st, a messenger from Jerusalem brought a telegram for me. It said Anna had died following complications. The child is dead as well. I don't seem to be able to think or act properly. Nothing makes sense, out here in the heat, this damnable wildness, nothing but flies and scorpions: the living dead, as these monks call themselves.

My first thought was to go back to Berlin. But I can't do that. Something is going on here. Von Meier and Keitel go into the mountains every day. Lorenz goes out of the monastery alone or with an Arab guide. I shall have to find a way of following them without attracting attention. The monastery feels claustrophobic, in spite of the spaces all around us. I feel trapped, useless. I want Anna, I can't believe she will not be there when I get back. If I ever get back. I have started to doubt that. . . .

28 September 1935

Ahmad's body was found early today at the bottom of Jabal Musa. Some of the Jabalis found him while gathering firewood for the bakery. They say his body must have been there for about a week. It was badly crushed—every bone was broken: they think he must have fallen from the top of the mountain, on the side away from the monastery. But why should he have gone up there? I sent him to Jerusalem on

184

the morning of the 21st, telling him to go there straight, promising him several Egyptian pounds on his return. He had no cause to climb the mountain, then or any time. I asked the men who found him if they had found any papers on him. They said no, there had been nothing on him. That settles it in my mind: he was pushed. But how did they know he was carrying my report?

Another discovery later on. Keitel and von Meier came back with a small stela covered in Proto-Sinaitic carvings. They'd gone to Wadi Beirak, on the way to the Temple of Hathor at Serabit al-Khadim. Keitel seems very excited, von Meier impassive as always.

30 September 1935

We're all to leave St. Catherine's. The order came down today from von Meier, and like a lot of dummies we ran around packing and getting ready. I shan't be sorry to leave. This place depresses me, with its great mountain always brooding over us. It has too many associations with Anna's death. But I'm not sure I like the sound of the place we're heading for. It's another monastery, by the name of St. Nilus', in a little defile not very far from here, the Shi'b al-Ruhban, the Defile of the Monks. . . .

2 October 1935

We arrived yesterday at St. Nilus'. I'm already starting to regret leaving St. Catherine's. By compairson it seems light and airy and spacious. We're hemmed in here by narrow canyon walls, we can't get in or out except by means of a primitive elevator that takes no more than two at a time. The monastery itself is a weird place on three levels: we've been assigned quarters on the "ground floor"—which is over 30 meters above the floor of the canyon—in a dark, rambling maze of cells that goes back deep into the cliff. There's a library on the next level, and a church with an ossuary above that again.

Von Meier has reached some sort of arrangement with the monks. I don't understand how. There are nine of them, six men of about thirty, one of middle age, and two older monks, who are the religious guides of the others. The younger men are fierce in their spirituality: dark-bearded, dark-eyed, gaunt, ascetic recluses who have set their backs firmly on the world. Our presence here is felt as an intrusion—I can sense it every time I pass one of them. What pressure has von Meier brought on them that they have agreed to let us stay?

3 October 1935

I have shared my suspicions with Hartmann. He agrees that something is going on, but he knows no more than I do. I told him about Ahmad so that he would realize the danger we are in. He does not understand why we have come to St. Nilus': his own work among the Jabaliyya has been left unfinished, and I have no function here since the monks speak Greek, not Arabic. Which, ironically, makes Lorenz more use than I.

Von Meier and Keitel went off today to search for more inscriptions, or so they said. I decided to take the opportunity to search their rooms. I went to von Meier's first and made a search of his belongings and papers. There was nothing of interest among them, so far as I could see. But just before leaving I glanced under the bed and caught sight of a small leather case. I took it out and tried to open it, but it was firmly locked, and I could not risk breaking the clasps. I put it back, in the hope that I can somehow obtain the key from von Meier. As I came out of the room, I thought I caught a glimpse of someone at the far end of the corridor. I am almost certain it was Lorenz.

I carry my Luger everywhere now, even when I am not in uniform.

5 October 1935

Nothing has been said about my visit to von Meier's room, but I am positive he knows. I don't see much of him, but when he's around he looks at me in a manner that says as much as "I know what you're up to."

Lorenz now spends most of his time in the library, reading Greek books. He seems to be looking for something, but whenever I ask him he just says he is sampling the collection. How does a banker like Lorenz know Greek so well?

This place gives me the creeps. It's always dark and dreary in the monastery, no matter how much sun shines up above. I feel cold, as if a deep chill is working into my bones. I spend the days reading Arabic works from the library or talking with Hartmann. He has agreed to try to follow von Meier and Keitel when they go out tomorrow. He has discovered that the monk in charge of the elevator has become lazy and leaves it on the ground to await their return, instead of winding it back up to the platform. Hartmann plans to climb down the rope once the monk has gone.

6 October 1935

Hartmann is dead. Von Meier and Keitel brought him back to the monastery late this afternoon. They said they had found him lying on the canyon floor, just where the small ravine comes out onto the plain to the west of here. He had been stripped and his throat cut—the work of bandits. But the monks say there are few bandits in the region now, and I believe them.

I have made a bolt for my door, two wooden holders for door and frame and a short stick to run between them. It could easily be broken, but it will deter a simple attempt to enter in the night. I look at Anna's photograph often and kiss it. Perhaps it is better she is dead. I cannot see any way for me to come out of here alive.

There was a knock at David's door. He started, alarmed. No one knew he was here. The rest of the house was occupied by *yeshiva* students and an elderly rabbi. They had never disturbed him before. The knock came again. He opened the drawer of his desk, took out the pistol, and stood up. He crossed to the door, put the gun on top of the wide, old-fashioned lintel, and took hold of the handle. There was a third knock. He opened the door.

Leyla Rashid stood there smiling at him. She was dressed in black and carried a traveling bag over her shoulder. He looked at her, unable to believe that she was there. She bit her lower lip and drew a sharp, nervous breath. Neither spoke.

187

A voice came from the next landing, the old rabbi upstairs.

"Who's knocking? Is something wrong?"

"Nothing's wrong," David called back. "It's a friend of mine. I didn't hear him knock, I was sleeping."

The old man muttered briefly and closed his door.

"Well," Leyla said. "May I come in?"

"I think you'd better," said David, still bewildered. He stepped aside and she came in.

"So this is it," she said. "Your hideaway." Her eyes scanned it: the narrow, unmade bed, the small sink filled with assorted pots and pans, the bleak, undecorated walls, the old furniture in need of repair, the threadbare rug in the middle of a worn linoleum floor, the rickety desk covered in books and papers.

"I don't think much of it," she said.

"You aren't supposed to," he replied, fumbling to take the gun down from the lintel without her noticing. She turned and caught sight of it.

"Who did you think I was?" she asked, smiling. "The Gestapo?"

He looked at her.

"You may be getting nearer than you think. How did you find this place?"

"Aren't you going to ask me to sit down? Offer me a coffee? I've had a long journey. Aren't you pleased to see me?"

He looked at her again. Yes, he was pleased. And worried.

"What's wrong, David? Shouldn't I have come?" She sat on the nearest chair. One leg was shorter than the rest and it rocked as she sat.

He put the gun away in the drawer before turning to her.

"I'm pleased you're here," he said. "Very pleased. But you shouldn't have come. You may be in danger."

"I know that already," she said. Her face had become serious.

He sat beside her.

"How in the name of God did you find me?" he asked again. "Nobody knows I'm here. Nobody."

She smiled again, a mysterious, infuriating smile that he had seen several times before.

"One person knows," she said. "Hasan al-Yunani knows. I went to see him this evening, to ask if he'd seen you. He said he had, that you'd asked him to find something for you. I can guess what that was. Anyway, he had you followed when you left his place today. He gave me your address. And he told me to tell you again that you're in danger, real danger. He said certain people are involved in this who shouldn't be tangled with. He wouldn't say who they are, but he looked worried . . . and frightened. He wants the book back tomorrow, David, as early as possible. I think he regrets finding it for you."

David felt angry at what he regarded as al-Yunani's betrayal and Leyla's interference. But when he opened his mouth to accuse her, he saw her smiling at him and the words would not come.

"Don't say it, David," she said. "There's no point. He needed to know where you were, what you were doing. He isn't concerned for you, but he's very worried about himself." She paused. "And I needed to know too. I'm sorry I was so . . ."

"That's all right," he said. He looked at her bag. "You've come from al-Arish today?"

She nodded.

"Have you eaten?"

She shook her head.

"I can't offer you much," he said.

"When you first met me," she said, smiling, "you said you'd be happy to take me to a restuarant. How would it be if I took you?"

She looked accusingly at his small stove and the dented pots on it.

"It looks as if you haven't eaten a proper meal in quite some time."

He shook his head.

"Thanks, but I can't go to a restaurant. I can't risk being seen in Jerusalem."

She shrugged.

"All right, we'll eat here," she said. "Show me how this thing works."

She got up and walked to the stove. He lit it for her and she set to work preparing a meal.

They ate from his one plate, scooping up meat and *hummus* with pieces of hot pita bread. There was enough for both. Just. They spoke very little as they ate. David did not ask why she had come to Jerusalem. She did not explain.

When the plate had been washed and the pots scoured, David

turned to Leyla.

"Where are you staying tonight?"

She looked at him and raised her eyebrows. She hadn't wanted it to be this quick.

"In my room at the university," she answered. "Where did you think?"

"I didn't. Nor did you. You can't stay there. Whoever these people are, they know you were with me down in Sinai. We can't take the chance that they may have someone watching your room. You heard al-Yunani. It could be dangerous."

"So people keep saying. Someday maybe you'll tell me just what's going on. In the meantime, if it's no inconvenience, I'll stay here." This was terrible. She had imagined staying, but not like this.

He shook his head.

"No," he said, "you can't do that either."

"Why not? It's safe, isn't it? That's why you chose it. Isn't that why you've had your hair cut in that ridiculous fashion? And don't worry about the bed. I've slept on floors before."

"Leyla," he said pleadingly, "I don't think you understand. Anywhere else you could stay without difficulty. But this isn't the university campus or one of your sophisticated new suburbs. This is Me'a She'arim. And that means trouble for someone like you. Nice girls don't walk about here unaccompanied. They don't wear makeup and pretty clothes. And they sure as hell don't spend the night in a strange man's room."

"You aren't strange," she said. "I've known you for several weeks now. You've even undressed me. Admittedly, I was unconscious at the time. Come to think of it, I've no idea what you may have got up to."

"Don't joke about it, Leyla," David retorted. She had hurt him somehow. "These people take this sort of thing seriously. They're fundamentalists, puritans. These are the real thing, Leyla, Jews with guts. They care about the Torah . . . and they make life unpleasant for people who offend them. I'm surprised you got in here without some kind of trouble."

"I got some odd looks in the streets, but nothing worse. Who knows I'm here, David?"

"I know you're here. The rabbi upstairs probably knows. They don't like this sort of thing. There's a group called the Committee for Guarding Modesty. Did you go through the marketplace as you came here?"

She nodded.

"Then you can't have missed the big notice they've got stretched over the street: 'Jewish Daughter—The Torah obligates you to dress with modesty. We do not tolerate people passing through our streets immodestly dressed.' That's the sort of people they are, Leyla."

"I'm not immodestly dressed," the protested. "And I'm not Jewish. So that takes care of their notice."

"If doesn't take care of being in Me'a She'arim or staying in this room. Even if I had an apartment you couldn't stay. People would talk, it would draw attention. The last thing we need is attention."

She said nothing, just looked at him.

"All right," she said at last. "I'll go. I half thought you wanted me to come to Jerusalem. Obviously I was wrong."

She stood, reached for her bag, and slung it over her shoulder. David watched her go to the door, watched her open it. She stepped onto the landing. He stood up and went to the door. She turned and looked at him. Her face was flushed and her eyes were shining.

"Good-bye again, David," she said. "Maybe I'll run into you sometime. If you ever need a guide to Sinai, maybe you'll look me up." She turned to go.

"Leyla." His voice was soft, little more than a whisper.

"I'm sorry," he said. "I'm tense. I'm worried. It's all right, you can stay." There was a pause. "Please stay."

She stopped and turned around slowly.

"Only on one condition," she said.

"What's that?"

"I get the bed."

191

TWENTY-TWO

David set out for the Muslim Quarter early the next morning. Leyla stayed behind in the room under strict orders not to venture out. As on the day before, he left his *yarmulkah* at home and tucked his hair back behind his ears. The sun shone, but his mind was elsewhere, back in the shadows of the Shi'b al-Ruhban. He wished he knew the name of the author of the diary he was reading. Somehow it mattered to him. He knew the man's wife had been called Anna, that he had been an Arabist and an SS Sturmbannführer—the equivalent of a British or American major—but beyond that he knew nothing. In his mind's eye, David had conjured up a face: blond, blue-eyed, in his early thirties, frightened. But it meant nothing: the face was a mere stereotype, Himmler's ideal Aryan, an exemplar of the master race, no more real than the *Ewige Jude* of the propaganda posters and films. This man had not been like that, David was sure of it. He wanted him to be different. But however hard he tried, he could only picture him as tall and blond, dressed in black, with a death's-head badge in his cap.

He came to the Shari' al-Najjarin. In his hand he clutched the *Tariq al-mubin* tightly, as if afraid it would be snatched from him. The street was almost deserted. No children played in the gutter, no old women leaned out of the windows. Only a handful of young men lounged about as ever. Above him, he heard a window close. Farther up, an old man came hobbling along, helping himself with a wooden stick. He wore a *tarbush* and a crumpled suit the color of ashes. His face matched it. He stopped and looked at David.

David knocked on the heavy door of al-Yunani's house and

waited. No one came. He knocked again, then noticed that the door was open. Gently, he pushed it further and looked into the tangled courtyard. There was no one inside. Puzzled, he stepped into the little passageway and closed the door behind him. He walked down to the courtyard; the inner door of the passage was wide open. Beneath his feet a tile rocked a little. He walked across the silent courtyard toward the door he had used twice before. Where was the old woman?

He knocked again at the inside door. Still no answer. Upstairs, a shutter creaked as it shifted back and forth in a thin breeze. The house seemed deserted, ghost-ridden, dead. David pushed the door and it swung open. He started as a white cat rushed past his legs and out into the courtyard. Had it cried as cats do, he would have been less startled. The corridor was in darkness. Farther along it more cats stood, eyeing him with fixed, baleful expressions. He opened the door to the room in which he had twice met al-Yunani. Weak dusty light crept through the windows, but apart from the furniture, the room was empty.

So was every other room in the house. One by one, David entered them, expecting at every moment to find the bodies of al-Yunani and his housekeeper, but he found only dust and cats. The cats watched him in silence. David wondered what went on behind those glittering, translucent eyes. There was instinct, of course, but also something more than that, something purposeful, something unfriendly. They did not want him there.

Every room was frozen somewhere in al-Yunani's past, in the days before he lost his sight. Curtains, carpets, and furniture hung suspended in a caul of dust and cobwebs, caught in a time warp. David felt as if he had entered an unopened tomb to find the body gone, leaving nothing but the artifacts that had been buried with him. But now it was as if time had reentered the house, to take back what al-Yunani had for so long held from it.

A body would have been better than this ambiguous emptiness. Had al-Yunani taken off on his own accord or had he been snatched? David had no way of knowing. But he was aware of one thing: the Greek knew where he lived. If someone made him talk, David's hideout would become a death trap. It was time to move out. He left the book in the first room. He did not need it now, and if al-Yunani came back he might still want it.

It took him time to find a taxi. During the short journey back to Me'a She'arim, he grew more and more nervous. Leyla was in his room alone: if anyone came, they would find her there. David did not have to use his imagination to guess what would happen to her then: he had already seen what these people could do. He told the driver to go faster, but the minutes still seemed to stretch out endlessly.

She was still there, reading the translation he had made of the SS major's diary, quiet and still, her mind fully occupied with the tragedy unfolding on the pages before her. She did not hear David come to the door, for he had climbed the stairs quietly and turned the handle slowly. He stood for a moment watching her, observing how her hair fell behind her ears, how the light from the open window played on her cheek and neck, shading and molding them. He knocked gently on the door and walked in. She looked up and smiled, but the smile faded when she saw the serious look on his face.

"What's wrong, David?" she asked.

He did not answer her at once. Instead, he walked to the desk and pulled open the drawer. He lifted out the gun, opened it, checked it was loaded, and closed it again. Slipping it into his pocket, he turned to Leyla.

"The Greek's gone. He may have been taken. We have to leave this place. Right away."

Leyla sized up the situation at once. She said nothing, just nodded and began packing. David piled his papers together and threw them into a large briefcase. There wasn't much else.

"David?" Leyla stood behind, holding her bag in one hand. Her eyes were wide open, anxious. She spoke in a tight voice touched with unease.

"David, I think it's time you told me what's going on. I've just realized that I hardly know you; I only met you a few weeks ago, and some pretty strange things have happened since then. I came up here because . . . because I would like a chance to know you better. I thought all the trouble we had in Sinai was over. But now I see I just don't know who you are, what you're doing here. I'd like to trust you, help you . . . but I need to know what's going on."

He walked toward her, took her by the shoulders. He looked into her eyes directly. He wanted to kiss her, but this wasn't the time or

194

the place.

"I'll tell you, Leyla. I'll tell you everything I know. But not now. Let's get out of here first. I have to find somewhere safe for you, then get a place for myself."

There was a sound of footsteps on the stairs. They both froze. The steps were slow, deliberate, careful. David held his breath tight in his chest cavity. He took the gun from his pocket, released the safety catch. Turning he made for the door. The foosteps drew level with the door and stopped. David raised the gun. There was a knock. David said nothing. He motioned Leyla to move to the other side of the door. She slipped across quietly. There was a second knock. Then a voice called out.

"Mr. Levi, are you there?"

Levi was the name David had been using in Me'a She'arim. The voice was that of the old rabbi from the next floor. David relaxed and signaled to Leyla that everything was all right. He pocketed the gun and opened the door.

The old rabbi stood on the landing. He was dressed from head to foot in black, relieved only by the white of his long beard.

"I heard voices," he said. "A woman's voice. I did not expect to hear a woman's voice in here. Is there a woman in your room, Mr. Levi?"

David nodded.

"Of course, *rebbe*. My cousin Miriam from Beit She'an. She came this morning with bad news. I have to leave at once."

"You've been here with her alone?" the rabbi asked in the stern voice he reserved for his less tractable students.

"She has not come here for frivolous reasons," David replied. "She has come with bad news about our family. We were about to leave." He turned and looked at Leyla, then back at the rabbi. "We're leaving now, if you will permit us."

Outside, they turned to the left and walked briskly down the street, past open market stalls, through crowds of jostling people who stared at them curiously as they went by. David turned to Leyla as they walked.

"You know Jerusalem better than I do, Leyla. Where do we go from here?"

She said nothing but walked on in silence for more than a block, an intense expression on her face as if she were struggling to come

195

to a difficult decision. As they came out onto Haneviim she stopped and looked at David, a curious expression in her eyes.

"All right," she said. "I'll trust you a little longer. But after this I want explanations. Agreed?"

He nodded.

"And I want you to trust me in return. Do you think you can do that?"

He nodded again, less confidently.

"Come along, then. I know somewhere we can go."

David started to look for a taxi, but Leyla shook her head.

"We'll walk. It's not far."

"Where are we going?" he asked.

"Ain Tur," she said. "Have you ever been there?"

"No," he answered, "but I know of it. What's there?"

She said nothing in reply. It was better not to. They walked down past the western side of the Old City, then east into Ain Tur, an Arab village that was now part of greater Jerusalem. The houses were old rural dwellings that had long since acquired the patina of urban decay. Ain Tur was crowded and ragged and tense, a hive of the permanently dispossessed. No one would fight for Ain Tur. No Arab armies would cross their borders to reclaim it. It was not the Haram al-Sharif, it was not the golden city of Arab revanchism. Ain Tur would pass back and forth between conquerors: Ottomans one day, British the next, Jordanians the day after, Israelis yet another day. It was matter of supreme indifference to them whether it was Arab or Jewish soil they were laid in at the end.

They walked through narrow, decaying streets to the edge of the district, where the shabby houses gave way to a dim wasteland. David looked about him and pondered on the irony of coming here with Leyla. In Arabic, Tur is the name for Mount Sinai.

Leyla stopped in front of a run-down house. It seemed as if it might be abandoned: paint had not touched its woodwork in well over a generation, its windows were grimy and partly shuttered, its wooden door hung, cracked and worm-eaten, on old rusted hinges. David looked at Leyla, puzzled, but he said nothing. Scab-ridden dogs watched them without interest from a weed-choked patch of earth nearby.

About to knock on the door, Leyla turned to David. Her face seemed troubled, uncertain.

"David," she began. "Before we go in, I want to ask you something."

"Go ahead."

"Afterward, when this is over, this trouble you're in . . . after it's finished, you won't have seen this house, you'll never have been here. Do you understand? Do you promise? We can't stay here unless you agree to that. I'm taking a risk, David. I trust you, but you must promise."

"All right," he replied. "I don't understand your reasons, but I promise. I'll be silent. You can trust me."

She looked at him with an intensity he had never seen in her face before, then pursed her lips and turned to the door.

The knocking sounded hollow in the street. David wondered that anyone lived here, in such a place. Footsteps sounded inside. Then there was a voice, whispering in Arabic from behind the door.

"Yes! Who is it?"

Leyla replied in a low voice.

"It's Leyla, Leyla Rashid. Open the door, Tawfiq."

There was an indistinct muttering, then the door opened, a crack only. Blurred by shadows, David could see a face and bright, steady eyes scrutinizing him and Leyla. The door opened further. A young Arab stood there. He was about twenty-five, of medium height and stocky build. Dirty hair straggled down to his shoulders and thick stubble covered the lower half of his face. The face itself was mean and angry-looking. There was no softness whatever in the eyes. In his right hand the man held a heavy pistol.

"Who's this?" He spoke to Leyla, but his eyes were on David, glaring with suspicion.

"His name's David Rosen. He's a friend of mine. We . . ."

"A Jew?" The hand holding the gun lifted a little. Enough.

"I'll explain," Leyla said. "Listen, Tawfiq, we need somewhere to stay, somewhere safe. David's all right, you'll be in no danger."

The man shook his head violently. His voice was angry. Angry and nervous, a bad combination. He made David uneasy: he was not wholly in control.

"It's impossible," he said. "You know it is. You know this place isn't for casual use. You shouldn't bring strangers here. Jew strangers. Not without permission. Not without speaking to the Council."

197

"There wasn't time for that," Leyla replied. She was beginning to lose patience. She pushed against the door, forcing Tawfiq back into the shadows of the hallway.

"Get out of my way, Tawfiq, I'm going to speak to Fatma."

She brushed past him into the house, calling Fatma's name. Tawfiq raised the gun in both hands, leveling it at her. His hands shook slightly.

Out of the darkness, a voice came, an educated woman's voice, severe and precise.

"Who is there?"

Leyla told her. The woman called to Tawfiq.

"Put down your gun, Tawfiq. Leyla wouldn't come here unless she had a reason. Or so I hope. Come inside quickly, Leyla, and bring your friend. There's already been too much disturbance."

Picking up their bags, David stepped through the door. Tawfiq slammed it behind him. He found himself in a dark passageway, at the end of which an open door revealed a dimly lit room. A woman was standing in the doorway. David walked along the passage, closely followed by Tawfiq and his gun.

The room was true to the house. The walls were damp. Patches of mold clung to the corners and adorned the ceiling. Plaster had come away in parts, revealing cold stone. In the center of the room a rickety wooden table held cheap plates and mugs.

When David turned he saw the woman for the first time. She was a striking contrast to Leyla. Tall and well built, she was dressed in slacks and a military-style shirt. Her face was pinched and hard, a man's face almost, but smooth. With cool eyes she appraised David, as if sizing him up at an auction. He noticed that she carried a gun as well. Unlike Tawfiq, her hand was steady: she was in control.

"You know our rules, Leyla," she said. "No one is to come here without Council authorization, except in an emergency."

"This is an emergency, Fatma. I'm sorry, but I can't explain why easily."

"I think you'd better try all the same."

"This is David Rosen," Leyla said. "An American, not an Israeli. A friend. He saved my life several weeks ago in Sinai. I owe him that. Now he needs my help. His life is in danger and he must have somewhere to hide. For a day, two days; until we can find

198

somewhere safer. All he asks, all I ask, is safety. Here, in this house."

The woman looked at Leyla. Cold, calculating, without a trace of emotion. Her voice when she spoke was flat, the voice of someone who had buried her feelings so far that they would never resurface to disturb her, like painful memories.

"This has nothing to do with us, Leyla. This man is a Jew, a stranger. You had no right to bring him here, no matter what the circumstances. Your behavior is unforgivable. I could have him shot: you realize that. As it is, he will have to stay here until I can obtain instructions from the Council."

"Don't be stupid, Fatma," Leyla protested. "He's no threat to us. I know him. He's an archaeology professor from America. He has no interest in politics. But his life is in danger and we can help. Sometimes you have to trust people. He has promised not to reveal the existence of this house."

Fatma held herself completely still. She eyed David, then returned her gaze to Leyla. In spite of herself, Leyla felt her confidence slip away like frost on a warm morning. Instead of safety, she had placed David—and possibly herself—in very real danger. Fatma spoke in a low, hard voice.

"Never call me stupid, Leyla. It is you who are stupid. The first rule you have to learn is never to trust anyone. Not a friend, not a parent, not a lover. And least of all a Jew. A Jew's promises are worth nothing. Less than nothing. You should know that, Leyla."

Leyla said nothing, but her face betrayed what she felt: anger, hurt, as if Fatma had slapped her on the cheek deliberately and hard.

Fatma turned to Tawfiq.

"Take them upstairs, Tawfiq. Put them in the small room beside mine. And stay on guard outside."

The surly Tawfiq said nothing. He had been vindicated.

David and Leyla preceded him up the stairs, stone steps that clung to one wall, with a broken banister listing outward on the other side. They hesitated at the top.

"To the right," Tawfiq muttered. "It's the third door along at the end of the corridor."

The room was tiny, about nine feet by nine. Its walls were covered in black patterns of long-established damp. The only window was a small, dirt-coated pane of glass set high up near the ceiling, just out of reach. Very little light managed to struggle through it.

Tawfiq checked the room briefly, then told them to come in. He examined their bags and frisked them both. He seemed not to notice that Leyla was a woman: his hands patted her body clinically, without noticeable tension. Taking David's gun, he went out without a word, closing the door behind him. There was no lock, but David and Leyla knew he would be outside, watching the door.

They squatted on the rough floor. For a long time neither said a word. Nor did they they look at one another. At last Leyla broke the silence.

"I'm sorry, David. I'm really sorry. I thought . . . I was just being naive, naive enough to think I could talk someone like Fatma into letting you stay here. Perhaps the Council will see sense. They aren't all like her."

David looked up from the floor into her eyes.

"Who are they?" he asked, his voice hardly more than a whisper. "PLO?"

She shook her head.

"PFLP," she said. "Popular Front for the Liberation of Palestine."

He looked down at the floor again, silent, brooding. Finally he spoke, without raising his eyes, staring at the dusty floor.

"You're a member?" he asked. "You belong to this group?"

She nodded.

"And since you came to Jerusalem, you've been working for them? A terrorist? Is that what you are, Leyla?"

She looked directly at him but said nothing.

"Answer me," he said, almost shouting.

"Look at me, David," she said.

He raised his head. He had been shouting at the floor.

"Yes," she said. "I'm a terrorist. If you like. I've never killed anyone, I've never planted a bomb or fired a shot. But I am a member of the PFLP and I do what I can to further its aims."

"Just what do you do, Leyla?" His voice was still rising. Anger and a sense of betrayal had begun to take control of him.

"Please, David, try to understand. I supply information. I'm

200

acceptable to Israelis. I'm a 'good Arab,' someone they can trust. So they tell me things and I pass what I know on to the group. Sometimes I act as a courier, sometimes I take people across the border into Sinai, sometimes I write articles for our publications."

"What difference does that make?" he sneered. "You don't pull the trigger or set the timer, but you're just as responsible for the murders people like Tawfiq here commit. Or don't you ever think of that?"

"I think of it," she snapped back at him. "Every day I think of it. And I think about Gaza and the West Bank and the soldiers on Bir Zeit campus and the Sabra/Chatilla massacres."

"That wasn't the work of Israelis."

"They stood by, David. They let it happen. As you said, it doesn't matter who pulls the trigger."

"All right," he shouted. "The army went crazy in Lebanon. Begin was a madman. What right does that give you to kill innocent civilians here in Israel, women and children who haven't harmed an Arab in their lives?"

"Begin was a terrorist. He belonged to the Stern Gang, he killed British civilians, he planted bombs. But that didn't stop him winning the Nobel Peace Prize!"

"That was years ago, before either of us was born."

"What the hell's that got to do with it? This will be years ago when your children are your age."

"Right," he argued, "perhaps you're not a regular terrorist. Perhaps you just run errands and supply intelligence. So what does that make you? A spy, that's all. A spy for a terrorist network. Using your safe position in the university to gather up information. Betraying people's trust. Is that something to be proud of? Is that . . ."

His voice trailed away. A spy, he had called her. And what was he? He had spied for Israel. He had betrayed his trust as an archaeologist. People had possibly died because of information he had supplied. What right had he to condemn Leyla?

"I'm not proud of it," she said in a quiet voice. "I despise it. The lies, the subterfuges. I couldn't be proud of that. But I am proud of my people, of the people who are fighting to win our country back. What I do may be despicable, but that doesn't matter if it helps my people find their dignity again. Not as refugees, as human beings with a land of their own. Surely you can understand?"

"Was your husband a member of this group?"

She nodded.

"Did he kill people? Did he plant bombs?"

She nodded.

"And you still loved him, knowing that?"

She did not answer at first; when she did, her voice was as tight as a drum.

"Yes," she said. "I loved him. He did none of those things for himself. He never took part in operations against civilians, only soldiers. He saw himself as a soldier: but because we don't have a country, our soldiers are called terrorists. I understand what he did and why he did it. He did it because he loved me, because he loved our people, our country. But I can't expect you to understand that."

"You're fooling yourself, Leyla. Palestine isn't worth all this bloodshed. Nothing is. You said so yourself back in Sinai. You said Palestine was a never-never land. What happened to all those doubts, or was that just another one of your subterfuges?"

She clenched her eyes shut, then opened them again. They were red.

"They were real, all of them. Don't you have any doubts, Professor? What about the secular Jew you claim to be? How come you're wearing a *yarmulkah,* how come you're growing a beard? Everybody doubts what they believe. I doubted everything after Muhsin was killed. But after Muhsin there were others. More arrests, more raids, more killings. Not every Palestinian is a terrorist, but sometimes you treat us as if we are. How many people at Sabra and Chatilla were murderers? I still remember seeing film of the camps on television. I cried then more than I'd ever cried for anything before, more than I even cried when Muhsin was killed. Little children, babies—how could people do such things? Don't things like that move you, David? Don't you love anything, anyone? Or do you just love yourself?"

He looked up, at her face, at her eyes, at the tears in them. There was nothing he could say, nothing that would not hurt her even more. All he could tell her was that he loved her. And after today, how could he tell her that? He looked away from her, toward the window high in the wall and the thin murky light that came through it.

TWENTY-THREE

In the evening a representative of the local PFLP Council arrived at the house. He was a man of about forty, slim, balding, and intellectual-looking. A portable gas lamp had been brought to their room. It sat in a corner, hissing and pouring out a cold white light. The newcomer introduced himself.

"My name is Qasim. Miss Rashid has met me before. I represent the PFLP Council of Jerusalem. I've been told that you, Professor Rosen, are in need of sanctuary and that Miss Rashid has brought you here in the belief you can stay here. Why do you need sanctuary, Professor? From whom are you hiding?"

Sitting on the floor, David felt intimidated. Obviously everything depended on how he impressed this man. He stood up.

"I don't know who it is I'm hiding from," he said.

"I see," said Qasim. "I think you'd better tell me more. Start from the beginning. Tell me what you're running from."

And David told him. What choice had he? To tell this man what happened or be kept here indefinitely or more likely shot? He had already promised to tell Leyla, but their argument had continued into the afternoon, quieting down, then flaring up again, petering out eventually in a long, unbroken silence. It was time to tell her.

When he had finished, no one spoke. Leyla seemed frightened, Qasim plunged deep in thought. At length he turned his eyes toward David. They were calm, serious eyes, not eyes that David would have associated with a terrorist. Qasim, he was certain, was a thinker, a writer, not a killer. Thoughts and words would be his weapons, not bombs.

203

"I believe you," Qasim said. "If you were lying, you'd lie better than that. Anyone would. I'm going to take you at face value, Professor. You'll stay here until I can check your story. That shouldn't prove too difficult. If anything else turns up—such as your being a spy—I'm afraid you know what will have to be done."

He turned abruptly and left the room as he had come. They heard him speaking outside the door. Two minutes later Tawfiq entered and told them brusquely that they were to be moved to other rooms. They picked up their bags and followed in his wake as he strode up the corridor and opened two doors, one beside the other on the right-hand side of the corridor. Qasim's words had had some effect, but they had not softened in any way Tawfiq's manner toward them. They were still his prisoners, and he would still be David's executioner if orders came to kill him.

Five minutes later there was a knock on David's door and Leyla entered. She closed the door behind her and stood facing him. He was sitting on the only object of furniture in the room, an old steel-frame bed covered with two thin blankets that had seen better days.

"I'm sorry, David," she said.

"There's nothing to be sorry about," he answered. He did not smile, however. It was too much of an effort to smile.

"Yes, there is," she said. "I got you into this without thinking. You were in trouble and I got you into worse trouble. You were running, now you're trapped, you can't go anywhere."

David shrugged.

"Maybe. Maybe not. This isn't a prison, you know. It's an old house with two people to guard us. They have to rest. They have to sleep. If we wait a day or two, we can break out. Or . . ." He turned on the bed and looked at the window. "We can try the window. We can go now if you like."

Leyla shook her head.

"No, we can't, David."

"What do you mean?"

"Go to the window."

Puzzled, he stood up and crossed the room. He looked through the window down into the piece of weed-covered waste ground behind the house. A man stood there, not looking at the house, but very clearly watching it. There would be no easy escape that way.

"Yes, I see," he said, turning away again. "As you say, I'm

trapped. But I don't understand why they want to keep you as well. You're one of them. You could just walk out of here."

She smiled oddly at him, the corners of her mouth turning upward at a gentle angle.

"For a man of your age, David, you're very naive. I've just brought a man who may be an Israeli spy to one of their safe houses, with a story one of them only half believes. How do you think Fatma would react if I said, 'I'm just going out to do some shopping'? She'll use her gun, David. The least provocation, the smallest excuse. She wants to kill you. It doesn't mean anything to her now. Killing. Perhaps you're right after all, David. Perhaps we are all tainted in some way.

David shook his head.

"Leyla," he said, the words coming with difficulty. "We're all tainted. I as much as you. I was dishonest with you back there. Well, less than candid anyway. I am an Israeli spy. I've worked for MOSSAD in Syria for years now, off and on. I don't think this business had anything to do with that. But when I condemned you this afternoon for being a spy . . . I wasn't thinking. Or I wasn't thinking straight. I've done my share of betrayal. I'm sorry. I should apologize. I do apologize."

She was silent for a while. When she spoke at last, it was in a changed voice, flatter, sadder somehow.

"It doesn't matter, David. I don't suppose any of this matters very much any longer. Let's forget the whole thing.

She paused briefly, then changed the subject.

"I wish you'd told me before about what really happened, all the details. It makes more sense now, the death in Sinai, al-Yunani's disappearance. I want to help. Isn't there anything I can do?"

He said nothing for a while. Then, abruptly, his expression changed.

"Yes," he said. "Yes, there is something you can do. You can read the *Tariq al-Mubin* for me. It would take me weeks, maybe months. You could read it in days, make detailed notes about everything significant, prepare a rough index. The copy's in my briefcase. Let me get it."

The room, the danger they were in, Fatma and her need to kill— all were forgotten as David took the Xeroxed sheets from his bag and passed them to Leyla. She leafed through them, checking the quality of the copy. There were about two hundred sheets, each containing twenty-five lines of sharp, legible Arabic script in a good modern hand. There would be little difficulty in reading the text unless the style itself was difficult.

"Here's paper and a pen," David said. "Now, make yourself useful, Miss Rashid."

"What do you want me to look for?" she asked.

He looked at her and his eyes became troubled.

"I wish I knew," he said, "but I don't. It could be anything. I have a hunch, or maybe it's just a wild hope, that my German diary will tell us. Otherwise we'll just have to work it out for ourselves. And the worst thing is that the answer may be staring us in the face all along, that it may be so obvious we'll never notice it. Take your time. Check anything you aren't sure about."

"And while I'm doing all this hard work, Professor Rosen, what are you going to be doing?"

"Don't worry. I'll be working too. I have to find out what our anonymous Sturmbannführer did next. There isn't very much further to go."

He reached down and took the diary and his Langenscheidt dictionary from the bag. It was time to go back to the past again.

8 October 1935

The monks brought Hartmann back yesterday. His body was kept in the church overnight, then brought out for burial this morning. They have a small cemetery at the far end of the defile, in the broad wadi into which it opens. All the monks, except the two most aged, came with us. Von Meier, Keitel, and Lorenz were there, which stuck in my throat.

The Greeks wanted to bury Hartmann according to their own rites, but I objected strenuously to that; I said he had not been a believer and that he should be interred in the proper Teutonic fashion. There was a bit of an argument about that, since some of our own party wanted the Christian ceremony. I insisted, with Fläschner and, curiously enough, Lorenz backing me. In the end, von Meier agreed to let me perform the SS rites for burial after the Christian nonsense. This will go on my report with everything else.

They say Hartmann's remains will be brought back to the

monastery in a few years, when they will be placed in the ossuary there. But I swear I will come back for them one day, to carry them to the Fatherland and bury them in German soil. I have seen the ossuary: it is a charnel house, a bone pit, unfit for one of the Master Race. But I now wonder if I myself shall ever set foot on German soil again. I still keep the bolt on my door fastened at night; and I sleep lightly.

9 October 1935

At last some light has appeared in the darkness. I still know very little of what is going on, but I have discovered something. Now, more than ever, I am glad I have been keeping this journal in code: my only fear is Keitel—he could read it if he took the time.

Yesterday, after the funeral, we all came back to the monastery. I went to my room to write my diary entry and think things over. At about five o'clock I came out into the corridor. I heard voices coming from von Meier's room and went quietly to his door. Keitel was speaking, then he stopped and I heard Lorenz. Finally von Meier himself broke in. They were all there, and it sounded as if they were arguing. It was then it struck me that Hartmann's room was directly next door to von Meier's and that it was empty. Without delay, I let myself into the room and closed the door. With my ear pressed hard against the wall, I could make out most of what was being said in the next room. They were arguing, that was clear. The first voice I heard was that of Lorenz. He said:

"I tell you for the hundredth time, Ulrich, it isn't here. I've been through the Greek histories of the place, I've spoken at length with the monks, and I've discovered nothing. Not a thing. The books know nothing, the monks even less. I say we should have stayed at St. Catherine's."

Keitel broke in at that point, already quite angry.

"St. Catherine's was a waste of time, and you know it. We scoured the place and there was nothing. People have been in and out of that region for centuries and nothing has ever been seen. And you know the text makes more sense if we read it as meaning this area. Ulrich and I haven't gone over half of this place yet. We need time."

"Time!" That was Lorenz again. "You've had plenty of time. How much longer do you need? You're looking for a city, for God's sake! That shouldn't be so hard to find."

It was von Meier who replied this time. His voice was lower than Keitel's, and much calmer, but I could still make out what he said.

"Listen, Heinrich. Walther is right. In archaeological terms, we've only scratched the surface around here. Cities can get lost very easily. No one in the West even guessed that Petra existed until Burckhardt stumbled across it in 1812—but once you've seen Petra you wonder how the hell anybody could have lost it! Anyway, I've already told you that I don't think Iram is a city, not as you imagine it. It was probably quite a small place, not even as big as Petra, some of it carved into rock perhaps, the rest of it made up by tents or maybe wooden structures. A place like that could easily remain hidden in this wilderness. And the text is quite clear, it leaves no room for doubt: 'The City of Iram is in the Defile of the Monks, which is in the neighborhood of Jabal Musa, in Sinai. I have seen it there with my own eyes, whoever wishes to behold it, let him go there himself.'"

David stopped reading and took several deep breaths. He noticed that his hands were shaking slightly and put down the book. After such a long search, it seemed scarcely believable that he had at last found the confirmation he had been looking for. Iram—Iram of the Pillars. The city about which Yigael Bar-Adon had discovered something just before his death, to which John Gates had devoted a chapter of his now missing Ph.D. thesis. The link in the chain.

He picked up the diary and began to read again. On the other side of the bed, Leyla sat engrossed in the *Tariq al-mubin*. Beyond the window, out of sight, the watcher in the yard had started to pace up and down. A whispering noise came from an electric motor in a workshop nearby, tense and trembling.

There was some muttering that I could not catch, then Keitel spoke again.

208

"Look, Heinrich, he's right. Honestly. We thought the 'Defile of the Monks' must be a reference to the Wadi al-Dair in which St. Catherine's is situated. You agreed with us. But when we learned about St. Nilus', we realized that it should be taken as a proper name, Shi'b al-Ruhban. The whole thing makes perfect sense. If anything, discovering this place was indirect confirmation that the text is accurate. We'll find it, you'll see. And we'll find what we're looking for in it. You must have patience in these matters. We have to proceed slowly, in case the others learn what it is we're really looking for. Another fortnight, that's all we ask."

There was a brief pause, then I heard Lorenz again.

"Very well," he said, "a fortnight. In the meantime, what about Sturmbannführer Schacht? Can we get rid of him?"

Von Meier replied. "No," he said, "he must be left alone if possible. He knows nothing, he only suspects. We can explain Hartmann's death, but not another one. It will create too much suspicion. Schacht must be kept in the dark, that's all. Keep him under your eye, Heinrich."

They broke up after that. Von Meier stayed in his room and I was able to get out of the cell I was in and make my way back to my own chamber without being noticed. It was time for dinner soon afterward, and I went to the refectory as usual. But I had already determined to get my hands on von Meier's case and see what was inside it. . . .

I had my chance this morning after he and Keitel went off exploring. I told Lorenz I was feeling ill and wanted to stay in my room and rest. Once the coast seemed to be clear, I made my way to von Meier's room. I looked everywhere for his case, but it was no longer there. Then, just as I was about to leave, I caught sight of something on the wall. It was an ordinary icon, a Virgin and Child, much like the one in my own room. But it was not hanging straight. It sat out at a slight angle from the otherwise perfectly flat wall. Curious, I lifted it down.

Behind it, von Meier—for I take it he had been responsible—had hollowed out a shallow cavity, in which he had placed a flattened roll of what appeared to be papyrus. I took it out, unrolled it carefully, and examined it.

209

It was quite small, about 30 centimeters by 20, and badly worn. The edges had frayed or been broken in places, and the papyrus was cracked and brittle. It had not been much improved, I thought, by von Meier's handling of it. The surface was covered on one side with large Arabic writing in the ancient Kufic script, written in black ink with a reed pen. Whatever it was, I knew I should have to read it, but first I would have to take it back to my room to make a copy.

That was, of course, easier said than done. This was a very primitive manuscript, in bad condition, in what seemed to be extremely early Kufic, perhaps as early as the eighth century. Since Kufic is enormously difficult to read at the best of times, even in its more developed form, I found it no easy task to transcribe the twelve or so lines of text. I'm still not sure about several words, but I have done the best I can. I think I understand now how Keitel came to be involved in all this. Kufic is an epigraphic script, used originally for rock carvings, and even though he is not an Arabist I suspect he knows enough to handle Kufic inscriptions.

I have replaced the scroll in von Meier's room, as nearly in its original position as I could manage. I shall attempt a translation of the text tonight.

10 October 1935

In general, the papyrus is not enormously interesting. It appears to be part of a longer work dealing with the various ancient cities and peoples mentioned in the Qur'an. It's just a suspicion, but from the style and content I would guess that this is a section of an early Qur'an commentary, one of several the names of which are known but copies of which have never been discovered. In the space of a few lines, the writer mentions al-Hijr, says it was the city of Thamud, and identifies it with Mada'in Salih in the northwest of the Arabian peninsula. That corresponds pretty well with modern theory. The "Overthrown Cities," he says, are Sodom and Gomorrah, which he locates near the Dead Sea. But just toward the bottom occurs the passage I overheard von Meier quoting yesterday. That's all there is, although I think the original text may have gone on further.

I can understand why von Meier is looking for Iram. A lost city is every archaeologist's dream. But why the secrecy? Does he want to be sure of having the credit for himself? Perhaps. But why go to such lengths as killing Ahmad and Hartmann? And what did Keitel mean when he said they would find what they were looking for in Iram? What else was there that the papyrus did not mention?

I shall have to keep my ears open. Unless I can find out more, my information is next to useless. All the same, something is bothering me, something about the text. It seems clear, yet somewhere in the back of my mind I keep thinking I have made a mistake, misread the Arabic. I shall have to look at von Meier's original again.

TWENTY-FOUR

11 October 1935

I have discovered the mistake—made by Keitel, made by me. They think they are looking for a city; in fact, they are looking for a book, only they do not know it. The city is there all right, somewhere, but almost certainly not here in Sinai.

I went to von Meier's room again this morning, took the papyrus out from its niche, and brought it back to my room. Reading slowly, I went back through every line, paying particular attention to the section dealing with Iram, together with the lines immediately preceding and following it.

The first thing I noticed was that the Iram section was incomplete. After the commentary on al-Hijr and Thamud, there came the Qur'anic verse referring to Iram: "Have you not seen how your Lord dealt with 'Ad, at Iram of the Pillars, the like of which had not been created in any land?" This was immediately followed by the words of the commentator: "'Ad were a people of the unbelievers, after the time of Noah, who lived among the sand dunes at Iram. The prophet Hud was sent to them, but they set their faces against him, wherefore God sent a storm upon them and drought. They perished, all but the pious among them, and became as nothing. Iram . . ." The text broke off at this point, with damage continuing for about a line.

The section I have noted earlier, commencing "The city of

212

Iram is in the Defile of the Monks," started at the edge of the page immediately after this, but some words at the beginning of the line had dropped out. On going over the previous commentary portions, I had noticed that, in most cases, the commentator had stated the location of the city or people concerned, followed by reference to a book or treatise dealing with it. Thus, after the account of al-Hijr, he had written: "The Book of al-Hijr was with Ibn 'Abbas in Medina, but its whereabouts are now unknown." Now, the word used there and in several other places for "Book" was the standard Arabic term, *kitab*. But Arab writers, especially in the early Islamic period, commonly use a wide range of alternative terms for "book," and at least one of these, *kurrasa*, occurred in one passage. *Kurrasa* is a very obscure word, so I was not surprised that it did not appear again. But I wondered why there had been no reference to a "Book of Iram" and asked myself whether the word "city" could have been a scribal error for "book." That seemed unlikely, though not impossible in a text dealing with both cities and books. And then I saw it.

Kufic is a primitive form of script. Letters that are perfectly distinct in ordinary Arabic hands are often written the same or in a very similar fashion in the Kufic style. Letters that ought to be joined are often separated, and vice versa. I looked more closely at the word I had taken for "city," *madina*. Now that I had thought of it, it seemed obvious to me that what I had taken for an *m* was, in fact, an *s*, the *d* was an aspirated *h*, and the *n* an *f*. No wonder Keitel had missed it. To the nonexpert, *madina* was the obvious word, bearing no strong resemblance to what I now saw. But to my eyes, once the link had been made and the psychological urge to read "city" removed, there could be no question. The word was *sahifa*, a very common alternative for "book," and the passage read: "The Book of Iram is in the Defile of the Monks which is in the neighborhood of Jabal Musa, in Sinai. I have seen it (or read it) there with my own eyes; whoever wishes to behold it (or read it), let him go there himself."

David laid the diary aside and looked across the room at Leyla.

She was still reading, bent unmoving over the book. The whining of the electric motor had stopped at some point. The room was still and warm.

"Leyla," he said gently, a strange feeling of excitement rushing through him.

She lifted her head and turned her face toward him.

"Yes, David."

"Have you had a chance to work out the general theme of the book yet?" He wondered if she could notice the excitement in his voice.

She looked at him oddly.

"Yes," she said. "Would you like me to tell you now?"

He nodded.

"Well," she said, "It's quite straightforward. Basically, it's this man al-Halabi's narrative of a pilgrimage from Damascus to Mecca. The odd thing—and it's very odd, come to think of it—is that most of the book, about half of it as far as I can tell, is about just one place, somewhere he visited on his journey."

"Iram," David said, his voice scarcely audible to her across the small room. She stared at him.

"Yes," she said. "Iram. How did you know?"

While Leyla began work on the translation of the lengthy Iram section of the *Tariq al-mubin*, David returned to Schacht's diary, eager to find out what had happened after his discovery that the Book of Iram was almost certainly in the library at St. Nilus'.

The SS major had returned the scroll to von Meier's room a second time without being observed. During the next few days he had spent all his time in the library, systematically checking all the Arabic books there. He had, of course, found none with a title resembling *Sahifa Iram* or *Kitab Iram*, and had gone on to read through the general contents of all the likely volumes, several hundred in all. He had found it in the end, an unlikely-looking book he had already glanced at and discarded, the *Tariq al-mubin* by al-Halabi. It puzzled him at first—he had ignored it because of the date in the colophon at the end: 10 Ramadan 574 (19 February 1179), which was obviously too late to have been referred to in what gave every appearance of being a very early papyrus. But on closer examination he had discovered that the twelfth-century volume was, in fact, a copy made from the original manuscript in the monastic library, which had been on the verge of crumbling to nothing after four centuries of neglect, worms, and damp.

But Lorenz had become suspicious. Schacht had been unable to hide his curiosity from the other man, who was still searching through Greek texts at the other end of the library. A few days after his discovery of the *Tariq al-mubin,* events began to take an unusual and unpleasant turn.

17 October 1935

I was told by von Meier this morning to expect important visitors from Jerusalem. He was very mysterious and said he could tell me nothing more until they arrived. I cannot understand how he knows about this: no regular messengers have left or entered the monastery in weeks. Have von Meier and Keitel contacts outside through whom they pass messages during their expeditions into the hills?

The visitors arrived at noon, much to my astonishment, for I immediately recognized A.H. and one of the members of his entourage whom I had met some years ago. The monks were understandably unhappy about the presence of Muslim dignitaries in their midst, but A.H. assured them his visit was purely a matter of courtesy toward his German friends. He smiled and talked a lot about his love for "his holiness Jesus, the son of Mary," and spoke about the little mosque in the middle of St. Catherine's, which he visited briefly. I have never seen a man look or sound more insincere. I don't think the monks were taken in by a word he said—they looked uneasy all day and went about with longer faces than usual.

A.H. remembered me from my first visit to Jerusalem, when I attended the 1931 Muslim Congress in an unofficial capacity and made our first representation to him. I learned that he had left soon after that for Iran, Afghanistan, and India, in order to meet members of his faith in the non-Arab regions. He talked with me for some time, but apart from expressing his admiration for the Führer and the Reich and reiterating his ealier sentiments about the Jew scum in

Europe and Palestine, he said nothing new. He had certainly not come to St. Nilus' to talk with me: an hour after his arrival he was closeted in the Archimandrite's room with von Meier, Keitel, and Lorenz. Even his own secretary and entourage were excluded. How they communicated I have no idea, since there was no interpreter.

I was certain A.H. was our man, but I am doubtful now that I see his intimacy with von Meier and his friends. This thing clearly goes deeper than I thought. A search for a lost city and something unspecified in it—treasure trove perhaps?—is, however mysterious, fairly innocent. But behind-the-scenes contact with foreign nationals—and important ones at that—is another matter and one that will have to be reported in full to headquarters. God knows how I shall ever manage to get word back to Germany.

Before turning to the next page, David pondered on the significance of the initials A.H., which had occurred once before, toward the beginning of the diary. Schacht had used the full names of all the other individuals mentioned in the pages of his journal, but from the very first mention A.H. was referred to by his initials only. Since the diary was already written in code of a sort, it seemed superfluous to encode the name further. Unless . . . It was, when he thought about it, perfectly obvious. A.H. was an Arab: that much was clear from the context. Had Schacht written out his name in full in Arabic script, it would have been perfectly legible. It was awkward for David, who felt it was somehow important to know who A.H. had been, but Schacht had had his reasons and the diary was unlikely to provide more than circumstantial evidence as to the man's identity.

18 October 1935

A.H. and his party stayed last night at the monastery and left early this morning after Fläschner had lined us all up to take a photographic record of the visit. The monks refused at first to be photographed, but the Arabs were quite happy to comply. Von Meier seemed unhappy about the whole business but said nothing.

Something serious has happened. I went to the library

after the Arabs had left. Von Meier and Keitel were nowhere to be seen, although I understood they had not gone out on their usual expedition. Lorenz was not in the libary as usual. There seemed to be an atmosphere in the monastery, a sort of tension.

The book was not in its place. I looked frantically through the shelves, thinking I must have misplaced it, but it was in none of them. I looked high and low, behind books, in dusty corners, everywhere. I spoke with the librarian, a man of early middle age named Gregorios. He speaks little Arabic, but I managed to make him understand what I wanted. He was very silent, very reserved. Several times he shook his head, to say he did not understand me, but I knew he did and that he knew the whereabouts of the book. After a little while I gave up. I did not have to ask further, for I knew where the book was by now.

19 October 1935

The horror of last night is still with me. I can scarcely stop my hand from shaking as I write. But I must set down all that has happened, all that I saw, even though nothing can possibly obliterate from my memory that weird scene.

I must begin at the beginning. After discovering the loss of the book, I tried to find von Meier and the other two, in order to have it out with them. I intended to ask, in my capacity as official Schutzstaffel representative on the expedition, just what was going on and why they had kept their search for Iram a secret from the rest of the group. They were not to be found anywhere. I searched high and low, but I could not find them, nor had anyone else seen them. The monk in charge of the hoist said they had not left with the visitors or after them. I went to the refectory, to the libary, to the church, but they were nowhere. It was as if they had vanished into thin air. But I think I now know where they were.

That evening I was in my room when I heard a door in the corridor outside open and close. I crept outside and entered the room beside von Meier's. They were there, talking together in low voices, a murmur filled with words too indistinct for me to make out. Did they suspect that someone might be listening to their conversation?

At last it grew late. I decided to leave my intended confrontation until the morning and returned quietly to my room. I was tired, tired and worried. The sense of isolation I had been feeling was greater than ever, and I felt threatened. I lay awake in the darkness for some time—an hour, two hours perhaps. Then I must have fallen asleep, though it cannot have been for long. I was awakened by the sound of someone trying to open my door. It shifted, but my makeshift bolt held, and in the end whoever it was gave up and went away. I was already wide awake, so I leaped out of bed, crossed to the door, and slipped the bolt open.

When I looked out I could just see the figure of a man slipping away into the corridors at the end of the corridor. Only a tiny lamp burned high up on one wall. When I looked again, he was gone, swallowed up by the shadows. There was no sound. It was early morning, dark and silent, the hours when everyone was asleep, even the monks. Quickly, I pocketed my Luger, closed the door, and followed the silent figure down the corridor out into the night.

It was dark outside, pitch-dark, it seemed at first; but as my eyes adjusted I could see stars up above, in the strip of sky visible between the walls of the canyon. They seemed unnaturally huge and bright, like baubles on a Christmas tree. I had never ventured abroad as late as that before, never seen the stars so gigantic and, it seemed, so close.

It was then I caught sight of a light somewhere above me, high up the cliff. I watched it for a while, but it remained still. I decided to climb the stairs. As I did so, the light vanished from sight, but I knew it must be somewhere at the top. My greatest fear was that whoever was up there might decide to come down again and that we should meet somewhere on the stairs face to face. I wish now that that had happened rather than what did happen.

The light reappeared as I came level with the top of the stairs. It took me some moments to orient myself in the darkness, then I saw that the light was shining through the open doorway of the ossuary beside the church. I had kept away from that place all through my stay here. It held a horrid fascination for me, but something—call it superstition—made me keep my distance. Its morbidness disturbed and unmanned me. When I saw that the light came from there, I wanted to turn around and go back.

Instead I steeled myself and crept up onto the upper level. I was fairly sure I could not be seen from the ossuary, there being no skyline at my back, but nevertheless I crouched low and moved around toward the little building by way of the church, coming at it obliquely and out of even deeper shadows.

As I came around the corner of the ossuary, I stopped dead in my tracks and held my breath. I could see two figures sitting together just outside the door, lit by the stars and the weak light that came from behind the open door. Pressing myself against the wall, I watched silently for a long time, trying to make out who they were. One of the figures was talking in a low voice, and I quickly realized that this was von Meier, although I could not at that distance make out what he was saying. The other man said nothing; he just sat motionless, listening to von Meier. Their figures were indistinct in that sepulchral light, but there was something about von Meier's companion that disturbed me exceedingly. Whether it was the intimate way in which he leaned toward von Meier or the rigidity with which he sat or the slightly bent, disfigured shape he presented to my eyes, I could not tell. But I watched him carefully.

Things remained thus for several minutes. Since neither man moved nor looked in my direction, I became bolder and moved step by step nearer to them in order to make out what was being said. As I drew close, I could hear von Meier quite distinctly, but I still could not grasp what he was saying. He was not speaking in German, but whatever language he was speaking, I was sure it was one I had not heard before. Then von Meier stopped speaking and the other man began to talk in the same incomprehensible language, in a somewhat higher voice. I crept a little closer.

All at once it struck me that I had heard the language before—often. As I realized what it was a cold shiver went up and down my spine. Von Meier and his companion were speaking in Latin, the Vulgar Latin of the later Roman Empire and the medieval Church. As they spoke it, it resembled the Latin I had heard at mass as a child and a young man, but it was more clipped and broken. It seemed not overly strange that von Meier, an expert on the late Empire, should speak Latin: it was, undoubtedly, an exercise he had often carried out at his school and, perhaps, with his own students at university. But who among us all living in the monastery, monks or visitors, could speak with any fluency at all that long-dead language?

Even as the question rose in my mind, it seemed to answer itself, for I realized with a chill of palpable, blinding horror that von Meier's bent companion was not one of us at all but a corpse he had carried from the ossuary. I had been told by Hartmann of the well-preserved bodies of saints kept at the upper end of the building, and now that I looked closely, I saw there could be no question but that one of those grotesque relics was sitting conversing with von Meier. I almost lost my senses out of fear, and I think I would have done had I not in the next instant realized that it was not the corpse that spoke but von Meier, projecting his voice in a higher tone as a ventriloquist will do with his dummy. And yet, for all that my realizing this helped calm my fears of something supernatural, beyond my rational understanding, it did little to diminish my sense of horror at the spectacle before me. If anything, to know that von Meier was seated here in the cold and dark, bathed in starlight, speaking to a corpse in Latin and answering himself increased my unease tenfold. But the worst was yet to come.

I began to inch my way back, away from the ossuary, intending to return below and spend the rest of the night bolted in my room with the light burning. Just as I started to go, my foot caught something—a stone, probably—and made a tiny, tinkling noise. Von Meier looked up, startled, and I realized with horror that there was just enough light for him to see me by. He seemed disturbed for a moment, and I thought he was about to stand up or speak, but he did neither. Instead he sat where he was, one hand on the upper arm of the corpse, holding it upright, his eyes wide open, staring at me. That was all he did. He stared, saying nothing, making no gestures, just looking at me as if from a great height. For a minute, perhaps two, he held me transfixed with his relentless stare until at last my nerve broke and I turned and ran back to the steps and stumbled down them, slipping and grazing myself badly several times as I fled back to the lower level.

I spent the rest of the night in a state of sleepless terror, certain von Meier and his friends would now seek me out. I sat up in my bed with my Luger loaded and pointed at the door. But no one came, there were no sounds outside until the monks rose before dawn and went up to the church to pray.

It is now midmorning, and I have not left my room since returning to it. My mind circles and circles through the scenes of last night: the lamplight flickering on von Meier's emotionless staring face, the leathery corpse sitting bolt upright at his side, the Latin conversation that almost broke my nerve forever, the faint smell from the charnel house. I have decided to visit the monk Gregorios in the library and to confide in him: his written Arabic is good, and I hope to be able to explain the situation to him. Surely, now that von Meier has desecrated the body of one of their saints, the monks will take some action against him and his cronies.

19 October 1935 (evening)

I thought the worst was over, but it was not. After writing my last entry this morning, I found Gregorios in the library and spoke with him for a long time, often writing things down to supplement my meaning. He understood me very well, he said, for he and his fellow monks had seen or suspected many of the things regarding von Meier and his activities about which I told him. But they had been unable to do anything, for it seemed that von Meier had some sort of hold over the Archimandrite, whom he had known many years ago in Thessalonica. I have an idea there was rather more to the matter than Gregorios said but, whatever the details, it is clear von Meier does have influence here and that the monks dare not go against him.

Gregorios was outraged and, I think, frightened, by von Meier's act of sacrilege in the ossuary. The use of Latin coupled with my vague description of the corpse made him think it had been the remains of St. Colum, an Irish monk from a monastic settlement at Glendalough who had died in the course of a pilgrimage to Sinai in the eighth century and been interred with the dead here since then. But, like myself, Gregorios could not guess the meaning or purpose of von Meier's pretended conversation, unless it was, as he suspected, some sort of satanic ritual whereby he may have hoped to raise the spirits of the dead.

I returned from my talk with Gregorios in low spirits. The moment I opened the door of my chamber I knew something was wrong. I lit the oil lamp and turned the wick up until the flame became bright. There, lying in my bed—not on top of it, but in it—was the body von Meier had been speaking to last night. I recognized it by its bent shape, the contorted set of the neck and shoulders. It seemed to give me a knowing look, leering at me with its shrunken, wizened features, and for a horrible, irrational moment, I thought it was going to speak to me.

I think I must have screamed or shouted, for there was a movement behind me as my door opened and someone came into the room. It was von Meier. He looked at the body in the bed, then at me. He said nothing at first, just stood staring from me to the corpse and back again.

"This is just a warning, Herr Schacht," he said at last. "If you continue to interfere with me and my work, you will have him as your permanent companion, up there where he belongs."

I had lost my nerve for a while, but his addressing me in those terms brought me to my senses. I remembered that I was an SS officer, that I was his political superior, and that he, like myself, was ultimately answerable to the Führer.

"And just what is your work, Herr von Meier?" I asked.

He looked at me for at least a minute without answering, with a contemptuous expression in his eyes. When he spoke at last, it was in a sneering tone, the sort of tone he must reserve for his less gifted students.

"Even if I were to explain it to you, Herr Sturmbann-führer, you would not begin to understand it. Not you, not your precious Heinrich, not even your ridiculous Führer." He paused, glanced at the body in the bed, then resumed, "I hope you sleep well tonight. With company that should not be too difficult. He will prove a better bed mate than your precious Anna ever was or will be again. She is worm meat, but he is a saint. His flesh is holy. It smells sweet. He was embalmed with oils and spices. Lie beside him, hold him close, lie naked with him, and think of Anna, dead and waiting for you in a cold German churchyard."

I hit him then. I hit his face and chest and belly, hard, stinging blows that dropped him before he could defend himself. And almost as quickly I stopped. I looked at him, cringing on the ground at my feet, and I felt loathing and disgust wash over me. Stepping over him, I opened the door and rushed out into the corridor and on out into the cool air of early evening. I sat outside for a long time, watching the stars come out all along the stretch of purple sky above. When I went back to my room at last, von Meier was gone. So was the corpse in my bed. I wondered if it had all been a dream. But my knuckles were grazed where I had struck him.

I shall watch the door carefully tonight. I dare not sleep.

But sleep he must have done, thought David, for it was the last entry in Schacht's hand. On the following page, there was a short inscription in Greek, signed by the monk Gregorios. David's Greek was limited, but he could read the passage without much difficulty.

I found this book among the other papers and belongings of the German Schacht, on the day after we found him in the ossuary. He had been pinned to the floor by spikes driven through his arms, legs, and groin, and the great spiders had covered him. He died two days later in great pain and in mortal terror, though I tried hard to comfort him. I have placed his things in two chests and shall leave them in a storeroom until the proper person comes for them. The other Germans have gone. They wanted to take the book that Schacht found in the library, but I refused to let them. In the

223

end, they made photographs of each page and took those away with them. May God protect us from them and their machinations. May Christ have mercy on us for our shortcomings and our vices.

Gregorios

David stared unseeing at the page. His thoughts turned at once to Ishme-Adad and his lingering fate in ancient Ebla. Centuries had passed since then and little had changed, just the victims, just the torturers. And if Sturmbannführer Schacht had lived, would he have stood over David's parents with a riding crop, would he have cracked his grandmother's skull with the butt of his pistol? And David's grandfather, that old partisan of Jabotinsky, would he not have driven the spikes even deeper if he had known?

It was dark and it was late, and David felt very, very tired. He closed the book slowly, as if the pages were large and heavy. He turned in his chair and saw Leyla on the bed, stretched out alongside the papers on which she had been working. She was fast asleep. David turned out the light and lay on the floor.

224

David dreamed that night, a long, wicked dream in which he was returned to the ossuary in the Shi'b al-Ruhban. And yet it was not the ossuary but the well in Tell Mardikh, much enlarged and engorged with corpses: the bodies of the Arab and the man he had killed there, both in the same well, his parents, John Gates, Michael Greatbatch, Leyla, pale and wasted, the seven dead monks, blood streaming from their wounds endlessly, a Christ figure, crucified with spikes to the floor, wearing a death's-head cap and jackboots, great spiders crawling from his wounds, and all the bodies from the ossuary: Nilus and Colum and the bones of hundreds more. They all sat up and stared at him and talked, gabbling incomprehensibly in Latin and Greek and Eblaite. He wanted to run, but his father held him by one wrist and would not let go. All along the wrist, the leather straps of *tefillin* bound him to his father's arm. His father was dressed in a blue and white prayer shawl, drawn up over his head, and he mumbled in Yiddish and Hebrew, lines from the *Targum*, verses of *Talmud* and *Midrash*, all jumbled and meaningless. His mother stood behind, speaking in Yiddish: "You don't understand him, David, but he understands you." Again and again she repeated the words, like an automaton, "You don't understand, you don't understand," until he wanted to scream to stop her. And then he looked away and saw that they were no longer in the ossuary, no longer in the well, but in a great city, like a graveyard, with long cavernous streets flanked by tall dark buildings. The streets were like canyons, like the defile of the Shi'b al-Ruhban, and silent figures wove in and out of tall doorways, crammed full of shadows. David broke away at last and began to run, but no matter where he fled he could not find his way out. He was lost in an endless maze and surrounded by the gray-robed figures of pale men and women. He asked for directions, but they only turned blank, sightless faces toward him and said, "This is Iram, this is Iram."

He woke bathed in sweat and shouting incoherently. It took several minutes for the disorientation and fear to subside, and when it did he saw Leyla standing over him, an expression of concern in her face.

"I heard you call out," she said. "In your sleep."

"I was dreaming," he answered. "A nightmare." His head felt fuzzy and his mouth was sour and coated. They had been given fatty lamb and stale bread to eat for supper, and now David's digestive system was registering its disgust.

"What time is it?" he asked.

She looked at her watch.

"Almost four." She paused. "Are you all right, David?"

He nodded.

"Yes, it's fading now. Just images, nothing concrete. I dreamed you were dead. Like the time I found you in the canyon, the time I thought you'd been drowned."

Leyla looked thoughtfully at him. It was dark in the room. The only light came from the corridor outside, a dull yellow light that became part darkness as it entered the room. The house was silent, yet Leyla thought Fatma must be awake somewhere, listening.

She rose and moved away from David, into the shadows, toward the light. Now that he was calm again, she could sense his presence in the room. The smell of his sweat, still mingled with fear, filled her. She moved to the door.

"Please," he said. "Don't go, Leyla. Stay with me."

She turned and looked toward him. He was partly hidden by the shadows, but she could make out his face, the paleness of his skin.

"Do you want me to sleep with you, David? Is that it?" Her voice was soft, slightly sad. The blood was making her cheeks warm. "I will if you want me to."

He shook his head, almost imperceptible to her in the darkness.

"No," he said. "Not now, not tonight. Just stay with me. Talk to me."

226

She shut the door and walked with him to the bed. They were in total darkness now. He climbed beneath the thin blankets, still warm from Leyla's body. She sat down on the edge of the bed, facing him. He reached out a hand and felt for hers, holding it tightly. For a long time they sat like that, neither saying a word, the world all around them dark and silent, their only contact the clasping of hands.

All the next day was spent working on the translation of the *Tariq al-mubin*, Leyla scribbling down her English version, David correcting and transcribing it. The text was clear and simple, without mystery or subterfuge, a direct narrative of a journey to a lost and hidden place. Al-Halabi had been to Iram. In the month of Shawwal of the year 75, corresponding to February 695, he had set out from Damascus with the *hajj* caravan, intending to travel directly south to Mecca for the annual pilgrimage two months later. The caravan had taken a route skirting the western flank of the Great Nafud Desert, intending to pass through Tayma' before descending to Khaybar and on to Medina, after which it was to take the coastal road to Jidda and finally to Mecca.

A Bedouin raid just south of the Wadi Sirhan had cut al-Halabi and several of his fellow pilgrims off from the rest of the caravan. They had become lost and entered an arm of the Nafud, where they were met by a more peaceful tribe of Bedouin, who took them farther into the desert in an attempt to outflank the marauders who had attacked the caravan. During a sandstorm al-Halabi had become hopelessly separated from his companions. Traveling alone, he had gone deeper and deeper into the Nafud in the mistaken belief that he should be heading east. With his camel on its last legs and his water running out, he had come to Iram.

He had found a strange people living there among the decayed splendor of what had once been a great city. They spoke a language that bore some resemblance to Arabic, but it was too difficult for him to understand, nor could they understand his speech. Later he was to learn that he was the first person from outside the city whom any of its people had ever seen or heard of. And then he remembered that the Bedouin had spoken in hushed tones of a sector of the desert they would not enter, even at peril of their lives.

Al-Halabi quickly found that the inhabitants of Iram were a primitive people, without culture or traditions. Their rich and tattered clothes they had purloined from the mummified remains of the dead in the great echoing catacombs underneath the city. They had no knowledge of their own ancestry, no legends of Iram or its origins, no religion, no laws, no political system that he could see. He spent three months with them, during which he learned enough of their language to ask the many questions that had arisen in his mind, though he was given few satisfactory answers to any of them.

In the end he had grown tired of the place and its inhabitants, whom he had tried unsuccessfully to convert to Islam. He had no hesitation in identifying the city as Iram and its people as the degenerate descendants of 'Ad, the people who had rejected the prophet Hud until God sent His punishment on them. At the end of his third month there, al-Halabi took offense when an Iramite woman offered herself to him and laughed at the notion of marriage. He had set off into the desert again—though the people of the city had warned him it had no end—and had been found there, delirious and wandering, many days later. No one would listen when he told them about Iram, attributing his story to the heat of the desert sun. But when he was told that it was not the month of Safar—early June—he knew his story had to be true, for he could not otherwise explain how he had spent three months in the desert alone and survived.

228

TWENTY-SIX

That evening around nine Leyla had a visitor, a young man of about twenty-five, dark-eyed, serious, and brooding. His name was Suhayl and he looked to David like a man who wanted to die. His eyes bore a haunted expression, as if he had internalized all the shadows of life around him and now lived in permanent gloom. He asked to speak with Leyla alone in her room. Half an hour later he left, as quietly and morosely as he had come.

When Leyla came into David's room after Suhayl had gone she seemed tired and thoughtful. The buoyancy that had been with her earlier was gone. It was as if Suhayl's mood had been infectious, as if the shadows he carried inside him had crawled into Leyla too.

"What's wrong?" David asked as soon as she entered.

She said nothing in reply, just crossed the floor to the bed and sat down.

"Bad news?"

She nodded.

"Well," he said, "tell me."

She drew a deep breath and let it out slowly before speaking.

"Suhayl's an old friend of mine. He's a distant relative, a third cousin. He came tonight because of that, because he's worried for me.

"He isn't a member of the Council, but he has close contacts in it. Early this evening he heard that the Council will probably vote to have us both executed. They've found out about your connections with Israeli intelligence. Suhayl says they haven't reached a final decision yet, but there'll be a meeting later tonight. They'll probably

229

send an execution squad here directly afterward, around midnight, maybe a little later. We have two, perhaps three hours.

"Fatma and Tawfiq have already been warned to keep a closer watch on us. The guard outside has been doubled. Suhayl wants to get me out, but he won't have anything to do with you. As far as he's concerned, you deserve anything you get. I'm innocent, so he can take me out until the fuss dies down. You're a Jew and a spy, so the sooner they put a bullet through your brain the better. I tried to convince him that you're as innocent as I am, that there are other issues at stake here, but he won't buy it."

David said nothing but went to the bed and started gathering up the papers scattered across it: the Xerox of the *Tariq al-mubin,* Schacht's diary, and the translations he and Leyla had prepared. He put them into the large bag in which he had brought them and set it on the floor.

"Leyla," he said, "whatever happens, these papers have to get to a safe place. You can get out of this alive. Get a message to Suhayl, tell him you agree to whatever conditions he sets, but be sure he takes you out of here. Once you're out, give Suhayl the slip and take the papers to Colonel Scholem at the MOSSAD offices on Haneviim. I assume you know where they are. Tell him I sent you, give him the papers and all the information you have. Leave things in his hands. I don't know if he can do anything. But we have to depend on someone, someone who can make sense out of all this."

Leyla shook her head.

"I'm not going to escape without you, David. Don't ask me to. For God's sake, I'm in love with you; haven't you realized that by now?"

He stood for a long time looking at her. She could not tell what he was thinking. She had not wanted to tell him like that, this had not been the right time, the right place. But when would be the right time, now they might both be dead in a matter of hours?

He spoke at last, in a voice rendered emotionless by the deliberate suppression of all emotion.

"Please, Leyla, don't argue. There isn't time. Take the papers to your room now, hide them somewhere, then come back here. When the time comes, take them with you. If I mean anything to you, you'll do that for me. I'll come with you if I can, but if I can't you'll have to try alone. We're the only people who know the whole story

230

now, the only ones who can make any sense of all this."

He bent down, lifted the briefcase by its handle, and handed it to her. She took it from him listlessly, not caring what it was or why she took it. Without saying a word, she went out.

When after five minutes she had not returned, David went in search of her. She was sitting on the bed in her room, the bag clutched on her lap, tears streaming silently down her face. He stood in the doorway watching her. What comfort could he give her? She knew as well as he, better than he, how little hope there was for either of them.

At that moment there were footsteps in the corridor behind him. David turned to see Fatma striding toward him, followed by Qasim. The woman seemed tense and nervous. She carried a pistol in her hand.

"Come with me, Professor Rosen," she said, stopping just in front of him. Her voice sounded rough to David, as if she had been drinking. There was a coarseness about her, behind the facade of terrorist sophistication. Or was she just an unhappy woman seeking to hide a sense of personal failure beneath a uniform, a veneer of callousness? David was churning inside. He wanted to hit her, to break through the barrier she threw up all around herself. Something in her manner, her voice, her face had disquieted him beyond toleration.

"What about Leyla?" he asked. "Where is she to go? We want to stay together." Asking for it seemed to be the best way to make sure they did not.

Fatma shook her head. Behind her Qasim said nothing.

"She is to stay here for the moment," Fatma said. "I only have orders concerning you. The Council wants to meet you. Qasim will take you there."

David looked at Qasim, but there was no response. No flicker of recognition, no acknowledgment of the thin but tangible bond David imagined had been forged between them. David felt for a moment as if he were an actor in some weird, unscripted play. Everyone had been given a role to play—female terrorist, terrorist intellectual, victim, traitor—and each of them was playing his part to the end. He half expected to see an audience beyond the lights of the dim corridor.

"Professor."

It was Qasim's voice, impersonal, cold, without the warmth of Fatma's hatred.

"Where are the papers you showed me yesterday. The ones we talked about? The Council would like to see them."

David thought quickly, like a boxer a little punch drunk but still weaving. He could see from the corner of his eye that Leyla had already managed to push the case out of sight underneath the bed. He had to decide immediately what to say. If there was any chance that Qasim's Council might change their minds in his favor on account of what was in them, then the papers must be shown to them. But if Suhayl had been correct and the decision to execute him and Leyla had already been taken, the only hope lay in the chance that Leyla might still make it out with the papers in her possession.

"I'm sorry," he said. "I gave them to Leyla's cousin Suhayl when he called this evening. If I'd known the Council would still want them, I would have kept them here. I asked Suhayl to take them somewhere safe, until Leyla and I leave here. You've seen them—can't you explain to the Council what I told you?"

Qasim pursed his lips. David could see he had lost interest, that it no longer mattered to him. The Council had decided, that was enough for Qasim.

"I've seen the papers," Qasim said, "but I haven't read them. We can get them from Suhayl if they are still of any interest. Come with me now."

David looked into Leyla's room. She still sat on the bed, rigid, her face impassive now. He wanted to say good-bye, but it would have sounded like an admission of something, he wasn't even sure what. He smiled instead, but she did not smile at him in return. He took a last look, then turned and walked away following Qasim. Behind him, he heard the door close as Fatma entered Leyla's room. All along the corridor and down the stairs he waited, every muscle in his body tensed, for the sound of a gunshot from the room, but none came and he went out of the house without knowing what was happening upstairs.

Outside, Qasim was joined by a second man, a stony-faced, heavily built creature, a small giant who seemed to walk on springs, as if unable to keep still lest he die from immobility, like a shark, who must swim and swim without ever ceasing, even to sleep.

Qasim held open the back door of a small, nondescript car. David stepped inside, followed by the lugubrious man-shark. Qasim got in behind the wheel. David expected a blindfold to be produced, but none was. He was to be allowed to see where he was going. That alone told him Suhayl had been right, that he was not expected to leave again after he had reached his destination.

The journey did not last long. They drove down past the railway station to Rehavya, where they stopped outside a house on Ibn Gevirol Street—not far, David noted, from the Jewish Agency on King George. Inside, David was taken straight to a ground-floor room toward the back of the house. The room was empty but for a dozen chairs lined up against the walls. The walls were white and blank: not even a photograph had been hung there. It was a sterile room, a room given to a cause, not to people.

"I thought I was to meet the Council," David said, alarmed in spite of his knowledge of how things stood. There was a form for such matters as execution; procedures had to be observed. He felt afraid to die without the formalities. They would make it easier somehow.

"That won't be necessary, Professor," replied Qasim. "We talked things over thoroughly. I did my best, I assure you, but you know yourself what secrets you carry. You can't be allowed to live. You may tell us of something of value before you die. You may know something we do not know already. Marzuq here will see to that."

He indicated the bobbing, restless giant by his side.

Even as Qasim finished speaking, there was a sound and the door opened. David looked up, toward the door. A fat man was standing there, staring at him.

Qasim stepped back to make way for the fat man, but the latter ignored him and stayed where he was, just inside the doorway. He closed the door behind him. The room seemed to grow smaller, as if the man, like Alice, had swollen out of all proportion into it or it had shrunk toward him.

The fat man said nothing to anyone in the room. He merely signaled to Marzuq by lifting one hand partly out of the sleeve of his vast robe. Marzuq reached into the inside pocket of his gray jacket and drew out a gun, a heavy black gun with a beveled handle that David could not recognize. David felt sick. A wave of real nausea passed through his stomach and he felt a shiver pass all along his

233

skin, as if every hair on his body had stood erect for a moment. His bladder felt suddenly full and weak; he was frightened he would wet himself, that he would die like a small boy, unable to hold back his water. It could not be happening—that was all he could think, that none of this was real. Suddenly, like an illumination, it came to him why so many people in history had gone calmly to the gallows: none of them had actually believed it was happening, it was something too enormous for the mind to cope with.

Marzuq raised the gun. David saw Qasim open his mouth as if to protest, but there was a singing in his ears and he could not hear what was said. Everything seemed to be happening in slow motion. He wanted to run, but where was there to go? There was only the room. Between him and the door stood the fat man. David's legs felt like lead.

Marzuq pointed the gun at Qasim and fired twice in rapid succession, two shots through the middle of the head, neat conclusive shots that carried bits of Qasim's brain to all corners of the room. David saw blood and fine gray matter on the back of his hand and wiped it off instinctively. As he did so, Qasim stood very still, as if the bullet had frozen him, then tilted and at last crumpled in an untidy heap to the floor. Rapidly, a pool of bright red blood began to form behind his head. His eyes fluttered like the wings of a dying moth. He jerked once, almost erotically, like a man climaxing, a spasm, nothing more. The spasm passed and he was still.

David waited for Marzuq to turn, to point the gun next at him, but he did not. He put the gun away in his pocket. It had been nothing, a moment's work, the least effort. He bobbed up and down as if awaiting a further signal. How strange, David thought, that one man's death might be no more to another than a casual movement of the fingers, an incident as trivial as trimming a fingernail.

"Leave us now," the fat man said to Marzuq. "And take him with you."

The shark-man, compliant, eager to please, lifted Qasim's slender body with what seemed practiced ease. He opened the door, dragging the body beneath one arm, and went out with it. All he needed, David thought, was a hunched back and a bell to toll.

The fat man stood facing David. He was a little man grown huge,

234

with tiny hands and feet, and a small bullet-shaped head set atop a grotesque torso of gargantuan dimensions. He seemed to dwarf himself; his extremities were victims of his centralized enormity, as if the great chest and belly and buttocks were slowly swallowing them down into their vast, insatiable girth. He was dressed in a voluminous brown *'aba* of the finest camel's wool. It hung around him like a tent, revealing underneath a brightly embroidered winter *farwa*.

The man's skin was sallow, a butter color, but the face was lined and cracked with wrinkles. David guessed he was a man of at least sixty, perhaps a good deal more. He stood at the entrance to the room for a while, looking at David, small, heavily lidded eyes scrutinizing him. Unlike the shark, David thought, a sharp intelligence lay behind these eyes. As if his terror of the past few minutes had been a mere fiction, David suddenly felt real fear. There seemed to emanate from the fat man a more complete, more chilling threat than he had so far experienced: he knew, as the man lumbered toward him, that his life was in terrible danger and that escape would be impossible.

The fat man reached into a low pocket and drew out a large white handkerchief.

"Here, Professor," he said. "There is blood on your cheek. Wipe it off on this." The voice seemed to rise up from somewhere deep inside the man's belly; it was a hollow, intestinal voice, edged with menace. As he spoke, his thick red lips sucked and nibbled at the words, moistening and fattening them before spitting them out. He handed the handkerchief across. David took it numbly and wiped his cheek with it in a stiff, mechanical action. The cloth was cambric of the finest quality, but the blood was only blood.

"Sit down, please," the fat man said.

David sat in the first chair he could find. Who was this man? he wondered. What did he want with him? What was going on?

The fat man crossed the room and eased himself slowly and patiently into a huge leather armchair that had evidently been built for him and placed there for his personal use.

"So, Professor," he said at last, shifting his bulk a little as if in perpetual search for an ever shifting center of gravity. "I am told you have a copy of a book entitled *Al-tariq al-mubin*. If I am not mistaken, it was obtained for you from a library that once belonged to a friend of mine. He is no longer alive, but he had many friends who would be distressed to learn that you had plundered his property."

The little hands vanished inside the wide sleeves of the outer robe. Only the tiny head remained visible, an old man's head that seemed to be perched on a huge pile of laundry. The lips opened and closed without any apparent relationship to the rumbling, often indistinct words that welled up from the depths below.

"Where is the book now, Professor? What have you done with it?"

"I've already told Qasim, the man you just had killed," David replied. "I gave it to someone called Suhayl, along with my other papers."

"No, Professor, you did not," he said. "We have already spoken to Suhayl. He was intercepted coming from the house in Ain Tur. There were no papers on him. They are still with the girl, are they not?"

David said nothing in reply. There was no point in lying.

"Well, no matter," the fat man said. "Someone has gone to the house. The girl and the books will be brought here."

"Then why all this nonsense?" David protested. "If you think you know where the papers are, why bother asking me? Why not just kill me like you killed Qasim and have done with it?"

The fat man leered at him.

"Come, Professor Rosen. You don't take me for such a fool, do you? I want to know whom else you have told about these matters. I know about al-Yunani: he has been taken care of. Who else knows?"

"Why should I tell you? I'll be dead soon anyway. I have no incentive for helping you out of whatever jam you're in."

"But of course you do, Mr. Rosen. 'Hope springs eternal . . .' Perhaps you may live after all. Perhaps I will let the girl live too. If you cooperate with me, tell me what I want to know, I may be persuaded that you are no further danger to me or to my friends."

"I don't believe you," David said. "If you have the papers, you won't want me. Or Leyla. Who are you anyway? Why is the book so important to you?"

The fat man squinted at David out of his flat, emotionless eyes. He redistributed his weight on the chair again.

"I was there, Professor," he murmured. "I was a very young man, a member of the party that visited Sinai to meet von Meier and his expedition. I learned of the book later, of course. In itself, it is not important: what matters is the information in it. And even the information is no longer of interest to us, except in so far as it remains hidden. We were careless: the original copy should not have been left at the monastery—that was von Meier's mistake. He thought it would help avoid difficult questions being asked. But now, after years of silence, the contents of the *Tariq al-mubin* have become known to too many people, people who have no right to know of such things. The young Englishman learned of it and copied passages from it; his teacher was informed, then his examiners. Fortunately, one of the two examiners mentioned the matter to a friend who was one of our close associates. And then it appeared that he had sent you a copy of his chapter on the contents of the book. When we failed to kill you, we heard that the chapter had gone to Haifa. Your parents' deaths were regrettable . . . but necessary. And yet you persisted, you went to Sinai, you found the name of the book, you returned here and located a copy. You are to be congratulated for your perseverence. But it's over now. There has to be silence. Great things are happening and you put us all in jeopardy. That is finished now."

David stood up, anger overcoming his fear.

"Why were my parents' deaths necessary? They knew nothing. Even if the chapter was in their apartment, they still knew nothing. The men who killed them didn't even know whether the package had been delivered."

The fat man shook his head.

"I assure you, they did."

"What about the monks, what sort of threat did they pose to you? They knew nothing either. None of them had ever read the book, I'm sure of that."

The man shrugged.

David felt outrage increase in him, then just as quickly evaporate. He felt useless, his emotions made redundant by the brooding presence of the fat man and his contempt for life.

"At least tell me this," David said. "The PFLP didn't exist as far back as 1935. Just what sort of interest does a group like yours have in archaeological documents discovered fifty years ago?"

Even as he spoke, David guessed something of the truth. The fat man gazed at him, the little round head bald and motionless, the blank eyes protruding a little from the aging flesh in which they sat, like raisins in pudding.

"The PFLP?" the fat man said. "They have no interest in this. By morning, their entire council will be dead. You will meet those who are interested in such matters elsewhere. They want to meet you, Professor. They would like to talk to you and make use of your talents as an archaeologist. I fear we have a long and difficult journey ahead of us. You shall see what you have longed to see, Professor. It will be more remarkable than you imagine. You are privileged; you are to be shown things few men have ever seen. Things you cannot begin to guess.

"Once the papers you stole are in my possession I shall make arrangements for our departure. In the meantime, I have other matters to attend to. Marzuq will keep you company here while I deal with them. I would advise you to rest, Professor. None of us will have very much rest for several weeks. We shall not be traveling by plane or Jeep. That would draw too much attention where we are going. I hope you have ridden a camel before this: if not, I fear you have some discomfort ahead of you."

The fat man smiled and stood up.

"Marzuq," he called. *"Udkhul wa khallik hawn."*

The door opened and Marzuq entered. The fat man went up to him, murmured instructions, and turned to go. At that moment another man came to the door. He was a younger man, and David noticed that he was not an Arab, that he resembled the man he had killed at Tell Mardikh. He seemed agitated.

Forgive me, sir, but I've just come from the house in Ain Tur."

The fat man looked at him.

"Well," he said. "Did you find the papers? Where are they?"

The younger man shifted uneasily.

"They weren't there, sir. The . . . the girl you told us to bring back . . . she's gone. I think she took the papers with her. We searched everywhere."

The temperature in the room seemed to fall. The aura of menace surrounding the fat man became intense, almost tangible. When he spoke, his voice held a ring of iciness that had not been present before.

"How did this happen? How did she escape?"

"The man Suhayl, sir. Apparently he returned and said he had orders from the Council to take the girl with him. The woman Fatma believed him. He took her about twenty minutes before we arrived."

"I see." The fat man paused. David could see that a deep anger was seething in him. "What have you done with Fatma and her subordinate?"

"They've been taken care of, sir."

"Very well. I want this Suhayl found, and the girl with him. But above all I want the papers. Do you understand?"

"Yes, sir."

"Spare nothing and no one: they must be found, and quickly. Do whatever has to be done. You have my full authorization for anything you require."

"Yes, sir. Thank you, sir."

"Well," the fat man said in a voice that rasped like a file, "what are you waiting for? There's no time to lose."

The young man turned abruptly and left. There was a long silence, then the fat man rotated himself in the doorway and looked at David.

"I suppose you will tell me you do not know where she has gone."

David nodded.

"That would be the truth. I told her to escape, but where she goes is for her to decide. If I had known a safe hiding place, do you think I would have let her take me to the PFLP?"

The fat man seemed to ponder that.

"Very well," he said. "She will be found. We have the resources. I cannot delay our departure. We shall leave as soon as everything is ready. Good night, Professor. Marzuq will find a room for you to sleep. Remember what I said about rest. You will regret it if you do not sleep while you can."

He turned and went out, leaving David alone with Marzuq.

239

TWENTY-SEVEN

A storm was building. Black clouds squatted low over the rooftops, the atmosphere was close, muggy and oppressive. An odor as of decaying orchids filled the air, a dense, cloying smell. The light was gray, edged with purple, dusklike and surreal. Leyla threw another half-smoked cigarette onto the ground at her feet. It lay there beside a dozen others, wasted, its tip growing dull as it died. She was edgy, nervous, impatient. Her skin felt clammy, and it crawled over her flesh, sensitive to the electricity in the air. She wanted to get up and leave, to walk forever, away from this street, out of Jerusalem, into the storm. Her face was pale and drawn, and there were dark, ugly lines beneath her eyes. Her lips were drained of all color, bloodless and unattractive. She had not slept properly in two nights, and exhaustion was catching up with her; the clammy air seemed to soak up her energy like a sponge. She lit another cigarette, a long Winston she had bought from a street hawker that morning. Her hand shook slightly as she applied a match to its end. It caught fire, and she gulped the smoke down greedily. The match dropped from her fingers and spluttered briefly on the pavement.

The street was a valley of tawny limestone, apartment houses and office blocks, gray, anonymous doorways for late night passersby to flirt in or knife strangers in. The district was run down, bleak, and unexciting. Old men lived there and old women and people who had little more to look forward to than growing old. The days were gone when the district had harbored intellectuals and artists, refugees from a thousand pogroms of the body and the mind. It was its own pogrom now, its own ghetto, a shell, a carapace in the center of Jerusalem. When the rain came, its gutters would fill with dirty water. Leyla sucked on the cigarette as if desperate for its warmth.

Music came from a transistor radio turned up loud, ragged popular music, raucous and unoriginal. It irritated her. There was no rhythm, no order, no meaning that she could make out. The vigor in it eluded her and made her unhappy. She felt no vigor in herself, no energy, merely a reluctance to let go. She had spent all of the day before outside the PFLP house on Ibn Gevirol. No one had entered or left the building. That evening she had gone in search of Suhayl again—he was nowhere to be found. Nor was anyone else she knew and dared to visit. It was as if they had all gone underground at a moment's notice. Their shops were shut, their seats in the cafes empty. Little shivers went up and down her back. Had David betrayed them after all? She felt nervous and cold. Would he never come? It was beginning to grow dark: the light was changing by the minute. The storm would break soon.

The door opposite opened and a man came out. She was not sure at first that it was he, then he bent to tighten his shoelace and she caught a glimpse of his face. She felt herself tighten, all attention focused on him now. Her fingers clamped hard on the cigarette, crushing it as a lizard crushes a butterfly, thoughtlessly. He straightened up and walked on. She watched him fade into the street, a gray figure in the early dusk, then she threw her cigarette down and crossed the road, falling in behind him, forty paces between them. A short distance behind her, the door of a parked car opened and closed soundlessly.

He walked down to Shivte Israel, headed south briefly, then turned onto Hmalka, heading toward Zion Square. He was wearing a long gray raincoat tied tightly at the waist, beneath which she could see gray trousers and heavy brown shoes. The raincoat flickered ahead of her, in and out of sight, as he passed through the crowds jostling on Ussishkim. People were hurrying to be indoors, out of the path of the coming storm. Somewhere far away thunder growled. The sky had an unhealthy look. She kept pace with him, blending with the crowd. Not far behind her a man's feet moved at the same pace.

He stopped abruptly to give money to a beggar on the corner of Keren Hakayemet. A drop of rain fell into the beggar's palm, heavy and cold like a silver coin. The beggar was blind, blind and past

241

caring about rain or silver. A cluster of *agorot* coins followed the raindrop. The beggar muttered something. Leyla paused to look in a shopwindow. Her reflection stared back at her, the hollow eyes dark in their sockets. She felt drops of wetness touch her head. Half a block away, a man stopped and looked at a display of sporting goods.

He left the beggar, his nightly beggar, and trudged on. In his right hand he carried a small black briefcase, the leather battered and scarred. All around him the pavement grew suddenly wet as the clouds opened. He fumbled at his collar, drawing it around him, quickening his pace. Leyla followed closely, frightened of losing him in the rain. People began to run in all directions, into doorways, across the street, in search of shelter.

He paused in the open doorway of a tobacconist's shop. Leyla looked around. There was nowhere else to go. She was afraid of losing sight of him. She slipped in beside him, soaking wet, her hair plastered against her head, her clothes wet through. Three other people stood in the doorway, two men and a middle-aged woman. They complained to one another about the rain, filled the doorway with small talk. Leyla looked away, nervous in case he should recognize her as having been outside his office. He stared out at the rain, heedless of her. The rain kept falling, steady now, a broad torrent of water that sprayed their feet. On the road, cars drove past in a flurry of wetness, their tires hissing loudly, their headlights useless against the slashing downpour. A dog huddled beside an empty *felafel* stand.

Leyla reached into her pocket and drew out her cigarette packet. It was empty. She crumpled it between her fingers and tossed it out into the storm. The rain carried it away, sweeping it carelessly into the gutter. The man beside her turned, his eyes on her. He put his hand into the pocket of his raincoat and brought out an unopened packet of Nelsons. With his other hand he deftly removed the cellophane and opened the pack. He held it toward her.

"Here," he said.

She looked away from his face, her eyes on the packet. She extracted a cigarette, mumbled, "Thank you," and looked out at the rain-swept street. He took a cigarette from the pack and put it in his mouth. From the same pocket he drew out a small Gauloise lighter. He flicked it once and a flame grew between his fingers.

Carefully, he held the flame out toward her. A small breeze took it and moved it sideways. She could not look into his eyes. With one hand, she held the cigarette between her lips and placed it in the little flame. He held it steadily until her cigarette was alight, then brought it up to his own and lit it too. She turned her face away again. In the street, the rain clattered down.

Leyla stared into the darkness, thinking. It had been easy getting away. Suhayl had returned of his own accord, soon after David was taken away. Fatma had not believed him at first, but he had blustered enough to convince her. He had pulled rank on her, in the best revolutionary style, and frightened her about the consequences of standing in his way. She and Tawfiq had let Suhayl take Leyla and drive her off. He had taken her to his own apartment. Making her escape had been easier than she had dared hope. Later that night he had tried to make love to her. Using her outrage and his shame as covers, she had stormed out of the apartment, making sure to take the papers with her. She had got well away on foot before finding a taxi and heading for Abraham Steinhardt's. The old professor had taken her in happily, and she had sat up until late with him, explaining what she and David had discovered. The papers were with him now; he was reading them, trying to find some fresh clue, something she or David had so far missed. He had already given the film to a friend at the university, someone who could be trusted and who would develop it in spite of its age and condition.

Steinhardt had wanted Leyla to stay and rest, but she could not. She had to find David or learn what had happened to him. And all she had found out so far was that something was wrong, badly wrong. People had gone into hiding or someone had taken them away. It might be coincidence, there might have been an Israeli clampdown, perhaps word of David's MOSSAD connections had made people jumpy. Perhaps David had betrayed them: the thought kept coming back to her. But none of these seemed adequate explanations to her, least of all the last. Instinct told her to look elsewhere.

That was why she was following Scholem. At first she had been reluctant to follow David's instructions about taking the papers to the colonel: she knew Scholem well by reputation and thought it much more likely he would have her arrested than that he would believe her story. But after some thought she had realized that, however much information Abraham Steinhardt could discover in the papers David had found, he had no resources to do anything about it. Scholem had those resources: she had to persuade him to help.

But she had decided against going to him in his office. A MOSSAD section was one of the last places she would enter voluntarily. It would be safer and more effective to talk to him at home. She paused and dragged deeply on the cigarette. The smoke seemed to fill her, creeping into her pores, like fine needles probing for her soul. She could still smell orchids beneath the damp odor of the rain. She remembered the flowers at Muhsin's funeral. Was that it? she thought. Was she running to Scholem now, another enemy? Was going to Scholem just another paradigm in the ugly grammar of self-betrayal she had been learning? She would give her body to him if necessary to enlist his help in finding David. What else would she give him? Who else?

The rain slackened at last, the final drops skittering down in their eagerness to be part of the flood. People shifted in doorways and some ventured early into the street. She let Scholem go ahead of her. It would be more difficult now. He had seen her. The streets were less crowded and it was too dark for her to allow him much of a lead. But there were shadows and she was small. She slipped out into the street. Up above, the sky was still heavy with dark clouds. There was a flash of sheet lightning. A minute passed, then thunder rolled, closer this time, heavy and frightening.

She could just make him out in the distance as he passed beneath a street light and took shape momentarily. His cigarette still burned between her fingers. She sucked on it once, then cast it into the stream of muddy water that chased down the gutter. Behind her a shadow moved and was still again.

She was worried lest he take a taxi or bus, but he continued walking in a straight line along Ben Yehuda. Then he turned off abruptly into a side street and she lost him. Panic caught her and she dashed to the corner, afraid he might have gone into a building or taken another turning. As she turned the corner, a flash of lightning lit up everything with a weird, eldritch light. He was caught in it, frozen in the act of opening the door of an old apartment building. The next moment he was gone, as if it had all

244

been a magician's act, with trick strobe lighting and dark mirrors. Leyla blinked and waited for the thunder.

It came on cue, a long, low rumbling that seemed to move about the sky, as if in search of something, like the roar of a questing beast. It grew almost silent at times, then rose again in volume, traveling in wide circles through the clouds. Leyla walked down the street to Scholem's door. The thunder covered the light steps of the man behind her.

The downstairs door was open and Scholem's name was on one of the rusty mailboxes at the foot of the stairs. She had expected him to live somewhere better than this. Wearily, she climbed the stairs. He lived on the top floor, eight flights up. Her footsteps echoed gently, falling like lost hopes into the stairwell. His door was like all the other doors she had ever known: old, battered, uninviting. She knocked three times, not hard, not soft. There was a sound of footsteps, then the lock was turned and the door opened.

He held a gun in his hand, a Colt automatic, small, metallic, and lethal.

"Come in, Miss Rashid," he said. "I've been expecting you. You must be soaking. That was a very heavy shower."

Leyla looked at the gun, then at Scholem. She had no choice. She stepped inside.

"You recognized me," she said as he closed the door.

He shook his head.

"No. Your face seemed familiar, that was all. When I got in my phone rang. It was one of our surveillance men; he followed you from Haneviim. It's standard practice—he saw you casing the offices. He's downstairs now, but I won't ask him up. Are you armed, by the way?"

She shook her head once.

"How did he know my name?" she asked.

"He didn't. When you knocked I'd just found your photograph. I keep files here. Yours isn't very large, but it does contain a very good photograph."

"Sit down," Scholem said. He was older than he had appeared in the photograph she had looked at three years earlier. His eyes were soft and kind, but they were lined and sad, and a dull film seemed to cover them.

They sat down together, Scholem with his little gun, Leyla

shivering from the rain. Outside, the thunder still rolled over the rooftops. He had already lit a fire, a small, two-bar electric heater that glowed dull red. With one hand he lifted it by its handle and brought it closer to them. Leyla wanted to crouch down beside it, to forget everything in its warmth.

"Why were you following me?" he asked. His tone was neutral, not angry, not solicitous. He had asked such questions thousands of times. This was just another interrogation. He felt bored. He would have them take her away soon.

"I wanted to speak to you," Leyla said. "I wanted your help."

His eyebrows moved up slightly.

"Why didn't you come to my office?"

"If you have my photograph, a file, you know why."

He nodded. He knew.

"What then?" he asked.

"I don't understand."

"What help? Are you in trouble? With your friends from the PFLP?"

She pursed her lips.

"Yes, but I don't want help for that. I want to find someone, someone who may be important to you."

He interrupted her.

"To me personally or to the people I work for?"

"I don't know. Perhaps to neither. But someone has to help."

"Who is it? David Rosen?"

"How do you know?"

He smiled, a little pleased by his own quickness.

"We know he went to Sinai with you. We lost track of him after that. Lost interest. I assumed he had returned to his archaeological preoccupations."

"You didn't know he was back in Jerusalem?"

He shook his head.

"No, I didn't know. I told you, we lost interest. He didn't visit me. I think he despaired of me. He was in trouble. There was a problem in Syria, then his parents were killed. He thought the events were related. It meant nothing to me. You say he's missing?"

"He's with the PFLP. Here, in Jerusalem somewhere. They were going to execute him."

Scholem's face clouded over. In the background the thunder continued.

"Was this your doing?"

She hung her head, shaking it. The room felt close, stale. Steam rose from her hair and clothes. The fire felt close but not close enough. She wanted to hold it to herself, to be consumed in it. A shiver ran down her right arm to her fingers.

"Yes, but not deliberately. We needed somewhere to go, somewhere to hide."

He held up a hand. The light of the fire caught it and reddened it.

"I think you'd better tell me everything," he said. "Start with Sinai. Did anything happen there?"

She told him about Sinai, about the deaths at St. Nilus', about the papers David had found there and in Jerusalem. And she told him about the house in Ain Tur and the events of two days before.

When she came to the end he only looked at her, uncertain what to say. It was outside his province, outside the normal horrors of his horror-saturated profession. An ancient city, stones, a desert: he left those things to others. His trade was guns and bombs and quiet killings by well-trained hands in back streets and deserted lavatories. But there had been guns and a bomb and quiet killings.

"Why did you come here?" he asked, hiding his uncertainty. "Don't you realize I could have you arrested, interrogated, put on trial . . . killed out of hand if I want to have you killed?"

She nodded silently.

"And yet you still came to me?"

"Yes." He could scarcely hear her, she said it so quietly.

He looked at her for a long time.

"You must love him very much," he said at last. It was rare for him to have such perception in such matters. But he knew he was right.

"Won't you help me?" she pleaded.

He got up from his chair and went to the window. Rain had started to fall again, as if a damn had burst high in the mountains, a rage of water against his windowpane. He watched it pour down in streams, as though it would never stop again.

"There was an execution," he said, his voice remote, his face still turned to the window. "A multiple execution. Some schoolchildren found the bodies this morning, playing on a building site on Mount Scopus. Seven men. Someone had taken them there, lined them up, and shot them one at a time through the head at point-blank range. There was a pit, a clay pit: the bodies had fallen into it. We've identified them. I have a list."

Leyla found it almost impossible to ask the next question. Her voice came in a whisper, her heart raced with it.

"Was . . . was David one of them?"

Scholem did not turn from the window. He watched the lights outside twinkling in the streaks of rain on the glass. He shook his head.

"No. They were all Palestinians, PFLP suspects. Some of them may have been Council members. Perhaps you would know."

"Perhaps," she said. She felt dizzy with relief. And yet, even as she breathed more easily, the realization came to her that it was not over. There were other building sites in Jerusalem, there was no shortage of bullets. Or executioners.

"What are the names?" she asked.

Scholem turned from the window and walked over to his desk. His briefcase lay on top of it, just as he had left it when he arrived home. He opened it and drew out a sheaf of papers. He leafed through them in silence, then extracted one and handed it to Leyla.

"This was prepared this afternoon," he said.

The sheet was carefully typed in Hebrew characters. Leyla found it difficult at first to decipher the Arab names in their transliterated form, but one by one they became clear to her, as if rising up out of their muddy pit into the light again. Seven names. Seven faces. She had known none of them well, but she had met them all and admired them once. The names were a part of her own past. She read the list again.

"Is this all?" she asked.

Scholem nodded.

"So far," he said. "Do you know any of them?"

"Yes. These are all Council members. Someone has done your job for you. You should be grateful. Perhaps the communication between your different departments isn't as good as you think."

He shook his head.

"This wasn't our work. I assure you. I don't mean we aren't capable of something like this. Why should I lie to you? If it was necessary, we would do it. That's the nature of my profession: necessity buys all, even Jewish scruples. But this was not necessary. We watch. We question. We suborn. But we prefer a single killing. Isolation is more effective than mass martyrdom. It was not our work."

Leyla looked at him out of faded eyes. It did not matter whether she believed him or not, whether he was telling the truth or not. There was no final truth in any of this, except death perhaps. In everything else men made their own truth. There was a Jewish truth, a Palestinian truth: Scholem's truth, Leyla's truth. And the rest was lies.

"It's not complete," she murmured.

He raised his eyebrows.

"The list," she explained. "Whoever carried out the killings didn't finish his job. There are seven names here. All Council members, all seven. But there were eight on the Council. There's one name missing."

Scholem's expression grew intense.

"Who is the eighth man?" he asked.

She returned his gaze.

"I don't know," she said. "I know of him, know that he is important, but I never learned his name, never saw. All I have been told is that he is an old man. And that he's fat, extremely fat."

Scholem's knuckles grew white as he gripped the arm of the chair beside which he stood. He said nothing, just stood staring at Leyla, his whole body tense. Without a word, he turned to the desk and picked up the phone. He dialed a short number and spoke almost immediately.

"This is Scholem. Give me Kahan in Section D."

There was a brief pause, then he spoke again.

"Arieh? *Shalom*. This is Chaim. Have there been any further reports following this morning's from Scopus? Yes, I'll wait."

There was a pause, then the receiver crackled again.

"Nothing? Are you sure? I see." He paused again. "Listen, Arieh. Put out an alert for al-Shami. He may be dead or he may be alive and active in Jerusalem."

Scholem fell silent for a moment as the man on the other end spoke. As he listened, his face changed. His cheeks seemed to grow pale and his eyes grew bright with concentration.

"What?" he said. "Are you sure? When? Is he there now? No, go on."

He listened again, this time for over a minute, and as he did so he showed signs of mounting excitement. When at last the other man was silent, he spoke again.

"Have Hasan Bey brought in for questioning. Yes, tonight, right

249

now. Keep Ahmad there. Don't tell him anything. Tell the patrols to keep a lookout. I'll be there soon. Wait for me. *Shalom.*"

He replaced the receiver and turned to Leyla. He was keyed up, on edge.

"The man you said was missing, the eighth man, is called 'Abd al-Jabbar al-Shami. He's one of the most wanted men in Israel. A man who has never killed in his life, so far as anyone knows, but who has been responsible for more deaths than you can imagine. For all his size, he's elusive. I met him once, ten years ago."

He paused, as if about to say more. There was a look in his eyes as if a dark, undesirable memory that he could not expunge had surfaced in his mind. He blinked and went on.

"We know almost nothing about him, and what we do know tells us very little. I've lived for years with his photograph, with the dream of catching him. And now there may be a chance."

His voice changed as he went on. Talking seemed to soothe him, to calm somewhat the strong excitement that had hold of him.

"This morning one of our informers reported seeing al-Shami in the Shaykh Jarrah Quarter. He saw him yesterday, around midday. Al-Shami was with a ruffian named Marzuq, a jailbird who earns his living cutting throats but has never been up on a murder charge in his life. They were buying provisions, enough for a long journey. Our informer followed them to a shop belonging to a man called Hasan Bey. We know Hasan well. He took the title "Bey" from his father, who was an Ottoman official in the days before the Mandate. Hasan inherited more than his father's title, though. He makes use of a network of contacts throughout the old Palestine region. He buys and sells almost anyone, so they say. He would buy you, Miss Rashid . . . and get a good price for you, I should imagine. In camels, probably."

He turned and looked at Leyla. His eyes glinted wickedly and the trace of a smile flickered at the edge of his lips. For a moment he had become a young man again, then the heaviness of sad middle age crept back over him and weighed his face down once more. He went on.

"Camels are a serious matter to Hasan Bey. He deals in them as far south as Najd and Qatar. The 'Aniza, the 'Utayba, the Shammar all do business with him. He has an entrepot on Ma'an in Jordan. He keeps the best bulls there—the tribespeople bring their females to Ma'an to stud. It's not the custom to pay, but he always has a price. The Bedouin dislike him, but he has the best camels: Sharariyya, Hutaymiyya, 'Umaniyya—all the finest breeds. I know all about it—I once turned him to work for me. Until I discovered he was still working for himself. I should have known better. I was younger then."

Leyla interrupted.

"What has all this about camels to do with what we've been talking about?"

Scholem shrugged.

"I'm not sure. Except that al-Shami arranged to buy five camels from Hasan Bey. Three riding camels, *dhaluls,* and two strong males with *misama* packsaddles for carrying food and gear. I don't know who the third rider is, but our man overheard al-Shami ask for an easy animal for someone who hadn't ridden before."

Leyla suppressed a thrill of excitement. She looked across the room at Scholem. He returned her glance.

"Don't put much faith in it. It could be anyone."

"Where are they going? Did they say?"

"No. They told Hasan nothing. All I know is that they were to pick up the camels in Ma'an today or tomorrow. They'll collect the bulk of their supplies there as well, from Hasan's entrepot. There's just one thing. Our man heard al-Shami give Hasan a particular instruction. He heard him say, *'Bi-lā wasma.'* Does that make sense to you?"

"Yes," she nodded. "'Without brands.' He wants unbranded camels. What would be the point?"

"I'm not sure. He may plan to brand them himself later. It depends on his destination. If he wants to travel in secret, tribal markings could be awkward."

"Can't you stop them?"

"I doubt it. They'll be in Ma'an by now. There are dozens of ways across the Jordanian border, even for a fat old man like al-Shami. I've asked my assistant to alert our border patrols, but I don't think they'll find anything. He'll go across by Jeep or truck, probably quite openly. I could send someone in after them, but I'd need clearance for that. My superiors will want hard facts. They'll have to be convinced it's worth the risk to try to take a man like al-Shami on Arab territory. Rosen means nothing to them. He's a victim, that's all. We have plenty of victims, the list can take another name. We don't even know he's with al-Shami. That's just a wild conjecture at the moment."

There was another silence. Scholem turned toward the window again, watching the rain form rivulets along the glass. Outside, the gutters sounded choked and full. How many nights had he stood at this window, looking out at nothing, trying to think about nothing, to lose himself in the darkness?

Leyla broke the silence in a low, dull voice.

"In that case, I'll go. I can ride a camel as well as a Bedouin. I can track in the desert: not well, but adequately. If it takes me a year, I'll find them. It will have nothing to do with you, nothing to do with Israel. If someone finds me, I'm a Palestinian. I'll be doing it for myself. You needn't worry, it won't embarrass you. You can add me to your list of victims. Or do you have a column for Palestinians?"

Scholem ran a finger down the glass. It came away wet with condensation. The room was warm. He wanted to sleep with the girl.

"What will you do if you find them?" he asked.

"I have a gun," she answered. "I know how to use it."

How long had it been since he last slept with a woman? Four years? Nearer five, perhaps. Not to touch, not to be touched. His fingers felt damp and cold. Every winter it was like this.

"How will you track them in the Nafud? You think they've gone there, don't you? That isn't ordinary desert. It's sand, miles of sand, the worst desert. You can't do it alone."

"I'll hire a guide," she said. "A Shammar *rafiq*. He'll take me in."

"Alone? A woman?"

She said nothing.

He wanted al-Shami. It was almost like wanting a woman, the intensity of his longing for this man. For years he had lusted to touch the fat man, to feel him between his hands, helpless, trapped at last. He looked out at the lights in the street. Al-Shami was out there now, traveling, heading away from him, perhaps forever. Now, if he wanted, he could find him, find him and take him. It only required the will, the decision. He turned his face to the room again.

"You can't go alone," he said. "Someone will have to go with you." He paused, weighing his next words, uncertain of them. "I can go. I have leave due to me. I want to find al-Shami, but if I wait

252

for my superiors to sanction a pursuit I'll lose him. He'll be in Ma'an by now, as I said. By tomorrow he'll be on his way to the Nafud, if what you suspect is correct. If he's to be caught at all, we must start tomorrow. I've asked them to bring in Hasan Bey for questioning. He'll supply us with camels and provisions. I'll make arrangements with the border guards. We can slip into Jordan without difficulty. I'll arrange for guides. We'll leave tomorrow night."

Leyla stared at Scholem, unsure what to say or how to say it. Suddenly, she felt afraid. It was as if she had, against her will, been sucked into a vortex of undesired action. Choice had been taken away from her. She felt as if she stood on the brink of a precipice and that Scholem had come behind her, pushing her. Was there no time to back out, to move away from the edge?

"How can you go?" she asked. "You of all people. What if you were caught? What if they recognized you?"

"I've been in Saudi Arabia before," he said, "many times. On missions. I can pass as an Arab. When I was a young man I spent years in the Negev, living with the tribes. Don't worry about me. This is what I do. I do it well."

She watched him, framed against the window, a gaunt man, burned out by a slow fire inside.

"What will you do?" she asked. "If you find al-Shami?"

He said nothing. His mind was made up. Al-Shami was everything to him now. He would have him, one way or another. He turned back to the window. Outside, the rain had almost stopped. The woman had unsettled him, opened something inside him that had been bottled up for too long. The storm was passing, but still he felt on edge. In the glass, he saw Leyla reflected, her skin red from the light of the fire, her eyes fixed on him. Then a large raindrop broke and ran down the window, cutting her image in half.

TWENTY-EIGHT

Leyla climbed the five flights to Abraham Steinhardt's apartment, dragging her weight with her as if she had grown old and heavy, or as if the rain had penetrated her pores and made her gray and sodden. The storm had gone, but the air was no fresher. The same stale closeness hemmed her in, the same dark odors caught at her throat and made her want to retch.

She knocked on the door, three times, slowly, as arranged. He did not come at first and she thought something had happened. Then she heard footsteps, the careful footsteps of a man not yet elderly, no longer young. He was wearing carpet slippers, an ancient pair with holes in the toes that he had worn when she first met him, six years earlier. The footsteps paused. There was a sound of bolts being drawn back and keys turned in locks. He had had the bolts fitted the day before, together with a spy hole through which he could see any callers.

He opened the door and stood back to let her in. Once she was inside, he locked and bolted the door again before turning to her.

"You look tired," he said.

"I am tired. Tired and sore."

"You need to sleep." He paused. "Have you eaten?"

She shook her head.

"No," she said. "I can't eat. I've no appetite. Don't ask."

Steinhardt frowned but said nothing. He knew Leyla too well to try to force her to do something against her will.

"Come inside," he said. "I've something to show you."

He had expected some interest, but she remained dull and impassive.

When she had sat down in his study he went to his desk and took a small packet from a drawer. All around them books climbed to the ceiling in dusty columns, the cases tall and almost menacing. Leyla was heartily sick of books—books and papers and manuscripts. She wanted to get away, to leave all this behind.

"Can I have a cigarette?" she asked.

Steinhardt reached into the pocket of his robe—a stained and threadbare garment that had come from Japan—and took out a pack of Europas, known to Israeli wits as "the cigarettes for nonsmokers." She looked at them contemptuously but held out a hand all the same.

"They're better than nothing, I suppose," she said.

"Yes," said Steinhardt. "A lot of things are better than nothing." He stood and crossed to a small table on which sat some glasses and a large bottle of calvados. He poured two generous glasses and passed one to Leyla.

"If you aren't eating," he said, "at least drink." He sat down. Picking up the packet, he passed it across to her.

"Here," he said, "take a look at these."

She opened the packet. It contained a small bundle of black and white photographs, snapshot size but clearer than anyone could have dared hope.

"My friend at the university tells me the film was remarkably well preserved considering its age and the conditions you say it was kept under. He was curious, but he didn't ask any questions. He'll keep his mouth shut."

Leyla examined the photographs one by one. She felt little interest in them. What could they tell them? They were just photographs, images from fifty years ago, faded gray shots of obscure events and people.

There were the monks, small, nervous men unused to being photographed, afraid of offending by refusing. The Archimandrite looked solemn and sad, a gray-bearded man wearing a huge crucifix on an ornate chain about his neck. Then, with a flash of recognition, she singled out the face of a somewhat younger man, in his mid-forties probably. The face seemed familiar, like that of someone she knew. And then it was apparent to her who he was: Gregorios, the librarian, who had gone later to live at St. Catherine's, the old monk who had helped her during her illness.

The next photograph was of a small group of Europeans. From their descriptions in Schacht's diary, she could make them out.

255

There was von Meier, small but with the build of an American footballer, with the sad, spaniel face and cold eyes. On his right stood Keitel, small and dried up, like a dehydrated mushroom grown out of all proportion and endowed with some sort of life. The man on von Meier's left must have been Lorenz: he was fat, grinned rather stupidly, and wore an expensive-looking suit of Bavarian manufacture. The man beside him was readily identifiable. Sturbannführer Schacht stood there, elegant in his black SS uniform, his boots polished, his cap straight on his head, his expression unreadable. Leyla wondered what thoughts had passed through his mind as he stood there, being photographed, knowing his life was in such danger.

There were several variations on the same group, with people in different positions and slightly altered poses. In one shot she could just make out the entrance to the church in the background. So the photographs had been taken on the small piazza outside the basilica. The next shot was of a larger group, the Europeans together with about a dozen Arabs. They were town Arabs, almost certainly Palestinians. Some wore *tarbushes* and European-style clothes, others traditional dress of a high quality. Otherwise, they meant nothing to her. She flicked desultorily through the remaining pictures, variations on the first theme. The last was a close-up of four men: von Meier, Keitel, Lorenz, and an Arab. Leyla recognized the Arab as the man at the center of all the larger group photos. He was a smallish man dressed in the garb of a religious leader, in a black robe and a tall *tarbush* around which was wound a slightly conical white turban. His face was thin and bearded and bore a smirking, cunning expression, especially in the tiny close-set eyes.

Something about the Arab's face troubled Leyla. She put the photograph on her lap and sat looking at it, her eyes filled with concentration. Steinhardt watched her, suddenly aware that her expression, her posture had changed. She lifted the photograph to examine it more closely, then went back through the larger group shots in which he figured. Something tugged at her deep down. She looked at the close-up again. And then she felt a shiver go through her body. She had seen that face before, she was certain of it. Yes, there could be no mistake. She recognized him, but she could not remember who he was.

She guessed he must be A.H., and somehow that triggered a memory too. A.H.? She was almost certain she knew his name.

"Is anything wrong, Leyla?" asked Steinhardt.

She looked up. She had forgotten him completely, forgotten where she was, what she was doing. It all came back to her, like a symptom in an illness that will not quite go away. David, Scholem, the pillars of Iram.

"No," she said, "nothing's wrong. But look. . . ." She handed the photograph of the close-up to Steinhardt, one finger on the Arab.

"I know him," she said. "I've seen that face before, several times; I'm sure of it. But I can't put a name to him. Is he someone well known, someone whose face appears in history books perhaps?"

Steinhardt stared hard at the photograph. Somewhere in the recesses of his own mind a memory stirred, but the face still meant nothing to him.

"Yes," he said, "perhaps. I'll show the photograph to some people at the university. Maybe someone there will recognize him. It's a possibility. But I don't see how it will be of any help to us all the same."

"I think," Leyla said slowly, "that he must be A.H. He's at the center of all the large group photographs. David thought the initials must stand for an Arab name. Something tells me he was right. Is it important, do you think?"

Steinhardt fell silent. A deep frown creased his face. He felt old. Life was hell, whatever you did. With a sigh, he got up and went back to his desk. He picked up a piece of paper and sat down again, facing Leyla.

"There was something else I had thought to tell you," he said. His voice sounded dull. He was still uncertain. "I didn't know whether or not to tell you; it could have been mere coincidence. But now . . . I think I know who A.H. was." He paused again. His fingers played nervously with the paper on his lap.

"Tell me," he said, "did David tell you where his copy of the *Tariq al-mubin* came from, the one al-Yunani found for him?"

She looked at him, puzzled.

"No," she said. "A library somewhere in Jerusalem, that's all."

Steinhardt nodded.

"I see. Yes, it came from a library here in Jerusalem. The library belonged to Hajj Amin al-Husayni. You know who I'm referring to? It was a private library, one that was left in Jerusalem after he was expelled from Palestine in . . . I don't remember exactly now."

"Nineteen thirty-seven," whispered Leyla.

"Yes," Steinhardt repeated, "nineteen thirty-seven."

"How do you know this?" Leyla asked.

Steinhardt held out the sheet of paper. It was a Xerox copy of the page of the *Tariq al-mubin* that carried the owner's seal, the one with the name Amin al-Husayni.

"This had got mixed up with David's other papers. I found it while I was reading through them today. I'd heard about the library before, and I guessed this must have been one of a number of books from the Greek Patriarchate that found their way into it."

Leyla fell silent.

"A.H.," she said, her voice still a low whisper.

Behind her, Steinhardt nodded silently. The sound of traffic came from the street below.

"You realize what this means?" Steinhardt asked.

Dumb, she nodded. She could see lights outside. White and yellow, they seemed to stretch for miles.

"What will you do?" he asked her. "Should I have told you? Was it fair of me?"

She put her hands on the window frame and leaned out into the night. She would have given anything for some fresh air.

"Yes," she said to the darkness. "It was fair. How could you not tell me?"

It was fair, if anything in life was fair. *"Maktub,"* her Bedouin friends said. "It is written." It was fate, the divine *qadar,* something intolerable that had to be borne. David, the book, the deaths in Sinai, the pillars of Iram, and now al-Husayni. Out of the past, he had come to haunt her.

She straightened up and closed the window. Abraham Steinhardt crossed the room and put his arms around her, holding her to him. She put her head on his shoulder, grateful for the thin, musty fabric of his old robe.

"Thank you for telling me," she said. "It has helped make my mind up. Tonight I agreed to go into the desert to look for David, to find Iram. When I came back here I had all but made my mind up not to go after all. And now this. I remember him now, the photographs I used to see. That's him, all right, there's no mistake. I've made my decision now. I'll go."

He looked into her eyes.

"Because of a photograph?" he asked quietly.

She nodded.

"Yes," she said. "Because of a photograph."

FOUR

. . in the waste howling wilderness.

Deuteronomy 32:10

TWENTY-NINE

A freezing mist lay over everything, as if the world had been wiped out. Nothing moved. There were no sounds. The mist had no beginning and no end: nothing came out of it, nothing entered it, it was a vast white grave in which all sights and sounds had been buried. The ground underneath was hard with frost, as if it had been turned to stone forever. There was no sky, no sun.

Somewhere deep inside the mist a light tinkling sound rang out in the crisp, trembling air. Silence closed in again, then the sound was repeated, the jangling of a camel bell. It was followed by the head and neck the camel itself, then the great beast loomed grotesquely out of a heavy patch of mist, a gray shadow ridden by another shadow. Camel and rider passed in silence into another freezing bank of fog and were swallowed up. A second camel followed, then a third and a fourth, until seven animals had passed, five with riders, two carrying baggage.

The mist had come down during the night, about an hour before dawn. It was already midmorning and there were still no signs of its lifting. The cold was white and piercing, well below freezing. The mist formed a thick hoarfrost on the clothes of the riders and the camels' matted coats. The damp ate into the flesh, penetrated to the bones.

There was a sharp cry as the lead rider reined in his camel and halted, gazing intently at the ground. One by one, the others drew up behind him, darker shadows in a shadowy world. Without a word, he stepped from his camel to the ground. He was a tall man, over six feet, with hard, piercing eyes, like those of a Hurr falcon.

He wore light clothes, a thin cotton *dishdasha,* and an old, well-worn *'aba'* but seemed impervious to the piercing cold. Around his head was wrapped a red and white checked *ghutra,* held in place by narrow headcords. Tense with concentration, he bent down and began to scan the frozen earth. Carefully he lowered his face to the ground, pulled the *ghutra* from in front of his mouth, and breathed hard on the frost. He fingered the earth, then picked up a small frozen lump nearby and held it between his hands, rolling and warming it. A minute passed, then he broke it open, looked at it carefully, and tossed it aside. He looked up at the second rider, in the mist behind him.

"Five camels," he said. "Three *dhalul* with riders, two *fahal* with packs. Batiniyya from Oman, not local beasts. I have never seen these animals before."

A muffled voice came from the second rider.

"How long ago?"

"I'm not sure. The ground is hard. But the dung is fresh. Five days ago. The camel had been watered six days ago. It was grazing at Ma'an."

"And the riders?"

There was a pause. The guide bent down.

"This one," he said, pointing at one set of tracks, "was a heavy man, extremely heavy. He has the strongest camel. This one was a man of average build, seventy, maybe eighty kilos."

He straightened.

"And the third man?"

The man on the ground looked hard at the speaker.

"The third man has never ridden a camel before. He shifts in his saddle, his back aches. It will be a long journey for him."

"Is that all?"

The guide grinned, his teeth flashing in the mist.

"One camel is black," he said. "They are carrying Iraqi rice and flour from Amman. The smallest *dhalul* is pregnant: about three months. I can tell you more when we find their camp."

Leyla did not ask how he knew and did not think for a moment that he was making any of it up. He had spent his life in the desert and was as educated in its signs as any university graduate in the country of his books. A single hair would tell him a camel's coloring, a grain of rice the origins of a shipment, the pitch of a camel's hoof its state of health and whether it was with foal or not.

Pulling his camel's head down by means of the guide rope attached to its headstall, the Arab used her long neck to scramble onto her back. He turned and knelt precariously on the thick sheepskin on top of the saddle. With a whisper, he set her in motion again. The swirling mist swallowed him up and all was silence once more as the party moved on through the bitter morning.

The mist cleared a little before noon. Fitful sunshine revealed a world of desiccated yellow earth and black stones, flat and immense, a great wilderness stretching away on all sides to a low, wintry horizon. They were on the flint-strewn uplands of the southern half of the Baidat al-Sham, the great Syrian desert that separates the fertile lands of the eastern Mediterranean littoral from the riverine country of the Tigris and Euphrates. The real desert, the sands of the Great Nafud, still lay ahead of them, two hundred and eighty miles away across the hills of al-Tubayq. From here to the borders of the sands the going would be tough: in the Nafud, worse, much worse, was waiting for them.

They had left Ma'an the day before, heading south in the darkness before dawn, five anonymous riders, four men and a woman in man's dress. If anyone had asked in Ma'an after them, they would have been told they had gone toward al-'Aqaba, carrying goods to trade with tourists there and across the border in Israeli Eilat. Near Naqb Ashtar they had turned east and headed out into the desert. Today, at last, they had picked up the tracks of al-Shami's small party. Their path to the Nafud lay before them.

Their party consisted of Leyla, Scholem, and three Arab *rafiqs,* guides known to the tribes through whose territory they would pass, who could guarantee their safety while they journeyed through. Their principal guide was the tall man who rode in front; his name was 'Ali, a Huwaytat whose tents were camped in Wadi Rumm, farther south. Scholem had met him two years earlier while traveling among the Huwaytat and had been overjoyed to find him at Ma'an. Scholem trusted him and knew his abilities. Aged about forty, 'Ali was one of the best and most experienced trackers in the region and could take them to the edge of the Nafud directly and with the minimum amount of attention.

On 'Ali's advice, they had also hired Suwailim and Zubayr, two friends who had come to Ma'an looking for work during the winter.

Suwailim belonged to the Bani Atiya, whose encampments lay to the west of their projected route. Zubayr's people, the Shararat, roamed the region to the northeast. 'Ali wanted to take them out of Ma'an, away from the desolation of work in the old railway depot or Hasan Bey's emporium. They were like dozens of other young Bedouin he had seen in recent years, living like ghosts between the desert and the town, drawn increasingly to the towns. There, they were used by men like Hasan Bey, chewed for a little while, then spat back out into the sands of the desert from which they had come. Even now, as they traveled through the relatively easy country south of Ma'an, 'Ali was growing concerned. He had watched them shiver in the mist: life in the town had already begun to rob them of the hardness of the desert.

'Ali and his two companions would accompany Leyla and Scholem only as far as the sands. They knew nothing of their purpose in going there, save that they were following three other riders who were going there as well. They were being paid well enough not to ask questions, and what with the cold and the risk of Saudi patrols, they had enough to worry about. The three *rafiqs* would turn back on the edge of the Nafud, after arranging for a Shammar guide to take Leyla and Scholem into the desert.

They stopped to eat at about two in the afternoon. Suwailim and Zubayr wanted to light a fire to take the chill out of their bones, but 'Ali would not permit it. They would need what wood they carried or could collect for the nights, when the temperature would drop even further and an hour or two of warmth might stand between them and death. They ate dates, *khalasi* from Hofuf, sweet and filling. There was no shortage of water with which to wash them down. Between here and the Nafud there would be wells and numerous rock pools filled by the rains of the past month and more.

When they set off again the cloud had broken and the sun became quite strong. Their spirits lifted immediately. Suwailim and Zubayr rode in front behind 'Ali; Leyla and Scholem kept to the rear, talking quietly. They spoke in Arabic rather than Hebrew in order to preserve the fiction that Scholem was an Arab from Sinai, like Leyla. For it to become known that he was a Jew could have been fatal. Perhaps none of their three *rafiqs* would have minded, but if they knew and were indiscreet, there were others who would mind to the point of murder. Each time they halted for prayers, Scholem

264

turned with the others toward Mecca: he knew the words and gestures of the *salat* as well as any *badu*. That was the only time Leyla went apart from the rest: they would not have her with them while they prayed. The rest of the time she traveled as Scholem's son, unbearded, thin, and taciturn, her small breasts hidden beneath the wrappings of her *dishdasha* and the heavy sheepskin *farwa* she wore against the cold.

"Why do you want al-Shami so much?" she asked Scholem. "Why him more than any other?"

He rode along beside her for a while without answering. She felt no impatience. In the desert, time altered in subtle ways. They rode at a slow pace, no more than three miles an hour. But the very slowness of their progress staved off monotony. There was time to think, time to talk carefully, time to watch the small things on their journey: the plants, the stones, the animals, the birds.

"Al-Shami's special," he replied at last. "He's not an ordinary killer. Most men kill because they have to: someone else orders them to, or there's a demand made on them by honor, or they feel threatened. Then there are others who kill because they're greedy or lustful: they want money or a woman, and if the only way they can get what they want is to kill, they do it. And then there are some people who kill for a cause: their country or their faith or maybe just a political notion; you should understand that. But I don't think al-Shami falls into any of those categories. I think he has an even deeper reason, I think killing and the need to go on killing are so much a part of him that he would die without them. The odd thing is he's a sadist who hates to inflict pain. He does so because he has to, and he does it well, I can assure you. But he needs to free his victims from their suffering. Since the best release he knows is death, he has them killed. He has a horror of killing with his own hands, or so I've heard; but he can sit and watch a man's throat being cut without so much as turning a hair. He can sit and eat a meal while watching his friends gouge out someone else's eyes. He's a monster, Leyla. If we find him he must be given no chances. Kill him if there is the slightest likelihood of his escaping."

They continued to ride as before, in a vast silence broken only by the quiet pacing of their camels and the voices of their guides up ahead.

"How do you know all this about him?" Leyla asked after

265

some time.

Scholem did not look at her as he answered. He stared ahead, over the neck of his camel, out into the empty forest.

"I was with him for a long time," he said. "Five days." He breathed the desert air deep into his lungs. It was cold; the sun had not warmed it.

"That doesn't sound very long," he continued. "But five days in al-Shami's hands could seem a lifetime. He wanted information from me, wanted it badly. Wanted it quickly."

He paused again to take deep breaths.

"I would have given it to him. By the second day, I think I would have told him anything, given him anything. I'm not ashamed to admit that. But I had nothing to tell him, I didn't have the information he wanted. I thought it would go on forever, the pain, the hopelessness. I have never wanted to die so much, I wouldn't have thought it was possible to long for death like that. On the fifth day there was a raid. One of my friends had tracked me down."

He fell silent again, then went on.

"My friend was killed in the raid, a bullet through his left eye. I made them take me to his funeral, but it was no use, it meant nothing."

Scholem did not speak again until after sunset, when they camped for the night.

They pitched their tent within sight of the Tubayq Hills, where they would cross the border into Saudi Arabia. It rained during the night, heavy, soaking rain that the little tent barely kept out. There was not enough wood to keep the fire lit after midnight. They lay shivering beneath thin blankets in the bitter cold, listening to the rain pour down. Leyla slept fitfully, waking at times in the night to peer into the gloom before turning over and trying to shut out the cold enough to sleep again.

They rose before dawn and huddled about a small fire for warmth. Outside, rain still drizzled down from a leaden sky. The desert was like paste, a waste of gray mud that stretched beyond the horizon. The camels would find the going hard until they reached the hills.

After breakfast they set off, walking beside their camels in order to lighten them. The rain soaked into their clothes and the mud clung to the soles of their feet, making every step an effort. Ahead of them, the Tubayq Hills lay shrouded in heavy fog. They entered them just after noon.

That night the temperature dropped to twenty-eight degrees, four degrees below freezing. They could not find anywhere to pitch their tent and were forced to huddle in the lee of their camels for shelter. About midnight a cold wind came down the gorge in which they lay; it howled like a pack of wolves through the fissures in the rocks above, writhing and twisting in its path through the hills.

"This is only a small wind," 'Ali said. "When you come to the Nafud, then you will meet with real winds, desert winds that can destroy you. Rest easy now. Conserve your strength. The Nafud will test you to your limits."

The wind abated by morning, but fresh fog formed on the hilltops and blotted out the sun. They went on, cold and damp and miserable. 'Ali had lost the track of their quarry early on the day before, not far into the hill country. It might be days before they found it again, if at all.

In the early afternoon 'Ali rode up beside Scholem and Leyla. From time to time during the past hour he had ridden briefly in the rear, sometimes dropping out of sight, stopping once or twice to climb an escarpment or ride into a side gully. Now, as he drew alongside them, they could see that he wore an unaccustomed frown on his face.

"We are being followed," he said. "One rider. *Badu.* He rides very quietly and he has tied the mouth of his camel; but I heard something this morning and went back to see what it was. He is tracking us. I think he has been tracking us since Ma'an. Someone there has told him about us."

"How do you know?" Scholem asked.

"There is mud on his clothes and on the legs of his camel. Some of it he picked up from the desert before the hills. But higher up there are traces of reddish mud that can only have come from around Ma'an."

"We saw no one then."

"He was tracking. Far behind. I am certain."

"How far is he now?"

"Not far."

Leyla broke in.

"What can we do? Can we challenge him, ask why he is following us?"

'Ali shook his head.

"He's armed. He might panic, shoot one of us. He doesn't look like the sort of man who would miss."

"What then?"

"We can look for a suitable spot up ahead and ambush him. It will be safer to take him by surprise."

Scholem nodded.

"Go ahead, 'Ali," he said. "Find a place. We'll join you there and wait for him."

'Ali rode off down the gully, taking Suwailim and Zubayr with him. Scholem and Leyla rode on, leading the pack camels. From time to time Leyla looked around, expecting to see their pursuer come behind them, but there was nothing except rocks and low-lying banks of fog.

'Ali was waiting for them a mile farther down the gully. He had found a spot where a broad side gully allowed them to hide the camels while they could climb up to a ledge about thirty feet above the ground. Suwailim was left with the camels. They were hobbled and strips of cloth tied around their mouths to prevent their calling.

Scholem and Leyla climbed to the ledge while 'Ali waited at the opening to the side gully with Zubayr. They all carried guns and were ready to use them at the first sign of danger. A great silence fell as they lay waiting for him to appear. There was no other way out of the gully: he had to pass by them, and when he did they would spring their trap, 'Ali and Zubayr in front of him, Leyla and Scholem behind.

The minutes crawled past without enthusiasm. No one spoke. The narrow gully was filled with the tension of waiting. Half an hour went by and still he did not appear. Had he been that far behind? They continued to wait, uncomfortably still in the cold. By the time an hour had passed they knew something was wrong. 'Ali signaled to Scholem. They climbed back down to the gully floor, where 'Ali and Zubayr were waiting for them.

"He must know we've seen him," 'Ali said. "Whoever he is, he knows what he's doing. He'll be more dangerous now, on his guard, taking precautions. He knows we'll be waiting for him. But he's in no rush. He'll wait for his moment."

'Ali looked back down the gully.

"He won't come now," he said. "We've wasted enough time.

Let's go."

They walked down to the side gully where Suwailim had been left with the camels. The animals were sitting quietly, hobbled and gagged as they had been left, but Suwailim was nowhere to be seen. They called his name, but there was no answer. Then Leyla noticed that one of the camels was nuzzling something on the ground. She went across to look and felt her stomach heave as she looked down. It was a human hand, drowning in a pool of blood. A trail of blood led down the gully. They followed it and as they did so discovered that it was more than just a blood trail: they found Suwailim's other hand, then a foot, then his penis, then another foot and both ears before they found the rest of him, just around a bend in the gully. He was still alive but horribly mutilated. He died soon after they found him, unable to speak, unaware of what was happening.

THIRTY

David lay on the cold, sterile ground, aching in every limb, wishing he could die or be reborn in a different body, now, at once—dreaming himself into another's flesh. But the dream evaporated as always and he felt despair return to lick at his wounds like a bitch in heat. He was freezing. He had been freezing for days, ever since leaving Ma'an for the desert. Al-Shami and the shark-man Marzuq dressed warmly during the day and had ample bedding at night, but David was clad only in the thing clothes in which he had been taken from the PFLP house. They ate well, al-Shami filling his gargantuan belly with tasty foods that Marzuq cooked for him over a fire of *ghada* wood, but David was given nothing but bread, and not enough of that. There were no scraps from al-Shami's plate, though by now David would have taken them had they been offered him.

Every day was the same as the day before. The grinding monotony ate into David, stultifying his brain in the same way that cold and hunger were wearing down his body. Twice he had tried to escape, but each time Marzuq had come after him and brought him back. They made surprisingly good time. Al-Shami, for all his weight, knew how to ride a camel well and could endure a long day's march far better than David, whose muscles were pummeled and torn by the constant rocking motion.

On several occasions al-Shami had ridden alongside David, engaging him in conversation. He declared Marzuq an imbecile and said he could not bear to speak with him. He asked David about archaeological matters, displaying a surprising knowledge of ancient Near Eastern history for a layman. His interests centered in one area in particular: the fates of the successive cities of Jerusalem. However much David tried to explain that the archaeology of Palestine was not his forte, al-Shami insisted on bringing the topic of conversation back to Jerusalem. What evidence was there that Abraham had prepared to sacrifice his son on the Temple Mount, on the spot now covered by the Dome of the Rock? Was the son Isaac or Ishmael, as Muslims believe? Were there no remains at all of Solomon's Temple, not even a stone, a jewel? What was the fate of the Jews taken into exile by Nebuchadrezzar, and what of those who stayed behind? How large had Herod's Second Temple been? Was the Wailing Wall part of that Temple or just a section of the platform on which it had been built? What had happened to the Temple when the Emperor Titus razed Jerusalem in A.D. 70? How much of the original Temple Mount was covered by the Muslim Haram al-Sharif?

The questions went on and on, like a test of some sort. David did his best to satisfy al-Shami. He assumed that the fat man's line of questioning was dictated by the perennial issue of who could best lay claim to Jerusalem, but he could not see what help most of his answers might be. For a while al-Shami would show intense curiosity, questioning David closely on some aspect of the excavations at Jerusalem (which David had often seen but never worked on), but then he would suddenly seem to lose all interest and shut off completely, riding silently alone or going up ahead to speak with Marzuq after all. In general the two Arabs talked very little together. Once or twice they argued, but out of David's hearing and in rapid, colloquial Arabic that he could not have understood. David had the impression that Marzuq knew very little of what was happening, though he seemed familiar with the terrain and must have made this journey more than once.

On a number of occasions David tried to turn the tables on al-Shami. He asked him about Iram, about the route there, about the purpose of their journey. But the fat man was uncooperative, telling David that he would in due course know everything—or, at least, everything he might be permitted to know. David's ultimate fate was not a foregone conclusion, al-Shami said. It would depend on how cooperative he was, how long he remained useful.

There were mist and rain on occasions. David felt ill. They let him sit by the fire at night, but it was only to keep him close, in the light where he could be observed. When the others slept, his hands

271

were tied, efficiently and cruelly, behind his back. He was unable to sleep properly in that position, aching as he did from the discomfort of riding during the day. The nights wracked him with cold and sleeplessness, with the hard, rocky ground, the days tormented him with exhausted wakefulness and the long, painful strides of his camel. His thighs and buttocks were ruined by the constant chafing of the leather saddle; what had begun as painful red weals had rapidly turned to open sores. His back was pulled by the unending effort to maintain his balance astride the camel. There was no respite, no proper sleep to restore his energy.

"Where is Iram?" he asked al-Shami once.

"In the desert, in the Nafud. You have read al-Halabi, you know."

"How do we get there?"

"Through the sands. You will see. You will see everything."

The journey became a catechism between him and the old man. Now one, now the other was priest, then catechumen.

David thought of Leyla often, afraid for her, knowing he would never see her again. He could not even be sure she was still alive. Al-Shami's ruthlessness seemed to know no bounds. Sometimes he would talk with David about death. He seemed obsessed with it, as if it was something he knew better, more intimately than life. David imagined that he carried the smell of it about with him, as a woman wears a favorite perfume on her skin. He was half in love with it, half terrified of it. When he spoke about it, it was with a mixture of delight and loathing. He told David of men he had seen killed or tortured, yet seemed innocent in his simple love for the thing. Almost, he was like a child: he played with death, taunted it, fondled it. And it seemed to love him in return.

"Who built Iram?" David asked him.

"Its builders," was al-Shami's only reply.

"Won't you tell me who they were?" asked David.

"You'll see in time," said al-Shami and rode on. "You'll see in time."

That was all he would say. Iram was a mystery, and the identity of its builders a mystery as well. But what preoccupied David's thoughts even more than the question of who had built the city was that of who inhabited it now. That, and why they had been so ruthless in ensuring that the existence of Iram remain a closely guarded secret.

THIRTY-ONE

Leyla, Scholem, and their two guides came out of the hills through a canyon known as the Shi'b al-Asad, past flat table mountains, into the open country to the east of the Tubayq range. It was about two hours before sunset. A sharp, irritating wind blew against them out of the east, gnawing them with icy teeth. They trudged on directly into it, feeling weary, ragged, and cold.

The sun set at last, a red ball of fire glowering out at them briefly as it sank through layers of thick, dust-laden cloud. They pitched their tent in the open, with its back to the wind, and lit a fire, using brushwood they had gathered in the last part of their march. 'Ali made rice, which he served with black beans and *hummus,* the best meal they had eaten since leaving Ma'an; but no one had any appetite and most of the food was returned to the bags. They were worried by the killing and uneasy about their chances of rediscovering al-Shami's track. In the morning 'Ali would have to scour the foothills, looking for a trace of the party ahead of them. If he left it until later, it might be impossible to find.

They set a watch that night. Their unknown pursuer could be anywhere, out in the darkness waiting for them to forget him for a moment, so that he could move in again. 'Ali volunteered to sit the first watch, until midnight. Wrapped in Scholem's *farwa,* he sat outside by a small fire, tending it through the dark hours.

Inside the tent, Leyla talked with Scholem in snatches during the night. He seemed to be able to go without sleep. She had seen him doze once or twice, but he never let himself fall into a deep slumber, as if frightened to do so.

"Don't you ever sleep, Chaim?" she asked.

273

He was silent for a long time. When he spoke at last, his voice came out of the darkness in a whisper, scarcely audible.

"I haven't slept properly for five years," he said. "I try to, but I always wake again. It began a few days after . . . the time I spent with al-Shami. I didn't tell you everything about that."

"Why don't you tell me now?" Leyla asked.

"When I was in the hospital, my wife and daughter didn't come to visit me. I was told at first it was for security reasons, but in the end it became obvious they were keeping something back from me. They told me at last, on the second day. While I was with al-Shami his people had kidnapped them; they'd planned to use them to put pressure on me. Then there had been the raid. Al-Shami had escaped, of course. Once I was gone, Hannah and Ruth were no longer of any use to them: he had them killed. They were . . . they were shot and their bodies were left on a rubbish heap just outside the city. I vowed then I would find al-Shami and kill him. Even if I die myself."

At midnight Scholem replaced 'Ali outside the tent. He discovered that there was still plenty of firewood: 'Ali had used scarcely any for himself. A sense of shame came over Scholem. He spent his life hunting Arabs as if they were all criminals, all killers with guns and bombs, and yet the Arabs he had known had shown him nothing but warmth and kindness. It was unimportant that 'Ali thought he was an Arab and not a Jew: he had still left firewood for him.

Shortly before dawn he came into the tent to awaken the others. There had been no trouble, the camels had not stirred all night.

He sensed that something was wrong the moment he set foot in the tent; there was a stillness about the place he did not like. In the dark, he could see nothing but the faint shapes of the sleepers on the ground. Quietly, he crossed to where 'Ali lay, his thin blanket clutched beneath his chin. He took him by the shoulder and shook him, but he lay on, as if in a deep sleep. A stab of fear pricked Scholem's heart. He reached for 'Ali's blanket, to draw it back. As he touched it, his hand felt something wet and sticky. 'Ali did not move.

Scholem moved quickly across to where Leyla lay. He grabbed her by the arm and whispered, "Wake up," in her ear. To his relief, she murmured and sat up.

"What's wrong?" she muttered sleepily.

"I don't know yet," he answered. "Just get up. I tried to wake 'Ali, but he won't move. I think I felt blood, but I can't see anything in this dark. Have you got matches?"

She scrabbled in the pocket of her *farwa* and brought out a battered box that she kept there with her cigarettes. Scholem grabbed the box, opened it, and went across to 'Ali. He struck the first match.

'Ali lay on his back, staring at the ceiling with wide eyes. His throat had been cut from ear to ear, a horrendous gash out of which pints of blood had gushed. The ground all about him was soaked with the stuff. Scholem heard a gasp behind him as Leyla came up. Then, across to his left, he heard Zubayr stir. He went to him.

"Are you all right?" he asked.

"Yes, what's wrong?" Zubayr asked. He had already been badly frightened by Suwailim's death the previous day.

"'Ali's dead. I've just found him. Someone cut his throat. Someone cut his fucking throat and I didn't hear a thing."

Scholem could feel the anger rising in him, the self-hatred that he knew too well from the past. "Why didn't I do something to prevent it? Why didn't I do what I was supposed to do?"

He lit another match and showed Zubayr what he had found. Leyla had gone outside, away from it. In the flickering light, Zubayr made out the mark of a gash in the tent's side, a long, straight cut through which 'Ali's killer had slipped under the cover of darkness, while they slept. Scholem cursed loudly and went outside to find Leyla.

A bilious light had begun to show over the eastern horizon, creeping toward them across the sands of the Nafud. Leyla stood stiffly near the tent, her hands clenched tightly by her side. Scholem came up to her and put his hands on her shoulders. She did not move.

"I must have frightened him," she said. "I remember being wakened, sometime in the morning, I don't know when. It was very dark. I asked if anyone had spoken, but there was no reply, so I turned over and went back to sleep. That must have been when it happened. I must have scared him off."

Scholem nodded. He took his hand away: it was still wet with blood.

Zubayr came out of the tent and up to Scholem and Leyla. In the dim light, it was clear that the man was terrified. In his right hand he held a handful of coins, the fee he had earned as a guide.

"This is your money," he said. "I don't want it. I'm not coming any farther. You can come back with me if you like, but this is as far as I go."

"Keep your money," Scholem said. "You've come this far. We won't force you to go on. Give us directions, that's all we need. The most direct route to the Nafud."

There was no point in arguing with Zubayr. He would be of no further use to them. It would be better to continue without him.

They shared out the provisions, giving Zubayr enough to get back to Ma'an with, taking the longer route around the side of the Tubayq range: he would find camps and hospitality on the way. He rode off, taking the two camels that had belonged to Suwailim and 'Ali, which he had promised to return to their families.

When he had gone Scholem and Leyla set about burying 'Ali. There was a spade in one of the packs, used for digging out wells that had caved in. They dug a shallow grave about four feet deep and made a niche at the bottom, in one side, where they would place the corpse according to Islamic custom. Scholem brought 'Ali from the tent, wrapped in the blanket beneath which he had been sleeping. As he came to the lip of the grave, Scholem raised a hand to close 'Ali's startled eyes, but Leyla held his wrist and shook her head.

"Leave them open, Chaim. It's not the custom."

He left them like that, open and staring, full of incomprehension and the single agony of the knife. Together, they lowered 'Ali into the grave. Scholem stepped down and rolled him into the niche.

Leyla brought brushwood and they covered the body in the grave. She recited some verses of the Qur'an—the *"Surat al-Fatiha"* and the *"Ayat al-nur."* Then they cast earth into the grave and filled it to about eight inches above the ground, in accordance with custom. It was enough. There are no lasting memorials in the desert.

They found tracks all around the small camp, but neither possessed the skill to interpret them with any certainty. There was no time to waste in pursuit of the killer. They had to make it to the Nafud and find a Shammar guide to take them across. Neither knew what "across" referred to. Where, in all that vast emptiness, was Iram? Without al-Shami's tracks to follow, they were like mariners in an open boat, drifting without oars or sail or compass to God knew what shore. If there was a shore at all.

276

THIRTY-TWO

Al-Shami, Marzuq, and David were met at the borders of the Nafud by a group of six silent, black-robed men who greeted the fat man with respect and treated the shark with indifference. David they ignored almost completely, as if he were not there at all. They spoke fluent Arabic and rode their camels with the natural ease of Bedouin, incomparably better than either the city-bred al-Shami or his shambling companion. But once David was able to observe them from close quarters he realized that they were not Arabs at all. He was reminded once again of the men in Tell Mardikh. Once he overheard some of them speaking together in what sounded like German, but when they realized he was listening they stopped and switched to Arabic.

In the sands, the going was hard for all of them, not least for al-Shami, whose great bulk slowed them down badly. They took a circuitous route in order to avoid the highest dunes. There was ample water for both men and beasts, though David was spared little of it. He became feverish and delirious at times, his mind and body driven beyond exhaustion and close to death. Death would have been as welcome to him as a draught of wine, heady, sweet, and warming. His hunger was intolerable, for it was daily exacerbated by the smell of cooking that wafted from al-Shami's fire. No one was deliberately cruel to him, but neglect in those conditions meant fearful suffering. His skin was raw and blistered, not just on his thighs, where his sores were healing a little, but all over, cracked and rubbed by the cold and the gritty sand. His lips felt swollen from lack of moisture, and his nose streamed constantly.

277

Al-Shami was by turns cold and kind. His basic instability became more and more apparent as the strain of the journey made its mark on him. Once, when David vexed him with an inopportune question, he lashed him with his *misha'ab,* the thin camel stick he carried in his right hand. The blow opened David's cheek, leaving him in agony that lasted for days until it subsided to a throbbing ache.

Now that the other men were with him, al-Shami was more guarded in what he said to David. Once David tricked him with a question about Ulrich von Meier.

"Was von Meier as brilliant as they say?" he asked.

"A genius," al-Shami protested, "a man of vision. Without him we . . ." He stopped and looked at David as if he would strike him again, then lowered his stick and giggled. Then he fell silent and an imprecise look came into his eyes—whether of cunning or glee or suspicion, David could not tell.

"You found a diary," al-Shami said, a statement rather than a question.

"Yes," David replied. What point was there in keeping it quiet?

"Who wrote it? What did it say?"

David nodded.

"A German," he said. "An SS major, Stürmbannführer Schacht."

A flicker passed through al-Shami's eyes.

"Ah, yes," he muttered. "The SS man. Schacht, you say?"

"Yes."

"What happened to him?"

"He died," David said. "He was murdered. By your friend von Meier."

"No doubt," al-Shami replied, smiling. He did not seem to object to this further reference to von Meier.

So there was a link between von Meier and al-Shami, between the Sinai expedition and this journey to Iram. And what about these Bedouin who looked like Germans and spoke German in private—where did they fit in? They were young, far too young to have known von Meier in the old days or even to have been involved in the war. How had they come to the Nafud, and what were they doing here?

They avoided other Bedouin with care. Once or twice a small

clutch of riders approached them, but when they drew close they invariably hesitated and then turned away at high speed. There could be no doubt of it: David's fellow riders were known in the desert, known and feared. Or loathed, perhaps.

The days spent crossing the sands seemed without number. And yet beneath everything David felt a curious excitement that at times became almost uncontainable. In spite of all that had happened, he was going to see Iram. He remembered the sensations he had experienced discovering fresh tablets at Ebla or uncovering the five or six really important finds he had made in his career. Important to him, that was, though they seemed scarcely valuable in any material sense. Now he was headed toward a place that the sands of the Nafud had covered for centuries, and which no archaeologist before him had ever seen.

No archaeologist, that was, except Ulrich von Meier. David could not doubt that the German had found Iram as he had set out to do. That in itself was an extraordinary accomplishment. But why had he kept its existence secret? What had he found there that had necessitated all these years of silence and so many deaths? Even as he asked the question, David found another on the edge of his thoughts: what had he found there . . . or what had he brought there?

THIRTY-THREE

It took Leyla and Scholem five days to reach the Nafud, trudging through wind and rain during the daytime, watching by turns at night by an open fire. Twice they saw Bedouin camped in the distance, but they passed by silently. If they were seen, no one came to ask their business or inquire after the news. Cold, windswept days they were, days in which life seemed suspended and time was meaningless. There was pasture for their camels and they found shallow *khabras*—little pools filled with rainwater—but the land felt dead and forsaken.

They never saw their pursuer, but they knew he was with them, waiting for his chance to strike again. He left signs for them, unmistakable tokens of his presence, like offerings laid on the altar of the region's pre-Islamic god. Each morning when they set off they would find his gift awaiting them, about half a mile from where they had camped the night before. He would build a cairn of small, ocher-colored stones shaped like kidneys, on top of which he would place his token: on the first morning, a bullet, polished carefully, set upright on the stones; on the second, a small *huardhi* dagger, its single cutting edge reddened with the blood of an unknown animal; on the third, a dead bustard, its soft throat slit neatly open; on the fourth, an entire gazelle with a tiny hole in the side of its head where a bullet had entered its brain; on the fifth, a camel's skull, whitened and bleached dry by last summer's sun. He was playing with them, as a trained falcon walks round and round its prey, waiting for the hunter to come and dispatch it with his gun or his knife.

It was on the sixth day, as they came within sight of the sands, them with his final and most gruesome trophy. a red, shimmering dawn, expecting to see the t of them before long, like day trippers anxious f the ocean. Then, at last, they topped a high y before them, a carmine band that stretched zon. They came down a long, rocky slope of tall sandstone outcrops, sculpted by aeons of grotesque, evil shapes. Then the sands lay at their feet, border sharply defined, as if a vast red sea had been frozen at a single moment of its flow, its great dunes towering above them like giant waves. And there, set precisely on the margin that cut the rock desert from the sands, stood his last cairn.

They approached it together, dreading it somehow, sensing that on it they would find his final warning to turn back from the Nafud. A sharp wind blew their robes about them, setting them flapping with a dull, hollow sound. The thing on the cairn became clearer until at last they recognized it. Birds scampered about it, flying off as they approached. Leyla felt her heart race suddenly and fought back an urge to throw up the coffee she had drunk an hour before. Scholem dismounted and approached the pile of stones.

The final offering was a human head. 'Ali's head, still wrapped in his red and white *ghotra,* the eyes bare holes where the birds had pecked at them after sunrise. The head had been sliced off cleanly at the shoulders, leaving a short stump of neck on which it had been set, facing west, away from the sands. It was as if they had come full circle, from the chill canyons of the Tubayq Hills to the edge of the inner desert. Scholem remembered 'Ali's eyes as they had lowered him into the grave. The beginnings of decay were written on the bloodless skin, the lips pulled back from the teeth in a rigid grimace. Unbidden, a line from the Book of Job flashed through Scholem's mind: "Come thus far, I said, and no further."

"He must have gone back to the grave and dug up the body," Scholem said to Leyla. She dismounted and came to where he stood.

"Who would do something like that?" she said, unable to control the trembling in her voice. Dust from the grave still clung to 'Ali's face. "A madman?"

"Not a madman," said Scholem. "This one is sane, his actions are thought out and careful. He does nothing out of madness."

281

"But it is madness, what he does. Surely it isn't sa█
Scholem shook his head.

"Sometimes the actions of a sane mind are crazier than █
lunatic. None of the defendants at Nuremberg was found i█

Leyla said nothing in reply. She could not believe in such sa█

They buried the head again, wrapped in the *ghotra,* deep in █
sand, with the pile of stones on top to keep out scavenging animal█
When they had finished, Leyla turned to Scholem.

"What do we do now?" she asked. "That warning was
unmistakable. Once we're in the desert, he can pick us off without
trouble. The dunes will give him cover, provide him with places for
a dozen ambushes."

"What do you want to do?" he said. "Turn back?"

She shook her head.

"We've no choice. We can go back and leave David with al-
Shami; or we can go on."

Leyla nodded.

"First we have to find a guide."

Scholem looked around, then pointed to the north.

"Do you see those hills? They must be the ones 'Ali told me to
look for on the west of the sands, at the northern end of al-Khunfa.
At a guess they're ten miles away. If I'm right, the Shammar camp
'Ali was headed for must be about five miles from here, to the
south."

Leyla looked at the desert, then at Scholem.

"What is there to lose?" she said.

They remounted and set off southward, skirting the edge of the
sands. Nearly two hours later they saw in the distance a series of low
black humps on the horizon: goatskin tents. They were seen and
welcomed to the encampment by the sons of the clan shaykh, Fahd
ibn Fawwaz.

Coffee was made in their honor, the skaykh's eldest son, Farhan,
ringing the mortar in which the beans were pounded with a loud,
rhythmic beat that drew the men from the surrounding tents to
meet the new arrivals. They gathered in the guest section of the
shaykh's tent, sipping coffee and asking for news of the world
outside. They were the Al Zubayr, a subgroup of one of the main
clans of the Sinjara section of the Shammar. Fahd ibn Fawwaz, the
shaykh, was a lean, hawk-faced man in his fifties, whose body and

mind had been honed since birth by the winds of the Nafud. As he served the coffee, pouring it with his left hand out of a tall brass pot into small ceramic cups, he displayed the ease of a man who rules by right and has the respect of his people, even if they numbered only fifty tents and lived from year to year on the edge of starvation.

'Ali had spoken well of the Al Zubayr and had provided Scholem and Leyla with plenty of information about them. Remembering what he had told them, they were able to inquire after the health of the principal members of the clan. They said little of themselves but told Fahd and his sons what they knew of the Huwaytat, from whose territory they had come. When they had spoken for some time, the shaykh turned to them and asked:

"What of 'Ali ibn Sa'd? Is he well?"

Scholem looked at Fahd without answering. The shaykh read the meaning in his eyes and lowered his own to the fire.

"*Rahimahu 'llah,*" he muttered. "May God have mercy on him. He was an old friend; a good friend."

The words passed through the tent like quicksilver, as one man after another heard and repeated them.

Fahd looked up from the flames.

"How did he die?" he asked.

Scholem answered in a low voice.

"Quickly," he said, "but unlawfully. I wish to speak with you in private concerning it."

Fahd looked hard at him, then at Leyla.

"When the coffee has been drunk," he said, "my sons and I shall hear what you have to say."

As was the custom, no one stayed beyond the third cup. When the guest quarters were empty of all but Fahd, his six sons, Scholem, and Leyla, they spoke of their journey and the circumstances surrounding the deaths of 'Ali and Suwailim. When they came finally to the tale of that morning's discovery on the edge of the sands, Fahd let out a cry and spat on the ground in front of him.

"*Astaghfiru 'llah!*" he bellowed. "I ask forgiveness from God! No human being could do such things. To cut a man in pieces. To dig up a dead man and cut off his head. It is not human. You were followed by a *jinni*, a spirit sent by Satan to lead you astray. God must have guided you."

One of Fahd's sons, a man in his late twenties with a long black mustache, turned to his father.

"Father," he said, "I would like permission to speak."

Fahd, still growling his disapproval of the outrage to his friend 'Ali, glanced up.

"Yes, Nazzal, you have my permission."

Nazzal turned to Scholem.

"Forgive me, but did either you or your son keep the *huardhi* that you found four days ago?"

Scholem nodded.

"Yes," he said. "I have it here." He reached inside his robe and drew out a tiny, curved knife of the sort used by a hunter to kill game birds, a miniature version of the larger *khusa*. He handed it to Nazzal, who turned it over, examining it closely before passing it to his father.

"It was no *jinni*, Father. 'Ali was killed by al-Gharib."

Leyla wondered at the name, if name it was. "Al-Gharib" meant "the stranger." Did Nazzal really mean "a stranger," someone from beyond their territory? Then she looked at the faces of Nazzal's brothers and realized they knew whom he meant.

Fahd handed the little dagger back to Scholem.

"Do you see the markings on the blade?" he asked.

Scholem looked and saw, beneath the dried blood, thin markings, like letters, but unreadable, like no alphabet he had ever seen.

"What are they?" he asked.

"His marks," Fahd said. "If you had looked closely at the stones you would have found others. He leaves them wherever he goes." The shaykh fell silent, staring into the fire. Nazzal spoke again.

"We call him al-Gharib," he said. "His real name is Talal ibn Qasim; but he is not a Bedouin, not an Arab. Since he was a child he has been known as al-Gharib. He lives in the sands; some say he is a companion of the wolves."

"If he is not Arab," Scholem said, "where does he come from? Is he Iranian? African? Solubba?"

Nazzal shook his head.

"None of those. We do not know where he is from. No one has ever seen one like him before."

"What does he look like?"

"He is quite small, with skin the color of an almond and little hair on his face. But strangest of all are his eyes. He does not have human eyes."

Nazzal lifted his fingers and pulled the sides of his eyes outward, slanting them. Leyla exchanged glances with Scholem.

"There are races of men like this," said Scholem. "Far to the east. Chinese, Koreans, Japanese."

A murmur went around the tent.

"Are they Muslims?" asked Fahd.

Scholem nodded.

"Some, yes. There are many Chinese Muslims. Indonesia is the world's largest Muslim country. Perhaps your stranger is Indonesian."

Nazzal spoke again.

"Do Indonesians carry swords?"

Scholem shook his head.

"Perhaps. But I have never heard of it. Why?"

"Al-Gharib has a sword. No such sword has ever been seen before in Arabia."

He bent down and, using the stick kept for stirring the coffee in the pot, drew a rapid sketch in the sand beside the hearth. The shape of the long-handled sword was unmistakable. Scholem leaned back and looked at Nazzal.

"He is Japanese," he said.

"Are they Muslims?" Fahd asked.

"No," said Scholem. "No, they are not Muslims."

Leyla broke in.

"How did he come here? And when? He knows the desert like a *badu*. He can ride a camel and track and hunt. You say 'since he was a child.' Was he brought up here?"

Fahd answered her, his voice low to prevent the women on the other side of the curtain from hearing. Such matters were not for their ears—though, had he known it, they were as well informed about al-Gharib as the men.

"Many years ago," he said, "a man from Palestine came among the Shammar. He traveled through the camps, bringing with him letters from Hajj Amin al-Husayni, the Mufti of Jerusalem. Of course, Hajj Amin was not in Jerusalem then. The English unbelievers had sent him into exile, may God curse them."

285

"When was this?" Leyla asked.

Fahd thought carefully before answering.

"Before Farhan was born. I was a young man, not yet married. I remember that my younger brother had just been circumcised. He is now forty-seven years old. It was at the time when the English had a great war in their country and their ships came to Aden."

"I understand," Scholem said. "That would make it around 1944 or 1945, if Fahd's brother had been circumcised at the age of seven or so.

"Please go on," he said.

"The letters from the Mufti asked me, in the name of Islam, to take children into our tents, male children. We were asked to take two or three in each camp. The shaykhs agreed, and some time later the boys were brought to us. It was not permitted to ask where they came from or who their true parents were. We were to bring them up like our own children, as Bedouin. They were to be instructed in the ways of the desert, every hardship, every suffering. Some died. The rest survived and grew into strong young men. When they were aged about fourteen, men came and took them away, without explanation. They also had letters from Hajj Amin. Then, soon afterward, more children were brought. Since then there have been many, but always they have been taken away from us at an early age."

"And al-Gharib was one of these children?" asked Scholem.

"Yes. He was one of the first, little more than a baby. He was brought up by the Al Shiha'."

"They were like him, then, these children?"

Fahd shook his head.

"No," he said. "He was the only one. That was why they called him al-Gharib. The others were less strange. They were like Europeans. Many had blond hair, others were dark. But none were Arabs. I think they came from Europe."

"All of them?" Scholem asked, excited and puzzled by this curious information. "Even the later ones?"

"I don't know," Fahd said. "They were brought to us from outside and taken away again, we don't know where."

"But al-Gharib is still here."

"Yes." It was Nazzal again. "He lives somewhere in the desert, but he appears from time to time to visit the Al Shiha'. Sometimes

286

others reappear like that, to visit their old clans for a day or two before vanishing again. But al-Gharib is different. People are afraid of him. They say he is a child of the Devil. Some call him that: Ibn Iblis—'Satan's Son.' He has killed several times, always with great cruelty, but no one dares to take revenge. They believe it would bring down a curse to lay a finger on him. He comes and goes as he pleases. He knows the sands better than any living man."

"Why does he want to stop us entering the sands? What is in there? Why did he leave 'Ali's head on the border as a warning?"

Looks were exchanged among the six brothers. No one spoke. Shaykh Fahd stared into the hearth of the fire again, as if he could read hidden messages in its flames.

Scholem ignored the silence and went on.

"My son and I have come from Jordan seeking three other men. We believe they have gone into the Nafud. To the center, to the very heart of the sands. What is in the center of the sands? Has any of you been there?"

Still no one spoke. Scholem could feel the tension rise within the tent. He sensed fear, palpable and fresh. He went on.

"My son and I found an old book in al-Quds, in Jerusalem. In it there was mention of a city in the Nafud, an ancient city. The author of the book wrote that the city was Iram, Iram of the Pillars that is spoken of in God's book."

It was Farhan who spoke at last.

"You are mistaken," he said. "There is nothing in the Nafud but sand. It is endless sand, enough to swallow cities and all the books in the world. What you have read about Iram is nothing but tales of the ancients. Perhaps the city you seek is elsewhere."

"Have you been there?" Scholem asked. "Have you been in the very heart of the desert, have you seen that there truly is nothing but sand?"

"In the Nafud," Farhan said, "the sun rises upon sand and sets upon sand. Perhaps the writer of your book saw a mirage."

The fire flickered on the hearth, burning low. No one moved to tend it or add more fuel. Fahd raised his eyes from the flames; the pupils seemed drained, lifeless, as if the will had been sucked out of him by the fire. He gazed at Scholem uneasily.

"You may stay tonight," he said. "You are our guests and may rest beneath our roof. But tomorrow you must leave. Return to

287

Jordan. Do not enter the desert, not even for revenge. You will find only unhappiness there, great unhappiness. Men go astray in the sands, they become lost and are never seen again. Forget al-Gharib. He has killed and he will kill again. We all come from God, and to God we return. Leave his accounting to God. Forget the men you seek. If they do not know the desert, they are as good as dead by now; you will never find them. If they have indeed reached its heart, they are in a place where you can never come to them. Let us not speak of this again. I shall order a sheep to be killed. We shall eat well tonight, in memory of 'Ali."

The shaykh rose, seeming older than when he had sat down. Some terrible burden seemed to weigh on him as he pulled himself wearily to his feet. The warmth, the conviviality had dissipated, the fire of welcome had burned low and was burning to ashes. The meal that night would be a gloomy one.

THIRTY-FOUR

The next morning Scholem and Leyla left the tents of the Al Zubayr and retraced their steps northward, along the crimson flank of the Nafud. The sands seemed to beckon to them, vast, silent, and, without a guide, impenetrable. No more had been said at the camp concerning their quest, and they both knew Bedouin etiquette well enough to be aware that the subject was closed for good. Their only hope now was to find another camp farther north, where they might be able to hire a guide to take them into the desert on a different pretext, hoping to persuade him, once alone, to take them where they wanted to go. The Shammar knew of Iram or, at the very least, of something in the desert, something that worried and frightened them and about which they would not speak.

"Who do you think these children are, Chaim?" Leyla asked as they rode side by side, huddled against the wind. "If Hajj Amin was involved . . ."

"Yes," he said, his voice hard, almost defensive. "I know. I know what you want to say, but I don't want to believe you."

"How did they get here? Where have they been taken? And why?"

He looked at her, a pained expression in his eyes.

"You're not a Jew," he said. "What difference does it make to you?"

She looked at him in turn, hurt by his rebuke.

"Would being a Jew make me any more human? They worry me, just as they worry you, and for much the same reasons."

The desert was beginning to eat at them, gnawing away at their fragile truce, turning them in on one another.

About three miles from the Shammar camp they heard behind them the sound of a camel being ridden at high speed across the rocks. Looking back, they saw a rider coming in their direction. He was dressed in black and rode a dun-colored mount with red trappings. Scholem reached for the rifle he carried on his saddle and held it in readiness. The rider approached, moving more slowly now as he drew near to them. He reined in his camel while still several yards from them and pulled the *ghotra* away from his mouth. It was Nazzal, Fahd's youngest son, who had spoken with them the day before. He was sweating and his breath came in rapid jerks. When he spoke, it was without the usual formalities.

"There is something out there in the sands," he said. "My brothers would not admit that it exists, because they are frightened. My father is growing old, and he is frightened too. It's the same everywhere, in all the tents of the Shammar."

"What is it they're frightened of?" Scholem asked. "Is it a place? A city?"

"I don't know," Nazzal replied. "No one knows. No one goes there or ever speaks of it. There is a region in the middle of the sands where no *badu* ever ventures. Among the Shammar, they say the place is haunted, that spirits of the dead and evil *jinn* walk the sands and lure unsuspecting travelers to their destruction. Some say there is a city where the *jinn* dwell."

"Is the city Iram?" Leyla asked.

Nazzal nodded.

"Yes, I have heard it called Iram. They say it was buried in the sand by God as a punishment."

"How wide is this region?" Scholem asked.

"Very wide. It would take a man riding in the sands for twelve hours a day about ten days to ride around it."

Scholem did a quick calculation, then looked at Leyla.

"That's about a thirty-mile radius, say around a thousand square miles. It's a large area to cover."

Leyla shook her head.

"We don't have to cover it. It sounds like a sort of exclusion zone, all the way around Iram. We just have to ride straight toward the center and Iram will be there, waiting for us."

Scholem nodded in agreement.

"But we still can't make it without a guide, Leyla."

Turning to Nazzal, he asked:

"Do you know of anyone who could take us there, at least as far as the beginning of that region?"

Nazzal smiled.

"Yes," he said. "I will take you. I don't believe in *jinn* or ghosts. I'm not afraid to go there."

"It may be dangerous," Scholem said. "There are greater dangers than *jinn*. I don't know what we will find there, but it won't be a warm welcome with coffee on the hearth. Al-Gharib will try to stop us, I'm sure of that. Think carefully before you decide to come with us."

Nazzal did not hesitate. His eyes shone as he answered.

"I made up my mind last night. When you left, I spoke with my father and told him my plan. He was angry, but he did not forbid me to go with you. I think he understands. He can remember the days when the tribes still raided each other, when we would fall on the camps of the 'Aniza or the Mutayr and take their sheep and camels. Now the government controls us with jeeps and planes and guns, and there is no adventure any longer. When I am my father's age, the government will have taken us from here and put us in towns, to live in misery in one place from season to season, never moving. I swear to you, I am more frightened of their oil wells than I am of Iram or al-Gharib. Take me with you. I will take the sands and empty them into your hands. Believe me: I will take you there."

A cold wind blew out of the desert. Above it, black clouds had formed, descending like vast, bloated beasts of pray come to gorge themselves yet further on its tracts of endless sand. They looked up at the tall, silent dunes that rose and fell into the distance until they vanished on the black horizon. Leyla's hands felt rough and cold, her eyes red and sore as she turned to face the wind. She looked at Scholem, at his anxious, troubled face. He nodded and they urged their camels on, over the threshold of the waiting sands.

THIRTY-FIVE

The sands swallowed them, silently, effortlessly, completely. The Nafud was an ocean whose red waters surged all around them in great crescent-shaped dunes, the lowest of which was almost two hundred feet in height, the tallest rising to six hundred and more. Progress was slow and difficult. There could be no simple forward motion through the sands. At a pace of about one mile an hour they rode or walked round and round the deep pits of crumbling sand that constantly barred their way. The knife-edged crests of the ridges gave beneath their feet, sending showers of loose golden sand tumbling away from them. The camels struggled on the yielding surface, making their way with great effort, dune after dune, until every step became hateful and they shook and trembled with the strain.

The clouds opened suddenly just before noon. Nazzal told them to dismount: they could not hope to move in the downpour. They sheltered in a half-erected tent at the foot of a dune while the camels stood shivering in the thick, icy sleet that gushed in heavy billows across the sand. Leyla wondered when she had last been warm and dry. "Last night," she thought, and it seemed like a dream. She had been wandering forever in this freezing cold and rain and mist, over flint and sandstone and sand the color of old blood.

Nazzal told them all he knew about Iram, the things he had heard from the old men of his clan or from his father. The city had been built, men said, in the days of Solomon by an *ifrit* called Sultan Mansur. Its walls were built of the skulls of unbelievers, and it was dotted with pits where their souls were kept for three days and three

292

nights before being taken to hell. Some said it was really an outpost of hell and that flames rose up into it out of the depths beneath. There was a constant sound of weeping and moaning.

"How long has this region been closed to your people?" Leyla asked. "Has it always been like this?" She remembered the comment by al-Halabi that the Bedouin of his day were afraid to enter the inner desert.

He nodded.

"Yes. The old men say their fathers knew of it and feared it, and their fathers in turn before them. It is an ancient place. But my father told me once that many years ago the desert around Iram changed, became full of *jinn* and evil things that had not been there before."

"What sort of things?"

"Tall *jinn,* in black robes, smelling of death. Lights that shine at night, red and green. Noises from beneath the ground. And other things of which no one will speak."

"How many years ago did these things begin?"

Nazzal frowned.

"I'm not sure. I think my father said it was about the time al-Gharib was brought here as a child. Later, many people associated his arrival with the things that happened in the desert."

Leyla turned to Scholem.

"About forty years ago," she said.

The sleet turned to rain and the rain to drizzle. During the downpour the sand had turned almost crimson. The clouds moved on westward, drifting toward the Shifa' mountains and the coast. They folded the tent and set off again, the wet sand hard beneath their feet as they climbed to the ridge of another dune. They seemed to be moving endlessly in circles as they circumnavigated the deep sand pits, but always their direction was eastward, and every dune they crossed brought them a little nearer their goal.

Here, at the edge of the sands, they could still find water in a number of wells known to Nazzal. But as they moved farther into the interior their supply of water would begin to run low, and unless they found a well in the vicinity of Iram they could be in trouble. Even in winter, when rain falls and pasture springs up, the sands can be treacherous, and fatal to the inexperienced. Scholem and Leyla were under no illusions: without Nazzal, they would die in

293

the sands.

They camped that night in the lee of a tall, high-crested dune, lighting their fire on the rocky floor that lay between it and the next. There was no shortage of firewood in the sands: the debris of bushes that had sprouted and died in former springs lay everywhere about them. There was a moon that night, the first they had seen in a while. It cast a flat white light over everything. The dunes seemed smooth and colorless, with stark black shadows where the wind had folded them. The wind whistled through the ridges of sand, its long, piping notes filling the night with images of sunless desolation.

They watched in turns during the night, but no one slept more than fitfully, in spite of the fire. They knew that al-Gharib was somewhere among the dunes, watching the flames burn, observing them, waiting for them to come more deeply into his lair.

At one point Nazzal spoke to them about the desert, about the things he had seen there, of what lay before them.

"We must cross several ranges of high dunes," he said. "The worst are the Kuthub Iblis, the Devil's Sandhills. They are very tall, like small mountains, and the sand is soft and treacherous. Your camels are already tired: they may not be able to cross them."

"Can't we go around them?" Leyla asked.

"It would take too long and take us far out of your way. I would prefer to cross them if possible."

"How long do you think it will take?"

He shrugged.

"It depends. The weather has been very bad. I am worried about it. With luck, about six days, maybe less."

"To the borders of the Iram region?"

"Yes. Perhaps three more days to Iram itself. I don't know. It depends on the surface. And the weather."

"What about food and water?" Leyla asked.

He thought carefully before answering.

"There's enough food, so long as we eat frugally. Provided conditions don't change deeper into the desert, there'll be enough pasture for the camels. Water's a greater problem. There are no more wells. We may be lucky enough to find a rain pool or two on a rock outcrop, but there won't be many outcrops on our route. The camels can go for about twenty days without water, possibly longer in this weather, but the Kuthub Iblis may weaken them. Our own supply will be enough to take us to Iram, but if we cannot find water there we will die. Once we have crossed the Kuthub Iblis, there will be no turning back."

"And if we cannot cross them?"

"Then we must turn back at once. Otherwise we will all die."

They came two days later to hills that seemed like small mountains, beginning as clumps of loose and heavy sand and rising by degrees throughout the day until they reached formidable heights, dark red and forbidding. Their camels had to be forced to climb, driven upward by pushing, pulling, and harsh words. They could not ride: the camels could barely carry the baggage, let alone riders as well. For hour after hour they clambered through the sand but seemed to make no progress. However far they went, there was always another dune to scale, and when they scanned the horizon from the top of one there seemed no end to them. They climbed until their legs ached and grew weak, as if they would no longer support them. Each time they reached the summit of a dune it was only to face the long, perilous descent, with the sand shifting under them in sliding streams, threatening at every moment to send them crashing down the slope. A broken leg here could mean death for all of them. Pain wracked and tore their muscles, a searing, abnormal pain that knew no cessation, that had neither beginning nor end.

They rested at noon, exhausted beyond all measure, aching in every limb, yet aware that they had to press on. Nazzal would not allow them more than an hour to eat and rest in. He had his reasons, he said, and made them get up when the hour was past. The camels would not move at first and tried to bite them when they came close. By midafternoon a heavy fog filled the lowlands, spreading out below them as they climbed, like a swirling gray lake out of whose waters they ascended into the dim light of an overcast day. When they came down, it blotted all but the nearest objects from sight, confusing and disorienting them until they had climbed again and found their bearings from the heights.

Leyla walked as if in a dream, her body and soul separate, her legs kept moving by an automatic reflex, past caring, past feeling pain. She wanted to lie down and sleep a long, dreamless sleep, to forget the sands, forget David, forget Iram. She imagined she was

295

home in Sinai, helping her mother in the kitchen, listening to her father recite his poetry, praying in the mosque with her sisters. She fell and was picked up several times, but she could not remember how she continued walking; the long march was blurred together in her head like a hopelessly tangled skein of wool. She tugged and pulled, but the threads remained knotted and would not come loose.

The grueling miles took their toll of Scholem's strength, stretching his lungs to their limit, making his heart pump blood at an alarming rate. He felt dizzy on the high summits, suffocated by the fog below. Only will power kept him going, will power and the lust for revenge that had burned inside him for so long.

At last the nightmare seemed to end. They descended a tall dune into a vast, curving depression, and Nazzal announced that it was over. They could camp and rest for the night. Leyla sank to the hard ground as if it were a feather bed. She watched Nazzal set light to the wood he had collected during the day's march and smiled feebly at him.

"Who will watch tonight, Nazzal?" she asked. "We all need sleep. What if al-Gharib is here?"

Nazzal shook his head.

"If he is here, he will be as tired as we are. He will do nothing before morning. We can sleep in safety."

Leyla sighed and turned over, then lifted her head again and spoke to Nazzal once more.

"You were right, Nazzal. The Devil's Sandhills are like hell. But we beat them. Nothing can stop us now. Nothing."

Nazzal looked at her, a curious expression on his face. He frowned and did not look at her as he spoke.

"The Devil's Sandhills? Did you think those were the Devil's Sandhills? Those were nothing, just ordinary dunes. We reach the Kuthub Iblis tomorrow. You will need all your strength for them. Sleep now. We have to rise before dawn."

THIRTY-SIX

The Devil's Sandhills lived up to their name. It took them seven hours to cross them, but it felt like seven days, seven monstrous days of unremitting nightmare. Midway they lost one of their pack camels. It collapsed on the summit of a steep dune and refused to move again. However hard they tried to bring it to its feet again, it would not budge, and in the end Nazzal pronounced it hopeless and put an end to its miseries with the sharp edge of his *khusa*. They redistributed its load, taking some themselves to spare the other camels, on whom they in their turn ultimately depended. Weighed down, exhausted, thirsty in spite of the cold, yet unable to spare water to drink, they went on and on, like Sisyphus toiling on the slopes of Tartarus with his ever rolling rock. Scholem and Leyla pleaded with Nazzal to let them rest, but he was adamant and paid no heed.

"We have to get across," he said. "If the camels rest, they will grow weak. There is no pasture here on the heights. We could lose them all, and if that happens now we are as good as dead ourselves."

And so they pressed on. The sand was dry again after the rain and their legs sank in it almost to the knee. Every time Leyla took a step she thought her leg would never come free again, that she would remain fixed there forever, trapped by the sands until her bones crumbled and became sand themselves. Nazzal was frightened. He knew he could cross the Kuthub, but these strangers were inexperienced and might not make it. If that happened, he would feel bound by his word to remain with them and if need be die in their company. To make matters worse, he was worried about the weather. Something was going to happen, something serious—he could feel it in the air. He wanted to have the Kuthub Iblis well behind him before it began.

In spite of everything, they made it to the other side and set up camp in the lee of a narrow, gently sloping dune. They drank greedily but had no stomach for food. Within minutes of their arrival they had wrapped themselves in their blankets. Heedless of the biting cold, they fell asleep at once, like children who have spent the day at a party and used up all their energy in wild, frenetic games.

With the morning came a strange, preternatural stillness. There was no wind, and the temperature seemed to have risen slightly. The sky was almost clear of clouds, but it seemed an unhealthy color: ashen, almost yellow in places. The light was sickly. The camels were unusually silent and appeared tense, as if they feared something. One of them was missing.

Nazzal woke Scholem and Leyla urgently. His face showed signs of stress and worry. He spoke in a low, anxious voice.

"Something's wrong," he said. "One of the camels has gone, the second *fahl*. Its baggage has gone too, along with most of the other packs. Only a few water skins are left and a little food."

"How did it happen?" Scholem asked. "Surely we would have heard something."

"Not last night, we were all too deeply asleep. No *badu* would have done this; no one would raid men crossing the sands, no one would take food and water. It can only have been al-Gharib. Only he could treat the old ways with such contempt. And only he would leave a little water and a little food for us to fight over when the time comes."

"How serious is it?" Leyla asked.

Nazzal looked troubled. His forehead creased, and in his eyes Leyla could see that he was not merely worried: he was badly frightened.

"It could scarcely be more serious," he replied. "We have enough food and water to last us a few more days. The camels will be all right from here: there is ample pasture everywhere. But if there is no water at Iram we cannot hope to leave the sands alive."

"Could we return if we started now?"

Nazzal shook his head.

"You've seen the Kuthub Iblis. You know what lies beyond them. It would be suicide to try. In any case, I haven't told you everything."

They looked at him, afraid of what he had yet to tell them.

"Have you noticed the weather?" he asked.

Scholem nodded.

"What is it?" he asked. "What's wrong?"

"A sandstorm is building up somewhere: a big one. It may pass us by, but I don't think it will. There's no knowing how long it may last: an hour, a day, three days. If it's more than a day, we're finished. We can't afford to lose so much time."

He paused. Leyla noticed that his face was grayish and that his eyes shifted when he spoke, like a man with something to hide or one frantically looking for a way out from where he was.

"Have you ever been in a sandstorm?" he asked.

Leyla nodded.

"Once, in Sinai, a small one."

"Then you've seen nothing. In the Nafud, the Bedouin fear them more than anything. Our worst nightmare is to be traveling in the sands when one comes. Everything will vanish: the sky, the earth, the light. All sounds will be blotted out by the wind howling. You can't feel anything, you can't see, you can scarcely breathe. When it comes, you'll know what true fear is."

A shiver crawled through Leyla's spine as if something living inside it had come awake. Al-Gharib had chosen his moment well. Even the elements assisted him, as if he were in league with them, as if he really were a child of Satan. And she was concerned about Nazzal. Something told her he could no longer be depended on, that he had stepped out of his depth and was on the verge of panic.

Their spirits were too low to eat, so they saddled and packed their camels and set off. It seemed easy going at first, by comparison with the last two days. Nazzal wanted to try to reach some sandstone outcrops, about five miles away, that would provide a little shelter from the storm when it finally broke. They pushed on, ever conscious of the tense, brooding atmosphere that heralded the madness that was to come.

They were within sight of the outcrops when Leyla called out. She sat with an arm outstretched in front of her, a finger pointing stiffly ahead. The eastern horizon was turning red, as if great flames

299

were licking it from below. It was as though the *'arfaj* and *ghada* bushes had caught fire and a gigantic blaze were roaring toward them out of the east. Suddenly a cold breeze hit them, utterly unlike anything they had experienced in the desert before. As they watched, dense black clouds formed above the reddened horizon, like smoke being thrown up by the distant flames. The camels shied in terror as the wind grew rapidly in strength and the blackness closed in on them.

Nazzal shouted to them to dismount and hobble the camels with their backs to the wind. The storm was bearing down on them with the speed of an express train, and now they could see it clearly: gargantuan clouds of black dust swirled high up, thousands of feet in the air, supported by great pillars of red sand, twisting and pulsating as they gathered strength and sucked into themselves more and more of the desert. Bright flashes of lightning jiggered and jaggered all across the clouds and through the pillars of red dust, like tongues of white flame licking their red and swollen skin.

There was a roaring sound as the wind became a gale, then in a matter of seconds the storm was on them, screaming, clawing, wrestling them to the ground, forcing them to hunker down low beside their camels, faces wrapped tightly about with their *ghotras*. The whole world was blotted out in an instant. Where before there had been earth and sky, now there was only a blinding darkness of crimson sand. It lashed everything in its path, tearing through the dunes like a living thing, monstrous and wholly without pity. The sound was terrifying: sharp cracks of discharged electricity followed by rolls of heavy thunder that boomed and echoed among the sandhills, and over all the incessant roaring, like demons howling for unnatural food.

It went on and on as if it would never stop. They lost all sense of time, each huddled separately in his own private nightmare, unable to talk or even think. They grew hungry and thirsty, and so knew that time was passing: otherwise, the storm seemed to have neither beginning nor end. It gave no signs of abating. The violence of the wind continued unchecked, the roaring and the crackling and the thunder went undiminished by the hours that passed. There was neither day nor night, just a constant, unrelenting murkiness in which men and animals were reduced to blurs on the edge of vision. If darkness fell, it fell within darkness and went unobserved. If the sun rose, it rose on darkness that had no palpable effect. They lay and listened to the storm rage or they slept, waking again to the sound of the wind and the thunder.

Nazzal crawled through the nightmare to Scholem and Leyla, bringing them food and water from his saddlebags, speaking with them, reassuring them. But even he was tired now almost beyond endurance, and in his hoarse whispers they could detect a quivering edge of raw anxiety that he was having more and more difficulty in suppressing.

"Is it bad?" Leyla asked him when he came to her.

"Yes," he croaked in answer, "very bad. The worst I've known. It may last for days. Our only hope now is God."

For the first time in many years, Leyla wanted to believe in Nazzal's protecting God. He was a desert God: the sand and the wind and the thunder were all His playthings. They were at His mercy here, in the middle of His oldest and most terrible terrain. Leyla wished she could believe in Him: He felt so real to her, dark and red and angry like the pandemonium that encompassed her.

Leyla had crazy dreams and waking visions that were like hallucinations. Nothing seemed real. She slept and dreamed, then woke into darkness and the beginnings of another nightmare. When she called out, no one answered, no one came. She clung to the camel as if it were the whole world, afraid to let it go for a second. It made no movement, uttered no sound: it sat in the face of the storm and it endured.

Leyla was not sure just what made her look up. She had been dozing again, dreaming about David and al-Shami, a terrible dream in which the fat man had grown four pairs of arms and turned into a bulbous white spider spinning David in an intricate and dirty web. When she opened her eyes, the storm was still raging as before, but she sensed that something was wrong. She strained to see through the red murk and could just make out the form of Nazzal standing a few yards away, near his camel. Even as she watched, he clutched his head as if in agony. She was certain that she could hear a scream, even above the high-pitched whining of the wind. Suddenly Nazzal whipped his head back and forth several times and began to run, heading away from her and Scholem, out into the storm. Within seconds he had vanished, swallowed up by the thick red dust.

Leyla staggered to her feet. Standing, she became a target for the driving sand. She was buffeted and slashed, her robes whipping away from her as if a giant hand were trying to tear them from her body. The sand stung any part of her that was exposed to it, lashing her with all the fury of a tormented creature thrashing about blindly in its hunger for revenge. She found it difficult to breathe and almost impossible to remain upright. Staggering, she fought her way to the spot where Scholem lay crouched against his camel's flank. Roughly, she grabbed him by the shoulder. He started as she touched him, staring wide-eyed at her.

"What is it?" he shouted. "What's wrong?" She could barely hear him above the racket of the storm. She bent down and put her mouth to his ear.

"It's Nazzal," she said, "he's gone."

"Gone? What do you mean?"

"He panicked. I saw him, a minute ago, no more." She paused for breath, panting with the effort of speaking.

"Where is he?" shouted Scholem.

"I don't know! He was screaming, as if he was having a fit. He ran off. We have to follow him!"

"We can't follow him. It would be suicide . . . in that!"

"We can't leave him! He needs help. I'm going after him!" Leyla knew she was being stupid, but she felt so near panic herself that only action, definite action, could prevent her giving in to it. She stood up and began to run in the direction she thought Nazzal had taken.

Scholem snatched at her, but he was too slow. He saw her running into the maelstrom, then she was gone. Where she had been a moment before, there was now nothing but swirling sand. He leaped to his feet and dashed after her. There was a chance, if he could reach her before she had gone too far.

Leyla staggered along like a drunkard, pitching and swaying as the wind rocked her to and fro. On and on she stumbled, oblivious of everything, wanting to run and run and run forever, in the vain hope that she could escape the claustrophobic darkness that was hemming her in. She had lost Nazzal, but she still pressed on in the direction she had first taken, though she knew it was no direction at all. There were no directions in this madness: for all she knew, she was heading directly away from Nazzal by now.

302

Scholem tried as best he could to follow Leyla by the brief tracks she left in the sand, before the wind ripped them to shreds or covered them up with fresh sand. He shouted to her, but the wind blew her name back in his face. His eyes stung badly and he felt sick with fear. Out here, away from their camels, getting more and more lost, they would just wander in circles until, one by one, they died. Suddenly, to his left, he made out a shape, a dark something within the all-pervading darkness. He ran toward it. It was Leyla, crouched on the sand, digging at it frantically and weeping. He shook her shoulders and she turned her red-rimmed, streaming eyes to him.

"It's hopeless," she shouted. "We can't get out! There's nowhere to go. Nowhere!"

He took hold of her hands and held them tightly.

"Keep steady, Leyla! Stay here with me. It'll be over soon."

She shook her head violently.

"No," she shouted. "Look." She held up a *ghotra* in her hand. "This is his *ghotra,*" she said. "I found it here. I thought he might have fallen, but this is all I could find. He passed this spot. He may be nearby. We've got to try to find him."

There was no use in arguing. It made little difference now. With Nazzal gone, with the camels God knew where, they had little hope of ever finding their way again, even if the storm stopped this moment. Scholem picked her up and held her as they staggered on.

They found nothing. The wind defeated them at last, forcing them to their knees, driving them to seek what shelter they could behind a thin *ghada* bush that had been ripped to shreds by the storm.

They fell asleep like that, worn out, half crazed by the ceaseless pounding of the gale. Neither slept well. When they woke at last, several hours later, the storm had passed. All around them, the sands stretched in all directions as before, silent and still and seemingly little changed by the great rage that had passed over them. It was late morning: a day had passed since the storm's arrival.

Neither knew which way they had come in the night. There were no tracks, no landmarks they could recognize, nothing but blank sand whichever way they looked. With the help of the sun, they established the direction in which the east lay, but beyond that they

303

could identify nothing. Their only hope was a clear sky that night and stars they could use to navigate by. Nazzal had been heading directly east. Hopelessly lost as they were, an identical route should take them to the edge of the region they sought. They would move more slowly without their camels, and their need for food and water would soon become desperate. In the meantime, they had no choice. It would be better to die moving than sitting in one spot waiting for death to overtake them. They turned east and began walking.

They found Nazzal shortly afterward, at the foot of a sharp incline down which he must have fallen in the storm. His neck had been snapped, and his face was twisted around at a dreadful angle, a look of terror and anguish on it. Too tired to dig a grave, they covered him with sand, sightless, silent, beaten by the very thing he had come to conquer, his own fear.

They left him and started on the final stage of their long journey.

FIVE

And he dwelleth in desolate cities, and in houses which no man inhabiteth, which are ready to become heaps.

Job 15:28

THIRTY-SEVEN

He was in a tiny room, lit only by an oil lamp high above his head. The walls, floor, and ceiling were constructed entirely of solid rock, uneven and devoid of any ornamentation. It was a cell now, but David suspected from the niches in the walls that it had at one time served as a tomb. It was certainly cold enough for such a purpose, and David feared it might not be long before it was returned to its former use. He had been there for over an hour, alone with his thoughts. They had brought him there directly on his arrival at Iram, blindfolded and totally disoriented. The blindfold had been tied over his eyes well before they came within sight of the city, so he had no way of knowing exactly where he was and how his cell related to its surroundings or to the outside—if there still was an outside, which he had already begun to doubt.

Suddenly there was a grating sound and the door opened. A tall man with faded ginger hair and a pronounced limp came into the room.

"Good morning, Professor Rosen," he said, speaking in clear, almost unaccented English. "My name is Dr. Mandl, Felix Mandl, from Geneva. I have been sent to examine you. They tell me you are in very bad condition."

So it was morning. David had lost track of time. He sat in the corner of his cell, mute, unmoving, not caring who Dr. Mandl was or what he had come to do. It was all the same to him now. If they abused him or looked after him, they did it for their own purpose, not his.

Mandl was a man of about seventy, pale-cheeked, lugubrious,

307

yet stern-looking, with sharp, critical eyes that seemed to bore into David. His hair was cut close to the scalp, and above his upper lip a thin gray moustache divided his face like a scar. He lit a small oil stove in the corner of the room and told David to undress. Slowly, without energy, David did so. His clothes were ragged and caked in dirt; he was conscious that his body was filthy and that it smelled horribly, but it did not matter. Mandl examined him with cold, waxlike fingers, prodding and probing the surface of his skin with delicate, palpating touches that sent small shivers of revulsion up and down David's spine. He looked at everything: the camel sores, the scar on David's cheek, the chilblains on his feet, the bruises he had sustained falling from the camel onto hard ground. After that, he sounded David's chest and examined his eyes and throat, and finally took his blood pressure and temperature.

"First," he said, "you will have to be bathed and given fresh clothing. Then I will send someone to dress your wounds and put some liniment on your bruises. In the meantime, I shall prepare some medicines for you. You have been treated badly, barbarically. I shall speak to my superiors about the matter."

"Who are your superiors?" David asked.

Mandl ignored the question, turning to pack his medical bag.

"Why have I been brought here? What do you want with me?"

The doctor glanced up, fastening the bag with small brass studs.

"You will find out tomorrow. Until then, get some rest. I am only a doctor. I cannot explain such matters to you. Rest assured: it is nothing to be afraid of."

"And when I'm done? When you've finished with me?"

Mandl said nothing. He picked up the bag and went to the door. He gave two small knocks and it was opened from the outside. Without looking around, he went out and the door closed with a bang.

Early the next morning—or so it seemed—David was slammed into wakefulness by the sound of the heavy wooden door being opened. Mandl had made him drink a number of evil-tasting potions and given him an injection that had knocked him out for the night. At first he could not remember where he was. He thought he must be in St. Nilus' again: the rough stone walls and the hard

308

bed on which he lay brought memories of the monastery flooding back. Then his guard entered, a man with a face ground out of cement, whom he had seen only briefly the day before.

"Get up," the guard said. "You're wanted."

David felt weak and groggy. He swayed as he tried to stand, but the man did not even reach out a hand. David fought back the giddiness, struggling to keep his balance and to keep the darkness from closing in again. It seemed an eternity that he stood there until the spinning in his head subsided and he could risk opening his eyes.

"Follow me," the guard said. David realized with a shock that he was speaking English.

He followed him through the door into a short, low-ceilinged corridor, dimly lit and smelling of refuse. A second warder was waiting there and, as David continued behind the first man, the second closed the cell door and fell in behind them.

At the end of the corridor they entered a narrow, sloping passageway that led upward past dark, empty side corridors and tall, vacant niches carved into the solid rock. Their footsteps echoed mournfully as they marched along in single file, ringing out into the distance and dying away in the darkness. The passageway was lit infrequently by flickering oil lamps that seemed to give more shadow than light. Once they crossed a narrow stone bridge over a drop of several hundred feet. Far below, David glimpsed lurid flames and remembered that al-Shami had once told him that Iram stood on a vast deposit of oil. It was the oil that had enabled the city's founders to render it inhabitable, carved as it was out of rock, for the oil had provided them with an inexhaustible supply of fuel for both heating and lighting.

They journeyed deeper and deeper into living rock, through a maze of caves and tunnels lit by small, dim yellow lights. The darkness grew everywhere, like a weed, a tangible thing that weighed on them relentlessly, as though it would choke them. A thin smell as of ancient perfumes or long-decayed spices pervaded every chamber and every passageway through which they threaded their way. David felt bewildered and disoriented, more lost than he had been in the vast spaces of the trackless desert. There was no way to tell whether they walked in one general direction or twisted about in circles, no way of gauging the true dimensions of the place.

They passed vast silent doorways, some wide and open,

ornamental openings of incalculable antiquity, others small and firmly shut. Stone staircases wound upward and downward into inky darkness, their treads worn by generations of passing feet. From time to time they passed great pillars, some single, others in clusters, their upper reaches concealed in shadow. At the entrance to one side passage, evidently long disused, David saw vast spiders' webs that stretched from floor to ceiling like curtains; they seemed as old as the city itself. Everywhere, dusty cobwebs were festooned like bunting from walls and ceilings, or tangled in the openings of niches and doors.

But nothing that David saw had as great an impact on him as his discovery of one startling and, in its way, profoundly disturbing fact: Iram had been a Jewish city. Everywhere he saw signs of the place's Jewishness: Hebrew letters, quaint and archaic in form yet readily recognizable to his trained eye, carved long ago into the walls of the passages down which he walked; biblical texts, familiar yet strange; Hebrew names cut into the polished stone as memorials of the long dead; drawings of a seven-branched menorah, the candlestick that had once graced the Jerusalem Temple; and representations of the tablets of the law that Moses had brought down from Sinai and that had vanished with the Ark when the Temple was first destroyed by the Babylonians.

And yet Iram had another side, sinister and even more disturbing than its Jewishness. In places, David caught glimpses of curious figures, statues of winged and hooded beings that stood in niches along the walls or on tall pedestals at intersections. Some had human features, others the heads of animals or birds; most were grotesque, some almost demonic. Had that been the sin of the people of Iram, the sin for which they had been destroyed by their angry God, that they had carved graven images for themselves? Statuary of any kind was strictly prohibited in Judaism, yet here in a Jewish city beings of stone leered out from web-encrusted shadows and guarded dark, secretive doorways. Had the lure of the stone and their love of carving it into ever more fantastic shapes become so great for the inhabitants of the city, buried here out of sight and the sun like troglodytes?

As David and his guards walked on, the nature of their surroundings began to change, imperceptibly at first, then with increasing sharpness. There were more lights, the walls of the corridors were smoother and in a better state of repair, the ubiquitous cobwebs were no longer visible. People began to pass them in rapidly growing numbers: men dressed in black Arab robes, like those who had met David and al-Shami in the desert; women in loose white garments tied at the waist with thickly braided cords of varying colors, their hair tied in plaits woven with white ribbons. Everyone they passed was European in appearance, but the women were paler than the men, as though they had spent their entire lives cooped up inside the rocks of the city. No one offered them a second glance, no one stared at David as he approached or turned to watch him after he had passed. All seemed bent on their immediate tasks, though David could not easily tell what those were. Some carried loads on their shoulders, others wheeled barrows or little covered carts, while yet others hurried along with books and papers.

At first, all seemed to David like a series of scenes from some weird fantasy, but the farther he was taken the more the grim reality of Iram was born in upon him. People lived and worked here, amid the relics of a vanished civilization, people no stranger in their own way than the Bedouin who roamed the deep desert beyond the city. He saw a dormitory and a dining hall, a gymnasium complete with equipment some thirty or more years out of date but still in constant use, a row of small offices with desks and filing cabinets, and a bakery whose blazing ovens had been carved out of the solid rock. Sweating men worked at the ovens with long-handled paddles, placing large circles of unleavened dough above the flames and pulling out loaves of freshly baked bread. At one and the same time it seemed both lunatic and normal, incomprehensible and ordinary.

They came at last to a tall door of beaten bronze set on broad hinges and patterned with wreaths of fruits and flowers—not those of Arabia, but the flora of distant Palestine: cassia and coriander, myrtles and juniper, hyssop and spikenard. On either side of the door stood two guards, short rifles slung over their shoulders. They nodded as David and his escort approached: they had been waiting for them. One of the men by the door turned and knocked, then stepped inside the room, closing the door behind him. A moment later the door was swung fully open and David and his guards were ushered into the room.

It took David a little while to make out the details of the room in which he now stood. In shape it was imperfectly circular, with a diameter of about fifty feet. It possessed a shallow domed ceiling and low, white-painted walls that were broken only by the door and by colored banners that hung at intervals all around the room. David recognized the banners as *thangkas,* Tibetan temple hangings depicting gods and demons whirling in a cosmic dance. Beneath each banner a lamp was lit, and on tripods set through the room flames burned in shallow bronze dishes, casting writhing shadows over walls and ceiling. At the exact center of the room a long chain was suspended from the ceiling, at the end of which hung a large ball of solid glass. Beneath the ball was a vast square bed draped in exquisite white linen. At each of the bed's four corners stood a tall figure of gold: four angels with bright, unfurled wings. One held a trumpet to pursed metallic lips, another raised aloft a thin two-edged sword, the third carried a flaming spear, and the fourth a book.

At first David could not make out whether or not the bed had an occupant, but as his eyes grew accustomed to the light and dimensions of the room he made out the head and shoulders of an old man propped up on finely stitched white pillows, over which long strands of silver hair cascaded in all directions. The old man was not the only occupant of the room: David could see the Swiss doctor, Mandl, together with four other men in black and two white-jacketed attendants. But the bed and the figure in it were the focus of all attention. Without him, the room would not have made sense: the angels at each corner of the bed, the Himalayan gods in their spinning mandalas, the glass ball turning slowly in the stillness, the hushed men standing in attendance, all in some measure drew from him their meaning and their place in the order of things. In some indefinable sense the old man was the room. He gave life to it, filled it with his presence as the host fills a church or a condemned man the cell in which he sits. Above his head the glass ball turned on the chain, catching and throwing back the reflected light from all the lamps in the room, like a ball of living fire, glowing yet cool and untouched by any flame. David stood and stared at the old man. Behind him, the door closed firmly with a soft but audible click. There was total silence in the room. No one spoke. No one moved. David stood frozen by the doorway, waiting.

There was a low cough, dry and splintered, then the man on the bed spoke. His voice sounded brittle and faded, an old voice, remote and lacking in timbre, flavorless almost, as if there was no savor in the words or as if what savor there had been had long ago vanished. He spoke without preamble, as though he and David had long ago been introduced and he merely continued a conversation just recently suspended.

"Time does not exist here, Professor. Here in Iram there is no morning, no noon, no evening. For over forty years now I have not seen the sun by day nor the moon by night. There have been no seasons, no years. And yet I have grown old. My hair has become white, my teeth have rotted and dropped out, my flesh is withering. How can that be?

"Come closer," the voice continued, changing the subject abruptly. "Come where I can see you."

Hesitantly David advanced to the foot of the bed, to the side of the angel with the burning spear. He stood there, staring at the old man, watching the shadows thrown by the flickering lamps move over his pale features. For a second he shivered uncontrollably, as if a deep chill conveyed to him by the acres of bloodless rock were penetrating every one of his body's cells. Then, as abruptly as it had come, the shivering fit left him and his body was quiet again, though he still sensed that baneful miasma crept to him through the very pores of the stone. The old man blinked pale watery eyes and began to speak again.

"Time passes here like silk through the hands of the weaver. It is all one substance, a single woven garment that we all wear. You too have put it on, Professor. Come close, let me see your face, let me look into your eyes."

David moved from the foot to the head of the bed. He could see the old man clearly now—the dark liver spots that freckled the folded skin, the vivid structure of the skull, the sunken lips, the pallor tinged with blue, the veins on the temples, the sharp, flared nose, the pale eyes within which a keen, hungry intelligence lurked, eyes that never left David's face for an instant. The cracked lips opened again. The old man spoke in English with a German accent, a little awkwardly, as if he had not spoken the language for a long time.

"Do you know where you are, Professor, what this place is?

There are few men living who have set eyes on our city, few men who have ever done so since it was first built. I know you are curious, I know you long to see more. You are an archaeologist, and this place is a paradise, something beyond your wildest dreams. But it is real, I assure you. Believe me, every stone is real. While you are here you will be shown the main parts of the city. I regret that you cannot be allowed to wander freely, but someone will take care of you. There is a great deal to see. You will not be disappointed."

David broke in, exasperated now by the old man's apparently purposeless discourse.

"Why have you brought me here?" he asked. "What do you want from me?"

The old face hardened and a light flashed in the watery eyes.

"Do not speak until I have finished speaking to you. I want your respect, not your questions. When I wish to do so, I shall tell you why I have brought you here. Until then, listen to me."

The voice lost its edge, the face softened a fraction, the eyes regained their customary paleness.

"You know that this place is Iram," he proceeded. "I am told that you discovered much by your own efforts: a diary kept by a man called Schacht, a book in Arabic by a writer known as al-Halabi, the fact of this city's existence. I congratulate you. And see how your persistence has been rewarded, how you have come here in person, to Iram of the Pillars."

The old man paused, a little out of breath. One of the white-coated attendants stepped forward, lifted a glass from a table near the bed, and helped the old man drink. David looked around him. The other men stood silently, reverently almost, as if awed to be in the presence of the wizened figure between the white sheets. David wondered who he was. One thought tugged at the back of his mind, one possibility that he at once dismissed.

"For all you have read, for all you have seen," the old man continued, "you know next to nothing of what this place is or what it has been. Even I, after all the years I have spent here, know only a small part of Iram's history. Even now there are parts of the city I have never set eyes on. It would take teams of scholars several lifetimes to sift through everything that the sands have preserved here, and even then they would only have begun the task of understanding Iram. There is a library here of twelve thousand scrolls, all in the most wonderful state of preservation. I have seen only a fraction of them. Everywhere there are inscriptions on stone: the whole city is like a book carved in rock. There are artifacts from every period of the city's existence; there are miles of tunnels filled with burial niches containing thousands of well-preserved bodies; there are whole sections of the city that have been left untouched since they were abandoned centuries ago. Iram is the greatest archaeological treasure ever known, the greatest that will ever be known."

He paused again. His voice had grown a little hoarse with the effort of talking. The attendant came forward once more and held the glass to his lips. He leaned forward a little and sipped twice, then his head sank back onto the pillows. He breathed deeply, then went on.

"But you know all this. You can see it or guess it for yourself. You want to know more; you want the answers to questions that have been on your mind ever since you heard of Iram. On your way to this room you will have seen things that have inspired further questions. Let me try to answer a few of them.

"As you will have guessed, Iram was built by your own people. They found the rock formation out of which it is carved here in the desert long ago and turned it into a city, one of the greatest cities the world had ever known.

"They came here during the exile in Babylon, in the sixth century B.C. I'm sure you know already that Nabonidus, the last Babylonian king, made his capital here in Arabia for a time, at Tayma', to the west of the Nafud. What is not known, though some scholars have guessed it, is that there were Jews among the people who accompanied him there. He brought Jewish masons, woodcarvers, craftsmen of every kind. He had plans to build a great city, but nothing came of it. After he died his Babylonian followers returned to Mesopotamia, only to be conquered by Cyrus the Persian, when he took Babylon in 538. But the Jews who had come to Tayma' had no particular desire to return to a land associated for them with forced exile. So they stayed. They remained at Tayma' for a while, but in their tenth year a tribe of Arab nomads raided the oasis. The raiders took everything and then proceeded to destroy the palms and poison the wells. The exiles were forced to leave, to seek somewhere they could live in security.

"It was winter, and so they made their way into the Nafud. Even then the Arabs on the fringes of the desert were frightened of the interior, regarded it with superstitious dread. That meant nothing to the Jews. They had their God and they had . . ."

The old man halted for a moment, his eyes shifting, as if he had been about to reveal something to David that he did not want him to know. He took a shallow breath before continuing.

"They had faith, they had the memory of the long years their fathers had spent in the wilderness with Moses, they had the desperation of exiles. And they found a place that seemed to have been put there for them by their God. There were deep wells of water beneath the rocks, inexhaustible stores of oil to provide them with heat and light, and, what was most important, whole sections underground where the original soil had not become desert. During their first winters they were able to take shelter in caves in the rock, but with time their stonecutters learned how to tunnel more and more deeply into the heart of the mesa. They built a small settlement inside the rock and called it Iram. Within two generations it had become a small city, self-enclosed, self-sufficient, impregnable. By the third generation they had begun to trade with Bahrayn and Yemen. There was silver in Iram, silver and precious stones. The people grew in numbers, and as they did so the city grew with them, honeycombing the rock, carving the stone, enriching its dwellings, embellishing its great Temple.

"But no one ever came to Iram from outside. It was like Mecca or Lhasa, a forbidden city. The people of Iram carried their valuables to the ports of Bahrayn and the cities of Hadhramaut and Yemen, and they brought back the goods they bought there: cloth from Persia and India, spices and perfumes from the south, iron and copper from the north. They made no contact with the Jews of Palestine, they had no idea the exile in Babylon had long since ended. After a time they forgot much of their faith. They knew nothing of the developments that followed the restoration of Jerusalem, nothing of the reorganization of Jewish life, nothing of the changes in thinking that went with it. They began to imitate the peoples they met on their trading journeys, to import their gods and goddesses, to worship them alongside their own god Yahweh. Manat, al-'Uzza, Hubal, Dhu 'l-Shara—they brought a host of alien gods into their Temple.

"For a time Iram prospered. For longer than most cities, in fact. It was an artificial environment, and its people led curious, strangely ordered lives. Only the men ever left the city—to guard its approaches in case the lure of its famed riches drew an invader from beyond the sands, to herd the camels on which their trade depended, to take the caravans to their destinations and back again to Iram. The women never saw the sun. From birth to death, they lived their lives among shadows and the light of oil lamps. They were pale, delicate creatures, like wraiths living out their days in a world of caves and tunnels. Like us, Professor, just like us."

He paused and looked about him, as though he could sense them in the room with him, the pale women of Iram's past. Then he sighed and went on.

"Almost from the beginning they had kings, a line of monarchs who claimed descent from Solomon and who ruled over their new Jewish kingdom as if Jerusalem had never been. And that, of course, was one reason why they never sought to return to Palestine. It is one thing to be king over a powerful desert city but quite another to live as someone else's vassal. Better power in solitude than servitude in a Promised Land that had become little more than a fable.

"But in the end Iram's isolation proved its downfall. The trade with the Bahrayn region declined early, but the city continued to flourish through its trade with Arabia Felix in the south. That all ended with the collapse of southern Arabia in the sixth century A.D. And then something happened in Iram itself. As far as I can tell, it was in the late sixth century, but it could have been a little later—the records aren't clear. I don't know what it was exactly. A plague of some kind probably; but whatever it was, it was sudden and it wiped out most of the population. Those who weren't buried were left where they died. Their bones are still lying where they were left.

"There appear to have been survivors, but if al-Halabi's account is to be believed—and I don't see why it shouldn't be—they forgot everything about the city and its history in a matter of two or three generations. There are no records after the sixth century. But at some point even the degenerate survivors of the original Iramites died out. And Iram was left abandoned down through the centuries. Until I found it again and brought it back to life."

The voice died away and silence filled the room. The gods in their

317

colored mandalas looked down impassively, as if they had heard it all before, or as though it meant nothing to them, these in-breathings and outbreathings of the unchanging cycle of earthly existence. The glass ball turned and turned. No one moved. Then the old man gestured with his eyes and the attendant brought him water to sip again.

"Well?" he said at last, almost in a whisper. David strained to hear him, bending a little further down to do so.

"What have you known to compare to it?" the old man went on. "Is there anything?"

David felt as though he were back in university, at a seminar where the teacher had explained the details of a site and was now waiting for an intelligent response. His mouth was dry, he felt dull and wasted, like a student out of his depth, wishing he were anywhere but where he was.

"No," he said, shaking his head. "I've known nothing like it. How could I have? It's like a dream. But how do you know all this about the city?"

"I told you," the old man whispered. "There is a library. There are inscriptions. There are histories of Iram from its foundation almost to its end. My colleagues and I have translated several of them. You can see them during your stay here: I guarantee you will be fascinated by them."

"And how long is my stay to last?"

The old man blinked his eyes. David could see the slowly rotating ball reflected in both pupils, lending them a borrowed fire from the lamps.

"That will depend on many things. A little while, but not long. It is too early to say. But surely you are not eager to go? I cannot believe that."

"Why have you brought me here?"

"To understand."

"To understand what?"

"That will be explained to you."

"And if I fail to understand?"

"You will not fail. Your life depends on it. You will not fail."

"You had no right to bring me here. You have no right to keep me here against my will." David's voice rose in spite of him. He felt agitated. Anger was moving in his veins like a poison.

318

"Please remain calm, Professor," the old man whispered. "When you understand, you will not be concerned with rights, with will. You will be glad we brought you here. You will want to thank me. But you are tired now. And I am tired. I have not been well for the past few days. There will be time later for explanations. Now you should eat and rest a little. Your journey has exhausted you."

The old man closed his eyes. David glanced around the room. The guard was waiting for him by the door. It made no sense, none of it. What sense could it make? He felt the rage rise in him.

"Who are you?" he asked tightly, his voice barely controlled.

The soft, bloodless eyelids lifted. Lamplight danced in the pale eyes like fire deep within. The eyes blinked and the old man smiled.

"Surely you know who I am," he said. He took pleasure in David's mystification.

David shook his head. He did not understand. He felt afraid of the strange old man in the bed.

"Then I must introduce myself. My name is Ulrich von Meier. Professor Ulrich von Meier. I am very pleased to make your acquaintance, Professor Rosen."

THIRTY-EIGHT

There was a deep silence in the room. David could feel his heart pounding in his chest. He felt disoriented again, as if he had somehow stepped into the pages of Schacht's diary and was floundering there, trying to tear free of the ink and paper, to rip a way for himself back to the real world.

"Professor." Von Meier's precise, dehydrated voice broke into David's thoughts, scattering them like flies. "I do not know what you have read about me in Sturmbannführer Schacht's diary, but I cannot imagine it was flattering to me or to my friends. I can scarcely expect you to believe anything I tell you now, if your mind has been poisoned by his opinions. But I do ask you to think carefully, to expose your assumptions to a little cold criticism. You have been trained to do so. You know what Schacht was, you know the nature of the organization for which he worked, to which he belonged. By 1935, when we were in Sinai, he and his fellows had already started their campaign of destruction against your people, their 'Final Solution.' They had stopped whispering and began to kick and bludgeon openly. They were thugs in the smartest of uniforms, immaculately groomed killers. Schacht was as devoted, as single-minded, as any SS man. I knew him. I assure you he was all you can imagine—the stereotype incarnated."

Had he not read Schacht's diary, David might have found in von Meier's words some sort of defense, some sort of justification, or at least grounds for the suspension of judgment. But he had read the diary, he had read the addendum by Gregorios.

"I see no reason in any of that," David interrupted, "for killing him the way you did. He was no threat to you."

A look of annoyance flickered across von Meier's features for a moment, then vanished as quickly as it had come.

"My dear Professor," he said, "I am hardly sure I understand you. I have not read the Sturmbannführer's diary, but I am sure it has misled you. And you must agree that not even an SS officer would be capable of describing his own death. Only Moses was able to do that. Schacht did not die at my hands or those of any of my friends. We were not murderers. His death was an accident. Regrettable but, I confess, not greatly lamented. None of us had cause to love the man. He was a typical Nazi, a strutting, vulgar fanatic bent on putting the world to rights according to his party's prescription. He objected to our work in principle. He believed the money spent on our expedition should have been used for the rebuilding of Germany, for guns or bullets to make the Fatherland strong again.

"And he was incensed by the fact that some of our party were Jews. I had insisted on hiring them myself; they were people I could trust. We almost came to blows on the issue more than once, but I refused to budge. To make matters worse, he discovered that the city I was looking for—this city, Iram—was a Jewish city. He almost had apoplexy when he learned of it. Do you begin to see why there was trouble between us? I don't ask you to believe me without proof. You are an academic, like myself. You are trained to demand evidence, hard evidence. Unfortunately, that is not very easy to provide, as you must appreciate. So I can only ask you to suspend judgment. When you have been with us for a while I think you will understand things better. You will begin to see many things from a new perspective. Then perhaps we can talk about this again."

David wondered why von Meier was bothering to lie, to go to such lengths in constructing his preposterous fabrication. Was it simply that he had not seen Schacht's diary, had not read Gregorios' account of the man's death? David could see in his mind the bloody figure nailed to the floor, the black and white spiders swarming over him. He shuddered, remembering some of the webs he had seen on his way through Iram.

"Do you want me to suspend judgment on my parents' deaths as well? On the deaths in Cambridge? On the attempt to kill me at Tell Mardikh? Or have I simply misunderstood those too? Perhaps you know a perspective from which they'll all begin to seem quite reasonable, the result of a minor misunderstanding."

Von Meier's face seemed pained, his eyes clouded as though troubled by a memory he wished to expunge.

"Please, Professor Rosen, you shame me, you humiliate me. You refer to things I should prefer forgotten. One of my aides made a mistake, no . . . a series of mistakes in the men he hired. All I wanted was to obtain certain documents, to prevent knowledge of Iram from leaking out to the world at large. We are not ready yet for such a revelation. The lives of many people depend on the continued secrecy of our existence here. I do not expect you to understand or forgive the wrongs that have been done to you . . . and to your family. All I can say it that the people responsible will be punished, severely punished, once they have been located. I give you my solemn word that it will be so."

David stared at the old man. His breath felt thick and stale. There was really no fresh air in this place, everything smelled and tasted as though it had circulated in these tunnels and passageways for centuries. Did von Meier take him for an imbecile that he even wasted time with these subterfuges?

"Why do you keep your existence such a secret?" he asked. "Why are you willing to kill in order to prevent knowledge of Iram leaking out?"

Von Meier smiled—a careful, constructed smile that lay on his face like a breath of warm air on a block of ice.

"Our need for secrecy," he replied, "is like our need for food and water, for heat in winter, for light in this perpetual darkness. Every day our young men draw water from wells beneath the city, put oil in the lamps and trim their wicks, tend to our flocks. Our young women grind flour and bake bread in ovens that were first used two and a half thousand years before they were born. We live here from day to day without knowing when it is day and when it is night outside. We have created a special community, a unique way of life. Should one word of this reach the outside world, it would all vanish like smoke. First the archaeologists would come, then the government officials with forms and censuses, and finally the tourists. Our experiment would be ended, our life here finished forever.

"You have seen nothing of that life as yet, nothing to this

community. You know nothing of our motives, nothing of our purposes. But until you have seen and understood these things you can judge nothing, least of all our need for secrecy. That will change. With time and patience you will understand. We will help you. There is plenty of time."

Von Meier stopped speaking and the attendant came forward once more with the glass. For all his apparent weakness, the old man did not seem to tire, and David sensed in him a strength of will and body that belied the fragility of the bones and the transparency of the flesh.

"It might help," David said, "if you told me just where and how this . . . community comes to be here. But first perhaps you can let me know what I'm doing here."

A frisson of impatience passed once more over von Meier's face and was gone.

"All in good time, Professor, all in good time. When you have been here long enough you will realize that time is nothing at all. It will pass, you will grow old, but that is nothing. You will not be aware of it. When you are ninety you will still feel a child and you will wonder where all the years have gone. The answer is that they will have gone nowhere. There is no such thing as time, only the aging of organisms and the birth of new ones.

"Do you see those banners hanging on the walls? They are *thangkas,* Tibetan temple banners, works of great antiquity. I had them brought here from the Drepung monastery in Lhasa just before the Chinese invasion closed the country. Look closely at them. Do you see the gods, the buddhas, the bodhisattvas? They have passed beyond time, beyond space, beyond illusion. They dwell in the eternal present. For them the wheel of *karma* has ceased to spin, for them beginnings have become ends and ends beginnings.

"That is what we are trying to accomplish here in this place. We have stepped out of time, out of the cycle of normal existence. In the city we toil and suffer, but through our actions we slow the wheel of *karma,* the spiral of death and rebirth. In a matter of generations, perhaps, the wheel will have slowed perceptibly.

"But I am rushing on. You know nothing yet. There will be much to tell you when you are ready. First, let me inform you how we came to be here at all."

Von Meier paused. Beneath the coverlet, his hands shifted, then lay still again. David looked at the *thangkas,* at the vibrant Tibetan colors, at the nebulous gods in heavens inaccessible to him. The other occupants of the room remained silent, as if the dialogue between David and von Meier were some sort of rite, as if the attendant with the water were an acolyte bringing a cup to the lips of the priest as he pronounced his benedictions. David remembered the monks at St. Nilus', the blood of the old monk like consecrated wine spilled in the sanctuary.

"There were a few of us before the war," von Meier began, "a small community devoted to the study of spiritual matters, seeking a retreat from the world. I played an active role in things, but my academic work prevented full-time involvement with the community. We avoided becoming entangled with the Nazis when they came to power. Their aims and ours were radically different. We wanted a community of spirit where men could live in peace; they wanted a strong nation that could wage war on other nations. Many of us were sent to camps and died in them. During the war our young men were conscripted, and many were killed on the Russian front.

"When the war was at last over there were only a few of us left, but we realized we had a job to do. Europe was crushed and exhausted: physically, mentally, above all spiritually. It had become a wasteland, a place more barren than the desert in which we live here. In the East, the Russians with their atheism and their scorn for tradition, in the West, the Americans with their material values and their boorish indifference to any but the most superficial realities. It was evident that we could not stay in such a place. But there were those around us who needed our help: widows, orphans, former prisoners of war. There were so many of them, people without homes or families or future, and we could do so little. We did what we could, of course, but it was a drop in the ocean. We began to despair: it seemed a hopeless course we were steering, to build a new community in the midst of so much devastation.

"And then I thought of Iram. I had discovered the city in the year after our expedition to Sinai. It had been my original intention to make the discovery public as soon as an agreement could be reached with the Saudi king, but by the time we had assessed the find, conditions in Germany had deteriorated to the point where I felt it prudent to let the city remain hidden. It would have been more than a little foolish to have announced the discovery of a major Jewish city at that juncture in German history. Don't you think so? Well, my colleagues certainly were in agreement.

"By the end of the war, most of them were dead. The few who remained joined our little group, and soon we were able to make discreet arrangements to transform Iram from an archaeological find into the home of an active community. We had Arab friends who assisted us and who ensured that our secret was kept. They still help supply us with essential items we cannot grow or manufacture for ourselves.

"Iram was to be our sanctuary. The seventh sanctuary. The final redoubt for a civilization under threat of destruction."

David interrupted.

"I'm sorry," he said, "I don't understand. 'The seventh sanctuary'?"

Von Meier seemed to contemplate before he answered.

"There have been seven sanctuaries," he said. "Seven sacred places where the long night of barbarism has been kept at bay. The first and the second were Jerusalem: Solomon's Temple and Herod's Temple. The third was Rome, the new Jerusalem. And in the East, Byzantium, the new Rome, the site of the Church of Holy Wisdom. Mecca was the fifth, the forbidden city. The sixth was to have been Berlin: there was talk of a new civilization, a new order. But even before it could be completed, one man's pride brought about its destruction. And so we came to Iram. To the seventh sanctuary.

"In the beginning, our community consisted largely of orphans, children who would have perished or been corrupted in Europe. We educated them, trained them in the ideals we had established for ourselves, helped them grow in body and spirit. We sent the boys to live for a time with Arab tribes on the borders of the desert, to learn the virtues of nomadic life. The girls were kept here to be schooled in the arts of civilization—in painting, in literature, in music. They had children at an early age. By now we are in our third generation—in a few cases, even, the fourth."

Von Meier paused again. David sensed that he had left much unsaid, that he had deliberately sketched only the vaguest outline of his group and the organization of the community here at Iram. But now that David was here, now he had seen Iram at first hand, what necessity was there for further concealment? Von Meier was still holding something back, that was obvious. The question was why.

"Such people," von Meier resumed, "are, you will understand, neither willing nor able to live in the world outside Iram or to become part of that world. As time passes and Western civilization decays more and more rapidly, the world outside becomes less and less attractive, more and more of a threat. Most of those living here have known nothing else but Iram. They would find adaptation hard, impossible perhaps. And what would they gain by reentering your world? In exchange for the security of this sanctuary, they would find nothing but fear and uncertainty. A massive buildup of nuclear arms, terrorism, unemployment, mental illness, divorce, rioting, a mounting crime rate . . . You see, I am not as isolated as I seem. I know what is happening. All our worst fears for the future are being fulfilled.

"But we have our own purposes, our own goals. You will understand them in due course. And when you have understood them you will share them. You will realize how essential it is that this place remain unknown to the world at large. And then, perhaps, you will help us recover the papers you have found and prevent their being made available to others. I want you to do so of your own accord, to give me the papers and tell me the names of anyone to whom you may have sent copies.

"But that will take time. Let us not speak of it again until you are ready. In the meantime, I have other tasks for you to perform. I chose you because you are an archaeologist, because you will understand my motives. While you are with us, I want you to study the city and its archives. I have already prepared a detailed archaeological record of the central sections of the city. You will begin by studying that: it will save you much time and effort. When you have completed it, I want you to supplement it, using your knowledge of modern techniques. Tell me what equipment you will need: I will see to it that you have it.

"Eventually a time will come—perhaps long after you have left Iram, but in your lifetime, I am sure of that—when it will be possible to reveal to the world the existence of the city. Not its location—that must remain a secret for an indefinite period—but the fact that it exists. When that time comes I want you to tell the world what you know, to publish a joint report in both our names, to provide examples of artifacts and documents discovered here. I had my reasons for concealing Iram after I found it, and I have even better ones for keeping its existence secret since then. But the archaeologist in me is ashamed that I have kept the world in ignorance of such an important discovery. It is the greatest archaeological treasure ever found, greater than all the pyramids of Egypt, greater than Troy and Ur and Pompeii all together. No archaeologist before me ever saw such wonders, not even in fantasy.

"But I have been here over forty years now in total obscurity. My name has been forgotten, my books and articles gather dust in the storerooms of libraries. The academic world is merciless, it allows no one to rest on his laurels. When I vanished no one asked where I had gone. New men and new ideas were waiting in the wings to take over. You have computers and electron microscopes and thermoluminescence apparatus now—I cannot compete with any of that. I am only an old man spending his last days in a forgotten city. But I have one claim to fame that cannot be dismissed or allowed to gather dust. I am the discoverer of Iram. The name of Ulrich von Meier deserves to rank with those of Schliemann and Carter and Woolley. You, Professor, are to see that it does so. My reputation is to rest in your hands. In return, I give you sole access to Iram for as long as you wish it. After my name, yours will ever be known as that of the man who unraveled Iram's secrets. Your books will become classics, standard works for many generations. The discoverer and the elucidator: our names will be carved together in archaeology's Hall of Fame.

"Before that happens, however, you have a long task ahead of you. You will have to study much and examine much. I will help you as much as I can. Come to me for advice whenever you need it. Before you leave here I shall introduce you to my assistants. I have instructed them to help you in any way you need. You will be housed near this room. There will have to be a guard at first, of course, until you recognize the importance of this work and the sincerity of our intentions. But within limits you will be free to go anywhere in Iram.

"There is, however, one other small task I want you to perform while you are here. In the library you will find photostats of all the tablets discovered at Ebla, together with the chief publications on the subject by Matthiae and Pettinato. I want you to go over the available material in order to establish what was the farthest extent of Ebla's empire when it was at its height. I have a theory that its borders extended far to the south, deep into what is modern Palestine . . . Israel, if you prefer. But I have no expertise in the matter, no real knowledge of Eblaite. When I heard that a real expert might be available to examine my theory, I was overjoyed. You cannot imagine how happy I was. And it will be of benefit to you, I am sure, to carry out work on Eblaite texts while you are here, to keep your hand in, as it were. Are you willing to do all this for me? Please say that you are."

"And if I say no?" David asked.

Von Meier smiled again, less warmly this time, if that were possible.

"Oh, that would be a pity, my dear Professor. You must understand your position here. Everyone at Iram works. There is nothing to spare for slackers. Even one extra mouth to feed is an extraordinary burden. The extent of cultivable land beneath the city is strictly limited: only a limited population can survive here without the import of extra food. The ancient Iramites could do that freely, but we are more restricted, there is a limit to what we can bring in from outside. In Iram, those who do not work do not eat. Even the sick do not eat if there seems to be little hope of their recovery. And those who do not eat die. Discipline here is strict, I must warn you of that. What might seem perhaps trivial offenses in the world outside are punished severely here. Last week we executed a man and a woman because they had conceived a child without permission. An extra mouth, you see. Unplanned for. You must be careful here. One of my assistants will explain. It will take a little while for you to adjust. We will be indulgent for a while, but I ask you to learn quickly—your survival here will depend upon it.

"Now it is time for me to sleep. You have met Dr. Mandl. I think I will allow him to introduce you to his colleagues outside. We will meet again in a few days, when you have had time to rest and recover from your journey. Good-bye for now, Professor. I am pleased to have met you."

Von Meier fell silent and closed his eyes. Mandl came forward and took David by the arm. An attendant began to dim the lamps. Darkness, unchecked, began to flood the room. A single lamp was left burning, like a small flame before an altar. With Mandl on one side and the guard on the other, David followed the other men out of the room.

THIRTY-NINE

After three days—days that were not days but alterations of light and darkness interspersed with sleep and meager helpings of food—David was taken for the first time to see the central sector of the city. He had been given black Arab robes to wear so that he would not stand out as he went about with his guard, but from time to time people glanced at him, conscious that he was a stranger, unable to understand the meaning of his presence among them. He was forbidden to speak with anyone, but he watched and listened as the inhabitants of the city carried out their tasks. Everywhere there was an atmosphere of intense seriousness. There were no smiles, and he heard no laughter anywhere at any time. People worked or rested after work or ate in one of several communal halls set aside for the purpose, large, drab refectories with kitchens attached to them, but there appeared to be no opportunities for recreation or entertainment. There were no displays of affection, not even between men and women or adults and children. He saw no one hold hands or embrace another person. Greetings, when they occurred, were somber and perfunctory. Everyone was dressed much the same as everyone else—black robes for men, white for women. Even the children were solemn and reserved. They watched with large eyes as he passed, their curiosity held firmly in check, neither whispering nor giggling among themselves.

He discovered that the people had no family life. There was no marriage in Iram and no love. Sexual relations were permitted—for girls from the age of fifteen, for boys from seventeen—but the forming of permanent or even temporary liaisons was strictly

329

prohibited. Partners were rotated regularly, according to a program worked out by an official known as the Geschlechtsver-kehrleiter, the Controller of Sexual Relations. Any attempt to infringe this arrangement was treated with the utmost seriousness. Unplanned pregnancies had to be reported to the Geburten-beschränkungsleiter, the official responsible for birth control, at the earliest possible moment. In the vast majority of cases such pregnancies were terminated, unless there had been a recent death in the infant population which had not yet been compensated for.

Women were permitted a total of three children, after which they were automatically sterilized. All children belonged to the city and were brought up communally, at first in nurseries, then in dormitories. Everyone slept in dormitories, segregated by sex. Meetings for the purpose of sex were carefully regulated, and permission had to be obtained in advance for every such meeting. Unsterilized women were particularly controlled. David was told that there were strict rules about the sexual relations of fertile women, so that their offspring would conform to certain standards, but he was unable to ascertain the criteria on which these rules were based. From certain hints, he concluded that any mentally or physically handicapped children were killed at birth and that euthanasia was also practiced in cases where handicap became apparent or occurred as the result of an accident at a later stage.

He also learned that the old, if they could no longer sustain themselves by some kind of work, were put to death painlessly in order to make room for a child. Sometimes this would be planned a year or two in advance. On three separate occasions David saw an old man and once an old woman struggling to keep up with a team of younger workers carrying provisions to the central stores. For the most part, however, he saw almost no one over the age of about fifty.

He had little opportunity to observe the children of the city. The youngest were kept in a dimly lit nursery not far from von Meier's room, where they were tended with emotionless efficiency by a group of scrubbed and cheerless women whose hair was pulled back hard into tight buns and whose faces were set in what seemed to be permanent scowls. At the age of four they began to attend school, boys and girls already segregated in preparation for later life. David was not permitted to visit any of the classrooms, it being

330

explained to him that it was not yet time for him to be exposed to the ideas and principles on which Iram was founded, theories that formed the basis of the curriculum taught in its schoolrooms.

On one occasion, however, David was able to hold a brief conversation with a child, a little girl of about eight who passed by while his guard, made careless by the easy routine into which they had slipped, was attending to a problem elsewhere. David called to the child, who looked demure and serious in her white gown and braided gold hair, and introduced himself.

"Hello," he said, "my name is David. What's yours?"

She looked at him curiously, half ready to run, yet intrigued by being spoken to by this unknown man who addressed her in German with such an odd accent.

"I don't have a name, silly," she said. "You know nobody has a name when they're a child."

"I'm sorry," David said, taken aback by this latest revelation. "There are many things I don't know. I'm new here, I came to do work for . . . Professor von Meier."

The girl's face, adultlike in its seriousness, wrinkled in a frown as if David's words were incomprehensible to her.

"What do you mean 'new'?" she asked. "No one is new here. We are all born in the city. We will die in the city. The only new people are tiny babies, the ones in the nursery. I'm not a baby any longer. Nor are you."

"But I wasn't born in the city," David tried to explain. "I came from outside, I was brought here. On a camel."

She frowned again, as if David were somehow mad.

"Outside?" she queried. "What is that? There is nothing outside the city. Only darkness without lamps."

He decided to leave the subject of where he came from, fraught as it obviously was with problems.

"I'll explain it to you when you're older," he said. "But first I'd like to know more about your name. If you don't have a name, how do people speak to you, tell you what to do? How do you know when your teachers want you to answer in class, for example."

She seemed almost offended by what must have appeared to her the obviousness of David's question, as though he had asked her what color white was.

"But of course I don't need a name for that," she protested.

331

"We all do the same things at the same time. No one does anything the rest don't do. When our teachers tell us what we should do, they tell us all at once. And in class we answer together. Why would someone want to answer alone? It would be a stupid thing to do. They would be wrong. We are only right when we answer together. Then we all know the correct answer. Weren't you taught that at school?"

"Then how are you alone today?" asked David, changing the subject slightly, disturbed by the image that rose up in his mind of a classroom full of children parroting set answers.

"Because it's a test day, silly. Don't you know anything?" she said, impatient of David's ignorance of the simplicities of life.

"And what do you do on a test day?"

"You don't know anything, do you? We have to travel the tunnels and find our way to Central Pillar alone. It's an important test, in case one of us should ever become separated from the others. Some people get lost in the old tunnels and die in the dark. It happened to a little girl in my class last year. I'm sure it isn't nice."

"Are you afraid of the dark?" David asked, wondering if she would admit to at least one normal childish emotion.

She shook her head.

"Of course not! Why should anyone be afraid of the dark? It's difficult to find your way if your lamp goes out, but sensible people don't go into the dark tunnels anyway. I like the dark most of all when we go through the Ancients with our lamps."

"The Ancients?" David asked. "What are they?"

"You are a strange man," she said, frowning again. "The Ancient Tunnels, of course, where the dead are buried. I love visiting them. It feels quiet and safe there. I shall go there when I die. It will be lovely."

The conversation had taken a disturbing turn. David tried to conceal the horror he felt.

"When do you visit the dead people?" he asked.

"Every morning, of course," she said. He knew by now that "morning" meant nothing more than the period after waking. Time was calculated by clocks. Otherwise, it was as von Meier had said: there was no day and no night in Iram.

"All the schoolgirls go to visit them," she continued. "I would have thought you knew that at least. We go to the Temple,

332

sometimes with flowers, to sing at the great altar. Then we leave by the Deadgate and go into the Ancients. We bring flowers with us and scatter the petals on the bodies. It makes a nice smell. I love the dead people, they're so quiet and so peaceful. The ladies look lovely in their long robes and jewels. The oldest ones have crumbled by now, of course, but some of them look just like living people, as if they're sleeping. Haven't you seen them ever?"

David shook his head. Dead people, yes, but not these dead, not the dead of Iram. Not yet.

At that moment there was a shout from nearby. The little girl looked around. David's guard had returned and was shouting to her to leave. She glanced once at David and then turned and ran off toward a nearby tunnel. David sighed. The nameless child stopped briefly at the tunnel's entrance and looked back at David, then disappeared into its entrance and was lost to him forever.

"You know better than to speak with anyone," the guard shouted, striding toward him. "I shall be obliged to report this incident to Herr von Meier."

David shrugged. What did any of their rules or regulations matter to him? They would kill him in the end anyway, he knew that.

His guard was a strange man, by name Talal and a fluent Arabic speaker, but Japanese by race. He was the only Oriental David had seen in the city, but he refused to explain how he came to be there other than to say he had been brought to Iram by von Meier as a child. He was now aged about forty-five, or so he said, but he looked much younger and was lithe and fit as a twenty-five-year-old. He was ascetically thin, clean-limbed, with not an ounce of excess weight anywhere on his body. Every muscle, every fiber, every inch of skin seemed charged with a raw energy that only a finely developed will held in check. The edges of his hair were flecked with gray, not, it seemed, as a sign of the onset of age, but rather as a token of hardships endured and inner battles won. Behind hooded eyes he concealed a quick brain and self-possession of a quality David had never encountered before in anyone. He seemed detached from all around him, not through indifference or a discipline of disinterest imposed on him from outside, but as a result of an inner control, a centering in himself that enabled him to dispense with the world of other men.

333

He was taciturn but willing to answer David's questions about the parts of the city they visited together. They were seldom parted during David's waking hours, though their enforced intimacy brought with it no real closeness and little understanding. At times when he could be persuaded to talk, Talal revealed enough about himself to enable David to construct a more rounded picture of the man. From the fact that he spoke Arabic as fluently as German, David inferred that he had spent a considerable time living among the Arab tribes in and around the desert, something Talal himself confirmed when asked about it. In fact it soon became apparent that Talal had vastly more experience of the world outside Iram than had the average inhabitant of the city. Not only had he lived for extended periods with a branch of the Shammar tribe on the borders of the Nafud, but he had even traveled to the Far East, where he had learned Japanese and studied several of the martial arts. It seemed that he was not subject to many of the restrictions imposed on other inhabitants of the city. He could, for example, choose to leave Iram almost at will, and often roamed for months at a time in the sands of the Nafud, alone and hungry, working at the twists and knottings deep within himself.

Wherever he went he carried with him a long-handled Japanese sword, its black lacquered scabbard laced with silk cords and chased at top and bottom with the finest silver. It was the one thing about which he was not reticent. He told David that it had been forged for him in Kyoto by the master swordsmith Gassan Sadakazu. The blade had been forged and reforged over a period of forty days until it sang like a glass bell when struck. All along it, fine Japanese calligraphy had been carefully incised. Talal translated the inscription for David. It was a *haiku*, a short poem he himself had written:

> In the steel, steel;
> In the blade, life.
> The clouds pass silently,
> The sword passes in silence
> Through still waters.

Often he compared himself to the blade. He had been forged and tempered many times, he said, until he had become like steel, firm

334

yet supple, sharp as a razor yet deadly only when he was drawn. Once he described himself as von Meier's sword, sheathed for long periods in the darkness of Iram, then withdrawn shining when the old man chose to send him out on a mission. But when pressed as to the nature of these missions, he would not even hint at them. It was only after he had spent more than a week in Talal's company that David remembered—vividly, now that the memory came to him—the Oriental face he had seen in the car racing away from the scene of his parents' deaths in Haifa.

When he was not being shown around the city, David spent his time reading in the library. In all his life he had never worked in a stranger place. Low-ceilinged and dimly lit, and only about ten feet wide, it seemed to stretch on endlessly until its farthest limits were lost in a cloud of darkness, as if the past itself were enshrined there, half visible, half lost in darkness. Along the walls on each side unending rows of small circular openings, each about six inches in diameter, ran down into a blur where they seemed to join before being swallowed up by hungry shadows. Twelve deep, they stretched from near floor level right to the ceiling, with only short gaps between them. Each one was found on examination to contain a parchment scroll wrapped in a cloth cover, sometimes sumptuous, sometimes humble. The general state of preservation of the scrolls was, David found, almost miraculous. Like the mummies he had seen in crypts on the other side of the city, following his conversation with the little girl, the parchments of Iram benefited from whatever preservative qualities it was that the place possessed. After only an hour there, David realized that the library alone represented the single most important discovery in the entire annals of archaeology, a discovery that made the Dead Sea Scrolls, the Ugaritic texts of Ras Shamra, the tablets of Ebla, and the Cairo Geniza fragments all pale into dull insignificance.

There were things in the library biblical scholars would kill one another just to touch, even to know merely that they existed. On the wall near the entrance at one end of the long room, a great stone tablet was carved with the titles of the major works contained there. Few of the titles meant very much by themselves, of course, since the names of the books that came to make up the Hebrew Bible were later additions. But it took only a few days and a handful of parchments to reveal the fact that here were located the earliest extant copies of all the principal biblical texts written before the exile in 586 B.C. Here too were works long considered lost, such as the History of Solomon, the Annals of the Kings of Israel, and the Annals of the Kings of Judah, that had served as sources for some of the historical books of what later became the Bible. David knew that, if he could publish the results of even six months' research among these scrolls, he could change the face of biblical scholarship, supporting or demolishing with hard evidence every theory and every hypothesis ever put forward in the last century or more.

But first he had to see to his own survival. Every day he read a little of von Meier's massive report, a detailed survey of Iram that stretched to over two thousand pages. Von Meier had carried out all but the very first explorations of the city single-handedly, and the report represented an astonishing achievement in respect to its breadth, its thoroughness, and its attention to detail. As he read it, David came to understand von Meier better and to like him less, if that were possible. The man had been obsessed with Iram to the point where he could not bear anyone but himself to study the city or report his findings. He had tolerated no collaboration and had no desire to share the fame he believed would ultimately be his. David could not believe von Meier was being honest when he said he wanted to share the glory of his discovery with him.

In the evenings David worked on the Ebla material, going carefully through the main references that indicated the extent of the city's empire at its height as far back as 2400 B.C. There were references to place names in Palestine: Hazor, Gaza, Lachish, Megiddo, even Jerusalem; references to biblical names like Abraham, Ishmael, and Israel; and numerous indications that Ebla had controlled most of the territories surrounding it for a period. David knew the question had been of interest ever since some biblical fundamentalists had sought in such references justification for the extreme view that the Eblaites had really been Hebrews, a view some Syrians had feared might lead to Zionist claims over modern Syria. Did von Meier harbor such opinions? David doubted it. But if he did, it would not be hard to demonstrate to him just how little substance there was in them, how, if anything, the same evidence could be used to argue the opposite, that the early Hebrews had been Syrians and that, therefore, Syria had a right to take and hold the Palestine region.

But David became quickly bored with the Ebla material. He had seen it so many times and worked on so much of it that it held no fascination for him, least of all here in Iram, where the smallest discovery lived more vividly and more poignantly for David than anything from Ebla had ever done or could do. No one kept watch over what he was doing in the library. Talal never came there with him, and instead one of the guards who had taken David to see von Meier was posted to remain in the library while he read. He was not alone, but he found he had complete freedom to read anything and make any notes he liked.

When he grew tired of reading tablets from Ebla he would walk past the rows of scrolls, picking them out at random, examining them, and returning them to their niches, ever more awed by the significance of what he had been given access to. The entire length of the library was lit by curious lamps quite unlike those elsewhere in the city. They were cut into the rock of the wall so that nothing could dislodge them, and each was supplied with a reservoir that led to a drainage hole at the back, to catch any oil that might spill and threaten to ignite the precious parchments it served to illuminate. After a few days David discovered that at one point over halfway down the library the openings in the wall were festooned with grimy cobwebs, evidence that they had so far remained untouched by von Meier or his associates. Though he had scarcely begun to make inroads on the vast quantity of scrolls at the upper end of the long room, he was intrigued by these rows of papyri that no one had touched and no eye read in who could tell how many centuries.

Overcoming his initial revulsion toward the thick, dust-choked webs that spanned each opening and his fear that the niches might not be empty of occupants, he brushed his way past them and retrieved scroll after scroll. On the eighth evening he was surprised to find, when he removed the webs that had been spun over one hole about three quarters of the way up the left-hand wall, that the opening had been plugged long ago with a large filling of wax, on which a seal had been firmly pressed. Cracked and dusty, the seal

337

was at first difficult to read in the dim light, but he brought a lamp and a glass from the table where he worked and finally deciphered it.

May the hand of whoever removes this waxen plug wither and may his eyes be blinded should he look on what lies within. Sealed by the orders of the High Priest Mattathias on the twelfth day of Tishri, in the fifth year of the reign of King Jehoahaz of Iram, may the Name protect and sustain him.

He hesitated for only a moment. No archaeologist was free of superstition regarding curses on tombs and funerary objects, but equally no archaeologist could afford to take them seriously. The wax had become brittle and the plug was not difficult to dislodge, but as it gave way it cracked and broke into fragments in his hand. He remembered suddenly the tablet that had crumbled at Ebla, the terrible events that had followed on the next day. Coincidence, mere coincidence, he thought, but a part of his mind felt uneasy.

His hand trembling slightly, conscious that he had stumbled across a find of real importance, David reached into the hole and felt about gingerly for its contents. His fingers felt the familiar touch of linen. Using both hands, he slowly extracted the roll from the niche, then, holding it carefully, carried it to the table and set it down.

The fine linen cover was the best preserved of all those David had seen so far, protected as it had been by the wax plug. It was lightly embroidered with gold thread and tied with a ribbon that appeared to be silk. Holding his breath, David eased the ribbon slowly off the narrow bundle. The cloth fell open as if it had been rolled only the day before, and David lifted out a scroll. With the utmost care, fearful that it might crack, he began to unroll it. Not one but three separate sheets of parchment lay before him.

338

FORTY

It took David just over half an hour to reach a conclusion as to what he had in front of him. There were three sheets of papyrus, each dating from a different period. The oldest, a small sheet rolled up between the others, was in a relatively poor state of preservation and appeared to date from a year or two after the deportation of the Jews to Babylon under Nebuchadrezzar—somewhere around 584 B.C. The next oldest, written on material of better quality but faded in places, could be dated by a reference in the text to the death of King Nabonidus of Babylon and Tayma' as having taken place in the previous year. According to a quick mental calculation by David, this meant it had been written in 538 B.C. The latest, which was wrapped around the others, had been penned at Iram "in the one hundred and twentieth year of the foundation of the city"— probably early in the third century B.C.

He spent the rest of that evening working on the first sheet, the shortest but the most difficult to decipher because of the condition of the papyrus and the awkwardness of the script. When he finished it, he rewrapped the documents in their linen cover and returned them to the hole in which he had found them, struggling to remain calm as he did so, lest the guard notice his excitement and report it to von Meier. He went to bed soon afterward but could not sleep for hours, his thoughts running excitedly over and over what he had read until he fell asleep at last through sheer exhaustion.

What he had found excited and troubled him as much as it perplexed him. It was a brief statement written by a priest of the Jerusalem Temple called Benjamin bar Hilkiah. During the siege of

Jerusalem, when it became apparent to him and certain of his friends that King Zedekiah would be unable to hold out much longer against the Babylonian forces, they had taken steps to remove several treasures from the Temple and hide them carefully throughout the city. When Nebuchadrezzar took Jerusalem and the mass deportations to Babylon began, Benjamin and his companions had somehow managed to disguise and take with them one of the objects they had previously rescued. Unfortunately, wherever this object was referred to in the text of Benjamin's statement, a later hand had heavily crossed out the word, as though its mention were something obscene or blasphemous. That fact alone had sent numerous tingles along David's spine. Benjamin and his fellow priests had succeeded in reaching Babylon with their mysterious burden and had hidden it in a cellar. The last portion of the statement consisted of a description of the location of the cellar and a prayer that the recipient of the letter might be led by God to find and recover it "when the sins of our people have been wiped away by the afflictions of exile and the heart of the Lord is softened toward us."

Throughout the next day David was restless for the evening and the revelation he believed would come when he read the remaining two documents. But he could not risk showing his eagerness and was forced to bottle it up while visiting yet another section of the sprawling underground city. Shortly after the midday meal, which consisted of dark bread and goat's-milk cheese, he was summoned to von Meier's room.

The old man awaited him as before, propped in his bed beneath the slowly turning glass sphere, attended by his aides, waited on by his two nurses. When David entered the room he was writing in a large leather-bound book and did not at first look up. David waited, watching the old man scrawl, watching the glass ball rotate, watching the bodhisattvas whirl as they danced their unmoving, eternal dance. Finally von Meier put his pen aside, closed his book, and looked up. The eyes seemed awash with memories today, thought David; there was a faraway look in them, as if he too joined in a silent dance somewhere beyond the visible confines of his room.

"I keep a journal," von Meier said, "like our friend Schacht, but not in code. It is here for anyone to read when I am dead. I write in it every day. Thoughts, memories, observations. You are in it now. Along with Schacht and Hartmann and all the others. You are part of the story now, part of Iram. Does that please you?"

David said nothing. He felt part of nothing, bound to no one. Had von Meier learned of his discovery of the evening before, had he been brought here to explain what he had found?

"Well," von Meier continued. "Tell me a little of what you have seen, what conclusions you have drawn. Is Iram to your taste? Has it lived up to your expectations?"

Relieved that von Meier seemed to want nothing more than an interim report on his survey of the city, David allowed all other thoughts to slip away as he settled down to providing a detailed account of his initial impressions. They passed the afternoon closeted together, and as they talked it became apparent to David why, above all the other reasons, he had been brought to Iram. For over forty years von Meier had measured and recorded, evaluated and described the stones and artifacts of his lost city, setting down his findings in the vast report David was still reading. In all that time there had been no one who was fitted to discuss the technicalities of his work with him, no one who could appreciate or admire the unquestionable achievement of the man. Von Meier was hungry for praise and recognition from another archaeologist, and as they talked David could not find reason to condemn him for that. None of us works alone, none of us can find meaning in life without the reactions of others. In his own career David had sought his father's blessing, his teachers' approval, his reviewers' praise. However extraordinary his circumstances, von Meier was an ordinary man whose lifework had gone unnoticed. For a while David considered telling him of the three scrolls he had found, since the credit for their discovery belonged ultimately with von Meier himself. But something told him not to do so, to keep their existence to himself, at least until he knew more clearly what they signified.

He dined with von Meier early that evening. A small table and chair were brought for him and set by the side of the old man's bed. There was wine, a bottle of 1945 Médoc claret that had somehow survived its journey to the heart of Arabia to mature perfectly in the caves of Iram. Von Meier told David that 1945 had been an unusually good vintage in the Médoc region, but he did not explain how he had come by the bottles he said were stored in the city. It was a privilege, von Meier said, for David to drink with him: the wines were his personal treasure trove, to which no one else was ever permitted access.

During the meal von Meier reminisced about his childhood and youth, telling David of his early studies in Hanover, of the great teachers under whom he had worked. He explained how he had found the Arabic parchment with the reference to Iram in a collection of early Islamic manuscripts deposited in the library of Tübingen University by Karl-Friedrich Hauser, the famous Islamicist of the late nineteenth century. Though conditions in Germany had been unpropitious, he had succeeded in organizing the ill-fated expedition to Sinai, in the course of which so many of his colleagues had died. Once the true location of Iram had been discovered by Schacht, von Meier had been able to organize a second expedition with the help of Arab friends and, in the autumn of 1936, he had come upon the city exactly as described in al-Halabi's account.

Iram had been utterly cold and dark then, its lamps long extinguished, its fires no more. Using hurricane lamps, von Meier and his colleagues had explored the black, winding tunnels and echoing chambers of the dead metropolis, slowly mapping out its thoroughfares, its sectors, its entrances and exits. Three had died, two by falling into unsuspected and unseen pits, the third as a result of wandering into side passages from which he had never returned. There were still such side passages, von Meier said, long unlit corridors crammed with mummified remains that honeycombed the rock and seemed to have no beginning and no end. From time to time children left unattended wandered into them never to be seen again.

David tried to get von Meier to say more about his subsequent return to Iram after the war, but on this he was far less forthcoming. The city was a sanctuary, he repeated, a place of hope where the wounds of war and the griefs of its aftermath could be healed and new generations brought into a world remote from civilization and all the evils it brought in its wake.

It was late when von Meier finally brought their conversation to

342

an end. David's usual guard was waiting for him and asked whether he wished to return to his room. He was tired but, having waited all day to return to the scrolls, he shook his head and told the guard he would prefer to go back to the library and finish some work he had waiting there. The guard shrugged his shoulders and led the way down empty corridors to the library. Minutes later David had retrieved the three parchments and unrolled them on the table.

The second scroll was more legible than the first and David found it easy to get the gist of it, even though several words meant nothing to him. It had been written by a priest called Baruch who had stayed on in Tayma' following the death of Nabonidus. Baruch had been a student of Benjamin bar Hilkiah, and it was to him that Benjamin had sent his letter shortly before his death. When King Nabonidus decided to leave Babylon for the Arabian wilderness, putting his son Belshazzar in his place as viceroy, Baruch and his family had been among those who volunteered to go with him, possibly in the hope of eventually making their way back to Palestine. Before their depature Baruch had gone with his father and three brothers to the cellar in which Benjamin had placed the treasure from the Jerusalem Temple. Again David felt frustration when he saw that whoever had effaced the name of the object from Benjamin's letter had done the same with the deposition left by Baruch.

The scribe and his family had taken the unidentified treasure from Babylon to Tayma', keeping its existence a secret even from the other Jews who accompanied them, and had buried it near the oasis at the foot of an outcrop of sandstone rocks. Baruch had written his statement for his son so that he would know where to look if ever the time came to retrieve the object from its hiding place.

At the end of Baruch's testament there was a short inscription in another hand, that of his son Ephraim, who stated that he had taken the treasure from its hole near Tayma' and brought it to Iram, where he had handed it over to the priests and Levites as a sacred trust from the ruined city of their fathers.

The third and final scroll completed the saga. It was written by Elihoreph, a priest who served as a scribe to King Jehoahaz, the third of the kings of Iram. As he wrote, the city was in danger from Arab raiders who had ventured deep into the Nafud during a season

343

of little rain, and the king had decided to remove the treasure to a place of safety. David's excitement mounted as he read on, for Elihoreph proceeded to describe the manner of the object's concealment and its exact location. But, like the others, Elihoreph's text had been tampered with. It began without preamble:

On the eleventh of Tishri of this year, when the Day of Atonement had passed and the High Priest had come forth from the Temple, my Lord Jehozhaz, king of Iram and master of the Inner Sands, decreed that the ****** be brought forth. He called into his presence Amariah bar Malluch, the High Priest, and Shemaiah bar Rahum, a priest of the Temple, a descendant of Aaron; and he brought before him Joiakim bar Johanan, Johanan bar Kadmiel, his father, and Judah bar Mattaniah, who are Levites; and he summoned me, Elihoreph, the son of Jozadak, that I might make a record of all that passed between them.

My lord Jehoahaz spoke of the famine that was in the land and the dearth that encompassed it, saying that he feared lest the hand of the Bene Qedem, the sons of the east, be raised against us and they overcome us. In a time when the future is hidden in mists and the fate of our people in darkness, it were better that precautions be taken lest that which we hold most precious and most sacred fall into the hands of the Ishmaelites and be lost to us forever.

In fear of such a day and in preparation for it, my lord's father, King Abishalom, had made ready a place deep beneath the city, a dark and hidden place, a hollow room cut into the living rock, six cubits long, four cubits wide, and five cubits high. When all had sworn themselves to secrecy by the most solemn vows, even I, Elihoreph, by vows to the Most High, my Lord the King described to us the place wherein it was to be kept. It was a place where none would go willingly, wherein the Bene Qedem would never set foot.

That same day, when many still slept on account of the fast they had kept the day before, the priests and the Levites (and I among them) brought the ****** forth from the Temple and covered it with gold cloth and silver cloth and cloth of fine silk. We carried it from the Temple through the Tall

344

Gate, into the tunnels beyond where the dead are buried. At the passage which is the third of those that are on the left side of the great tunnel, we turned, carrying the ****** with us. Amariah bar Malluch, being an old man and of much dignity, went before us bearing a lamp, and Johanan bar Kadmiel, an old man also, came behind us with a lamp like that of Amariah. We walked between them in shadows, and the dead lay on either side of us, in dark rows, seeming to move at times in the flickering of the lamps. There was an opening on the right after two hundred paces, and we turned therein and went deeper into the darkness, with a light ever in front of us and a light ever after. At the end of the tunnel in which we then walked, there was a wall beyond which we could go no farther.

According to the king's instructions that he had given to us when we met with him, Amariah bar Malluch bent down and searched in the dust for a metal ring that had been placed there and covered over that no man might find it unawares. Yet indeed it was there as the king had said, laid into the stone skillfully by a master mason that had built the place beneath. So we set down the ****** that the younger priest, Shemaiah bar Rahum, might try to raise the stone that had been set there, that covered the entrance to the place beneath. So cunningly had the stone been laid that he raised it, not without effort, yet by his own strength. For it had been made that way, that a single man might raise it and take shelter beneath, even though he were the last of his people and had no one who might aid him or give him help.

And so we brought the ****** and laid it in the small chamber below and so sealed the doors and put the name of Amariah upon them, and the name of Jehoahaz. When it was done and we had sealed it there and prayed over it prayers of protection, we came up again into the tunnel where we had been and placed the heavy stone in its place once more, covering it with the dust of the earth, even as it had been covered.

I have taken two epistles that I have had in my possession, that were handed down to me from my grandfather Ephraim, in which the story of how the ****** came to be in Iram is recounted, and I have given them to Amariah the High Priest, that he might preserve them with this scroll, that the history of this thing be not lost to men forever. And I have completed this writing on the twelfth day of the month of Tishri, in the fifth year of the reign of King Jehoahaz, may the Lord of the Universe preserve him and lengthen his reign.

As he laid down the parchment, David's heart was beating rapidly, and he felt sure the guard must hear it pounding in the close silence of the ancient library. But the guard was dozing in his chair, oblivious of David or anything else. David put his hands flat on the table to stop them shaking and strove to calm himself. He guessed that Amariah, the old priest, had been responsible for the erasures in each of the three documents. But he also thought he knew by now what the unnamed object had been. If he was right and if it was still there, it would prove a discovery that would eclipse the whole of Iram by itself.

But he reasoned that there was little likelihood that it would be there any longer. Iram had survived whatever threat had been posed that year by neighboring Arab tribes, the Bene Qedem of Elihoreph's account, that he knew already. Once the danger had passed, it had to be assumed that Amariah and the others would have recovered their treasure from its hiding place and restored it to the Temple. Unless . . . David wondered. Why had the scrolls never been removed from their niche? Could the secret have inadvertently been lost and the treasure never recovered? David felt his heart begin to beat again. It was a possibility.

He could at least check something, he thought, rising from his seat and going to the stone tablet where the names of the principal manuscripts and the positions of their niches were recorded. Von Meier's report mentioned a particularly detailed history of the city arranged according to the reigns of its first fifteen kings. David quickly found the title on the tablet and was able to locate the scroll in the appropriate niche. It was a thick scroll in good condition, written in a legible hand with dark, clear ink.

The reign of Jehoahaz, Iram's third king, was near the beginning of the scroll. With a shock, David saw at once that he had ruled for only five years. Shortly after the Feast of Tabernacles, which lasted from the fifteenth to the twenty-third of Tishri, a confederacy of seven Arab tribes from a mountain region to the south of the sands (presumably the modern Jabal Shammar) attacked Iram but were beaten off, though with heavy losses, including King Jehoahaz himself and Amariah, the high priest. Jehoahaz' death combined with the unstable conditions in the city to create confusion and a growing state of anarchy, in the course of which a man named Abishai, a blacksmith, deposed and killed Jehoahaz' young son Jerimoth, and put to death everyone who had been associated with the late king's court, including, it was said, priests and Levites. The chronicler then went on to say that, as a result of his blasphemies, Abishai was struck down within one year by a wasting disease from which he never recovered and which dragged him down rapidly to the grave. Another son of Jehoahaz, Naphtali by name, whose teacher had rescued him from the slaughter of Abishai, ascended the throne of Iram, and order was restored to the city.

Thoughtfully, David rolled up the chronicle and replaced it in its niche. It was indeed possible. It was very likely that all those involved in the removal and concealment of the Jerusalem treasure had died suddenly and unexpectedly within a short time of that incident—the king and the high priest in the battle with the nomad tribes, the others following Abishai's coup. It was still a remote possibility, but David thought it was worth a try. He was going to find the object if it was still in its place. But if he was right as to its identity, he had no wish for von Meier to learn of its existence. He would find it, but he would find it alone.

347

FORTY-ONE

If he was to keep his discovery to himself—assuming, that was, that there was anything there at all—David would have to give his guard the slip. He did not think that would be unduly difficult, but the real problem would be getting back afterward without arousing suspicion. He thought he knew a way and decided to try it that night, to take advantage of the guard's drowsiness.

Replacing the scrolls in the opening in which he had found them, he collected his papers together and spent some time poring over charts in von Meier's report, copying details onto a sheet of paper. When he had finished, he closed the file and roused the guard.

"It's late," he said, pretending to yawn. "I can't work any longer. Take me back to my room."

The guard nodded, still drowsy, eager to return to his dormitory to sleep, leaving David locked in his room for the rest of the night.

They left the library, the guard in front carrying a lamp, and headed in the direction of David's room, about three corridors away. At the end of the first corridor there was an abrupt bend to the right, shortly followed by a second to the left. Before reaching the first turn, David allowed himself to fall behind by about five yards, almost the distance of the short interval between the right- and left-hand bends. When he came to the first turning he glanced around and saw that the guard, still half asleep and oblivious of the fact that David had fallen so far behind, was about to take the second turn. At that moment David turned and ran as quickly and as quietly as he could back along the first corridor until he came to an unlit side tunnel on the left-hand side. He paused only long

348

enough to snatch a lamp from a niche in the wall opposite, then lunged into the tunnel.

From here on it was largely guesswork, assisted by the rough map he had made from von Meier's charts. He had seen enough of the city and studied sufficient of von Meier's diagrams to know the basic layout of the place, but he was also aware of Iram's very great complexity, its interlacing networks of tunnels and corridors, both natural and man-made, that added up to well over one hundred miles of underground passages. Not every opening was shown on von Meier's plans, which concentrated only on the main arteries. A man could indeed become irretrievably lost there, wandering the maze of tunnels until strength gave out and he was forced to lie down among the dead, knowing he was already one of them.

The tunnel into which David had run was no more than that—a plain, unlit channel bored through solid rock to provide a short cut between two larger thoroughfares. It was not shown on any of von Meier's charts, but the logic of the city's layout at this point made its purpose and its extent reasonably clear. The real problems would come later, when he reached the necropolis region beyond the Temple, an area virtually uncharted by von Meier. If there had been any radical changes in the disposition of the mortuary tunnels in the area of his search since the reign of Jehoahaz, he might never locate the underground chamber and might conceivably lose himself in trying to do so.

He came out, as expected, into a lighted corridor, empty at this hour of passersby. From there it was but a short distance to the Temple, a place he had visited briefly only once, intending to examine it more carefully at a later date. He entered the Temple abruptly by a low doorway set in its upper end.

It was a vast hollow of cathedrallike proportions, a natural cavern that had been formed with the rock itself, then further cut and shaped by the hand of man and buttressed in its center by a single massive pillar of reinforced stone. Only the bottom half of the great chamber was permanently lit, by means of flames kept burning in tanks of oil in a hollow space below the floor, the light shining into the Temple through shafts cut in the rock between the two levels. The upper portion, into which David stepped, was shrouded in its own primitive darkness, hooded in the grim sanctity of unlightedness, like a pantheon dedicated to the gods of the underworld. He passed through it nervously while his small lamp burned without effect, merely serving to accentuate his smallness and fragility in that place.

When he came to the illuminated portion of the great cavern he breathed more easily, as if the darkness had somehow congested his lungs, rendering the vast open space claustrophobic to him. He was conscious of his vulnerability, walking there at a time when most inhabitants of the city were asleep, knowing he could find little explanation for being in the Temple were he challenged. There was something about the place that had made Talal uneasy bringing him there, as though it contained some secret it were better David did not know. Talal had allowed him only a few minutes inside and had restricted him to the lower part. When David had asked to return there in order to make a thorough examination, he had been told that it would require von Meier's express permission and that, until then, he should regard the Temple as out of bounds. It was tempting, now that he was there, to spend some time exploring the place, but he was pressed for time and eager to move on.

He left the Temple through a large carved gateway without doors and found himself in a broad, unlit passage flanked on either side by large niches, in each of which lay the mummified remains of a man or woman. The niches stretched from floor to ceiling. In the light cast by his lamp David could see only scraps of cloth and flashes of dried skin, exposed bone, or matted and cobwebbed hair, the everyday accouterments of ancient death. Uneasy memories of the ossuary at St. Nilus' flooded back, memories that he tried to suppress but could not wholly shut out from his consciousness. His tiny lamp shed only a small pool of light before him, allowing only a few feet of visibility. The true darkness began here.

From its size and the fine quality of the carving on the niches, David assumed he was in the "great tunnel" referred to in Elihoreph's text. He watched carefully for openings on his left and, when he reached the third, turned into it. The darkness seemed to intensify, though he knew it could not in reality have done so. The niches here were less well constructed and packed more closely together than those in the main tunnel. A curious musty smell mingled with spices came to David's nostrils out of the darkness, evoking memories that were not his memories. The floor was rough and uneven, making it difficult to keep his footing, threatening to betray him and hurl him forward, extinguishing his light. He walked carefully, counting the steps he took, keeping a close lookout for a tunnel branching off to the right. When he got to two hundred paces, no opening had yet appeared, and he began to fear that he had mistaken the directions after all or that the entrance had been blocked up, perhaps by orders of Jehoahaz himself, before his death.

Then, all at once, it was there, narrow and cobwebbed and utterly dark, like a mouth gaping into Sheol, the abode of the dead. As he stared at it, the cobwebs shook briefly as a denizen of the eternal darkness scuttled from the light. Suddenly he remembered the dream he had had in Jerusalem, the Christ figure with spiders crawling from his wounds, the bones in the ossuary, his father holding him transfixed, the great, funereal city filled with gray, silent figures whispering, "This is Iram, this is Iram." He could feel cold sweat break out on his forehead and his flesh creep. He felt as if he were reliving the nightmare and wondered if he were not, after all, asleep in the library. But the light flickered and shone on a sliver of yellow bone and he knew he was awake and alone in the darkness with the silent ghosts of Iram.

Ducking under the thick cobwebs, he entered the tunnel. Little sounds came to him, the scurryings and scuttlings of rats and cockroaches disturbed by his passing. The only human beings such creatures knew were their playgrounds: David's presence threw their black world into turmoil. Here too the floor was unfinished. What use, after all, had the dead for polished pavements or marble floors? Cautiously, David advanced through the dark, a step at a time, straining to make out the path in front, fighting down an old fear that someone or something crept along behind him, stalking him, waiting for him to pause.

He came at last to the blank wall that marked the end of the tunnel. The floor here was covered in a thick layer of dust that had been much disturbed at one point, but not, it seemed, for a very long time. David laid his lamp on the ground, knelt down, and began to scrabble about in the dust. The ring was there, as Elihoreph had said it would be, recessed in the stone. It lifted free and David positioned himself to pull on it. He heaved back with all his strength. Nothing happened.

Over the centuries, whatever mechanism had permitted the slab

351

to pivot had locked itself into position. David sighed. It would probably take several men, if not a block and tackle, to dislodge it now. He bent and and pulled again. Still nothing. Then he noticed a small hole set at a little distance from the ring. Brushing aside some of the dust around it, he noticed that the hole lay at the end of a short, angled channel. It was possible, just possible that . . . Carefully, terrified lest he extinguish the light, he tipped his lamp gently toward the little runnel in the stone. A thin stream of oil ran out, along the narrow channel, and into the hole.

He waited for the oil to take effect, then heaved hard again on the ring. There was a slight movement. He rested, easing his hands, flexing his fingers, then resumed work, bracing his legs, throwing all his strength into the backward pull. There was a low grinding noise and he felt the stone shift momentarily beneath his feet. Redistributing his balance, feet astride, he pulled again. This time the movement continued, and suddenly he felt the slab give and begin to slide with his pulling, freeing itself of the accumulated dust under which it had lain for so long. It came easily now, pivoting on a stone axle, counterweighted somewhere below the surface.

David leaned the edge of the slab against the side wall and picked up his lamp. At his feet a flight of narrow stone steps led down into a dark shaft. Awkwardly, he turned and began to descend the steps backward, uncertain of his balance should he go down directly. There were nineteen steps in all, ending in a stone floor at the bottom of the shaft. At the foot of the steps the opening widened out considerably, and when David turned and raised his lamp he found himself standing in a vestibule of sorts, in front of a double metal door about seven feet high.

The door had been fashioned from beaten copper in which Hebrew lettering had been incised and inlaid with gold and silver. The lettering was ancient and difficult to read, but it was not hard to translate the wording of the well-known biblical verse: "Draw not nigh hither: put off thy shoes from off thy feet, for the place whereon thou standest is holy ground." David recognized the words as those addressed to Moses by God on Mount Horeb, when he saw the burning bush and heard the voice of the divinity for the first time. In the center of the door, just below the incised verse, were two wax seals, one bearing the name of the High Priest Amariah, the other that of King Jehoahaz, together with curses on whoever violated them to pass the door and enter the chamber beyond.

David felt at one and the same time a sense of awe that made him want to retreat, as if he were about to violate the holiest of his father's religious laws, and a surge of excitement impelling him to open the door. He knew now he had not come in vain, that the chamber would not be empty. But it was as if his father stood beside him, whispering in his ear, warning him against the blasphemy he was about to perpetrate. David was neither a priest nor a Levite, he had no right to stand here so close to the holiest of holy things. But he was an archaeolgist and a disbeliever, and surely he had come to deliver what he had found into the hands of his people. He reached out his right hand and touched the seal of Jehoahaz. It came away lightly and he set it on the ground. Then he reached out again and touched the seal of Amariah. Like an ill omen, it broke and crumbled at his touch, falling in shards to the floor. His hand shook. He was trembling. Fear and excitement mingled in his veins, unsettling him, making his heart race. The roof of his mouth felt dry and his breath came in short gasps. The air in the vestibule was stale and heavy, scarcely fit to breathe. His lamp burned dangerously low, starved of oxygen. He set it to one side and pushed against the door.

The dry hinges protested loudly as they were made to turn. The door opened slowly. It had settled over the centuries, and the bottom edges of its leaves scraped against the stone floor. The left-hand leaf stuck halfway and would not be budged another inch, but that on the right continued to move, albeit with some resistance, until it was fully open. David waited a little for the air to improve, then picked up his lamp and held it high at the opening.

The chamber into which he gazed was small, as Elihoreph had described it: six cubits by four by five—about nine feet by six by seven and a half. The walls and ceiling were bare of any decoration—unpainted, uncarved, unfrescoed. The marks of the chisel could still be seen here and there, raw wounds that centuries had not healed. Time could not, after all, heal all things, David thought. His light flared and flickered in the foul air, casting weird shadows on the formless rock.

On a stone plinth, raised about two feet from the ground, stood an object swatched in precious cloths. It was rather smaller than he had expected, almost four feet long, two wide, and four high. He knew what it was even before he stepped forward to remove the cloths. No longer frightened, yet still filled with a sense of awe and trepidation, he lifted the first cloth, the cloth of silk. Beneath it was a cloth embroidered with silver thread, and beneath that another into which strands of pure gold had been woven.

His hand shook as he drew away the cloth of gold and let it fall where the others lay upon the ground. He felt a tightness in his chest and a constriction in his throat and his eyes blinked as he gazed on the object he had uncovered. He did not have to ask what it was. What else could it be? What else? He felt the breath leave his body and his heart come almost to a standstill. It was beautiful and frightening and heavy with age. He thought he had never seen such antiquity in an object before, though he had observed and handled things much older than it many times. It was as if it was the oldest thing in the world, yet utterly new, reborn before him in this tiny chamber: the Ark of the Covenant and, above it, the Mercy Seat.

The light seemed to multiply, leaping and dancing, refracted a thousand times in a river of gold. On the bottom was the Ark itself, a chest of lambent, coruscating gold in which were placed the tablets of the law. On top of it stood the Mercy Seat, at either end a golden angel with its pointed wings upraised. The angels faced each other like lovers eternally parted, and their gold wings over-shadowed the chest beneath, as the branches of a broad tree shadow the ground.

He could not tell how long he stood there transfixed, gazing on the Ark. Hours might have passed, or days, he had lost all consciousness of time and place, all awareness of self. There was nothing but the Ark, it formed his whole world, his whole being, his past, present and future. He saw himself reflected in the gold, his thin body, his tangled hair, his staring eyes, yet he felt unaware of his own existence, as if he had somehow merged with the Ark and become one with it, losing his separateness in its shining, translucent depths.

It was the light that roused him in the end. It began to tremble, a signal that the oil was burning dangerously low. There would be enough to get back to the lighted regions of the inhabited sectors, but only if he left right away. Reluctantly, he covered the Ark once more in its cloths, the gold underneath, the silk on top. That done, he turned and left the small room that had served for so many centuries as the Holy of Holies, unknown and undisturbed. He closed the double doors behind him, but as he left his foot trod on the shards of Amariah's seal, breaking the fragments yet further. He hoped the old priest, if he were watching him, would understand and forgive.

Once at the top of the stairs, he debated whether or not to close the slab. He feared that, if he did so, the mechanism might not operate a second time and the Ark would be sealed inside its tomb forever, unless he could bring a team of men to raise the stone. Who, after all, would come here? he reasoned. It would be safer to leave the slab as it was.

He turned to go and, as he did so, his foot slipped on a patch of oil that had spilled there when he had poured some into the hole in the stone. He pitched forward and the lamp left his hand, landing several feet away and breaking into fragments, like Amariah's seal. The flame sputtered for a moment, then died. Darkness filled everything like water running into an empty pool.

FORTY-TWO

When the desert bites, it bites hard. There is nothing soft about it, nothing facile or blandly redemptive. It is merciless because it is lifeless and soulless. Nothing goes into it or comes out of it unchanged, yet it itself remains changeless and aloof, self-sufficient in sand and rocks and thorns. It gives no second chances and precious few first. An inch off course becomes a yard, a yard a furlong, and a furlong a mile—distance enough and more for a man to pass the last well unawares, heading deeper and deeper into the final sands. There are no margins in the desert, no fat, no residue— just lean flesh and bones. It kills you when you have your back turned, creeps up behind you with its mirages, its dried wells, its scorpions, its flash floods, its piercing frosts. It crawls inside you, deep beneath the surface of your skin, with its heat and cold, its dust and silence, its vast distances and its tiny narrow places where nothing, not even a spider, can breathe, gnawing, consuming, eroding.

It took them three days to reach the borders of Iram. Three days of unrelieved misery as cold and thirst and hunger took their heavy toll. They each had a few dates in their robes, kept over from the handfuls Nazzal had brought them during the storm: they hoarded them avariciously, eating a tiny amount once a day, enough to provide a little energy, not enough to stave off the pangs of hunger. Once they found a small *khabra*, a pool of rainwater at the foot of some rocks, covered with a thin crust of red sand. The water was bitter and slightly salty, but they drank it greedily until they could take no more. They had nothing in which to carry the rest with them, so they left it behind and carried on, plodding eastward through an unchanging expanse of dead sand.

There was no mistaking it when they reached it. They woke on the third day, huddled together for warmth, dirty, foul-smelling, covered with sores and blisters. Like automata, they began to walk, hour giving way to hour of dark monotony. There were heavy clouds that day, and everything looked washed out, sullen and transparent. They were reaching the edge of their strength. It was almost noon when Scholem stopped and looked around, his eyes scanning the desert.

"Leyla," he called. His voice was weak and cracked.

She stopped, a few paces ahead of him.

"Yes, what is it?"

"Look at it, Leyla, look at it! That is it, I'm sure of it!"

She looked. Imperceptibly, the landscape about them had changed. Where there had been foliage, there was now nothing, not even *ghada* or *'arfaj*. In place of bushes, harsh rocks protruded from the sand. The dunes had given way to a flat region interspersed with outcroppings of sandstone and occasional salt flats. A thin wind hissed across the surface of the sand, causing it to rise like a fine, drifting smoke. There were no birds in the sky, not even the ubiquitous bustards. The color of the sand had changed: it seemed paler here, drained of its rich redness as a corpse is drained of blood. The rocks had a beaten and weathered look, pitted and scored by endless ages of eroding wind and rain. A brooding silence hung over everything, deeper and more menacing than the silences of the outer sands.

Leyla turned to Scholem. He was still staring around him, unable to tear his eyes away from the extremity of desolation that stretched on every side.

"It feels old," she whispered, her voice subdued, awed. "It started here: the sand, the desert . . . everything."

It was an ancient place, older and more worn away than any they had yet been in. They could feel it in their bones, the dark, abiding antiquity of the primeval wasteland. Nothing lived here, nothing had grown here for long, windswept millennia. Even the bones of the dead and the fossils of whatever creatures had walked here at the dawn of time had been ground to dust and scattered among the sands.

"This is the place al-Halabi wrote about," Leyla murmured. "He said that Iram was set in the midst of a dead place, the Valley of Barhut, where the souls of unbelievers are assembled before being

357

cast into hell. We're in the right place, Chaim. Iram is in here somewhere. All we have to do is find it."

They walked on, alert now, watching for a sign, for anything that would give them a clue to the whereabouts of Iram. But all they saw was sand and rock and salt. They spent the night in each other's arms again. There was nothing sexual in their embrace. The desert had erased all inessentials. They craved nothing but food, water, and warmth. There was no firewood to be found, and even if there had been, they had nothing with which to light it. Even before dawn broke, they set off again.

They found the airplane midmorning. At first they thought it was another outcrop of red sandstone, then, as they came closer, they saw the unmistakable outline of the tail plane sticking up into the sky. Something about the plane's shape seemed wrong, so they approached it cautiously, watching all the time for signs of movement. There were none. They drew nearer. The plane had obviously crashed: it was sitting with its nose partly buried in the sand, its tail at an angle. One of the wings had sheared off on impact and lay about three hundred yards to the rear of the plane.

At about fifty yards, they could make out the rest. What they had taken for the redness of sandstone was, in fact, the color of rusted metal. Less anxious, they walked up to the wreck. When they were still about thirty feet away Scholem suddenly froze and stood staring at the tail. Leyla came up behind him.

"What is it, Chaim? What's wrong?"

"Don't you see it?" he asked. "Up there, on the tail plane." He pointed and she followed his finger.

Eroded by years of sand and rain, a faded decal could still be seen. Pitted and rust-stained though it was, it was unmistakable: a plain black swastika tilted at an angle and outlined in white. Lower down, on the side of the fuselage, they could make out the shape of a broad black cross with equal-sized arms. They could just make out letters and numbers beside it: C8 on the left, BF on the right.

"I don't understand this at all," said Scholem. "I recognize this plane. It's a BV-144, a passenger and transport plane developed by Blohm und Voss in . . . oh, somewhere around 1943. They built some prototypes in occupied France, but nothing ever came of it in the end because the Germans had to abandon the factory in 1944. It makes no sense for one to be here. No sense at all. There was no fighting here. Not even near here, except for Iraq during the Rashid Ali coup—and this plane was only on the drawing board then."

"What do the letters stand for, do you know?" Leyla asked.

"I'm not sure exactly. They're Luftwaffe unit codes, of course. The ones on the left—the C8—identify the unit the plane belonged to. I think C8 was a transport unit, but I'm not sure: it's a long time since I read about such things. BF stands for the Staffel, the squadron."

They walked around the plane, as if by doing so they could find some meaning in its presence here in the heart of the Nafud. The windows were intact but grimy, covered with a thick coat of sand. Scholem hauled himself up onto the one intact wing and crawled along it to the fuselage, where a door was set. Leyla followed him.

The door was closed tightly and rusted on its hinges. They heaved and pulled at it, but it resisted all their efforts. Leyla climbed down and found a small rock a short distance away. Walking up to the nearest window, she smashed it. When the sand and dust had settled, she peered inside. She could make out dark, inchoate shapes, but there was too little light to tell what they were. Still carrying the stone, she clambered back onto the wing, where Scholem was still vainly attempting to force the door open. She handed the rock to him, then skimmed down over the edge in order to find another for herself. This time she took a larger one and heaved it up onto the wing before pulling herself up after it.

Together they pounded the heavy rusted lock until their hands were raw and their breath came in ragged gasps. Long years of successive burning heat and freezing cold had acted on the aircraft's metal, stretching and tightening it like the skin of a drum. Steel that had been pressed and welded to withstand the pressures of high-altitude flight had been weakened severely. It was rust more than anything that blocked their way into the fuselage. A last cracking blow forced the door open a fraction. It opened inward, and all they had to do was push. Putting their shoulders against the flat surface, they heaved. The hinges protested loudly, but in the end they gave way for the first time in forty years. The door moved inward slowly, blocked partially by something that lay behind it.

With a final screech, the door shuddered open. A cloud of dust billowed, then settled slowly, letting what light there was stream into the plane's dim interior. Scholem stepped inside, followed closely by Leyla. A heavy, fetid smell clawed at his throat and nostrils, causing him to gag. It felt airless, stale, like an unopened tomb. He breathed more slowly, taking in a little fresh oxygen from the air that was now coming in through the doorway. Gradually, his eyes adjusted to the weak light. He took his rock with him and smashed several more windows near the door. It helped a little, but not much.

As he stepped further inside, his eye was caught by something on the floor behind the door. A skeleton, wrapped in the tattered remains of a German military uniform, lay sprawled and partly broken where it had been pushed by their forced entry. Patches of hair and flesh still clung grotesquely to the bone head. It grinned up at Scholem, as if apologizing for having tried so hard to keep him out. He stepped gingerly past it and went deeper into the fuselage. Leyla came with him, fighting down a growing panic, an urge to run back out into the desert, where, in spite of everything, the air was clean and fresh.

In some ways they were both grateful for the lack of proper light. Horrible as the semidarkness was, it mercifully concealed as much as it showed. The plane had been converted into a private passenger aircraft, spacious and luxuriously appointed. They could make out a dining table and chairs toward the rear, a small desk, a couch, and several easy chairs, all bolted to the floor and covered in a fine layer of dust. The rest of the fuselage was taken up with regular aircraft seating, widely spaced and comfortable, with enough seats for about twenty people. All but one of the seats was occupied. Nothing had been touched. Everything was as it had been on the day of the crash. Leather straps dangled helplessly from the ceiling, as if awaiting a passenger's hand. Two rows of lights stretched the length of the fuselage, intact, canopied in glass, as if a touch on a switch would serve to set them alight again. Beneath its cover of sand, a dark blue carpet ran between the rows of seats, ready to be swept and walked on once more. A glass that had been in someone's hand before he died lay on the floor, curiously unbroken, as if put there to be picked up and filled with wine.

Scholem walked slowly down the aisle, between the two rows of seats, ten on either side in pairs. The bodies lay sprawled in the seats, still held in their places by broad canvas straps. The desert air had preserved them well. Tight leathery skin still covered their bones; coarse, matted hair dressed their shrunken skulls. Their clothing had rotted badly, but it was still recognizable. Three of them were women, dressed in faded cotton frocks, their bodies twisted and turned by their final agonies. The rest were men, several in Wehrmacht or SS uniforms, three or four in civilian garb. Scholem had once worked on an assignment that involved the arrests of former Nazis, and he knew a little about the uniform and insignia of the Third Reich. As he walked between the rows of seats he quickly reached the conclusion—obvious enough from the furnishings and layout of the aircraft itself—that these had been unusually important passengers.

Leyla found him near the front of the fuselage, staring as if mesmerized at the remains of a man and a woman. The man was dressed in military clothes, but without visible regalia or decorations, except for a single Iron Cross, above and below which were two small circular badges; an eagle with spread wings had been stitched to the left sleeve. Scholem could not tear his eyes away. Leyla joined him, puzzled at his behavior, then, as she looked, she realized why he was staring, who the man and the woman were, and understood why he stood there, as if nailed to the spot. Only one man in the Third Reich had worn that uniform, that calculated simplicity that spoke in muted terms of absolute power. They stood there side by side for a long time without moving, then Leyla put an arm around Scholem and held him tightly to her side.

"We have to go, Chaim," she said softly. "They're dead now. He's as much a corpse here as he would have been in Berlin. Nothing's changed."

He nodded and drifted back to her out of his reverie.

"First I want to look in the cabin," he said, turning and opening the door that divided the cockpit section from the passengers.

It was dark in the cabin, shut off almost entirely as it was from light that came from the rear of the plane. Scholem trod carefully through the heavy dust that covered the cabin floor. The windows at the front had shattered on impact, letting sand in. The pilot and copilot were sitting hunched over their controls, as if still vainly trying to pull the aircraft out of its last dive. Scholem turned and came back into the body of the fuselage.

The dead sat in their seats, row after row, staring at him with innocent, accusing eyes, eyes that were not eyes at all but mere sockets of bone. He closed the cabin door behind him and walked on down the gangway again, to where Leyla stood at the back.

She had gathered up some papers from the floor beside the desk and was thrusting them into the fold of her robe. As Scholem approached, she stood up and gestured toward the dining area.

"Look," she said. "The table was laid. They'd just finished their last meal."

A tattered cloth hung on the table. Several plates, dirty and covered in mold, still lay on it, but the bulk of the tableware had crashed to the floor during the crash and lay there in a tangled, filthy heap: crystal goblets, bone china, silver cutlery, all smashed or covered in the red dust of the Nafud.

Scholem made his way over the debris, past the table to the rear inside door.

"There must have been a galley in there," he said.

He opened the door and forced his way in. Everything was a mess. Four bodies lay twisted on the floor amidst a heap of pots, pans, and cooking utensils. From their clothes, or what was left of them, Scholem guessed they had been a chef and three orderlies. He picked his way through the mess and opened the cupboards along the side, one after the other.

The food, like the flesh, had rotted or dried up long ago. But in the third cupboard along Scholem found something he had been looking for: five unopened bottles of white wine, along with something he had hoped for but not really expected to find: two bottles of Apollinaris mineral water. Ever since he had left the corpse at the front of the plane, he had wondered whether there might be any spring water on board. The dead man had always taken some at meals.

In the next cupboard along he found soemthing he had not anticipated: a stack of metal boxes, each about seven inches by five and two inches deep. On the lid was the word *"Notproviant* [Emergency Rations]," alongside a stylized eagle holding a swastika. The boxes were vacuum sealed and had not been opened. Scholem took a box from the pile and pulled a tag on one end. It opened silently. Inside, sealed in foil, he found a variety of foodstuffs, all decayed now, with the exception of some hard crackers wrapped separately, that had somehow survived the years without visible deterioration. Carefully, he bit into one. It tasted a little like sawdust—or at least what he thought sawdust would taste like—but it was edible. One by one, he took down the boxes, opened them, and extracted the packs of crackers. This little hoard he then transferred to two empty boxes.

In a nearby drawer he found a corkscrew, rusted but still serviceable. He pocketed it and carried the bottles and boxes out of the galley to where Leyla was waiting. Handing them to her, he removed the cloth from the table and tore it roughly in two. It was rotten, but it would hold. He prepared two bundles of boxes and bottles, handed one to Leyla, and set down another for himself.

"Wait here," he said, and went back into the galley. Leyla saw him fumble about again among the debris. A minute later he returned carrying a small box of matches and two rusty carving knives.

"They're not very sharp," he said. "But we need weapons of some sort. These will have to do for the moment."

"Will the matches work?" Leyla asked.

"I don't know. They seem dry enough."

He opened the box and, taking out a match, struck it on the edge. It flared up at once, illuminating briefly the musty interior of the plane and sending a multitude of shadows scuttling in every direction. Scholem looked, surveying the scene. Suddenly he felt cold and uneasy, an intruder among the dead, himself too close to death now to be comfortable there.

"I think we should go," he said as the match burned down and died. Leyla nodded mute agreement. They made their way to the door and stepped outside. Though it seemed an action with no purpose, they closed the door again as best they could. Perhaps they were afraid of ghosts, ghosts that were better left in their iron tomb until the patient desert in its own time reclaimed what belonged to it.

When they had walked a distance from the plane, Leyla turned to Scholem and asked, "How do you think they died?"

"I'm not sure," he replied. "Not in the crash, that's obvious. They were all seated, except for the man at the door. They may have flown too high by accident and died from lack of oxygen. Or perhaps there were fumes after the crash landing. The man at the door may have been trying to open it when he died."

"But here, here in the Nafud. It doesn't make sense. Nothing makes sense any longer."

Scholem stopped and looked at her.

"On the contrary," he said, his voice tight and earnest, "it's all beginning to make a lot of sense. And the more it makes, the less I like it."

FORTY-THREE

They mixed the wine with the water and drank it slowly, without gratitude. Neither believed in God, neither believed in the man whose water it had been—who else was there to thank? The crackers tasted dry, a little sour and very old, but they stayed down on a second attempt. They hoarded the bottles like misers, afraid to squander them, aware of the miles that might yet lie between them and the nearest well—if there was a well. They were in the presence of Death, so they went quietly and with great circumspection, lest they disturb him. They never used the matches: there was no firewood anywhere, and even if there had been, a fire might have been dangerous, might have brought unwanted company. They felt conspicuous in the open sands, without cover or the least place in which to take shelter. Their every move was watched, or so they felt, their footsteps left a straggling, visible trail in the sand behind them.

Late on the second day they crossed what appeared to be a permanent track, the nearest thing they had seen to a road since Ma'an. It had clearly been in use for some time and was deeply imprinted with hoofmarks and footprints. Sand had blown across it in places, probably during the recent storm, but it was too well established to be wholly obscured.

"The yellow brick road," said Leyla.

Scholem smiled, then frowned in quick succession.

"Yes," he said. "But just who or what is waiting at the other end? It won't be the Wizard of Oz."

"I think we should take it all the same."

He nodded.

"I agree. We have very little choice."

Following the track, the going became easier for them. Easier, but more dangerous. If anyone were to travel along it, whether coming or going, they could not fail to see Scholem and Leyla. The path went almost straight, winding at times only to avoid large obstacles, like dunes or hollows. It was more ancient than they had at first thought. At intervals they passed pillars of weathered sandstone, on top of which stood tall figures, whether of men, angels, or demons it was impossible to say, so badly had they been worn away.

That night they lay huddled together in a small hollow of sand about seventy yards from the road. There was a moon, flat and deathly pale in a coal-black sky, but they were too tired to continue walking. Scholem held Leyla tightly from behind, his breathing shallow, unable to sleep. A shaft of moonlight revealed her to him: dirty, her face pinched and colorless her hair unwashed. She seemed almost squalid, her beauty turned to ugliness by hunger and exhaustion. The desert had thinned her, burning away the soft flesh, reducing her, taking away all that was superfluous. He felt desire for her but, like her body, it had been thinned and weakened by the desert until there was no strength left in it. They lay wretchedly on the cold, dark sand, bereft even of passion, their minds and bodies drained of all emotion and all sensation. A mood of dark despair came over him, torn between desire and the inability to express it even as a need. The desert had entered him: he no longer moved in it, it moved in him. He held Leyla in his desperation, his hands on her narrow, jutting hips, his head pressed against her back. They lay like that until the night took away all feeling and all pain. If there was a God, He preferred to skulk in the darkness, out of sight.

In the morning they ate and drank a little before setting off once more down the camel track. Toward noon Leyla saw something in the distance. For some time the sand had been rising again in dunes, and at first she took it for taller hills. After that it vanished for a while as the road wound its way through a range of high dunes, only to reappear, sharper and larger than before. Whatever it was, it was not hills and it was not sand. From the distance, it appeared black in color and very large.

The pillars became more frequent, one appearing every hundred yards or so. Some of the figures could now be seen to have folded wings, but on none of them were the features discernible. It was like an Egyptian tomb in which the priests had effaced the features of a king whose blasphemies had outraged the gods and condemned him to everlasting oblivion.

They walked on, listening carefully for the sound of feet or voices that might alert them in time to the approach of a rider or a group of riders from the other side of the next dune. Once or twice the pillars vanished and the track twisted abruptly to the left or right, evidence that here and there the sands had shifted over the centuries.

As they drew closer, Scholem suggested that they leave the road and make their way indirectly around the dunes. It would slow them down badly, but they were both beginning to feel uneasy. Whatever lay ahead of them could be guarded.

It was. As they rounded the base of one tall dune, Scholem grabbed Leyla and threw her down heavily, dropping behind her with a soft crash.

"What do you . . . ?" she began, breaking off as she caught sight of Scholem's face.

"Shhh!" he hissed, gesturing at the top of the next dune. He crept toward her and whispered quickly in her ear: "There's someone up there. I don't think he saw us. Stay down. I'll go up again."

He crawled to the corner of the dune, then, carefully scraping sand away, formed a small hollow through which he could peer. The man was standing sideways to him, against the horizon. He was dressed in Bedouin clothes, entirely in black. Over his shoulder he carried a submachine gun on a strap, and in his left hand he held a walkie-talkie, into which he was speaking. He appeared calm, and Scholem was confident he had not seen them.

Scholem slipped back down the dune to where Leyla was waiting.

"It's a guard of some sort," he whispered. "He's armed and he has a radio. At a guess, there'll be one like him on every dune from here on. If this is Iram, it has a cordon around it."

"Can you see the city?"

"Not yet, but it must be close."

"How do we get past the guards?" Leyla was tired. She wanted to come to Iram now, to know that her journey was over. If being here meant death, she wanted to embrace it, just as she would have

366

embraced Scholem the night before had he asked her to—directly, without caresses.

"Let's wait for darkness," he said. "We may be able to slip past or take the guard from behind. If al-Halabi's correct, we'll never be able to cross the open country around the city in daylight."

Leyla sighed. She wanted to see the city. It had obsessed her for so long now, lain in her blood like poison, invaded her dreams.

"Shouldn't we reconnoiter," she asked, "see what's ahead of us before going on?"

It made sense. If they lost their way or encountered an unexpected obstacle, it could prove fatal. So far they had evolved no plan, no firm idea of what to do, other than to find a way into Iram, locate David, and attempt to get him out. Their weapons were with their camels, hopelessly lost in the sands; they had no means of transport, no way of effecting an escape: if they were tackled, they could not fight back; if pursued, they could not get away. It was a futile gamble: but what else was there to do, where else could they go?

"All right," Scholem said. "We'll take a look. Any ideas?"

"We could take out the guard," she answered. "But if we do we'll have to go right in before someone raises the alarm."

"Too risky. Can we distract him?"

Leyla thought. It seemed impossible, but there must be a way. Then she remembered something she had seen once in Sinai, a boy's trick. It would mean taking a risk, but it might work.

"Did you see a camel?" she asked.

"No," said Scholem. "If he came on one, he'll have left it at the foot of the dune."

"I'll go around. Have you still got the box of matches?"

He cast her a puzzled look.

"Yes," he said. "Here." He reached into his robes and drew out the box. Leyla took it.

"Wait here," she said. "If you think he's seen me, get away from here."

She said nothing more. Like a shadow, she moved off along the rest of the dune, careful, careful, inching her way. The guard would not be too alert. It surprised her that there were any at all in a place that no one ever visited. She came around the side of the dune. The camel was there as she had expected, hobbled, squatting quietly on the ground. But the animal hardly attracted her attention; it was an irrelevance, a distraction. She froze, rooted to the spot. It lay before her: Iram and the great plain around it. It was vaster, taller, and more cruel than she had ever imagined. She tore her eyes away, frightened to waste time now.

Cautiously, she approached the animal from behind. She took the matches from the box, held them together in a bunch, and tied them with a long thread torn from her *ghotra*. Taking care not to startle it, she touched the camel gently on its hindquarters. It turned its head, staring at her, half alarmed. It had been hobbled with a rope tied around its left rear leg. She reached over and undid the knot, letting the rope fall loose to the ground. Grabbing the camel's tail with her right hand, she lifted it with a jerk and eased the bundle of matches into its anus. The beast grunted in protest but remained still. Leyla took a last match from the box and struck it against the side. It would not light. She struck it again, but still it failed to catch. The camel brayed loudly. Leyla took firm hold of the box and ran it against the bunched heads of the matches beneath the animal's tail. Three or four sputtered, then caught fire, igniting the rest in quick succession. She let them burn for a moment, then let go of the camel's tail. As the tail touched the flames, the beast roared loudly and staggered to its feet, Leyla slapped it hard on the flank and dashed back behind the dune.

Her heart beating wildly, she lay there, peering around the edge of the low hill.

"Run, you bastard!" she whispered. "Run!"

The camel ran, lifting its tail away from the flames, roaring and kicking as it dashed across the sand, away from Leyla. Moments later she saw the guard run down the slope, shouting and waving his arms. The matches would burn down in a moment or two, but the camel would keep running. If it was frightened enough, it would void its bowels: there would be no trace left of the matches.

Leyla ran back to Scholem.

"It worked," she said.

"What did you do?" he asked.

"I'll tell you later," she said. "Come on, we may not have much time."

They turned to the spot where Leyla had just been.

There was a light mist on the ground, writhing, low down. A

burgeoning wind took it and stirred it all across the plain. For more than two miles in every direction the salt plain stretched out, gray and flat and cold, and in the center of it was Iram. A freak of nature, a mesalike formation of black, weathered sandstone rose about four hundred feet into the air. It was perhaps a mile and a half in length and half that in width. It was irregular, in both height and outline, cracked and fissured in places, immeasurably ancient. In the distant past, regular floods had eroded large sections of the rock's lower half, carving it in the shape of rough, uneven pillars, some of them with a girth of many yards, others thin and fragile-looking: the Pillars of Iram.

Even from a distance they could see how the hand of man had transformed the living rock, terracing and buttressing it, bejeweling it with porches and cornices and pilasters, old wind-shaped caves opened up and embellished with doors and gateways. Staircases wound about the thickest pillars and ran along the face of the rock, cut deep into the body of the sandstone, steep and perilous. Grooved channels lay ready to take the rains of winter down to deep tanks far below, where they could be stored for use in summer. The red stone had been worked and polished and tunneled, the elaboration of centuries. The style was a complex mixture of ancient Babylonian and Hellenistic, like a combination of a ziggurat and Petra, gigantic yet refined.

All about the central rock of Iram the plain was dotted with small buildings, erected from stone quarried in the course of tunneling out the city itself. Most had fallen into ruin and lay in confusion, partially covered by little heaps of drifted sand. The camel track ran like an arrow to the city, ending at the opening to a massive stairway, each side of which was flanked by great lions of pitted stone. For its entire course, as it crossed the plain to Iram, the road was flanked by tall, winged statues, similar to those encountered earlier but in better condition and with their broad wings unfolded. The gray mist rolled sickly at their feet and they seemed suspended, as if hovering in the air on their outstretched, unmoving pinions. Beyond the figures Scholem and Leyla could make out rows of what appeared to be pits: wells possibly, or excavations of some kind. Near them, small pylons stood here and there, the purpose of which they could not guess. A few camels roamed about, feeding on vegetation that had been left for them in ancient sandstone basins

369

or drinking water from troughs.

They scanned the plain for as long as they dared, imprinting on their memories the layout of the pits, pylons, and buildings, the configuration of the rock itself. Only close and prolonged observation could tell them which were the least used entrances, which would be the easiest and safest way into the city. Only the Devil could help them find a way out again. The guard had caught his camel at last and was riding it back; it seemed jittery and roared from time to time. That was understandable. Leyla and Scholem scuttled back out of sight, taking shelter behind a more distant dune, well away from the edge of the plain.

Their water was almost gone and the vinegary wine was too strong to take on its own. In their weakened condition, it made them sick and lightheaded. They mixed a little of it with the last of the water and took it in sips. If they ever drank again, it would be within the confines of Iram.

Night fell rapidly and completely, covering them in damp, stifling darkness. They prayed there would be no moon, otherwise they could not hope to cross the open plain undetected. For hours they waited, biding their time until activity in Iram might have ceased or at least died down. Toward midnight they began to move. Cautiously they returned to the dune from behind which they had gazed into the plain earlier that day. The guard—or a replacement—was still there: a black silhouette against a black skyline. He should not have been visible at all. Leyla slipped to the side of the dune and looked out. All across the plain, small fires burned on the pylons, red and green and white, casting an eerie glow over everything, giving a semblance of life to the winged figures and an aura of hellish anger to the salt flat. In the windows of Iram yellow lights burned, ghoulish and unreal, like candles in a Halloween pumpkin face.

There was no real option: they would have to take the risk. By taking a winding route that could keep them at the maximum distance from the pylons, they might still hope to avoid detection. One at a time, they stepped out into the red darkness and began the last and most perilous stage of their journey. They felt naked and exposed, prepared at every moment to hear a challenging shout. Yard by yard they crept through the flickering dark. Leyla's heart was beating wildly and her mouth was dry. She tried to swallow and could not. She felt as if she was walking through molten glue, held to the spot at every step, unable to break and run for cover.

How they did it neither could guess, but after what seemed an eternity they reached the shadow of a thick pillar near the north end of the city. Iram towered above them, its black bulk blotting out the sky. They had headed in this direction because there seemed to be fewer lights. The stairway that wound up above their heads was unlit, leading by a gradual ascent into blackness, a blackness deeper and more menacing than that of the night through which they had just passed.

Scholem led the way upward. The stone steps were rough, cut deeply into the pillar, without rail or handhold of any kind. They had to press themselves tightly against the face of the pillar, climbing by touch, like blind mountaineers without ropes or grappling irons. At the top a wooden hatch barred the way. Scholem pushed upward, fearing it would be locked from inside. It was not. It gave to his push, creaking on unoiled hinges, and rose. A thin light shone in the opening above, yellow, like a corpse light on a winter marsh. Scholem put his head through the opening. He could see a long passageway stretching away on either side of the opening, lit at long intervals by curious lamps set in the walls. It seemed empty. He climbed through the opening and stepped out onto a smooth, flagged floor. Suddenly he froze. Behind him, he heard the sound of a heavy footstep. A voice rang out.

"Was machen Sie da?"

Something curdled in Scholem's heart. Dark childhood memories rushed out from concealment and pinned him to the spot. The question snapped out in those tones, in that language! That voice came again.

"Drehen Sie sich herum!"

All down the long passageway he saw nothing but lights. His mother had walked down a long corridor like this one, freezing, tiled with white, and he had never seen her again. The voice insisted. He did as it asked. He turned.

A man in black robes was facing him, a short gun cradled in his hands. The robes were Arab, but unusually neat, more like a uniform than the casual garb of the Bedouin. And the hair was blond—a dirty shade, much tinted by the sun, but unmistakable. Blue eyes stared at him. The man walked toward him, holding the

371

gun in tight, nervous hands. A delicate tremor passed through his left cheek once and vanished.

"Woher kommen Sie? Sprechen Sie Mal schnell!"

Leyla's hand snaked out from below and gripped the man's ankle tightly. She pulled back hard and he staggered forward, falling heavily on top of Scholem with a pained grunt. Scholem felt momentarily stunned, then, as he collected his wits, the frozen horror of the previous moments left him. He grabbed for the man's gun, snatching it from him by the barrel and sending it skidding across the flagstones with a metallic screech. The man drew breath to shout for help. Before he could let the breath out again, Scholem rammed his right hand into his open mouth. The guard gagged and struggled to get to his feet. Scholem wriggled desperately, throwing his weight across the other's chest, his hand still pressed into his mouth.

Leyla clambered through the opening and launched herself onto the man's legs. He was not a big man, but he had a wiry strength that took her by surprise. His face was contorted with pain and frustration, his eyes big and popping as the pressure of Scholem's hand prevented him from exhaling properly.

"Your knife!" Leyla hissed. "For God's sake, use your knife!"

Scholem had never killed a man at close quarters before. In a gun battle with terrorists three or four times, in border raids often, in war many times—but with a knife, face to face, skin against skin, never. He reached inside his robe and drew out the carving knife. The man saw it and renewed his efforts, kicking, trying desperately to scream. He bit down hard on Scholem's right hand, his teeth tearing through the flesh, all his frantic strength in the bite. Scholem put the edge of the knife to his throat. The throat seemed so innocent, so undeserving of butchery. The man brought a knee up hard and caught Leyla in the ribs. She reeled but pressed down harder with her body. The man was grunting like a pig that knows it is being slaughtered, chewing on Scholem's hand in his frenzy. Scholem wanted to scream with the pain of the bite, but he fought it down, like bile, sour and bitter.

He cut with the knife against the desperate, straining throat, across the tight, purple veins. The blade was rusty and blunt, virtually useless. It cut a shallow gash into the side of the neck, little more than a surface wound, out of which a watery line of blood started oozing. The man's face was growing purple, and sheer panic filled his bulging eyes. His arms jerked convulsively, but Scholem lay on them, binding him like Abraham binding Isaac as he sawed crazily at his neck with the dull-edged knife. It began to cut more deeply, but slowly. It slipped on the smooth skin, without penetrating it. The thin blood seeped onto Scholem's fingers as he carved hopelessly, cursing the knife and the victim in the same breath.

"The point!" Leyla cried to him, desperate, knowing she could not hold the man down much longer.

Scholem brought the knife back and put the point against the side of the neck. It was difficult to find enough leverage. He pressed. The point refused to go in at first, the taut skin seemed to resist it, then it gave and the knife plunged in, not easily, sticking in the tightly bunched muscles. The guard's body heaved and horrible sounds came out of his mouth. Something thick and slimy was spewed over Scholem's hand as the man threw up. He pressed the knife harder, gaining some purchase, driving it down deep into the neck. The limbs jerked convulsively. Suddenly the man's hands were free, reaching up and taking Scholem by the neck, pulling his face down to his own. Scholem's right hand came away from his victim's mouth. He let go of the knife, leaving it dangling from the bloody mess in the neck. The man retched and tried to breathe in, wanting to live, wanting to scream in his agony. He choked, drowning on blood and vomit, dying. His hands fell away from Scholem's throat, lifeless.

They lay across the body for what seemed an age, though it was no more than a couple of minutes. When Leyla looked up she saw Scholem bent over the corpse, as if embracing it. She lifted him away and helped him to his feet. His hand was bleeding badly where the man had bitten him. Leyla tore a strip of cloth from the hem of her *dishdasha* and made a crude bandage, winding it tightly around the hand.

"That's the best I can do," she said. "Can you move the hand?"

"Not very well, but it'll serve."

"Let's get rid of this," she said, taking the body by the legs and pulling it toward the aperture through which they had entered the city. With his left arm, Scholem helped her. They dropped the guard through the opening, then lowered the wooden trapdoor into place. With luck, the body would lie undisturbed until morning or even later. Someone might miss the guard in a while, but there would not be a hue and cry immediately. Unless that someone also saw the blood, which lay in a gory pool on the floor.

Scholem picked up the knife, which had fallen from the dead man's neck, then stepped across to the submachine gun he had carried.

"Here," he said, handing it over to Leyla, "you'd better take this. My hand's next to useless for anything of that kind."

Leyla took the gun, then looked up and down the long, featureless corridor.

"Let's get out of this passage," she said.

They headed to the right, in the direction that would lead into the city. They were inside Iram, but they still had to locate David. And get out again.

Behind them, the pool of blood congealed in the cold night air.

FORTY-FOUR

Scholem's hands were still sticky with half-dried blood. He wiped them on his *'aba,* but the blood did not seem to come away, not wholly. His right hand throbbed with growing pain, his own blood mingling with that of his victim. He could smell the sweat that adhered to his body and clothes, its scent intensified indoors, combining with the curious odors of Iram itself. The city exuded a host of undefinable smells, the ghosts of perfumes and spices, traces of cinnamon, cassia, frankincense, and myrrh. Had Iram once been an entrepot on the trade route from the "aromatic south" of Arabia to the north, a depository for perfumes from Yemen and spices from distant India? Scholem inhaled deeply, but he could not free his nostrils from the acrid smell of sweat. Nor could he avoid the feeling that the delicacy of the phantom odors, at times so subtle that they seemed almost not to be there at all but to be merely impressions in his mind, concealed a deeper, darker perfume, a sweet scent of decay, of corruption, of ancient death.

The corridors along which he and Leyla walked were hollow and empty, devoid of life. Their feet made no sound on the cold stone. At every twist and turn of the passageways, they expected to be challenged, but there was no one. Evidently there were guards on the entrances but nowhere else . . . so far. From the outside, Iram had seemed vast and impregnable. Now they were inside, it had become a complex maze of lit and unlit passageways in which they were helplessly lost. Had it not been for the guards outside, they would have thought they were alone.

They had taken oil lamps from the wall near the spot where they had entered the city, and now the light from them was proving increasingly necessary. Leyla was the first to notice that the wall lamps were growing more and more infrequent. Presumably some parts of the city were used less often than others.

They could not say exactly when it occurred, but it finally became apparent to them that, apart from the small lamps in their hands, they were in total darkness. The passage they had entered seemed older and narrower than any of those they had passed through before, and a damp chill came from somewhere. Leyla held the lamp up high and cast the light around. They were in an ancient bazaar of some sort, with shops on either side, simple openings cut deep into the wall and raised up several feet above the floor, like the shops in the market of any traditional Arab city. Leyla went closer and looked into the first shop on her left. She gasped with astonishment.

The shop was still filled with goods. Tall pots and jars, flat dishes, small vials for oil or perfume, clay lamps—all the offerings of the potter's trade. There was the stool on which the shopkeeper had once sat, still in its place, a little rotten but intact, and there was what appeared to be an ancient water pipe, in which something other than tobacco must have been smoked. There was almost no dust. Everything seemed virtually pristine, untouched by either man or the centuries. The next shop was the same, and the next, each stocked with goods as if waiting for the owner to return and resume trading, for the customers to come and haggle. The lamps in their hands flickered over the assorted wares—figurines, jewelry, instruments for writing, knives, baskets—and conjured up shadows among them, like ghosts. Leyla shivered. In one shop there were tiny models of animals, little figures of men and women, tiny houses, and brightly coloured tops—toys for children long, long dead. Leyla turned to Scholem.

"I don't like it here," she said, "it gives me the creeps."

"Me too," he said. "It's like one of those museums in which everything's arranged to look as if you've stepped into the past, into an old room or a shop. . . . Except that this is real." He picked up one of the toys, a miniature camel with leather saddlebags. His daughter Ruth had once had a toy zoo, complete with lions and tigers and a long green crocodile that opened its jaws. There had been a camel too, with a long neck and two humps. The animals in

Ruth's zoo had been made of plastic and the one he held in his hand was carved from wood. But they were all the same: the abandoned playthings of dead children. He put the camel down.

They hurried on, guarding their fragile lamps from the moving air. The shops gave way after a while to what appeared to be living quarters, the doorways broken here and there, revealing dark, gaping openings. They went into one house, crossing the threhold with a sense of being intruders. As in the shops, everything was intact: chairs and tables and low, gilded beds. There were cooking utensils in a small, box like room at the back, and ashes still lay in the tiny hearth, above which there was a narrow opening, probably a chimney that wound through solid rock to the outside. Leyla stood mesmerized in the room; it was as if she had stepped directly into the past, as if the twentieth century and everything in it had been swept away. She crossed the room to a low connecting door and opened it.

In the next room the last inhabitants of the house lay huddled in one corner, as if they had died slowly in one another's arms. The flesh had rotted long ago, but fragments of clothing still clung to the still white bones. The smell of decay was very strong in the room. Leyla closed the door and walked away from it, out of the room, out of the house.

They entered a half dozen houses, each with its melancholy array of domestic trivia suspended in time, unchanged as if incorruptible, each with the bones of its former inhabitants and the sour smell of their death lingering in the background, like a vapor in the flat, stale air. A sense of brooding emptiness pervaded everything. What had killed the people of Iram? A plague, a virus brought into the city in a shipment of frankincense, the stench of disease smothered beneath tremendous heaps of the sweet-smelling resin? Mass suicide, whole families sharing a draught of poison? Leyla felt depressed. The city seemed like a vast rock tomb, a necropolis swept clean of everything but softly decaying bones. What could she achieve here? Who would care?

"There's nothing here, Chaim," she said, her voice echoing dully in the cold chambers of chiseled rock. "We have to find a way out, we have to get to David. We could die down here and no one would ever know."

"They'll be looking for us soon enough," he said, "as soon as they

377

find the man I killed. We can't waste time here. But we can't just rush in either. Let's try to get out of this section, then we can get hold of someone who can tell us where David is."

Before long they left the living area behind and entered an even stranger world of dark, natural passages, extended and widened to no obvious purpose. Perhaps this had been a region being prepared for habitation when disaster struck. Perhaps better light would reveal a function that the dark concealed. There were sinister, scurrying sounds and vague distorted echoes that seemed to come from far away and yet sounded at moments near at hand and menacing. Leyla came hear to panic, frightened that their lights would go out and leave them permanently lost in this maze of tunnels. It would have been wise to extinguish one lamp in order to conserve its oil, but the risk of proceeding with only light between them and final darkness appalled them both. They held hands tightly, more for comfort than out of necessity.

Suddenly, there were niches in the walls, horizontal niches that rose in tiers to a high ceiling out of sight. Their size and shape made it grimly apparent what their use had been. A little farther, Leyla discovered the first of the bodies, mummified and dressed in a plain white shroud. They passed between row after row of them, shriveled, cobwebbed things without eyes, pile upon moldering pile, stretching away forever. Side passages held more of them, hundreds, thousands, generations of forgotten dead. Small stone plaques carried inscriptions in a form of Hebrew script that neither Scholem nor Leyla could read, indecipherable as the bodies they commemorated. On some of the bodies small jewels caught the light and fine bands of gold coruscated like ripples as they passed with their lamps: in all the long centuries of Iram, the bodies of the dead had remained inviolate, immune from the depredations of tomb robbers, perfect in their ornamented decay. On others, small bunches of dried flowers still lay in withered hands. Leyla wondered where the flowers had come from, here in the inhospitable depths of the sands. She saw a child with a wooden doll, its face a contorted mask of panic, as if it lay in an unending nightmare, like the Mexican mummies Leyla had seen in photographs.

The sense of panic began to grow stronger within Leyla. The combination of ubiquitous darkness, tall, oppressive passageways, and endless rows of grimacing dead worked on her to produce a stifling, constricted sensation. She felt claustrophobia grip her and a desperate urge to run, to run until she broke free of the blinding darkness. She gripped Scholem's hand convulsively, clinging to him for some sort of support or comfort. He walked alongside her, ill at ease, superstitious in spite of himself, anxiety gnawing at him, as if he had been condemned to walk these dark, sweet-smelling corridors forever.

Suddenly Leyla stiffened and tightened her grip on Scholem's hand.

"I see a light," she whispered, "somewhere up ahead."

"I can't see anything."

"It's very faint, but I'm sure it's there. Let's keep moving."

They hurried now, ignoring the silent sleeping cohorts on either side of them. At last Scholem too could make out the light, a pale reddish glow on the edge of vision. The light grew in intensity as they went on, until they could finally make out what seemed to be a great monumental doorway out of which the red gleam was shining. With increasing caution, they approached it, as nervous now of the light as they had previously been of the darkness. The doorway rose up into shadow, fifty feet or more, flanked by flat pillars faced with glazed ceramic tiles, and topped by a massive entablature whose details could not be discerned. The tiles were decorated with numerous motifs—bulls, dragons, and flying figures like those on the pedestals they had seen earlier. Leyla unslung the machine gun and held it pitched ready to fire. Like toy soldiers, dwarfed by the great pilasters, they passed through the doorway.

The chamber into which they stepped was out of all proportion to everything that had gone before. The doorway had been a mere herald of its dimensions. They both knew instinctively—and David, had he been there, would have confirmed their view—that nowhere else in antiquity had there ever been such a hall. In its center, a massive pillar rose up into the shadows that concealed a ceiling high above. It must have measured at least twelve feet in diameter, like the trunk of a giant tree. Tall, undecorated pilasters flanked the walls. At the foot of each pilaster was a small, semicircular opening in the floor, out of which a reddish-golden light came from somewhere deep below. The light flickered and changed, casting mad shadows on the walls, now revealing, now concealing a series of small statues that stood in niches just above head height. Faces appeared and disappeared at random, eyes stared out momentarily and were veiled again, the great chamber was a shifting shadow play of nightmare images. It stood empty and silent, its lights flickering, as if it had been waiting for their arrival.

A flight of about a dozen steps took them down to floor level. As they descended, they felt smaller and smaller, rendered insignificant by the echoing hugeness of the place. The far end was in virtual darkness, for the subterranean lights did not extend that far. It made Leyla dizzy to look up toward the ceiling. She felt lonelier here than in the deserted streets or the long passages of the dead. Something in the place chilled her. All around her the bleak walls frowned, darkened and stained by age and soot from the fires below. It was all grandeur without feeling, cold, mathematical arrogance without warmth. It felt worn out and faded, like a graveyard long ago disused and left entirely to the elements and the dead. The walls had crumbled in places, revealing fresh stone beneath the blackened surface.

Leyla wanted to turn back, to retrace her steps through the long dead passageways until they found the entrance once more and returned to the fresh air of the desert. Her lungs felt coarsened by the stale, drowsy atmosphere of this place, and she was uneasy, as if a brooding presence hung over them in the vast and shadowed chamber. She was not superstitious. She believed in nothing outside herself: not in God or angels or ghosts or *jinn*. But here it was as if the place itself derided her unbelief and introduced small intimations of a diseased afterlife into her brain. Her reason felt corrupted by the indelicate hugeness of her surroundings. With one hand, she reached out for Scholem, linking her fingers lightly with his. His bandaged and bleeding fingers felt damp to her touch, a thin trace of blood lying like a secret between his skin and her skin.

They moved uneasily through the flickering dark. Something behind the shadows menaced them, but however Scholem moved his lamp, they could uncover nothing but deeper shadows, pale gestures against the red and troubled darkness. The true dimensions of the cavern were invisible to them, but they sensed its awesomeness and its stillness as if they were tangible things, old and sleepless and measurable. As the shadows leaned and tilted around them, they caught glimpses of curious shapes hanging from the walls, high up, like tattered regimental flags hanging in the perpetual twilight of an ancient cathedral. Other forms, that seemed to be figures carved from the rock, loomed above them just out of sight, sinister presences that watched their every movement. The skin of Leyla's neck tingled, as if she could feel their stale breath sliding across it. Their footsteps were swallowed up into the darkness as though they had never been. The tall, echoing chamber diminished them as the darkness diminished the light of Scholem's lamp. They were encased in blood-red shadows and a dim, nervous silence. The desert, with its wind and sand and eternal cold, was gone forever, as if it too had never existed, as if it had been a feverish dream and they had been walking all the time in these corridors, in this silence, in this half-light.

The farther they penetrated into the vast hall, the dimmer the reddish light grew, until only their small lamps remained to mark out a path for their tired feet. But now they could make out the shape of a second doorway in the far wall, much smaller than the one through which they had entered, rendered just visible by dim light somewhere behind it. As they drew closer to the back of the huge chamber they could make out a curiously shaped structure not unlike a small, roofed temple or oratory that jutted out from the wall, rising to a height of perhaps ten feet. In front of the structure and set partly within it stood a low, square-cut block of stone that might have been an altar. Dimly, they could discern the outlines of deeply incised markings and carved figures all along the sides of the stone block, and Leyla thought she could make out the softer texture of a dark-colored cloth laid on the upper face of the low slab. Scholem lifted his lamp higher and they moved toward the strange structure, their curiosity drawn to it after the long emptiness of the hall behind them.

At that moment Leyla heard something. It was faint at first, like leaves falling in a forest at the close of autumn, but even as she listened it grew and gathered force, thin, reedy voices rising and falling in unison. Her fingers tightened on Scholem's hand, hurting him.

"Chaim," she whispered sharply, afraid of her voice in the silence. "Can you hear it?"

For half a minute he stood, listening intently. His ears were duller than hers, older and less accustomed to detecting small sounds in vast spaces. But at last he too heard the voices. He shivered. It was cold in the chamber, but it was not the chilliness of the atmosphere that made his skin crawl. In the dark immensity of Iram he could hear little children singing in voices that lifted and dropped gently, a little out of tune, in a trembling chant. He remembered the toy camel he had seen, the tiny huddled skeletons in the houses they had entered, the mummy and its wooden doll tucked into their niche for all eternity. Did the fragile ghosts of the infant dead still wander these bleak stone corridors, singing together as they sought the parents who had abandoned them all those cold centuries ago? The voices grew louder, like a tide rising. They came from the direction of the small door to their right.

Leyla pulled on Scholem's arm.

"We can't stay here, Chaim," she hissed, her voice urgent with fear and uncertainty. The weird chanting increased in volume.

"Hurry," Scholem whispered, "get back into the shadows farther down the hall!"

He extinguished the unsteady flame of his lamp with a quick, nervous puff. The world became darkness again, tense, unrelieved, and crowded with black, abandoned centuries. Light was a dream and an illusion. Not even a memory of it remained. And in the swelling darkness little voices grew and the sound of lightly shod feet rang out ever more clearly against the bone-heavy flagstones of the city.

Holding one another by the hand against the blind dizziness of the dark, Leyla and Scholem shrank back into the shadows, as lovers flee discovery or thieves arrest. From the direction of the open doorway they could hear it distinctly now: a murmur of children's voices raised in a mournful, dreamy melody that raised goose pimples all over Leyla's flesh. By the side wall they paused and turned. Through the doorway they could now see a pearly, flickering light playing on the smooth stone walls and growing in intensity as it approached the opening. Crouching in the shadows by the wall, they watched the doorway apprehensively, like foxes with their eyes fixed on the entrance to their earth, listening to the hounds baying outside. The voices echoed weakly, as if in a corridor beyond the doorway, a pale, plangent sound like the wind in reeds on a gray evening.

There was a sudden flicker of yellow light, then a figure appeared in the opening. Leyla shivered. It was the figure of a little girl carrying a tall wax candle in her right hand. The light from the candle threw a flat illumination all around the child, cradling her gently within the surrounding blackness. She seemed to be about five or six years old, with fine blond hair that fell to her shoulders in a golden stream that shifted in the moving light. Around her brows a thin chaplet of white flowers had been tied. In the middle of winter, in the heart of the desert, in a city of stone she wore pale spring flowers like a bridal crown. She was dressed in a long white robe that fell to her ankles; below the hem small feet could be seen, shod in light sandals. As she walked, her mouth opened and closed and she sang in a thin, high-pitched voice. Her eyes were half closed and the skin of her face was pale, almost translucent, as if the white bone shone through. She walked on, carrying light into the darkness, her tapering candle in front of her, and behind her came a second child of about the same age, dressed in identical clothes and singing like the first.

One after the other, about thirty children passed through the door, the youngest above five, the oldest fourteen or fifteen. They were all girls, mostly blond, and dressed alike in white, with flowers in their hair. They all held candles in their hands and sang the same song over and over, like a mantra, repeating it in a dirgelike fashion, as if to keep the darkness at bay. At the small oratory they gathered at the altar in a semicircle, swaying a little as they stood in line. There was a pause in the singing, followed by an eerie silence. The children stood erect and still as statues, even the tiniest ones, then one by one removed the bands of flowers from their hair and laid them on the altar. At either side, one of the oldest girls stepped forward and lit a lamp hanging by the stone slab. Then more lamps were lit until the altar seemed to swim in a gently swaying pool of light.

Its surface was devoid of all but the chaplets of white flowers that lay on the stone like wreaths on an old tombstone, pale and already dying in the flickering light.

The girls stood their candles in front of the altar, stepped back, and joined hands, pale waxen fingers white as ivory linking them like ghosts seeking comfort in one another's presence. They began to sing again, a new song this time, slow and measured, the words low and indistinct at first, the melody simple yet somehow disturbing, then the voices rose and the words became clearer. Scholem started as he heard them and realized what they were. The language was German, the song an elegy of some sort:

"We are all children of the world of dreams,
forged in the darkness out of flesh and steel;
we rise up golden in the early dawn
with flowers for the dead and newly born."

For verse after verse they sang, pretty children in a nightmare. As he listened, the lilting voices startled old memories in Scholem. Sounds of a vanished childhood came back: the voices of young girls in brown uniforms singing Party songs, members of the Bund Deutscher Mädel marching in the streets. He could see their flaxen hair tied in plaits and ringlets, their smiling faces, their bright eyes. And behind them he could see their brothers in the uniform of the Hitler Youth, marching to adult tunes and adult destinies. And behind the singing voices he could hear the ringing of boots on stone and the growl of shunting locomotives.

He glanced up, and as he did so a candle flared suddenly and lit up a dim shape at the back of the altar. It was a golden swastika, etched against the darkness like the spinning rays of a torch, plain, unadorned, confident. In the hollow, crumbling hall, among the ancient shadows and the trembling lights, its stark symbolism held unwavering sway over past and present. The candle sputtered and returned to its original state; shadows folded about the swastika like black wings.

Scholem turned to Leyla, his hand gripping her own tightly.

"Did you see it?" he asked, his lips close to her ear.

"Yes." Her voice was almost inaudible. She wondered if she had died after all in the desert, as if all this were really no more than a nightmare of death.

At the altar, the song was finishing. One of the older girls bent down and picked up a small wicker basket shaped like a cornucopia and began to break up the flowers from the altar into it. When she had finished, she stepped away from the others, facing the far end of the long hall, then waited while they picked up their candles and fell into line behind her. Two of the tallest children lifted tapers fixed on long poles and lit them at candle left by the first girl, then moved toward the two sides of the hall. Leyla and Scholem moved away from them, away from the light, back down into the darkness of the Temple. The girls lifted the tall tapers and lit two oil lamps set about ten feet up on the walls. They began to walk down the hall, lighting more lamps as they went. Down the center of the chamber, now dimly lit from either side, the line of girls began to move again, intoning a new song as they went, a dirge this time, dreary and funereal:

> *"We bring flowers for the dead,*
> *and lights for the darkness."*

Scholem turned to Leyla, panic in his voice. He gripped her arm tightly with tense, nervous fingers.

"We must get away from here," he said. "They'll find us if we stay."

Treading lightly on the stone, they moved on tiptoe through the shadows by the wall, then, as they drew within range of the red light that still flickered up from below the pilasters at the far end, they went out into the dark center of the great chamber and made silently for the door. The tall central pillar stood between them and the approaching file of singing children, but as they reached the entrance the first of the girls passed it, then the next, her bright candle held aloft in a tiny hand.

Outside the hall, all was darkness. They did not dare relight Scholem's lamp. But they could not risk the winding passages ahead of them without light. If they once become lost, they might never find their way again, might wander for days in the lightless tunnels until they grew weak from thirst and hunger and were forced to die down with the dead in order to join them.

"Where can we go?" asked Leyla desperately. "We can't stay here. Can we risk going a little down this passage?"

"No," replied Scholem. "The song they're singing is all about bringing flowers for the dead. They're coming here, I'm sure of it." He looked around in desperation. His hand ached. He felt tired and beaten, all life, all energy driven out of him by the desert and the cold stones of this place. The swastika, above all, had woken in him a kind of mute, senseless despair that threatened to overwhelm him. Dimly, he could see the long passage behind them stretching back far into the darkness, the niches of the dead the only openings on either side.

"Quick!" he cried. "Into that niche! Get behind the body and lie flat. I'll take this one."

Leyla stared at the niche. There was just enough light from inside the Temple for her to be able to make out what was in it. It was like an open coffin, cobwebbed and dark and rotten. An ancient corpse

385

lay on it, shriveled and inhuman, dry flesh on dry bones, a thing that might crumble if it were touched. She could not move. She could not lie beside it, not in that darkness. The voices of the children were near them now.

"Hurry!" Scholem hissed. "They'll be here in a second."

If she didn't move, they would come upon them cowering by the doorway and find them there. The revenge Leyla had come to take for her family would never be taken. Scholem too would die without exacting his revenge. David would be lost. The desert and all that had happened there would have been for nothing. If she did not move in another few seconds, David and Scholem would certainly die and she would follow them just as certainly—and where would her revulsion for the dead be then? In the grave with her, rotting? She ran to the niche and closed her eyes tightly as she clambered over the brittle, papery flesh. A smell of faded spices filled her nostrils. Graveclothes crumbled at her touch, a dried limb came away as she struck it with her arm. She was festooned in dusty webs. The sound of footsteps reached the door. The song made echoes among the stone:

"We bring music for the silence,
and breath for the unbreathing."

Leyla lay down, and as she did so she felt something move against her leg. Footsteps sounded beside her and the thin singing of the children came to her like voices heard in a dream.

The light of candles filled the darkness, revealing to Leyla the horror by her side. There was a brief movement just beyond the niche and something fluttered for a moment. White petals had been scattered over the corpse and lay like discolored snowflakes on the crumbling shroud. The voices echoed among the burial niches as the children passed on to the next, to strew their petals over the dead. Leyla remembered the posy of withered flowers she had seen in the hands of a corpse and wondered again where they had come from. She shut her eyes tightly, blotting out the sight of decay beside her, holding back the screams that rose in her throat. The thing on her leg moved again.

FORTY-FIVE

The footsteps and the voices receded into the distance and were gone. The light of the last flickering candles faded and grew dim and vanished. Silence and darkness gathered strength again and returned.

That was the worst part: waiting through those last minutes to be certain the girls had all gone and it was safe to venture out into the passage again. Leyla brushed her face and neck with shaking fingers. She had to force herself to continue to lie still. One minute . . . two minutes. The spiders—if that was what they were and not something even worse—still crawled over her flesh with stiff, quivering legs. She had squeezed herself against the wall at the back of the burial niche, to be as far from the body by her side as possible. She wondered if she could bring herself to climb back over it or whether she would simply stay here in the darkness, paralyzed, unable to move again.

A sharp whisper intruded into her horrors.

"Leyla! You can come out now. They've gone."

She shifted and the moving things shifted with her. They had been with the unmoving dead for so long, they could not relate to anything that stirred in the darkness but themselves. Stifling her revulsion, she climbed over the corpse. For a horrible moment she thought it looked up at her, resentment in its eyes at this disturbance of its long, untroubled sleep.

Scholem was waiting for her in the passage, near the gaping doorway. In the dim light from inside she could see the cobwebs in his hair. Nervously, she brushed a hand through her own and swept it across her robes. A large black spider fell from her clothes and scuttled away across the floor. She shuddered and bent down beside Scholem. They glanced around the edge of the doorway into the hall beyond.

Lights still burned at the top end of the long nave. Whatever the purpose of the ritual performed by the little girls, it seemed likely that it was in part intended to prepare the way for further visits to the Temple by yet more whispers. If Scholem and Leyla were not to be forced to spend many more hours hiding in the shadows of the tombs, they would have to move quickly.

They stepped into the Temple again, dwarfed by its unforgiving hugeness, like insects on a table. It was safer to stick to the middle, where the shadows were thicker and the chances of detection a little narrower. Leyla went ahead, glad to be out of the tomb and moving once more, but strangely unsettled by what she had seen of the little girls and their strange ceremonial. She had not understood the words of the songs, but the queer, lilting melodies kept repeating in her brain like a dark nursery rhyme chanted again and again by children at play. If only she could believe that these children had been playing, that their songs and their strewing of flowers on the dead had been no more than a game; but she had heard no laughter and sensed no mood of levity. There was a more serious purpose behind what she had seen.

For the second time they reached the top end of the nave. No sounds came from beyond the small door to the side, and they approached it with caution. On the far side of it lay another corridor, lit with oil lamps, with doors instead of niches in its walls. There was no one in it. But from its appearance, which was relatively clean and cared for, this seemed to mark the beginning of the inhabited part of the city, as though the Temple was a sort of no man's land between the living and the dead.

They had no choice. They could remain in the Temple, imperfectly hidden, not knowing what part, if any, constituted a safe hiding place. Or they could try to find somewhere secure in which to rest and wait for nightfall—or whatever passed for nightfall in this realm of perpetual darkness. Iram must surely be up and stirring soon. They had no time to wait.

Leyla headed down the corridor, holding the gun at the ready, though she knew it would be of precious little use if they were confronted. Scholem followed her, still dazed a little by what he had seen and heard, as if he had stepped unwittingly and unrehearsed into one of his own nightmares, nightmares in which his childhood returned to haunt him like a malign and swollen ghost. They moved stealthily, their eyes and ears straining for the slightest movement or the least sound.

They were about halfway along the passage when they heard voices and footsteps in the distance, as though a large party of people were headed in their direction.

"Quickly," said Scholem, "in here!"

He pushed open a door on his left, praying it was not occupied but reasoning that, if it was, they could handle its occupants more easily than the crowd out in the passage. Leyla turned back and followed him, shutting the door quietly behind her.

She thought for a moment that she had gone insane or stepped into a nightmare. In the light of the lamp she saw eyes staring at her, monstrous, distorted faces, leering mouths, a crowd of men who were more like demons standing watching them. She started and almost dropped the gun in panic, but Scholem grabbed her arm.

"It's all right, Leyla! They gave me a fright too, but they're just statues, that's all."

The room was full of statues like those they had seen on their way to the city and here and there inside it—the deformed monsters of a warped religious imagination, denizens of someone's private hell made flesh in stone. Leyla shuddered and took a deep breath. Outside, the sound of footsteps reached the door, but the voices had fallen silent as they neared the Temple.

The statues had clearly been stored in the room as part of a collection. Each carried a number and label in German describing its precise origin and the date it had been removed and placed in the room. Some went back to the early 1950s, others were quite recent. Leyla estimated that there were about sixty in all, varying in size from around three feet to over ten. Some had wings, a few three sets of them, others held weapons or strange devices in gnarled hands; some were clothed, others naked, some obscenely so, with huge, erect phalluses swollen beyond nature; all appeared to be male, although one or two seemed androgynous or even gave the impression that they belonged to a third sex altogether, a supernatural gender conveyed by every means at the sculptor's

389

disposal, from the turn of the mouth to the shape or number of the genitals.

Leyla and Scholem agreed that they had hit by chance on an ideal hiding place. It was extremely unlikely, so they thought, that anyone would come here in the course of the average day. The statues were dusty and conveyed the impression that they sat here over the years untouched, awaiting the arrival of the next member of their coterie. To minimize any risk of discovery, however, they squeezed past the crowded statues to the back of the room, where there was sufficient space for them to stretch out in, invisible to anyone who might by chance open the door and glance in. They extinguished one lamp and placed the other inside the fold of a demon's wing so that it was almost completely shaded.

They tried to sleep. At first it was difficult, their nerves had been set on edge so badly. But in the end tiredness and the dark took their toll and they fell into an uneasy slumber. Scholem had long since ceased to use his wristwatch, so meaningless had time become in the desert, where only the days and the nights mattered, and where the hours could be better endured if they were not numbered. But before falling asleep he set it arbitrarily at six o'clock and wound it.

It was early afternoon when he woke. Leyla still slept heavily. He sat for a while, deep in thought, then ate a few crackers. As he was putting the box back in the bag, he noticed the bundle of papers Leyla had brought from the plane. They were in poor condition, crumpled and worn, but still quite legible. He lifted down the lamp from its place behind the demon's wing and moved a little away from Leyla so that the light would not disturb her.

He read with mere curiosity at first, to pass the time before night and the probable consummation of their ill-advised venture, but soon his curiosity passed to real interest and that in its turn grew to a gross excitement. When he had finished he began at once again, lost in the intricacies of what he read. Iram and the room in which he sat, with its cohort of demons all about him, faded and were gone. When he had finished reading for the second time, he sat there with the papers on his lap, staring into the darkness where it mingled with the light, thinking thoughts that left him even more worried and distressed than he had been. What he had read had filled him with a gnawing fear that was swelling in the pit of his stomach.

Leyla's voice broke into the silence, like a stone dropping into a dark, weed-filled lake.

"What is it, Chaim?" she whispered. "What have you found?"

He held out the papers to her.

"The papers you found in the plane. I've been reading them."

"Are they of any interest? You seem disturbed."

He nodded slowly, pensively.

"Yes," he said. "They're disturbing. I wish . . ."

He looked away from her, down at the stone floor.

"Yes? What do you wish?"

He stared at the floor as though hoping to see something there that would help him answer her. But there was nothing, just rock, hard and silent.

"I wish I'd never come, that I'd never heard of this place or these people. I wish we hadn't stumbled upon that plane or these papers. It all makes sense, forms a pattern. And the picture that's beginning to take shape is"—he paused, groping for a comparison—"like these statues. It's grotesque, a little insane. It's like a sickness that works inside until it comes to the surface in a deformity."

"Why don't you tell me what you've found? Can you translate some of it for me, give me some idea of what's in them?"

He hesitated, then nodded and moved back beside her.

"Very well," he said. "You have a right to know what it is you found."

He separated two sheets of typewritten paper from the pile in front of him.

"We'll start with this. It's undoubtedly the most important. It's a letter from Henrich Himmler addressed to Adolf Hitler in person, in which he gives the details of a meeting held in the early part of 1944. I'll make a rough translation for you.

"It's dated 28 April 1944 and headed 'Reichsführung SS,' SS High Command. Underneath that, someone's written the words 'Schloss Wewelsburg' by hand. That's Wewelsburg Castle, Himmler's country retreat in Westphalia. He used it as a sort of temple for the SS: kept all sorts of ritual paraphernalia there, held special ceremonies. Up here in the right-hand corner it says 'Geheime Reichssache,' which means this was regarded as a top-secret state document. It starts out with the usual phrases like 'Beloved Führer' and then gets down to business in the second paragraph. I'll start there."

He paused, brought the lamp a little closer, and looked at Leyla. It seemed almost cozy, crouching together in the light of the little lamp, all darkness excluded from their tiny circle. Scholem began to read.

"As I reported in my last communication (RfSS 897/7/2/44), I was summoned recently by Professor von Meier to consult with him on a matter of great importance. I . . ."

"Just a moment," Leyla broke in. "I thought you said this was a letter from Henrich Himmler."

Scholem nodded.

"I don't understand," she said. "You read 'I was summoned.' Wouldn't it be the other way round?"

Scholem shook his head.

"That's what I thought at first too. But it's quite clear: *war ich auffordert*, it says, 'I was summoned.' The rest of the letter backs up that reading. You'll see. I'll continue.

'I can now reveal to you the content of that discussion. He asked me, in my capacity as Reichsführer SS with ultimate responsibility for the RuSHA, to . . .'"

Leyla started to interrupt, but Scholem anticipated her.

"*Rasse und Siedlungshauptamt*, the Race and Resettlement Bureau. It was one of the principle departments of the SS, with responsibility for ensuring the observance of absolute racial purity within the organization. I'll go on.

'He asked me . . . *et cetera*, to establish whether it was possible, in case of further reverses in the war effort, to provide for the future of the race by providing an elite group of the best racial specimens to be given sanctuary outside the Fatherland until such time as circumstances permit the creation of a new power base from which to set about the reestablishment of the Reich. I told him at the time that I could see no obvious obstacle to such a scheme, but

392

expressed my misgivings as to the feasibility of finding a location sufficiently remote for such a purpose and yet practicable as a place of refuge for what may turn out to be a very protracted period. He simply smiled and told me the Bund had already something in mind. As if I needed telling! They always have something in mind, don't they?

'I reported back to him last month, outlining the main problems about selection and how I thought they might be overcome. The basic racial criteria established previously by Professor Schultz and used until now as the basis for admission to the SS remain fundamentally valid, although I have suggested a more restricted policy of accepting only those in Schultz's first category, the pure Nordic, without any trace whatsoever of bastardization. I recommended independently to von Meier that we could draw on the children currently housed by the Lebensborn Institution in order to provide an immediate pool of pure genes for the next generation.'"

Leyla broke in.

"I'm sorry," she said, "I've never heard of this Lebensborn Institution before. What was it? An orphanage?"

Scholem shook his head.

"Not really. It was more of a breeding institute, designed to give SS officers a chance to produce racially pure offspring, though surprisingly few took advantage of it. They may have been murdering, cold-blooded bastards, but they were very moral in sexual matters. Basically, the Lebensborn was a foundation for unmarried mothers, providing homes where they could have their children free of charge in amenable surroundings. Marriage sometimes got in the way of perfect breeding, but they had to preserve appearances. Girls got pregnant for the sake of the state, but if the father was unacceptable, they had no problems. They and their children were taken good care of. I'll go on.

'Von Meier took my recommendations to the Bund Council, and I heard nothing more until a few days ago, when he asked me to convene a meeting here at Wewelsburg. The meeting was held last night in my private study. Von Meier was there, together with Lorenz and Schmidt as representatives of the Council. Also present was the Grand Mufti, who had come with von Meier from Berlin, apparently in a personal capacity, although I have a suspicion that he may already be a Council member. Do be careful when you next see him.

'Let me tell you about the meeting. We dined first and talked about affairs in general. I may as well tell you, since you have no doubt been told this already by von Meier, that there is much dissatisfaction about the conduct of the war, coupled with extreme pessimism about its outcome. They've already started calling Bund members back to Munich before sending them out of the *country*. Did you know that? They're worried, and they're panicking—but not, of course, the way anybody else panics. They panic like blocks of ice melting in December. The Sanctuary Project is just part of this organized panic.

'Von Meier had his sanctuary ready all the time. It's called Iram. It's a city somewhere in the middle of the Nafud Desert in Arabia, a place he discovered after a long search in 1936. He says it can provide shelter for at least one thousand inhabitants for an indefinite period. There are deep artesian wells and oil for fuel. Crops can be grown in one section, and there are ample storerooms where enough food for ten years can be kept. The Mufti says his people will be able to ensure regular supplies without jeopardizing the secrecy of the city. In return for his cooperation, he wants an assurance that an Arab Reich will come into existence, ruled by him or his descendants. Von Meier has given him that assurance.

'We have worked out a preliminary scheme for the organization of the Sanctuary. The core leadership will be drawn from senior members of the Bund, including some of the present Council. They will be assisted by SS officers drawn from above the rank of Obersturmbannführer and members of the present Reich leadership, including myself, Göbbels, Bormann, and Speer. You will, of course, retain the office and functions of Führer, subject to the present conditions and possibly some new ones to take account of the alteration in circumstances.

'There will be a large contingent of RuSHA-approved

394

females of the highest racial type, to provide breeding stock for the next generation. In addition, the Lebensborn homes will be instructed to supply two hundred male children sired by SS fathers, who are to be trained to the highest standards of excellence as the first of the new race of men it will be our destiny to bring into existence. As they reach manhood, some of them will be sent back into the world in order to play a role in laying the foundations for a new Reich. They will be the vanguard of the new world order, working side by side with my Valkyrie units for victory. I understand that the Mufti is to be involved in some way with their early training, but I have yet to be given details of this.

'It is von Meier's belief—and one that I personally share—that the British will have exhausted themselves by this war. He predicts their rapid political and economic decline in the years following any so-called "victory," with the loss of their colonies and the evaporation of their prestige in the world, concomitant with the rise to global power of their supposed allies, the United States. It is, accordingly, to the latter country that we must direct our attention in the coming years, and it is there that the majority of Bund members are now being sent or will be sent on the cessation of hostilities. Von Meier does not think there will be any major impediment to the movement of even large numbers of people through postwar Europe, and I support him in this. Intelligence reports already show that neither the British nor the American authorities are eager to pursue a serious or far-reaching war crimes program in the aftermath of the war. The Russians are, for their own reasons, more likely to insist on purges, so we have to do all in our power to ensure that our people are in the areas under the control of the Western powers at the time of the cease-fire. A history of anti-Soviet activities will probably prove one of the best covers, with even the possibility of easy entry to the American or British intelligence organizations.

'The purpose of the Sanctuary is to provide even deeper cover where long-term projects can be planned and executed without fear of external interference, and where future generations may be trained properly in the attitudes, theories, and methods of service to the Reich and to the work of the Bund.

'In the end, we have no choice in this matter. The Council has decided in favor of the Sanctuary option, and they merely ask us to assist in the implementation of the scheme, through the provision of facilities and funds. I have already arranged for the transfer of an adequate sum of money for the initial financing of the operation. Von Meier will be contacting you directly with instructions as to the role he expects you to play in this. If I may offer a word of advice, try to convince him that, however much you may have been let down by the Wehrmacht and the mass of petty officialdom, you are still in control of yourself and your own destiny. You are, after all, still the man they chose, and I for one still have abiding faith in you and in what you can and will accomplish. By all means let there be a *Götterdämmerung*, let the dogs of war wreak destruction while they may. The German people have shown themselves unworthy of the high destiny to which we called them. It must be for another generation, a generation of racially perfect beings, to usher in that glorious epoch of moral and physical perfection of which you and I have dreamed for so many years. We will go into the desert, like Abraham, like Moses, like King Heinrich, who built his fortresses in the frontier wilderness, and we will lay the foundations for a new Reich, a Reich of infinite duration. Believe me, my Führer, it will be for the best.

'Signed,
'Reichsführer SS und Chef der Deutschen Polizei
'HEINRICH HIMMLER'"

There was a long pause as Chaim laid down the paper and leaned back into the shadows. He rubbed his tired eyes with his knuckles and blinked hard.

"Can it be genuine?" breathed Leyla, still unable to accept the implications of what she had just heard.

"I see no reason for it not to be. It was found in a place where such a letter might be found. The style appears to be that of Himmler. There's even a reference to King Heinrich. He means his hero, Heinrich I. Heinrich was a Saxon king who conquered the Slavs back in the tenth century. Himmler was obsessed with him. He had his bones brought back to Quedlingburg Cathedral. It's said he used to stay down in the cathedral crypt alone at midnight every year on the anniversary of Heinrich's death. He said Heinrich's spirit appeared to him in his sleep. And in the end he actually believed he was Heinrich himself, reincarnated. I think the letter's genuine."

Leyla thought of the great Temple through which they had just passed, of the swastika looming above them at its upper end, of the little girls performing their daily ritual in front of it. Yes, there was a pattern, a disturbing one.

Scholem held up two smaller sheets.

"This will be of interest to you," he said.

Leyla raised her eyebrows.

"It seems to be a part of a letter or statement written by the Mufti, probably to Hitler. Here."

He held the bottom sheet out to her. It had the Mufti's signature at the bottom, the initials "A.H." over the typed words "Amin el-Husseini, Grossmufti von Palästina."

"I see," she whispered, handing the sheet back to Scholem.

"Shall I read it to you?"

She nodded.

"Let's see," he began. "It starts in the middle of a sentence. There must be an earlier section missing." He began reading.

". . . in our long and glorious history. The Arab people have a great destiny, a destiny that until now has been frustrated by the machinations of inferior peoples, by the Jews and by the Christian races of the Mediterranean. We ruled the world's greatest empire once, and one day we shall rule it again, side by side with a Germanic empire in the north. You yourself have said on more than one occasion that it would have been better for the German people to have been converted to the Muslim rather than the Christian religion, since the faith of Islam is a warrior's creed, in which the struggle for victory by the sword is sanctioned by holy law.

"I cannot speak too highly of such noble perception. There is a weakness in the Christian faith, a fatal flaw that few inside it have ever seen. It is that emphasis on meekness, on passivity, on turning the other cheek that the Church has so cunningly propagated through the centuries. They have made the heart of their religion something shameful, a defeat, pain and suffering. They have made their symbol a cross and proclaimed a God who lets Himself be taken and put to death by His own creatures. How can strength or enduring greatness come out of such false beliefs?

"The Qur'an teaches that Jesus never died on the cross. It preaches holy war as a duty incumbent on the community, and it urges all believers to offer up their lives in the path of God, not as willing victims, but on the field of battle. Nor does Islam fall into that other great Christian error, that the Church and the State must be separate, that religion is an affair of the next world, not of this. For a Muslim, there is no distinction, no demarcation between religion and politics. The law of God instructs us how to organize the perfect society as well as how to pray or bury the dead. Every area of life, from international relations between states to the most intimate relations between a man and his wives, is governed by the one system, ruled by the one set of laws.

"Hence my proposal that the children brought to Arabia from Germany, as well as every child born at Iram, be brought up in the faith of Islam, trained from birth to serve both God and the State. The male children will be given to the Bedouin of the inner sands to be trained in the ways of the desert. There is great wisdom in this. Your own *völkisch* writers have stated time and again that it is the cities that corrupt, where the vices congregate, where whole races are rendered degenerate. We Arabs have known that for centuries, ever since the first days of the Islamic conquests, when the pleasures of Damascus and Ctesiphon beckoned our rulers and our young men. From that day to this, it has been a practice among many of us to send our children for a time into the desert to live with the tribes, to breathe the pure air of the sands, to be hardened in every fiber, to return immune to the lusts and distractions of the city.

"That is what we shall do with these heralds of the master race. Their bodies and spirits will be purified like those of the Bedouin. They will be German in blood, Bedouin in spirit,

398

able to withstand any hardship, trained to endure any suffering, utterly loyal to their tribe, to their race, to their blood. They will be taught the pride of ancestry, they will learn the meaning of honor and duty, they will worship a God Who has never given Himself to the cross or crowned Himself with thorns. They will be capable of killing without mercy or pity and of dying without fear or regret. No one will ever have seen their like in the world, they will be perfect in mind and spirit and body, ready to accept the leadership of the world. Only a man who possesses mastery of himself can be the master of others. Only . . ."

Chaim stopped reading and put the papers down.

"It goes on like that for another couple of paragraphs," he said. "But I think you've got the gist."

Leyla nodded.

"There are one or two other things," Chaim went on. "Some documents from Dr. Gregor Etner, the head of Lebensborn, saying that he has personally selected the children who are to be sent to the Reichsführer SS for what he calls 'special placement.' I don't think he knew anything about their real destination. A letter from von Meier telling Hitler the time has come to get everyone out of Germany and into the Sanctuary; it's dated 10 April 1945—that's only twenty days before Hitler's supposed suicide. A list of names, apparently the passenger roster for the flight: it makes interesting reading, very interesting reading indeed. It looks as if some of us have spent years chasing after people whose bodies have been cooking out in the Nafud for the past four decades."

He paused and picked up a small blue folder that had been tied with string. It contained dozens of sheets that had been stapled together at the top. The staples had rusted and stained the paper in which they rested, but the folder had kept the pages relatively clean and legible. Scholem passed the sheets to Leyla without saying anything.

She looked at them and frowned, unable to make sense of them. It was simply an alphabetical list of names with numbers alongside them, nothing more. She began to read down the list.

Adler, F. (Valk.III): 12944 / D7139-V

Abshagen, H. (Valk.III): 12944/BE9412-V
Angren, K. (Valk.IV): 121044/D7294-V
Auerbach, J. (Valk.I): 12544/A7381-V
Abetz, P. (Valk.III): 12944/BE9843-V
Ampletzer, K. (Valk.II): 121844/D7157-V

The names went on and on, page after page, each one different and yet somehow the same as the rest, dehumanized by the numbers that followed them. Leyla handed them back to Scholem with a frown.

"Do they make any sense to you?"

He shook his head.

"Names. Numbers. There were so many in the Third Reich. Sometimes it seems that is all it ever was: an endless linking of names and numbers. Identity cards, passes, clearances, camp registers, arm tattoos . . . everyone was numbered. And so many of them for death: these for the front, these for the ovens. The whole thing was about regimentation. If it ever happened again . . ." He sighed. "Just think of it," he said. "Computers, data banks, fingerprint decoders, voiceprint machines . . . The Nazis were like primitives compared to what governments have now. But they managed with what was available." He gathered the papers up and replaced them in the folder. "They managed very well." He sighed and looked at Leyla. They had been enemies, but now that seemed trivial, almost childish.

Leyla gazed at the little pile of papers on the floor. Things that had previously made no sense were now beginning to seem clear to her. She understood at last where she was, what the meaning of Iram was. She looked up at Scholem.

"You want to leave, don't you?"

He said nothing, but she saw him nod gently.

"To tell people about this."

He nodded again.

She was silent for a while.

"I understand," she said. "But I can't come with you. I came here for David. Everything I went through I went through for that purpose. I can't turn back now."

"He may not be here," Scholem said without looking up.

"No," she said, "there's no need to say that. He's here. I know he is. I want to find him, Chaim. You can go; you must go. I'll stay and look for David, try to get him out. I'll keep the gun if I may."

Scholem sat for a long time without answering. At last he looked up and found Leyla's eyes. They were small, thin tears on her cheeks, making pale lines in the dirt. He reached out and took her hand.

"You're right," he said. "We have to stay. We came for David. It's suicide whatever we do. At least we can try to do what we came for. Let's not discuss it any further. Eat a little, then we'll talk about what to do tonight."

He would stay. But it frightened him to do so. He had to get back. He had to warn anyone who would listen. Himmler had referred to his Valkyrie units. The list of names used the abbreviation "Valk." He had heard of Valkyrie: rumors, idle talk. But enough to frighten him to the core. And now he had evidence that the Valkyrie units had not been someone's fantasy, that they had existed. And if what had been happening recently was any indication, they were about to be activated.

FORTY-SIX

The darkness was total, all-embracing, inescapable. Sometimes he thought he saw lights, but when he looked again he realized they were in his own head. Somehow he had managed to cross the first branch tunnel, continuing down another opening that led off it, growing more confused and lost with every step. He fought to keep down the panic, aware that it would be fatal if he gave in to it. He was tired and needed to sleep, but he feared to do so lest he become more disoriented. As he walked, trying to retrace his steps, he used the niches to keep his path straight and to warn him when one passage ended and another began. The main thing, he told himself, was to avoid getting any deeper into the labyrinth. He could not be far from the main mortuary tunnel that led back to the Temple. If only he could get that far he would be safe.

But darkness and silence do strange things to the senses and the mind. The blind manage well enough in their own homes and streets, but in a strange place, deprived of sound and the touch of familiar objects, even they become hopelessly lost. A man in a dark room is less likely to panic than one in a lightless forest or a vast, empty house, however small and claustrophobic the room in daylight, however spacious the forest or the house. David suffered the worst of both worlds: he felt hemmed in, trapped by the rock walls on either side, as if they pressed slowly in on him, and yet he also sensed the vastness of the maze in which he was wandering, the endlessness of it.

In the end he slept, tired out by the exertions of the day before and the long night that had followed and that now continued without any hope of day to succeed it. He did not choose where to sleep: one place was like another, just as one grave is like any other grave. It was cold in the tunnels, and he lay shivering for a long time before total sleep took him. His dreams were bad, filled with dead things that rattled and spoke, the voices of spiders and the hands of centipedes.

He had no idea how long he slept. It might have been hours, it might have been a day. When he woke, his body felt stiff and cold, and he ached all over. A foul headache throbbed behind his left temple, and he felt a vast, sickening hunger that ravished his stomach and left him nauseous. Twice he threw up, filling the tunnel in which he sat with a bitter, acrid stench. His head spun, and for a long time he dared not stand. But it was death to go on sitting there, and in the end he did move, trying to bring back feeling to his limbs by walking.

In sleep, he had lost all notion of where he might be. It was like one long tunnel to him, a tunnel of bones, spider-eaten and lonelier than the face of the moon. One thought returned again and again to distress him, though he knew it was irrational: that he might, in the madness of hunger and the fear of death, be driven to eat the mummified flesh that lay in such abundance on every side. He prayed for a fast way to die, for a madness that would overcome the insanity of a slow death. He had no way of knowing how far he walked or for how long he did so. Sometimes a step seemed to take hours, sometimes he felt that only seconds had gone by since he left the chamber containing the Ark.

He was tiring rapidly now: his feet faltered and he was compelled to stop and rest from time to time. It was the hopelessness of his situation more than anything that weakened him. It sapped his will and undermined his strength. There seemed little point in walking on and on through the tunnels when it would make no difference in the end where he lay down to die. For all he knew, he had passed within inches of the right turning, perhaps more than once. But whether by an inch or by a mile, he was still trapped.

He remembered how, as a child, he had loved to play blindman's bluff, stumbling with hooded eyes after his tiny, shouting friends, delighting in the strangeness of a world that consisted only of sound and touch and smell, secure in the knowledge that a flick of the blindfold would restore him to the world of light and color. He recalled too how he had played at mazes, his pencil tracing the winding pathways that led the hero out of the enchanted forest, the forking lines that brought him to the buried treasure. Here, he had found the treasure in reality, but he had lost the way out.

Or had he? In a flash, another memory came to him, something he had been told when he was about twelve, a method for finding one's way out of any maze. It was simple, and it was effective—he had tried it several times and lost all interest in mazes thereafter, because it had taken away the challenge. All you had to do, he recalled, was to keep your hand—or your pencil—on one wall, the left-hand wall, let us say. However far it took you, you were never to remove your hand from it, and in the end, even though you went into every dead end and crossed your own tracks several times, you would emerge from the maze.

He realized that to follow such a course where he was would be difficult. He had no idea how far the tunnels stretched, how many twists and turns they had. But it was a chance, and he knew he had to take it. Using his left hand, he ran his fingers along the continuous ledge of stone between two niches at about shoulder height and began to walk a steady pace. Before long he reached a turning, then another, but he kept moving, his hand on constant contact with the wall. From time to time the level of the stone would shift, but it was an easy matter to resume contact and continue. Once he stumbled against something blocking the passageway. A quick examination showed it to be a body, presumably that of someone who had strayed into the tunnels as he had and died there.

In spite of this grim reminder of his plight, the fact that he had adopted a positive course of action did much to revive his spirits and restore his strength. His only fear was lest he grow tired and fall asleep again, in case he should wake unsure of his direction and start back the way he had come. As he walked, he marveled at the extent of Iram's catacombs, at the trouble to which the city's inhabitants had gone just to house their dead.

He could not be sure, when he saw the light, that it was not a hallucination, his tired eyes playing fresh tricks on him. But he closed his eyes and opened them again slowly and it was still there in front of him, a dim glow in the distance, luring him toward itself.

He had come out a little farther down the main catacomb tunnel that led into the Temple. The rest was easy. He found his way through the Temple into the quiet corridors immediately beyond, and from there it was only a short distance to his room. No one was there. The room was quite empty, as he had left it . . . when? The day before? Two days ago? He had no idea. There had been no one in the corridors on his way there, and he assumed it was "night" again. A wave of utter exhaustion flooded over him. He sank onto his bed and fell into a deep, untroubled sleep.

He was wakened by a hand roughly shaking his shoulder. His eyes opened a fraction, struggling to see. The dim light of the lamp felt unusually bright. Talal was standing by the bed, looking down at him, his face set hard, an unsmiling Buddha displeased to have been dragged away from his contemplation of the infinite in order to attend to mundane trivialities.

"How long is it since you returned?" he asked.

David shook his head, groggy from sleep and tiredness.

"I don't know," he said. "I don't even know how long I was away. Or when it is now."

"It is the first period after waking. You disappeared two nights ago."

David nodded. Not as long as he had feared. He felt terrible.

"I want to eat," he said, "and to drink."

Talal ignored him. His eyes were implacable and his voice as hard as the rock against which it echoed gently.

"Where have you been? What have you been doing? What have you seen?"

David felt impatient. His mouth was like sand, as if he had been outside in the desert, swallowing it down like a raw delicacy.

"Can't we talk later?" he protested. "I'm tired, I'm thirsty, my throat is agony."

Talal insisted.

"I want to know where you have been, what you have been doing. Why did you run away?" His voice was like a blade now, bright and calligraphed, its keen edge honed to an almost perfect sharpness.

"I've been nowhere," David snapped, his patience wearing quickly thin. "I got lost, I took a wrong turning. The guard left me behind, I was tired. I got lost in the catacombs. For God's sake, can't you see the condition I'm in? I need rest, not an interrogation!"

"I don't believe you," Talal snapped back at him.

"Then that's just too bad, because it's true. I slipped and my light went out. I'm lucky to be alive."

Talal looked at him curiously, evenly.

"Perhaps not," he said.

David swung his legs onto the floor and sat facing Talal.

"What does that mean?"

Talal said nothing.

"Well, I'm sorry," David went on, "but I just don't want to talk about any of this now. I want some food and I want some time to rest. After that I'll tell you anything you want to know—if I'm able to. Where's Boris?"—it was David's name for his usual guard. "I want him to bring me some breakfast."

"Heinz is dead," Talal said. "I am your guard now. We will see much of one another, you and I."

David looked into Talal's eyes, as if he hoped to read something there. The other man stared back at him, his dark eyes unreadable, like two characters in Japanese script.

"Dead? How dead? I don't understand."

"He had been ordered to watch you closely, to control your movements. He let you slip away. Herr von Meier ordered that he be executed."

David's mouth fell open. An acute horror of the place ran through him, as though its cruelty were only now becoming clear.

"But that's absurd," he said at last. "Nothing . . . no harm came from my absence. It wasn't his fault I took a wrong turn."

"Please, let us say no more about his death. He was a soldier under orders: he knew the consequences of failure. That is enough." Talal paused, as if uncertain whether to broach another subject. "You say no harm came from your absence," he went on at last. "How far did you go into the tunnels? Where did you get to?"

David shrugged.

"How should I know? They're all the same. I had no light. God knows where I got to. I may have gone round and round in tiny circles for all I know."

"Weren't you at the west end of the city? Last night?" Talal asked.

"I've told you, I don't know where I was. I may have been, I really can't say."

406

"If you were lost, how did you find your way out again?"

"That's easy to explain, though not quite so easy to do. I followed the wall. I kept one hand on the damned wall and I walked. Try it sometime. It works, but it isn't pleasant."

"Then you know nothing of the body?"

"The body? I was surrounded by bodies. Which one did you have in mind?"

Talal eyed David closely, as if by such scrutiny he could detect deceit.

"The body of the guard," he said. "The one we found at the change of watch, at the west entrance to the city."

"You mean you think I killed a guard."

Talal hesitated only briefly.

"Yes."

"And then came back here and waited for you to come for me?"

"I don't know. I don't know what your reasons were, why you came back."

"And I didn't try to escape? I was at the entrance, you say, I killed the guard there . . . and I just turned around and walked calmly back to this room?"

"You had nowhere to go. There is only the desert outside. You know what it is like. You have no food, no water."

"Then why would I kill a guard?"

"I don't know. Perhaps he found you doing something else, tried to stop you. That's for you to tell me."

"And suppose I tell you I don't know anything either? That I've spent the past two days crawling about in the dark with some very unpleasant company? Maybe you've got a renegade. Have you checked on who's missing?"

Talal shook his head.

"That will be done, don't worry. In the meantime, Herr von Meier would like to see you. He's very disturbed by everything that's happened. Be very careful what you say to him. He tolerates you because you serve a purpose and . . . you amuse him, I think. But after what has happened, he will not find you so amusing. I advise you to take great care."

Without another word, Talal went to the door and opened it, waiting for David to accompany him. David sat for a while on the edge of the bed, his eyes fixed stubbornly on the other man, unwilling to move. In spite of his sleep, he was drained, physically and emotionally. A fraught interview with von Meier was the last thing he felt he could cope with at the moment. Talal's eyes remained locked on him, urging him to stand, but David stayed put, matching his will against the other's.

Talal's next movement was so sudden that David saw only a blur that exploded suddenly in pain. The man's hand moved to the hilt of his sword, he altered his stance and swung toward David, the sword whipped out of its scabbard, flashed momentarily, and was drawn diagonally across David's chest, to the top of his stomach. Where the sword had passed, a stream of crimson blood oozed in a long line. David clutched his chest in agony, then wondered why he was not dead. He looked up and saw Talal wipe the blade and replace the sword in its sheath with a slow, practiced motion, passing it between the fingers of his left hand as it entered the scabbard. He looked down again at the red line of blood that flowed along his chest. The cut was skin-deep, like the incision of a razor passing over the surface of the flesh.

"Do not force me to cut you more deeply," Talal said, motioning David to the door again.

His wound still stinging sharply, David stood and went to the door without another word. He would have to brazen it out with von Meier. At the door he turned to the left, in the direction of von Meier's room, but Talal took him by the arm and pressed him in a different direction, away from the room. He looked at Talal, the puzzlement evident on his face, but the man said nothing, merely indicating the path David should take, following a pace or two behind him. David walked on in silence, along the corridor in which his room was situated, then down a flight of steps he had not seen before.

They came to a lower level where David had never set foot. It seemed darker and older here, uncared for, primeval. The passage through which they walked was low-ceilinged, causing David to stoop slightly. Old cobwebs hung at intervals on the walls. They entered a second passage, a downward-sloping tunnel that stretched into the distance, bleak and empty. There was no one else but David and his custodian. Shadows clung to them here like old friends clustering around returning travelers.

This was the old heart of Iram, almost empty now, a place of grim, bloodless shadows and decaying dreams. Every city has its heart of darkness, that abandoned wasteland that was once its core, a place of derelict streets and dank, rotting warehouses, a place left to decay in the shadow of its own deformity. Iram's deformity was here, in these drab passages, in crooked statues and crumbling ornaments, a black leprosy that ate the stone away with remorseless simplicity. The walls crowded in on them here as if a million tons of stone were pressing down, jealous of the little lives that scuttled through their narrow cavities. They entered a last tunnel. Leprous winged statues lined the route, like stone guardsmen lining a road for a procession. Or a funeral.

The tunnel ended in a short flight of steps. Light came through the opening, a garish red light unlike any David had seen elsewhere in the city, with the exception of the lights at the lower end of the Temple. There was a strong stench, and David sensed weak fumes drifting up from below. Talal prodded him in the back and he descended the steps, one at a time, fearful of slipping into unknown depths.

They came out into a low-ceilinged cavern that stretched across the central section of the city, a wide area where the sandstone had not been carved into pillars by the wind. The cavern was filled with a throbbing blood-red light and masses of taut shadows that writhed and undulated across blackened walls. The air was hot and close, but breathable. The floor of the cavern was dotted with pools of burning oil that varied in size from a few feet to one huge basin almost forty feet long. Ages ago, in the spring of Iram's first settlement, the pools had burned all winter and been extinguished for the duration of the hot summer months. When al-Halabi visited the city in the eighth century, the barbarous descendants of the original inhabitants had lost the old knowledge of the oil pools and warmed themselves in winter by means of wood collected in the desert during the summer. Now, for over forty years, the pools had burned again in winter. No one knew how deep they were, but they seemed inexhaustible, as undying as the city itself. However much they burned, the level never appeared to sink, as if they were constantly replenished from endless fields of oil in the depths far below Iram.

At the edge of the nearest pool, his back turned toward David and Talal, a tall figure stood, dressed in a long black robe. It was von Meier, all odor of the death-bed departed from him. He stood, a little bent, his white hair falling wearily to his shoulders, as if he were lost in meditation, like an old king alone in the deserted cellars of his abandoned castle. Light and shadow moved across him in equal measure, as though in a game or slow, undulating dance. He was lost in thought, lost in memories, lost in dreams. In his mind he walked out of the mortuary tunnels of Iram, out of the cold encircling desert, out of Arabia into a world made soft and vulnerable by long years of peace and prosperity. In his dreams, he and his children rebuilt the earth: they draped white flags on the buildings of Washington, London, and Paris; they planted runic symbols on the spires of great cathedrals; they marched along the broad, tree-lined avenues of a dozen cities; they cleansed and purified the nations. The earth would be clean again, redeemed by their exile and suffering, by his nearly fifty years of incarceration, pain, and loneliness. He breathed the acrid air of the dim cavern and sighed.

Near him, propped up against a stone pillar, a sightless mummy stood, flames and speckled shadows coruscating across its dried skin and tattered shroud. David recalled the incident recorded in Schacht's diary, von Meier's midnight colloquy with the dead. The old insanity, he thought, in a new place.

David looked away from von Meier and the mummy, out into the depths of the cavern. A winged statue stood on an island of rock, phoenixlike, flames licking it like angry, diseased tongues. It had a bland and untransfigured face, like an angel so long fallen it has forgotten bliss and converted the pains of hell to daily inconveniences. Like the Sinaitic bush, it burned but was not consumed. David turned his face to Talal and away again. He stood slightly behind him, his eyes fixed on von Meier, waiting.

Out in a dark corner of the cavern something soft and white moved. Then a second movement and a third. Through a gap in the wall to David's right, pale things like giant maggots came lumbering into sight. David shuddered involuntarily. He could not see the white things clearly, but something in the way they moved repelled him, as though they were indeed maggots seething in graveclothes. Neither von Meier nor Talal appeared to pay the creatures any attention. David strained to see more clearly what they were. And then the first of them came into view, outlined by flame. They were pigs, huge white pigs rooting on the floor of the cavern.

Suddenly von Meier turned, though David could not be sure he had heard him and Talal enter. He seemed not at all surprised to see them there, and stood for a while looking at David. Raising one hand, he crooked a finger and beckoned David to himself.

"They stray here sometimes in search of warmth," he said. David realized he was referring to the pigs. "Not light, you understand. They are quite blind. We found them here when we discovered Iram, a breed of white pigs living in the darkness of the caverns. They ate anything that grew down there: even the remains of their own dead. They were the last abomination of Iram, the great blasphemy. From time to time we kill one and eat it; the meat is pale, but quite sweet."

Von Meier paused and looked away from David again, out toward the corner where the pigs were nuzzling the rock with soft, obscene lips.

"Why do I not have you killed?" he asked.

David said nothing. He knew it was in von Meier's power to do so. Like the pigs. Were reasons necessary? Here, in a place like this?

"You will answer me," von Meier said, turning. The menace in his voice was naked and raw like David's wound.

"What do you want me to say?" David looked at the old, lined face, at the cold eyes. "I've heard the charges from your man Talal. I can't refute them, not with evidence. I wanted freedom to see the city without a guard for once, so I slipped off my leash. As a result, I got lost. Very nearly permanently. But I know nothing about your dead man, the man you found by the entrance. As far as I know, I wasn't anywhere near there. One of your own people must be responsible. If you don't believe me, you're taking a risk. You've got a killer among your people. Or someone is missing."

Von Meier said nothing at first. He had fine, soft hands that he held together in front of him, white hands that made David think of a surgeon rather than an old, withered man in a flame-filled cavern. He looked past von Meier and saw the pigs again. Their flesh was white as well.

"What did you see? Where did you go?"

"I saw almost nothing. I went through the Temple, but most of it was in darkness. I took the third—no, the fourth opening turning

411

into the catacombs. I must have gone quite far, then I slipped on something and lost my lamp. After that I tried to find my way back, but I took a wrong turn somewhere and became lost. Nobody saw me. Believe me, I'm not lying."

He knew that precious little stood between him and sudden death. The hand that had wielded a sword like a razor could as easily sever his head from his shoulders with a single blow. Von Meier looked at David for a long time, his face impassive but for his pale, searching eyes. He was the king of Iram now, thought David, a Solomon reigning over a kingdom of the dead.

"Very well," von Meier said at last. "You are to be taken back to your room and placed under strict confinement. Inquiries will be made. If anyone is missing or there whereabouts are unaccounted for, I shall assume your innocence unless further evidence comes to light. You will still be punished for slipping away from your guard. But let me tell you now that I do not believe you. I have already given orders for your execution tomorrow, in the first period after waking. It will not be quick or painless—I reserve that privilege for my own people, for men like Heinz, whose death you caused. You will wish you had died like Schacht or that you had never found your way out of the catacombs. And when it is done I shall have your body cut up and fed to these pigs."

He waved a hand at David, as if brushing him away, and turned back to contemplate his subterranean realm.

"Leave me," he muttered. "I have no further use for you."

David turned and followed Talal to the steps. He looked around briefly and saw von Meier standing still before the flames. Behind him, the leprous shapes moved silently across the rock, licking and sucking it with loathsome tongues.

FORTY-SEVEN

Near the small doorway that opened into the Temple there was an empty vertical niche that had once held a tall statue. The nearest light was a little distance away, and the niche lay in permanent shadow. Leyla had been waiting inside for what was beginning to seem like a very long time, watching for someone to pass. Soon after she had taken up her position, a group of about ten people had gone into the Temple and stayed for about half an hour, finally returning the way they had come. She wanted someone on his or her own if possible, but now she began to think that no one else was going to come at all. She was stiff and tired. The sleep she had taken that afternoon had not refreshed her. She felt unable to relax until she was out of Iram—and that now seemed an utterly remote possibility.

There was a sound of footsteps farther down the passage. Leyla looked carefully around the edge of the niche, hoping the shadow would conceal her. A man was coming, alone and, as far as she could tell, unarmed. He was rather taller than she and burly-looking, but she would have the element of surprise. Scholem had told her what to say in German, and she rehearsed it now in her mind as she drew back into the niche waiting for the man to pass.

Suddenly he was there, then he was past. She stepped out lightly behind him, the knife in her hand, moved behind the man, and threw one hand over his mouth as she brought the knife around to his throat.

"Don't move!" she whispered.

He stood stock still, stunned into immobility by this attack from nowhere. He could see the knife pointed at his throat, could feel the tip of it lick his skin. Leyla's breath was hot and heavy on the back of his neck. She hissed another command. Scholem had taught her the words.

"Turn slowly!"

He began to turn, while she kept her hold on him, pressing the knife in until she knew it must hurt. The point had already nicked the man's skin and drawn blood.

"Walk!" she ordered. He began to walk back down the passage, slowly, awkwardly. Now that the first shock had passed, he started to think of how to dislodge his attacker without giving her a chance to use the knife. His hands were free, and if he judged the moment right he could break loose and turn to the offensive before she had a chance to strike. But first he had to lull her into a sense of security, let her drop her guard a fraction. Where was she taking him anyway? Who was she? What did she want?

They reached a door at the far end of the passage. He recognized it as an old storeroom, little used now.

"Open the door!" she ordered.

He put his hand to the handle and pushed. The door opened. A light was burning somewhere inside. On a box facing them, a man sat holding a gun. He had left his bid for freedom too late.

Leyla pushed the man inside and closed the door behind them with her foot. She took her hand from the man's mouth, then stepped away from him abruptly, out of reach in case he thought of making a grab and using her as a shield. There could be no second chances if they made a mistake now. When every step is a risk, it is easy to grow blasé.

Scholem looked at the man intently, holding his gaze for a long time.

"Come here," he barked in German. The man moved toward him.

"That's far enough. Stand there." The man stopped and stood in front of Scholem, his arms hanging loosely by his side.

"I want to know where the American is, the man they brought here recently."

The man said nothing. He stared at the wall behind Scholem. Scholem stood. He gestured to Leyla. She came to his side and took the gun. Scholem went close to the man, almost touching him.

"Where are they holding the American?"

No reply. Scholem struck the man across the face with the back of his good hand.

414

"Where is he?"

No answer. Another blow. The slap seemed to ring out in the small room like a gunshot.

"Where?"

Nothing. A third blow. And a fourth. Crack, crack. Leyla wanted to turn away, but she could not show the man her weakness. Scholem felt sick with himself, but he knew there was no time for patience.

"Wo ist der Amerikaner?"

The man was in pain, but he gritted his teeth and said nothing. Scholem hit him again, his open hand like a flail, back and forward. He kept it up for half a minute until the man was reeling from each blow, his head spinning. Scholem paused and repeated the question. The man opened his mouth and spat out blood, a long red stream mixed with sour saliva.

"I don't know," he said, coughing. Scholem hit him again.

"I don't know!" the man repeated, more loudly this time. Scholem raised his hand.

"I swear I don't know!" The man was pleading now, cringing before the coming blow. Scholem hit him. Then again, twice. Weeping, the man repeated what he had said before.

"I don't know where he is, I swear. I've seen him once, that's all. He had a guard, Heinz, but they executed Heinz yesterday. I don't know where they keep him."

"He's telling the truth, Chaim. I'm sure of it. Don't hit him again." Leyla could not understand why the desert had not destroyed all feeling in her.

Scholem's hand was raised, ready to strike again, but he lowered it.

"Very well," he said. "You," he said to the man, "take your clothes off."

The man looked at Scholem, then at Leyla. He hesitated.

"Do as I say!" Scholem ordered. "Or I'll hit you again."

The man stripped. Under his black robe he wore nothing. Summer and winter, the robe was all he ever wore.

"Throw it over here!" Scholem snapped. "Leyla, keep him covered while I put on the robe."

Scholem picked up the garment and put it over his head. It was a loose fit and a little long, but he tied it at the waist with the cord from his old robe, which he wore underneath, and decided it

415

would do.

"What do we do with him?" Leyla asked.

Scholem turned to her and, almost casually, said, "Shoot him."

Leyla looked at him in horror.

"Just like that?" she said. "In cold blood, the way they kill?"

Scholem came up to her, put his hand on her arm.

"What else do you suggest?" he asked. "We have no rope, nothing to tie him with. This door has no lock. Do we just let him walk out of here and alert his friends? We might as well not bother with all this"—he tugged at the robe he had just put on—"and just go out and tell them we're here."

She knew he was right. But it was impossible for her to kill the man or let him be killed. She had seen enough to convince her that, were the positions reversed, their prisoner would probably not hesitate to kill both of them. She looked at the man. He stood returning her gaze, naked and sullen, not cowed by his situation. His face was red and swollen where Scholem had struck him. His thin, tightly muscled body disturbed her. She would have to stand by while Scholem pumped a bullet into his frightened brain.

"I can't do it," she said in a small voice. "I can't let you do it. Can't we just knock him out?"

"For how long? An hour? Two hours? How long will it take to find David, get him out of here? Less time than that? Longer?"

"Then we'll tie him as well," she said. "Give me your waist cord."

Scholem hesitated.

"It's the only difference between us, don't you see? If we kill him like this we undermine everything. In the desert you told me about your wife, about your daughter. Kill him and you join the killers, you perpetuate their deaths. He's nothing to you. Don't make him something, don't turn him into a victim you can't explain to yourself afterward."

"You watched me kill the guard," Scholem exploded. "Why didn't you stop me then?"

"That's wasn't in cold blood. It was you or him. This isn't like that, can't you see? Give me the cord, for God's sake!"

"It won't hold him."

"I'll make it hold him, don't worry about that."

Scholem fell silent. He looked at the man, then back at Leyla.

"Here," he said, loosening the cord.

Leyla took it from him and gestured to the man to step close to her and turn around. She felt it again as he came close, the lean masculinity that disturbed her. It was not the man's nakedness that troubled her so much as the man himself, his silence, his intensity, his possession of himself.

She tied his wrists tightly and expertly behind his back, then unfastened her own waist cord.

"Lie down," she ordered. He looked at her, uncomprehending.

"Niederlegen Sie sich," repeated Scholem.

The man lay down and Leyla bound his ankles together, joining the cords at feet and hands together in the middle, where he could not reach. It was a skill she had been taught at a PLO training camp once. She knew the man would not escape if someone else did not come for him.

When she had tied him to her satisfaction, she used the knife to cut the hem of her robe and that of Scholem's. It was a ragged enough job, but it would prevent them from tripping—and it gave her a cloth with which to gag the man on the floor.

"Are you happy, Chaim?" she asked when she had finished.

Scholem bent and examined the knots, then straightened up and nodded.

"It's fine," he said. "He won't make trouble. I'm sorry I seemed callous."

"You were willing to be callous," Leyla replied.

"Yes. But if it had been the only way, if there had been no cord, no alternative, what would you have done? In the end?"

She shook her head. There was no answer she could give. Not to Scholem, not even to herself.

They went out into the corridor, Leyla in front, like a prisoner, Scholem behind her with the gun.

They passed a series of open doors, but the rooms beyond lay swathed in darkness and revealed nothing of their interiors. Then a closed door, with a single word written on it in red paint. Scholem paused and drew Leyla's attention to it, explaining in whispers what it was. They would have to come back here, if they could, after they had found David. If they found David. Leyla nodded grimly and they went on.

Only the central passage in which they walked was lit, and that dimly. There was an intersection, then, abruptly, another, but they kept to the main path. All was quiet. There seemed to be no one abroad.

At the next turning Leyla heard something. They stopped, listening carefully. Someone was washing pots and pans nearby. They crept on down the corridor toward the sound, their senses strained to the limit. From a doorway on their right a pale light shone into the passage. Pressing themselves to the wall, they edged toward the opening, ready to fight or run if need be. The sound of cleaning was louder now, coming from the lighted room. Leyla reached the edge of the door and looked inside.

A single woman stood in a large kitchen facing a high stone sink. She was about halfway through a huge pile of pots and dishes. On a stove near her, water was boiling in a large kettle. Leyla turned and gestured to Scholem. Together, they stepped quietly into the room and approached the woman. She continued her washing, oblivious of them.

Scholem stepped behind her, slipping one hand over her mouth, overpowering her even as she reacted to the sudden intrusion.

"Don't make a sound," he whispered, turning the woman around to face him. She was a young woman of perhaps seventeen or eighteen, and her eyes were wide with fright.

"Are you alone?" Scholem asked, putting his mouth close to her ear. She smelled of spices, as though her skin had acquired the odor over the years. Frantically, she nodded.

"Is there anyone near, anyone who could hear us?"

She shook her head. Her eyes were still wide with panic.

"I'm going to remove my hand. Do you understand? Don't shout or try to scream or I'll be forced to stop you. Do you understand?"

She nodded. Scholem took his hand away and she breathed in deeply several times, then started to cry in reaction to the shock. Her hands were still wet with dishwater. On the stove the water boiled, releasing steam in a gentle cloud.

She was quite a pretty woman, Scholem thought, but her features were marred by a dullness, a blankness of expression that came, he inferred, less from an innate lack of intelligence than from a lifetime sequestered in a world of rocks and shadows.

"I won't hurt you," he said, "unless you call for help or try to escape. Just answer my questions and no harm will come to you."

Leyla watched him without saying anything. She wondered why he did not hit her to make her talk. Or was that to come?

"Have you seen the man they brought here a little while ago, the American?" Scholem asked.

The woman nodded, tears still streaming down her cheeks.

"Do you know where he is kept, where he is now?"

She nodded.

"Tell me, then. Don't be afraid."

The woman gulped and tried to speak. Her voice was hoarse at first and wobbled from fright.

"He . . . he comes here every mealtime . . . to eat. I . . . I have served him . . . a number of times." She paused, not sure what to say next.

"And where does he sleep? Is it near here?"

She nodded.

"Yes," she whispered, "near the ruler's quarters."

"Where is that?" Scholem pressed.

She took a quick breath and wiped her eyes. She was beginning to calm down a little. But she was still frightened. Who were these strange people? Where could they have come from? She had never seen them in the city before.

"Outside, not far. . . ."

"But which way, for God's sake?" Scholem grabbed her by the shoulders and shook her violently. She began to cry again. Leyla pulled Scholem aside roughly.

"Please," she said, "can't you see the girl's frightened? You won't get anywhere by making her worse. You have to do it, only you speak German, but at least try to be more gentle."

Scholem's voice was quieter as he turned and spoke to the girl again.

"I promise not to hurt you," he said. "But it's important you tell us where we can find him."

"You leave here," the girl said, grasping at last what was wanted of her, "and go . . . right. At the end of the passage, go left. It's one of the first doors in the next passage. I don't know which one. There may be a guard outside, I don't know."

"Thank you," said Scholem, smiling to reassure the girl. "Now, you say David . . . the American . . . comes here to eat every day. Where do you keep the food for the meals you cook here? Is there a larder or a storeroom?"

The girl pointed to large cupboards in the wall.

"There," she said, "we keep what we need for a week at a time, then we are sent more from the stores on the next level below here."

Scholem told Leyla what the girl had said. She nodded and went to the cupboards. The doors were locked, and she asked Scholem to tell the girl to give them the keys if she had them. He did so and the girl drew a set of keys from her pocket and handed them to him. Her hand shook as she did so and her eyes constantly shifted toward the door, as if contemplating a dash for freedom. Scholem passed the keys to Leyla without taking his eyes off the girl. He still had to think what to do with her.

Leyla opened the largest of the doors, revealing not a mere cupboard but a deep larder cut directly into the stone wall. Inside were jute sacks and pottery jars of several sizes. She opened several and found rice, flour, and a variety of pulses. The staple diet of the people of Iram was monotonously plain, though well enough balanced and in most respects much healthier than that of the average American or European.

Leyla turned to Scholem.

"Ask her where all this is grown, Chaim. Surely they can't supply their own produce in this place."

Scholem asked the girl, but she nodded.

"Yes," she said, "we grow everything we eat. What else could we do? Where else will food grow? The men say there is only sand outside the city, sand that stretches the length of hundreds of passages in every direction. Perhaps they are lying, I cannot imagine anything as vast as that. But beneath the city there are six fields and many rooms for . . . hydro . . . I'm sorry, I don't know the word.

"Hydroponics, is that it? *Wasserkultur?*"

Scholem translated the gist of what the girl said for Leyla.

"Ask her where the flowers come from," Leyla said.

Scholem asked.

"From the hydro . . . ponics. There is a special room for them. They grow only the one flower, they call it edelweiss, I think. They grow it for the dead. And for the ruler."

Scholem explained all this to Leyla and added, "The edelweiss was Hitler's favorite flower."

He turned his attention to the girl again and asked:

"Who is this ruler you speak about? What is his name?"

She shook her head.

"He has no name. He is just the ruler. He has always been here, before I was born, before any of us were born, except the oldest perhaps. We see him very seldom. Mostly he lives in his room, but sometimes he comes to visit us. He is very old, there is no one as old as him in Iram. But they say he will never die. Not until the world is made new. Then he will die and return to us in a young body."

While Scholem spoke with the woman, Leyla had started emptying a large jar with a lid that screwed shut. It would do for water. When it was empty, she tipped some flour out of a sack, then found a pitcher of water in the corner and filled the jar. She then placed the jar in the sack, leaving enough room to tie it once at the top and again at the bottom. Taking a second sack and a second jar, she did the same, turning the sack into a sort of bag with knots at either end. Turning to Scholem, she said:

"Tell her to give me her waist cord. I think it's long enough for what I want."

The girl wore a plaited cord that had been wrapped three times around her waist. At Scholem's request, she undid it and handed it to him to pass to Leyla.

Leyla took the cord, found its middle, and cut it raggedly in two with the knife. She took one of the two cords, tied one end at the top of one bag, the other end at the bottom, and repeated this with the second cord and the second bag. She picked up one bag and threw the cord over her head so that it ran over her left shoulder, with the bag hanging diagonally across her back. It was a lot less comfortable than a rucksack, but it would have to do.

She handed the other bag to Scholem, covering the woman while he put it on.

"What do we do with her?" Leyla asked. There really was nothing with which to tie someone up this time.

Scholem cast a glance toward the larder.

"We'll lock her in there. Someone will let her out eventually. With luck we'll be gone by then."

He told the girl to clear a space for herself in the larder, then ordered her inside. Reluctantly, she climbed in and crouched down, submissive, as if all her existence were focused in the act of crouching down under menace, under the threat of violence. Scholem wondered what sort of life it was for her in this place. He looked away, then closed the door and locked it.

Leyla was waiting for him at the door. She held the gun tightly in both hands.

"It's time to go," she said.

He nodded. It was time.

FORTY-EIGHT

David lay half awake, half asleep in the remote darkness of his room. There was a lamp beside his bed, but he preferred the comfort of the dark. In the light he could see where he was; he would lie flat on his low bed staring at the ceiling, at the blank walls, at the presence of Iram all around him. He could feel the city breathing through its long, unlit tunnels, tightening its coils about him, suffocating him. In the dark he could be anywhere and nowhere. His thoughts were muddied: nighttime thoughts of death without peace, without resurrection. He wondered why von Meier bothered to keep him alive at all. And he wondered who had killed the guard at the west entrance.

There was a small sound at his door, then it opened and al-Shami entered, fat and mournful and sinister all at once. He carried a lamp. Flickering gray shadows played over his face. He seemed tired and edgy, less full of the élan of cruelty than David remembered. He had lost weight. After a moment's hesitation he stepped into the room, wheezing slightly in the cool air. There was a small stool beside the narrow truckle bed. He lowered himself onto it carefully: it seemed absurdly small for his bulk, like a child's stool.

Since he had come to Iram, David had seen al-Shami only twice. Neither occasion had been a comfortable meeting. Al-Shami, rebuked perhaps for his treatment of David during the journey to Iram, had tried to be conciliatory, but David had been unable to make the transition to a more relaxed relationship. He still feared and distrusted the fat man, felt uneasy in his company, sensed the underlying evil of the man as freshly as he had sensed it the first time. More profoundly, he could tell that al-Shami was not at home here in Iram, that he disliked, even feared the place, and could not be trusted on that account. David was of the opinion that the fat man had sensed some advantage in him, that he had sold him in some way to von Meier, in return for precisely what David had no means of knowing. And he was sure that whatever bargain had been struck had not, in the end, been entirely to al-Shami's liking. Had David been an ace in a protracted game of poker between the two men, an ace al-Shami had played too late or too ineptly? David could not guess what deep relations existed between the Syrian and the German, he only knew that, whatever they were, von Meier would always have the upper hand. And al-Shami, for all his bluster, must have known it too.

The fat man put the lamp down on the floor and looked at David.

"Were you sleeping?" he asked.

David shook his head.

"No," al-Shami said. "You would not be sleeping. I find it hard to sleep here too. In spite of the darkness. Or perhaps because of it." He paused, watching the long shadows gather beyond the range of the lamp.

"They say von Meier never sleeps," he went on, "that he hasn't slept for seven years. I find it hard to imagine that. Seven years without rest, without dreams. Thinking, always thinking. Unable to get away. I don't think I could bear that, to be always awake." He sighed. The shadows seemed to cluster in the highest parts of the room.

"And yet," al-Shami went on, his pudding face creased tightly, "I think I understand. When a man grows old, sleep is a terrible thief. When so little of life is left, to spend so much of it in sleep . . ." He stopped abruptly and looked at David.

"Is that why you do not sleep?" he asked.

David shook his head. He had hardly thought of death since von Meier pronounced the sentence on him.

"I heard what happened," al-Shami continued.

David said nothing. There was a cautious silence.

"Did you kill the guard?" the fat man asked at last.

David shook his head. Was it that simple? he wondered. Was al-Shami just hoping to get a confession from David, something else

423

he might give to von Meier?

"I think you're telling the truth," al-Shami said. "It's a mystery, then, his death. Perhaps someone wanted to leave the city. They say it has never happened, but I could understand it."

He paused again. From a pocket he took out a small strand of worry beads. They were made of amber and had a fine green tassel of silk at one end. The fat fingers began to play indolently with the beads, clicking them gently along the cord.

"Where did you go?" he asked, breaking the silence again. "When you left two nights ago. You must have had a reason to slip away. Were you trying to escape? Was that how you became lost? Or were you looking for something? Is that what happened?"

David kept silent. He would tell al-Shami nothing, not even to bring the Ark to light after his death. It had lain underground for close on two and a half millennia, it could endure a longer stay. Perhaps it was better that way. He remembered the curse on the wax seal, the warnings on the door in front of the Ark. He remembered the lamp spinning out of his hand in the tunnel, the descent of the darkness. Old superstitions stirred in him, childhood memories.

"You're very quiet," al-Shami prodded. "Don't you want to talk? Am I disturbing you?"

"Why are you here?" David asked.

"To speak with you. To keep you company. If they don't find another suspect von Meier will have you executed tomorrow after the city is awake." He paused. "But if you are open with him, if you tell him where you went, what you saw, he might reconsider. You're useful to him, he had you brought here for a purpose."

"I'll have to disappoint him, then. He'll have to find someone else."

"Yes," said al-Shami. "There will be someone else."

"What is it he's afraid of my seeing?" David asked. "Does it matter what I see, what I know? I can't get out of here, I can't tell anyone. Why so many secrets, even now?"

Al-Shami fiddled nervously with his beads.

"There are no secrets," he said, half in a whisper, "only . . . things it would be better for you not to see. If you help him, if you cooperate as he asks, all will be made clear to you in the end. There is too much room for misunderstanding. And there has been too much of that in the past."

"And what about you? What are you to him?"

Al-Shami seemed taken aback by the question, unable to answer for a moment.

"His friend," he said at last.

"Does he have friends?" David asked. "Do you?"

"I have known him for a long time," al-Shami ventured. "Helped him. Kept him safe. Lied for him." He paused. "Killed for him."

"Would you kill me tomorrow if he asked?"

Al-Shami began to speak, faltered.

"Yes," he said quietly. "Of course."

"Quickly?"

The little eyes shifted, watching the shadows. Al-Shami shook his head.

"I could not promise that," he said lamely.

"When did you meet him?" David asked, returning to the subject of von Meier.

"A long time ago, when we were much younger, though we did not think we were young then. As I told you, I was in the party that went to Sinai in 1936. In those days I was an aide to Hajj Amin al-Husayni, the Mufti of Jerusalem."

David nodded. That made a little sense at least.

"I came to Syria from Palestine in the early thirties and became involved in politics there. My family had connections with that of Hajj Amin, and I joined his staff. He had met von Meier several years before our visit to Sinai. They had an understanding of some kind, there was something between them . . . even now I'm not sure exactly what it was.

"Hajj Amin helped von Meier find this place in 1937, just before he was forced to flee Palestine by the British. I was involved in that too. Just before the war ended, when von Meier decided to create his Sanctuary here, he spoke with Hajj Amin about it. The Mufti was in Berlin then. I was with him. When an agreement was reached, I was sent here to make part of the city habitable, to arrange ways and means of providing supplies, to establish camel routes that no one else would know about. We had to use camels: motor vehicles or airplanes would have been conspicuous.

"In those days I was thin. I could ride in the desert for weeks without tiring. I made a refuge here. Von Meier came first, with the

425

children and a few others. Later, more came. We kept the way open. We have kept it open ever since."

"And what have you had in return?" David asked, still probing.

The answer was simple, unfeigned.

"Hope," al-Shami said.

"Hope of what?"

"Of a future for my people." The fat man sighed. 'You think of me as a vicious man, a thug, a killer. Perhaps I am all of those things. The years have made me brutal, coarsened me. But I started differently. And anything I did I did for my people. To free them, to give them their liberty."

"But you are free," David said. "All the Arab states have independence."

"Not the Palestinians. Your people still occupy what was once their country. As for the other Arabs, they are not free. The West has made them prisoners, vassals, just as effectively as if it still ruled their territories. You think of us as children—immature and fanatical, incapable of self-rule, useful only as suppliers of oil. The Arab is still a stereotype for you, something from the *Thousand and One Nights*, from a Valentino film. At best a noble savage in exotic robes. But not someone you would invite for dinner or let your daughter marry.

"So, you see, we aren't really free, Professor. You keep us on a leash, you let us roam so far, and then you pull on the cord to keep us within our limits, limits that you have set for us. Our civilization is older and deeper than yours, but when we try to keep it alive, you call us backward. Our language is a hundred times subtler and more expressive than yours, yet we have to speak English when we want to trade with you or discuss political affairs. How many of your statesmen or businessmen speak even a word of Arabic? Your culture is like a cancer that is eating into our society. Israel is only the most visible manifestation of the disease, the tumor that must be cut out before we can begin any other treatment. Yet when we try to treat ourselves you accuse us of selfishness.

"So, you see, we need some hope that things will not always be this way. What von Meier wants for his people we want for ours: dignity, freedom, a chance to grow without the interference of others. In spite of what your statesmen imagine, we aren't children any longer. We don't carry magic lamps and expect *jinn* to come

426

pouring out like smoke: we use electricity, just like you. We use carbines instead of scimitars. We fly in airplanes and helicopters, not on the wings of giant birds or on magic carpets."

"You still haven't told me what von Meier gives you in return for your help," David pressed. "How does he give you hope? Don't you require something more substantial than that?"

Al-Shami's eyes clung to the shadows, as if looking in them for something he had lost.

"If you live," he said, "you will know in time. His people have helped us in many ways. With money, with men, with equipment. And when the time comes, we will repay that help. There will not be long to wait. I leave tomorrow for Jerusalem. I want to be there when the leash begins to slip. I have waited a long time, but not much longer now."

David felt the intensity, the eagerness of anticipation. Something crawled evilly in his bones. Al-Shami was not dreaming, he was planning.

"What will happen in Jerusalem?" David asked, knowing that it no longer mattered what he knew.

"If you live, you will find out. If you die, what will it matter to you?" The fat man shivered. "I am tired of this place. This will be my last visit here, I am too old to come again." He lifted his lamp and stood looking at David. The sickly light cast his shadow hugely on the wall behind, like the shadow of a misshapen Pleistocene beast.

"Good-bye, Professor," he said in a quiet voice. "I will do what I can for you. I will ask him to make it a quick death, a clean death. A last favor."

He turned toward the door. As he did so, the handle turned and the door opened. The guard was there, not Talal, but another man assigned to watch David's locked door for the night. He stepped into the room. Behind him came a woman in ragged Arab robes carrying a submachine gun, and after her a man in black.

FORTY-NINE

The man closed the door behind him and smiled at David, then at al-Shami, two very different smiles. David stood up slowly, his eyes on the woman, unable to breathe or think. It was Leyla and yet it was not. She had changed: her body, her face, her eyes. Above all the eyes. They bore a distant, haunted look, more pain than anything. In a matter of weeks she had become almost a stranger again. She said nothing, offered nothing. He tried to smile at her and found he could not.

Scholem was the first to speak.

"David," he said, "will you please frisk Mr. al-Shami and take from him any weapon you find? As you can see, my right hand is a little damaged." Scholem's voice sounded brittle, as if he spoke and acted under enormous strain.

David did as he asked, as if in a dream. He turned and began to frisk the fat man, his hands moving over the great torso like little birds on the body of a hippopotamus. Al-Shami stood in silence while David thus reversed the roles in which they had previously stood. His eyes were locked on Scholem, as if in recognition. In one pocket of al-Shami's robe David found a gun, a Luger automatic, old but well cared for and lethal. He took it and held it out to Scholem. The Israeli shook his head.

"You keep it, David. I want to leave my hand free."

Al-Shami's eyes still held Scholem's firmly in their gaze, but it was clear that he did not, in fact, recognize him. He had seen him before somewhere, he sensed it, but where and when and under what circumstances he could not remember. Scholem stepped

428

forward until he was immediately in front of the fat man. The rusty knife was still in his robes. He had kept it for al-Shami, as a lover keeps a delicacy for his beloved. The fat old man stood before him at last, fatter than he remembered him, oily and sweating and afraid, the eyes haunted by a thousand tortured ghosts. "Vengeance is mine, saith the Lord." Scholem had wanted vengeance for year upon dreary year. The thought of it had kept him alive through hot summers and cold winters. It had staved off final despair with life. It had sustained him in the desert. But it would be nothing to kill al-Shami now, he realized: just a simple action, an act of mercy, empty of meaning, sterile. He could use the gun, make it fast. But that would not given meaning to the act. Not like this, not in cold blood, not after so much death, in the cold darkness. He spoke to Leyla.

"Leyla?"

She shook her head wearily without looking around. She had no use for al-Shami either. Her blood was cold as well. She realized she had come here for David, not for revenge.

"Then let me have your gun, Leyla," Scholem said, "while you and David make some ropes for our friends here." He took the outstretched weapon and leveled it at the two men, who were lined up against the back wall of the room. David pocketed al-Shami's Luger and began to help Leyla tear strips from the thin blanket on his bed. The fabric was poor but, twisted and tied, it would hold long enough.

They tied al-Shami and the guard in the same fashion as the man in the storeroom and gagged them securely. With luck, they would have time to get out of the city before David's disappearance was discovered. When they had finished, David and Leyla looked at one another again. They still had not spoken to each other.

"You made it, then," David said. It was all he could think to say. Leyla nodded. She managed a smile, a little wan perhaps, but enough. From near the door, Scholem spoke.

"Time for reminiscences later. We've got to get out of here first. Come on. Leyla knows the way, she'll go in front."

He opened the door a crack and looked out carefully. The coast was clear. David followed Leyla to the door, still wondering if it was all a dream. At the door he turned and looked back at al-Shami on the floor. The fat man lay on his side like a beached whale trussed for some inconceivable purpose, yet in his grotesqueness and helplessness there was nothing either humorous or pitiable. He eyed David with all the viciousness and rage of a leashed dog that seeks only the opportunity to bite again.

They went out quickly and locked the door behind them, using the key Leyla had taken from the guard. Leyla went first, leading them down the empty passage, back the way she and Scholem had come. They moved along in silence, hearts racing, pulses throbbing, mouths like rough cloth, certain someone must spot and challenge them. But there was no one. David carried the lamp al-Shami had brought, and Scholem had taken the one belonging to the room as a reserve.

They entered the passage that led down to the Temple. Halfway along it, Leyla stopped. Opposite her was the door she and Scholem had passed earlier that night. Scholem nodded and Leyla tried the door. It was locked. David looked at the small notice printed on the door and frowned. What did Leyla and Scholem want here? The notice was simple: *Achtung: Sprengstoffe* (Attention: Explosives), it read. Beneath it in smaller letters was a warning: "Extinguish all lamps."

The lock had been designed more from the angle of safety than as a serious means of keeping anyone out. Discipline in Iram was strict: the lock was there merely to remind the careless of what the notice said. Scholem kicked the door hard and it gave at once.

The room inside was permanently lit by means of a row of oil lamps behind glass in one wall, to which access was available from a small chamber next door. Scholem and Leyla set down their lamps and entered the room. David hesitated, then put down his own lamp and followed them, closing the door behind them. All around the walls, boxes were stacked in careful piles. David could make out containers of gelignite, TNT, nitroglycerine, and ammonium nitrate. There were smaller boxes of detonators and timers, all stacked carefully away from the high explosives.

"I don't understand," David said. "Why have we come here? They'll soon find al-Shami's missing or the guard's not at his post. We haven't much time."

Scholem turned and faced David. He nodded.

"I know," he said. "We'll have to work quickly. Look, David, I've talked this over with Leyla and she agrees with me. Our chances of getting out of this place alive are slim—you know that. And even if we do make it out of Iram, I don't give much for our chances of surviving the desert a second time—without transport, with only the provisions we've got in these two sacks. That means we may not get back to Jerusalem or anywhere else with what we know, and there isn't going to be any way of sending a message back. Not to Jerusalem, not to anywhere. That leaves only one option. We have to destroy what we can now, while we can. If we make it, all the better. Someone can come back here and finish the job, if it needs finishing."

David shook his head. He was finding it hard to take in what Scholem was saying.

"I'm sorry," he said, "but I don't understand. Destroy? Destroy what?"

Scholem stared at him.

"Iram, of course. What else? I've worked it out. I think there's a way we can do a lot of damage, maybe a hell of a lot. It's worth a try."

David stared back, the truth of what Scholem was saying sinking in.

"Surely you can't be serious," he said.

Leyla came and stood beside Scholem.

"Yes, David," she said, "he is. We are. He's explained it to me and I think he's right. I don't know much about explosives, but I think it can be done. And Chaim's right when he says we have to do it now. We can't take the risk that none of us makes it back. If that happens and we've left this place intact, God knows what will happen."

To David, it seemed as though they had both lost their senses. They wanted to destroy the greatest archaeological discovery of all time. He had seen things beyond his wildest dreams. The library alone was worth more to mankind than a dozen collections twice its size. There were statues, wall paintings, artifacts from every period of Iram's existence, treasures from every culture the city had ever been in contact with, robes and jewels and weapons and cooking utensils, an entire society in aspic. There would be enough here to occupy a thousand scholars, each for a lifetime. There would be answers to innumerable unsolved questions, keys to thousands more. And they wanted to reduce all this to rubble, to bury it forever beneath a mountain of dust and sand.

"I can hardly believe this," he said. "Are you seriously suggesting we destroy this place? Do you realize just what we've got here? It isn't ours to destroy. Iram belongs to mankind, everything in it. What harm does it do to leave it? Von Meier and his crowd are harmless. The whole thing won't last another generation or two."

Scholem glanced at Leyla, then back at David.

"Von Meier? He's here in Iram?"

David nodded.

"He must be a very old man," Leyla said.

"He is," replied David. "But he still runs this place like a king."

"'The ruler,'" Leyla whispered.

"All the more reason, then, for what I plan to do," said Scholem.

"What, because a crazy old man lives down here with a crowd of people who don't know any better, you want to blow everything up?" David paused. "Do you realize just what's down there, what's been hidden here all this time?"

"I'm sorry, David, but it doesn't matter. No matter what it is. I don't think you understand. Von Meier and his people are a threat, a real threat. This place is a threat."

David held Scholem's eyes. It was vital to get across to him just how devastating the destruction of Iram would be.

"Chaim," he said. It was the first time he had used Scholem's personal name. "Please, listen to me. Even if you don't care about the rest of Iram, you've got to care about this. I found it a couple of days ago. I still find it hard to believe, but I know it's there. They brought the Ark here, Chaim. After Babylon. Do you understand? The Ark of the Covenant."

It was as if a chill passed through the room. Scholem's face went gray. However unobservant he was, however impatient of tradition, he knew it was something he could not bring himself to do. It was the holiest of all holy things. He could not be the instrument of its destruction. He looked at Leyla. Her eyes were fixed on him, uncomprehending.

"What is it?" she asked. "What are you talking about?"

"The Ark," Scholem said. "The Tabut al-'Ahd, that's what you call it in Arabic, isn't it? It contains the tablets of the law. It's been lost ever since the Temple was destroyed two and a half thousand years ago. David's right, we can't let it be destroyed. We have to think of something."

"Are you serious, Chaim?" Leyla protested. "You're willing to

432

leave this place intact just because David found some ancient Jewish treasure? You know what we found, what this place is. Tell David. He's been here, but I don't think he actually knows what's going on."

Scholem looked at her, then back at David.

"Just what do you know about Iram, David?" he asked.

David pursed his lips.

"Not very much," he said. "The city's a sanctuary set up by von Meier after the last World War. I don't know why, exactly, they wouldn't tell me. I think it's some sort of religious community."

"You don't think they're dangerous?"

David hesitated.

"Yes," he said, "I suppose I do. We've seen what they can do. But I don't think they pose a big enough threat to anyone for us to destroy this place. We don't have that right. We have a responsibility."

Scholem exchanged glances with Leyla, then returned his gaze to David. He shook his head slowly.

"You're right, David. We do have a responsibility." He paused. It was not easy. "Iram is a sanctuary as you said; but not for a religious commune, not as such. It was planned toward the end of the war by von Meier in conjunction with Heinrich Himmler and other officials in the Third Reich. Amin al-Husayni, the Grand Mufti, was involved somehow or other. They brought children here from the Lebensborn homes. They brought teachers to indoctrinate them in Nazi ideology. It's a nursery, David, a last refuge for seeds transplanted from Nazi Germany. I don't know what their plans are or how they mean to carry them out, but I do know they set this place up for a purpose. If von Meier is still alive as you say, then I don't doubt that purpose has not been forgotten."

David stared at Scholem in bewilderment.

"How . . . how do you know all this?" he asked. "I've seen no sign of it, nothing." But he thought of the parts of the city declared out of bounds to him, of the restrictions placed on speaking with its inhabitants, of the prohibition on visiting the city's classrooms.

"We found papers, David. There's no time to explain now. Later, if we're still alive. The papers are in Leyla's bag."

Leyla herself broke in quietly.

"Just near here, in a sort of temple, there's a huge swastika. It *is*

433

like a sort of religion, with the swastika as its symbol. You've got to believe us. This place is the center for something much more dangerous. We have to put it out of action somehow. It has to be done."

It sank in at last. The Temple. Talal's uneasiness. The upper end of the long cavern in darkness. He thought of al-Shami's words: "I leave tomorrow for Jerusalem. I want to be there when the leash begins to slip." David took a deep breath, then nodded.

"Very well," he said. "I understand. You're lucky . . . you haven't seen this place, you don't know what it's like. But if what you say is true, I don't suppose we have much choice, do we?"

Scholem shook his head.

"I'd like to say, 'Yes, let's leave it as it is and hope for the best,' but it's just not possible. We may regret it for the rest of our lives—if we live long enough—but that's something we'll have to cope with when it happens. I'd rather not have to live with the alternative."

"What about the Ark?" David asked. "Can't we do something about it? I think we could carry it out between us, it isn't very large."

"It would slow us down a lot," said Leyla.

"She's right, David," Scholem urged.

David looked at them, knowing what he asked. He wanted to risk their lives for the sake of something he did not even believe in.

"It's for you to decide, Chaim," he said at last.

Scholem remained silent, lost in thought. Time was passing. Finally he turned to Leyla.

"Go on ahead," he said. "David and I will lay the explosives and set a timer for . . . let's say an hour. Then we'll find the Ark and see if it can be carried out. If it can't, we'll just have to leave it."

Leyla shook her head.

"We go together or not at all. I brought you here. I came to get David out. Do you really think I can just go on and leave you both behind?" She paused. "Is it really that important, this Ark?"

Scholem wondered how he could explain.

"Yes," he said. "I think it is. It's a symbol. It stands for something. I don't think I could destroy it, not knowingly."

"Very well," she said in a quiet voice. "I'll come with you. Please don't argue."

Scholem smiled.

"In that case, let's get a move on. We haven't time to waste. There

434

seems to be plenty of gelignite. A box each should be enough."

"I don't understand," said David. "What can we do with three boxes of gelignite? Even the entire contents of this room wouldn't be enough to do serious damage to Iram. It's getting late. People will soon be moving about. There isn't time to put explosives in enough places."

Scholem put his hand on David's shoulder.

"Have you looked closely at the central pillar in the Temple?" he asked.

David shook his head.

"I've only seen it a couple of times," Scholem continued, "but if I'm right, a powerful charge will break it clean in half. Once it goes, the Temple will go. And if the Temple gives way, this whole place will start caving in. It may not work. But it's the only chance we've got."

FIFTY

Silence lay on the Temple like a shroud. From shafts high up in the ceiling near the pillar, rays of moonlight struggled to bring life and a memory of the outside world into Iram. Lozenges of watery light lay dappled like beached fish on the upper sections of the pillar itself. Caught between light and shadow, the pillar seemed like the great World Tree of northern myth, Yggdrasil, the cosmic pillar joining heaven and earth.

David scrutinized it with an archaeologist's careful eye, observing how the stones from which it had been constructed had been cut and shaped and laid one on the other with almost perfect precision, with absolute horizontality, growing upward like a living organism as the cave itself had been enlarged. Scholem, he thought, was right. Everything depended on the pillar now: the walls of the Temple, its roof . . . the whole of Iram ultimately. The city had been carved out of sandstone. It was old and pitted and weathered, and for unnumbered centuries it had been splitting and cracking. The Nafud subjected it to terrific changes in temperature: from day to night and from season to season, the stones ran the gamut of heat and cold. If the pillar gave way, destroying the precarious balance at the city's heart, the great, echoing Temple would indeed collapse. And if that happened, David was certain, from what he had seen and read, most if not all of Iram would go with it. He remembered the words of Jesus concerning the Temple in Jerusalem, the Temple of Herod: "There shall not be left here one stone upon another, that shall not be thrown down." Jesus had been a Jew, but he had prophesied the destruction of his Temple. And the prophecy had

436

been fulfilled.

They opened the boxes and carefully unwrapped the gelignite, laying it gently along the base and up the sides of the pillar. Leyla and Scholem both knew what they were doing, each having learned for quite opposite purposes how to handle and detonate explosives. Now they worked together, quickly and expertly putting the gelignite in place while David kept watch. It took only minutes, though it seemed much longer.

When they had finished, they set off in the direction of the great gateway—the Tall Gate of Elihoreph, the Deadgate of the little girl David had spoken to. They were headed for the tomb passages and the hiding place of the Ark. As they reached the gateway, David looked back down the long nave of the Temple, illuminated as always by the fires from below, spangled at its apex with flecks of moonlight struggling to enter Iram's dark interior. He watched the moonlight play on the upper reaches of the pillar and thought that it had been this way month after month, year after year, since the small apertures in the roof had been opened. He realized that the same apertures must let in daylight to a limited degree, but he had only ever been in the Temple after darkness had fallen outside . . . or so he surmised. He wondered what the Temple would look like with shafts of sunlight stabbing down, capturing the dust that floated in the stale air of the city, the dust of stone and dry flesh mingled as it rose. His eyes fell to the base of the pillar, but he could not make out the packed explosives or hear the timer ticking away the last minutes of the doomed city.

He turned to go, but as he did he caught sight of a movement out of the corner of his eye. He hissed to make the others stop, then stepped cautiously in the direction of the movement, holding his lamp in front of him. With his free hand he felt for the Luger in his pocket. He strained his eyes, trying to make out shapes in the darkness, but the banners and the gargoyles confused him and made him see movements where there were none, mixing their darker shadows with those thrown by the fires. It was impossible to tell if anyone was there, and they had no time to waste on a search. He turned and rejoined the others at the gateway.

"I thought I saw someone," he said, "but it may have been the light playing tricks. I think we should go on."

Scholem nodded and they hurried out of the Temple, along the

437

main tunnel of the necropolis. David went in front. He was nervous. He could not be sure that there had not been someone lurking in the Temple watching them. They would have to hurry.

They reached the turnoff that would take them deeper into the mortuary tunnels. David paused and said:

"It's this way. It isn't far, but for God's sake be careful with your lamps. If we get trapped in here we won't have a hope in hell of getting out again."

They hesitated for a moment, then Leyla and Scholem followed David into the blackness. Even with three lamps, the tunnel was claustrophobically dark. David led them slowly past the sleeping hosts on either side, down through the inky blackness until they came to the right turn that led to the Ark. They filed into the narrow passage. No one spoke. David experienced once more the sense of awe that had gripped him the last time he had been here. He wondered if Scholem felt it. Perhaps it was something almost tangible that anyone who came near the Ark would feel. Perhaps it was merely his father's voice out of his childhood, speaking in hushed tones of the Ark of God and what it contained.

The slab was open just as David had left it. There was an oily streak on the ground, where David's lamp had spilled: he warned Leyla and Scholem to avoid it. One by one, David leading, Scholem in the rear, they descended the stairs and collected in the tiny space before the doors. Though he now knew what to expect, David was no less anxious than he had been the first time he had stood there. He paused, his hand on the door, ready to open it. Leyla stood beside him, awed in spite of herself, infected by David's trepidation. She wanted to hold him suddenly, to cling to him here in the dark, to draw him down into the darkness with her to sleep.

David pushed open the doors. Nothing had changed. The Ark stood beneath its cloths as if waiting for them. He stepped inside and removed the cloths, one by one, until the Ark was uncovered. In the light of three lamps it shone more brilliantly than before. Age had not tarnished it. The acacia wood from which it had been built had not rotted, the gold with which it had been covered had not grown dull.

Scholem did not step forward at first. He stood in the doorway as if transfixed there, unable to take in what he saw or to cope with the emotions he felt. In the end David stretched his hand out to him and urged him to join him by the Ark. They stood close together like children bowed down by the weight of all their fathers resting on their shoulders.

Leyla stood outside, unable to enter the tiny room. She felt she had no place there. The Ark belonged to them, lived through them. She would fight them over the land, over Palestine, but not this. The mere memory of this object had kept their people together over countless centuries. It was a symbol more potent than bombs or bullets. She felt that it diminished her, not all at once, but in fragments, as if she were atomized, as if it made her dust and sand. She and her people were ancient like David's, more ancient if anything; but for them history was the desert, flat and bleak and ageless, the long endurance of wandering, whereas his people saw everything from the summit of a mountain ringed with fire and smoke. It was the difference between them. They had both built civilizations, they had both heard God speaking to them, they had both been crushed by exile and foreign conquest. But here, in this room, stood the symbol of all that clove them apart, the token of an unbreakable covenant with a jealous God. She hated the Ark for all it represented, for its mastery of her and her people. And yet, in loving David, in the same moment that she hated it, she found herself loving the Ark as if she belonged to it.

"How did it get here, David, do you know?" Scholem asked in a hushed voice, as if afraid to fracture the silence.

David explained as briefly as he could his discovery of the scrolls and outlined their contents. Somehow, knowing the details of how the Ark had reached Iram did not in the least detract from the mystery of it. When he had finished speaking he turned to Scholem and suggested they try to move the Ark. Scholem hesitated, then nodded and went in front of the structure. With the cherubim seated above the Ark on a low platform—the Mercy Seat—the whole thing was a little unwieldy and looked as though it might be too heavy for them to manage. But once they found proper handholds, it proved possible to lift the Ark with little real difficulty. Ideally, there ought to have been two long poles inserted through the rings at the four corners of the box, but these had evidently been lost or abandoned at some point during the Ark's transfer from Jerusalem. David followed him, supporting the Ark from behind. Leyla slung Scholem's bag across her shoulder and

439

picked up the lamp he had set on the floor. They would have to leave the third lamp behind.

It was awkward work getting the Ark up the stairs and through the narrow opening. At the top they laid the Ark down at the back of the tunnel and waited for Leyla to come up with the lamps. She left David's lamp behind, still burning in the chamber where the Ark had stood, as if in remembrance of its presence. David bent to lower the slab in place again—it seemed wrong somehow to leave it open. As he did so, his blood froze. A voice came out of the shadows a little distance down the tunnel, an old man's voice, hard and vibrant in the enclosed space.

"Please don't bother, Professor Rosen. I shall want to examine whatever is underneath myself. Please tell the young lady to put her gun on the floor. I am aiming a pistol directly at her head; please don't make me use it."

David straightened and put a hand on Leyla's arm.

"He wants you to drop the gun, Leyla. You'd better do as he says."

Leyla unslung the machine gun from her shoulder. For a moment it seemed as if she were about to swing it into a firing position.

"I would advise against it," the voice said.

Leyla looked at David. He shook his head. She dropped the gun at her feet, near the edge of the opening.

"Very good. Now, Professor, please put your hands on your head. Ask your friends to do the same."

"That won't be necessary," Scholem said in German. "I understand you very well. I have never forgotten how to obey commands in your language." He put his hands on his head slowly, insolently. David whispered to Leyla and they followed suit.

A match flared in the darkness, sudden and violent, throwing shuddering shadows across the faces of the dead. A hand lit a lamp and held it up. Von Meier stood there, the lamp in his left hand, a Mauser pistol in his right. Beside him stood his Japanese companion, Talal.

There was a sharp intake of breath. Leyla stared at Talal, guessing at once who he was, sensing a climax here in the pinched darkness. He had waited for them after all, had known they would come to him in the end. She felt her blood run cold. Her feet and her hands grew icy as if a chill wind had blown on them. Somewhere in

440

the Temple, she knew the timer was ticking its minutes away remorselessly.

As the light steadied, von Meier saw properly for the first time what David and Scholem had carried out of the underground chamber. He stood gazing at it in astonishment, realizing slowly what it was, unable to grasp that it was there in front of him, that it had been in Iram all this time, unknown and unsuspected by him. When he spoke at last, it was in a dry voice, a voice that seemed to have grown suddenly old.

"So this is why you came here. I congratulate you. It eclipses everything I have ever found, I freely admit that. It makes Iram . . . ashes. I had suspected it, of course. There were references in the histories—hints, allusions. But not the slightest clue as to its whereabouts. And then you come here and in days you track it down. You impress me very much. I was not mistaken when I had you brought here." He paused and fell silent again, his eyes on the Ark.

"Well," he said at last, "there will be time to see it properly. I would prefer to be alone with it, to think my own thoughts as you must have thought yours. But I am extremely curious to see what is down those steps. If you would be so kind as to lead the way."

"How did you find us?" David asked. He could not believe von Meier had appeared there by chance or that he had simply followed them all the way.

"You were seen. A worker in the Temple caught sight of you. He followed your lights to this spot, then came to lead me back here."

David sighed. He had been right: there had been someone in the Temple.

Von Meier gestured with the gun. Leyla was nearest the steps. Reluctantly, she went down, followed by David, then by Scholem. Talal drew his sword and stepped toward the opening. The blade glinted in the light cast by the tiny lamps, as if stealing fire from the Ark. He reached the top of the steps and started down them. Von Meier came behind, waiting until they were down.

Just as Talal reached the fourth step, Scholem turned. He held the rusty knife he had found in the plane. With a cry of rage, he leaped upward toward Talal, lunging with the knife. The Japanese leaped backward lightly, and as he did so swung his sword in a quick slicing motion that seemed almost effortless. The blade caught Scholem on the left shoulder and passed on through his torso in a diagonal line, like a wire slicing cheese. For a second, Scholem seemed to stand frozen on the steps. The cry on his lips snapped short as though a switch had been pulled. The knife dropped onto the steps with a clatter. Then the top portion of his torso, including his head and right arm, slid off the lower part and toppled backward on top of David, while the rest of the torso and the legs fell forward onto the steps. Torrents of bright blood cascaded everywhere, washing the stairs. Leyla screamed. David fell, knocked back by Scholem's head, then twisted on the bottom step, pulled the Luger from his pocket and fired upward blindly, three times in quick succession.

The bullets caught Talal in the chest, throwing him back and sideways. Von Meier started forward, grabbing for him. As he did so, Talal's sword arm jerked in a spasm, severing the rope that held the counterweight for the slab. As von Meier rushed forward to catch Talal, his foot slipped in the oil that had been spilled a few days earlier. He toppled forward, and as he fell the slab teetered and crashed down, catching him in the middle of the back and snapping his spine. He hung trapped in the entrance, half in and half out of it, as the slab crushed him beneath the inexorable weight.

David pushed Scholem's head and arm away from him. Leyla stood by the door of the Ark chamber trembling. Somehow she still held the lamps in her hands, though they shook terribly. The stairs were a mess. Scholem and Scholem's blood seemed to be everywhere. At the top, Talal lay twisted on top of his sword. The upper half of von Meier's body hung down on top of the Japanese. Blood dripped down from the entrance. David felt sick and turned his face away.

For a long time he and Leyla stood holding one another in the semidarkness, unable to speak or move. The explosion caught them unawares, as an alarm bell whispers insidiously within a dream and claws the sleeper back to wakefulness and the depression of a new day.

FIFTY-ONE

The passage sounded as though it had come alive, as though the day of resurrection had come at last and the dead were awaking. They had managed to climb out of the underground chamber only to face the threat of being buried alive in the tunnels. Everywhere there were sounds of cracking and splitting as the walls groaned under the strain they had previously shared with the great pillar in the Temple. The floor beneath their feet shook suddenly. Tiny pieces of rock broke away from the ceiling and landed in their midst. Near them, a body in one of the niches crumbled with a gentle, whispering sound, like a sigh. Another followed it.

Against the wall the Ark sat unblemished, as though defying the rocks to crush it. It had been born in rocks, in words uttered by thunder at the summit of a mountain wreathed in cloud. In its belly it had carried those words, carved in stone, just as generations of the pious had carried them carved in their hearts. In spite of everything, it had endured, not only here in its forgotten sanctuary, but in the minds and memories of those generations.

David crouched by the side of the Ark. There was no way they could take it now, even if they could escape themselves, which he doubted. But perhaps . . .

"Leyla," he said, "please help me. Quickly."

"David, we have to get out of here. There's no time."

"Please. This is important."

She joined him by the side of the Ark. On his instructions, she helped him lift the Mercy Seat with its cherubim off the top of the structure. Underneath was a flat, golden lid. David pushed hard

443

and it slid open effortlessly.

Behind them, something fluttered in the darkness. A corpse returning to dust.

David lifted his lamp and shone it into the Ark. At first it seemed empty, then he made out the shape of a cloth rolled carefully and bound with leather thongs. He reached inside and lifted it out. The dried leather snapped as he touched it. His hands trembling, he unrolled the cloth. It contained two smallish rocks, each weighing about two pounds. They were rough, as though they had just been picked up from the ground, but one side of each stone had been chipped away slightly to flatten it. On the flat surface there were lines of writing. David recognized the style as the ancient Sinaitic script.

He held them in his hands, near the lamp he had set down on the edge of the Ark. The tablets of the law, two crudely incised stones picked up from the ground and placed here as symbols of a God of fire and carnage Who had made a covenant with a troop of ragged nomad tribes crossing His desert. They were baetyls, sacred stones, abodes of the deity, repositories of His word, the earliest form of Semitic religion.

He held one of the stones out to Leyla.

"Can you carry this?" he asked.

"I think so," she said. She took one of the sacks from her shoulder and placed the stone inside. It was pointless, she thought, but she did it.

"I'll take the other bag," David said. Leyla passed it to him and he placed the second stone inside it. In the distance, rocks cascaded into an abyss.

"It's time to go," David said.

They hurried down the side passage into the secondary tunnel that would take them back to the main corridor. At the end they turned and looked back. Though they could not see it, the Ark was there in the darkness, waiting to be crushed beneath a thousand tons of falling masonry. In the room below Scholem lay, buried in the darkness with the Ark and the whispering shrouds. They turned and headed for the main passage.

Within yards of it they heard a heavy crashing sound, then a deep-throated roar as the ceiling ahead of them caved in. Ton upon ton of rock tumbled down in front of them, filling the tunnel down which they were running. The passage shook and one by one the corpses in it disintegrated in a long row of dust.

Leyla sank to the floor and put her head in her hands. It was as if some malign fate were chasing them down these tunnels, determined to hound them into abject surrender before burying them forever in the depths of Iram. David slid down beside her, feeling beaten as well. He had done everything possible, he could do no more. He had delayed unnecessarily to find and carry away the tablets of the law. Now the city itself had claimed them. He remembered the curse on the wax seal he had broken, the other seal that had crumbled in front of the Ark chamber. He had presumed too much. He held Leyla's limp hand in his. Above them, a last mummy became dust.

The soft sound made David look up. As he did so, he remembered something he had read in von Meier's report, something he had forgotten until now. At one stage in his exploration of the city, von Meier had discovered a series of shafts at the back of the mortuary tunnels. He had at first thought they might possibly have been used as chimneys for some sort of cremation, but closer examination had showed that that had not been the case. Later, a reference in one of the histories of Iram had disclosed the fact that the shafts had been constructed as avenues for the souls of the dead, passages through which they could escape the unending darkness and return to the upper world.

David explained to Leyla about the shafts.

She sighed. It seemed such an effort even to contemplate moving again. It was so much simpler, so much more comfortable to sit here in the half-dark and let the city decide their fate. David pulled her around to face him. Hope was rising in him again. Or perhaps it was merely defiance, a sense of outrage at the encroaching dark and a refusal to let it conquer him.

"It's our only chance," he said. "We've nothing to lose by trying it. Come with me. Please."

She looked at his eyes, at his pale, tormented face in the half-light. With one hand she touched him gently on the lips.

"Yes," she said.

David led the way into the writhing darkness. The sounds of crashing rock were all about them and growing in volume. The whole place was coming down. The builders of Iram had burrowed

445

and dug and tunneled through solid rock for centuries, carving the city out of the old sandstone. The great plateau was a warren of passages and side passages, halls and chambers, wells, staircases, pits, and cesspools. It was giving way at last, and each section that caved in put an intolerable strain on what remained.

They ran, shielding the lamps, threading their way through blackness in search of escape. The floor leaped and became still again. Behind them, a shower of rocks came down, blocking off any possibility of return. Heavy cobwebs lay thick across their path. No one had been down here in centuries, perhaps not since the last dead had been laid in their niches. If they were in a wrong passage, one without a shaft at the end of it, they would never get out of Iram alive.

The passage turned and twisted several times, then leveled out. Suddenly it ended against a blank wall. They could go no further. They were trapped in a cul-de-sac. This must have been one of the earliest burial passages: the bodies in the niches were no more than skeletons, as old as Babylon. But the air smelled fresh. David lifted the torch.

High up in the wall above, he could make out what looked like an opening, narrow, but just wide enough to allow a human being, if he were thin enough, to go in.

"That must be one of the shafts," he said.

"How can you be sure?" Leyla asked. "It could be anything, a natural hole in the rock, anything at all. We could get trapped."

"We are trapped," David answered. "But there has to be a shaft here. Air's coming from somewhere. This is the only opening I can see."

"Shouldn't it be straight? Shouldn't there be light?"

"I don't know. Perhaps they weren't cut straight. We've got to try it. There's nothing else."

The whole passage shook.

"How do we get up there?" Leyla asked.

"Use the niches," he said. "Follow me."

They put the lamps down. Now they would be of no use to them. But they continued to burn, giving a little light. Gingerly, he placed a foot on the bottom ledge of the first niche, then stood up, grasping for the ledge of the one above. He touched rotten cloth and bone. With both hands he hauled himself up, leaning forward into the dark niche. He had no idea what was in there, and he preferred not to know. He knelt and put a hand down for Leyla to grasp. She pulled herself up and stood beside him, both feet on the ledge. The light from the dying torch fretted her with shadows. He bent forward and kissed her, a light, trembling kiss on parted, frightened lips. She squeezed his hand, once, then turned to climb again.

He helped her up to the next niche, then she pulled him after her, scrabbling among the dead for a handhold. They got their breath, then began again. A low rumbling passed through all the passages. Part of the wall opposite them disappeared.

There were five niches, then they were at the opening to the shaft. If it was a shaft.

"I'll go first," David said. It seemed the right thing to say, but it took all his courage to put his hand into the dark opening. His shoulders went through and he pushed up into the narrow gap with the rest of his body. The shaft ran at a shallow angle, allowing him to slide inside and move forward, his arms out in front of him, inching his way like a snake. It was pitch-dark. He could feel the walls of the tunnel hemming him in on all sides, thousands of tons of shifting rock.

He fought down the rising panic and squirmed forward. Behind him, Leyla was already in the shaft, pressing hard on his heels. There was a shudder, and through the rock all about him he heard a sound like an express train. A sudden jolt sent his shoulder crashing into the tunnel wall. There was a sound of falling rock somewhere. It was unimaginably black. He felt his heart race. A childhood fear of being buried alive resurfaced somewhere in the recesses of his mind. He wanted to break free, to stand up, to move his limbs. He felt constricted, choked.

Leyla could not see David, but she knew he was there in front of her. The sound of his breathing came to her down through the darkness, harsh and fast. He was wrought up, she thought, giving way to claustrophobia. If he panicked, they would both be finished.

"David," she called. "Breathe more slowly. Take deep breaths. Try to relax."

He heard her voice as if it came from miles away, remote and detached. He breathed in deeply, holding his breath, then exhaled slowly, then in again. Gradually his pulse rate slackened and he felt himself grow calmer. He inched forward again. There was another heavy crashing sound, very close this time.

"David!" It was Leyla again. "That was just behind me! I think the entrance to the shaft collapsed. We've got to get out of here!"

David realized that the whole tunnel could cave in on top of them. Or that, even if there had been an exit at the end of the tunnel, it might be blocked by now. He pushed and pulled himself forward with renewed desperation, clawing his way through darkness toward light that he only hoped might be there. It was difficult to tell, but all the time he had the distinct impression that he was climbing up a gentle but definite gradient. It seemed to go on forever. His hands, elbows, and knees were raw, the skin scraped away on the rough rock. From time to time he heard sounds like thunder, sometimes far off, sometimes frighteningly close.

Without warning, his fingers touched something. His heart stopped beating. Gently, he slid forward, then stretched out his hands further. They came up against rock. Frantically, David scrabbled in front of him, above, below, on every side. It was rock. Solid, impenetrable rock. The shaft went no farther. It was no longer a shaft: it had become their tomb.

...

FIFTY-TWO

"What is it, David? Why have you stopped?" Leyla's voice reached
him from behind. He breathed deeply several times, trying to keep
his answer calm.

"I've come up against a wall," he said. "I can't go any farther. I
think we're finished."

There was silence, then. "Are you sure? Maybe it's just a small
obstruction."

"No, it's solid rock. A rock face of some kind."

"What about the air?" Leyla called from behind.

"What do you mean?"

"The air, in here. Where's it coming from? And what's the point
of this shaft at all? It can't be a dead end. The air has to come from
somewhere."

She was right. In his stupid panic he had forgotten to think. He
willed himself to be calm; gradually he collected his thoughts
together. There was more to it than just the air. The shaft was man-
made, he was sure of that. It seemed to be straight and regular in
construction and came out at a convenient place below. But why
dig a shaft that went nowhere? Even if it was only intended as a path
to Gehenna, it made no sense for it to finish in a dead end. The
shades of the departed might be able to get out through a pinprick if
they were agile enough, but there did not seem to be even that here.
The ancients had not interpreted death in very spiritual terms. They
put pots and food and weapons into the tombs with their dead. They
thought of life after death as a semiphysical existence, not one
of disembodied spirituality. A dead end made no sense.

Somehow the idea of a shaft that led nowhere was familiar to him. Archaeologists often came across blocked passages and walled-off tunnels in their digs, but this was different: it was meant to be like this. And then it came to him. Some of the tombs in Egypt, including the Great Pyramid itself, employed closed shafts as a means of foiling would-be tomb robbers. Heavy stone portcullises, slabs, or rock plugs were used to shut the passages off, often leaving an escape route for the workmen who put them in place.

But there would be no escape tunnel here; the shaft they were already in would have served that purpose. Perhaps it had even been built to do so. More seriously, David doubted if tomb robbery had been a very common crime in a closed society like Iram—where could a robber have sold his loot? And surely the tombs were at the other end of the shaft, not here. Unless . . .

He began to explore the rock in front of him, running his fingers along the joint where it met the wall of the tunnel. His heart gave a small jump. It was not continuous with the rock of the shaft. There was a tiny gap, hardly enough to insert a finger into, on the bottom, at both sides. This was a slab or plug of some sort. The question was, just how big was it? Some of the plug blocks in Egypt stretched for as many as ninety yards or more. Then he realized that the gap must be the source of air in the tunnel.

He dragged himself closer to the rock and pushed with all his strength. Nothing happened. He had very little purchase, lying at length on the stone floor. He shifted, wedging himself between the walls. There was a rough area against which he was able to lodge one foot. He pushed again. There was a grating sound, stone moving over stone. He put his fingers to the gap. It had widened by a fraction, he was sure of it. The slab was movable.

"I can move it!" he shouted.

"Save your breath!" Leyla called back. "Keep pushing."

The floor shifted and another part of the tunnel collapsed. David pushed again, gritting his teeth in desperation. The stone grated again. A soft glow appeared in the gap, a dim light. He redoubled his efforts, willing himself to use the last of his strength. The stone shifted yet further, letting two thin bars of light into the darkness. The rumbling sound was constant now. Iram was disintegrating. He heaved, the muscles on his arms and back standing up like ropes, the veins in his neck like wires. Sweat poured down his face.

450

The stone shifted, then rocked and began to tilt backward on some sort of counterweighted bracket. Light came flooding into the shaft. David closed his eyes against the glare, then opened them cautiously.

He was facing into a low-roofed stone chamber of regular construction. Here lay the final secret of Iram, a secret so well kept that, in all the long centuries, no one had even suspected it was there. David was the first to set eyes on that place in over two millennia. The chamber was illuminated through cunning shafts in the ceiling that let in light yet allowed rain to be sluiced away to the outside again. But David's eyes were not on the ceiling and his mind was not concerned with light.

All around the room, on high stone chairs, sat the kings of Iram. Dressed in the finest of brocades, in richly embroidered robes of red and gold and purple, the heirs of Solomon sat enthroned in the heart of their desert kingdom. Precious stones and ornaments of gold filigree, clasps of silver, and rings of amethyst winked and shone beneath the light dust of centuries. There were chests of ivory and figurines of ebony and cedarwood, delicately carved and painted to resemble living men; camels carved from alabaster, model ships from Yemen, swords from Babylon. Slumped in their chairs, the royal mummies held court to the centuries, their faces concealed behind pale masks of alabaster, fastened with ropes of gold, the unseeing eyes tinted with antimony.

David crawled out of the shaft and jumped down into the tomb chamber. He saw the figures of gazelles, ivory falcons, winged demons like those in the dying city below. The light seemed dim, now that his eyes had grown accustomed to it, but it shone on everything it touched. He looked around as Leyla's head appeared in the opening of the shaft; he saw the amazement in her eyes. Until this moment he had not had leisure to look properly at her face. It had changed, but it was still her face, and her eyes were still her eyes. She saw him looking at her and looked away, unable to return his gaze.

She came down from the shaft and walked across the chamber to the throne opposite her. The shriveled mummy hands and the faded, rotting clothes spoke of death, but the mask and the colors of the ancient fabrics and the jeweled pectoral on the breast still held echoes of a vanished majesty. She wanted to kneel. David's voice woke her from her reverie.

"We've got to get out quickly," he said. "Everything's collapsing around us. This room could go any second."

"How do we get out? This isn't much better than the tunnel—it's just bigger. We can die in comfort, that's all."

David looked around desperately. There must be a way.

"We're at the top of the city here," he said. "Those shafts lead directly to the outside."

"But they're far too narrow, we could never get out through them."

"Then what about the souls of the kings?" he asked. "Those shafts were built to let light in, not souls out. The tunnel we came through was the only link between this chamber and the city, as far as I can see. But al-Shami said there were dozens of the shafts he originally mentioned. The one we came through must have been a blind, constructed to look like the others, but actually allowing them to bring the bodies of their kings here at frequent intervals— hence the counterweighted slab. Assuming the other shafts exist, as al-Shami was told they did, why isn't there one for the kings? They need to get to heaven too, don't they?"

"But a large shaft would let the rain in during the winter."

"Unless it could be kept covered."

They began to scour the ceiling, looking anxiously for any trace of a larger opening. Ominous crashes sounded below them. Suddenly the floor bulged in the center of the room. A crack appeared and began to widen. One of the kings collapsed in a heap, a bundle of bones and yellow gold. The mask slipped on the face of another, revealing ordinary death, stark and unroyal. The room vibrated.

Inch by inch, they scanned the plastered surface. It seemed so smooth, so untouched. Geometrical patterns had been painted on it in gold and silver.

"Here!" David shouted. His practiced eye had caught sight of the fine, rectangular lines of the opening. Leyla rushed to his side.

"How do we get to it?"

"The boxes! Quickly!"

They grabbed chests, tipping out their contents and stacking them in a tottering pile. David was taller; he went up first.

There had originally been a pulley, but the rope had rotted long ago. David rammed the trapdoor with the heel of his hand, but it refused to budge.

"The counterweight!" Leyla shouted. "It's down here!"

There was still a length of rope attached to it. She picked it up and passed it to David. A heavy vibration rocked the room. One of the thrones tilted, sending its occupant flying into the center of the room. His head rolled across the floor, stopping beside Leyla's feet.

David stood on tiptoe, wiggling the rope through the ring to which it had originally been attached. The weight was heavy, threatening to throw David off balance. The room shook again. He teetered for a moment, then righted himself. The rope slipped through the ring and he tied it, nervous that it would break again.

This time the cover began to move, with infuriating slowness. Suddenly another crack appeared in the floor, widening rapidly as the room began to tear apart. Leyla was on the other side.

"Jump!" David shouted. "For God's sake, jump!"

She looked into the crack and saw the yawning space below. It dizzied and terrified her. She looked at David. The gap was widening every second.

"Don't wait any longer, Leyla! Jump!"

She closed her eyes and leaped, clearing the gap with about a foot to spare. David scrambled up through the opening and eased himself out onto the roof. He was on top of Iram, on the very summit of the rock formation, which he had only heard described before by al-Shami. He reached down and helped Leyla through. The tower of chests gave way and crashed to the floor. She hung for a moment by one arm, then David found a firm purchase on the rock and hauled her through.

They stood and listened as Iram died beneath their feet. Far off, at the other end of the mesa, a whole section caved in, leaving a gaping hole hundreds of yards wide.

"We've got to get off this rock," said David. "It could all go."

They climbed down slowly, scrabbling in the crumbling rock for handholds and footholds. The rock seemed alive, roaring and screaming in its dying agonies, trembling from time to time like a sick animal trying to hurl them off. One slip would be fatal.

It seemed like hours, though it could not have been more than fifteen minutes. At last they lay at the bottom, too tired to move, their bones aching, their muscles burning as if on fire, their skin bruised and bleeding. They knew they had to get away from the rock before it finally collapsed, but neither could move or even speak. They lay in the shelter of one of the pillars, feeling safe in the

453

shade. Up above, the whole of Iram creaked and groaned and thundered.

Leyla came to with a start. The voice came again.

"Was gibt's? Was geschieht?"

She looked up. One of the guards was standing over them. He had come riding up on his camel. Posted far out, he was the last to get back to the city since the strange crashing noises had begun.

David stood up, ready to throw himself at the man. The guard looked at him, then at Leyla.

"Wer sind Sie?" he asked. *"Was machen Sie hier?"*

He unslung his submachine gun and pointed it at them.

"Who are you?" he asked again, this time in Arabic. "What are you doing here?"

Almost at the same instant there was a sound as if a store of high explosives had been detonated, then a low rumbling began, rising in volume with incredible speed. The pillars around them shook violently. The guard looked up, terrified. David fired through his pocket, twice in quick succession. He watched the guard fall, quiet and inconspicuous. Why was death so easy, David asked himself, when everything else was so hard?

They ran now. The final throes had come upon Iram at last. Around the rock, men were still milling in confused bunches, shouting to one another above the noise. No one was even aware of their presence. They ran farther until they reached a shallow pit and jumped in. They looked back across the plain, past the dark pits and the pylons, past the winged statues. Iram was finished now. The pillars had begun to buckle under the shifting weights above, first the thin ones giving way, then thicker ones, then whole sections. It was like divine wrath. The whisper in the night, the dark wings, the music of sudden death, here now in the roaring of rocks and the breaking of mammoth pillars. A legend crumbled and fell to the sand. David thought of Samson in Gaza, in the Temple of Dagon, the pillars buckling and the building falling on the Philistines. He could hear the roaring of Iram, like the sea on rocks in a storm. He thought of the kings in their high chamber turning to dust, of the treasures of the city, of the library, of the great Temple, of the Ark. He turned his face away and clung bitterly to Leyla in the rank-smelling pit.

454

FIFTY-THREE

David and Leyla stayed in the pit all that night. When they came out in the morning the plain was deserted. There did not appear to be any other survivors. Iram was a pile of rocks from which smoke and flames occasionally issued. They found an abandoned camel, possibly the mount of the guard David had killed the day before. They came across water in a rock pool and food in the camel's bags, enough for two or three days, eating frugally. They still had the little food and water Leyla and Scholem had taken from the kitchen in Iram. Leyla thought about the girl they had locked in the cupboard there: had she guessed what was happening when the world caved in on her?

Even now, they went on, as if driven by a force stronger than themselves. It would have been so easy to lie down in the sand and never rise again, to accept the end of Iram as an end for themselves as well. They knew they were close to death and that every step they took brought them nearer to it. They rode the camel by turns, one walking, one riding, taking a straight line to the north. It seemed pointless, but what else could they do? They spoke little of what had happened. Leyla wanted to forget, to leave behind the memories of her journey to the Nafud, of all that had taken place in Iram.

At night they lay together, huddled near the camel in the dark. Leyla thought of the cold nights she had spent in the sands with Scholem, of his despair and bitterness. She wanted to hold David, to touch his face and hands, convince herself that he was real. She longed to make love to him but was afraid to, afraid to give herself to him in the cold, sterile sands. She did not repeat the admission of love she had made in Jerusalem, and David did not refer to it. Did he think she had been prompted by the fear and uncertainty of those last days in Jerusalem? And would he think, if she said it again, that it was not her speaking but the sands and the fear of things ending?

David watched her sometimes when she went ahead of him, a solitary figure beneath a pale sun, small, fragile, dwarfed by the towering dunes. When he lay with her at night, he wanted her, but something indefinable held him back, and all his passion ebbed out into the cold and the dark.

They talked in bursts, with long silences between. Both were looking for forgetfulness in the sands, but talking reminded them of where they had been and why. David was preoccupied by the loss of Iram, by the destruction of the Ark. He brooded on it constantly, like a man who has killed something precious to him, though he knows she would have brought him untold suffering. What is undone is undone, and David could not imagine the evil of Iram in an impossible future. He remembered only the dark beauty of its corridors, the light entering the pierced roof of its Temple, the Ark emerging from beneath its veil. And he thought constantly of the little girl to whom he had spoken, whose body he had crushed beneath tons of grinding rock. At such times he felt a terrible guilt, a revulsion toward himself.

But Leyla showed him the papers she and Scholem had found in the plane, and he remembered al-Shami's boast that something was about to happen in Jerusalem. The conspiracy did not begin and end in Iram. There was more, perhaps much more, that was as yet concealed. And he still did not understand why von Meier had brought him to Iram, why the collation of the tablets from Ebla had been so important. Something told him that there were deep reasons behind von Meier's interest and that they were connected to a wider and more terrible plan than the one they had uncovered.

They continued their hopeless journey, spurred on by new fears that overshadowed their own personal dread. Unless they could make contact with some Bedouin, they would die here, and if they did, they feared that nothing could hope to interfere with whatever plans were afoot.

That night they lay in the darkness, holding hands as if they were lovers, shivering from time to time, out of harmony with the night

456

and the desert and each other. There was no way to measure love in those remote distances; no nearness seemed enough to undo the vastness of the sands.

"Why did you come, Leyla? You were free; why trap yourself again?"

She told him about the reel of film, about the photograph of the Mufti.

"Al-Husayni was a wanted man long before he went to Germany," she said. "In Palestine during the twenties and thirties, he organized anti-Jewish riots and attacks on Jewish property. He became the leading power in the country: president of the Supreme Muslim Council, head of the Arab Higher Committee. He was greedy and ambitious, and he allowed no one to stand in his way. He wasn't content with killing Jews. His men killed Arab politicians who stood up to him, and ordinary people who took a more moderate line than he did. Dozens of innocent people were murdered. Whole families were shot or beaten. My family lost ten members, all gunned down by the Mufti's henchmen.

"I knew he was dead. But when I learned that he'd been involved in . . . all of this, I couldn't stay in Jerusalem. It seemed significant, like fate or something. I'm a Muslim, I was brought up to believe in fate, in God's will. I can still remember my father talking about him to us, when we were children. He would show us his photograph, then photographs of my uncles and cousin who had died. What the Jews did to us later was nothing to what the Mufti did then. He set Arab against Arab, family against family. I don't know, David, it makes no sense to me, to have so many hates."

The sky was clear. A shooting star stroked the blackness for a moment with its light, then vanished.

"Was it worth it?" he asked.

She looked up.

"Going go Iram," he said, "finding what you found. Was it what you wanted?"

She shook her head.

"No, it wasn't. How could it be? I realized it long before I got to the city. I didn't go to find al-Shami: I went to find you. That was more important to me than avenging old deaths. You tell me al-Shami's dead, buried back there in the rocks. But it means nothing to me. Even if I had killed him with my own hands, it would still mean nothing. Some wrongs are so old, revenge makes no sense."

"The Bedouin think differently."

She nodded.

"Yes, the Bedouin think differently. But they carry their past in their heads, keep it alive around their campfires. We have books and newspapers and films; we write histories, we rewrite them, we select, we edit, we amend. How do I know what happened in the thirties? Fifty years ago, before I was born?"

"Don't you believe in anything, Leyla?"

She looked around her, at the stones, the sand, the fretful camel, David.

"No," she said, "not any longer."

458

SIX

We weave, we weave the web of the spear
as on goes the standard of the brave.
We shall not let him lose his life;
the Valkyries have power to choose the slain.

Njal's Saga

FIFTY-FOUR

An early spring had opened the first flowers in Jerusalem. On the Mount of Olives the winter green of the cypresses was relieved by flashes of red and purple. The scent of jasmine filled the air. The late morning sun shone on the golden domes of the Church of Mary Magdalene and, below it, the Dome of the Rock.

David and Leyla walked along Herzl Street, heading for Abraham Steinhardt's apartment. Three days from Iram, they had found a Bedouin encampment. The shaykh had escorted them himself to an Aramco exploration base camp four day's journey to the north and they had persuaded the men there to help them get out of Saudi Arabia undetected. The camp's transportation included a light aircraft, a Cessna 414, and the pilot had agreed to fly them to a place near Haql on the Jordanian border. They had crossed the border into Jordan without difficulty and made their way to Aqaba. Leyla had relations there, people who knew not to ask questions, who had supplied them with clothes and money and taken them late that night across the Gulf of Aqaba to Eilat in Israel. From Eilat they had taken an early *sherut* to Jerusalem. So far they had been exceptionally lucky. No one had asked to see their papers.

Steinhardt lived in a new block not far from Jerusalem's Central Bus Station. It was past noon when they reached it; with luck Steinhardt would be at home for lunch. They had brought a present, a bottle of French calvados. Leyla had drawn everything from her bank account that morning: they needed money as much as they needed luck.

They climbed the stairs to the fourth floor. David knocked on Steinhardt's door: three times, the old code fixed between him and Leyla. There was silence. He knocked again, harder. Still nothing.

"What do you think we should do?" he asked. "I could ring the university, perhaps, see if he's there."

"He hardly goes there now, David. A few lectures, visits to the old library on Mount Scopus. He works at home mostly."

"So we wait."

The door opposite Steinhardt's opened a crack. Someone looked out at them from a shadowed interior. Two pale eyes scrutinized them. There was an asthmatic cough, followed by a wheeze. They turned.

"Looking for Steinhardt?" an old man's voice asked from behind the door.

Leyla nodded. There was a long pause. The crack in the door did not widen.

"He's gone," the wheezing voice said. Another pause for breath. "Dead. Died about . . . two weeks ago. Fell down the stairs here . . . broke his neck. Poor bastard had low blood pressure. So they say. Giddy spells. Stairs are steep. Too damned steep . . . for old men."

They listened in stunned silence to the voice, the unseen neighbor telling his woes. Then he stopped speaking and began to cough again, his old lungs throwing up the rains and mists and vapors of the long winter. For a long time no one spoke. Leyla held David's hand, fighting back tears. It was cold on the dim, beige-painted landing. Winter had taken its toll of the building, as of the inhabitants. The paint was flaking in one corner. Leyla looked at the stairs. They seemed hard and uncomforting, not a deathbed to choose.

The door closed and they were left alone with the landing. David began to go back down the stairs. Leyla looked at Steinhardt's door, remembering that last evening when she had come there from Scholem's. She shut out the memory and made for the stairs.

Suddenly the door opposite opened again and a head peered around it. Tufts of gray hair floated above a bald pate. Little red-rimmed eyes peeped myopically at Leyla without the benefit of lenses. Thin bloodless lips were set in motion.

"Are you Leyla?"

462

She nodded. There was no response. She said, "Yes."

"And you," the voice went on, speaking to David, "you must be David. David Rosen."

"Yes, I'm David Rosen."

"Wait here," the old man said. "I have something for you. For you both. It has your names on it."

He went away, closing the door behind him. They waited on the stairs, in the pale beige light. Leyla felt haggard. She wondered if she had enough strength left to reach the foot of the stairs. She sat down on the top step. A long time passed.

The door crept open and the withered head sprang out again. A long arm reached forward. A thin, bent hand clutched a white envelope, creased and grubby. Leyla stood and took it. Her name and David's were written on it in Steinhardt's hand, carefully, in old-fashioned Hebrew script. She could not accustom herself to seeing her name in Hebrew.

"Thank you," she said, her voice muffled in the long, deep landing.

"He left it here," the little man murmured. "Said I was to give it to you if you came, if anything happened to him." There was a pause and a pale cough. "He must have known. They sometimes do. Know, I mean. Know they're dying." Another pause, another cough, more a spasm really, dry, deep in the chest.

"How long was this before he died?" Leyla asked.

The old man thought. His wasted cheeks were drawn in, like the skin of a collapsed balloon. He breathed spasmodically, as if about to give it up after all. It would take so little effort to die, thought Leyla.

"Two days," he said, "maybe three. No more. Do you think he knew?"

"Yes," she said quietly, "I think he knew."

The old head nodded cryptically. He looked at her out of the side of his eyes.

"Yes," he agreed. "Old men know."

The head was withdrawn and the door closed with a soft, unhappy click, like the lid of a coffin shutting.

They went downstairs and out into the bright spring air. There was a cafe nearby, filled with people eating lunch. In a daze, they found a table and sat down. Waiters and customers buzzed around them busily, talking, calling orders, arguing; but they seemed to sit away from everything, in a cocoon of silence and sadness, unable to act or speak. The bottle of calvados stood on the table, an incongruous symbol of mute grief. Then a waiter came and asked for their order. Automatically, they asked for *kreplachs* and two Nesher malts. The food took awhile to come. While they were waiting, Leyla opened the envelope and took out the letter it contained. Sitting close to David, she read it in a low voice. It began abruptly, without preamble.

Dear Leyla and David,

If you ever read this, I shall be dead. I pray that you will both still be alive, although I fear for both of you. I am being followed, I am almost certain of it. There was a man outside my apartment block three days ago. He was there again yesterday and again today. He watches and waits, for what I do not know. When I go out, he comes with me, at a discreet distance. I haven't seen him behind me, but I know he is there, I can feel him at my back.

I think my apartment has been broken into and searched, at least once. There were small signs that someone had been there. They won't have found anything. I have sent all your papers—the book, the diary, the photographs, and your translations—to a friend. Don't worry, they will be safe with him. I posted them, so no one will know where they have gone. I'd better tell you a little about the man I gave them to.

His name is Harry, Harry Blandford. He's an Englishman, but he has lived in Israel since 1947. He converted to Judaism about ten years ago, though his observance of the *mitzvoth* still leaves a lot to be desired. The Chief Rabbi wouldn't approve of him at all. Not that I need criticize! But he eats bacon for breakfast when he can get it—which is quite often.

Harry Blandford's a strange man, but he's the best man in Israel to have your papers. He came to this country as a young man, and he's never set foot outside it since. After the war he was appointed to a post with AG3, the section of the British War Office's Adjutant General's Department responsible for the investigation of war crimes. After a while he was transferred to CROWCASS, the Central Registry of War

Criminals and Security Suspects, where he worked under Palfrey in Paris. By 1946 he was thoroughly disillusioned because he felt nothing serious was being done to apprehend former Nazis, by either the British or the Americans. The Russians seemed to be the only ones doing anything very much, and he hadn't a great deal of sympathy with them for other reasons. He resigned his commission and found work as a journalist with the Manchester *Guardian*. In 1947 his paper sent him to Palestine, and when the country became Israel a year later, he stayed on. He continued to learn a living as a free-lance journalist, but his real obsession was identifying and hunting down ex-Nazis. He's worked with Simon Wiesenthal and a few others in Europe, but mostly he goes it alone. He has very little money, and what he has he spends on his files and correspondence.

You may be wondering why I have sent your papers to such a person. Or perhaps by now you have worked it out for yourselves. In case you have not, let me spell it out for you. You found a diary written by an SS major which describes a prewar German expedition to Sinai. That expedition was headed by someone obviously in close relations with Hajj Amin al-Husayni, a man who later became the Third Reich's linchpin in the Arab world. I have just learned from another source that the man al-Shami who may have kidnapped David and taken him off to the Nafud was one of the Mufti's closest associates, before, during, and after the war. Whatever links existed in 1935 may still exist. Harry spent a long time during the fifties and sixties trying to have al-Huysayni arrested and tried. He knows as much about him as anyone alive. If there are links, he'll find them. The rest will be up to you.

I write all this on the assumption that you are both safe, or that you will be if you ever read it. One of you at least. I have no right to make such an assumption, of course, but the alternative is to despair. Life has to mean something, even if it is only an interval. Perhaps Harry will find something, perhaps you will be able to contact him, and perhaps someone in high places will believe you when you tell them what is going on. What about Colonal Scholem? Is he convinced? You will find Harry Blandford at Apartment 7, 15 Nissim Behar St, in Makhane Yehuda. Tell him I sent you, tell him who you are—I gave him your names.

I'm leaving this with my neighbor Potok. He's been old for so long, he thinks young people are another race. He probably won't even notice I've gone, if anything happens. But he'll keep the letter: he never throws anything away. When his wife died, they had to fight with him to get her body out of the apartment. Potok saw bad things in Russia; I hope they won't hurt him if they come for me.

Take care. If I see the Lord of the Universe, I'll tell him what's going on. He probably won't pay any attention; I think He's bored or annoyed with us. Still, He could try harder. Don't be fools: be nice to each other. When you get to my age, it won't matter . . . whatever it is that seems to matter now. *Shalom.*

Abraham

Leyla fell silent and folded the letter, replacing it in its tired envelope. The waiter brought the *kreplachs* and the beer. They ate and drank in silence. When they had finished, David called the waiter and asked for two small glasses. When they arrived, he reached for the calvados and poured a shot in each glass. He looked at Leyla, at her thin, worried face, at her sad eyes. Softly, he reached out and took her hand in his. With his other hand, he lifted his glass.

"*L'chaim*," he said. "To life."

Leyla raised her glass.

"To Abraham," she said.

FIFTY-FIVE

After almost forty years in Israel, Harry Blandford still knew only enough Hebrew to order a meal and direct a taxi home when he was too drunk to make it on foot. He paraded his Englishman's disdain for any language but his own with a swaggering air of gleeful indifference. When he had come to Israel, it had still been Palestine and English had been the *lingua franca;* as far as Harry Blandford was concerned, it still was, and forty years of Semitic gutturals in trains and buses, cafes and bars, had not convinced him otherwise. In the past ten years he had made things worse for himself by sporting a bright red *yarmulkah* and attending synagogue regularly. He wasn't a very religious Jew, but he made up for his impiety during the week by rigorous observance of *shabbat* and by getting religiously drunk during Purim.

He received David and Leyla in a room so crammed with papers that they felt as if they were stepping into an outsize filing cabinet. Nothing had been spared: not the chairs, not the tables, not the floor, not the sagging old couch that crouched beneath a heap of files in one corner. Even the doors had been unscrewed from the cupboards to allow free access to the shelves, and the stepladder that made it possible to reach the highest files had itself been commandeered for service, with boxes perched on every rung. A smell of dust and aging paper filled the place. From the ceiling a single light bulb presided dimly over the chaos below. A large tabby cat surveyed them sleepily from the back of one of the chairs.

Harry went across and picked up the cat, putting him under his arm and offering the chair to Leyla.

"He's called Sammy," he said, meaning the cat. "A bugger when he was young. Used to knock my files all over the damned place. Never seemed to make much difference, though. But he settled down in the end. Had to. It was settle down or be bitten to hell. I used to bite his bum, you see, just to show him what it was like. God, he had teeth in those days! Eats porridge now; getting old like myself."

He cleared another chair for David, then stood facing them near the window. Beneath his *yarmulkah,* which made him look like a cardinal, a tangled mat of unwashed white hair stuck out at improbable angles, as if trying to throw the red cap off. He had a high white brow, lined with thought and age. A very English-looking mustache set off a round, pink face that made David think of retired majors and bulldogs. The lower part of the face did not seem to match the upper, as if they had been joined together by accident. He wore a faded college summer jacket, with light stripes and no elbows. His white shirt had seen better days. The stripes on his tie matched those on his jacket. The outfit had lasted him a lifetime: there would be no parting from it now. David noticed that he had a young man's eyes. Sharp, inquiring, intelligent eyes that gave his name away. Harry Blandford was no doddering eccentric: he was a falcon, a bird of prey set to go after field mice and when he found them tear them limb from limb.

He offered them tea and they foolishly accepted, thinking it polite. In all his years away from England, he had never lost the knack of transforming the world's most civilized beverage into something almost poisonous. In a back street somewhere in the Old City, he had long ago found a supplier who could provide him with all the materials necessary for persisting in his vice. He dropped bags of something called PG Tips into a large brown earthenware pot, scalded them with boiling water, and stewed them until a liquid had been brewed that was almost black in color. When it had stood long enough, he poured the foul-looking liquid into chipped china cups, added milk before he could be stopped, then looked up with a pair of silver-plated tongs in his hand and asked:

"One lump or two?"

They shook their heads and he brought them their cups, complete with saucers and some round things called digestive biscuits. Smiling politely, they munched the biscuits and sipped the milky drink. Harry cleared some papers from an old, overstuffed armchair and sat down.

"So," he said. "Abraham Steinhardt sent you."

David looked at Leyla, then back at Blandford.

"Not directly," he said. "He gave your name to us in a letter. I . . . I'm afraid Abraham's dead. He . . ."

"Yes, I know," said Harry. "He fell down some stairs outside his flat, I heard about it soon afterward, from a mutual friend."

"The thing is," David went on, "I don't think his death was . . ."

". . . an accident?" Harry broke in. "I've known that for about two weeks now. Those papers you left with him led to some pretty strange connections. He wrote me a letter, telling me about the killings. It makes sense. Not a lot, but enough. There isn't much to go on as yet. But my old friend Hajj Amin seems to have been involved. Anything he's been involved with interests me."

"Why?" David asked.

"Why the Mufti?"

"No, not just him. Why any of them?"

"Ahhh!" Harry sighed. He sipped his tea. He seemed to enjoy it, like an addict with his fix. "You see around you the tokens of obsession, and you ask yourself, 'Is he harmless, or should I make a bolt for it?' Well," he went on, tapping his cup with a small spoon on which the tiny figure of an apostle stood, "I'm not harmless. I may look it, I may even smell it, but I assure you I'm not. At first I was, of course, like any eccentric with his hobby. I would collect my information, prepare my files, write up my reports, and pass them on to what I considered the appropriate authorities: the Allied agencies in West Germany, then the West Germans themselves, then the Israelis. I had polite letters in reply telling me that my information had been 'filed for future action' or even just 'future reference.'

"I gave them files on men responsible for the deaths of tens of thousands of people. *Einsatzgruppe* commanders, concentration camp officers, industrialists, Wehrmacht generals—and all they could ever say was 'pending further investigation.' Their key word was 'normalization.' They wanted Germany back on its feet again. They wouldn't have anything to do with trade unionists, socialists, people who had been opposed to the regime. Expertise and re-spectability, those were the things they wanted. The Nazis have been laughing up their sleeves ever since the war ended. We put on a few show trials—and that was after the British Foreign Office put up a hell of a fight to stop even those—and then let everyone else off the hook. We just wiped several million deaths off like bad debts and got down to business as usual.

"In the end, I started giving my papers to other people. People who cared. Groups of young Jewish activists mostly. You want to know what they did? They put bombs on doorsteps; they fired bullets into men they'd only seen before in photographs; they arranged for certain people to have unpleasant accidents. It wasn't much, I admit, but it made me a dangerous man. I'd wanted a better kind of justice, of course, something cleaner, more open: trials and public exposure, a proper accounting. Well, there wasn't going to be any of that, was there? So I had to make do with second best. But they know. Every time one of them has a mysterious accident, word gets around. They worry a little, maybe even a lot. They lie awake for a night or two, wondering if the doorbell's going to ring. They swear every time a car slows down when it's passing them."

David lifted the china cup to his lips. The handle was small and awkward to use; he could not fit any of his fingers through it. He'd heard somewhere that in England they extended the little finger of the right hand as they drank. That seemed risky. He took another sip.

"Aren't you afraid that will happen to you?" he asked. "That there'll be a knock on your own door one day?"

Harry leaned forward in his chair. Old springs creaked.

"Do you think I'm naive, Professor?" he asked. "I haven't stayed alive this long by behaving like a child. I told you I deal in information. In digging up one sort of past, you inevitably dig up other sorts as well. There are men and women, some of them very important people, who will freely own up to a Nazi background, as if they have no shame: 'I was young, I didn't understand what I was doing' or 'I stayed within the system to help as much as I could, to rescue Jews.' You know the sort of thing. It seems to do them very little harm. In some circles it's even an advantage. But let these same people know that you have information concerning, let us say, a marital infidelity or a homosexual liaison or a business swindle, and you will find them eating out of your hand. Provided, of course, that you have taken care to place the information in question in a very secure place with instructions to reveal it should you meet with any harm. The very people who would like to see you dead for other reasons become your most assiduous protectors, like mother birds watching over their fledglings. I assure you, Professor, that even today people are more embarrassed by sex than they are by violence, even murder. A man will more readily confess to a crime of violence than to one of sexual passion."

He leaned back in his chair and drained his cup. He looked inside it with seeming disgust, as if he too was appalled by what he had drunk, then set it down.

"That's the problem with tea bags," he said. "No leaves at the bottom of the cup. Cleaner, I grant you. Tidier. But you can't tell your fortune."

David looked quizzically at him.

"An old British custom," Harry explained. "You used to tell someone's fortune from the patterns of the tea leaves at the bottom of the cup. A ship was a journey. A house was good luck. A dying art. Mumbo jumbo, of course, like horoscopes; but a way of passing time. There used to be such a lot of it to pass.

"Still," he went on, as if shaking himself out of some fit of reverie, "that's another world and another era. We've more pressing things to talk about. You've come about your papers."

"Yes," David said. "Did they mean anything to you?"

"Oh, yes. Yes, indeed. They're most interesting. But then I'm interested in anything concerning my old buddy Hajj Amin. He was always up to tricks, God bless him. A regular bastard. No, take that back. Not regular at all. A most irregular bastard. Slimy, devious, double-crossing . . . He made Adolf seem like a fractured saint. Old Adolf was never really in his right mind; but Hajj Amin . . . He was the most calculating little turd of the century. He's dead now, of course. Copped it back in '74, in his villa near Beirut. Something nasty, I believe; hope so, anyway. But 'the evil that men do lives after them,' as the Bard put it. Words to that effect. You think he still has little friends doing nasty deeds?"

"Big friends," David said. "Friends of more than passing interest to you. Friends from the old days in Berlin."

The old man sat up very straight and very still. He stood up, crossed to the window and looked out, then drew down a dark roller blind. He walked back to his chair and sat down on the edge of it again.

"I think you'd better tell Uncle Harry what it is you know," he said.

David told him. Leyla filled in some further details.

When they had finished, Harry sat deep in thought for a long time. Silence filled the room. For the first time David noticed the ticking of an old, heavy clock. A vague chilliness haunted the air. Leyla shivered and looked at David. Their eyes met and drifted apart again. The clock went on ticking remorselessly. In the cups, their tea had long ago grown cold.

The old man looked up at last. He seemed to have aged. His shoulders sagged and his drawn face looked gray.

"I see," he said. That was all. The minimum response, but it said all that had to be said. It was precise. He did see, he saw all too clearly the pattern that was now beginning to take shape. And what he saw frightened him, so much that he wanted to be sick. He stood up and walked across to a desk in a shadow-filled corner of the room and returned carrying an armful of old files. He sat down again, setting the files on the floor beside him.

"What do you know about the origins of the Third Reich?" he asked.

They both shrugged.

"A little," David said. "The basic facts, I suppose."

"I'm not interested in facts. At least, not bare facts. It's the mood that concerns me. What do you know of the mood?"

David thought for a while. He sought for the right words.

"Frustration," he said at last. "Economic, political frustration. Resentment about Germany's treatment after the First World War. Dissatisfaction . . . with the Weimar Republic, with its politics, with the standard of living, with wages. Paranoia about Jews and Reds, a sort of moral panic, a feeling that decadence was sapping the nation's fiber. Deep feelings of uncertainty, a desire for national greatness, for self-assertion. Looking for a scapegoat: Jews again, communists, homosexuals, Jehovah's Witnesses. I suppose, a feeling of helplessness, that only a total change could take away all the miseries and transform society. People wanted a savior, someone who could lift them up out of the mire. I don't know really, there must have been so many things. But an overall air of mass neurosis, a sense of something being about to snap."

472

Harry nodded.

"Not bad," he said. "And, of course, something did snap. At least that's the way it often seems. The truth is, there was no moment you could put your finger on now and say, 'That was it, that was when the Germans lost their reason.' What happened in 1933 was nothing more than a formality, it just put the seal of approval on something that had been going on for some time. The mood deepened after that, of course, and changed; but the neurosis was still in control.

"But you missed out on one thing, one really central thing. Irrationality. An English writer called James Webb gave it a name: he described it as a 'flight from reason.' It started in different parts of Europe in the second half of the last century and it reached its height in Germany in the thirties. In a way it's still continuing. People get easily frightened by too much reason. For most people, it's the emotions that count, the feeling in the gut. Anti-Semitism isn't rational, but try telling that to a right-wing fanatic. Will it make any difference to him? Anti-Semitism feels good, it gives you someone to kick in the face when your wife walks out on you or you've just been put out of work by an economic system you can't really understand.

"But, of course, not everyone wants to kick a Jew in the face or burn down his synagogue. We leave that sort of thing to the proles. We're above that sort of thing, we're civilized people. At the same time, being irrational isn't a prerogative of the uneducated working classes. Far from it. If Hitler had depended solely on the rednecks, he would never have got into power. Educated people can be as frightened of reason as illiterates, sometimes more so, because they know the tensions it causes at first hand. By 1931 there was twice as much support for the Nazis in the universities as among the rest of the German population put together. Does that surprise you? It shouldn't. I'm speaking proportionately, of course. Academics were beaten up or thrown out of their institutions because they held unpopular opinions. There were riots in some universities. And you won't have forgotten the bonfires of books in 1933. What had happened to the Age of Reason? What had happened to Progress and Science and the new Liberal Culture? It had been flushed down the loo and the toilet door had been closed, that's what happened!"

The anger, mixed with a long-unhealed sorrow, broke through in Blandford's voice and caused him to pause for breath. David took advantage of the pause to break in.

"This is all very interesting, Mr. Blandford. I mean it, I'd like to know more of what you have to say. But I can't see its relevance to what we've been talking about. All this theorizing about origins won't help us find out what's going on now, what plans these people may still have."

Harry looked at David with his sharp, appraising eyes.

"You can't see the relevance?" he asked, then smiled. "No, perhaps not yet. But you will. Wait and see. What about you, Miss Rashid?"

"I feel the same as David," Leyla said. "It's fascinating, but it gets us nowhere."

"It will," Harry said. "Try to be patient. What I've been saying was by way of an introduction. Perhaps I digressed a little. But some of the things I'm going to tell you may appear . . . let's say, a little strange. A little hard to believe. Hence the preamble, hence the apparent irrelevance. But I do promise you it will all make sense in the end. May I go on?"

They nodded.

"Very well. We've established that too much reason produces a reaction. Faith in reason gives way to faith in the emotions. To romantic yearnings. To a belief in irrational forces. Hegel and his unstoppable processes of world history; Nietzsche with his superman; Wagner and his myths of Teutonic grandeur come to life. All heady stuff, all very appealing to intellectuals in search of something transcendental.

"The Germans weren't alone in this. If you'd gone to Paris or St. Petersburg or New England in the late 1800s you would have found any number of people in a similar fix. They'd had enough reality in their lives; they wanted something more, something to lift them out of themselves. Séances, table rapping, magic, the Hermetic sciences, the Kabbalah—anything and everything that promised new insights, an escape from the pettifogging demands of reason. Spiritualism, Theosophy, Freemasonry, a host of new religions and cults and occult orders—a whole bunch of groups sprang up offering instant enlightenment or access to 'rejected knowledge,' knowledge that the Establishment had 'suppressed.' Everywhere you went there were new messiahs, oriental seers, occult masters: a mixture of saints, rogues, and charlatans, with a decided bias toward the latter."

David broke in again.

"Are you saying this was all like . . . well, like the sixties and seventies, with the hippies and the Maharishi and the Moonies, astrology, tarot cards, all of that?"

Harry nodded.

"Precisely the same. Even some of the same groups were involved. Krishnamurti started out as a Theosophist messiah. Vivekananda visited Europe and America around the turn of the century. Abdul Baha, the Baha'i leader, followed him a few years later. Nothing much changes. Similar problems, similar responses."

"But I still can't see . . ."

"I'm coming to that," Blandford snapped, a little impatient. "Please," he said more gently, "I assure you this is important. There's a pattern here, but it isn't easy to get across. What you've seen is only a fragment, a piece of the pattern. Let me at least try to fill in the other details for you."

"At any rate, let's get back to Germany. The Germans had their fair share of occult obsessions. The occult fitted in well with Wagner and all those romantic yearnings about a pure German life that could only be lived away from the decadence of the cities, what they called the *völkisch* philosophy."

David stopped squirming in his chair. Blandford *was* beginning to make sense after all. The Nazis had been deeply influenced by the *völkisch* philosophy, the belief in the German "folk," in blood and soil and racial purity. *Völkisch* thinkers had extolled the virtues of the countryside and condemned the decadence of the big cities. Like the hippies, the German "wandering birds" of the twenties had dropped out in favor of a return to a simpler way of life. Hitler had dreamed and written of a *völkisch* state. David listened as Harry went on.

"By the 1920s the occult was enjoying a boom in Germany. There were any number of movements: little cliques like the Society for Modern Life in the Munich suburb of Schwabing, large groups like the Weissenbergers, with one hundred thousand members by 1930. All the usual crowd were there, of course: Theosophists, Gnostics, Taoists, Neo-Buddhists, often mixed up with nihilists, collectivists, syndicalists—a whole underground network.

"But the Germans had their own contribution to make to all this. There were German prophets like Bö Yin Râ, whose real name was Joseph Schneiderfranken, or Ottoman Zar-Adusht Ha'nish, otherwise known as Otto Hanisch. There was the Gottesbund Tanatra, founded by a businessman called Feder Mühle: by 1929 they were getting as many as two thousand people at a single meeting."

He paused.

"Am I boring you with all these details?" he asked.

"No," said David. "You're beginning to make sense. At least I think you are."

He was thinking of Ulrich von Meier as he had seen him in the underground cavern at Iram, about the Temple and the little girls Leyla had told him of. Harry was doing rather more than guess in the dark.

Harry smiled.

"You will think so when I've finished. I'll go on. A lot of these people were what you Americans call 'weirdos.' In my day we called them 'headcases.' Now, most of the time, when a nutter arrives on your doorstep telling you the Venusians have landed in his back garden, the best thing to do is tell him to bugger off. Begging your pardon, Miss Rashid." He seemed to blush.

Leyla looked up and smiled.

"I'm sorry," she said. "I've never heard the expression before." Blandford reddened visibly.

"Oh, in that case . . . It's a not very polite British way of saying 'f— off,' which is really . . ."

"I get the idea," she said, laughing. She liked Blandford; he was like an overgrown schoolboy. But if David thought he was beginning to make sense, she couldn't see it at all.

"Where was I?" Blandford asked. "Oh, yes . . . nutters on the doorstep. Well, the thing is, it doesn't always pay to ignore weirdos. Today's weirdo may be tomorrow's big noise. There's no easy way of telling. In retrospect it's easy enough, but never at the time. Still, it happens enough to make a sensible person worry. Jesus' family tried to have him put away in the local loony bin. Muhammad was chased out of Mecca by the city worthies, who said he was possessed by spirits or something. They both got their own back in the end, though. Muhammad actually conquered Mecca eight

476

years later. It's enough to give a man pause next time the doorbell rings.

"I'll get to the point. As long as occultists stick to table rapping or debating where Atlantis was situated or trying to project themselves onto the astral plane, they're quite harmless. They may even do some good for some people. It's a lot better than kicking Jews in the face. It allows people to be irrational in a pseudorational way. So far so good.

"But it doesn't always end there. After all, if you think you're privy to some special knowledge that the people around you don't have, it isn't long before you start thinking, 'My friends and I could organize things better for the good of mankind.' Or perhaps you think you and your little clique are really the nucleus of a new race of men, the germ of a regenerated society. Or maybe the messiah has come to usher in a new age right here on earth. The old order has to make way for the new order. *Die neue Ordnung*. Occultism gives way to politics. Séances make room for rallies. Table rapping paves the way for Jew-baiting.

"You only have to look at the ideas of some of the German occult groups to see how easy such a transition would be. From dreaming about a new world to building one. I mentioned the prophet Hanisch. He founded a religion called Mazdaznan. Among other things, he taught that only pure-blooded Aryans with blond hair and blue eyes could be the bearers of the truth. Sound familiar? Quite a few other occult groups in Germany taught the same thing.

"Even before the First World War some sects were talking about the advent of a new age. By the twenties, millenarianism was all the rage. The Gottesbund Tanatra was preparing for a thousand-year Reich. So was a group in Saxony called the Laurentians. They got their name from a man called Hermann Lorenz. In case it's of interest to you, Hermann had a brother called Heinrich."

David looked up. He caught Blandford's eye but could read nothing there.

"I'll come back to Heinrich later," Blandford said. "I'm still filling in background. Some people weren't content with waiting for the Utopia to come in God's good time. They set up colonies everywhere, mini-Utopias where they could practice the good life. The best-known was Monte Verita, at a place called Ascona in Switzerland. Everybody went to Monte Verita. Writers like

Hermann Hesse and Stefan George, painters like Arp and Klee, Isadora Duncan the dancer, and politicans like Lenin, Trotsky, Bakunin. Monte Verita was linked to a magical society called Ordens Tempel der Ostens—the Order of the Templars of the Orient.

"There was another group with a similar name, the Order of the New Templars, run by Jörg Lanz von Liebenfels. Members were to be racially perfect. They wanted to found colonies of the pure-blooded out in the countryside, to establish castles where they could develop their new race. Von Liebenfels bought real castles to serve as centers for his 'Aryan heroes,' starting with Burg Werfenstein on the Danube. He wasn't the first. A lot of people left Schwabing after the First World War to found similar colonies. One of them was a prophet called Ludwig Derleth. He wanted to build an ideal city, the Rosenburg. The task of the inhabitants of the Rosenburg was to train the younger generation as an elite, the seed of the future new order."

David and Leyla exchanged glances. Bit by bit, like a painting that takes shape as you walk back from it, Harry Blandford was beginning to make a great deal of sense. Harry looked at them, smiling.

"So far a lot of hints," he said. "But we're getting somewhere, aren't we? Colonies away from towns, cities in which to raise a new generation of the racially pure, plans for a thousand-year Reich."

David broke in again.

"Just a moment," he said. "I want to get one thing straight. Has all this been sparked off by what I told you earlier about Iram? It sounds to me as if you're making a lot of connections just to fit what I said. It's interesting. It makes sense of a lot of things. But it isn't what we came here for, if you don't mind my saying so. You say the papers Abraham sent you were significant. Can't we get on to those?"

Harry sighed and pursed his lips gently.

"Would you like more tea?" he asked.

They both shook their heads.

"Tea helps," he said. "It sharpens the mind. Keeps the thoughts clear." He paused. "Did you think I dredged all this information up out of some unfathomable, unfailing store of memories? That I carry stuff like this around in my head all the time, just waiting for someone to bring up something remotely connected with it so I can spout off and show how much I know? Like some bloody Mr. Memory in a circus? Good God, man, I'd have no room for anything of importance if I stored up trivia like this. I was already going to tell you most of this, even before you told me about what you found in the Nafud. I've changed my emphasis a little, selected some points and left out others, that's all. But I did my research on all of this before you came, because of what I read in those papers. Do I make myself clear?"

He paused again.

"Shall I go on?" he said at last.

They nodded. Something like fear had taken hold of them.

"What you're waiting for," Harry said, "is for me to make some sort of link between what I've just been talking about and the Nazis." He paused and breathed deeply. "Well," he said as he let his breath out slowly, "that's not altogether easy. A lot of people have tried to prove links that just didn't exist. There's been endless speculation and very little hard fact. Most of the people doing the speculating have been occultists themselves, people who have believed in the mysterious powers and secret knowledge our prophets and seers laid claim to. And that has tended to cloud their minds.

"But there are facts. For one thing, there's the general atmosphere. Even where there aren't direct links, all these groups and ideas merge together to form a sort of mystical background to Nazism. It comes out most strongly in Himmler and the SS. The rituals, the *Ordensburgen* or order castles as training places for the elite, the obsession with racial purity. Himmler modeled the SS on the Jesuits: they were to be to the German people what the Society of Jesus had been to the Catholic Church.

"But I'm interested in origins at the moment. Bits and pieces again, I'm afraid—but all suggestive. First: when Adolf Hitler lived in Vienna he attended public lectures on occultism. He was interested in astrology, graphology, and number mysticism. In Munich he visited Lanz von Liebenfels—you remember him?—and regularly read his racist magazine, a thing called *Ostara*. But this is all a bit vague, rather circumstantial. Hitler wasn't much of an occultist by the time he came to power. But what is well known is that, in 1919, he joined an organization called the German

Workers' Party. The Party had, as you probably know, been founded a year earlier by a man called Anton Drexler. Later it became the NSDAP—the National Socialist German Workers' Party. The Nazi Party. Now, Drexler's original party had unusual origins. It started as a 'workers' circle' founded by Drexler and a journalist named Harrer, Karl Harrer. And Harrer in turn was a member of an occult society known as the Thule Bund. Several other early NSDAP members were also Bund affiliates. The Thule Society itself was a branch of an anti-Semitic organization known as the Germanen Order. Wheels within wheels, Professor. Circles within circles."

David shrugged and shook his head. He had heard much of this before.

"I still don't see . . ."

"Where all this is leading us?" Harry paused. "To the center, Professor. Right to the center. Who do you think was the head—the real head—of the Thule Bund in Germany? Shall I tell you? You know him already. You've even met him. His name was Professor Ulrich von Meier."

David sat bolt upright. Leyla stared at him.

"And who," Harry went on, "was the head of the Bund in Berlin? I've already mentioned his name. It was a certain Heinrich Lorenz, the brother of Hermann, the founder of the Laurentians. Heinrich was a banker, a very wealthy and influential man. Do I begin to interest you?"

David nodded. What could he say?

"It was von Meier and Lorenz who caught my attention when I read your translation of the diary," the little Englishman continued. "I already knew a fair bit about them, and I wanted to know more. I knew, for example, that neither of them ever became a Party member, neither before nor after 1933. Neither held public office, nor, indeed, any very prominent position outside of the Thule Society—and that was kept pretty quiet. Neither was related to anyone within the Nazi power cliques. And yet their names keep coming up. At little soirees with the Führer, on weekend visits to Berchtesgaden, in Himmler's entourage, at dinners with diplomats in the Reich Chancellery.

"In 1941 the Nazis rounded up all the occultists in the Reich and had them hauled off to concentration camps. Theosophists,

480

Anthroposophists, faith healers, astrologers, spiritualists—they all went. Except, perhaps, for some fortunetellers who may have foretold what was about to happen and went into hiding in time. Strangely enough, there seem to have been very few of those. But von Meier and Lorenz went on as before. I've often wondered about that. The Thule Bund had long disappeared, of course. But there's plenty of evidence in my files that von Meier and Lorenz kept up a very indiscreet interest in matters occult. There are records of séances held in the presence of Himmler and other ranking SS officers. Von Meier even published articles on occult themes. All this at a time when people like him were being put in the camps.

"Actually, I've also wondered about the change in official policy. It goes back to 1936, when all the major sects and cults were proscribed. I've never understood why it should have happened. It makes very little sense, unless you think of the sects as competition that had to be crushed. A bit like a communist government suppressing its left-wing rivals after the revolution. The question is, who were the occultists in competition with? On the surface, the Nazis were a political party pure and simple. I've asked myself many times whether there wasn't something else beneath the surface.

"And now I'm starting to think there was. I'd always assumed von Meier had died in 1945. There are no reports of him after that, no rumors, no Mengele-type stories. And now you tell me he was alive until a few days ago. That's immensely interesting. But it's not the most interesting thing you've told me. Let me tell you something else about von Meier. He had an obsession. Articles written by him from the late twenties through to the mid-thirties keep returning to a single topic. He believed that the Ark of the Covenant was still in existence somewhere and that a proper study of certain ancient texts would reveal its location. Some of these articles appeared in serious academic journals and were quite innocuous. But in occult publications—including Von Liebenfels' *Ostara*—he said a little more. He argued that whoever found the Ark could destroy forever the influence of the Jewish people. The Elders of Zion, he said, still exercised their power through the Ark. But if it could be wrested from them, that power would pass to its new owners. It was essential for the future of the Aryan race that the Ark be found.

"His articles on the subject ceased abruptly in 1936. The year he found Iram. The year the Nazis began to round up the major cults. The year Hitler sent troops into the Rhineland and started the slide toward war."

Harry looked at David, then at Leyla.

"I think he knew—or suspected—that the Ark was somewhere in Iram, but he didn't know exactly where. I would hazard a guess that it was the belief that they had control of the Ark that gave the Thule Bund such influence. They'd brought the Nazi Party into existence: now they could guarantee its success by occult means. I'm only guessing. But one thing is certain, I think. From 1936, von Meier and his Thule Bund were the real power in Germany, the hidden masters of the Third Reich."

David remembered the letter from Himmler, referring to von Meier. *I was summoned recently by Professor von Meier. . . . Von Meier took my recommendations to the Bund Council. . . . It is* [to the United States] *that the majority of Bund members are now being sent or will be sent on the cessation of hostilities. . . . In the end, we have no choice in this matter.*

He looked up. Blandford was gazing at him. An Englishman become an honorary Jew, an old man in a blood-red *yarmulkah*, trapped in history like an old fly struggling in a nacreous, sagging web.

"There's something else," he said. He looked at David with eyes that had seen too much. "Something I'd known but ignored until recently. It had seemed irrelevant. But I don't think it is. Von Meier had a son."

FIFTY-SIX

It was growing late. Harry Blandford was tired. In a matter of hours the world had tilted, and he was still trying to regain his balance. He rose and brewed himself more tea. David asked him to make a little for them, weak, without milk. Under his breath, Harry muttered something about "Americans and Orientals," but he made the tea and presented it to them with that look of pity the best of the English reserve for the rest of benighted humanity. Out of a battered and shapeless tin with a worn photograph of the young Queen Elizabeth II on its lid—a gift from his early years in Israel— he produced a lump of fruit cake: cherries, almonds, and raisins held together in a brown, crumbling medium of uncertain origin and even less certain wholesomeness. He sliced it—or, more accurately, crumbled it with the aid of a knife—and passed it around on small, chipped plates decorated with flowers resembling roses. He sat down again, holding Sammy on his lap. For a while he sat there, glancing through his files, then he closed them again and resumed speaking from where he had left off.

"The boy was born in 1940," he said. "His mother was von Meier's second wife, an Arab woman from Beirut. Her name was Khadija. Khadija al-Husayni—a relative of someone else we've been talking about. Through her mother, Khadija was a direct descendant of the Prophet. And she bore the name of the Prophet's first wife. For such a woman to have been married to a non-Muslim is almost unheard of.

"Khadija died soon after the boy's birth," Harry continued. "Under circumstances very similar to those in which von Meier's first wife died. She was drowned during a boating trip on Lake Starnberg, where Ludwig II was drowned. His first wife was lost at

483

sea in 1937, on a cruise to Egypt.

"During the war the boy, who was called Friedrich, remained in Berlin with his father. Von Meier did not marry again, not, at least, before 1945. After that, who knows? There had been talk, of course, but nothing seems to have come of it. I don't believe he lacked for female companionship. His sister Julie looked after the boy until she was killed in an air raid on Berlin in 1944. After that, nothing very clear is known about his movements except that, after the war, he turned up in Iraq, where he was given protection by former sympathizers of Rashid Ali."

David interrupted.

"I'm sorry," he said, "but I'm not very well up on these things. What Rashid Ali was that?"

"Al-Ghailani," Harry said. "He led a pro-Axis coup in Baghdad in 1941. Only lasted a short time before the British took over again, but he left a lot of supporters. Al-Husayni was mixed up in the coup, but he got out and ended up in Rome before anyone could lay their hands on him. The Scarlet Pimpernel had nothing on our Mufti: he always knew when it was time to scarper." Harry paused and crammed some lumps of cake into his mouth, moistened them with a generous intake of tea, and sat chewing on the mixture until it had gone.

"Of course," he continued, "I knew nothing about the boy until recently. He wasn't of interest to anybody . . . not then. He was brought up in Iraq by a family related to the al-Husaynis. He took an Arab name, cut off all links with Germany, became an Arab boy in every respect."

David broke in again.

"You haven't told me what he was called," he said.

"Oh, I'm sorry. Friedrich, I think. Friedrich von Meier."

"No, you did tell me that; I mean his Arab name."

Harry looked at David and smiled. He raised the cup to his lips and sipped noisily. More tea went after the cake to ease its path through his intestines.

"We'll come to that," he said. "All in good time." He belched suddenly. "Beg pardon," he muttered. "Now, where was I? Oh, yes, he was brought up as a good little Iraqi boy. Went to school, spoke Arabic, learned to recite the Qur'an, read stories about Abu Bakr and Umar and Salah al-Din, all of that. He was dark-haired, like his parents, and his features were quite Arab from his mother.

Everything went quite smoothly until he was eighteen.

"That was in 1958, when General Kassem took control and proclaimed a republic. The family young Friedrich belonged to were royalists, or at least they had had close links with Faisal and the court. They'd made a lot of money after the war. When Kassem came to power they decided it was time to get out. The al-Husayni blood, I suppose, the Pimpernel instinct. Most of them headed for Saudi Arabia, but the boy had other ideas. He crossed the border into Syria and made contact with another branch of the family in Damascus.

"He enrolled at Damascus University, where he studied engineering, though I believe he never actually graduated. While he was there he became involved with a Syrian branch of the Muslim Brothers, a fundamentalist political organization that had been started earlier in the century in Egypt."

It was Leyla's turn to interrupt.

"You mean al-Banna's Ikhwan?"

Harry nodded.

"He moved up in the movement very quickly, and by the time he was twenty-five, in 1965, he'd become a regional leader for the Hama district. At the same time he was coming increasingly into conflict with some of his superiors. He was less concerned with religion than they were, more of a secular Arab nationalist who thought he could use Islam to gain popular support. There were a few incidents when he was accused of disrespect toward the Prophet. He became increasingly left-wing and wanted direct action against the Baathists. Finally, about 1969, he broke away or was thrown out and formed his own party."

Leylas eyes were fixed on Harry. Her heart was thumping. She knew Arab politics. She knew who von Meier's son was.

Harry looked at her, a little sadly.

"You've guessed," he said.

She nodded.

"You know what the party was called?"

"Hizb al-Qawm al-Watani. The National People's Party," she whispered. She closed her eyes.

"Quite correct," Harry said.

She opened her eyes.

"Mas'ud al-Hashimi," she said.

Harry nodded.

David sat frozen for a moment, then burst out:

"I don't believe it. I . . . can't believe it." He paused as if for breath. "Are you seriously trying to tell us that Mas'ud al-Hashimi—the President of Syria—is von Meier's son? I find that hard to accept."

Harry sighed. A long painful sigh.

"I sympathize," he said. "But surely by now you've begun to realize that whatever's going on here doesn't fit the usual categories. At first I thought al-Hashimi was as liberal as everybody thought he was, but then I heard that some of the old al-Husayni group in Syria had been seen in contact with various members of his government. Your friend al-Shami was seen in Damascus about two months ago, and he seems to have met with some of the key figures in al-Hashimi's cabinet—General Ahmad Subki and Ibtisam al-Bakri, al-Hashimi's right-hand man and the person most likely to succeed if anything happens to the leader. So I asked questions here and there, spoke with friends . . . and discovered what I've just told you. It worried me a little. And then I received the materials you gave Abraham. Please, let's not argue about whether any of this seems logical or sane. It's the way I've told you. Al-Hashimi is von Meier's son. It's that simple. It may be mere coincidence, or it may have some deeper significance. I'd like to find out."

David looked across at Leyla. Harry was right. In a situation where nothing made much sense, it was a form of craziness to insist upon it, to go on looking for it as if you could make the world a sensible place merely by forcing rationality upon it.

"I think it's time you showed Harry the papers you found," he said to Leyla.

Harry glanced at him.

"There are more?"

David nodded.

"Here," Leyla said, lifting out of her bag the bundle of papers she had found in the plane in the Nafud. She passed them to Harry. They were creased and dirty, ravaged by the long years in the airplane, further damaged by their subsequent treatment, wrapped in Leyla's robe or in a sack.

Harry took them and unfolded them on top of the file that lay across his knee. He leafed through them carefully, then looked up at Leyla.

"Where did you find these?" he asked.

"In a plane that had crashed near Iram, in the desert. It had been there since the end of the war. A German plane. There were bodies inside. We recognized two of them by the clothes. One was Hitler, the other was probably his mistress, Eva Braun. The papers were on a desk at the back of the fuselage. I didn't take all of them, only a few. Chaim read them when we got to Iram. He translated most of them for me."

"You say Hitler was on the plane?"

"Yes."

"Adolf Hitler?"

"Yes."

"You're sure of that?"

"It was dressed like Hitler, Chaim said. But it was only a skeleton. We might have been mistaken."

There was a deep silence. When Harry spoke again, his voice had changed.

"I see."

He said nothing more but began to read the papers. Though he would have affected not to speak the language, he read German with an ease born of long use. He asked no questions, made no comments, but as he read Leyla could see his color change. Once he shivered as though a cold wind had passed through the room. He read everything, then he began at the beginning and went right through the papers a second time. When he had finished he sat staring down at the papers on his lap, as if ghosts had gathered about him in the shadows of his rough-and-tumble room and he were in a trance, communing with them as they circled. One hand hung by his side, stroking the cat with the tenderness of age, yet absent-mindedly. The young Harry Blandford was marshaled within him, whose eyes had seen storm clouds on earlier horizons, whose ears had listened to the irrational as it marched in jackboots across Europe.

For a long time no one spoke. The air was heavy with an undeclared tension. In the end Leyla broke the silence.

"There was only one thing we really couldn't make sense of. Chaim said it meant nothing to him, but I had the feeling there was something there he recognized, something that frightened him. I'm talking about the papers in the blue folder, the ones with a list of names and numbers. Do they mean anything to you?"

He looked at her. Such a look. She wanted to hide, it seemed so like anger. Then she realized it was more like fear . . . fear and terrible sadness.

"Yes," he said, "I think I know what it means. If I'm right those papers make the rest of this stuff almost innocuous. For years now I've heard hints and rumors, but until now I've refused to believe them. Now I'm not so sure any longer."

He raised a hand to his forehead and brushed back a strand of hair that had fallen into his eyes. Leyla noticed that the hand trembled. Slowly, he lowered it again.

"In January 1944," Harry continued, "SS High Command formed a special detachment made up of men specially selected from the best units then stationed in Germany and abroad. A large proportion were from Einsatzgruppen, the murder squads used in Eastern Europe to carry out the killing program. They were all young men, none over the age of nineteen. They formed a regiment called the Valkyrie Standarte. Himmler gave them his personal approval and supervised their training. Unfortunately, no one knows what that training consisted of. None of them were captured after the war, no one knows why. All we do know is that they were split into four groups, Valkyrie I, Valkyrie II, and so on, and sent to the four *Ordensburgen,* the SS 'order castles' for the training of the elite, at Sonthofen, Crössinsee, Vogelsang, and Marienburg. They were quite a bit younger than the other men at those places, but it's said they were given special privileges and separate quarters. They stayed in the *Ordensburgen* under close security for several months at least. No one knows what happened during their training or what became of them after they left. All records of them cease after November 1944.

"This," Harry went on, picking up the stapled sheets, "is, if I'm not mistaken, a complete list of the names of members of the Valkyrie regiment. That much is merely interesting. It's what follows the names that worries me. The numbers. They're quite clear. The first part consists of a date: December 9, 1944, and so on. The second section begins with a letter, an abbreviation for a concentration camp: 'A' for Auschwitz, 'D' for Dachau, 'BE' for Belsen. The actual figures are simply the registration numbers for camp inmates—the number they tattooed on people's arms. The 'V' at the end obviously refers to 'Valkyrie,' and, of course, 'Valk. I,' 'Valk. II,' and so on are the original unit numbers." Harry paused again. He closed his eyes tightly, as if in pain, then opened them again.

"I think these young men disappeared into the camps. As inmates, not as guards. I think someone wanted them there for some purpose I can only guess at."

"What would that have been?" asked David.

"To give them new identities, impeccable identities. They would be reborn after hostilities ceased. Reborn into a new world, with new names and histories."

"Can you prove any of this?"

Harry shook his head.

"No, not easily. But there's someone I'd like you to meet. He told me about this years ago, but I never believed him. There was so little evidence to go on. But this . . ." He held up the sheets again. "This gives us more than evidence. It's something concrete, something we can ask questions about. I'll get started on that tonight.

"In the meantime," he continued, "let's sort out more practical matters. Where are you staying?"

David shrugged.

"Nowhere as yet. We can't go to my old place or Leyla's, they could be looking for us there. I thought we'd check into a hotel."

"No need," said Harry. "Stay with me, at least for tonight. I want you both where I can contact you easily. We have a great deal more to talk about. I haven't much space here, but if you're tired enough you'll sleep without too much difficulty. I've got an old camp bed somewhere. That can come into the bedroom with me; we'll argue later about who gets it. Miss Rashid can sleep in here with Sammy; he won't mind. That thing over there"—he pointed to a dubious-looking item of upholstered furniture covered in papers—"is called a sofa. When it's clear of bits and pieces it's tolerably comfortable to sleep on. I'll get some blankets."

Just as Harry turned to go, David called him back.

"Harry," he said, "there's just one thing. Before we left Jerusalem, there was talk of al-Hashimi coming here. There were plans for some sort of conference. He was going to sign a peace treaty. Has anything come of that?"

Harry looked around.

"You mean you haven't heard?"

"Heard what?"

"Everyone's talking about it. It's hard to avoid it: in the papers, on the television . . . He's coming to Jerusalem to sign a treaty as planned on the third of March. In four days' time."

FIFTY-SEVEN

God had not smiled for a long time. Perhaps He had never smiled; it was hard to remember, it had been so many years. But Marcus Bleich still waited. He had been born patient, he had learned every kind of patience life had to teach him, he would die patient. It was the only way he knew.

He lived—or existed—in a single room on the top floor of a tall tenement in the Romema district. He had lived there for over forty years, almost since his arrival in Palestine after the war. It took him twenty minutes every morning to walk down the stairs to the street and forty minutes every morning to climb back up them again. His chest was weak, his breathing cracked and painful. It had not always been that way. Some mornings he lay in bed, dreading the walk down, the climb back, longing to stay where he was. But he knew that once he gave in to that urge it would be the beginning of the end for him; he would stay in his room the following day and the day after, until he never left it again on his own feet. Social services had promised him a new place on the ground floor of a more modern block, but that had been several years ago and he was still waiting. He treated it for what it was: another lesson in patience.

Most days he went to *shul,* then on to a nearby day center where he played chess or backgammon and ate an indifferently cooked lunch. It was his life now, he had accustomed himself to it. That was what life was about, after all—accustoming oneself. He could see little point in it otherwise. He had no relatives, unless he counted some few he had left behind in Europe and others who had gone to the Goldener Medineh; none of them were close, he knew little of

490

their lives, cared almost not at all. There had been a marriage, children too, a long, long time ago. What few keepsakes remained—a stained photograph, a comb, a lock of hair, a letter taped where it had come apart from constant opening and closing—sat on the table by his bed, the only treasures he had brought out of Europe. He touched them every night before he slept and every morning they were the first things his eyes fell on.

They found him in the day center playing chess with another old man, pawnless and knightless, his glazed eyes fixed on the little wooden pieces as if they betokened something beyond themselves: a pattern, a strategy . . . or as if they merely waited for a hand to pick them up and move them around the squares. He was thin and stooped, like the back of an old spoon, and seemed to hold his body as though it were a shield in front of his real self, as though he stood unbent behind it, peering out through dark interstices at a crooked world. His clothes were shabby and stained, and his chin had not felt a razor in several days. Everything about him seemed threadbare. He reminded Leyla of an old carpet or a rug on which countless feet had trodden until the nap had worn through. But she sensed something else as well, a hardness, a resistance, a durability that belied the flimsiness of his appearance.

Harry went up to him and introduced himself. He spoke in German with a distinct English accent.

"Good morning, Marcus," he said. "Do you remember me? Harry Blandford, the Englishman you spoke with a few times back in 1975. Salomon Pinkes introduced us. We talked about . . . the past."

Marcus nodded. Yes, he remembered. Harry had listened to him at least, which was more than most people did. He had not believed Marcus, of course, or had assumed that he had misinterpreted what he had seen; but he had not been the first to disbelieve.

"I'd like to talk again," Harry said, "if you have time. I've brought a couple of friends who'd be interested in hearing your story."

"Time?" snorted Marcus. "What else do I have?" He leaned across to his chest partner and asked if he would mind if he abandoned the game.

"I'm winning for once and Bleich has to leave!" the other old man grunted. "But go, I can wait. I'll beat you later."

Marcus took them to a small room in the day center where they could talk in private. The room, like the center of which it was part, possessed that drab cheeriness that is endemic to all such places: bright yellow paint that leaned more to bilious than cheerful, posters of luxurious foreign scenes that none of the old folk would ever visit now, plastic flowers in plastic pots on a table marked with cigarette burns, red, vinyl-covered chairs in which one might sit but where one could never relax.

They talked desultorily for a little while, touching on nothing of importance, allowing Marcus to grow accustomed to his visitors. His eyes never left one or the other of them, as if he were weighing them, probing them, sifting them. He had been a gem cutter by trade, first in Germany, then in Eretz Israel, until his sight had grown too weak and his fingers had lost their precision. Since then he had lived on his tiny pension, supernumerary in the land of the promise. But his eyes, though they lacked the strength and acuteness needed for the precision cutting of a diamond, retained their power of penetration in the art of evaluating men and women. No one had ever believed his account of what had happened at Dachau, but he knew, deep inside himself, that he had not been mistaken.

At last Harry turned to the subject that had brought them there.

"Marcus," he said, "when I spoke with you before, we talked about a lot of things. You gave me some valuable information: the names of Wachtruppe guards, descriptions of SS officers, details of incidents. I've never thanked you properly. But I do now. What you told me was a help, a great help. Now I want your assistance again. When we last met, you told me about . . . inmates who were not inmates. At the time I told you that I believed you had seen what you described but that I thought you had placed a false interpretation on it. I regret that judgment now. I should have been more careful, given it more thought. But I was unusually busy at the time and got sidetracked.

"Now I think I have evidence that you were right. Leyla and David found it recently. Please forgive me if I don't tell you where or how. Let's just say that it's authentic and . . . disturbing. I'd like you to tell them what you told me. Leyla doesn't understand German, but we'll explain to her what you tell us later."

There was a brief silence while Marcus looked first at David, then at Leyla.

"Very well," he said. "But still you may not believe me." He breathed as deeply as he could, wondering for the thousandth time why his lungs refused to take in air as easily as they had once done. He waited, letting the breath sink in, then closed his eyes, forcing himself to see it all again: the huts, the towers, the frost-speckled wire, the hungry birds pecking.

"It is cold in the camps," he said. "Even in summer there is a coldness, a chill on everything. It comes from inside, from lack of food, from lack of hope. I don't remember ever being warm. But that winter was the worst. The water froze—not just water in the rain pools or in the taps, but every trace of moisture. The huts were damp, so the walls froze, blankets, clothing . . . anything in which the damp had settled. People were dying in every way possible for them to die. What wasn't officially decreed, the guards invented; and what they didn't invent, the weather did, or sickness.

"You know all this, of course. Everyone knows it, or thinks he does. That's what's wrong: we know and yet we don't know. Especially here in Eretz Israel, where memories of the Holocaust are nothing unusual. I know because I was there, I saw it with my own eyes: you think you know because you've seen things in books or films, because people like me have told you. Your parents maybe." He glanced at David.

David nodded. His parents, yes. Marcus looked into his eyes, then went on.

"But you don't know, of course. Not really. So what I tell you is hard for you to judge. Not for me, it's not hard for me; not for others who were there—they understand at once. So you must try to understand more slowly.

"We had little idea of time, of course. It was winter, that was all we knew. The war was going badly for them, we could tell. They tried to hide it from us, but it was so, we could read it in their faces. But the killing never stopped. Perhaps it increased, it's hard to know, there was so much of it.

"But you want me to talk about what I saw that winter, so I'll try to tell you. I was in Hut 19 of Block 36. There were over four hundred of us in the hut at that time, even though it was meant to hold only eighty. It got much worse later, when they brought people in from the east, from the camps they had to abandon to the

493

Russians. Every day people died; less often, new arrivals were brought in. Whatever happened, it was crowded—a few less, a few more, it made no difference. Not until they brought them from the east.

"One day, it must have been in December, they brought seven new men to our hut. From the very beginning I knew something was wrong. On the surface they seemed like the rest of us—heads shaved, striped uniforms, numbers on their forearms. But there was something about them, something not quite right. They looked disoriented, frightened, anxious, but . . . it was as if they were acting, as if they played a role. I kept a close watch on them, but discreetly. They were scattered around the hut, but it didn't take long for me to notice that they met with one another from time to time. Never in one group, always two or at the most three, and seldom the same two, never the same three as far as I could tell. But always some combination of the original seven. Do you follow me?"

"Yes," David said. "But I still don't quite understand what it was about them that drew your attention."

"I'm not quite sure myself," the old man admitted. "I'd been in the camp longer than most by then. I was young, reasonably fit. I'd learned how to play the game, how to survive. Perhaps I had an instinct for the place, the people in it. Listen . . . you see the photographs, everyone in them looks the same: thin faces, huge eyes, arms and legs like sticks, hair shaven—all standing there, staring remotely at the camera. Or the bodies in the pits, like so much flesh, indistinguishable. The most you might say is, 'This is a man, this is a woman,' if they were naked. And not always even then. Otherwise, only the children stand out.

"But it wasn't that way in reality. All sorts of people were there. Religious Jews and unbelieving Jews, rich Jews and poor Jews, clever Jews and stupid Jews. They made no distinctions, of course: we were all *untermenschen*, the best of us and the worst of us. But we could distinguish, we could tell. The moment someone arrived at the camp, I knew how long he would last. You always knew. Some carried their deaths into the camp with them, as though they themselves willed it. Others had whatever it took to see them through. Cooperation was the key. If a man was selfish, looking out only for himself, not willing to share his food, for example, or a tool

494

he might have found, you knew he wouldn't last long. If you helped other people, they helped you. And in the camp there would always be a time when you needed help. It wasn't strength or weakness so much as humanity that made a survivor what he was.

"That was the only distinction that mattered in the end, whether you were a survivor or fuel for the ovens. In a way they had eroded all other distinctions. A few rich bastards were able to smuggle things in with them, diamonds, perhaps, or bank account numbers. They bought a few privileges with them: a fortune for half a loaf of bread. But it didn't stop them going to the ovens when the time came. In the end nothing else counted but that inner distinction. It wasn't courage or spirit or defiance or anything like that—just the ability to endure, nothing more, nothing less. And a willingness to share.

"These men didn't seem to have either of those qualities. But they just as clearly weren't marked out for early death. It was as if they didn't really care, as if they knew somehow that they'd make it, that their survival was guaranteed. It showed in little things. The survivors were the ones who made sure they got the food they were entitled to. Not someone else's share, not more than their share, but what was theirs. They might share it, of course, with someone who was sick that day or someone who'd been beaten. But the first thing was to get your ration. From the start. If you let someone else take your share by force, there were those who would treat it as a weakness. The Kapos would take advantage of it. The *Blockalteste* would make a mental note of it. There wasn't any margin: once you let that weakness show, you were finished. Not the first day, not the first week perhaps, but quickly enough.

"I never saw one of them fight for food or assert his claim to a hunk of bread or go to trouble to get extra rations. They grew thin, very thin, like all of us, but they still seemed strong, like men with no fat, just hard muscle. Somehow they were getting more food, better food, something that didn't put on fat but gave them strength. I was sure of it. That was after a few weeks, of course, maybe a month or more, but it grew to a certainty.

"One night I decided to watch one of them, to see what he did. I was convinced they were given extra food during the night, you see; it was the only time anyone could have done it without being observed. I stayed awake that night until it was early morning.

495

Everything was dark, almost too dark to see. I almost gave up; in that freezing cold it was so tempting to fall asleep. But it paid off. The one I was watching got out of his bunk—it was a top bunk—and made quietly for the door. He stumbled across people a few times, of course, but no one really noticed. It happened when people got up to pee in the night if they had to.

"I decided to follow him. I don't know why. It wasn't a sensible thing to do: he might have seen me, or I might have lost my way in the dark and been unable to get back to my bunk. That could have been serious. But it didn't seem to matter somehow, it had become so important to me to discover what was happening.

"He went outside, and after a few moments I followed him. That was extremely dangerous, there were strict rules about remaining in the huts at night. If I'd been seen I would have been shot: they didn't ask questions. But I didn't have to go far. The sky was overcast, which made it harder to keep track of him, but it also kept me in darkness. He walked away from the hut for a little distance, then whistled twice, quite softly. About a minute passed. He didn't move, just stood there waiting. I stayed in the shelter of the hut, well out of sight. The next thing I knew, a guard came out from between two of the huts opposite and walked up to him. It was too dark to see exactly what went on, but I could tell that the guard passed him something and that he was eating and drinking. They spoke together a little in low voices: but I couldn't make out anything. They remained there about ten minutes, then he handed something back to the guard. I guessed he was about to come back, so I slipped inside the hut and made my way back to my bunk. He came in about two minutes later and visited each of his friends in turn. I guessed he must be taking them food he had obtained from the guard."

The old man stopped, as if expecting David to challenge him.

"Did you tell anyone about this?" David asked. He believed the story. Wishing it untrue would not make it so.

Marcus shook his head.

"No," he said. "Not then. I've told you I was a survivor. That was a major part of surviving: you never drew attention to yourself. You kept things to yourself, especially things that seemed dangerous. You couldn't afford to trust anyone too far. That could be fatal. You couldn't afford the luxury of close friends—that took up emotional energy, cut down your powers of resistance. And you didn't talk. What I had seen might have seemed worth something to somebody. They would have told a Kapo that I knew something in return for a bowl of soup: there were people like that. The fact is, they would have been killed along with me, but some people were stupid, they didn't think that far. Only survivors thought ahead . . . and they kept what they knew to themselves."

"What about the resistance in the camp?" David asked. "Couldn't you have told them?"

"I didn't know who they were. I didn't even know they existed then. If I had known . . . yes, I would have told one of them."

"And after that, did anything else happen?"

"Yes," Marcus said. "I'll come to that. But first, there were other things, other signs that something was wrong. I was on a working detail with two of them. We went out every day to dig ditches. I never knew what for. Slacking was severely punished. The guards with our detail were particularly brutal. Most days saw several deaths. People who didn't pull their weight were often clubbed to death. I saw several people collapse or just stop work and wait for the guards to come and beat them until they were finished. Well, those two never slacked exactly, but they never really worked either. I'd seen people whipped for working harder, but the guards never touched them. Except once, that is, when a guard laid into a group of workers and one of them happened to be among them. I watched it. The guard knocked him down and kicked him. But he was holding back; I swear. I'd seen guards kick men before. They made their kicks count, every one of them. They enjoyed it, it was a sort of sport. But this one let the man roll with the kicks. I saw enough of it before another guard knocked me down for ignoring my own work.

"After the business during the night, I decided to try to get to know the man I'd followed. It wasn't easy. It never was very easy in the camp, but I persevered. He told me his name was Gershon, Gershon Neusner. He was originally from Baden-Baden, he said, but he and his family had escaped to France before the war and had been living in hiding there until recently. They'd been split up, he didn't know where to. That was all he would tell me at first.

"But I made it difficult for him to avoid talking to me. I engineered situations where we would be thrown together. I asked questions. And as I got answers I found he wasn't telling me very much at all. I told him I'd had relations in Baden-Baden, asked him about them. Of course, that was a lie, I knew no one there. But I wanted to make him talk about the place, to draw him out a bit. He always said no, he hadn't heard of this uncle or that cousin. But then one day I said that surely he'd heard of Eli Schumacher, the cantor in the main synagogue, the one who was so well known. Oh, yes, of course, he said, he remembered him well; he'd heard him sing at Yom Kippur when he was a child, the Kol Nidre. He shouldn't have said that. There never was a cantor called Schumacher at Baden-Baden. Eli Schumacher was the name of the old cantor at my own synagogue in Bremen.

"Now I knew for certain Neusner was lying, I laid further little traps for him. I talked about religion, it seemed the best way. You see, I wanted to know whether he was a Jew or not. I would refer to the Talmud, giving the names of tractates that don't exist, that I had made up. He never contradicted me, and once he even said, 'Yes, I remember that passage.' I made little mistakes in my Hebrew, enough to make an educated Jew correct me, but he never did."

David broke in again.

"Did you ever challenge him outright about any of this?"

Marcus shook his head vigorously. A strand of white hair dislodged itself and fell across his left temple. He brushed it back.

"No," he said emphatically. "I was taking a big enough risk as it was. If I'd even hinted that I'd guessed he was masquerading, he would have had me killed. I'm sure of it."

"Why didn't he? You were asking a lot of questions, getting close to him. Wouldn't that alone have made him nervous?"

Marcus smiled, revealing teeth that would have made a dentist cringe.

"I don't know the answer to that. In a way, I think he liked me. I've often thought about it since. It's curious, but in a way I think he found it harder in the camp than the rest of us."

He saw David's expression and raised a hand.

"Don't misunderstand me. He could eat some proper food, he was never beaten—that was easy for him. But for all that, he had to live in the camp. And yet I'm convinced that he could have walked out of there any time he chose. We had no choice. We knew we were there until we died and we had learned to make the best of it. But for him and his friends it was a matter of daily choice. We willed ourselves to survive: they willed themselves just to be there. And I think Neusner needed some friendship, even from a Jew. Perhaps, in some strange fashion, especially from a Jew. Maybe I don't make sense to you."

David shook his head.

"No. I think you make a lot of sense."

"Thank you." He paused. "There's not much more to tell. They brought in the people from the camps in the east after that. And then a few months later they started to go crazy. Killing, killing, as if they had to kill all of us as quickly as possible. We knew something was happening. Of course, what was going on was the final push toward Germany, but we didn't know that then. That was the most insane time of all—their obsession with carrying out the extermination program even though they knew they were finished, that in a matter of weeks it would be all over anyway.

"And then it was over. The Americans entered the camp and we passed from being prisoners to being displaced persons. I was sent to a DP camp in Hanover. I don't know where they sent Neusner or his friends. I never saw him again." He stopped briefly, then added in a slightly lower tone:

"Until a few years ago."

Harry started. This was something new.

"You didn't tell me that," he exclaimed. "That you'd seen Neusner again."

Marcus smiled his decayed smile again.

"No, it was after I met you, a few years later."

"Why didn't you get in touch, let me know?"

"I'm not sure. It seemed so long ago, I wasn't certain."

"That it was him?"

Marcus shook his head.

"No, it was him. I couldn't be certain that I'd understood. It made no sense, seeing him the way I did."

"Where did you see him? Was it here, here in Jerusalem?"

Marcus nodded.

"On Jabotinsky. I was walking. I walked a little better then, this chest problem is more recent. And it was summer."

"It was daylight? You saw him in daylight?"

"Yes. Oh, it was him. I wasn't sure at first, he was so much older.

But he hadn't changed that much."

"What did you do? Did you speak to him, show yourself to him at all?"

Marcus shook his head.

"No, he . . . I wasn't sure then, I wanted to be certain. I followed him. I don't think he saw me. He didn't go very far, just to Giv'at Oren, to a house there. It was his house."

"How do you know?"

"It had his name on the gate, on a little plate. When I read it I knew I hadn't been mistaken. It was him all right."

"Gershon Neusner? It had that name?"

"Yes," Marcus said. "Gershon Neusner." He looked directly at Harry. At first it seemed as though he were harboring a joke, as if there were something amusing about the name. Then his eyes seemed to cloud over with some inner uncertainty, some deep misgiving. He opened his mouth to speak, then closed it.

"Yes?" Harry asked, sensing there was more.

"His name," Marcus said. "That wasn't all. He had acquired a title. He wasn't just plain Gershon Neusner any more. He was General Gershon Neusner."

They all looked at him. They recognized the name.

"My God," said Harry, almost inaudibly. That was all.

FIFTY-EIGHT

The lost are still lost, the silent still hidden in silence. David stood with Leyla and Harry in the diffused light of Yad Vashem on Har Hazikkaron, the mountain of remembrance. They were in the Ohel Yiskor, a square hall with a tent-shaped roof and a wall of large rounded stones. Between the wall and the roof a narrow gap let in the quiet light of the day outside. At the top end of the hall a flame burned behind a low plinth on which four wreaths had been laid. But their eyes were not fixed on the flowers or the bobbing flame. Set at intervals in the floor were black slabs on which large letters spelled out in Hebrew and Roman script twenty-one place names in Germany and Poland. Simple names belonging to simple places, places where ordinary men and women had lived, where they still lived. Villages, small towns, decent municipalities . . . turned into the death factories of the Third Reich. The names lay there in the stone, stark and uncompromising, the bleakest of statements for the bleakest of memories: Belsen, Chelmno, Auschwitz, Majdanek, Bergen-Belsen, Dachau . . .

In all the years she had lived in Jerusalem, Leyla had never been here before. Palestinians did not go to Yad Vashem. Did they not have their own memorials in the refugee camps, their own names to remember? Deir Yasin, Tell al-Zatar, Sabra, Chatilla. Standing here now, she did not forget. If anything, it made her more conscious of what her own people had suffered, were still suffering. But in the stark simplicity of the hall, in the restraint of the black, chiseled stones, she found something she had not looked for: a sense of the vastness of the evil that had been done, a realization

501

that the mind cannot take in suffering on the monumental scale. What matters in the end is the individual, his suffering, his death. In another hall the names of two million victims were recorded, but it had meant nothing, nothing at all. But here, for the first time, Leyla had come face to face with the hot blast of the furnace, had felt in her stomach the anguish, had understood the people who had taken her home from her. She could not forgive them. She could never forgive. But she could no longer condemn. She knew now that they were doomed to live like that forever, side by side, unable to forgive one another, condemning a world that had set its victims at one another's throats. She held David's hand and stared at the dim, exhausted sunlight as it washed the stones.

Marcus Bleich had asked them to go there on his behalf, before beginning their work at the Institute for Holocaust Studies, also at Yad Vashem. He never went to the memorial himself. Like other survivors, he carried his own memorial with him every day of his life. And the photograph, the lock of hair, the broken comb were to him more evocative than anything at Yad Vashem. But he did not affect to despise the memorial for that. If anyone went there, he would ask them to remember his family, to look for them in the Hall of Names.

David watched Harry standing in thought in the Ohel Yiskor, listened to him recite the Kaddish for the dead. As they turned to leave, he looked at him again. Their eyes met.

"You want to know why, don't you? Why I come here, why I converted."

David said nothing.

"Don't you understand?" asked Harry. "Here of all places, do you need an explanation? We're all Jews now, David, every one of us. Not just you and your people, that's only in the blood. There's more to it than that. When they killed so many, they made Jews of everyone. Whether we wanted it or not, we were made children of Abraham by the Holocaust. It's so simple, David. Surely you can understand. Once they did it to you, they could do it to anyone. How many did Stalin massacre in Russia? The Cambodians after Year Zero? How many are in camps today, or in torture chambers? God has taken the foreskin from every man on this planet. It took me a long time to understand it, David, but it made sense in the end."

502

It was early afternoon when they left the Ohel Yiskor and headed for the Institute, a low limestone building about five hundred yards farther down the hill. They were expected: Harry had telephoned early that morning to ask for help on an urgent matter. He was a frequent visitor at the Institute, liked and respected by its staff. But his visits were never officially recorded, he was not known formally to anyone there. If somebody were to ask about him, they would be told that he had never been there, never been helped in his work by the Institute or its staff.

They were met in the hallway by a small, thin woman in her late sixties. Katje Horowicz was the second survivor they had met that morning. She had survived because she had been pretty as a girl, and she still carried the inward scars of that prettiness. Leyla noticed almost at once that she had a number tattooed on her left arm, just visible where it protruded from below the sleeve of her woolen cardigan.

Katje held out her hand and took Leyla's in a firm grip, without waiting for Harry to perform the introductions. She had always been impatient, and the older she grew the more impatient she became. Since leaving the camp she had lived as if there was never enough time. Every day there had seemed like the last. And every day since then had been the same. It was the only way she knew how to live.

"I'm Katje Horowicz," she said. Her English was good, but heavily accented. "Assistant director of the Institute. You must be Miss Rashid. I understand you were a student of Abraham Steinhardt's. So. Very good. I liked Abraham; there was no nonsense about him. None about you either, I see."

Leyla felt uncomfortable beneath that direct gaze, as if she were being scrutinized and judged. Though she did not know it, Katje was indeed observing her closely. She was the first Palestinian ever to visit the Institute: her presence made the older woman uneasy, in spite of her apparent briskness and confidence. Then Katje turned and took David's hand.

"Professor Rosen? How do you do? What brings an archaeologist to this place? Surely we are not yet so old. Or has so much digging among the dead made you morbid?"

David looked around the painted hallway.

"This doesn't seem such a morbid place."

503

Katje shook her head.

"No. The place is cheerful. It has to be to keep our spirits up, working here every day. The morbidity is in what it enshrines . . . in the very fact that it exists. But let's get on. I won't say hello to Harry, I see too much of him as it is."

Behind a locked gray door lay a brightly illuminated corridor. There was a gentle hum of machinery somewhere behind the walls. Someone came out of a door near the other end and crossed to another door opposite. Katje led them down the corridor, talking with Harry about a mutual friend.

The room into which Katje showed them was a stark modern room lined with the most up-to-date computer consoles and VDU screens. Everything felt clean and sanitized, a million miles away from the death camps whose obscenities had been encoded and stored in the bowels of the central computer's memory banks.

"What have you got, Harry?" Katje asked when they had sat down at the table in the center of the room.

"Some numbers," Harry said, drawing a sheaf of papers from his briefcase. They were not the original sheets found in the plane—he did not want to show those to anyone just yet—but simply a copy of the numbers he had prepared the evening before.

"Numbers? That makes a change." It was usually names. Katje took the papers from his hand. "Hey!" she went on. "What have you got here? This is no shopping list, Harry: a maintenance manual is what this is. Days. It will take days to run!"

Harry shook his head.

"No, I don't think so. I think they'll either be straightforward or you won't get anything at all. Please, try a few. See what you get. Would I waste your time, Katje?"

Katje snorted, then turned to David and Leyla, who were sitting together at one end of the table.

"Has Harry explained to you just what all this involves?"

They shook their heads.

She snorted again.

"Typical! The imbecile thinks these machines are just magic. Tap in a number . . . and out comes the information you want." She turned to face Harry again. He tried to look away. They had had this conversation before.

"Look, Harry, it isn't that simple. To get output, you need input.

504

If you want information out, someone has to put it in. It's as simple as that. Look at these numbers. What's this 'V' at the end of them? Since when have there been V's? You've found a whole new category of numbers. Or am I being obtuse? Are these what they look like or are they something we haven't handled before at all?"

"They're what they look like. I'm sure of it. Ignore the V's, just feed in the numbers. Please. It's important."

"To whom? Look, Harry, I love you. I help you every way I can. You are such a nice old man, we all love to help you when we can. But here you come to me with hundreds and hundreds of numbers and you sit there and wait for me to pull a pile of names out of a hat." She turned back to David and Leyla again.

"Let me explain," she said. "Maybe you'll understand. We keep files here on the camps: concentration camps, displaced persons camps, POW camps. We've got names, numbers, personal data on guards, other SS personnel, and inmates. Harry's usually interested in the guards. Do you know what that involves? We've stored the complete files of CROWCASS, JAG, ACID, the UNWCC, UNRRA, the She'erit ha-Peletah, the Jewish Agency Mission, the IRO, the American Jewish Joint Distribution Committee, and dozens of smaller agencies and committees. That's every agency ever involved in investigating war crimes or assisting refugees. That's a lot of files, but even Harry knows they aren't complete. In addition, we've got a set of the complete *Fragebogen,* the questionnaires filed in by all adults in the U.S. zone of Germany after the war. There are over thirteen million of them for 1945 alone."

She paused.

"Am I confusing you?" she asked.

"Yes, but go on." David smiled. "We're listening."

"I wish Harry would listen. Anyway, that's the easy part. Keeping files on the Nazis or survivors is nothing to keeping a record of the victims. We've got two million names of definite victims here at Yad Vashem. But we know that at least five million Jews were killed—some in the camps, some by SS Einsatzgruppen. Three million of those were from Poland alone. So many families were wiped out entirely, we have no way of ever knowing all their names or identities.

"After the war the Allies obtained camp records, but very few of them were complete. The SS destroyed as much as they could before they surrendered. We have camp registers and *Totenbuche*, the 'death books,' but it's all a bit like a jigsaw without most of its pieces. Inmates were generally placed in DP camps after they were fit to be moved, and we've got records for those, as I said. But people were moving around Europe, in and out of the DP camps, in enormous numbers. There were eight million DPs at the end of the war. Six million were repatriated by the end of 1945. After that it got very complicated. Jewish survivors started making for the DP camps in Germany. Some of them had been in hiding, some had been with the partisans, and quite a few had succeeded in posing as Aryans. Who was who? What sort of records could you keep for that sort of confusion? You can follow someone here, then he turns up somewhere else, then he's gone and there's no further record. The Allies knew there were Nazis among the DPs, trying to avoid detection. People used false names, forgot their real names, used odd spellings of difficult Eastern European names, trying to help out some GI clerk.

"Look, nobody's ever going to pick up the pieces left behind by that war: it's just too much, even with computers. And now Harry hands me numbers and expects miracles! Am I mad or is he mad?"

"Katje," Harry said in a quiet voice, "don't talk so much. They understand. I understand. We all understand. But please, please do what you can. It is important, I swear. Feed the numbers into your little machine and see what comes out."

She sighed, picked up the papers, and went across to one of the consoles. Ignoring Harry, she keyed in instructions, then fed in the first number. In less than a second a message flashed across the screen.

RESTRICTED INFORMATION
PLEASE KEY CLEARANCE CODING

Katje darted a look at Harry, frowned, then turned back to the screen. Looking somewhat annoyed, she reentered her personal user code. Again a message flashed at her.

CODE INADMISSIBLE

"What's going on?" she exclaimed. "Restricted? There's no such thing. I have access to everything in this place."

"Try the next number," Harry suggested.

Katje looked down at her list, cleared the screen, and entered her original instruction followed by the number. Again the screen flashed.

RESTRICTED INFORMATION
PLEASE KEY CLEARANCE CODING

Angry now, Katje proceeded to key in a string of numbers, one after the other. And each time the same message flashed across the VDU. When she reached the tenth name she pushed her chair back and swore loudly.

She stood up and turned to face the others.

"Something's wrong," she said. "Well, of course you can see that for yourselves. I'm being refused access to the data banks. There's no reason this should happen. There are only two categories of access in the Institute. Staff have open access to all material. Outsiders coming to us for information are given restricted access—and even that's quite broad. But I keyed straight in as if I wanted the information for myself, like I always do for Harry. This has never happened before."

"What sort of material's normally restricted?" David asked.

Katje shrugged.

"It depends. Personal details about survivors or their families, speculative reports, some of the evidence from the *Spruchkammern* —the German denazification tribunals. Of course, we use our discretion. If we know someone like Harry, or have good reason to believe they're reliable, we extend the access. Normally they have to go through one of us, of course, but there have been cases where researchers have just been given unrestricted clearance."

"Is it possible this involves the kind of information that's normally held on restricted access, only someone's programmed it incorrectly so that there's a sort of blanket restriction?"

"That shouldn't happen. If it did, no one could retrieve the information again. No, the computer expects to receive a clearance code of some kind. I'm going to ask Saul to come down. Maybe he'll be able to get through."

Saul Bernstein was director of the Institute, an elderly German-American who had fought with the Allied forces after his escape

507

from occupied Europe and had come to Israel ten years earlier to take charge of research at Yad Vashem.

Harry shook his head.

"No, Katje. Not yet anyway. I think it's best we keep this to as few people as possible for the moment."

She eyed him suspiciously.

"I see," she said at last. "I think," she went on in an abrasive tone, "we'd better sit down again. And then one of you had better start explaining just what this is all about."

"I'd rather you didn't know, Katje. For your own good," Harry muttered.

"I'm sure you would. And you know I'm not going to listen to you. I'm an old woman. They did everything they could to me when I was a girl, now they can do nothing. Nothing at all. Let's sit down."

They sat down and David began to explain. It took a long time.

FIFTY-NINE

It was cold in the little room. Cold and comfortless. Marcus Bleich sat in his chair staring at the wall ahead of him. Outside, it was night, and small stars listened to the darkness in the remoteness of space. Marcus was unaware of them, unaware of any of his surroundings. He had been sitting like that, in one position, his eyes fixed on that single spot, for hour after hour, as if frozen into immobility by some terrible frost in his soul. His silence was like the muteness of death.

He was back in the camp, digging, sweating, hurting, surviving. All around him, braided wire hung in complex loops, twisting its way into every segment of waking life. There were huts in long rows like railway sheds, stinking with excrement and filled with stale, unusable air. Watchtowers and chimneys held the horizon fixed, like pins or bayonets stabbing the sky. Everywhere men, women, and children walked and crawled, all on a single journey whose destination was the ovens.

He hugged himself in his muteness, against the cold, against the dark. A small light burned on a low table near the window, enhancing the darkness with a dim, ethereal glow. He was oblivious of it as of everything else. Only the darkness seemed to matter now, the darkness and the man from the camp. Neusner. Somehow or other, without his really knowing it, Neusner had been buried inside him all these years like a living corpse, waiting to be reawakened, to be clothed with humid flesh again. Seeing him had been the first stage of the alchemical process. His conversation that morning had been the elixir, distilled and potent at last. Neusner was alive again and dangerous. His very existence threatened Bleich. In a remote sense, Neusner had become the camp, waiting out there in the darkness for him with his coils of stinging wire and his monstrous, gaping ovens.

The Englishman had said nothing at all in explanation of his visit, but Marcus knew who he was, what he did. Marcus could guess what was happening, even if he did not understand what lay behind it. He had come to the Holy Land looking for some sort of promise and had found nothing but dry ashes, like Dead Sea apples. A Gentile hunted the killers of Marcus' people. Blandford was a convert, but in Marcus' eyes he was still a *goy*. He had not undergone the circumcision of the camps or donned the phylacteries of death.

Marcus shivered. It would not be long before he rejoined Marta and the children, all the sweet damned. In all these years he had taken no revenge, repaid no wrongs. There had been so many wrongs, he would not have known where to begin. No one would. And now, here in Jerusalem, an Englishman came digging in his memories, here in Jerusalem the Devil was loose.

He remembered an incident in the camp, the execution of a child, a ten-year-old boy who had stolen food during an air raid. They had lined up the other prisoners in still, silent rows to watch. No one had wanted to watch, but SS guards and Kapos had stood all around them, the former with machine guns trained on them. The gallows had been tall and painted black, and he remembered that the rope had been too short at first, that they had been forced to send someone to look for a box to place on the chair, to make it high enough. They had had to lift the boy up bodily to the noose while he balanced precariously on the box, not on tiptoe exactly, but poised more than standing, like a dancer or an acrobat, his tiny feet teetering between life and death, ready to soar into darkness.

Suddenly Marcus remembered, as if it was important, that Neusner had been near him that day, in the row in front of him, about five rows from the gallows. He had seen the back of Neusner's head and . . . yes, he remembered it now, he had wanted to see his face, to look into his eyes when they killed the boy. The child had shivered on the box while the commandant read out the sentence, citing the law by number and paragraph. All the time a Kapo kept the boy steady lest he fall prematurely, lest he die without sanction of the law. The platform, the chair, the wooden box together formed a sort of tower, at the apex of which the boy stood white-faced in the bitter cold, in a thin shirt, shivering his last moments of life away into the even thinner air. Marcus had wanted to see Neusner's eyes but, like everyone else, his own eyes were fixed on the boy's, willing him to hold fast.

In the moment that they kicked away the chair, he had felt such rage and pity rise in him that he had nearly cried out with the pain of it. To have done so would have been fatal, but it had taken all his willpower, all his learned instinct for survival to dam up the words that had crowded onto his tongue. The box had clattered away and the boy dropped into the noose like a stone, then jerked like a toy monkey as the rope bit into his neck and began its slow work of strangulation. It took a long time. His body, emaciated by the hunger that had driven him to steal, had been like a feather to the rope. They had filed past while he was still alive, and Marcus had sworn as he looked into the dying, pain-wracked eyes that he would take revenge. There had been death all around him, he had witnessed the deaths of thousands, but it was this death he had vowed to revenge. Nothing else made sense. One death or ten million, it was all the same.

But on leaving the camp and coming to Palestine, his thirst for revenge had become a dryness in the throat and then an occasional taste on his palate that grew less and less irritating as the years went by. He had done nothing, said nothing. He had come away from Dachau with wet eyes and an aching heart, but the tears had dried in time and his heart had found its ways of coping with its pain, grown scar tissue to cover it. He had reasoned to himself that there would have been no sweetness in revenge. It seemed too abstract, too remote from him. There had been reports of the trials at Nuremberg, there had been the excitement when they brought Eichmann to Jerusalem. But he had remained untouched by it all, it had meant nothing to him. He had never met Streicher or Ribbentrop or Eichmann, never suffered at their hands, and neither in the judgments passed on them nor in the sentences carried out could he find satisfaction or relief.

But today . . . today was different. Today he felt ashamed. He had seen Neusner in Jerusalem and said nothing. He had skulked in his room and closed his eyes and his ears. He still did not know who

Neusner was or what he had done, but he knew the Englishman was looking for him. And all day he had seen in his mind's eye the boy's face and the back of Neusner's head. What had it been? The angle of the head, the stance, the bearing? There had been something implacable in Neusner, and Marcus sensed that that implacability had been there on that day, that if he had been able to look into his eyes . . .

He stood up and walked across the room to the bed. Bending down, he scrabbled under it for a while, then drew out a small bundle, an old bundle that had lain there for years gathering dust and cobwebs. He straightened slowly and placed the bundle on the bed, then began to unwrap it. The cloth that he unfolded was an old Israeli flag, the star of David faded, the fabric torn and moth-eaten. It was a Palmach flag that had flown over Hebron in 1949. The flag had belonged to Yaakov, a friend who had come to Israel with Marcus straight from the DP camp where they had met. They had been part of the Aliyah Bet, the clandestine immigration movement into Palestine. Yaakov had died in the fighting at Hebron, and the flag had been retrieved and given to Marcus by another member of the Palmach brigade with whom he had fought.

Out of the folds of the flag he drew Yaakov's pistol. It too had been given to him in memory of his friend. It was a Webley .45, heavy and unwieldy in his unaccustomed hands. He knew it still contained six bullets. They would be more than enough for the job he had in mind.

He put on his coat and scarf and placed the gun in his pocket. It was strange, but he could not remember Yaakov's face any longer. So many things faded. But the gun felt solid, the gun felt reassuring, as if Yaakov were somehow present in it after all this time. He looked around the room and his eyes came to rest on the photograph by the bed. Without thinking, he walked to the bedside, picked up the photograph, and put it to his lips. It felt heavy, as if it were a gun, loaded with memories. They could kill a man as surely as bullets, such memories. He put the photograph down and breathed hard, like a man who has been running and needs to rest.

It was cold outside, a deep cold that penetrated the lungs and seemed to travel on even further, into the veins. Marcus walked with his scarf fastened around his mouth. It warmed the air a little, but at the same time it felt tight and suffocating. The streets were almost empty of people, though it was only nine o'clock. He walked down to Nordau Square, then to the corner of Nordau and Zalman Shazar, where he stopped by a bus shelter. There was no one else around. His hand caressed the gun in his pocket. Yes, it felt solid, like the anger that had begun to live in him again.

The bus took half an hour to arrive, but he scarcely felt the cold now. He was in another world, the world of the camp, and there he had become inured to winter. When the bus finally drew alongside him he did not move at first. Two people got off, but he still stood there.

"Are you getting on, Grandfather?" the driver shouted. The doors were wide open and cold was seeping inside.

Marcus glanced up, as though he had been a thousand miles away. He nodded and made slowly for the steps. Inside, someone muttered, the impatience in the voice quite undisguised. Marcus did not notice. He paid and found a seat as the doors hissed shut and the bus roared off, turning right into Yitzhak ben Zvi. It was not a long journey, and there was little traffic on the road to cause delay. Fifteen minutes later Marcus disembarked at the first stop on Tchernichovsky, on the west side of Giv'at Oren, a modern quarter southeast of the university. Ha-Poretzim was only a few streets away, but Marcus walked slowly, as ever. Something told him there was no need to hurry, that Neusner would be there, as though he expected Marcus' arrival.

The house was low, set back from the street, quiet. Lights burned in an upstairs room. But in a way Marcus did not see the house. His vision was focused inwardly, and he saw instead a low concrete hut out of which a pale light shone onto the snow. He felt prickles of fear as his hand reached for the gate. Surely there would be alarms, searchlights, voices. Behind him, a car went by in the dark and passed into the night: he froze as its headlights grazed him, then relaxed again as the darkness returned. He pushed the gate open and stepped inside. Until now he had not even thought how he was going to get into the house. But all at once it seemed simple, simple and obvious.

He walked up to the front door. Beside a small *mezuzah* set on the frame, there was a bell push. He pressed it hard. A bell rang somewhere in the distance, muffled and musical. He remembered the bells in the camp, directing, ordering, controlling their existence. In particular there had been the bell that signaled the end of selection, when SS officers had culled the inmates, plucking out the *Muselmänner*, the irreparably weak, noting down their numbers for extermination: "These for the ovens, these to be spared another week, another month." He pressed the bell again. Footsteps sounded. A light went on.

Gershon Neusner had not changed visibly since Marcus last saw him, on the day he had followed him here.

"Yes?" asked Neusner, puzzled by the strange old man in a soiled overcoat standing like a tramp on his doorstep.

Marcus looked at Neusner without speaking. He had made no mistake. It was the same man, though much altered since the camp.

"Gershon," he said at last, "I want to speak to you. Let me come in."

Neusner frowned. Why was the old man speaking in German? Who was he?

"You have me at a disadvantage," he said. "You know my name, but I'm afraid I don't know yours."

The general was dressed in a well-tailored silk robe, beneath which he wore an open-necked shirt and trousers. He looked robust for his age. His eyes were clear, his skin firm and evenly tanned, his stance erect. Two old men from the same camp, the same hut . . . but a world of difference between them.

Marcus was wheezing. Even with his scarf he could not keep the cold air from invading the soft tissues of his lungs.

"You know me," he said, then drew in a quivering, rasping breath. It was a torture to speak.

Something very like fear tightened in Neusner's chest. Who was the old man? What did he want? He stared at the lined face, the rheumy eyes, the sunken cheeks. And as he did so a ghost flickered into sight and was gone again.

"You," he whispered. Bleich the questioner, Bleich the curious. He had wanted to have him sent to the ovens, but Schultz had dissuaded him. Bleich might prove useful, he had said, his friendship would provide additional credibility. Gain his trust, Schultz had argued, make him believe you, and if there are any questions afterward he'll vouch for you. It was strange, thought Neusner, that Bleich the young man and Bleich the old man were really not that different. It was age that lay between them, not pain or hunger or emaciation.

"Are you alone?" wheezed Marcus, his hand tight on the gun in his pocket.

Not thinking, mesmerized by the thin ghost from his past, Neusner nodded.

"You have . . . no wife? No children?"

"Except for one, my children have their own homes now. My wife is with our youngest child in Germany, visiting relatives." Neusner paused. What should he do? What did it mean, this reappearance?

"You'd best come in," he said. "It's cold outside."

Perhaps it was nothing, mere coincidence. Perhaps the old man had recently discovered that he lived here, guessed he was his old friend from the camp, and decided to visit. Or perhaps Bleich was down on his luck and needed help, help he thought a general might give . . . even a poorly paid Israeli general.

Marcus stepped into the hallway and waited for Neusner to shut the door. He remembered his first day in the camp, the steel door closing behind them, the finality of the sound. Neusner turned and smiled, as though this were, after all, a social visit from an old friend.

"Please . . . Marcus," Neusner said, "let's go into my study. It's on this floor." He had had difficulty in remembering Bleich's first name.

He led the way to the study, a small, book-lined room hung with photographs, an intimate room with soft leather chairs and cut-glass decanters of fine spirits. Marcus thought of his little room, no bigger than this, of the low, uncomfortable bed, the single chair, the single, faded photograph.

"Let me take your coat," said Neusner, reaching out for it.

"No, thank you," said Marcus. He kept his hand in the pocket.

"As you wish," Neusner said. "But at least sit down. You must be cold. A drink would warm you up. What will you have?"

"No, thank you," Marcus repeated. The warm air had begun to make its way into his lungs, softening them, making it possible for him to breathe.

"If you don't mind," Neusner said, "I think I'll have one myself. It was a shock to see you there. Like a ghost." He tried to smile, but

515

nothing happened. This was hardly like a meeting of old comrades, he thought. His hand shook very slightly as he removed the stopper from a decanter of brandy and poured himself a generous glass. When he turned, Bleich was still standing there exactly as he had been, staring at him.

"Well." Neusner was the first to speak again. "You've taken me by surprise. I didn't know you were in Eretz Israel. How long have you been here?"

"Since 1946," Marcus said. To hear the words "Eretz Israel" on this man's lips . . .

"But that's incredible," said Neusner. "I've been here as long myself. I came on the *Hannah Szenes* at the end of '45 and joined the Haganah right away. I've been in Jerusalem since 1955. I'd no idea you were here, no idea at all. And all this time we've been so close. How long have you lived in Jerusalem?"

"Almost as long. I came here in '57, from Rosh Pina."

It was beginning to sound so cordial, like a college reunion: "Where have you been living? What have you been doing?" Marcus caressed the gun in his pocket.

"When did you learn I was here?" Neusner asked.

"A few years ago. I saw you in the street. I recognized you, but you didn't notice me. I followed you here, to your home. Your name was on the gate, I knew it was you."

"Why didn't you say something? Why did you wait so long?"

What did the old man want in his tattered coat and worn-out shoes? Money? A job? Why was he standing like that with his hands in his pockets? He should have sent him to the gas chamber while it was still possible. There were no chambers here, no ovens, no chimneys. One day, perhaps, but not now, not in his lifetime.

"I had nothing to say to you," Bleich said.

"And now you do?"

Marcus wanted to cry "No!", to get it over with. He had not come to talk but to act. But his hand would not move. The gun was like a stone in his pocket.

"Who are you?" he asked. His voice felt thin and remote to him, as if it came from a long distance away. He could see the boy on the platform shivering—had it been cold or fear that caused him to tremble most?—and beside him Neusner in his striped suit with a death's head pinned to his breast, pushing away the chair.

"Who am I?" In all the years since he had been here no one had ever asked him that question.

"You know who I am," he said. "I'm Gershon Neusner. You recognized me. I'm the same Gershon who lived in Hut 19 with you. Why need you ask?"

Marcus shook his head.

"Your name's not Neusner," he said in a whisper. "What is it? You can tell me now, the past is far away. We're alone. No one else need know."

"What is this nonsense?" Neusner protested. He almost stammered in his haste. So Bleich had guessed all along. He had thought as much. His carelessness in sparing the man had come home to him after all these years. But what had brought him here tonight? And why did he keep his hands stuffed into his pockets? What was he hiding?

"It's not nonsense," said Marcus quietly. "There is no nonsense here. All the nonsense is done with, long ago. We were children, don't you remember? Children in men's bodies. But you knew things the rest of us never knew. You weren't one of us at all. You and your friends who came with you. They all left with you, didn't they? Every one of them. None of you died in the camp. How many of you were there altogether?"

"I don't know what you're talking about," shouted Neusner, his voice rising. He was trembling now. Who else knew? Who had Bleich spoken to?

"It doesn't matter," Marcus said, taking the gun from his pocket as if it had been magically released. It felt heavy, but it was not a burden any longer. He raised it slowly, pointing it at the other man. Neusner stepped back instinctively, backing into the table with the decanters. Glass tinkled as the table shook.

"Marcus, please . . . what are you doing? Explain to me what's wrong, but for God's sake put that gun down!" For the first time Neusner looked directly into Bleich's eyes. He found nothing there to reassure him.

"Do you remember the boy they hanged?" asked Marcus. "He was ten years old. They put him on a box, kicked it from under him. They say he took half an hour to die."

Neusner shook his head. So many deaths, how could he remember one?

"You were in front of me. You watched him."

"I don't remember. I'm sorry. There were so many."

517

"Not like that." Marcus shook his head. "Not like that." He looked into Neusner's eyes. They were blue and soft and menacing, and he knew he had to pull the trigger. For the boy. He held the pistol steady. He felt so calm now, calmer than he had ever felt in his life. The pistol seemed to lose its weight, it became light, as though it were nothing. He pulled the trigger.

Nothing happened. Neusner had closed his eyes. There was a click, but the gun refused to fire. Marcus pulled the trigger again. Nothing. Frantically he pulled back on the trigger again and again. Nothing but the sound of metal striking against metal. The blood roared in his head like a torrent, dizzying him.

Neusner opened his eyes. He saw the old man standing opposite him, desperately trying to fire his useless gun. He took a deep breath and walked toward him, right up to the gun, and put his hand firmly on the barrel.

"Please, Marcus," he said. "Give me the gun."

Marcus' fingers went limp. Neusner took the gun from his hand like a teacher confiscating a forbidden toy from a child. Great tears welled up in Marcus' eyes. He looked at Neusner through them, saw him swim in front of him, saw the boy spin on his rope, felt the blood rush through his brain, felt the room spin, the blackness claw at him, the box and the chair drop from beneath his feet.

Neusner caught him and helped him to a chair. He loosened the old man's coat and checked his pulse. It was abnormally fast, yet weak. He straightened up and walked across the room to his desk. As if it had been no more than an empty glass, he set the gun down on top of some papers and picked up the phone. He dialed a short number and stood with the receiver to his ear, listening to the ring. Someone answered.

"Heinrich?" he said. "It's Walther. Listen. We may have trouble. I can't explain now. Come over straight away . . . and bring Paul with you. Be here in half an hour."

Without waiting for an answer, he put down the receiver, then turned and walked back to the old man in the chair. He looked down at him for a long time, wondering, remembering. And at last it came to him, the small boy on the box. He and the others had laid bets how long the child would last. He had won a cigarette from each of them that day.

518

SIXTY

They came back to the Institute late that night. Katje thought she could break through the block on the computer if she had time, but she wanted access to it when there was no one else around. She often worked late in the computing lab anyway, and the security guard accepted her presence there as normal. While he was on his rounds she let Harry, David, and Leyla into the building by the rear entrance. They made straight for the computing room. Katje sat down in front of a terminal and ran a check of the system.

"No problems," she said. "Let me have the list."

She keyed in the first number:

D7139-V

At once the screen flashed as it had before:

RESTRICTED INFORMATION
PLEASE KEY CLEARANCE CODE

She keyed in her code.

CODE INADMISSIBLE

"You may as well sit down," she said, looking up at them. "This may take some time."

"How risky is it?" David asked. "Will the system be booby-trapped?"

"I expect so, yes. What would be the point of creating a data block and then putting no alarm on it?"

"What about this last attempt? Will that have raised an alarm?"

Katje shook her head.

"I don't think so. Most probably the computer will log the request and the code, but that won't matter unless someone is checking every entry. Please, just sit down. You're making me nervous."

Time seemed to crawl. Katje sat at the terminal, pressing keys, reading messages, keying in further commands. Forty minutes later she sat back in her chair and sighed deeply.

"I've tricked the computer into supplying me with all its current passwords, all one hundred and twenty-eight of them. None of them works. I've tried to go around the block rather than straight through, but all I've done is set off a couple of alarms somewhere. Probably not in this building. If there's anyone monitoring those alarms, though, we'd better get out of here quickly."

"How long do you think we have?" asked David.

"It's impossible to say. It all depends on how alert these people are. But someone could be here in five minutes . . . or less."

"Are there any other ways past the block?"

Katje shook her head.

"I've tried every way I know. This is one of the best-guarded systems I've ever encountered. Somebody really wants to keep us out."

"What about the names?" Leyla said. "The names on the original list. Would they work?"

"Let me see," asked Katje.

David gave her the list. She returned to the keyboard and keyed in the first name:

ADLER, F.

The screen flashed:

NOTHING CORRESPONDS TO THIS ENTRY

She tried the name followed by the bracketed code:

ADLER, F. (VALK. III)

The screen flashed:

NOTHING CORRESPONDS TO THIS ENTRY

Then the whole line:

ADLER, F (VALK. III): 12944/D7139-V

The screen flashed:

NOTHING CORRESPONDS TO THIS ENTRY

She reversed the order, giving the number first, then trying the name as a password, but it was rejected as inadmissible.

"We've just tripped another alarm," Katje said. She seemed untouched by the growing tension in the room, as if it were all a game to her, as though it did not matter whether she won or lost.

"Is there any other way of finding the password?" Leyla asked.

"Not in the time available, no. It's probably quite arbitrary, as arbitrary as the numbers themselves."

"What did you say?" asked Leyla, her voice tight with tension.

"I said it's probably quite arbitrary."

"No, after that."

"Arbitrary . . . like the numbers."

"But they aren't arbitrary," she said. "The first half stands for a date, then a letter for the camp, then the actual number. . . . And a V at the end. It never varies, it's the one item that's constant." She took a deep breath. She had just realized what she had said.

"Key in the word 'Valkyrie,'" she said in a quiet voice.

Katje turned back to the screen and keyed in the word. The screen flashed.

YOU HAVE FULL ACCESS
PLEASE KEY IN DATA REQUEST

Katje leaned back.

"We have our password," she said.

Some of the tension seemed to slip away from them. Harry squeezed Leyla's arm and she smiled at him. They were through.

"Key in the first number," Harry said.

521

Katje did so. This time the response was totally different. Line after line of hard information flickered onto the screen and hung there, each letter like a tiny green ghost brought to life out of the strange interworld of the computer's microcircuitry. And what appeared was in every way consistent, a ghost from the distant past, growing more and more like flesh:

ADLER, FRIEDRICH ARTHUR
BORN: DÜSSELDORF, 7/12/26
JUNGVOLK: 1936-40
HITLERJUGEND: 1940-42
SS-STANDARTE VALKYRIE III: 1942
ORDENSBURG SONTHOFEN 1943
DACHAU KL 12/9/44
OPERATIONAL NAME: MOSHE ABRAMS
KL NUMBER: D7139-V
MAUTENDORF DP CAMP: 1945-46
ARRIVED HAIFA, PALESTINE 2/11/46
HAGANAH: 1947-49
OPENED IMPORT-EXPORT BUSINESS, TEL AVIV, 1949
MEMBER OF TEL AVIV BRANCH HISTADRUT
(FEDERATION OF LABOR) 1955
SECRETARY OF TEL AVIV HISTADRUT 1957
MEMBER OF MAPAI PARTY 1958-68
MEMBER OF ISRAEL LABOR PARTY 1968-
ELECTED TO KNESSET 1970

There was more.

"Can you get a printout of this?" David asked.

"Of course." Katje pushed a button and at once a printer to her left clattered into life, filling a sheet of paper with row after row of data.

There was a sound of cars drawing up outside, then car doors opening and shutting. Footsteps sounded on gravel.

"We'll have to go," shouted Katje.

"We can't go," David protested, feeling despair clutch him with heavy hands. "We've scarcely started. For God's sake, we've got to get more information!"

"Do what you can to keep them off," said Katje. "Make a

barricade at the door. We'll get out through the window once we've finished. Hurry!"

David and Leyla began to move a filing cabinet toward the door. Katje turned back to the keyboard and typed quickly. The machine responded immediately:

VALKYRIE FILE AVAILABLE ON REQUEST
PLEASE KEY IN INSTRUCTIONS

"There's a file," said Katje. "But even with a high-speed printer there isn't time."

They could hear running footsteps in the corridor outside. The filing cabinet was in place behind the door. David and Leyla began to push a second one beside it.

"Does it have to be printed?" Harry pressed. "Isn't there a way of just taking it out of the system?"

"I could dump it onto a disc or . . ." Katje spun around in her chair. "Quickly!" she shouted. "Bring me a magnetic tape from the rack behind you."

Voices sounded outside the door. Someone banged on it heavily.

Katje's fingers flashed over the keyboard. The screen flashed a message:

DRIVES 5 AND 7 FREE
RESPOND WITH DRIVE NUMBER
TO MOUNT TAPE

She pressed the number 5, then got out of her chair and took the tape from Harry. Which was drive number 5?

A pane of glass shattered in the door. A voice called loudly:

"Open up! This is the police! Open this door at once!"

Katje found the drive. She was growing nervous and her fingers fumbled as she tried to insert the tape.

There was a shot, high up, through the broken pane. David ran to a corner where there was a large metal filing box, lifted it and, with Leyla's help, heaved it on top of the filing cabinet, blocking the opening in the door.

The tape slipped into place. Katje dashed back to the keyboard and typed out the final command:

There was a sound of whirring as the tape spun. Seconds later it was finished. She instructed the computer to rewind, then got up and retrieved the tape.

At the door there were loud crashes as the men outside hurled themselves against the barricade. The lock snapped and the cabinets gave slightly. Someone inserted the barrel of a submachine gun into the gap and fired wildly. Lights and equipment smashed, but the shots were wide.

"Here," said Katje breathlessly, pressing the tape into Harry's hands.

"Get out of here now!" she shouted. "I'll hold them as long as I can."

"Don't be a fool, Katje," Harry protested, but she overrode him angrily.

"Please, Harry, I know what I'm doing! They already know I'm here. I'm the assistant director. I'll keep them talking while you get away with the tape. For God's sake, don't argue with me. There isn't time!"

Reluctantly, David went first, taking the gun from his pocket, ready to shoot if there was anyone outside. He pulled himself flat onto the windowsill and climbed out.

There was a heavy crashing behind them. The cabinets rocked. A coarse voice shouted incoherently. Harry got to the window. David helped him through, then turned and leaned across the sill into the room.

"Leyla!" he shouted. "Lie flat!"

He raised his gun and fired at the door.

"Now, Leyla! Hurry up!"

She dashed to the window. David grabbed her by the wrist and hauled her over the sill.

There was a crash behind them. The cabinets had toppled over. Without waiting to see what was happening, they turned and ran into the darkness.

524

SIXTY-ONE

He was in hell again, or hell was in him, he could no longer tell which. Hell was a place, not a condition, not an abstraction, not a dream: it had size and shape and dimension, it possessed color and light and sound. He had learned the truth of that the first time, and now he was learning it again: hell is a definite place with up and down, left and right, front and back—the only directions in an otherwise insane and directionless universe. Above all, it possessed pain, red, immeasurable pain. Here, he was the center of hell, as though it existed for his torment alone and he for its greater glory.

They had brought him back to the camp. He had not thought it possible, but he was there now, no doubt about it. All the old smells, all the old sounds, and yet he felt alone, dreadfully alone. In the camp there had been other people, and it was in and through them that he had survived. It was a basic tenet of the place, that no one got through on his own. But here it was as though the camp existed solely for his destruction. They had burned six million in their ovens and yet they had not finished, they had to have him too, they had to take his death back into their employ, as though it embarrassed them to lose it. Had he once sold his soul to them? Was it possible that, like Faustus, he was with his black-coated Mephistopheles at last? He screamed, but he could hear nothing. Not a sound.

Neusner leaned over the prostrate form of Marcus Bleich. The old man lay stretched on a white-sheeted bed in the basement of Schultz's house. Schultz had insisted they move him from Neusner's at once, and Neusner had agreed. Others might know where Bleich had gone, might follow him there. They needed time and space to work on the old man, extract anything he knew. Schultz had long ago prepared a room in his basement in case such facilities were ever needed. From time to time it had been useful. Soundproofed, hidden, self-contained, it provided an ideal environment for interrogator and victim both. There were tools and chemicals at hand, a cool washbasin, clean towels, even a shower if things got messier than expected.

Bleich had gone into some sort of coma, although he gave every impression of being conscious. He seemed impervious to questions or blows, as if his mind were trapped in a world of its own. But they had to get through to him. Alone, he would never have confronted Neusner, or so Neusner felt. Bleich had known something was amiss ever since the camp and had known that Neusner lived in Jerusalem for several years, but he had done nothing about it. So something must have triggered off the visit. And there had been the alarm at the Yad Vashem Institute. Someone had tried to penetrate the Valkyrie file. Now, within days of Ragnarök. And there was a rumor—it was still no more than that—that something had happened at Iram. The old man was nothing, a cipher, no more . . . but what if there were others, people with guns that fired?

Heinrich Schultz left the bed and came up to Neusner.

"He's conscious, but he isn't aware of his surroundings. He mutters things in German. Disconnected, but I think he's talking about the camp, about Dachau. I think he imagines he's back there now. He may be reliving the first time, or he may think he's been taken back again, that it's starting all over."

"Good," snapped Neusner. If Bleich thought he was in the camp, he could capitalize on that fact. He'd make the old man believe it, put him right back there among the shit and the mud and the corpses, give him another taste of hell. And then he'd make him talk. He went across to the bed.

"*Wie ist ihr Name?*"

No reply.

"*Wie ist ihr Name?*"

No reply.

Neusner raised his hand and slapped the old man hard across the face. He repeated the question.

"What is your name?"

No reply. The hand moved again.

"*Antworten Sie mir!*"

526

No reply. Another slap. Bleich would remember. The questions, the slaps. Neusner called to Heinrich, who stood to one side watching. Watching and remembering.

"Help me to make him stand," Neusner called.

Schultz came over and lent a hand. They dragged Bleich upright, then hauled him out of the bed and onto his feet. He tottered, unable to hold himself straight.

"Hold him," Neusner ordered.

Schultz held the old man from behind. Bleich would remember. Neusner began to recite numbers, a long string of numbers he made up as he went along. The old man swayed, remembering.

He was at the *Appel*, the morning roll call—or was it the evening call? He could not tell, but perhaps it was morning; he had been in bed. He must be ill, he thought, or they would not be holding him up. This was the most dangerous time of the day. During the *Appel*, people had to stand for hours on the parade ground, row after row of silent dummies, waiting for their numbers to be called. SS guards patrolled their ranks, watching for those who were ill, waiting to snatch those who fell, to take them to the ovens or even shoot them on the spot. Every day hundreds died here. But the others would help, they would hold you up if you showed signs of being faint. The danger lay in a sudden swoon, in an unpredicted blackout. But he was all right, he was being held. He felt his legs sway as though they were jelly.

"Siebentausendachthundertsechsundfünfzig."

It was his number, the one on his arm. He had to answer or they would think he was missing. If he failed to answer at once, he was a dead man.

"Hier!" he called.

The man behind him let go. He had no strength, he was falling. He collapsed on the floor like a rag doll, limp and cold.

"Put him back on the bed," ordered Neusner.

"How do you intensify hell?" he asked himself. Bleich carried it in his head, he knew that. They all did. Even himself, the whole Valkyrie mission, none of them had escaped. Bleich and the others had been the lucky ones. They had been liberated, given their land, their freedom. But what about those who had given their lives to permanent incarceration? Walther Nebel had been Gershon Neusner for almost fifty years now, like someone trapped in another man's body, unable to escape. His Aryan purity had been wrapped in a dirty cloak of Jewishness for so long now, he knew he would never get the smell of it out of his nostrils. Every time he peed, every time he bathed, every time he made love to his wife, he saw the evidence of his sacrifice.

And he had never forgotten the camp. Their training had not prepared them for it: nothing could have prepared them. The stench still haunted his nostrils. No one had been immune to it, not even the guards. But they at least had their leave and their own quarters in which to sleep. He had been steeped in it, forced to share the latrines, forced to sleep with the sick and dying, forced to eat from dirty bowls with his fingers. Not all of them had survived, but there were no memorials to their dead, no Yad Vashems, no famous books. They had known there would be none, at least not yet, but it still rankled. For now, his hatred must be a monument.

He spat in Bleich's face.

"Stehen Sie auf!" he bellowed.

Bleich stirred but did nothing. He could not move. He wanted to move, desperately wanted to get up, but his limbs would not obey. His body felt sapped of all strength, he could do nothing but lie there broken.

"Get up!" The voice rang in his ears like a klaxon. Something struck his cheek with bewildering force, then again and yet again. He could not believe the brutality of the blows, the savagery with which they were stung. He had to get up. His life depended on it. Those who could not get out of bed were taken away by the Kapos. He tried to make his legs move. They were not his legs any more. His body was no longer his body. And yet it was: he could feel it, every ache, every stabbing pain, the feces and urine that clung to his skin, their stench in his nostrils. He felt hands on him, pulling him to his feet again. He wanted to sleep, wanted to find some sort of oblivion, but they would not let him.

Neusner leaned across the old man and whispered to Schultz.

"How high can you turn this boiler?"

"High. Very high."

"Turn it up, then. Leave the door open, though."

In a louder voice, he yelled at Bleich.

"You're sick, old man. We've no room for the sick here in Dachau. This isn't a rest house, it's a work camp. If you can't work, you can't take up valuable space. You're excess baggage, Grandfather. We'll have to lighten ourselves of you."

528

Schultz had already opened the door of the old oil-fired boiler in the far corner of the basement. He added more oil and adjusted the controls. Red and yellow flames climbed upward. The heat began to rise.

Neusner walked the old man round and round the room, dragging him like something already dead. Bleich had never felt so sick. It wasn't just the usual breathlessness and weakness, it was deeper, more fundamental than that, as if his heart had stopped functioning. His head spun and he wanted to throw up, but he seemed to remember having done so already; his stomach heaved, but it was empty, it had nothing more to disgorge. Hell lasted forever, but this couldn't last that long, it was impossible. There had to be oblivion, nothing could endure this.

It was growing unbearably hot in the basement. The pipes that led from the boiler to the rest of the house seemed to throb with heat. The opening of the boiler gaped like the mouth of a baker's oven, eager for bread.

He remembered the ovens. He had passed by them more than once, shivering. In the winter the guards joked about it to the inmates. "If you're feeling cold, we can always warm you up in here." This one was smaller than he remembered them, but perhaps each had his own oven in hell. He had seen babies thrown into the flames, living babies, living mothers. Flesh made bread, like the Christian God. They had grown into smoke, gray wandering smoke. He wet himself again, a warm, gentle stream that reminded him of childhood.

There was a man in front of him. He remembered him. Gershon. But it wasn't Gershon, it was someone else, someone dressed in Gershon's body. A dibbuk, a spirit of the irredeemably evil dead, had entered the body and was masquerading as him. But Gershon was the dibbuk, he remembered that now.

The dibbuk grabbed him by the shoulders. He could feel the terrible heat behind him, taste it on his tongue. He could hardly breathe. The weight of the heat seemed unbearable.

"You can escape the oven," the dibbuk said. "Just tell me who sent you, who else knows about me. That's all I want to know. Then you can go. Then you can sleep. Sleep as long as you like. Just tell me the name. Even one name, that's all I ask."

It had never been that simple, Marcus thought. They wanted to trap him, they wanted his own name. Of course, they had his number, but his name would let the dibbuk take him as well. Without the name, the dibbuk could do nothing, it was powerless. He stared at the figure holding him.

"Walther!" It was Schultz.

"You're going to kill him!" Schultz shouted. "He's weakening fast. His breathing's getting heavier. He won't last. Then you'll have thrown it away. If you want information out of him, keep him alive for God's sake!"

"He's breaking, don't you see? He knows I'm here, he can hear me; he understands. Another minute, that's all it'll take. Another minute!"

"Leave him, Walther. Bring him back to the bed. Or else you'll lose him."

The dibbuks were arguing over him. He could hear their voices piping like birdcalls in the depths of a pine forest. There had been a forest when he was young. A forest with calling birds and a carpet of fine needles on the earth. And a second forest when he was a little older, where they had taken people to die, a dim place loud with birdcalls. Or had they too been dibbuks?

"What is his name? Who is looking for me?"

The Gershon-dibbuk shook him. Then he began to shake of his own accord. His whole body started to shake, as if the spirit had already entered him. Great shudders ran up and down his frame. He was on fire, he could feel the flames sucking at his flesh. His stomach heaved. He had thought it impossible, but a great ocean of bile poured out of him, then blood, clot after clot of it. The room started spinning, wilder and wilder, as if freed of the earth. His body quaked. He had become glass, fine-spun and fragile, transparent as the light in the forest. He was falling. He would break, he would shatter like dust. The dibbuk had drawn away from him.

He crashed onto the ground, not even trying to break his fall. The bright blood continued to pour from his mouth.

"He's dead," said Schultz in a low voice. "I told you it would kill him."

Neusner said nothing. A trail of mixed bile and blood ran down the front of his shirt. They would have to burn the body, he thought, remove all trace of it. He looked up at Schultz.

"I want the woman," he said. "Tell them to bring her here as soon as they've cleared up at the Institute. I'll see to it that she talks. Depend on it."

SIXTY-TWO

They found the car where they had left it on Ha-Zikkaron, near the
entrance to Yad Vashem. David had hired it earlier that day from
Kopel on King David Street. It was a new Citron BX, fast and
sturdy, with good suspension, well suited to Israeli roads. They left
at once, without waiting to see who would come out of the building.
Whoever had come for them, they could be sure it had not been any
of the people they were looking for. Neusner and the rest, whoever
they were, had been too well hidden and for too long to risk
coming out from concealment now. They were somewhere else,
watching and waiting. The men at the Institute had been hired
thugs. Or, just possibly, real police acting under orders to prevent a
serious breach of security.

Nobody spoke as they drove back. Harry held the flat disc of the
tape on his lap, like a discus on the knees of a defeated athlete. He
prayed that Katje had made no mistakes in the flurry of those last
desperate minutes, that she had transcribed the file onto the tape
correctly, that she had taken the right tape from the correct drive at
the end.

Above all, he prayed that Katje was safe. He had known her for
so long and bickered with her so often, he had almost forgotten how
much she meant to him. In a strange and unexplained way, he
realized, he loved her. A lifetime of self-sufficiency had made him
tie and saddle his emotions lest he find the animal too strong, the
ride too painful. And Katje for her part had learned even harder
lessons and held an even tighter rein. But now, as it began to sink in
that she was in terrible danger, he felt the bridle loosen. He wanted

to force David to stop and turn the car. But the tape lay in his lap, the tape and everything it contained.

Leyla looked out the window of the moving car, at the emptiness on either side of the unlit road. David had deliberately taken an out-of-the-way route that avoided built-up areas until they reentered the city at Kiryat Shmuel. The Hebrew University lay somewhere to their left, hidden by distance and darkness, to their right Bayit We-Gan was a string of uncertain lights just out of reach. They seemed as far away as the moon or the stars, shining in silence. The road was empty. No one followed them. Nothing. Then out of the corner of her eye Leyla caught sight of a cold white shape, followed by another. It had begun to snow.

By the time they got back to Makhane Yehuda the snow was coming down in earnest. Dense white flakes encrusted the car, while others not yet corrupted by the heaviness of matter flashed in the headlights like moths in a luminous storm. The streets lost their gray and unkempt appearance and took on a sudden glory, as if a veil had descended, thick and gorgeous. Spring was suddenly as far away as ever. Leyla wondered if warmth would ever return to the city. She shivered gently as they drove the last blocks to Harry's apartment. The snow was beautiful, but it could not lay a veil over her thoughts or her feelings. She felt grimy inside, dingier than the old streets through which they passed.

When they got to Harry's apartment David was moody and uncommunicative. Harry made tea as before, but he acted mechanically and made no remarks about pouring cups without milk for his guests. Sammy curled up on his lap as always, but the old man seemed hardly aware of him. Leyla drank her tea in silence. David would not sit or drink tea. He could not stand still. Tonight's events seethed in him like a slow-acting poison, filling his cells to exhaustion. He felt irritable and morose at the same time, suppressing an overwhelming urge to strike back at these people. But how do you strike at shadows?

"I'm going out," he said abruptly, making for the door.

"David . . ." Leyla stood up.

"Please," he said. "I want to be alone for a while." He opened the door and went out.

It was still snowing heavily. In less than a minute he was dressed in a cold white cloak. When he looked up toward the sky, all he could see was a haze of gray blobs hurtling down. He walked westward through dark silent streets, his footsteps muffled by the soft layer of snow that had already formed on the ground. He headed for the main road to the west of Makhane Yehuda. Beyond lay Sacher Park, a dark expanse into which the pure white snow drifted, light yet inexorable.

He crossed the road and entered the park. He knew there would be sentries somewhere: the Knesset and several other government buildings lay to his left, out of sight. But he needed space in which to walk. The snow had erased the pathways and wiped out all sense of direction. He headed in a straight line, not caring where it went. Here in the white blindness it was all the same. He wanted to run, to lose control and throw himself into the swirling confusion, lose himself in it until he felt calm again. His brain felt as though a blizzard were raging inside it, independent of the one outside him. Images flashed in and out of sight like sharp, white flakes: the man at Tell Mardikh screaming in pain, the explosion at his parents' apartment, the bodies in St. Nilus', al-Shami, von Meier, Talal in the shadows at Iram, Abraham falling on his stairs, Chaim Scholem on the stairs below the Ark. Flake after glistening flake, they hurtled in a storm through his head.

There was a voice calling his name, then someone touched his shoulder. He started and realized he was standing in the middle of the snowstorm, staring into space.

"David." Leyla was holding something toward him. "Here, put this on. You'll freeze in this snow."

It was an overcoat belonging to Harry. Leyla brushed away the layer of snow that covered him and draped the coat over his shoulders. He could scarcely see her in the darkness. The swirling snow blurred her. He felt dizzy, as though he spun in a maelstrom without heart or center. He fell against her, clumsy and aching.

"I'm cold," he said.

She said nothing, touching him lightly, holding him to her. She stared into the rushing darkness behind him, cradling him awkwardly. Her frozen fingers stroked his hand numbly. It was as if they had become a tiny world, cocooned with each other against night and cold. He kissed her forehead with icy lips, then lowered his mouth until it met hers. For a second their lips touched like ice on ice. Her hand moved on his head, pulling him down to her, then her mouth opened, warm and moist. As though her breath had thawed him, his lips parted and he took her outgoing breath into him. Her light raincoat was still unbuttoned. He pulled it aside and took her to him, feeling Harry's overcoat fall from his shoulders, aware only of her body touching his for the first time. His hands slipped behind her, drawing her more tightly to him. He drew his lips away and kissed her face, covering her cheeks and eyes with tiny strokes.

"I almost lost you," she said. "When you came into the park. There were lights until then." She reached up and held his face in her hands. "What would you have done if I hadn't found you?"

As if in answer he held her hard, looking out into the darkness, though he saw nothing there but snow cascading into the freezing air. Leyla was darkness in his hands, the night made flesh, air and snow become blood. In the cold he grew warm. They stood in an embrace that seemed to last forever, as though night were enshrined within the city for all time. There were no sounds, no cries, no whispers . . . nothing but their slow breathing, softer than the snow. But even into that tiny world the elements intruded at last. Leyla shivered. The cold was beginning to eat into her.

"We'd better go," she said. "Harry's been on his own long enough."

David picked up the coat, shook snow off it, and draped it around his shoulders again. Arm in arm, he and Leyla found their way back to the main road, then walked slowly back to Nissim Behar Street. The snow still fell, but it seemed gentler now and more in harmony with their mood. They clung to one another as though afraid of drifting apart again into the darkness, like swimmers who know and fear the currents that may sweep them out to the emptiness of the ocean. There was no need for words: the silence was filled with each other. David felt as though he could reach out and find Leyla anywhere in the darkness, as if he could snatch her to him from the snowflakes, like a magician making matter out of the wind and the stars.

Harry was waiting for them when they got back. He made them change at once, dredging up old off-white towels from a chest in his bedroom. When they were dry he sat them by the fire and poured hot tea into them until they could take no more. It was growing close to dawn and they were all tired. Sammy had gone to sleep in his cat house, clearly disgusted with the antics of the humans who shared his home.

"We'll have to leave at daybreak," Harry said. "Katje won't talk, I'm sure of it. But I was seen there yesterday. They'll make the connection soon enough, then they'll be here. And I don't think my insurance policies will work with these people, whoever they are."

"Where can we go?" asked David. He was tired; he felt as though he had been running since November.

"We have to stay in Jerusalem if we can," said Harry. "I want to get the contents of this tape printed and copied tomorrow. Then I want to lodge the copy with my other keepsakes. In itself, it's evidence of nothing, but people who know me will believe it's genuine." He paused. The problem was, he knew, that those who would believe him were precisely those who had no personal power actually to do anything.

Harry's reference to the fact that only certain people would believe the evidence they had obtained made David think of one person he was sure they could take refuge with. His oldest friend in Israel was a fellow archaeologist called Etan Benabu. He'd married a classmate of David's from Chicago, Beth Isaacs. Now he taught at the Hebrew University in between fathering children and writing. Etan was one of the weirdest archaeologists David had ever known, and one of the most likable. He was more human being than academic: he could even tie his shoelaces without consulting a manual.

"Harry," David said. "I think I may know someone crazy enough to give us all a place to stay at short notice. And maybe even crazy enough to believe our story."

"Does he like cats?" Harry asked.

"Hates them," David replied. "But his wife is mad about them. They have about six."

"What's his name?"

David paused, then said with a smile, "Damien. Damien Wise." Harry's eyebrows rose.

"I've heard of him," he said.

"I thought you might have."

Etan Benabu had worked out one of the most extraordinary sidelines David had ever heard of. Under the name "Damien Wise," he'd written three or four books and God knew how many articles of the "Spaceships of the Gods" variety, using archaeological evidence to "prove" that spacemen had visited the earth thousands of years ago and that they had been responsible for just about every odd artifact or inexplicable legend there was in existence. Then under his real name he had published even more articles debunking his own books and demonstrating just how cavalier Damien Wise was with the evidence at his disposal. Only two or three people, David among them, knew that Damien Wise and Etan Benabu were one and the same, and they very sensibly kept the secret and enjoyed the ongoing joke.

They spent the rest of that morning packing and sorting through Harry's papers. He knew someone would come before long and that they would turn the place upside down looking for the missing tape. There were too many sensitive documents to leave lying about for such people to read. But the more they sorted through his files, the more irritable Harry became. He lived in chaos, but he hated disruption in any form. The best chaos takes long and careful planning; it is the work of months and years of elaborate disorganization. Harry's was a work of art. But now he had visions of dull, thickset men coming to his apartment, ripping it apart in what would prove a useless search for items long removed. It would take years to get it back into a proper mess again.

Just before eight, David telephoned Etan. He spoke with him for five minutes and then hung up. There was no problem: the Benabus would take them for as long as they needed to stay.

Ten minutes later they carried the luggage to the car, checked that Sammy was safely stowed in his wicker basket, and drove off.

SIXTY-THREE

The Benabus lived in the artists' quarter of Yemin Moshe, just to the west of the Old City. David drove there directly along Yafo. Jerusalem was like another city, starched and white and silent, the buildings looking very prim and proper in their coat of snow. On their left, the Old City rose up, its crenellated walls white and gleaming; just beyond it, Mount Zion was pinnacled in ice.

They were met at the door of the Benabus' apartment by Etan's wife Beth. She was a small woman, with compact, refined features and an air of quiet reflection. Thoughtful green eyes met the world head on. Even at such an early hour, not yet properly groomed or made up, she conveyed an impression of serenity coupled with sensual awareness that in many women is at best a contrivance of the late evening. There was a long silence while she looked at David, the smile on her face half suspended as she tried to come to terms with his sudden reappearance.

"How long has it been, David?" she finally asked.

"Three years."

"That long?" She sighed. With some friends, the absences are longer than the short times in between. Then the mood lifted and she let the smile take over her face.

"Aren't you going to introduce me to your friends, David?" she asked.

"Of course. This is Leyla Rashid, Harry Blandford. And that's Sammy."

"Hi!" Beth said, reaching out to shake their hands. Sammy looked at her balefully. "I'm Beth. Come on in, Etan's waiting inside."

The man's face clouded. He had large eyes with bags underneath.

"I see," he said. "Look, would you mind telling me what you know? My name's Rabin, Major Rabin. I've been attached to D Section since Scholem went missing. We've been extremely anxious about him. Wait a minute, though. Did you say your name was Rosen?"

"Yes. David Rosen."

"Aren't you the American professor who had all the trouble up in Syria?"

David nodded.

"Well, in that case we really must talk. I've done some work on your case and I think I've discovered one or two things. If I can be of any help with whatever it was you wanted to talk to Kahan about, I'll be glad to lend a hand. Why don't you come on up to my office?"

David gave in. What more could he do? Now that he thought of it, he was sure he had heard Rabi's name mentioned more than once in the past. If this man already knew something of what had happened, if he could be persuaded of the basic truth of Scholem's fate, perhaps he would believe him—enough, at least, to give serious attention to the papers David had brought.

David was thoroughly searched by the desk officer and his time of arrival logged. Rabin led him up a flight of stairs along a musty corridor painted in a vile olive green that came only halfway up the walls. His office was at the end, tucked away in a small cul-de-sac as befitted a temporary attachment. David recalled that Scholem's office had been somewhere nearby. There was a smell of fish from somewhere, a smell that made no sense to David.

The Benabus' children were at school, so they were free to talk. After a general chat during which people got to know one another a little, the conversation turned to David's brief and cryptic request for sanctuary. Slowly, death by death, David described in the sparest of language the events of the past few months. As he spoke, it sounded to him as though his voice issued a long way off, down a tunnel filled with wind. Yet telling seemed to help. The tunnel shortened and disappeared. He was alone in a bleak landscape, explaining it all to himself once more. When he finished, no one said a word for a long time. It was Beth who finally broke the silence.

"I think I'd better show you to your rooms," she said. "I'll take the children to stay with my mother tonight. There's plenty of room."

She stood up and went to the door. Just as she reached it, she turned and looked at David. There were tears at the corners of her eyes.

"I'm sorry, David," she said. "About your parents. About everybody. Don't worry; you can stay here as long as you like."

Leyla had a user's code registered with the central computer of the Hebrew University. It would mean taking a risk to use it, but on balance the risk seemed small and worth taking. While Harry stayed at the Benabus' getting his papers into a more acceptable disorder and introducing Sammy to his new home, David accompanied Leyla to the campus.

After a slight delay a terminal and printer became vacant and they set to work. Leyla logged on and was relieved to find that her code was still registered as valid. David put the tape into the first available drive and Leyla instructed the computer to supply a printout of its entire contents.

Like doctors presiding over a deformed birth, they watched the printer type out the names and biographies of the men from the Valkyrie file. It took over an hour. Name after name rolled out of the machine, a continuous catalogue of evil. Twenty to twenty-five per cent were dead, some in the camps, others in various ways since then. A few had failed to do anything much with their lives and were of little consequence to David or Leyla. But the names and identities of the remainder made anything that had gone before seem trivial in the extreme. As the wheel ran back and forth across the paper, the breadth and depth of a frightening conspiracy was fully revealed for the first time.

The majority of names were those of men living in Israel. Neusner was not the only high-ranking military man. Abrams was not the only politician. No fewer than ten held positions of trust in Israeli intelligence—six in MOSSAD, four in Shin Beth. Three were influential academics, men whose opinions weighed heavily in the framing of national policy. Five held important posts in the police, two in the customs service. Over a dozen were involved in industry and commerce, eight in banking, fifteen in the civil service—all in positions of power.

539

Many of them had been active in ensuring not only that they came to Palestine but in so arranging things that their future there might be guaranteed. Several had belonged to executive committees of the She'erit ha-Peletah, the central organization of Jewish refugees in the American Zone of Germany after 1946. Others had been prominent in the clandestine immigration movement, helping other refugees and finally themselves to leave Europe for occupied Palestine. A few had even joined in the struggle for independence. After that, no one had ever questioned their credentials or disputed their place in Israeli society.

But the names did not end there. When, in 1948, the United States Government had, after much dispute, passed the Displaced Persons Act permitting refugees from war-torn Europe to enter America, almost fifty members of the Valkyrie regiment had joined them. David recognized only a handful of the American names reproduced by the computer, but that handful was enough to make him feel sick with apprehension. Wherever they had gone, the men from the Valkyrie regiment had gone single-mindedly about their task of infiltrating their host societies at the deepest and most sensitive levels.

When the computer finished its task of printing out the names, they took the sheets to a Xerox machine and ran off three more copies before leaving the laboratory. They also made copies of all the materials that Leyla and Scholem had found in the crashed plane, which they added to the rest. Though not unduly heavy in themselves, the papers seemed to weigh in their bags like lead. Not even when he was taken to Iram had David realized the true proportions of the thing in which he had become ensnared. It was in the clinical austerity of the computer laboratory, a shrine to human reason made perfect, that he had come face to face with the true dimensions of modern irrationality. To have poured so much talent and so many resources into what could, in the end, prove nothing more than a harebrained scheme to destroy whatever had been built up from the ashes of an insane conflict seemed to him the greatest lunacy of those he had met so far.

They made two stops on their way back to Yemin Moshe. The first was at a solicitor's office, Van Leer and Wassermann, on King George, the second at the main Yafo Street branch of Bank Leumi. They deposited a sealed copy of the list together with the other materials at each location and left instructions with the solicitors that, if David, Leyla, or Harry Blandford failed to report in person to the office every three days, the contents of the packets should be sent simultaneously to the heads of Shin Beth and MOSSAD. When that was done it was already almost noon. They traveled by a circuitous route back to the Benabus', taking care they were not followed.

When Leyla got out of the car David leaned across the front seat and handed her the bag containing the original printout and the materials from the plane.

"Keep these safe till I come back, will you, Leyla?" he asked.

"I don't understand," she said. "Where are you planning to go?"

"I want to take these papers to someone who can do something about them. We've got to act soon. That peace conference is in two days' time. We have to warn the people involved to be on their guard in case they're planning something."

"Who are you planning to see? Who'll listen to you?"

"They'll listen—when they see these." He patted the bag that held the third set of copies.

"I'd like to come with you, David. You shouldn't go alone. I can confirm your story, back you up."

He shook his head.

"I'm afraid not, love." It was the first time he had called her that. "I want to see someone at MOSSAD, one of Chaim's colleagues. He knows me and I think he'll believe me. Sufficiently to look into things, at least. Your being there might complicate things. I wish it wasn't that way, but you know they've got you on file. And the last record they probably have of you is your meeting Chaim that night before he disappeared."

He looked at her. The need to touch her was almost overwhelming.

"Please," he said. "Let me do this alone. I won't be long. I'll come back for you soon, I promise."

She said nothing. She remembered another time when they had spoken like this, when he had set her down at al-Arish and driven off toward Jerusalem. It seemed so long ago, like childhood. The car pulled away and swung out to meet the traffic coming up from the railway station. She picked up the bag and turned to go into the Benabus'.

David drove slowly as if, now that he had begun to act at last, he no longer felt able to continue. He wanted to retreat from the position in which he now found himself but felt as though he were on a moving walkway with no room to turn, borne inexorably nearer and ever nearer to the dark consummation at its end. For he was sure now that there would be a denouement, that an end would come, whether by his own seeking or without it. He longed to be set free of it all, to walk on his own feet again in a direction he himself had chosen, not to be taken like this, whether he willed it or not.

He parked the car near the MOSSAD offices out of which Scholem had operated. The man he wanted to see was Arieh Kahan in D Section, Scholem's old second in command, a man whom David knew and trusted. In the foyer of the little office block he approached the duty officer manning the broad desk. Security seemed slack, but David knew that that was a false impression, that no one got past the desk without the most careful of checks. Anyone who tried to rush past—a PLO terrorist, for example— would not make it farther than the foot of the stairs. There were guns in shadows here, and watchful eyes.

David asked for Arieh Kahan but was told he was off duty. Would he like to speak with someone else?

He hesitated. He had counted on Arieh being there. Arieh knew him, would accept his story without demur. He knew no one else there well enough to risk his story with.

"Can't you get Kahan at home?" he pleaded. "It's important. Tell him it's David Rosen, that I have news about Colonel Scholem. He'll come in."

"I'm sorry, sir," the duty officer manning the desk said. "But Captain Kahan's on leave. He's up in Galilee somewhere. I don't think he's contactable. He's not due back until the weekend."

Someone behind David spoke.

"Excuse me." It was a man of about fifty, someone who seemed slightly familiar. David thought he had seen him around on an earlier visit.

"I couldn't help overhearing," the man said. "You mentioned Colonel Scholem. Did you mean Scholem from D Section?"

David nodded.

"You have news of him?"

"Yes. Not good news, I'm afraid."

542

The man's face clouded. He had large eyes with bags underneath.

"I see," he said. "Look, would you mind telling me what you know? My name's Rabin, Major Rabin. I've been attached to D Section since Scholem went missing. We've been extremely anxious about him. Wait a minute, though. Did you say your name was Rosen?"

"Yes. David Rosen."

"Aren't you the American professor who had all the trouble up in Syria?"

David nodded.

"Well, in that case we really must talk. I've done some work on your case and I think I've discovered one or two things. If I can be of any help with whatever it was you wanted to talk to Kahan about, I'll be glad to lend a hand. Why don't you come on up to my office?"

David gave in. What more could he do? Now that he thought of it, he was sure he had heard Rabi's name mentioned more than once in the past. If this man already knew something of what had happened, if he could be persuaded of the basic truth of Scholem's fate, perhaps he would believe him—enough, at least, to give serious attention to the papers David had brought.

David was thoroughly searched by the desk officer and his time of arrival logged. Rabin led him up a flight of stairs along a musty corridor painted in a vile olive green that came only halfway up the walls. His office was at the end, tucked away in a small cul-de-sac as befitted a temporary attachment. David recalled that Scholem's office had been somewhere nearby. There was a smell of fish from somewhere, a smell that made no sense to David.

The office was tiny, with room for a desk and a couple of chairs. The window looked out onto bare wall; it was cracked in one pane, and grime had accumulated over its surface until it made every day seem overcast and cloudy and days like this one unbearably bleak. Rabin tripped the light switch, an old metal one in a circular box beside the door. A weak yellow light bulb glimmered over the desk.

"Sit down, Professor," Rabin said, speaking in English now.

David sat. He was feeling tired. All he wanted now was for someone to take the whole thing out of his hands, tell him to rest while they sorted things out.

"Now," Rabin went on, "tell me what you know. We have information that Scholem was followed by an Arab terrorist, a

543

woman called Leyla Rashid. He made a call to his assistant Kahan, the man you wanted to speak to, then came to headquarters here to question a suspect called Hasan Bey. He left just before midnight. That was the last anyone saw of him."

David took a deep breath, then began to explain what had happened after that. He spoke carefully, filling in the details as he had heard them from Leyla. Rabin listened to him with increasing attention, interrupting from time to time to ask a question, to clarify an obscure point.

"But Iram's been destroyed, you say," said Rabin when David had finished the first part of his story.

"Yes. I don't think anything or anyone survived. I don't see how they could have. Except for a few who were outside the city. And Leyla and myself."

"Thank God for that," said Rabin, though David thought he seemed nervous about something. "At least they're finished, these people in the Nafud. I'm grieved to hear about Chaim. But his death . . . served a purpose, don't you think?"

David nodded. If deaths could serve purposes, yes, Scholem's had served one. But if he had lived, the same purpose might still have been served, he thought.

"Yes," he said. "But I'm afraid that isn't the end of the affair. The people in the Nafud are finished, but they had associates in other places. And, if anything, their associates are much more of a threat than the group at Iram ever were."

David lifted the packet of papers he had brought and laid them on the desk in front of him. Rabin sat up straighter. David noticed that he had green eyes. His smooth-complexioned face registered little emotion, but in one corner, just under his left eye, a tiny tic betrayed anxiety.

"Do you believe what I've just told you?" David asked. He realized, now he had related the general outline of his story, that it sounded farfetched. Perhaps Rabin would think he was making it up or that he had lost touch with reality.

Rabin nodded.

"Yes," he said. "I believe you. I've worked with MOSSAD for most of my adult life. I've heard stories almost as strange as yours before. Believe me, I have. More than once. Nazis, ex-Nazis, neo-Nazis. For most people, they're just a memory or characters in

544

fiction. Not for us, I assure you. They're real people, flesh and blood—and often very dangerous. A lot of us think: they lost the war, their wickedness was exposed. Any reasonable man would admit defeat, confess he'd been wrong, even try, perhaps, to make amends—that's how we reason. But it isn't human nature to think or act like that. When people have invested their lives, their beliefs, their deepest hopes in something, it's very hard for them to admit they were wrong, that all the sacrifices they made were for nothing. They look for explanations, justifications. I've heard them all in my day. You're not the first with such a story, Professor, believe me.

"Now, let me see what you've brought."

David explained briefly about the Valkyrie list and how it had been found. He showed the printout copy to Rabin, then bent forward and leafed through it until he found the names of the men belonging to MOSSAD. One by one, in silence, he showed them to Rabin.

The major said nothing. He did not have to. His eyes registered his amazement, his horror. The tic beneath his eye twitched rapidly. Page by page, he looked through the file, then at the other papers David had brought. Half an hour passed. Finally he looked up at David. His face was grim and serious.

"May I keep these, Professor?"

David hesitated.

"I assure you," Rabin urged, "they'll be safe with me. I won't show them to anyone else at this stage. But I need to study them more carefully. Where have you kept the originals?"

"They're . . . safe," said David. Even now he wanted to be careful. The originals were the only real insurance they had. He trusted Rabin, but he knew he worked for MOSSAD. An intelligence agency. They were not above stealing the originals if they decided they could be useful.

"I don't like to push you, Professor, but don't you think they'd be a lot safer with us?"

David shook his head.

"I can't get them at present," he lied. "But you can have them when the time comes."

"I hope so," Rabin said, clearly annoyed by David's refusal to cooperate. "If we're to prepare a case, we'll need them. But first we'll need more than these, more concrete evidence. What you have

545

so far is circumstantial. None of it would hold in a court of law."

"What about the Valkyrie file?"

Rabin shook his head.

"A forgery. You programmed it yourself."

"But the original file on the Institute computer?"

"I think you'll find that there is now no such file stored there. Nor will there be any evidence that it ever was."

"But why would I do that? Why would I concoct such a story?"

"Fantasies sparked off by your parents' deaths. Perhaps Iram really existed. That increased your fantasies, gave them a focus."

"Is that what you think?" David asked.

Rabin shook his head again.

"No. I believe you. But I think a clever attorney could get around your story as it stands. We've no hard evidence of anything, except for the papers you found in the plane. But they only lead us to Iram, not to actual people in important positions in this country or the United States. We're up against powerful people, Professor Rosen. I don't know if you understand what that means. Academics lead sheltered lives. I don't wish to sound platitudinous. But there are . . . certain realities that seldom impinge on the world of academia, certain political truths that people in other walks of life understand only too well. I guarantee that, if you went to court with the evidence you've brought me today, with that and nothing else, it would be you who'd be facing a prison sentence at the end of the day. For defamation of character, for slander . . . they'd pin you to the wall. If you got as far as a courtroom, that is. If you want my opinion, unless you go about this the right way, this information of yours will never even see the light of day."

"What about the press?" asked David. "Couldn't I take this to them? They'd be sure to be interested."

"Of course they'd be interested. But when they saw how little hard evidence you really have they'd refuse to print a word. An individual reporter might want to go to town on the story. Even his editor: it would sell copies, no doubt about it. But newspapers have owners. And the owners have friends, friends in high places. No newspaper boss is going to print allegations about people who are his bridge partners or about people who guarantee his own place in society. Not only that, but newspapers rely heavily on advertising, and the big advertisers will have friends on that list of yours. If you

546

had schoolteachers on your list or minor officials, the newspapers would print anything you told them. But what you've got could ruin any paper that ran the story."

Rabin paused and closed the file. He hoped he had made his point.

"So," he went on, "please be frank with me. Is there anything else, anything at all you're holding back, for whatever reason? If there is, it's best you tell me. I'll have to be responsible for this investigation. I can tell you now, it's going to be messy. Messy and dangerous. I'll need every scrap of evidence I can lay my hands on. Even things that may seem insignificant to you."

David shook his head firmly.

"There's nothing more, I assure you."

"Then we shall have to find it," Rabin smiled.

"Except . . . ," David began.

Rabin leaned forward.

"Yes?"

"I wasn't going to mention this. Not yet. I have no real evidence for it at all. And it seems even crazier than the rest. . . ."

"Go on."

"The . . . the new President of Syria, Mas'ud al-Hashimi, is only half Arab. His father was German." He took a deep breath. "The name of his father was Ulrich von Meier."

Rabin said nothing. Small beads of sweat stood out on his brow.

"Go on," he said, his voice tense and hard.

David told him what he knew. He wished he knew more about Harry's source.

"Where did you learn all this, Professor?" Rabin asked when David had finished.

"From Harry, Harry Blandford. He didn't tell me his sources, just that he had relied on them. I believe him."

"Yes, yes, I'm sure. It seems hard to swallow along with everything else."

"What worries me," said David, "is the signing of the peace treaty in two days' time. I think something's going to happen at it. Al-Shami said they were ready for something, here in Jerusalem. Isn't there anything you can do to stop it? Have it postponed until we know more?"

"You're quite right," Rabin said, but he was still sweating. "I'll do what I can. But don't expect anything. The conference is a major

547

event. They aren't likely to stop it just on my say-so, not without hard evidence—which is what we don't have. And if I tell them what I know, I'll have blown the whole thing. I'll simply have to make up some story about a threat to the conference, something to justify extra security. That won't be too hard. But you, Professor, you must promise me you won't try anything foolish. We can't afford to jeopardize this whole operation at this stage. Do you understand?"

David nodded.

"That's fine," Rabin said. "Now, where are you staying, so I can get in touch with you?"

"I'm at . . ." David hesitated. He had almost told Rabin about the Benabus. But they would guess that Leyla was there too, and Harry. Leyla was still on their wanted list. And they might decide that their maverick activities were a threat of some kind. He did not know Rabin well enough yet to trust him not to want to take them into custody. It was the way intelligence agents operated.

"I'm staying at the university," he said. "You can get me there, I'm in the Rabbi Aqiva Hall of Residence."

"Fine. I'll be in touch as soon as I've had a chance to look at your papers more closely. I'll take care of them, don't worry. But at some point I'd like you to bring in the originals of the papers you found on the plane, so I can have our forensic people go over them."

David nodded. One thing at a time, he thought.

Rabin accompanied him to the desk downstairs and saw him signed out. When David had gone, he turned to the duty officer and said:

"I'd like Professor Rosen followed, please. Let me know where he's staying, as soon as possible."

He turned and went up the stairs again. There was still a smell of fish in his corridor.

548

SIXTY-FOUR

David waited long enough before driving off to be sure he was being followed. He would have been surprised if Rabin had not sent someone to tail him. He had lived in the shelter of academe all right, but the past few months had rubbed off at least some of his innocence. Jerusalem, fortunately, is one of the worst cities in the world in which to tail someone, being surpassed only by Fez, Cairo, Istanbul, and Bombay. David knew a dozen places where he could lose his tail without much difficulty. He had left the car at the Damascus Gate and plunged into the Old City, through the twisting *suqs* of the Arab Quarter. Half an hour later he was sure his pursuer had lost him. He left by the Jaffa Gate and walked down to the Inter-Rent office on Shlomzion Ha-Malka, where he hired another car, a Volkswagen.

He drove west, along the open road toward Tel Aviv, for a distance of five miles. There was no question: he had lost his tail. He headed back to town and drove straight to the Benabus'. Leyla was waiting for him. Harry had gone to bed, unable to stay awake any longer. Beth had gone to pick up the children at school in order to take them to stay with her mother in Petah Tikva. Etan was in his study, reading over the papers David had left with him. The large apartment was quiet, as though the morning's silence still lay over it. Without exchanging a word, knowing instinctively that it was time, David and Leyla made their way to Leyla's bedroom.

They sat for a while on the edge of the bed, tense, afraid to touch. Somewhere outside, a radio was playing. Not very loud, not very soft. The sound rose and fell intermittently, as if a storm a long way off was interfering with the radio waves. David recognized the song, remembered the words. An English band was playing.

The singer was dead, like an offering to his own music, seeking in suicide an authenticity he had been unable to reach in song. David thought of the young men at Iram, of the young men sent into the camps, now grown old, still knocking on the doors of their lifelong hell.

He reached out for Leyla's hand. The slatted blinds were drawn but soft patterns of late afternoon light crept into the room and decked the bed with stripes and spangles. A bar of light fell across Leyla's face. She looked at David and the light fell like a cone across her body. Tiny specks of dust quivered and danced in the honeyed alembic of the light. Leyla let go of David's hand and silently removed her sweater. The light lay softly on her sudden nakedness. One breast lay cradled in shadow, the other washed in light. She put the sweater down on the floor and looked at David.

She felt frightened in her nakedness after so long. Though she longed to be touched, she feared the onset of passion. Suddenly, she felt, she and David were strangers again, for they had as yet to meet one another naked flesh to naked flesh, and even as she turned to him a part of her hung back. He sat beside her, watching her, as though it were enough to do so, as though to watch the light touch her breast were enough. She stood and removed the rest of her clothes, and bars of whirling light turned her flesh to fire as David watched.

"I wanted this," he said, "but now that it's come I'm afraid."

She nodded, reaching for his hands.

"I'm frightened as well," she whispered, putting his arms around her. He drew her to him and rested his cheek against her belly. Her skin was warm and scented, soft to his touch, delicate.

The music had stopped. Silence filled the room as David drew Leyla down to the bed, coming to her in the softness and the light. Her lips met his and the room dissolved into fragments of light and darkness. She helped him undress, then held him to her breast, feeling him enter her without words. He felt everything slipping away as his body merged with hers.

David woke to find himself in darkness. The light had slipped away somewhere between sleeping and dreaming, leaving the room in the dominion of shadows. The bars of sunlight that had lain across Leyla's body like threadless ribbons were gone, as if forever.

David shivered and reached out for Leyla but found only emptiness and an elusive fragrance in the bed where she had been. He called out softly:

"Leyla, are you there?"

Her voice came back to him out of the darkness.

"It's all right, David, I'm here. By the window."

She was sitting with a sheet draped around her shoulders, looking through the partly opened blind at the lights of the Old City. He came across to her quietly and sat beside her. She wrapped part of her sheet around him, cocooning them inside it like children who have just come from a bath.

"I've never seen the city quite like this before," she whispered. Outside, the sky was clear. A full moon hung like a vast globe of light above the Dome of the Rock, surrounded by streamers of quietly throbbing stars. The moonlight fell, solemn and nebulous, over stark fields of snow and frost out of which towers and domes, spires and minarets grew like stalagmites into the shimmering air. It was as if a single icy breath had changed the very substance of the city, like Lot's wife changed into a pillar of salt.

David held Leyla tightly, his flesh finding comfort in her nakedness again. Watching her as she gazed out at the city, he understood for the first time what Jerusalem meant to her. He had always felt the city to belong exclusively to him and his people, but somehow it was difficult to feel that exclusivity as more than an illusion tonight. If only they could share the stones outside as easily and as gladly as they shared one another's flesh, he thought.

"We'd better join the others," he said.

She yawned and nodded.

"Have you been awake long?" he asked.

"No, not very long. I watched you sleeping for a while; you seemed very tired."

"I was dreaming about you," he said.

"You're lying," she protested, pleased that he had said it.

"No, it's true," he said.

But he didn't tell her what he had dreamed. He could not remember exactly, but it had not been a good dream. He had woken from it sweating and uneasy.

After a large meal cooked by Beth, who had returned almost an

551

hour before, they went into the living room to discuss what they should do next. Harry picked up the printout David and Leyla had brought back from the library.

"Is this the only copy?" he asked.

David shook his head and explained about the copies they had made. He went on to explain about the visit he had made to MOSSAD, about his conversation with Rabin.

Harry said nothing for a while, then nodded.

"You did the right thing," he said at last. "It was too much of a risk keeping all of this to ourselves. But I'm afraid Rabin's right. The papers we have won't be enough on their own. By now, they'll have removed all trace of the Valkyrie file from the Institute's computer. I'm willing to bet no one at the Institute knew it was stored in their data bank in the first place."

"Then why keep it there at all?" Leyla asked.

"I've been wondering about that," Harry said. "I think the answer's obvious. The numbers had to be on file somewhere in the Institute's records, since those were compiled from official lists kept by the Allies and refugee organizations—the ones Katje mentioned to you. Just taking the numbers out might have drawn attention to them. It was easier to hive off all the V-coded numbers into a separate file and have that reserved under a restricted-access listing. They knew it was a thousand to one that anybody would ever come looking for all the V numbers as a group, but there was just a chance that a casual search might have turned up too many coincidences. And since the file was now inaccessible to anyone but themselves they used it to keep their own information about one another."

"And you think Rabin's right—that the list won't be enough to convince anyone about what's going on?" David broke in.

Harry nodded.

"That's right. You could have faked the whole thing. We have the papers from the plane, of course. I think we could convince someone higher up than Rabin, given time. But we can't assume we have time. Even supposing Rabin did get to one or two people in the right places, they'd have to convince others if anything very serious was to be done about the matter. We're dealing with powerful people: don't fool yourself by thinking otherwise. We've lost the element of surprise—ever since last night they know someone's on to them. They'll be making their moves already. And don't imagine they don't already have all sorts of fallback systems in existence for just this sort of emergency. The minute they get a hint that someone has information about Valkyrie, things will start to happen. I don't have to tell you how ruthless they can be. At this stage of the operation they can still afford to be almost reckless in disposing of people. Just as long as the right connections aren't made, they can kill almost anyone in order to cover things up. Even if we went to the very top with these papers, there's no guarantee it would lead to anything."

"Why not?" interrupted Etan. During the day the full implications of what was happening had dawned on him. From bewilderment he had passed to outrage. "I have friends who can help, people in government circles, in the police. My cousin Ben is one of the country's leading lawyers. He has access to all the top judges, public prosecutors, people like that."

Harry shook his head.

"There isn't time, Etan. If these people have some sort of plan, they'll bring it forward. David, Leyla, and I are the only witnesses who can tie all the loose ends together: before any case ever came to court we'd be dead. Anyone else who threatened to pursue the matter would suffer the same fate."

"But you have the papers," Etan protested.

"They're not enough. I'm a Nazi hunter, a maverick. If I came up with a file incriminating some of this country's top people, I'd be asking men like your cousin to go after their friends: people they knew in the camps or in the War of Independence. Good men, good Jews, good husbands and fathers.

"Listen to me, Etan. The Valkyrie project was the cleverest thing the Nazis ever dreamed up, because it turned their victims into their helpers and protectors. If I put the finger on the men in this list tomorrow, for each one I accuse a dozen, two dozen genuine, honest Israelis will come forward to testify that I'm just a crazy old man whose obsessions have run away with him. I'm British, and you know what that means here. We did some bloody rotten things to the Jews, and they haven't entirely forgotten it, have they? Some of the people on this list got to Israel by running British blockades. They probably helped genuine refugees get into this country when the British were trying to keep them out or put them into internment camps all over again. And now I start accusing them of being Nazis."

He paused. This time it was Beth who interrupted.

"But if you could get real evidence, evidence tough enough to convince the hardest skeptic? Would you go to Ben with that?"

Harry looked at her for a while before nodding.

"If it was cast-iorn, yes. But where do you imagine we can get that sort of proof? In the time there may be left?"

"You said earlier that they'd be looking for you at your apartment. Wait for them there. Follow them. Let them lead you to the evidence themselves."

554

SIXTY-FIVE

The men hesitated coming out of the apartment house, then turned abruptly left and walked slowly down the street. David watched them as far as the black Volvo parked a hundred yards along. He was in his own car on the other side of the road, a bit down from the street door. Once the men were inside the Volvo and had their backs turned to him, he started his engine. He let them turn out into the light, early morning traffic, then moved out himself, leaving about six cars behind them.

He had gone straight to Harry's apartment and checked that no one had been there. All night he had waited in the car, watching the entrance to the apartment house. The men had arrived just after 5 A.M. There were two of them, one tall, one of medium height, but David had been unable to make out their features in the dark. They had spent almost three hours inside. Now it was a few minutes before eight.

They were in no hurry to get where they were going, and David had to take care not to allow himself to come too close. They headed north briefly, then turned left on Nordau down to Herzl and drove south toward Yefe Nof. The traffic grew even lighter, and trailing the Volvo became increasingly difficult. David had to hold back so far, he feared several times that he had lost them, but they always reappeared somewhere up ahead on the main road. In spite of the bright sun the snow had thawed very little. The tires seemed to burn on the tarmac. Bit by bit the city dissolved on both sides. Yad Vashem was coming up—were they going there? David looked to his right. Frost sprinkled Mount Herzl like a precious thing that had been squandered on the grass. The Volvo forked to the left at the crossroads ahead, taking the road down into Kiryat Ha-Yovel. He followed it.

They stopped outside a large house on Zangwill, not far from the Jerusalem Sports Club. David drove on past without even glancing and turned in at the entrance to the club. If they'd seen him following, his going there might serve to calm any suspicions. In his rear-view mirror he caught sight of the men going into the house. Once they were inside, he drove out of the club entrance once more, turned, and parked his car a little farther down the street. This was a quiet district—modern, respectable. Someone important lived in the house. David wondered which of the names on his list it was.

He walked past the house just once, scanning it. It lay a little back from the road, with a small garden in front. A narrow driveway led to the front door and continued on past the side of the house to the back. Approaching from the front would be difficult—there were too many windows and no cover. He walked back up to Tora wa-Avoda. A driveway led down to a large school, and off it was an empty space that stretched between the school and the backs of a row of houses that included the one he was interested in.

There was no one on the street. The children were already at school; their parents had dropped them off and gone on to work or back home. David slipped through an open wire fence and walked slowly to the wall. He knew which wall he was looking for—his house was the only one with a green roof and a double TV aerial. There were no obvious signs of a security system. He would risk it.

Getting over the wall was easy. On the other side was a larger garden full of shrubs. David dropped gently to the ground, coiled immediately for flight at the slightest indication of an alert. A dog barked nearby, then fell silent. Curtains were drawn across all the windows at the back of the house. Moving from bush to bush, David approached the house. Even now he was wondering what he should do. Better to leave entering the house until late that night, he thought. But now he should at least check it out in daylight.

He watched the back of the house for a while, but there was no movement at any of the windows, and no one entered or left by the rear door, just to his left. There was no sign of a burglar alarm or wiring of any sort, and he thought the house might prove easy to enter. Then he caught sight of a light he had missed before, just above ground level, in what looked like a basement window. Curiosity overcame him, and he crept forward to the window. It was about three feet long and two high and was clearly set high up near the ceiling of a basement. He lay flat on the ground and looked in.

A naked light bulb illuminated a stark, brooding scene. The basement was large, occupying perhaps half of the area of the house itself. It had plain white walls and a concrete floor; here and there patches of moldy damp disfigured the purity of the walls, like blemishes on fair skin. The light of the bulb did not quite reach into the corners, leaving masses of intense little shadows lurking in them. There was a tall boiler on one side, and something that David took to be the motor for an air-conditioning system.

Five men stood beneath the light—the pair he had followed and three others. He recognized the man in the tweed coat as one of those who had been in Harry's apartment. He was about sixty, close-faced, with eyes and lips that gave away nothing, red, slightly protruding cheeks, and a nervous smile that came and went like a faulty light. The man beside him had his back to David, but he recognized him by his raincoat. The third man was thin and driven-looking, with wispy, dirty gray hair brushed back to cover a balding head, a taut, veined neck, and dark, haunted eyes beneath which heavy lines sagged into hollow cheeks. Beside him stood General Gershon Neusner. David recognized him from photographs he had seen over the years in the Jerusalem *Post*. The fifth man stood, like the man in black, facing directly away from David, but there was something about him that seemed uneasily familiar.

They were speaking together earnestly. Though they appeared calm, the thin man seemed to be growing slowly more and more agitated—presumably by the news that his friends had arrived at Harry's only to find that the bird had flown. David could hear the voices of the men below, rising and falling as they argued about what to do, but he could not make out what they were saying. Neusner seemed to say the least, but when he did speak he commanded the most attention. David knew they were debating their next move, and he wished he could hear what they decided, but it was impossible from where he was. Should he try to get into the house after all, see if he could listen from the basement door without their seeing him? He rejected the idea as uselessly dangerous and went on watching the scene below.

Suddenly the figures broke up as though some sort of decision had been reached. The two men whom David had followed moved toward the steps that led back into the house proper. Just behind the spot where they had been standing there was now revealed what looked like a white hospital bed with a painted cast-iron frame and crisp white bedding. Crisp and white, that was, everywhere except in the middle, where something red and shapeless lay. David could not make out what it was at first, but he could see that, whatever lay there, it was not human. He looked closer, then wished he had not done so. The thing on the bed, he now realized with a nauseated shudder, had been Katje Horowicz. He felt a wave of dull sickness hit him; vomit rose into his throat, thick and uncontrollable, and he turned away to throw up. He knelt on the snow by the window, his stomach heaving, shaking from head to foot. He could only guess dimly what they had done to her, but he prayed she had been unconscious for most of it. Even after the things he had seen at St. Nilus' and Iram, he found it hard to believe that one human being could do something like that to another.

When he had finished, he steeled himself and looked through the window again. He wanted to see the face of the last man, the one who had kept his back to him throughout. As far as possible, he kept his eyes averted from the thing on the bed. Why didn't they cover it up? Then, out of the corner of his eye, he saw it move and realized she was still alive, though he knew that whatever lived in that . . . body, it was no longer Katje Horowicz.

Even as he watched, the man with his back to David took something from his pocket and moved closer to the bed. It was a pistol. He raised it to what had been Katje's head and pulled the trigger. David heard the light explosion, saw the thing on the bed twitch once and lie still. The man put the gun back in his pocket and turned around to face his accomplices. David had seen the face before. He had seen it only the day before. It was Rabin, the MOSSAD major to whom he had given the printout of the Valkyrie file and the other papers.

The list of names in the Valkyrie file was not complete. There were others. The brood of Iram had not died with the city.

558

SIXTY-SIX

David could scarcely remember running from the house, climbing the wall, returning to his car. Everything was a blur as he pushed down on the gas and swung into the road, narrowly missing a child on a bicycle as she went past him. He slammed the car forward and roared away at top speed, as though possessed by devils. But no one followed him. The road behind was quiet, almost empty of traffic. He had reached Giv'at Oren by the time his nerves calmed. Five minutes later he drew up outside the Benabus' and turned off the engine. He had decided what he was going to do.

The door was opened by Etan. He took one look at David, saw that something was badly wrong, and ushered him inside. They went straight to the living room. Beth and Harry were sitting in front of a low table drinking tea. Harry stood up as David came in.

"David. We were worried about you."

"So I can see," snapped David.

"Please, David, that's unfair," said Beth, turning angrily. "Harry has been concerned. So have I. But we haven't been able to do anything."

"I'm sorry," David said. "I'm on edge. Could I have a drink, please? Something strong."

Beth glanced at him. His hands were shaking.

"Yes, of course," she said. She glanced at Harry and Etan, then went to a small table in the corner and poured a helping of whiskey into a finely cut glass.

"Where's Leyla?" David asked.

"It's all right, David," Harry said. "There's nothing wrong. I'll

559

explain in a moment. But first tell us what's happened. Why are you so worked up? And sit down, for God's sake, before you have us all on edge."

David sat down. Beth brought him his drink. He took it in an unsteady hand, glad she had not added ice to it. He told them the main details of what he had found, sparing Harry the truth of what had happened to Katje—though, indeed, he realized that even he could not guess the full enormity of what must have been done to her. Harry said nothing when David had finished. He wanted to ask what had happened, but there was something in David's manner that prevented him.

"What about Leyla?" David asked.

"After you left," said Harry, "she had an idea. We were talking about tomorrow, about the signing of the treaty. There was an article about it in this morning's Jerusalem *Post*. Apparently the plan is for al-Hashimi to stay in Jerusalem tonight. He's been provided with a private residence somewhere in the city—the authorities aren't saying where, of course. In the morning he goes to the Dome of the Rock at eleven o'clock to pray and meet with the Egyptian delegation and local Arab leaders. After a brief speech there he'll be taken to the Knesset, where he delivers an address to the Israeli parliament and invited dignitaries, mostly diplomats. Then he's expected to sign the treaty, shake hands with everyone, and head back to Damascus. It seems simple. There isn't even a banquet. All straightforward and to the point."

"So?"

"So Leyla thought someone should try to get close to him tonight, in case there's a chance of overhearing something. She used to work for the Government Translation Bureau as an Arabic-Hebrew interpreter. She thinks she can find out who's been given the job of interpreting for al-Hashimi, and if it's one of her old friends she should be able to get them to do a swap."

"What's the point of that? She won't get anywhere near his residence."

Harry shook his head.

"She thinks she will. She says it's standard procedure in a case like this. She's done things like this before. He'll be speaking in Arabic, but there'll be Hebrew speakers at the Knesset. He'll want to go over his speech with his interpreter well beforehand, to rule

560

out any possibility of there being misunderstandings. Since he doesn't arrive until this evening, he'll probably have the interpreter there after dinner."

David felt nervous. She would be taking a tremendous risk.

"What if they recognize her?" he asked.

"She's thought of that. She went out to buy a wig and some glasses. The chances of there being anyone there who knows her are slim anyway."

"I wish she'd waited until I came back before going off," David protested. He felt it like a premonition, as if he would never see her again.

"If she comes back," he said, standing up, "ask her to wait for me here. Please. I'd like to see her."

"Where are you going?" asked Beth.

"To Neusner's," David said. "I realized when I was leaving the other house that, if Neusner was there, it might be safe to try to get into his own house. If I can lay hands on just one piece of evidence linking him to the Valkyrie setup, it may be possible to do something tonight before the conference." He turned to Harry.

"Have you got the printout of the Valkyrie file? I want Neusner's address."

Etan stood up. "I'll get it," he said and went out to the study.

David was on edge, unable to sit down, unable to rest. Leyla's unexpected absence had rattled him badly, coming as it did on top of what he had witnessed that morning.

"I'm sorry I was so rude when I came in, Harry," he said. "But Katje's death upset me. She needn't have been involved at all. So many people have been killed who had nothing to do with this."

Harry shook his head gently.

"That isn't true, David. There are no innocent bystanders. No one can stand apart from a matter like this. Just saying, 'I don't want to be involved,' brings down a sort of guilt."

"He's right, David," Beth broke in. "I'd rather not be involved in all of this. I have children, parents. I'm frightened for Etan. But I don't know how I can stand back either."

Etan came back carrying the file. David took it from him and found the entry for Neusner. The address on Ha-Poretzim was listed clearly. He wrote it down, along with the telephone number, and closed the file.

"Harry," he said, "while I'm gone, will you please look through the file for the house on Zangwill, see who it belongs to. It was number 73."

Harry nodded and picked up the file.

"Take care, David," he said. But his thoughts at that moment were with Katje Horowicz.

Beth took David to the door.

"Be careful, David," she said. "Don't take any unnecessary risks."

He walked to the car, then looked back at Beth standing in the doorway. "There are no innocent bystanders," Harry had said. But what else would she be if they came here and killed her like the others they had killed? He opened the door and slid behind the wheel.

SIXTY-SEVEN

Neusner's house was silent. David watched it for a while but saw no
sign of movement. The morning paper had been delivered but not
picked up. He drove farther down the street and parked the car.
There was a grocer's shop nearby, on the corner with Kovshe
Qatamon. He went in, picked up the telephone, and dialed. The
phone at the other end rang and rang, but no one answered. To be
certain, he dialed Neusner's number again. Still no reply. He put
down the phone and went out. The snow was thawing in small
patches, but it was still cold and treacherous underfoot.

Either Neusner had gone on to Harry's, he thought, or he had
asked the two men David had seen there to return and bring him the
files. As long as they stayed at Zangwill, he would be reasonably
safe in the house.

Getting in was easier than he had hoped. Perhaps Israeli generals
counted on public esteem to keep them safe from burglars. A back
window on the upper floor had been left open, allowing David to
climb through without much difficulty. He found himself in a large
bedroom expensively but tastefully furnished, with a wide bed that
looked temptingly soft. He had expected something more spartan
somehow, something more in keeping with the SS ethos of a
toughened elite. A deep carpet cushioned his footfalls, enhanced
his feeling of being an interloper by imposing silence on his
movements.

He padded to the door, opened it, and looked out into an unlit
corridor. The house was silent. There was a light switch on the wall
by the door. He flicked it down and a soft pink light filled the

corridor. Immediately opposite him, a large Impressionist painting hung on the wall, a scene of what he took to be a Paris park on a warm summer's afternoon. He stepped closer: the painting was an original and, judging by the signature, it must have been worth a fortune. Neusner had clearly not lost out on the good things of life. What sources of income did he have above and beyond the strictly limited salary of an Israeli general?

One by one, David examined the rooms on the upper floor. They consisted of five bedrooms, two bathrooms, a small television room, and a large linen closet. Neusner had children, two girls and a boy, as far as David could tell. Two of them had obviously left home, but David thought the third, a little girl of about ten from the look of her room, was still living there.

He had stood in the child's bedroom, filled with Barbie dolls, soft toys, pretty frocks, and posters of pop stars, thinking about the thing on the bed in that other house, the thing that had been Katje Horowicz. And he had thought about Neusner's hands, the same hands that must have tortured Katje, stroking his little girl's hair, his lips kissing her on the cheek at bedtime. The burning hands, the freezing lips. And he thought then that there were so many children with such fathers: the children of SS men, the children of torturers in South America, the children of executioners, the children of secret policemen, the children of Mafia gangsters. Their soft skin was petted, their golden hair was stroked, their eyes were closed with soft kisses, and in the parks on Sundays they walked with trusting hands held in Daddy's big, gentle hand that he had washed clean of blood and sweat on Saturday evening.

He shuddered and went downstairs. The second room he entered was a study, a quiet, book-lined room warm with the glow of polished leather, agleam with well-rubbed brass. David switched on a lamp over the desk and crossed to the far wall. The books sll dealt with military history and included volumes in Hebrew, English, German, and French. They had been rebound in fine leather and stamped in dull gold, row after quiet row of them, each one an antithesis of its subject matter, the muted voice of carnage.

Carefully, David began to go through the documents on the desk, then those in the various filing cabinets that stood alongside it. The longer he looked, the more hopeless he knew it would be. "Why would Neusner keep anything incriminating here?" he

thought. "But where else would he keep things he might need?"
Time passed, and David grew nervous, but everything he read
seemed utterly innocent.

At last he decided that there must be a hidden safe, but there was
no sign of one on any of the walls. He looked behind the paintings
and photographs that hung on the wall facing the desk, but none of
them concealed a safe of any description. He felt near despair,
knowing he had no time to scour the house for something that was
either very well hidden or not even there at all. And then he recalled
a basic truism of archaeology—treasure caches are usually to be
found in floors, not walls, because walls collapse, but floors remain
more or less intact. He began to roll up the edges of the fine Persian
carpet.

The safe lay near the desk. A section of floorboard lifted out to
reveal the recessed lid, in the middle of which was a dial bearing
numbers and letters in concentric rings. He went back to the desk
and began to search for a diary or notebook that might contain the
combination. Nothing. He knew there was no way he could
possibly guess the numbers, no way he could work them out
logically. For a would-be burglar, he had come pathetically ill
equipped. Had he really expected to find the sort of evidence he was
looking for just lying around waiting for him or anybody else to
pick up? He thumped a fist on the desk in frustration, knocking
over a photograph of Neusner that stood there.

It was hopeless. He would have to leave, obtain drilling tools or
explosive, and come back again, as soon as possible. It would mean
that he would be powerless to do anything about the following
day's meeting, but he would have to take that risk. Perhaps nothing
would actually happen, perhaps the purpose of the visit was merely
to set something in motion. The leash would start to slip. He wished
he could be sure.

As quickly as possible, he began to clear up the study,
straightening files and papers, replacing the rolled-up carpet,
putting chairs back into position. He acted numbly, like a man who
has been defeated but keeps on moving because there is nothing
left to do. He finished clearing the desk and stood Neusner's
photograph up again. Cold eyes stared at him, as though mocking
his failure. The general was dressed in a khaki shirt with his arms
folded in front of him, smiling and confident. David tried to

imagine him as a young man taking the SS oath of allegiance:

> "Ich schwöre Dir, Adolf Hitler, als Führer und Kanzler des
> Deutschen Reiches, Treue und Tapferkeit. Ich gelobe Dir
> und den von Dir bestimmten Vorgesetzten Gehorsam bis in
> den Tod, So wahr mir Gott helfe [I swear to thee, Adolf
> Hitler, as Führer and Chancellor of the German Reich,
> loyalty and bravery. I vow to thee and to the superiors whom
> thou shalt appoint, obedience unto death, so help me God]."

And then in Dachau, a master posing as a slave, the blue eyes
pretending a humility the heart had never felt. The row of numbers
on the forearm were a mockery, like cheap fun-fair tattoos
proclaiming eternal love. He turned off the lamp and the face
vanished.

He got as far as the door before the thought took shape. Seconds
passed, then he turned and went back to the desk. He switched on
the lamp again and looked at the photograph. The numbers were
too small and indistinct to read. He remembered that there had
been a magnifying glass in one of the drawers. Hurriedly, he opened
and shut them. The glass was in the fourth. He held it to the
photograph.

D7932-V, he read.

He bent down, rolled back the carpet again, and lifted up the
loose piece of flooring. Holding his breath, he dialed the letter and
four digits, then the V. He pulled back on the handle. The door
remained firm. David slumped back. It had seemed such an
obvious idea, extremely neat, satisfying. Then he remembered the
way the numbers had been set out on the pages of the original
Valkyrie list. He could not remember Neusner's number exactly, of
course, but he knew he had gone to Dachau in December 1944. All
he had to do was go through the possible dates one by one. He
started with 12144-D7932-V.

Gershon Neusner had arrived in Dachau on December 12. At
David's twelfth attempt the door swung open as though he had
whispered, "Open, sesame," in its ear. He reached in a hand and
drew out a stack of papers, then another and another. He took the
papers across to the desk and put them down. With shaking hands,
he untied the string that held the first bundle.

A letter of commendation from Heinrich Himmler, handwritten. Letters from Ulrich von Meier, from Iram. A photograph of twenty SS men, among whom a young Neusner could be recognized with little difficulty. A grotesque and, in its way, obscene photograph of young Neusner being circumcised by an SS surgeon, a grin on his face, beneath a banner bearing an anti-Semitic cartoon and caption. Letters from other members of the Valkyrie regiment, presumably forwarded through a central clearinghouse somewhere, notifying Neusner of their whereabouts, their progress, or their plans, or asking for information about his activities. A list of Valkyrie operatives alive in Israel. SS insignia, some old, some evidently of more recent origin, the oak leaves and star of an Oberstgruppenführer—matching his rank of general in the Israeli army. Medals, again both old and new, in stiff packets of buff cardboard.

Neusner had signed his own death warrant. For whatever motive—pride, nostalgia, mere bravado, a sense of history—he had taken an unconscionable risk bringing such materials into Israel at all. If David could succeed in putting even a few of these items into the right hands, Neusner and all of Neusner's associates were washed up. It was unlikely that anyone would ever know of what happened: to reveal the full dimensions of the conspiracy would serve only to undermine public confidence severely. At the moment, what the Israelis needed was an injection of morale, not an increase in insecurity.

He opened the second bundle. It contained more letters, handwritten in Arabic script, with a German translation clipped to each one. David glanced through them rapidly. They went back several years, and each one was signed by the same hand: 'Abd al-Jabbar al-Shami. He picked out the most recent, dated about two months ago, and began to read it:

Dear Walther,
When we last met, we agreed that I should check on the situation in Damascus. I have been here for two weeks now and am satisfied that all is as it should be. Al-Hashimi is popular, with few challenges to his leadership, and none that he cannot handle. The peace plan goes ahead without interruption. There are several elements violently opposed to

it, of course, but when I spoke with al-Hashimi, he assured me that they can be contained.

I had interviews with General Subki and Ibtisam al-Bakri. Subki has been appointed general in charge of the Golan sector as planned, with three divisions under his command at present. Please inform Heinrich Schultz that he must ensure Israeli intelligence understand these to be the fifth, ninth, and fourteenth divisions currently located along the line from Quneitra to Butmiya. By March 1, Subki will have replaced these with three fresh divisions made up of men from crack regiments drawn from the Iraqi border, including the Intisar, 'Anaza, and Sayyaf regiments from Baalbek and Aleppo.

At 11 A.M. on March 3, General Subki will start to move his troops back to the positions agreed in the treaty document, just as al-Hashimi begins his speech in the Dome of the Rock. There will be international observers in place to report that the Syrian forces have been moved in preparation for the fixing of the new borders by the afternoon's agreement.

At 11:30, just after al-Hashimi finishes, but just before Schultz makes his move, your command headquarters in the Golan sector will receive an intelligence report transmitted from Aleppo to the effect that Syrian troops are moving toward territory under Israeli control. You should order two battalions to advance in readiness for a possible attack. I think you should let your staff know you are notifying Jerusalem immediately of what is happening, but our people will make sure that your message is intercepted. At 11:45, a message will be relayed to your command post indicating that the Syrian force has launched an assault on Israeli forward positions to the south of you. At that point, I suggest you experience a total communications blackout. Mausbach tells me he can arrange something along those lines without much difficulty. At 11:50 you will order your men to attack. Once the two sides have exchanged fire, Mausbach can reestablish communications for you.

From that point on, everything will go according to the plan worked out between us in December. Please ensure that Hacker, Wüstenfeld, and Thiess are all certain of their duties.

I am particularly concerned that Wüstenfeld be one hundred per cent sure that all Israeli nuclear weapons are inoperative by that date—if he cannot guarantee this by March 1, we may have to fall back on Plan B, but as you know I would prefer to avoid the delay this would involve. Al-Hashimi may be popular, but his control is still too uncertain to allow us to waste time. There may not be a second chance if we fail to move on March 3.

Please be sure that the timetable for that day is adhered to scrupulously. Once Schultz has acted, there can be no going back. The Israelis must be shown to be the aggressors from the start. Al-Bakri will ensure complete control in Damascus by 11:30, but it is vital that Syrian troops be in control of as large a portion of Israeli territory as possible before other Arab forces enter the war. The invasion will have moral legitimacy, but without actual possession of territory, this will amount to nothing in the subsequent negotiations. We must have enough land to be able to offer concessions to the Jordanians and the PLO in the east, while retaining all other regions for our exclusive use. Ideally, we need to keep overall control of all regions currently inhabited by Jews, since they will be essential to us as our labor force during the first phase of occupation and Syrianization.

As you may know, Ulrich von Meier has been looking more closely at the question of legitimation. Our best argument, he feels, will be to reverse the Zionist claim to the region, which is based on nothing more than biblical texts. He understands that some of the materials found in the Syrian archaeological site of Ebla indicate a much earlier occupation of Palestine by Syria. In his last communication, he told me that he has recently heard that an expert on the Eblaite texts is in Israel at present. He thinks he might be persuaded to help him compile references in the texts to Syrian hegemony in the Palestine region. He wants me to bring him to Iram. Our biggest problems are going to be justification and control, as I said in my last letter. I heard a few days ago from Schneider in Washington. He and his associates are optimistic about the present situation of the Arab lobby there, and he thinks the Zionists have been considerably weakened in the past year or so. It will not be easy, of course, but he thinks that, if we can manage the initial takeover without too much bloodshed, the Americans can probably be persuaded to accept the whole thing as a fait accompli. The Jewish lobby will go crazy, that's obvious, but they've made a lot of people there impatient recently, especially since Lebanon, and they'll find it an uphill push, that's certain. What American politicians lose in Jewish votes, they'll get back in deals with the Arab world. The main thing will be for us to insist on a pro-Western, anti-Communist stance from the beginning. That way our victory will be seen as a plus rather than a minus. In fact, we'll soon be regarded as having removed a long-standing thorn in everyone's flesh. If Syrian control puts an effective end to tension in the region, there's no reason why the entire world—and I include the Soviets—should not feel grateful to us for what we've done.

But control will be more difficult, I predict. You know the Israelis better than I do, and I think you're right when you say they'll take a Masada-top view of the situation: better go out fighting to the last man than let yourself fall into the hands of the enemy. Please be careful about how you set up internment camps. We can't afford to give the wrong impression, otherwise we'll lose the goodwill of all the people we're trying to make see our action in a favorable light. No hints of concentration camps. Internees should be restricted to known terrorists, and there must be provision made for the rapid trial of cases. The labor camps should be guarded discreetly and made to look as much like simple continuations of the existing *kibbutzim* as possible.

We will, of course, have to transfer a certain percentage of the population. Can we consult at greater length on this once control has been established? I'd like to work out a scheme for bringing back Palestinian refugees direct from the camps or from places like the Gaza Strip and displacing Jewish settlers who have taken what was clearly Arab land in 1948. That will make a good start. I'd like the Jewish refugees to stay within Arab jurisdiction if possible, however, since they could cause problems if allowed to go to Europe or America and join forces with other Jews there.

The main thing at this stage is to be sure everything is ready for March 3. There must be no hitches. Your people in the air force must ensure that the sabotage operation goes ahead smoothly, otherwise we may have problems. If you still think that's a weak spot, see if you can do something to remedy it even at this stage. I know you are still unhappy about the young men sent to you from Iram recently, but I have worked with others from the city for several years, and I assure you they are well trained and absolutely reliable. They need time to adjust to their environment, that's all.

I will see you before I leave for Iram. If only Hajj Amin were alive to see this day. In his name, then: this year in Jerusalem.

'Abd al-Jabbar al-Shami

For several minutes David sat stunned as the grim truth of what he had read settled like lead in his stomach. He did not want to believe it, not a word, not a syllable of it . . . but it hung in front of him like Banquo's murdered face, dark, inescapable, and bloody. He could almost smell the blood; it was pungent and tangible, waiting to be shed. And he knew what would happen if al-Shami's and Neusner's plan succeeded. With Israel gone, there would be nowhere to escape to. The old anti-Semitism would flare up again, in France, in Germany, in Britain, in the United States. Politics had already moved far to the right: it would take only a nudge here and a push there to move them even further. No one would help, he was as certain of that as he had ever been of anything. Israel gone would mean a weight off the backs of the Western powers. They would be free to court the oil-rich Arabs as seldom before. Only a handful of people had had the courage to speak out before the Second World War, while governments and churches had sat back, turning a blind eye to the events in Germany. It would happen again. They would be told of the camps and would pretend they did not exist. Those with firsthand stories of them would be accused of willful exaggeration, as their predecessors had been. They would be implored to take in refugees and would respond by imposing rigorous entry quotas or none at all. With high rates of unemployment in all the developed countries, an influx of educated and often highly skilled refugees would be unpopular everywhere.

Backed by state power at last, the Valkyrie organization would grow in strength. It would creep and creep until it held the ears of powerful men in all countries. David shivered. In the early thirties, no one would have believed the scenario of the forties possible, but it had happened all the same. Now, people said, it could never happen again. No? He knew it could and that, unchecked, it would. There would be no black flags, no swastikas, no jackboots—that would be much too blatant. A new style and a new fashion would inform the dress and mind of the next generation of fascists. They had learned their lessons from the mistakes of their own past. David knew that they were there waiting, always waiting—the SS men in each one of us. They were a tide in mankind's blood that, if it were not constantly watched and barred, would at first seep back and finally come crashing into all the corners it had once vacated.

There was a sound somewhere outside the door. Absorbed in the documents and his own thoughts, David had failed to notice that someone had entered the house. He heard the murmur of voices, men's voices. Desperately, he looked around for a way of escape. The study was windowless: the only way out was by the door. He looked at the papers on the desk. At all costs he had to ensure that they were placed in the right hands. Almost without thinking, he swept them up and tossed them back into the safe in the floor, reclosing the door and spinning the dial. He replaced the piece of floorboard that concealed the safe and drew back the carpet over it. Returning to the desk, he picked up the telephone and began to dial a local number.

SIXTY-EIGHT

The door opened. Gershon Neusner stood there alongside Rabin, the major from MOSSAD. Behind them stood the third man who had been with them at the house on Zangwill. David wondered who he was.

"Just who the hell are you, and what do you think you're doing?" Neusner barked. Rabin leaned forward and whispered something in his ear. Neusner's face changed. The sudden flash of anger drained away and he grew calm.

"Please," he said in a softened voice, "put the phone down, Professor Rosen. If you have anything to relate, I'd rather you related it to us. I'd like to hear about what you think my friends and I are doing."

David put the phone down but said nothing.

Neusner sighed audibly.

"Why be so predictable, Professor? I only want you to tell me what you're doing here. What's so terrible about that?"

David felt wasted and defeated. They had stymied him at every turn, as though a fallen deity watched over them, leading them on to victory.

"Unfortunately," Neusner said, "you've come here at a difficult time. I expect visitors shortly. You can't stay here." He turned to Rabin.

"Can you take care of him?"

Neusner turned back to David.

"I think you know Major Rabin. He tells me you had an interesting conversation with him yesterday. But I don't think

573

you've met the gentleman standing behind him. Allow me to introduce Colonel Isserles, Major Rabin's departmental superior."

Neusner and Rabin made way for Isserles to step forward into the room. He looked at David briefly, then turned to Neusner.

"What do you want done with him?" he asked.

"I want to know who he's working with apart from Blandford. I want the whereabouts of Blandford and anyone else involved with him. I want to know who else they've given copies of this file to, and the details of any safeguards they've taken to protect themselves and their information. Concentrate on anything that could endanger things tomorrow."

"I can't take him back to my house," Isserles said. "There's been too much activity around there in the past few days."

"All right, what about one of your MOSSAD interrogation rooms? You have all the equipment you need there."

Isserles nodded.

"There's a room in a block near my office. We use it for emergencies, if the normal facilities are full. I have keys."

Rabin stepped forward toward David. He reached inside his coat and brought out a heavy pistol.

"Please stand up, Professor," he said. "We have a short journey ahead of us."

David stood. He looked at the photograph of Neusner on the desk, at the numbers tattooed on his arm, then at the man himself, standing in the doorway. All it required was one last effort and he could still bring Neusner down. David knew it as surely as he knew that they would not give him the slightest chance to make that effort.

He moved toward Rabin, wondering if he should not at least try. Rabin saw the look in his eyes, the tensing of his body, almost imperceptible though it was. He drew back his arm and struck David across the face with the gun, knocking him backward against the desk. David coughed out blood and felt a tooth go with it. Rabin stepped toward him, raising his hand for a second blow.

"Leave him," Isserles said. "You'll have time for that later. I want to get him to Room 19 in one piece."

He held Rabin's arm, restraining him. To withhold from violence for the sake of a greater violence, there lay Isserles' gift. Like Neusner, who stood impassively beside him, he was in control, as always. In a little while he would help Rabin find pain in David Rosen, find it and nourish it, encourage it to take root and spread.

Rabin helped David to his feet, offered him a handkerchief. David put it to his gum and winced with pain. The tooth had broken. There was still part of it embedded in his gum, a focus of growing agony, a shrill, red torment.

Isserles and Rabin escorted him outside. Neusner watched them go, still impassive. Parked by the curb was a back Volvo, blunt and purposeful, built for strength. He was made to sit in the back with Rabin, the gun still pointing at him through the pocket of Rabin's coat. Isserles got behind the steering wheel.

It was a short drive from Giv'at Oren into town. They stopped on the corner of Haneviim and Shivte Yisrael. Haneviim was full of people: men rushing back to their offices after a late lunch, early tourists walking from the Bus Station to Me'a She'arim, an old rabbi leading a line of schoolboys back to their studies.

"Get out slowly," said Rabin, taking hold of David's arm. David opened the door and slid across the seat. Awkwardly, he stood up, Rabin still holding him. As Rabin bent to get through the door, David knew it had to be now. There would be no second chance once they reached the interrogation room.

At that instant, as the balance shifted, David swung backward, sending Rabin against the car. He fell onto the pavement heavily. David broke and ran, away from the car, toward the old rabbi amidst his charges.

"Reb Katzir," he shouted, dashing toward the bewildered old man, giving him a name, any name. He pushed through the flock of black-coated boys, right up to the rabbi. Behind him, he heard a shout as Isserles ran toward him, followed by Rabin. David grabbed the rabbi, embracing him as if holding a dear friend long lost to him.

"*Rebbe,*" he murmured urgently in the old man's ear, "for God's sake, help me. These men are trying to kill me. Pretend you know me."

It hung in the balance for a moment. David thought the old man had not heard him, then there was a whisper.

"What's your name? I should know your name."

Isserles was there, almost on him, pushing through the frightened boys.

575

"David!" the rabbi shouted. "My old friend!" And in his turn he embraced David. Isserles hesitated, caught off guard. Rabin was behind, drawing his gun. He had lost his head. There was nothing he would not do now.

The old man saw Rabin raise the gun.

"Get behind me," he whispered to David. Out loud, he shouted to Rabin, "There are children here. Put your gun away!"

Rabin fired, hitting the old man in the chest.

The boys screamed, people turned. Someone began running toward them. The old man collapsed in David's arms. There was blood on his caftan. David looked up and saw Rabin standing, petrified by the sound of the gun in the open street. Isserles snatched the weapon from his hand and aimed at David. He too would do anything now. He knew what was at stake.

"Run," said the rabbi to David, his voice weakening. David hesitated and Isserles fired, catching him on the left shoulder. There were more screams. The rabbi moaned and coughed blood, a crimson stream of it running down his beard. David let go of him and ran. Another shot sped past him, slicing into the wall by his side and tearing part of it away. He found an opening and ran.

He could hear Isserles running behind him. At the next opening he turned, then again. He had come into Me'a She'arim, among the caftans and the broad-brimmed hats, the beards and the flowing locks. Every man he passed reminded him of the old rabbi spitting up blood in his arms. He felt helpless, hunted, like a rabbit pursued by a mad dog. His shoulder was aching badly and his tooth gave him no respite. It felt as if his whole mouth was inflamed, swollen unbearably and pierced with red-hot needles.

He had lost Isserles. People glanced at him curiously, but he stayed among them, secure among the throng. Using small, unfrequented alleys, he made his way to the street in which he had lived briefly after his return to Jerusalem from Sinai. He stood just outside the entrance to the apartment house where he had lodged, watching the street. Half an hour passed and Isserles did not appear. He felt weak from loss of blood. The bullet had passed through his shoulder, but it had torn a nasty hole on its way. It would require treatment.

Unsteadily, he climbed to the top floor and knocked on the door of the old rabbi who had lived above him. He realized with a shock

576

that he did not even know the man's name. There was a sound of shuffling footsteps, then the door opened. The old man stood there for a moment framed in the doorway, looking at David, seeing the blood and the pale, pain-wracked face.

"*Riboyne Shel O'lem,*" he exclaimed. He reached out for David and helped him through the door. David tried to say something but found that his mouth was too painful.

"Don't speak," the old man muttered as he walked David to a couch in the far corner of the room. "Leave speaking for later." He helped David sit on the couch, then raised his legs until he was lying flat.

"It's Mr. Levi, isn't it? What happened to you?"

David struggled to speak, but the rabbi put a hand to his mouth.

"No, you shouldn't speak. I shouldn't ask questions. I'll go for a doctor. Will you be all right? Don't speak. Nod, if you have to answer."

David nodded. The old man smiled, then frowned and went to the door. David watched him go out, touching the *mezuzah,* mumbling prayers as he hurried off. A wave of nausea hit him, then another. He managed to sit up partly before the vomit came, a hot, sour-tasting wave of foaming bile that forced itself out across his chest. Sweat broke out on his forehead. He felt dizzy, on the verge of blacking out. It would have been a relief to do so, to lapse into painless unconsciousness, but he could not afford oblivion, not now. He had to fight it off. He lay sweating, biting back the pain, tasting the vomit in his mouth.

And all the time his brain pounded with phrases from al-Shami's letter to Neusner, as though a broken tape recorder whirled round and round inside his head: *The invasion will have moral legitimacy . . . We must have enough land . . . need to keep overall control of all regions currently inhabited by Jews . . . control will be more difficult . . . be careful about how you set up internment camps . . . The labor camps should be guarded discreetly . . . this year in Jerusalem.*

The rabbi returned ten minutes later with a doctor, a fresh-faced young Hassid whose bag and stethoscope seemed curiously out of place alongside his *pe'ot* and caftan.

"Who did this to you?" the doctor asked while he helped the rabbi clean away the vomit and the blood. "When did it happen?"

577

"He can't talk, Doctor," the rabbi said. "Don't make him talk. Give him something for his pain. Something to make him sleep."

David looked frantically at the doctor. He shook his head violently. Pain shot through it like fireworks in darkness.

"No," he murmured, "no sleep. I . . . must stay . . . awake. . . . Believe me. . . . It's important. . . . Life and death . . . Please."

The doctor shook his head.

"You're injured. You've lost a lot of blood. You need to sleep, even if only for a few hours. I'll give you something to take away the pain and relax you. You'll wake up in two or three hours feeling a lot fitter, I promise. Whatever you have to do, you can't do it in this condition."

"But there isn't time," David protested. He tried to sit up, but the violent darkness howled at him. The doctor's hand pressed him back against the couch.

"Please, don't try to sit up. Relax." He reached into his bag and drew out a hypodermic. David looked pleadingly at him. The doctor rolled up his sleeve and inserted the needle in his arm. The darkness howled again and he felt thick arms reach out for him, warm and smothering.

578

SIXTY-NINE

When David woke he found himself on a bed. For a moment he had no idea where he was and had to fight down a feeling of panic. He remembered being in the study with Neusner and the others, the threat of interrogation, the short journey into Jerusalem. And then the rest of that day's events flooded back to him. His head ached terribly and there was a raw pain in his mouth. He rolled over and caught sight of someone sitting on a chair near the bed, watching him. It was the old rabbi. David remembered that his name was Gershevitch.

The old man looked at him but did not smile. He stood up and went to the door, then opened it and called someone. A moment later the young doctor came into the room.

"He's awake," Reb Gershevitch said in a low voice.

"Yes, so I see." The doctor came across to the bed and, without speaking, examined David.

"How do you feel?" he asked at last.

"Not too good," David replied. His voice was hoarse, and he realized that his throat had become painfully dry. "My head aches . . . and my tooth, the one I broke."

"I'll give you another shot for those," said the doctor.

"I don't want to sleep again."

"Don't worry. You've slept enough for the moment. I want you to sleep properly tonight."

"What time is it now?" David asked. A sense of urgency had begun to flood back. There was so much to do.

"Just after seven," the doctor said. Like the rabbi, he did not smile. David seemed to remember that he had smiled before.

"What's wrong?" asked David. His heart felt light, as though a wind had scoured it and left it empty. "Is something wrong?"

The doctor nodded.

"Yes," he said.

Had something happened already? David wondered. Had Neusner put forward his deadline? Had there been further instructions from Damascus?

The doctor bent down and picked up something from the floor. It was a copy of *Ma'arev,* an evening newspaper published in Jerusalem.

"After I left here," the doctor said, "I had to make calls on other patients. But about half an hour ago I decided to come back and check on your progress. On my way here I saw a copy of this on the newsstands."

He passed the paper to David, folded so that the top of the front page was facing him. David sat up slightly. The doctor did not try to stop him. The first things David saw were five photographs. In the first, he saw his own face staring back at him from . . . how long? Three years ago, when MOSSAD had taken a fresh picture of him for their files. He recognized the suit, the tie he had been wearing. Beside it was a photograph of Harry Blandford, taken, David guessed, ten or twelve years earlier, but still a good likeness. The third photograph was directly beneath that of David. At first he did not recognize the man, then he knew and understood. It was the old rabbi Rabin had shot that afternoon. There was a caption underneath the photograph: "Rabbi Avram Wise," it said. Lower down the page were photographs of Isserles and Rabin.

Above the photographs was a banner headline:

JERUSALEM MANHUNT FOR KILLER OF RABBI

David felt a surge of vertigo. His bowels constricted and loosened, and he felt a terrible urge to defecate, then the sensation rushed upward and he wanted to throw up. He leaned his head forward and breathed deeply. The nausea left him and he leaned back again. With the paper close to his face, he began to read.

Details are now beginning to emerge about today's tragic shooting on Haneviim. Shortly after 3 P.M. a suspected terrorist, David Rosen, was being escorted along the street by two MOSSAD officers, Colonel Ephraim Isserles and Major Moshe Rabin. Taking advantage of a distraction, Rosen, who was not handcuffed, snatched a gun from Rabin, struck him, and made a dash for freedom. He was pursued by Colonel Isserles, who was unable to use his gun for fear of endangering passersby. In his hurry to escape, Rosen collided with a group of schoolchildren from a nearby *yeshiva* and, finding his way blocked by their teacher, Rabbi Avram Wise, shot the old man and ran off. Colonel Isserles followed Rosen for some distance, but eventually lost him in crowds in Me'a She'arim.

Rosen, aged 34, is an American university professor known to have close links with Palestinian organizations, including the PFLP. When interviewed this afternoon, Colonel Isserles stated that Rosen is suspected of involvement in a PLO plot to prevent tomorrow's signing of the peace treaty by President al-Hashimi of Syria. A second suspect, Harold Blandford, an English resident of Jerusalem, is still at large and is being sought by police.

Both men are known to be armed and dangerous. Any member of the public sighting them is asked to avoid tackling them directly but to report the matter immediately to the authorities. Anyone knowing of Blandford's whereabouts is requested to contact his local police station without delay.

The murdered man, Rabbi Wise, was a well-known figure in Me'a She'arim. He . . .

David could not read any more. He put the paper down on the bed beside him. When he looked up he saw that Rabbi Gershevitch had come closer to the bed.

"Is it true?" asked Gershevitch.

David stared at him, as though struggling to see himself through the old man's eyes, a killer, a terrorist. He shook his head. The pain in his tooth stabbed at him viciously.

"You did not kill this man? Avram Wise?"

David shook his head again. Again the pain attacked him.

"Do you know who killed him?"

"Yes."

"Was it this man Blandford?"

581

David shook his head gently.

"It was Rabin," he said, "the MOSSAD major."

Gershevitch looked at the doctor.

"Why would he do that?" he asked David.

"He was firing at me," David answered. "I was standing beside the rabbi. The bullet went wide, it hit Rabbi Wise."

"Why did he fire at you? Were you running from him? Trying to escape, like it says here?"

"Yes," said David. It was so hard to explain, so hard to convey the truth.

"You admit you are a terrorist, then?" It was the doctor who spoke this time, his voice hard and impersonal.

David shook his head in defiance of the pain.

"No," he sighed. "I worked for MOSSAD," he went on, "not for the PLO. Isserles and Rabin, these two men they write about, they work for MOSSAD too, but in reality they belong to another group. It's hard to explain."

"How do you expect us to believe you? If you're telling the truth, surely the police will know. You know I have to tell them."

David closed his eyes. There had to be a way. He opened them again and looked at the doctor. If this man did not believe him, the result would be war.

"What about the children?" David asked. "They saw the incident, they can tell you what happened. Why hasn't anyone asked them?"

The doctor looked at Gershevitch.

"It would help settle the matter," he said.

Gershevitch nodded. The doctor turned back to David.

"The only reason I haven't gone for the police so far is that the newspaper report doesn't mention your being wounded or hurt in the mouth. It says Isserles wouldn't fire his gun in the street. And Reb Gershevitch tells me you weren't armed when you arrived here." He paused. "I'll go and see if I can find one of the boys who were with Rabbi Wise this afternoon."

Gershevitch shook his head.

"It's better you stay here," he said. "They know me at the *yeshiva*. I know the families of several boys. They trust me. Keep an eye on our friend. I won't be long."

The doctor remained with David. Neither man spoke. There were no words for such a situation. David closed his eyes and tried to rest, but the pain in his head and the thoughts that raged through it made him grow agitated.

"May I have something for the pain?" he asked at last.

The doctor stood up.

"Of course, I'm sorry. I forgot."

He opened his bag and took out some tablets.

"Take two of them," he said. "They should work quickly and last for an hour or two." He looked down at David as he took the tablets with small sips of water. He had to be sure he was doing the right thing. Instinct of some sort inclined him to believe David's story. But he had to be certain. It was not a light matter.

Gershevitch returned half an hour later trailing a small, visibly frightened boy of about ten. The child hung back, his hand in Gershevitch's. The events of that afternoon had disturbed him. Now Rabbi Gershevitch wanted him to identify a man for him. He trusted the rabbi, but he felt confused by everything, confused and frightened.

He came into the room behind Gershevitch. David saw that his eyes were red from crying. The doctor stood up and went over to the lad, attempting to reassure him.

"This is Nachum," Gershevitch said. "His mother and father agreed to let him come here with me." He turned to the boy. "Now, Nachum," he went on, "please try not to be frightened. You're safe here with me. I just want you to tell us if you recognize the man in the bed, if you've seen him anywhere before."

The boy stood rigid for a while, staring at David, then he turned his eyes away and nodded.

"You have seen him?" the doctor asked.

The boy nodded again.

"Can you tell me where you saw him?"

"In Haneviim," the boy whispered, almost inaudibly. Gershevitch bent down to listen.

"When was that?" he asked.

"Today," the child said. "This afternoon, when Rabbi Wise was shot."

"I see," said Gershevitch. There was a pause. Then he went on. "Did this man kill him?" he asked finally.

The boy shook his head. Gershevitch raised his eyes and looked at the doctor. He wondered if the other man felt the same fear that was starting to crawl through his veins.

"Did you see who shot Rabbi Wise? I'm sorry, but it's important.

I wouldn't ask you if it wasn't."

The boy nodded.

"Yes," he said.

"Would you recognize him?" Gershevitch felt the boy's hand tighten in his. "It's all right," he reassured him, "he isn't here. But I have some photographs I'd like you to look at."

The doctor picked up the paper and took it across to the boy.

"Was it one of these men?" he asked, holding the page open flat in front of the child. Without hesitation, the boy put his finger directly on Rabin's picture.

"This man," he said.

"Can you tell us what happened?" asked the doctor.

"Yes," said the boy, his confidence growing a little. "We were walking with Rabbi Wise when this man"—he pointed at David— "came running toward us. He spoke with the rabbi. I didn't hear what he said, but Rabbi Wise said *'Shalom,'* and held him as if he knew him. Then the other man, the man in the paper, came running. He had a gun. He lifted it and fired. The bullet hit Rabbi Wise. Rabbi Wise fell down. The man in the bed ran away then. And then another man came up and took the gun from the first man and ran after the first man."

The doctor indicated David.

"Did this man have a gun? Did he fire at anyone?"

The boy shook his head.

"No, I saw no gun. Only the other man had a gun. This man was running."

"I see," the doctor said. He looked at Gershevitch.

"Will there be trouble?" asked the boy.

"Trouble?" Gershevitch asked. "Why should there be trouble?"

"Because I came here. I wasn't supposed to say anything. The man said we were to say nothing to anyone."

Gershevitch and the doctor exchanged glances.

"What man was this?" asked the doctor.

"I don't know who he was. He came to the *yeshiva* late this afternoon. He called all of us together, the boys who had been with Rabbi Wise, and he said he had been given orders to tell us that we should not speak to anyone about what happened today. I think he was from the police, but I'm not sure. He was a big man. He frightened us."

"It doesn't matter," Gershevitch said. "It will be all right. There won't be any trouble, I promise you. Come. I think it's time to go home. I'll take you back to your parents."

The boy nodded, then turned toward David.

"Are you all right?" he asked. "Did they shoot you as well?"

David tried to smile.

"Yes," he said. "They shot me too. But I'm better now. The doctor's been looking after me."

"I'm glad," the child said. "I hope you get well."

When Gershevitch and the boy had gone, the doctor sat down beside David.

"I'll have to leave soon," he said. "I have some serious cases to attend to, people who need me. You'll be all right, I think, once you've had that tooth looked at." He paused and sighed. "But I don't suppose you can do that very easily, can you?"

David shook his head. The pain had diminished to a dull sensation.

"I'll see what I can do. It requires someone I can trust. Do you plan to stay here? You'll be safe, for the moment at least."

"No," David said. "I can't stay. I have things to do. I can't explain. You'll have to trust me."

"Yes, I trust you," the doctor said. There was a pause. "Is your friend in danger?" he went on. "The Englishman?"

"Yes," David said. "But I think he's safe for the moment. After tomorrow it won't matter. If I don't succeed in what I have to do, none of us will be safe. Not you, not Gershevitch . . . not the boy who just came here."

The doctor said nothing. He could tell from David's voice how serious it was.

"Is there nothing I can do to help?" he asked.

"No," replied David. "You'd have to explain how you came by certain information. It would take too long."

"At least I can help you keep that pain at bay." The doctor reached for his bag and took out a bottle of the painkillers he had given David earlier.

"Take two of these whenever you feel you need them. Try not to overdo them, but if it's necessary to keep you going, take them."

He put the bottle on the little table beside the bed. A few minutes later Gershevitch returned.

SEVENTY

It was not until the doctor had gone that David realized he had not learned his name.

"Yaakov Gaster," Gershevitch told him. "He's young, but he understands our ways. You can trust him."

"And you. Why didn't you go straight to the police when you read the newspaper report?"

Gershevitch snorted.

"The police! The newspapers! That is the first newspaper I have ever read. And what happened has confirmed my belief that they serve no other purpose than to spread lies. As for the police, they belong to the Zionists, not us."

David understood him. For the ultra-Orthodox, the state of Israel, its laws, and its agencies were no more than blasphemy. There could be no Israel until the coming of the Messiah. Prayer was of more profit to them than the screech of a police siren.

"You would have kept me, then, believing I had killed a man, a rabbi?"

Gershevitch sighed and shook his head.

"No. Crime deserves punishment. But I would have gone to others for advice. Now I am glad I did not."

"So am I. Very glad."

Reb Gershevitch smiled.

"Now you should rest. You've been through a lot today."

David shook his head tiredly.

"Later, perhaps, but not now. Please don't try to force me. I want to get up. There are two important telephone calls I have to make.

586

Can you help me find a telephone?"

The old rabbi sighed.

"My son-in-law has a telephone. They have children, he says they need one in case of emergency. You can use it. But first we have to find clothes for you. When I first met you, you were dressed in proper clothes. You had *pe'ot* and a small beard. You wore a *yarmulkah*. A little fancy, perhaps, but a *yarmulkah*. Now . . . now you look like a *goy*." He sighed. "My son-in-law is about your size. You will have to dress like a Jew. A Jew with an arm sling. Will it do?"

David smiled.

"Yes," he said. "It will do very well."

It seemed appropriate that he should dress as a Jew again.

At the son-in-law's, after he had changed, David rang the Benabus'. Etan answered the phone.

"David! Where are you? What's happening? We've seen the paper and we're worried sick. Do you know what they're saying about you?"

"Yes," David replied. "I've seen it. But I'm all right. Everything's fine. I'm safe for the moment."

"Is it true what they wrote? That you . . ."

"No. Rabin killed the rabbi. He was trying to kill me at the time."

"We knew it couldn't be true. Harry says Isserles is on your list. His real name is Schultz. He was with Neusner in Dachau. David, Harry says it's become too dangerous, that you have to pull out."

"Let me speak to him, Etan. Or to Leyla."

There was a brief silence, then Etan spoke again.

"Harry's right here, David. I'll pass you over."

At once Harry's voice came on the line, tense and quivering.

"Thank God you're safe, David. What's happening?"

"Listen, Harry. This is important. I went to Neusner's this afternoon. I found papers, a safeful—all the proof anyone could want. But Neusner and two of his pals came in and found me. Isserles and Rabin, the men in the paper. Rabin's the same man I saw yesterday. They knew who I was right away. But I managed to put the papers back before they found me, so they don't know I've seen them.

"Harry, you've got to get somebody in there to see those papers, somebody you can trust. There's a bundle of letters from al-Hashimi in Syria. They contain details of a plot to invade Israel. It starts tomorrow, Harry. Right after al-Hashimi signs the treaty."

There was a long silence at the other end. Then Blandford's voice at last, tight and gray.

"Oh, Christ!" he whispered, the unredeemed Gentile rising in him like a tide. "How? Where?"

"It's in the letters, Harry. All the details. Read the last letter, the one dated about a month ago."

"You're sure of this?"

"I've read it. There's no mistake."

Harry drew a deep breath and let it out again in a long, shuddering gasp.

"Where are the papers, David?"

"In Neusner's study. To the left of the desk, under the carpet. There's a loose board, then a safe. The combination is Neusner's Valkyrie number, you'll find it in the original file or in the printout. It's the whole number, date, letters, everything."

"I understand. I'll find it."

"Good. But be careful who you go to for help. If they arrest you, it could take days to sort things out. If Isserles and his chums don't get to you first. We don't have that sort of time. I think Leyla should make contact first. Can I speak to her?"

There was an uneasy pause.

"I'm sorry, David. She isn't here."

"Where is she?"

"She . . . she rang about two hours ago. She fixed the interpreting job for tomorrow. But that means she has to be briefed tonight. She's at al-Hashimi's residence. All she knows is that it's somewhere in Jerusalem. The security people won't let her leave. She'll be taken from the residence with al-Hashimi in the morning: it's standard procedure."

David felt cold inside, like ice. He would have to do it alone.

"Harry, if she gets in touch, ask her to leave. Say she's been taken ill—anything. But tell her to get out. I'll be back soon. Wait for me."

David replaced the receiver. His hand shook, but he sat immobile, like an Egyptian statue, a stone god staring into the strange room as if he had always been there. It was growing late.

588

Even time was turning against him.

David sighed and got to his feet. He went into the next room, where Rabbi Gershevitch and his son-in-law were waiting for him, deep in conversation. They looked up as he came in.

"Rabbi," David said, "I have to leave."

Gershevitch stood up and came across to him.

"You're sick; you should rest. You've done what you can—let someone else finish this thing for you."

David shook his head.

"I'd like to do that, but I can't. I have no choice. If I stay here and wait, something dreadful will happen. Innocent people will die. I'm afraid, Rabbi. I'm afraid for myself, I'm afraid for you, for all of us."

"There will be more killings?"

"Many more. The Holocaust all over again. All that darkness. And this time it will be worse. I've seen things, *rebbe,* terrible things. Things my parents have seen, things you have seen. Papers with swastikas, badges with lightning flashes . . ."

The old man shivered.

"Don't speak of such things!" he said. He spoke sharply, as you might rebuke a child who chatters carelessly about death on the day of a funeral. He looked around, at his son-in-law, at a collection of photographs on a low table—his daughter and grandchildren. He looked at them for a long time.

"What do you need?" he asked finally.

"A car," said David. "Someone to drive me to a friend's house. I can't take a taxi, there's a risk I'll be recognized."

The son-in-law stood up.

"I have a car," he said. "I'll take you. Where do you want to go?"

SEVENTY-ONE

The idea had formed in David's mind as he lay in bed waiting for Gershevitch to bring the boy. It still sounded lunatic to him. And it all hinged on something that might prove to be nothing more than yet another of Damien Wise's hoaxes. Etan came to the door alone. David pushed past him and, without waiting to explain what had happened, asked Etan to talk with him in his study. When they had closed the door and settled into chairs by the desk, he came straight to the point.

"Etan," he said, "you told me when I was last here that you knew of a way into the Dome of the Rock, a way nobody had ever discovered. Was that a Damien Wise exaggeration or were you telling the truth for once?"

Etan looked pained.

"David, would I lie? Damien always tells the truth. It's what he does with it that causes problems." He paused. "Yes, there is a way in. I've been saving it for my next book, *Secrets of the Crusaders*. It was to be a big revelation. You aren't going to spoil it, are you?"

"I'm afraid so, Etan. Does anyone else know about it?"

"I doubt it. I found out just before your last visit. You know the old caves down near Herod's Gate, the ones they call Solomon's Quarries or Zedekiah's Cave?"

David nodded. He'd been there.

"The story goes that it's the place where Solomon found the stone for his Temple. According to the Masons, it's where their order started. A perfect place for Damien Wise to poke about in. Now, the quarry travels about seven hundred feet down into the Old City,

590

but there were rumors about additional galleries going even farther. I'd read that the Crusaders, or, to be more precise, the Templars, had carried out excavations under the Temple Mount. Did you know that, David?"

David smiled.

"Yes," he said. "I even know about the Copper Scroll."

The Copper Scroll was one of the Dead Sea scrolls discovered at Qumran. It referred to the existence of bullion, sacred vessels, and other treasure, and spoke of twenty-four hoards buried right beneath the Temple in Jerusalem—beneath the site, that is, where the Dome of the Rock now stood.

"That's a pity," Etan said. "I was saving that up."

"Sorry, Etan. It's been done. But go on about the Templars."

"The Templars. Well, I thought they might have tried digging in the quarries as well, especially if they thought there was a link with Solomon. I got permission to scout around a bit. No actual digging, just a trowel and a flashlight. I found what I was after, though. It had been walled over very carefully, but I made a way in. Covered it up afterward, of course. It was a long tunnel, and it went right through to the Temple area, underneath the Mount."

"You think the Templars dug it?"

"Oh, no, it's older than that, I think. But there were Crusader emblems on the walls. I think they may have been the ones who walled it off."

"Where does it come out?"

"Inside the Dome. David, you aren't planning to go in there tomorrow, are you?"

David nodded.

"May I ask why?"

"I have to kill al-Hashimi. There's no time for anything else. Not if we want to stop this thing."

Etan breathed deeply several times.

"I see," he said at last. "All right, I won't ask any questions. What can I do to help?"

"Three things, Etan. I want you to help me find the tunnel into the Dome tomorrow. Then I want you to help Harry get the papers from Neusner. And I want you to lend me your rifle."

Etan, like most healthy Israeli men his age, was an army reservist. He spent about forty-five days out of every year on military service.

And he kept a rifle at hand in his home in case of an emergency call-up.

He got up and walked to the window. It was dark outside, he could see nothing.

"All right, David. You can have the rifle. I'll take you right into the tunnel. It goes under the rock, right underneath. It comes out in the little grotto beneath the rock, the cave called the Well of Souls. Will that help? Can you do it, David?"

David pondered. The rock was a large, almost rectangular outcrop that stood exactly at the center of the building, which formed an octagon around it. It was said to be the rock on which Abraham had prepared his son Isaac for sacrifice, from which Muhammad had ascended to heaven mounted on a winged creature named Buraq. The grotto below it had been thought by many to be the Holy of Holies of the original Temple—the place in which the Ark had been kept.

"I don't know," David said. "I need a plan of the Dome. Have you got some sort of diagram?"

"Yes, of course. Just a minute, I think there's one in my study."

He went out, then came back in about a minute carrying a massive folio volume bound in green, Cresswell's *Early Islamic Architecture*, the first volume. Going over to the dining table, he cleared it and put down the book. David joined him. There was a clear plan in the first chapter devoted to the building.

"Look," Etan said, pointing at the outline of stairs on the south side of the rock. "You'd come out of the grotto there. Then what?"

David thought.

"That depends on where al-Hashimi is. They could hold the speech almost anywhere: for God's sake, it's a circular building."

"But it would be logical to orient things toward one of the sides. I'd go for the west. It's the normal entrance. It faces toward the Wailing Wall, which is the only part of the Herodian Temple still standing. Or of the platform at least. But it would allow people to face east, which might be regarded as symbolic, even in Jerusalem."

"All right. Let's assume it's on the west. Al-Hashimi will probably face the door, with his back to the central pillar in the rail that goes around the rock. There'll be a platform or a plinth of some kind for him to stand on, I'm sure. If I can get on top of the rock I should be able to crawl across to the balustrade. I seem to remember the rock's flat on top. It isn't too far to the floor. I should be able to get over it if I lie flat. Those are metalwork screens between the pillars, aren't they?"

Etan nodded.

"Then I'll fire through the screen. It ought to work."

Etan looked unsure, but he said nothing.

"When can we go there?" David asked.

"They open the quarries to tourists at eight-thirty. Of course, there won't be anybody there that early, not in March, but I'd prefer not to open up that wall while there's a chance we'll be seen. I suggest we go early, about six. That'll give us time to get in, find our way through, and cover up the wall again from inside."

Etan stood up.

"And now I think you'd better go to bed. You need to sleep. You can tell us what happened tomorrow, when it's all over."

David looked up at his friend. Would it ever be over?

"Etan," he said, "will you fetch my black bag, the one in the bedroom?"

Puzzled, Etan went out. He came back a minute later with the bag and handed it to David.

From the bag David drew out a small canvas sack containing something heavy. It held the two stones of the law. On the way back to Jerusalem he had managed to decipher the ancient script. In somewhat altered language, but in the essence of the thing, they contained the basic laws of the Decalogue, the Ten Commandments Moses had brought down from Sinai.

David took the stones out of the sack and cradled them in his hands briefly before handing them to Etan.

"Here," he said. "These are for you. Not Damien Wise but Etan Benabu. They're genuine. They are precisely what they seem to be. I want you to have them."

Slowly, Etan began to read the thinly incised inscriptions. It took him a long time, but his archaic Hebrew was better than David's. When he finished, he put the stones down gently on his desk and looked at David.

"Where did you find these?" he asked.

But David had fallen asleep, exhausted, in his chair.

SEVENTY-TWO

David had been dreaming of the desert. He woke up sweating, his arm and shoulder competing angrily for his attention. It had been a cold dream, bleak and full of winter. The desert had symbolized something: society itself, the brave new world of modern man. All tracks, all direction signs had been wiped out, there was only a vast expanse of endless, shifting sand. Like nomads in a true desert, people wandered in search of a path, quartering the empty sands for signs of life. They wanted a savior, someone to lead them out of the wilderness to the promised land. Any promised land would do, as long as it was a land of plenty; and any savior would do, as long as he gave them what they wanted.

It was five o'clock. David felt stiff and tired. His short, troubled sleep had not refreshed him. He got out of bed and tiptoed out of the room. Etan and he had arranged to meet downstairs in the kitchen at five-thirty. In his hand he carried Etan's rifle, which he had kept in his room throughout the night. He put on a light and sat down, loading and unloading the rifle, testing its actions. Later he would have to fire a few rounds to adjust the sights. David knew he would probably have only one chance, two at the outside. Two bullets to stop the darkness returning.

His main worry was his left arm. The right was painful, but he could pull a trigger without difficulty. He needed the left to support the stock, but his shoulder constantly threatened to give way. It would be vital for him to get into a position where he could support the arm. He had been trained by MOSSAD, but his training had been limited, and he was far from being a good shot.

Beth opened the door, unnoticed by David. She stood in the doorway watching him, her green eyes sad and thoughtful. David looked up and their eyes met. He had known Beth for years now. He had dated her for a while in school, before the spaceman came on the scene. They had called Etan that even then, their private name for him. David tried to smile, but his mouth stayed rigid, as though locked in place. She said nothing but came and sat near him on a stool.

"You're going through with it, David?"

He nodded.

"Etan told me last night in bed. This morning, I mean. I wish you didn't have to do it."

"So do I," David said quietly.

"And there's no other way?"

He shook his head.

"I always hated guns, David; since I was a little girl. They frightened me."

"They frighten me too," he said. "Don't you remember, we were together on those antiwar demos? I hated war. . . . I still hate it. Such a stupid way of settling differences. I'd still protest if there were demonstrations. But this isn't war, Beth. It's worse than that in a way. It forces your hand to the point where you have no choice any longer. If I don't kill a man this morning a lot of people will die, maybe millions. This isn't like dropping a bomb on Hiroshima, to defeat an enemy who's already been beaten. These people are fresh, fresh and quite deadly."

"And you think you can stop them all alone, David?"

He shook his head sadly.

"No. It needs all of us to do that. To be watchful, to keep our wits about us, develop an awareness of their methods, their ideologies."

"You sound like McCarthy, David. You'll find them everywhere if you look hard enough."

David smiled.

"I'm sorry, Beth, I didn't mean to sound . . . fanatical. McCarthy went about things the wrong way. Every liberal became a Red, every radical a threat to society. Keeping watch means watching for the McCarthys too, because they create an atmosphere in which these people thrive. It's happening today, Beth, Darwin banned from schools, books by homosexual authors thrown out of public libraries, antiabortionists planting bombs in public places. What better conditions for a right-wing revival can you imagine?"

"You think there'll be a revival?"

"Of course. Don't imagine it will stop here, in Israel, in the Middle East. They have people in the States, probably some in Europe as well. It wouldn't take much to push things in that direction. In the past decade or so, things have gone wrong back home. You don't know, you haven't lived there for so long. But this is the Rambo generation, Beth, the generation that acts tough and doesn't much care who gets hurt as long as they can prove their virility."

"It's because of Vietnam, David, because we lost. People are insecure. We thought we were the strongest nation on earth . . . and we were beaten by a nation of peasants. People need to feel strong again. It's the only way they know how."

"Like the Germans after Versailles. When people are in that mood, all it needs is for the right man to offer them what they want. Build up your armaments, fight little wars abroad, scare people into being patriotic."

"You think we're that stupid, David? We'd let ourselves get conned?"

"Beth, the Germans were intelligent people. They didn't have the mark of Cain or anything. They won't use swastikas or wear jackboots. They'll wave the Stars and Stripes and talk like good ol' boys from Texas. There won't be any concentration camps, not at first—just little bits of legislation and a tougher regime in existing prisons. A hard line on immigrants maybe, ship loads of Mexicans back over the border. Some hard-line laws on abortion, pornography, marijuana, then maybe a backlash against the gay community. The Moral Majority will go wild with pleasure. Bring back the electric chair in every state, reintroduce the draft. Then some big newspaper reveals that the Jews are in league with the Commies, that muggings by blacks have got out of hand so that no one white is safe, that Hispanics are destroying our kids with dope. A small riot in Washington, a handful of lynchings in Alabama, one day a gay Jew sets fire to the White House."

She listened in silence while he talked and she remembered. She remembered the Kennedys and Martin Luther King and Kent State and the end of the war, and she wondered where it had all gone—all those dreams, those beautiful dreams. She saw Jack Kennedy going down in Dealy Plaza, and Bobby Kennedy going down in the Ambassador Hotel, and Martin King going down in the Lorraine Motel, like skittles, white and black skittles tumbling, and she knew they could do it, that it had already started years ago. Like everybody else, she had kept her eyes closed or focused on other things.

There was a sound at the door. Etan came in and sat down. Beth set about preparing a light breakfast, more because it seemed the proper thing to do than because anyone was really hungry. A few minutes later Harry came in with Sammy under one arm.

At a quarter to six it was time to go. They kept the good-byes short. Everyone was tense.

"Take this, David," Harry said, taking something from around his neck. "It's a good luck charm. Had it for years." It was a *Magen David*, old and tarnished. David remembered the star he had bought for his father all those years ago, the one he had kept without telling him. He slipped it over his neck without a word.

They reached Sultan Suleiman Street just after six. There was a small garden, and at the back a small iron-grille door. The lock was easy to force—no one imagined a break-in here. There was nothing to steal but rock. They shut the door behind them and moved off down the first passage, their flashlights playing on the dark, eroded walls. David felt as if he were back in Iram again and experienced once more the stifling claustrophobia he had known in the final stages of his escape. They walked down through the galleries, their footsteps echoing eerily in the darkness. Etan went in front, his flashlight swinging on the walls and ceiling, a long white cone like a rod of ice.

The section of wall Etan was looking for was right at the back of one of the deepest passages, one seldom entered by tourists. The tunnel had been cunningly concealed by stones cut on the outside to resemble quarried rock. It had taken Etan's trained eye to see the one stone laid wrongly, as if it had been worked from an impossible angle. Together, they pulled the rocks away, opening up a great darkness behind. There was a smell, as of cloves or coriander, faint but unmistakable in their nostrils. They passed through the

597

irregular opening they had made, going from one darkness into what seemed an even deeper one, heavy and luxurious. Once through, they replaced the stones they had dislodged, rebuilding that section of the wall well enough to escape casual notice.

They worked their way along the tunnel. It was low and narrow, about four feet high, forcing them to stoop, half walking and half crawling. More than ever, the nightmare of Iram came back to David, and that moment of dark horror in the corridor at the monastery, and the terror of waking in the charnel house. It was as if a network of interconnecting tunnels, low and dark and filled with monstrous and unspeakable things, had brought him in the end to this destination, this rock at the center of the world, this *omphalos*. He had read once in the *Mishnah* that the Temple stood directly over *tehom*, the waters of chaos below the earth, and as he crawled through the darkness, it was as if he could hear them surging, though he knew it was only the blood pounding in his head. He had cut down on the painkillers, because he needed to be alert, and now the pains in arm and shoulder and tooth were shooting in spasms that drew him up at times with a sudden jolt. His whole mouth ached, and his cheek felt numb up to the eye. He craved the tablets that would provide relief but steeled himself to endurance. He would take some half an hour before the deadline, but more than that would slow his responses.

The tunnel ended abruptly at a blank wall. Etan pointed upward. Set in the roof was the outline of a stone slab. Etan twisted himself around somehow to face David.

"It leads directly into the grotto," he said. "The other side fits perfectly into the pattern on the marble floor. As far as I can tell, no one has ever suspected that this is down here."

"Can we move it easily?" David asked.

"Yes, I did it myself. I had to come here on a Muslim holy day, when there was no one in the cave."

"Will it make a noise?"

"Not if we do it together. Do you want to go up now, see what's happening?"

David hesitated, then nodded.

"Yes. It's just past seven. It should still be fairly quiet."

Together, they pushed the slab up and to one side. No light came from the chamber above. With Etan's assistance, David heaved himself up into the grotto. He flashed the light on briefly to get his bearings. Whitewashed walls gleamed for a moment, then darkness returned as he switched off the lamp. He went to the foot of the stairs and looked out into the space beyond. High above, some lights were lit in the Dome itself. He went up a little higher. He could hear voices, the sound of furniture being moved about, orders being given. A second later he ducked down again as footsteps came in his direction along the inner ambulatory. When the feet had gone by, he climbed the first few steps again. There were eleven altogether, the last three beyond the edge of the balustrade that encircled the rock.

He went up farther, pulled himself onto the edge of the balustrade, which was wide enough to hold him at this spot, and crawled along it until he was able to slip down onto the rock just below. A mere shadow in the dim light, he crawled over the flat surface of the rock until he came to a long hollow between the main area of the rock and the western side of the balustrade. From where he crouched he could see men working at that side, setting up chairs in a semicircle along the outer edge of the ambulatory. Brighter lights shone beyond the finely worked metal screen. Satisfied, he climbed back to the upper surface of the rock and retraced his steps to the stairs. In half a minute he was back in the tunnel with Etan. They left the slab up, to give them warning in case someone decided to enter the grotto.

"It's on the west, as you thought," he said. "I can get across without much difficulty, but there's likely to be a problem once they put on all the lights. I'd go over now and wait if I thought I could stay there without being detected, but there'd be a risk. There could be a complete security sweep just before things begin. The best time will be once everyone's seated."

"Isn't that cutting it fine?"

David nodded.

"So what do we do now?" Etan asked.

"Nothing. Except wait. And I want to adjust the sight on this rifle to suit me. I'll go back down the tunnel and set up some targets."

David took the rifle and several rounds, crawled back fifty yards or so along the tunnel, and erected a cardboard box he had brought folded up. He went back about thirty feet, the maximum distance he expected to fire, and started the slow process of setting his sights correctly. These were far from ideal conditions. Each time he fired he had to crawl back to the target to check the shot. The flashlight showed him the target clearly enough, but it strained his eyes aiming along its beam. In the end he got it right and even scored several near bull's-eyes. But his left arm was causing him more and more trouble. He went back and sat with Etan. The long vigil began. Dim sounds floated down to them where they sat, but no one came to see what was happening in the Well of Souls. David prayed that none of the visitors would be pious or exhibitionist enough to want to visit the grotto. At least it was still in darkness— obviously nobody else was expecting that eventuality either.

Time had never seemed so slow to David. The minutes seemed to drag on endlessly, hoarding their seconds as a small boy hoards marbles, taking them from his bag one at a time, setting them up in colored rows before skittling them and starting again. Nine o'clock came, then ten. Sitting cramped in the little tunnel, David feared his arm was going to seize up. He moved it deliberately from time to time, ignoring the pain in the hope of keeping it mobile enough.

At a quarter to eleven David climbed gingerly into the grotto. "Good luck," whispered Etan. A voice in the darkness.

He could hear the sound of other voices far away. Many of them. The cave was cool and dark. He listened to the sound of his own breathing as he stood there, steeling himself. He wondered whether this really was the Holy of Holies, whether he was committing the greatest of blasphemies by being here. No Orthodox Jew would set foot in this place.

Cautiously, he went to the foot of the stairs. Lights had been lit all around the building, low-hanging chandeliers swinging in the narrow passages of the inner and outer ambulatories. The voices seemed to come from a distance, on the west side of the building. He went up the stairs one at a time, pausing on each step to listen for the sound of voices or footsteps coming near. Nothing. Near the top he slipped onto the balustrade and slid forward to the rock. The rifle felt heavy in his hands, like a dead weight he had been condemned to carry. Bit by bit he inched his way across the rough face of the rock, then eased himself down into the long hollow on its west side. He knelt by the balustrade and peered over cautiously.

Through the open ironwork between the three slender pillars he could make out rows of men seated in chairs facing the rock. Others stood around, some quite still, others gesturing or speaking quietly into walkie-talkies. David could make out a low podium with a lectern directly in front of the central pillar, precisely where he had predicted it might be. To the right of the lectern stood a second microphone in a stand.

There were lights everywhere. In addition to the old-fashioned candelabra that hung by chains from the ceiling, tall electric lamps had been erected on both sides, lighting up the area between the railing and the balustrade behind which David was crouched, as if it was the perimeter space around a high-security prison. David dared not set foot in there. The least movement would be seen. Trained eyes were all around him. Men with guns stood at regular intervals, men trained never to relax or be lulled into false security by the calmness of their surroundings.

There was a sudden bustle at the rear of the seats. It was eleven o'clock. The Syrians were arriving from the Aqsa Mosque, where they had been praying along with members of the Egyptian delegation and representatives of the Arab community in Israel. Those in the seats were foreign diplomats and journalists. They rose and applauded as al-Hashimi entered, side by side with the Israeli President. David realized that an enormous concession must have been made to allow the President to be present at the meeting, along with members of the Israeli Cabinet: he remembered the outcry there had been early in 1986 when Israeli MPs visited the Aqsa Mosque.

The new arrivals were escorted to seats while al-Hashimi went straight to the lectern. David started as he saw a woman step forward and stand behind the second microphone. It was Leyla. The murmur of voices in the audience ceased. An expectant hush fell over the gathering. History was about to be made.

It could not have been worse. Leyla was standing directly in his line of fire, and there was no other angle from which to hit al-Hashimi. If David moved to the right he would be blocked by the pillar, if he shifted to the left the left wing of the door would deflect his shot. If he fired, it had to be through the narrow aperture or not at all.

There was, of course, one simple solution to his dilemma, but he

601

did not even want to think about it. That was to shoot Leyla. She and al-Hashimi were close enough to allow a high-velocity bullet to pass through her and hit him. Even if the first shot did not actually kill al-Hashimi, there would be a good chance of getting in a second, maybe even a third, if al-Hashimi was immobilized. The main thing was to put al-Hashimi out of action. But to do that he would have to risk killing Leyla. The very idea was horrendous to him.

A microphone crackled briefly, then al-Hashimi's voice came, speaking in Arabic. He paused every few sentences to allow Leyla to translate his words into Hebrew and English. Her voice came to David, the words mostly incomprehensible to him, the tone painful in its familiarity. He remembered how she had sounded two days before, when they had made love at last, nestling beside him, telling him again and again how she loved him. He gritted his teeth against the memory.

"Gentlemen," al-Hashimi said, "today is a historic occasion. We have met together in the holiest of holy places to talk of peace. Behind me is the rock on which Abraham stood when he came to sacrifice his son. From that same spot the Prophet Muhammad ascended to heaven when God brought him from Mecca to Jerusalem in a single night. Over this rock stood the Temple that Solomon built, and beneath it is the spot in which he placed the Ark of God's Covenant. In the Second Temple built on the ruins of the First, Jesus Christ was blessed as a boy by Simeon, and as a man he taught there and performed miracles."

David eased his arm out onto the balustrade and brought the rifle into position. Surely Leyla would move. His shoulder ached, but the painkillers had started working. He put the butt to his right shoulder and steadied the barrel with his right hand.

"But Jerusalem has become a place of strife, a symbol of contention," al-Hashimi went on. "The Jews call it Yerushalayim and claim it for their own. The Arabs speak of it as al-Quds and seek to repossess it."

David looked through the telescopic sight. It was out of focus, the image blurred. He adjusted it slowly. Leyla came into view, close, as if she were beside him and he could reach out and touch her.

"For years now, people have talked about peace, written about peace, prayed for peace. And it seems further away than ever. For man is incapable of bringing peace on his own. Man needs war, man needs struggle, man needs conflict. Only God can bring peace."

David felt the rifle, the polished wood, the cold metal. Leyla's image hung there in the sight, like an icon graven on the glass. He lowered the sight, aiming at her neck. Al-Hashimi's head was immediately behind. His fingers tightened on the trigger. There would be no option. "Forgive me," he thought. But his finger would tighten no further. It was physically impossible. He could not bring himself to do it. He lowered the rifle.

"I am not a man of God," al-Hashimi continued. "Far from it. I am a politician, and that has involved me in innumerable compromises with moral values. Some of you listening will understand what I mean. I came to power as the result of a coup d'état. I am not proud of that fact, but I swore when I came to power that I would rule for the good of my people or not rule at all. I swore that I would prove a man of peace or nothing. I have come here today to honor that pledge.

"On my mother's side," continued al-Hashimi, "I am an Arab. But my father was a Jew—a German Jew who was afraid to be known as one, who changed his name and created a new identity for himself. This is something I only learned a few years ago, but learning it changed my life. In my own body I carried blood from both sides of a bitter struggle. I wanted to proclaim my heritage from both parents, but how could I do so?

"Today, however, I do proclaim both those heritages. I come to make peace in the name of one God and one ancestor, Abraham. Let this peace be eternal. Let it be said loudly and clearly that those who oppose this peace oppose the will of God and mock the memory of their father Abraham. There is no shame in peace, nor is there disgrace in reconciliation."

David put down his rifle. He did not understand. Had he made a mistake? Had al-Hashimi really come to make peace after all? Von Meier had really been a Jew. Thus his obsession with the discovery of the Ark, with finding Iram. But if al-Hashimi was sincere, was there a plot at all? And in a flash David realized that there had been no evidence to show that al-Hashimi was actually involved in the conspiracy. The plot was al-Shami's and Neusner's. They were using al-Hashimi. They wanted to destroy the peace treaty by starting a war. And something had to happen to trigger off that war.

Al-Hashimi ended his speech and stepped down from the podium. David watched, his mind churning. Schultz—otherwise Isserles—was going to do something. But what? He looked through the narrow opening of the door and saw Leyla follow al-Hashimi from the platform. And then he saw her hand move to her pocket and draw something out. A small pistol. She didn't believe al-Hashimi, she thought it was yet more lies. She was going to shoot him!

David leaped up and shouted:

"Leyla! For God's sake, Leyla, he's telling the truth. It isn't him, it's Neusner!"

Leyla spun, frightened, looking for David's voice. There was a glint of metal in her hand. Al-Hashimi turned back toward her.

Someone rushed forward from the crowd. A man in Israeli uniform. He raised a gun and pointed it at Leyla. Without pausing, he fired, twice in quick succession. The bullets tore through her head. Her body jerked and fell, and as it did so a square compact— not a pistol—flew from her hand and struck the railings with a rattling sound.

Al-Hashimi dashed toward Leyla. No one else moved. And then, as if in slow motion, David saw it all. The man in uniform, still standing with his gun raised, was Isserles. Schultz. Al-Shami's words came screaming out of the darkness at David: *just after al-Hashimi finishes, but just before Schultz makes his move . . . Once Schultz has acted . . .* He looked at Schultz. He was raising the gun again, but he was not aiming at David. The gun was pointed at al-Hashimi.

That was the legitimation. An Israeli colonel would shoot the Syrian President, an Israeli army would attack retreating Syrian troops. And when the war ended the Syrians—under a new leader already chosen by al-Shami—would be covered in glory and self-righteousness.

David lifted the rifle to his shoulder. It winced in pain, but he ignored it. Schultz was in his sights. Everyone's eyes were on al-Hashimi bending over Leyla's body. David fired. The bullet hit Schultz in the forehead. The gun jerked in his hand and fired, a wild shot that ricocheted from a pillar and was lost. He toppled backward into the crowd.

David dropped the rifle to the ground. He had finished with it. He did not care what happened to him now. A man appeared in the doorway, a soldier holding a gun. David held his hands in the air. Another man appeared.

"Come out," he shouted in Hebrew. "Come out or I'll blow your fucking head off!"

David stepped toward the balustrade. The men held their guns leveled at him. He climbed over and jumped to the ground. Holding his hands behind his head, he walked to the door. The men grabbed him, then others made for the door. Just in case there was someone else there. Just in case David had an accomplice.

They brought David out into the pandemonium and bustled him through the pillars, toward the western door. He saw al-Hashimi staring at him as he went past, surrounded by security men. Then he caught sight of Leyla, a pale, bleeding doll, frozen forever like that in his memory, the blood still pouring, like a libation, from her head. The wig had fallen and her own hair lay soaking in the pool of blood. Someone rushed up and threw a coat over her.

They took him out into the sunshine. The clouds had broken up and a pale blue sky covered Jerusalem like a mantle. A church bell was ringing the Angelus on the slopes of the Mount of Olives. Before they hustled him into the back of a car with tinted windows, David looked around at the Dome of the Rock. Blue and white tiles shimmered in the sunlight, the Dome rose golden into the sky. But he could see nothing but dark blood trickling over it, red and warm like newly pressed wine. A hand took him by the arm, the fingers hard and unyielding as they pressed him toward the waiting car. He looked around at the man holding him. He did not recognize him, but his eyes noticed the number tattooed on his arm, just above the wrist. It was an ordinary number in every respect, except for the letter V at the end. The man's eyes were cold and bleak and dead. David tried to struggle, but other men surrounded him and he was drawn farther away. The warm blood trickled over everything, over

605

the domes and the steeples and the houses and streets of old Jerusalem, bathing them in its sweet baptismal fluid. David opened his mouth to drink it, but there was nothing, it was empty. He called out loudly once and was silent again. Hands held him on every side, pressing him, pushing him, pulling him down. They put him in the car and took away the sunlight and the blood and the blue sky.

ACKNOWLEDGMENTS

I would like to express my thanks to the numerous individuals and bodies who have assisted in different ways in the writing of this book. It could not have been written without my wife Beth: her love, her much-tried patience, her bright ideas, and her keen sense of style and proportion kept me writing when the going was toughest. My thanks are due to the trustees of the David Rosen Trust for permission to make use of and to quote from the various journals and other materials originally in his possession and now incorporated in my text. Copies of these materials were kindly supplied by the library of the Institut für Orientforschung of the Akademie der Wissenschaften in Wiesbaden, the Avrum Davidson Library in Haifa, and the Rosen family of Los Angeles, to all of whom my sincere thanks are due. I am grateful to Dr. Denis MacEoin of the Oriental School at Durham University for his translation of the Arabic texts used and for his comments on the text of the *Tariq al-mubin*. My thanks are also due to Mr. Ahmad Rashid of al-Arish for permission to quote one of his poems, originally published in Arabic in *al-Ahram*. Several people read and commented on the book at different stages of its presentation: Adrian Zackheim, Patrick Filley, and Patricia Parkin all helped change it out of recognition; John Dore helped with the archaeology; Graham Harvey and Professor John Sawyer helped me avoid some blunders relating to Israel. I am particularly grateful to Mr. Harold Blandford for agreeing to meet with me at his home in Jerusalem, and for supplying me with several important

607

documents. Professor Richard Halstead of Cambridge University gave me the details of several incidents. Jeffrey Simmons did everything an agent should do—and a great deal more: thanks for everything.

DANIEL EASTERMAN